The Dragon Nimbus Novels

THE DRAGON NIMBUS NOVELS

VOLUME 1

THE GLASS DRAGON

THE PERFECT PRINCESS

THE LONELIEST MAGICIAN

Irene Radford

DAW BOOKS, INC.

DONALD A. WOLLHEIM, FOUNDER

375 Hudson Street, New York, NY 10014

ELIZABETH R. WOLLHEIM
SHEILA E. GILBERT
PUBLISHERS

http://www.dawbooks.com

First Paperback Printing, October 2007
1 2 3 4 5 6 7 8 9

DAW TRADEMARK REGISTERED
U.S. PAT. AND TM. OFF. AND FOREIGN COUNTRIES
—MARCA REGISTRADA
HECHO EN U.S.A.

PRINTED IN THE U.S.A.

Introduction

Welcome to a world where dragons are real and magic works. If you are new to the Dragon Nimbus, pull up a chair and join us as we revel in tales that have touched my heart more than anything else I've written under any pen name. If you are returning after an absence, I am very happy to have you back.

This is a world that began with a Christmas gift of a blown glass dragon. The dragon sat proudly on the knick-knack shelf for several months, loved and admired, reluctantly dusted, and totally inert. Then one night at dinner my son remarked, "You know, Mom, I think dragons are born all dark, like that little pewter dragon, then they get more silvery as they grow up until they are as clear as glass." The dragon came to life for me.

Out of that chance remark came first one book, then three, five, seven, and finally ten. I built a career on these books and loved every minute of the process. These characters still live in my mind many years after they jumped into their stories and dragged me along with them.

Many thanks to DAW Books and my editor Sheila Gilbert for reviving *The Dragon Nimbus* a lucky thirteen years after they first debuted.

With this omnibus volume and the two that follow, you can read about the dragons with crystal fur that directs your eye elsewhere yet defies you to look anywhere else. Wonderful dragons full of wit and wisdom. Magic abounds. Magicians and mundanes alike learn about their world and special life lessons as they explore dragon lore past and present. The books will be presented in the order in which they were written, and the order that makes the most sense of the entwined tales.

So, sit back and enjoy with me.

And may reading take you soaring with Dragons.

Irene Radford
Welches, Oregon

THE
GLASS
DRAGON

This book is dedicated to
Karen, Judith, Laurie, and Barbara,
who taught me how to search for dragons.

Prologue

Coronnan is dying. Isolation, imposed upon us by the magic border, is the cause. This kingdom needs to be jolted out of its lethargy. No one is willing to grasp the tremendous power of this land, save me.

Our king is spineless, incapable of decision. My father was just as useless. So I killed him. My brothers, too. I used the king as long as I could. But he is so weak he cannot act, even with my prompting. The time has come to eliminate him for good.

Only I have the resolution to save this land. The great winged god Simurgh shall guide me. I shall make a sacrifice to him. What shall it be? A spotted saber cat? A great gray bear? Or perhaps a kahmsin eagle.

No. I shall offer up the greatest sacrifice of all. The last female dragon.

Chapter 1

"The only way to catch dragons is to hunt 'em when they're young. Still silvery, you know," said a one-eyed derelict.

A half dozen heads nodded in the dim, cavelike pub.

Jaylor sucked in his breath, as shock drained what little energy he had left from his thin spell of delusion. Didn't these people know that dragons provided everything that was good and safe and free in Coronnan?

He'd encountered suspicion and distrust of dragons before. But never out and out hatred. The University of Magicians needed to know about this strange little village.

"Yeah, if you wait 'til dragons're growed, there ain't no way you can see a *s'murghin'* one of them." The middle-aged man next to Jaylor smelled of stale fish and salt brine. "About ten years ago we had to root out a whole nest of the blasted monsters. They was eatin' all our fish."

Green smoke from the crude hearth burned Jaylor's eyes. He kept them half closed, avoiding direct eye contact with the half-drunken men who shared his table in this cave that served as the tavern. As long as these local gossips viewed his body and not his eyes, they would see only a long lost friend. A different friend to each man.

"Lord Krej has the right of it. Told us we didn't have t' provide nothin' for dragons. They can feed elsewhere. Can't afford a tithe to the dragons and another tithe to lord, too." The derelict's one eye glittered and probed from the depths of his grizzled and wrinkled mask of a face. Jaylor looked away nervously.

"We can't afford to anger the dragons though. The witch-woman's in league with them," another man added. He was covered in wood dust and wore an apron with more pockets than Jaylor bothered to count.

"Netted a big male in the nets last time we hunted. Couldn't kill him, but after he escaped he never came back." The fisherman leaned across the table toward the carpenter. "The old witchwoman deserted us then, and we did fine without one for nigh on ten years. Then last summer a new one shows up, and the dragons came back. I say we burn 'em both out."

"Without a witchwoman we have to depend on University healers. Who among us can afford a healer? If we could even get one to leave the comfort of Lord Krej's castle to come all the way down here," the carpenter argued.

Shouts of agreement and argument rose around Jaylor. The noise covered his recitation of a strengthening spell.

"Young'uns are cunning hunters. Only feed at night." Old One-eye continued to stare at Jaylor's unkempt appearance.

Nervously the young magician finger-combed his unfamiliar growth of new beard and long hair. It was so unlike his habitually clean face and fashionably restrained queue, he wondered if he'd ever get used to it.

He halted the gesture in mid-comb, afraid to call attention to his discomfort. He wished he could see the old man's aura, but the delusion blocked his inner sight.

He turned his combing gesture into a signal to the man tending the cask of ale. Somewhere across the bleak cave, the barkeep caught his gesture for more ale.

Awful stuff. It tasted more like . . . Jaylor decided he didn't want to think about what it really tasted like. It slaked the thirst of weeks on the road. That was all he asked.

"Young dragons're the same color as moonlight, slip in and out of shadows like a dream. Make a more interesting hunt that way." Old One-eye's intense stare drew Jaylor's gaze once again. The spell of delusion slipped a little more.

Stargods, he was tired. Carefully, he reinforced the spell. Just a little longer. He had to keep these provincials believing he was a local just a little longer, until he had the information he needed. Then he could slip away and rest his depleted body in preparation for the next stage of his quest.

"Sometimes you have to go after dragons at the source. Clear out all the juveniles and sucklings in the nest and the ma goes away, too." One-eye continued rubbing his grizzled jaw with a scarred hand. Jaylor's own chin itched in sympathy. He resisted running his fingers through the new growth again. "If you let 'em get too big, they'll rob the whole province."

"Worse than Rovers stealin' our young'uns."

Jaylor sat up straight and listened closer. There hadn't been Rovers in Coronnan in, oh, three hundred years. At least. Not since the magic border had been established. So, why were these people familiar with Rover habits?

Jaylor willed the conversation back to dragons. He needed to hear about the dragons.

The barkeep finally wound his way around the darkness of the cave interior. "Heard tell of a new nest up in the mountains."

"Last year's little'uns ought to be coming out for their first hunt right about now." One-eye threw out that information as if it were bait. For Jaylor or the rabble-rousers beside him?

The fisherman grabbed it, like the voracious fish he snagged out of the cold, blue depths of the Great Bay. "If'n they start robbing our catch again, we'll have a merry hunt. Soon as the snow clears the pass. This time we'll get the *s'murghin'* beasts 'afore they starve us out!" the fisherman laughed.

Chills radiated out from a tired place where Jaylor stored his magic. He knew he didn't like the viciousness of his informants. The disturbance in his magic convinced him not to trust them either.

"Odd season for first sight of the young." Jaylor found his voice after coughing out the acrid taste of the ale. "Most animals birth in the spring and have the young weaned by fall."

"Not dragons." The natives of the place chorused.

The equinox had just passed, though it still felt like winter outside. The last of the snow was still crunchy in the shade. Mud mired the roads so badly the huge, splayed feet of sledge steeds sank up to their hocks. Now was the time for birthing not weaning.

Jaylor quaffed more of the hideous ale. It was starting

to taste good. He'd had too much. Pretty soon he'd lead the dragon hunt with his drinking companions.

The king's magicians gathered magic generated by dragons, to be used only for the good of the kingdom. King Darcine ruled by Dragon-right. He sat upon the Dragon Throne and wore a crown of precious glass forged by dragon fire.

Yet, according to village sages Jaylor had encountered on his journey, no one in his right mind went to see a dragon with less than murderous intent.

Who ever said a journeyman magician on quest was in his right mind?

"Go see a dragon," Old Baamin, the senior magician had ordered Jaylor.

But how did one see an invisible creature?

"The dragon nimbus is dying," said Baamin, defining the quest. "During your search you must listen very carefully for clues to the cause."

Jaylor had his answer. These locals hunted dragons for fun and for protection of their livelihoods and their lives.

Jaylor was also to keep his eyes open for any youngsters with signs of magic talent. University recruits were fewer and fewer each year. Of course (his youthful wisdom dictated), with fewer dragons left to emit magic, there naturally were fewer men to gather that magic.

"The rest of Coronnan reveres the dragons," Jaylor prompted the men around him.

"More fools they. *S'murghin'* predators they are." The barkeep grumbled. "More'n enough dragons in the north to keep them *magicians* happy. They're as mean a predator as any dragon."

"But if we hunt dragons again, the witchwoman will go away. None of you are sick right now, but who'll help my Maevra when her time comes?" the carpenter interjected. He looked as if he wanted to agree with his companions but didn't quite dare.

"Dragons used to fly over nearly every week during the summer, until we stopped planting the Tambootie for them. You could catch sight of their rainbows now and again. Too bad something so pretty belongs to a creature so evil."

"Rainbows?" This was the first Jaylor had heard of a dragon having anything to do with a rainbow; though ancient sources said good weather was the result of a strong nimbus of dragons.

"When the sun hits a dragon's wings just right, a rainbow arches out and touches the ground." The barkeep sat to join the conversation. He swilled a huge mouthful of the poisonous ale. "If we see more'n one or two a week, we know it's time to go on a hunt again."

"Prism effect." Jaylor mumbled.

"Whism effect?" The one-eyed drunk looked up from his cup. His left eyelid was permanently closed, but it twitched with an emotion Jaylor couldn't read. He wondered if the eye were really gone. Perhaps, behind the scars, it glittered with the same malice as its undamaged mate.

Just for a moment Jaylor's magic vision penetrated the eyelid. He caught a brief image of a tall vigorous man with bright red hair. University red hair. Then the image faded. At one time the old derelict might have been an apprentice magician at the University. If so, he'd know about precious glass and prisms.

"Prism," Jaylor explained, "when sunlight hits clear glass at a precise angle the light refracts into a rainbow." He twisted the crude pottery mug in the firelight. Had these villagers ever seen enough glass, even the muddy colored stuff that was common in the capital, to understand its properties?

"Glass? Do you suppose a dragon is made of glass?" the barkeep murmured with awe. No one from this village in the back of beyond had probably ever seen true glass.

But they might have seen a dragon.

Jaylor wondered what kind of reaction he'd get if he pulled his tiny shard of viewing glass from his pack. They'd probably hang him, or throw him into the deepest part of the Great Bay as fish bait. The glass was barely as large as two of his fingers pressed together. But the mere possession of it identified him as a magician.

"Glass?" the one-eyed drunk laughed maliciously. "Another privilege for the Twelve and their greedy magicians. Wouldn't surprise me if dragons and glass come from the same hell. We're expected to provide food and shelter and cursed Tambootie trees under their orders, for their profit. And what do we get from it? Poorer by the day. I say we kill 'em all, magicians and dragons."

The little bit of magic left in Jaylor quivered in reaction to the derelict.

"I need to find the road into the mountains." Jaylor started to push back his stool. He'd had enough of the smoke and the steed-piss ale. It was time to move on.

One-eye stopped Jaylor's retreat with a look. The undamaged organ gleamed black in the dim light. The smell of Tambootie smoke tickled Jaylor's nostrils and lifted the top of his head to the cave roof. He silently mumbled an armoring spell before the odor sent him into the void between the planes of existence.

This old man suddenly reeked of the aromatic smoke. The old books in the library cautioned, repeatedly, to beware the stench of burnt Tambootie wood. A rogue magician intent on evil usually lurked behind it.

Old One-eye cast off his semblance of inebriation. The stench of Tambootie smoke intensified.

Jaylor tasted copper on his tongue. Tambootie trees always grew near veins of copper. The smoke must be infiltrating his entire body!

He pushed away his natural panic while he reached into the well of magic within him. It was dry. He was too tired to think. Instead he blinked his eyes, shifted his feet to a stronger position, and found another source. He strengthened the spell with a silent image, more precise than the formula of words.

In his mind he clothed each portion of his body in armor. He began with his vulnerable torso, spreading the protection upward and outward. Iron could douse a Tambootie wood fire. Iron would smother the smoke. His head cleared. He felt stronger, more alert now that his protection was complete.

Not precisely a traditional answer to the problem, but the University needed any magician they could find, even one who used rogue methods to accomplish traditional quests.

"Someone's got to find the dragon nest, keep track of it until we see if we need to hunt them out." Jaylor sought desperately for an explanation for his actions.

"Can't find a dragon without the witchwoman. She guards the path into the mountains."

Silence greeted that statement. None of the villagers looked too happy, least of all the carpenter.

"What witchwoman?" Jaylor dismissed the concept of *witch*. Women just couldn't gather magic.

"Our witchwoman, the one who guards the dragons," One-eye explained.

"She'll sell you a potion for the coughing disease or help your woman get with child." The barkeep was looking into his mug rather than at Jaylor. "All she asks in return is some new thatch or help with the plowing."

"Or a piece of your soul."

Jaylor had seen plenty of old crones during his wandering, forgotten widows living on the outskirts of villages. Most did midwifery. Some were skilled herbalists. That was the extent of their so-called magic.

Inside his head he heard cackling laughter. The high-pitched mockery denied his University trained assumptions. Tambootie smoke drifted around him once more. Jaylor's magic armor shriveled. He slapped a patching spell into his protection. The holes spread, the metal dissolved.

He shifted his feet once more. Energy and power seeped upward through his body. Stability and sanity followed the renewed magic.

'I've dealt with witches before." He turned on his heel to leave the cave before anything else stripped him of more magic.

"I'll bet you have, magician."

"What did you call me?" Jaylor swung back to face One-eye. The other men seemed frozen in time and space.

"I called you what you are. Magician. Watch out for the witch and her familiars. She has a wolf who will tear out your heart while she shreds your soul and leaves you living. You'd best kill the beast right off."

Noon sunshine shattered into a thousand bright colors around Brevelan. She looked up through the shade of a leafy tree into the brilliance. One hand sought the silky ears of the wolf at her heels while the other shaded her eyes. The huge canine sat blinking his yellow eyes in contentment as he eased his injured foot. Brevelan cuddled the weight of the animal against her side. Affectionately, he grasped her hand in his mouth. No tooth penetrated her skin.

"Good morning, Shayla," she called to the fleeting shadow that streaked across the blue sky.

'Tis past noon. The pragmatic words formed in Brevelan's mind, just as the magnificent image of the speaker did. A swirl of all colors, that were really no color at all, formed into a faint winged outline. Shayla might be as small as an insect or as large as Krej's castle. Brevelan had no idea which.

"Did you have a good hunt?" She spoke openly for her own benefit while she threw the thoughts to her friend.

The picture of a fat cow appeared in her mind.

"Oh, Shayla," she sighed. "Some farmer is going to be very upset when he finds the carcass."

We didn't leave enough for him to find.

"We? When did you hunt with other dragons? You've been alone longer than I have." Something akin to loneliness snaked through her. Her golden companion whined to remind her that she wasn't really alone.

"You're right, Puppy. I have more friends here in the forest than I ever did at home." She stooped to hug the wolf. "Still, it would be nice to talk to someone who talks back occasionally."

I talk back.

"Too much sometimes. Who joined your hunt?"

The image of three huge male dragons appeared. One had blue tips on his transparent wings, another was red-tipped, the third still had the silvery gloss of adolescence clinging to the delicate wing vanes. One day soon those silver vanes promised a green glow.

The images hovered in a background of erotic purple. "Shayla! You shameful thing. Three at once."

The more fathers, the larger and stronger the litter. There was no embarrassment in the dragon's thoughts. She merely communicated a fact.

Suddenly the clearing around Brevelan's hut filled with children. A gangling blond teenager stood by her side, a babe suckled her breast. She felt the tug of its tiny mouth relieve the aching pressure of heavy milk. Off by the door, twin girls, with mops of red curls, giggled while plaiting a basket of fragrant grasses. Another boy, also red-haired, chopped wood while his younger brother built stacks of kindling. Only the oldest was blond.

As blond as the golden wolf whining in distress.

Brevelan sagged with relief when the illusion vanished as quickly as it had come.

Did that ease the thing you call loneliness?

"No! It made it worse." Brevelan's entire body ached with grief for the babies she would never have. She looked up once more. She couldn't lie to Shayla.

"I thought we were too close friends for you to spin your dragon dreams on me. Haven't you led enough innocent wanderers astray?" Brevelan forced indignation. Inwardly she wept for the figure of a dead man she had found last fall. Shayla's illusion had danced him through the forest until his skin hung from him like rags.

Stargods, but the man's death-smile haunted her still.

Perhaps my visions prepared you for him.

"Who?"

The one who comes.

"The barkeep," she mused. "He promised me an ell of good cloth for the infusion I prepared." She'd caught him sneaking a glimpse of her breasts as she bent over the hearth. That had probably helped him satisfy his wife more than the tea.

Not the swiller of poison. Shayla was emphatic. *You should have given him a tincture of wazool root.* The dragon named a powerful laxative. Her thoughts were bright pink with humor. Then, still in a lighthearted tone, the dragon added: *Prepare yourself for the one who comes. Him.*

The image of a tall man carrying a gnarled walking staff flashed through Brevelan's mind. He appeared in the distance with the sun behind him. The glowing light of sunset outlined his long frame while it hid the details of his features.

Brevelan forced herself not to tremble in memory of the same image waking her in a cold sweat from deep sleep.

"Him."

The one in your dreams.

"The one who brings destruction." The vision had come to her three times. Only terrible portents of the future came in that number.

Her mind was empty. Shayla was gone. Back to her lair to sleep off the exertions of mating and hunting.

Chapter 2

Jaylor dumped a bucket of water from the village well over his head. Icy droplets penetrated his unkempt hair and beard. His eyes cleared as some of the smoky stink washed away. Removing the stench from his clothing and hair would be another matter.

He drank long from the next bucket, rinsing the rancid taste of ale from his mouth. The air around him was clean and cool after the closeness of the cave.

When he had arrived in this village, he was too relieved to find habitation with drink and hot food to pay much attention to the place. Slowly he turned to survey the homes of the men who'd been in the pub.

Hovels. All the dwellings were as poor and as ragged as the men. A scrawny pig rooted around the edges of the village. He'd never seen such a skinny creature!

Now he felt guilty for eating the hot pasty and drinking their horrid ale—even though he'd paid good money for them. He felt as if he'd robbed the villagers of basic sustenance.

It had been a hard winter for everyone. Food stores rotted from too much rain. Privation always brought out diseases that thrived in the cold damp. Yet the weather was never cold enough to kill the pestilence and stop the rot.

Surely this village was in a better situation than most. The Great Bay lapped the foot of the cliff below the village. Fishermen had easy access to the bounty of the bay that fed Coronnan. Heavily forested foothills rose behind the rooftrees of the cottages. Wood should be plentiful for fishing boats, housing, furniture, and heat. Behind the houses he spied extensive fields and pastures spreading out beyond the village.

In the center of the village stood the ceremonial Equinox Pylon. A cluster of five poles, sparsely decorated with oak branches and faded ribbons. Where were the fronds of ever-blue, bright with new life, the first shoots of grain and new garlands of ribbons to celebrate the coming of the most fruitful season?

This was the first village he had encountered where life was so tenuous they didn't sacrifice the best of the new for the equinox or even have garbage for a pig!

Was this the result of a dragon stealing their food supply, too heavy taxation, or evidence of a neglectful lord?

Krej, lord of this province, donated thousands of drageen every year to the poor, to the study of healing arts, and to the priests of the Stargods. The nobility in Coronnan City considered him a good and generous man. Perhaps he should have donated some of that money to his own province.

Jaylor put aside his questions. His quest came first. Where was he, and where should he go next? "Go find a dragon, indeed." He snorted. "As if they grow under rocks. More likely they roost on the top of the blasted Tamboo-tie trees."

From memory he drew a map of the kingdom in the air before his eyes. Green lines glimmered in nothingness as he sketched the sweep of the Great Bay on the east, a long chain of mountains curving from northwest to southeast. Coronnan River wound from those mountains through the central plains to open out into a wide delta filled with islands and aits. Entrenched among the largest islands created by the river's merging with the bay, Coronnan City presided over all shipping and commerce in the kingdom. Twelve provinces, equal in resources if not area, radiated out from the capital.

He had started his quest at the University in Coronnan City. A blue dot appeared on the map at the head of the bay. A line wandered away from that dot on the map to track his journey east and south. At each stopping place, the blue line widened a tiny bit. He dredged from his capacious memory every detail of every village along the way, the size, wealth, location, and the number of poles in their Equinox Pylon. Most Pylons consisted of three poles, scrupulously maintained with flowers and fruits in due season.

Five poles denoted ancient prominence. So why wasn't this Pylon revered?

As Jaylor had wandered south through Faciar, the groups of dwellings had become farther apart. The trader-roads had been well maintained, and usually there was enough to feed a stranger. Especially if he had news from the capital.

A stranger wasn't turned away as long as he wasn't a magician. Distrust of that elite order of talented men ran rampant beyond city and castle walls. No wonder Baamin had ordered Jaylor to guard well the nature of his quest and his status as journeyman magician. The secretive old sot knew the mood of the country better than Jaylor had expected.

Conditions were worse here in the south. Hostility toward everything from the capital was so strong Jaylor could see waves of hatred almost without magic. No one cared about news from Coronnan City, the king's waning health, or their obviously absent lord—Krej, first cousin to the king.

Something was very wrong here. He hadn't even had to ask about local dragon lore. These people seethed with it. As if the winged creatures embodied all of their problems. Had they even seen enough of their lord to know that he should be taking care of them?

Rumors in Coronnan City said that Krej's latest philanthropy was sponsoring sculptors. He collected life-sized figures of rare creatures to display to deprived children who had no other way to view the wonders of Coronnan. Did Krej have a dragon? One made of precious glass perhaps? No. Even Lord Krej, second in line to the throne, couldn't afford an entire dragon made of glass.

"Stranger." A soft feminine voice broke his concentration.

With a word and a quick gesture the glowing map, evidence of his magic talent, disappeared. Only then did he turn to face the owner of the voice, the barmaid.

In the dark cave of the pub, the girl's dirty face and ragged clothes revealed little but too thin limbs, hollow cheeks and sunken eyes. The noon sun revealed a lush bosom.

"Stranger, my da sent a pasty and some ale to see you on your road." She arched her back so that her breasts threatened to burst through the threadbare homespun of her bodice.

This girl was so thin and bedraggled that all she roused in him was outrage that she had been reduced to such a level.

Women, girls, always they tempted him; with their loveliness, their scent, their generous curves. Their mere presence usually made him forget he was a magician born and bred, and as such forbidden to take any woman. If he gave into temptation, he would lose his magic. And because he was forbidden to lie with any woman, all of them became more desirable.

"Give my thanks to your da," he replied politely. It would probably be considered an insult to refuse, even though he knew they couldn't afford to be so generous.

"Must you leave so soon?" Her eyelashes fluttered.

"My journey is a long way from ending."

"It's festival tonight." Her finger traced the neckline of her garment.

Stargods! Last night, not tonight, had festival. The girl was lying. For while he'd heard that some barbaric peoples celebrated on both the night of the equinox and the first full day of spring, no one in Coronnan followed that custom.

Slowly, she outlined the dip and curve of her breasts with a lingering fingertip. Her lips pouted prettily while her eyes wandered toward the sparse decorations on the Pylon.

"Aren't you celebrating a little late this year?" Jaylor asked through clenched teeth. Her invitation touched him with panic rather than desire. A close regard for the movements of stars and planets, sun and moon was among the most sacred duties of magicians and priests alike.

He had spent the night in the hills outside of town, determined to avoid the temptations of festival. If the celebration had gotten out of hand, he might have awakened in the morning to find his magic reduced or gone altogether just because he hadn't resisted what spring and the fertile women offered.

"Tonight is festival," the girl insisted. Her eyes traveled to the cave opening of the pub as if seeking answers. She avoided looking at the Pylon. She couldn't lie while her eyes rested on this ancient symbol of the movement of sun and moon and stars.

"Does your da think me so simple I can't read the skies? I learned to follow the passage of sun and moon as an infant. Either your priest is lax or the world spins in a different path here in the south." He glanced at the cave opening, too, with his mind. There was a shadow there his eyes couldn't see.

"You must stay." The girl's color rose and she twisted her hands in her skirt.

"Why?"

Her voice rose to a whine. "I . . . I was told you must stay." She swallowed and dropped her voice to a purr that might have been seductive in a whore less desperate, less pathetic. "I can make the evening quite pleasant."

Jaylor squinted in the first stage of a truth spell. Shock waves rolled back on him. Echoes of his own magic reverberated against his body. He gritted his teeth until his toes stopped tingling and he could stand upright without effort.

The girl was armored!

Who in the village was powerful enough to throw such a strong spell? The same person who had ripped holes in his armor earlier. The person in the shadows of the cave. Was the one-eyed derelict a rogue magician?

He whirled to face his adversary but found only sunlight flooding the doorway. The shadow was gone. Where did it go?

The voice of his inner guidance hummed a warning. He needed to get as far away from here as possible, and quickly.

A cloud of roiling, red-orange fog, that was trying to be green as well, erupted from the doorway of the cave. Gathering speed, the magic mist flowed over the ground. It passed the rooting pig. The animal stilled, its life frozen in time until the cloud moved away. Jaylor knew that if he were caught in the magic mist, he, too, would be imprisoned by it.

The ground beneath him reached out and grabbed his feet. Frantically he searched his memory for a spell of release. None of the spells he'd so painstakingly memorized came to him. In desperation he tried to picture the books in the library. There was one on the back shelf that should help. In his mind he saw the book float from its shelf. The cover opened, pages turned. They were all blank.

His body recoiled in fatigue. He'd held the delusion spell too long, then wasted more energy with his useless map.

The cloying clay mud thickened and threatened to solidify around his worn boots like fire-case pottery.

His brow and chest were clammy with cold sweat. He forced his mind into a meditative trance. Breathe in three counts, hold three, out three. Breathe in. His mind stilled. The fog appeared distant and unreal through his refocused eyes.

With a dragon-sized effort he pulled one foot free, then the other, shattering the images that bound him. One foot in front of the other, he measured his paces on the muddy road to the southern mountain pass.

One step farther away from the evil that followed him. One step farther on his quest. One step closer to his master's cloak of deep blue wool with the silver markings of the Stargods on the collar.

Jaylor quickened his pace.

Baamin gathered his bright magician's robes tightly around his rotund figure as he squeezed through the side door of the University to welcome the king. 'Twas the study hour. The time when the senior magician and his king took advantage of the quiet to engage in a brisk game of piquet.

But King Darcine hadn't been well enough to venture out of the palace for many, many moons.

Leave it to his rather perverse king to prefer a quiet entrance through this little-used passage rather than at the wide front door. As if his arrival in a steed-drawn litter with a full military escort could be kept quiet.

The soldiers ringed the courtyard. Baamin noticed that many of the men were developing a bit of a paunch. They didn't have enough to do.

"Have you heard anything about my son yet, Baamin?" The slight frame of the king trembled as he wheezed the words.

Baamin paused to allow his friend and ruler to catch up. The pace the monarch set these days was still woefully slow. It was a miracle he'd survived the miserable winter.

Perhaps he had some good news for King Darcine after all. "Last night I had a vision in the glass. The dragon Shayla has bred." The ruling monarch of Coronnan was magically linked to the nimbus of dragons. In return, the people of Coronnan were pledged to plant and maintain enough Tambootie trees to feed the dragons' needs and to provide a tithe of livestock. Shayla's vitality should impart some strength to this ailing king.

But the peasantry rebelled against obligations they no longer understood. Precious few of the magic trees, and fewer dragons, were left these days. It would take more than one litter of dragonets to restore Darcine's damaged lungs and weak heart.

"As for your son, the glass is clouded," he whispered. So far they had managed to keep the prince's disappearance a secret.

Darcine's tall shadow wavered against the stone walls of the little used passage. In his youth, the king had been as tall and as strong as any warrior in the kingdom. But his illness had wasted muscle and mind. A strong gust of wind, or the loss of one more dragon. . . .

"The men you sent on quest, do they know they are looking for the errant crown prince?" The king coughed.

Baamin placed a chubby hand on Darcine's shoulder. He could feel the king's bones sharply defined beneath the layers of rich fabric. King Darcine wouldn't notice the small strengthening spell he added to the touch.

"Each journeyman's task is designed to teach him the full use of his talents, and to overcome his weaknesses." As any quest should. "I was careful to word each assignment so my students would cover the entire kingdom while they seek new recruits and the source of distrust of magic." Baamin didn't add the report that yet another healer magician had been stoned out of a village when he failed to save the last of the dairy herd from a mysterious wasting disease. It was the third such incident in Lord Krej's province of Faciar this winter.

"My students will also cover the hunting grounds of every dragon left in the nimbus. The beasts will instinctively protect the prince."

"You're certain, then, that my son was kidnapped by magic. He isn't on some wild caper with Jaylor and his hooligans? He used to take great joy in slipping away from the palace when I needed him most, to indulge in mischief with his common friends. I thought he outgrew his base preferences. Perhaps my son has just wandered into the mountains following a dragon dream."

"Others might wander aimlessly while in dragon-thrall; wander until they starved to death or broke their necks. But a true dragon of the king would never harm one of the royal family," Baamin asserted. "We are certain of the kidnap, Your Grace. The glass tells us he is alive, but we cannot be sure where. His face, figure, and location are lost in a mist of colored magic. All we can see is the essence of his soul. We can't even pin down the color of the mist and thereby identify the magician," Baamin sighed. "But I do know Jaylor's magic isn't sophisticated enough to blur the glass so well."

He hoped. Jaylor's talent was so unpredictable he might be throwing delusions while he and the prince devised some practical joke.

"Do the people really believe my son is at a monastery reconsidering an inappropriate dalliance?"

"Of course." Baamin smiled reassuringly. "Each of the Twelve thinks the prince will eventually marry one of his daughters. So, naturally, they believe you disapprove of every other romantic entanglement." And there were many, if rumors were to be believed. Baamin didn't believe in rumors. He knew the truth behind the numerous ladies who claimed to have bedded the prince. Most of them lied.

The official pretense for the prince's absence must end soon. Some of the Twelve were grumbling about his lack of leadership. The crown prince should be leading an army to control raiders on the disintegrating western border.

"How many journeymen did you send?" The king seemed slightly recovered as they proceeded down the dark corridor to the main hallway.

"Every journeyman who was anywhere near ready." Seven young men. Every journeyman in residence. There should have been a hundred.

"Including Jaylor?"

"Even Jaylor."

"Was that wise?"

"He never got the hang of why a spell works. At best I

Irene Radford

hope he'll stir something into action so that a more accomplished magician can follow through. I had no choice but to send him. I don't have enough journeymen to cover the entire kingdom otherwise." The boy was creative and powerful, but there was no proof his methods would ever be reliable or repeatable. And his magic tended to slip beyond the control of the Commune of Magicians.

"Did Jaylor pass any of his exams?" They moved beyond the main hallway and into the residential wing. Baamin's private study was just around the next corner.

"A few. Master Maarklin devised a test that allowed Jaylor to qualify for his quest. But we of the Commune cannot accept that he is master material." *But we'll use his strange talent for our own purposes,* Baamin thought.

"I've heard Jaylor was drunk much of the last two years. The families of his friends complained constantly that he was corrupting their sons." The king dodged a book that came flying down the corridor from library to dormitory.

"Your Grace, you and I both know there is only one way for a journeyman to get drunk." Baamin pointed to a mug gliding slowly toward them. Its progress was steady, about a finger's length above the stone floor and very close to the left-hand wall.

"Someone is making progress." The first day of class new apprentices were invited to drink their fill of the fine wine in the cellars. The catch to this license was the magically sealed door. The wine cups could pass through the seal, apprentices could not. When the students could levitate a full cup of wine from the cellar to their rooms, without spilling any, they could drink all they wanted. By the time they figured out how to do that, they were usually ready to become journeymen. "Have you had to change the spell on the door to the wine cellar yet?"

Baamin chuckled. "Not since Jaylor left. He managed to break it with little or no effort. But then he didn't need to."

"He kept your potter working overtime for several weeks at first." King Darcine seemed to find the antics of the apprentices amusing. When he was well, everything in life was amusing to him.

"Only until he discovered he could make the cup appear in his hand." Another example of his imagery becoming magic. "Then he smashed the spell on the lock of the cellar door so his classmates could share his celebration. But since he couldn't tell his master how he had accomplished the feat, he was denied promotion."

"At least he didn't teach his classmates how he performed that little trick."

"I heard he tried. They were smart enough not to listen to him. Jaylor's magic is too unorthodox for anyone else to follow." And without being able to keep his spells within traditional parameters, Jaylor was of no use to the Commune.

"Shall we follow the cup to your next prodigy?" King Darcine smiled at the wobbling cup as it slowly neared the dormitory wing. It was a weak smile that appeared more like a grimace on his gaunt face.

"Perhaps we should. I need to know who will have a hangover come morning." They watched a moment as the traveling cup connected with the floor while the unknown apprentice rested. He was a smart one. Most boys thought their levitations at eye level where a mishap resulted in shattering the mug and splashing the wine. On the other hand, cups traveling as close to the ground as the one they followed ran the risk of being kicked. Whoever moved this cup had solved the problem by keeping it close to the wall and out of the way.

The cup paused again by a closed door. It settled to the floor while the door was opened for it.

"He hasn't figured out how to suspend it while he performs another task, or to open the door before he begins the spell. Still, he shows caution," Baamin whispered to his companion.

The cup rose a few inches and slid through the opening. There was the ominous thud of pottery hitting the floor and shattering, followed by a string of curses. "*S'murgh* you, Marcus! You broke my concentration," an apprentice yelled to his roommate.

Baamin sighed with relief. "That's one promotion I don't need to worry about. Yet." Baamin reached into one of his deep pockets for an ever-present flask. He downed a swig and grimaced.

"Tsk, tsk, Baamin. You know you shouldn't drink so much of your cordial." King Darcine shook his head.

"My sacroiliac is killing me today." Baamin deliberately screwed the cap back onto the flask and repocketed it. In

almost the same gesture he popped a mint into his mouth
to disguise the telltale odor of his medicine.

"I have put a terrible burden on you, my friend." The
king looked contrite. "You have enough worries keeping
the University under control."

"I am Senior Magician, Your Grace. It is my place to
help you in this dire adversity."

"I sincerely regret that you are the only person I can
fully trust. No one but you is in a position to coordinate
the search for the prince in secret." Darcine slammed his
fist into his open palm. "*S'murgh it,* Baamin, I need my
son here to negotiate the new treaty with Rossemeyer. The
palace budget has become a mess since he's been gone, and
the servants have become lazy."

Baamin touched his king's arm, feeding him strength
once more. *Stargods,* he wished he could give his king
health and determination as well. He didn't need the healing
talent to know Darcine was dying, along with the dragon
nimbus. Shayla was the only breeding female left, and her
lair was kept secret even from the king. Baamin hoped
Jaylor wouldn't be the journeyman to find her. Who knew
what kind of trouble he'd stir up if he did.

"Why do we have to be so devious? Why was my boy
kidnapped in the first place?" Darcine moaned.

Baamin wouldn't tell him the reasons. The crown prince
had already proved he would rule with strength and wisdom.

None of the Twelve or the Commune would tolerate a
strong king after years of noninterference. Especially Baamin.

Chapter 3

The journeyman knows nothing of real magic. He only plays with his spells. Still, he can be useful. I shall drive him forward, make him lead me to my dragon.

The witchwoman will help. Her wretched thirst for love will drive her to betray the dragon. My dragon. There is no lasting power in love. The love she relies on will drag her down. Maman taught me to purify my power with love for no one but myself and the power.

I am the only one who can save Coronnan. But to do it, I must keep those inferior lords and meddling magicians in their place. Their loyalty to Darcine and his son will be their undoing.

The day was late when Jaylor awoke from his nap under a sprawling oak tree. With an appeal for protection to the broom of mistletoe in its highest branches, he had decided to sleep off the effects of his magic duel in the village.

He also had to make up for his lack of sleep the night before. Even a league away in the hills he had heard the cries and shouts of festival ringing in his ears.

They'd called to him, urged him to join the revelry. The voices had torn at his sanity and swelled his body with desires he dared not explore.

He knew of ten young magicians who had lost their powers. All because they took a woman too early in their training. Jaylor wasn't willing to risk his magic for the temporary pleasures of a woman.

In the fading light he stretched and pushed stiff muscles. A nearby stream enticed his parched throat. The skin of ale given to him in the village bumped against his side as he stood again. Ale would taste better than plain water. If ale was all the girl had put into the skin. He sniffed the ale cautiously. No obvious poison or spell.

Better to be safe. He drank deeply from the crystal stream and thought of the fine wines in the University cellars.

If he were still within the walls of the University, one quick image would place a cup in his hands. Mischief brightened his mind. What if he could bring wine from the University cellars to this forgotten corner of nowhere? Old Baamin wouldn't miss one more cup. The current batch of apprentices was probably breaking several right now.

Magic wasn't supposed to traverse such great distances. Still, he'd never allowed someone else's limitations to stop him from trying—especially if his stunts would irk the drunken old coot at the head of the University. Eyes closed, with the magic already gathered in his body, he formed an image in his mind.

In the cellars, halfway across the kingdom, a cup slid off its shelf and glided to the barrel. The spigot turned. Wine flowed into the crude pottery. Dark red wine, full of fruit and light.

Jaylor's mouth watered again. Using the magic that flowed through his being, he reformed the image of the now brimming cup. It appeared in his hand. He nearly dropped the cup in surprise, spilling some of the precious liquid.

His magic had crossed half the kingdom!

He took a gulp to soothe his confusion. Then he laughed out loud, long and hard. He couldn't pass any of the Commune's infernal exams, but he could transport a cup of wine across three rivers, two forests, and a small mountain, without spilling a drop.

He gulped again, then paused to savor the flavors. It was good wine. The University kept the best cellars as an incentive to the apprentices.

His second sip was more leisurely. Jumbled thoughts crowded his mind. He used the process of sip and taste to sort them, just as he had in his student days.

He knew his magic was different from the ritual sort prescribed by the Commune, stronger, too. When it worked. Time and again Jaylor had proved that magic didn't have to be limited by convention and approved methods. He

could accomplish any task the masters set for him, as long
as he could work the spells his own way. It was only when
they forced him to limit his work to traditional methods or
join his magic to another's that he faltered. Over the years
he'd learned to fake traditional spells. Most of the time he
got away with it. The times he was caught had cost him
promotions and the right to pursue his master's cloak.

But he was on quest now. All he had to do was figure out
the riddle of Old Baamin's command. His master wouldn't
have given a single task, no matter how farfetched. Something else was cloaked in the wording.

"Go see a dragon." A dragon was invisible, so he'd have
to use his magic sight. What else was he supposed to see
while looking for a dragon?

This quest was turning into one of those incredibly boring story problems that were cloaked in archaic symbolism.
Jaylor hated those tests. He always failed because he couldn't
blend traditional spells with ancient language, or he looked
at the problem from a twisted angle and saw too much.

The wine finished, he sent the cup back to the University.
Not to the cellars. To the kitchen, where it could be washed
and returned to its proper place.

He wished he could see the faces of the scullery drudges
when the cup appeared on the counter. Would they tell
Baamin? Serve the old wire-puller right if they did. Let
him stew over the whereabouts of his least favorite student.

Jaylor stretched again. His leather journey clothes creaked
with dirt and hard use.

The sun was still above the horizon, though the air was
not truly warm this early in the season. The creek burbled
happily, swollen with snow melt. Jaylor shivered in the light
breeze. Just perhaps he could wash off some of the travel
dirt from his shirt and body.

Another sip of wine, perhaps, to help him decide. Wine.
If he could transport the wine why not a tub of hot water?
He stirred his brain into trance mode.

No, he was still tired and drained. He might need some
strength when he confronted the witchwoman and her familiar. Those old crones knew non-magical tricks that could
fool some of the best master magicians.

Perhaps just a basin of hot water and some oil to condition his boots and trews. From Baamin's private bathing

chamber? The old man wouldn't be there now in the middle of the afternoon. So why not?

As soon as the thoughts formed, a basin of steaming water, perfumed with sweet stellar petals, appeared before him along with a small flask of oil from the pantry. He set them in the nest of tangled roots that had been his bed.

The wash worked wonders on his mind and body. He'd forgotten how light and free one felt when newly clean. The restorative power of a wash was worth the drain on his magic.

Invigorated, he sent the basin and the flask back—to the kitchens. In his mind he watched them settle onto the washing counter. Returning his used vessels to the kitchen was his signature. By tonight the entire University would know that Jaylor was alive and well. They'd think he was back in the capital instead of nearing the southern border.

Baamin had taught him to hide his tracks, if nothing else.

He chuckled and set his staff on the road. As soon as he stepped away from the protective branches of the oak, the hairs on the back of his neck stood straight up. They almost hummed with tension. Was someone from the village following him?

He extended his senses around him.

Nothing. Whatever followed him was gone, or just the product of his imagination. He shouldered his pack and set the staff back on the path of his quest.

"Is that where it hurts?" Brevelan gently probed the huge paw of the golden wolf. He whimpered slightly and tried to withdraw the limb she held. She had no fear of the long teeth he kept muzzled.

"It's never quite healed, has it, Puppy?" He whined again and rested his head on her knee. His golden eyes looked up in adoration. A low moan, the canine equivalent of a purr, erupted from the back of his throat.

Ever so gently, Brevelan continued to probe the paw while she hummed a little tune of her own making. Her song rooted out the sore spot and soothed it. The golden eyes drooped in contentment.

"You old faker!" she exclaimed, but continued to rub the paw. "You limped in here just so I would give you some attention. With her free hand she ruffled his ears.

The energetic caress roused the wolf from his near slumber. His tongue caressed her healing hand in response. Then he grasped it gently with his mouth.

"Well, off with you, Puppy. Go find your dinner." The thought of lives ending to feed his vigorous appetite made her shudder in revulsion. Yet she knew he needed meat, just as Shayla did.

In the early days of her association with the wolf and the dragon, his injured paw and leg had prevented his hunting. Shayla had magnanimously dropped rabbits or a haunch of something larger for the wolf every day or two. Now, after most of the winter had passed, he was nearly healed and able to fend for himself.

Somewhere in the wild forest that spread around the mountains, he must have a mate about to whelp. He was an adult wolf in his prime. Yet he showed no inclination to assume his family duties, something inborn in wolves. They mated for life and were devoted parents. If he had come to her as a pup she could have understand his attachment to a human.

A squirrel chittered to the wolf from the doorway of the hut. He ignored the scolding and continued to beg caresses from Brevelan. She ran her hands through his winter-thick fur, drawing as much comfort from the touch as he did.

"That's enough for now. I have work to do. Didn't you just hear Mistress Squirrel? There are roots to be dug, and seeds to be started. The floor needs to be swept and Mistress Goat needs a milking." If she kept busy enough, she wouldn't think about her dreams of portent.

She stood to separate the wolf from her hand. The stool wobbled when relieved of her slight weight.

"Someone remind me to ask the carpenter to fix this chair when his wife needs help with her birthing," she called out to the various mice and birds that scurried around her bare feet. The only other response to her command was a petulant meow from Mica, the cat curled up beside the fire. She didn't like her nap being disturbed, even by such a simple request. For a brief moment Brevelan thought Mica's eyes appeared round and hazel, like a human's. Another blink and the illusion was gone. The cat's eyes were yellow, slashed vertically by a very feline pupil.

Brevelan stepped out of her one-room cottage into the

bright clearing. Her eyes wandered to the pathway. No tall man carrying a pack and walking staff. She breathed a sigh of relief.

"I'm not going to tell you again, Puppy, go get your dinner." She swatted his behind lightly. He trotted off, tail high, nose low, to begin his hunt. "And don't bring any of it back. I don't want your bones cluttering up my house." She shuddered again at the loss of a tiny life to feed her friend. He'd dragged a carcass back only once. Every crunch of a bone felt like her own limbs breaking. His sensual pleasure at the noise stabbed her through the heart. Since then she reminded him to eat his hunt in the woods. He'd never disobeyed again.

"And if you get muddy again, you sleep outside tonight," she called after his retreating tail. "Shayla may have given you a princely name, Darville, but you get too dirty and disheveled to be a royal pet."

A flusterhen dashed out from the cover of saber ferns at the edge of the clearing. Her sisters followed. They pecked at Brevelan's feet, and she shooed them away. "I'll feed you later. When the sun sets," she promised them.

As she went about the mundane chores of digging and milking, feeding and soothing, Brevelan sang. Music flowed and swirled around her, reflecting the beauty and serenity she found in her isolated clearing. Trees and plants, ground and hut seemed to hum in harmony with her song. She lifted her voice a note higher into a descant to the natural sounds. As she reached the apex of her voice she sensed the clearing sealing itself against intruders.

Less than a year ago her life had been devoid of music, just as the solitude she craved had been denied her.

Households were large in her home village. Many generations lived in each house. Excessive noise, like singing, was banned, lest it disturb the elders or the babies, or the fathers concentrating on their work. Girls were married off early to make room for the brides of the younger men. Babies abounded everywhere.

She missed the babies. Memories of Shayla's dragon-dream returned. A compelling delusion. Once more she felt milk-heavy breasts ache for a baby's suck. She shook it off. If she hadn't run away last summer, she'd have a child of her own by now. A soft, small creature with her own ruddy hair and pale skin. Her imagination would never allow her to supply that unborn child with the coarse black hair and angry disposition of her husband.

Sometimes in the night, when she was alone and her body ached for contact with another human being, she wondered what her life would be like now if she had stayed.

That was the trouble with dragon-dreams. They seemed so real it was difficult to return to the light of day. A day when she must be alert to word from the village. Maevra was close to her time and might deliver early.

Brevelan just wished the villagers would accept her help without the frequent use of garlic and gestures meant to ward off evil. She had never told them how much she liked garlic.

Jaylor followed the road as it curved and dipped into a hollow. He jumped a narrow creek where it crossed his path. Green meadows spread out around the road in all directions. A little farther along the stream, away from the road, would be a good place to camp.

As if he'd conjured an encampment, Jaylor found several tents nestled beside the water. Traders usually welcomed strangers. This far south, the traders could come only from Rossemeyer. Those stalwart desert dwellers were even more suspicious and insular than Coronnites.

He paused behind another protective oak tree. From its shadows he surveyed the scene ahead of him. In the creeping twilight he should be invisible until he decided to be seen.

Sturdy pack steeds grazed behind a picket line. Wary dogs zigzagged around cook fires and brightly colored tents. Purple, red, black, and blue shelters for unseen campers.

Who but Rovers would live in such garish tents? Certainly not traders from Rossemeyer who sought to blend into their environment. Rovers were homeless wanderers who worked no honest trade, were beholden to no lord, and obeyed few man-made laws. And they fascinated Jaylor.

The Council of Provinces had outlawed Rovers when the Commune of Magicians established the magic border three hundred years ago. Jaylor had read every enticing word about their forbidden lifestyle.

No band of Rovers should be within the boundaries of

Coronnan for any reason. Where had they learned the
spells to open a hole in the magic wall? Or which magician
had they bribed?

Jaylor knew from his secret reading that Rovers weren't
above robbing travelers of their purses, packs, and clothes.
Mercifully, they slit the throats of their victims so they
wouldn't freeze to death or be attacked by wild animals.

He checked his appearance. Worn and dusty journey
clothes, provincially uncombed hair and beard, small pack
and walking staff. He could be any benighted traveler. Except that few people journeyed through the kingdom these
days. The Twelve lords were supposed to provide homes
for their dependents. Traditions and superstitious fears established during the Great Wars of Disruption kept almost
everyone in those homes.

The Rover camp was suspiciously quiet. No voices called
out. Dogs didn't bark. No person stirred the savory smelling stew cooking over the fire.

Jaylor pressed his back into the tree as he scanned the
landscape. Whoever had been here was not long gone. He
hoped no one stood ready to plunge a knife into his back.

Chapter 4

Brevelan interrupted her root digging. Her inner sight tingled a warning. Someone was on the back path that sometimes led to her clearing. She faded into the shadow of a tree. Mastering the urge to run from a pursuer, she forced absolute stillness into her body and her mind. Every wild creature of the forest knew that predators saw only movement and disruptions in the patterns of light and shadow.

"Brevelan?" Maevra, the carpenter's wife, called. She was in the last weeks of her pregnancy and frequently sought Brevelan's counsel as a midwife.

"Coming." Brevelan breathed deeply once more.

With a wish and a firm image in her mind, she opened the path to the clearing.

"Oh, there you are," Maevra sighed wearily. "I forget how steep the back path is." She rubbed her protruding belly.

"You shouldn't walk so far on a steep track so close to your time, Maevra." Brelevan urged the woman onto a convenient stump. She sat heavily and awkwardly.

"I needed to walk."

Brevelan masked her concern. This woman, so near her own age, had lost three babes before they were fully formed. Under Brevelan's careful guidance, this pregnancy looked as if it might run to term.

"Why?" Brelevan asked. She rested one hand on the swell of the child, the other upon the woman's shoulder.

"Because the house was stuffy, the sun is shining, and Garvin is away for the day."

Good. It was just boredom and loneliness, not the compulsion that forecast an early labor.

Energy flowed through Brevelan's fingers, seeking the child. A personality shifted beneath the heavy folds of the woman's clothing and the taut skin of the mother's belly. A strong and steady heartbeat tingled up Brevelan's fingers. The dark comfort of the womb enveloped her. A soothing world of water and nourishment rippled against her skin.

She curled her back and ducked her head. Just before her knees bent and drew her into the same posture as the unborn, the same awareness as the babe, she clutched at her own identity and withdrew.

"Bold and restless, strong, too. I think it's a boy." She shook her hand to free it of the lingering link with the child. Her back wanted to continue to curl, so she arched it in defiance. The utter loneliness of being only one person, where a moment ago she had been two, left her dizzy.

"He's strong, but not yet ready to come out and face daylight."

"How do you know from just a touch?" Maevra looked utterly amazed.

Brevelan shrugged. "I'm a witchwoman."

"Don't let the others hear you say that." Maevra looked over her shoulder anxiously. "They may not call you that to your face, but they still make a gesture of warding." She held her right hand tightly in her left preventing herself from initiating the cross of the Stargods.

Brevelan covered Maevra's hands with her own and smiled at her patient. "Give them time. They must learn to trust." Brevelan released her hold on her patient's hands.

Maevra opened and flexed her fingers. "Soon, I hope. I need you with me when little Garvin is born."

"I will be there. I promise." Brelevan hugged Maevra reassuringly. "Come, rest in my clearing. I've baked fresh oat cakes, and I think there's still a little cider left." She guided her guest a few paces. The path opened and revealed the entrance to the clearing.

"I'll never understand why this place is always hidden, unless you show the way," Maevra laughed nervously. Her hand twitched again.

"I don't know myself," Brevelan admitted. "The clearing

was waiting for me when I came here last summer. It protects me and provides for me."

"That's good. Then the magician won't be able to surprise you."

"What magician?" Fear lumped in her throat. Had her family sent a magician to find her and take her back for judgment?

"A wandering one. He was in the pub earlier asking questions. He was disguised, but Old Thorm saw through it. I swear he sees more with that one eye than the rest of us do with two."

Old Thorm, the wandering, one-eyed drunk who was always nearby when there was trouble.

"What did Old Thorm do to the magician?" Brevelan listened to the clearing. No one came. She was safe for now.

"Oh, you know Old Thorm, filled him with dragon lore. Then he sent the young man on a wild lumbird chase. Told him to come by way of the road. He'll never find you."

"I hope you're right, Maevra. But magicians have a talent for dropping in when you least expect them." The dream image of a man approaching at sunset haunted her.

Suddenly she saw the clearing from a second set of eyes. Eyes that approached from the west, the image they saw overshadowing her own. Chill dizziness swamped her senses. Her gram used to say that kind of feeling was a hand from the grave reaching out to remind you that all in this life is temporary.

"Baamin always said I was more stubborn than smart," Jaylor mumbled to himself. "I want answers, and I intend to get them. Besides, I may never again have the chance to visit with a real Rover." The magic he'd gathered and stored as he walked quivered anxiously. He should avoid this place, these people.

He listened to the power growing inside him for a moment. The warning was stronger than ever. Jaylor moved forward anyway.

The lone figure of a tall middle-aged man, nearly as big as himself, appeared before him. Silver wings of hair at his temples made the black mane seem darker, oilier.

Jaylor caught a whiff of the man almost as soon as he

saw him. Musky sweat, days old, with just the faintest hint
of Tambootie underneath. His instinct was to recoil from
the faint scent of evil. His armor snapped into place.

He sniffed again to make sure he had caught it correctly.
Definitely Tambootie, but not unpleasant. Mixed with the
other pungent smells of bruised grass, fragrant stew, evening dew-fall, the essence took on a haunting hint of exotic
adventures rather than danger.

"Welcome, stranger." The Rover's voice boomed out
over the camp. He held his arms open in greeting.

"Have you hospitality for a lonely traveler?" Jaylor asked.
In ancient times when passage across the border was easy
and the people of Coronnan chose to travel, there were
traditions of hospitality. Jaylor presumed that Rovers still
held to those old rules.

He leaned heavily on his staff, as if he needed the stout
wood to bear much of his weight. Thus anchored to the
ground, the staff channeled his extended magic as he continued to scan the area with the extra senses available to
him. The staff vibrated and tried to twist away every time
Jaylor looked directly at the Rover.

"The camp of Zolltarn is always open to fellow travelers." The Rover's loud voice filled the stream's hollow with
camaraderie. "Come share our evening meal and rest your
weary bones on soft furs. In the morning we leave. Perhaps
we follow the same roads?"

"Perhaps." Still wary, Jaylor slung his pack to the ground
in front of him, keeping one hand on the strap. The other
clutched his staff.

A woman emerged from the tent. Tall and handsome,
with blue-black hair, she carried a basin. She wore the tent
colors, red and purple with black trim. Her skirt and petti-
coats swirled about her ankles. The colors drew Jaylor's
eyes upward to nearly bare shoulders and the sharp shadow
of cleavage. She, too, carried the musky odor of Tambootie.

Jaylor felt himself drawn forward to see more of her,
smell more of the enticing mixture. His gaze rested on the
just noticeable swell of her belly. She carried a precious
life there.

He took a step back lest his magic influence the unborn.
One of the many superstitions he'd encountered on his
journey claimed a magician could capture and command

the soul of an infant. Jaylor knew he, personally, wouldn't do such an evil thing. Who knew what the rogues of old had done? Rural memories, he discovered, were long, much longer than in the fashion-conscious capital city.

His glance shifted to Zolltarn. Somewhat old to be the father. Yet the woman was none too young either.

"My wife." Zolltarn rested his arm about her shoulders possessively. He smiled into her upturned eyes with warmth and pride.

Other members of the tribe emerged from the security of the garish tents. Each woman carried a bowl of food for the evening meal. All were dressed in wild color combinations similar to Zolltarn's wife's. Many showed the same degree of pregnancy. Jaylor reeled in the tendrils of magic that fed his senses. No point in chancing that his personality might influence the unborn.

"From where do you hail, fellow traveler?" Zolltarn led Jaylor to a stump beside the largest fire.

Caution, Jaylor warned himself. Rovers had a talent for reading thoughts. He couldn't allow this barbaric chieftain to suspect he was a magician on quest. He'd come this far without violating any of the rules of secrecy that surrounded such tests.

Except that in the last village a one-eyed derelict had called him "magician" as he left the pub.

"Here and there. Over the next hill and beyond." It was the truth in a way, just not the whole truth. Another of the rules on this endless journey.

"Your accent speaks of education. Why is it you rove when you could be usefully employed? Why is it you bring with you no trading caravan when only merchants follow the roads of Coronnan?"

"The only goods I have left are in my pack," Jaylor said truthfully.

"Your hair is ruddy brown, not black, your eyes are soft and your skin pink like that of a city dweller too long in the sun. You have not the look of a Rover." Zolltarn's eyes squinted in the smoke from the fire.

"One roves. One looks as one looks." Jaylor avoided Zolltarn's probing gaze. "Was there no magician at the border to grant or deny you entrance?" he parried Zolltarn's question with another.

Several Rover men moved closer. Jaylor felt his armor strengthen. His magic didn't trust these people.

"In this forgotten corner of Coronnan? No one bothers with a border. Not since Lord Krej inherited the province, anyway." The Rover snorted as he fingered the wicked blade in his belt. "Your question tells me you did not cross the border at this point. Perhaps you never crossed it at all."

"The people of Coronnan do not rove, as you said. Therefore, I must hail from elsewhere." Did that qualify as a lie? He was concentrating so hard on keeping Zolltarn at bay with words that he didn't care if he spoke the truth or not.

"Magicians wander on quest." Zolltarn eased his body closer to Jaylor. "Magicians whose hair almost always shows traces of red." The smell of Tambootie now dominated the camp odors. "Your aura, too, bears the colors of magic, traveler of Coronnan."

"If I were other than a weary wanderer, would I tell you?"

"No answer tells me all, magician." He laughed loud and long. The men joined him in the momentary revelry.

Jaylor stiffened his spine. He didn't see anything funny about being a magician. It was a talent he held with pride. Most of the time. As long as more adept magicians didn't ridicule him because a traditional spell failed.

He scanned the hollow nervously. The women were busy around the fires. He caught the eye of a girl just barely of marriageable age. She smiled and ducked her head flirtatiously. Her eyes continued to seek him through long lashes.

"It takes the strength of a sledge steed to become a magician." Zolltarn's mirth eased. "I imagine you need much food and wine to maintain your powers. We'll feed you well, magician."

Why did his statement seem unfinished?

"Are you going to share this handsome stranger, Papa?" The girl who had smiled at Jaylor stepped into the light of the fire. She was tall, like her mother, with a majestic carriage that showed her splendid bosom to advantage.

The men behind Jaylor moved back a half pace. Each man drew a knife from his belt and toyed with the overlong blade. Jaylor's spine tingled with expectation of a killing blow at any moment. But he couldn't concentrate on the men. The girl's presence drew his mind and emotions.

Shifting shadows enhanced her beauty. Jaylor's bones melted as his eyes traced the clean lines of cheek and nose, full mouth, snapping eyes. She had the blacker-than-black hair of her tribe, the wild-colored skirts and deeply dipping bodice of the other women. But she was younger, slimmer, more beautiful. Much more beautiful.

Suspicions faded from his mind, along with Zolltran, and the other men with their wickedly long knives.

Once again Jaylor caught the enticing smell of musk and Tambootie. He felt himself falling into the alluring spell of the girl's dark glance and blossoming womanhood.

"Ah, Maija, you find this stranger pretty?" Zolltarn laughed as he pounded Jaylor's back heartily.

Zolltarn shouldn't have been able to touch him! How had he penetrated the armor?

"Pretty enough." The girl slid onto the narrow piece of stump on the other side of Jaylor. Her bare arms brushed against him. The smoothness of her skin sent shivers to his groin. She, too, was touching him when her hand should have been repulsed. "And strong. He will breed sons with strong magic. We need strong men with stronger magic in the tribe."

This beauty presented a greater danger than any of the armed men. They could only deprive him of his life.

Stargods! She could deprive him of his magic.

Once more he scanned the scene, this time estimating his chance of escape. The men continued to ring the log where he sat.

He stood, separating himself from the girl and her hypnotic beauty. "My road is long. I cannot afford to linger with you." He stepped toward his pack and staff. When had he allowed them out of his grasp? A young Rover with broken teeth and a malicious grin stepped in front of the gear.

Maija edged closer to him. The heat of her body penetrated the worn leather of his journey clothes. He felt his neck and face grow equally warm. Her breath whispered across his nape. Desire for her masked the danger of the men and their knives.

He longed to enclose her in his arms, to fit her close

against his body. Her womanly scent, heightened by Tambootie, clouded his senses.

When did a magician know if his magic was strong enough to withstand an encounter with a woman? Was it before or after he achieved his quest?

Did he dare take the chance?

Not yet! He was too close. With a tremendous effort Jaylor pushed her away. A knife blade across his throat stopped any further movement.

"Sit, magician. You will stay the night. You will provide us with what we need," Zolltarn hissed behind him.

But it was Maija who wielded the sharp blade that tickled the sensitive skin beneath his half-grown beard.

No wonder his armor had broken down. His own lust had lowered his defenses. Reluctantly, Jaylor sat. Maija's knife disappeared, but he had no doubt she could draw it again and slit his throat faster than he could escape.

Jaylor searched for idle conversation that would engage them all until his mind cleared. Something he could concentrate on other than Maija. "You've wandered far. Have you had any trouble with dragons?"

"Dragons! The curse of us all. Do not speak of them, lest they hear you and come again." Zolltarn and Maija both made a superstitious, and useless, gesture of protection, wrists crossed and hands fluttering like wings. A gesture that was older than the cross of the Stargods. Perverted magic was the only evil. Gestures couldn't help against a rogue magician.

"Come again? You've seen them?" Jaylor pressed. This was great news. He was closer to the end of his quest than he thought. The information gained during a night in Rover company could shorten his journey considerably. He'd learn what he could from these people, but he wouldn't give them what they demanded.

"Nay. Who ever sees a dragon? They toy with us instead, sending their *s'murghin'* dragon-dreams." Zolltarn shook his head in grief. Maija pouted.

"Dragon-dreams?" Old Baamin had evaded discussion of that undefined term with great dexterity. "Of what nature are these dreams? I presume they are dangerous."

"Dangerous! Nothing less than murderous. May the

Gods who descended from the stars protect us." This time he crossed himself in the accepted manner.

Zolltarn's wife thrust bowls of stew into their hands, then gestured with her head for the girl to come away with her. "Wait until he has eaten," she whispered to her daughter.

Sad silence hovered around them. The older man stirred his dinner absently with a horn spoon. The other Rovers turned away from Jaylor and ate with grim determination. Their knives were still too lose in their sheaths for Jaylor to risk running.

Jaylor tasted his meal. The spices burned his tongue. A welcome discomfort if it kept his mind off Maija. She sat with the women, her back half turned to him. Restlessly, she shifted her position, hiking her bright skirt to her knees.

"Why are dragon-dreams so dangerous?" Jaylor spoke softly, enticing an answer from a preoccupied Zolltarn. His eyes strayed to Maija's shapely calves and ankles.

"My clan is murdered and you ask why the dreams that delude are dangerous!" Zolltarn shouted again as he leaped to his feet. The others stared. He sank back to his seat heavily. "Six men and three boys, nearly men. One night after moonset they were caught in some grand vision of bliss and just wandered off. By the time we found them, some had fallen, their bodies crumpled at the bottom of a cliff. Others were lying facedown in small creeks too shallow to be a danger to anyone. They all died with beautiful smiles on their faces. Two men we never found. I hope they died before wild beasts got to them." The man looked older, his shoulders slumped.

"When? When did this happen?" Jaylor pressed while Zolltarn was still vulnerable.

"At the solstice, just after the big storm."

No wonder so many of the women were breeding. This Rover clan desperately needed to replace the lost men and boys.

As soon as he'd eaten he'd find a way to escape. He had a knife of his own tucked into his boot. Staying the night looked more dangerous than the value of their dragon lore.

He took another bite of stew, savoring the sizzling seasoning. A drum and a string-gamba sounded on the other side of the fire. Jaylor felt the vibrations of the primitive music through the ground against his thin boots. The hot spots on his tongue thrummed an answer to the beat.

Two huge gulps finished his meal. Its fire made his eyes and ears swell and throb in tempo with the rising music. He cast around for a place to put his empty bowl while he watched the camp celebrate the first full day of spring. Perhaps when they began drinking and singing, he could slip away. The bowl vanished into willing hands, the same hands that pushed him closer to the ring of fires.

Maija stood, swaying freely to the music. Her skirts swirled about her ankles and bare feet, her hips undulated in a rhythm suggestive of a more primitive, more intimate dance. Her feet stamped out the music as she circled the camp, once, twice, a third time.

Jaylor's teeth throbbed, his blood sang with her steps. Each spin lifted her skirts higher, revealing more and more of the length of her lovely legs, drawing his eyes and imagination into the secrets of her body. Her movements grew faster with the increasing tempo of the music. She circled and spun widdershins around the fire in a parody of a planet around the sun.

All thought of magic and defense drained from Jaylor. He could only think—feel the dance. When a slender, feminine hand reached for his, he needed to extend his arm, to touch her in order to complete the pattern of sun and moon and stars. He became the music, swirling, pounding, undulating. One more note, one more beat in the rhythm of time.

Chapter 5

"**Y**ou put too much timboor in his stew, Maman!"

Jaylor heard Maija's strident complaint through the fog that numbed his tongue and made jelly of his limbs.

Timboor. The fruit of Tambootie was a dangerous drug avoided by all, even a master magician. It could calm a hysterical child, ease a racing heart, or put one to sleep—forever.

As part of his training Jaylor had had to spend a night and a day in a closed room with only a Tambootie wood fire for heat and light. It was a rite of passage as well as a test of his abilities to control his magic under the drugging effect of the smoke.

There had been only one door in that cold stone room. It, too, was stone and securely bolted from the other side.

He'd left that stone room dizzy, sick, hallucinating. In his delirium, his heart had beat irregularly for weeks afterward, while his newly awakened loins ached for release.

One obscure text in the University library claimed that in the right dosage, timboor gave a man the stamina of a wild steed in rut. Or at least enough to satisfy a small harem.

This band of Rovers must be very desperate for his seed if they'd dosed him with timboor.

As he puzzled over the implications of his predicament, Jaylor found a spell deep in his memory. If he could just lift his leaden hand to form the proper gesture with the murmured words of the traditional spell. Hair's widths at a time, he moved his hand into view. It was so heavy he needed the other hand just to lift it. But that hand was heavier still.

In the end, it was easier to roll onto his side and leave the weary hand resting on the pounded dirt beneath him.

He placed an image in his mind of his hand following the prescribed gesture.

"He's not dead," the voice of Maija's companion announced. "See, he rouses."

Jaylor froze in mid-thought.

"Rouses. Not rises." Maija spat. "He's useless!"

"Useless now, perhaps." The older woman cajoled. "Later, while he's still docile, he'll be more than ready to give you his seed, again and yet again." Her chuckle was rich with lusty possibilities. "He'll give us the child who will insure us a homeland at last. No magician's border will stop such a child. Fifteen years we've searched for a magician whose strength could overpower the Commune. Fifteen years since your sister was lost and her babe with her."

The women turned their backs on him once more.

He had a few moments, Jaylor mused. No more. He had to hurry the spell.

Smoke from the fires pierced his nostrils with unusual pungency. He could hear the pacing of one of the men outside the tent as if he were standing beside his head instead of yards away, outside this tent. If he thought about it, he could identify the man by his smell. Jaylor sorted through the odors—the rich spiciness of the stew, the dankness of wrinkled clothes, and bruised grass—to find the unique smell of the youngster with the malicious smile and broken teeth. Jaylor recalled the features of the last man to sheathe his blade after Maija had approached Jaylor. A man whose own lust for the young beauty was strong, even without timboor.

A second man joined the first, his footsteps loud on the moist grass. The passage of wind as he swatted at an insect sounded like the raging thunderstorm at the solstice that had flooded an already drenched Coronnan. His senses were magnified; why couldn't he move? He had to escape before Maija joined him on this crude pallet. If he waited much longer, his quest and his magic would end forever.

Slowly he manipulated his hand, mouthing the spell.

Feeling rushed with painful tingles back into his fingers. Each grain of dirt rasped against his sensitive palm. Concentrating on that hand, he reinforced the spell. His body responded.

He needed a focus. Something to channel the energy of his overactive mind to his limbs. His staff and pack lay nearby. Someone had moved them into the tent with his body when he blacked out. How long ago? Carefully, lest he alert the women, Jaylor reached for the staff. It was too far from the end of his fingers to grasp. He stretched as far as he could and only succeeded in pushing it farther away.

"Come here," he commanded as he strained to reach it again. The staff obeyed, appearing in his outstretched hand almost before it disappeared from its resting place.

Jaylor grabbed the instrument and tapped each foot as he whispered the proper words.

Again, control and strength returned with a painful rush. He flexed and twisted his muscles until the pricking subsided. Now if he could just sneak past the two waiting women without being seen.

He gathered his energy slowly and levered himself into a crouch. The women's conversation rose in distress. He froze in his uncomfortable position. They turned and stared at him.

"See how heavily he sleeps!" Maija wailed. "We're running out of time. We have to move again at dawn or risk discovery."

She didn't see him, saw only what she thought she should see. Or rather what Jaylor wanted her to see. How could that be? He hadn't thrown a delusion at her. He shouldn't have the energy for it. Any normal man would have been brought to the brink of death by that dose of timboor.

Cautiously, he stood. Maija continued her conversation as if nothing had changed. Jaylor summoned his pack. It thumped against his shoulder. He grabbed it with his left hand before it fell. Still the women saw nothing unusual.

He must be invisible! He looked back to the pallet. A shadowy form reclined there. In his need to escape he'd projected that shadow to delude the women.

Outside the canvas walls, pack steeds snorted, birds awoke, insect chirps faded. He smelled the dawn dampness and knew he must move quickly, before sunlight revealed his shadow and the women decided to investigate the form they thought they saw lying on the ground.

One bold step after another Jaylor paced to the tent flap. No one stopped him. He saluted the camp with his staff in relief as he silently slipped into the protection of the woods.

Large hands, callused, with splotches of dark hair on the back reached for Brevelan. They grasped her arms, cruelly. Bruises would form in the shape of his fingers. She screamed and screamed again. Desperately, she tried to wrench herself away from the hot breath of the black-haired man who held her. Each movement only tightened his grip, brought the heat of his body closer. One last scream and twist of her body. She was free!

She was awake.

Brevelan breathed deeply, trying to calm her racing heart. Cold sweat covered her face and back. She was so tangled in her blankets she couldn't break free to clear her mind and body of the nightmare. She rolled off the oversized bed onto the hard-packed earth of her own cottage deep in the woods.

The cat, Mica, lifted one round-pupiled eye in mild curiosity then settled back into a sleeping ball at the foot of the cot. The wolf by her side lifted his head. His warm tongue darted out to lick her hand.

"It's all right, Puppy. We're safe here. No one will find us and make me go back." Her pet caressed her again with his tongue. She scratched his ears and lay her head on his neck. The long winter-thick fur comforted her as his gentle warmth replaced the evil memory of her dream.

"It's almost dawn. Puppy. We might as well get up and begin working the garden." The wolf responded by leaping up, his tail wagging so hard his hind end moved.

"You're too eager." She laughed at his antics. He stood by the door, waiting to be let out.

Mica mewed in protest. Her half-open eyes showed the vertical pupils of a cat again. She settled back into the warmth of the blankets.

Brevelan reached out with her mind and checked each of her charges. The rabbits emerged one by one from their holes for early grazing; the goat still slept. The flustercock stood and strutted for his first crow of the day. Somewhere above, Shayla circled.

You were frightened.

"Only a dream." Brevelan shivered as she shed her damp shift and pulled on a clean one. Her woolen overgown added warmth. She slipped her feet into thick stockings and clogs against the dawn chill. Later, when the sun found the clearing she would discard them.

More than a dream. A memory.

"From a long time ago, almost a year. I don't need to worry about it anymore."

You will.

"Now what is that supposed to mean, Shayla?" For the first time, Brevelan allowed anger to tinge her conversation with the dragon. Just once, she wished Shayla would explain her thoughts.

You will have to face that man again.

She didn't say mate or husband, just "that man." That told Brevelan something. In Shayla's mind the black-haired man was not her husband. The law said differently.

"That man is dead. Isn't he?"

Blankness. Shayla did not deign to respond.

Darville is well?

"Of course. The wolf thrives." She wondered why Shayla doted so on the wolf. Dragons usually hunted wolves and other creatures of similar size, rather than feed them and ask after their welfare.

You must protect him. Trust the one who comes to help you.

"Shayla?"

But the dragon was gone. Where, Brevelan had no idea. Somewhere up in the mountains to her lair probably. Someday she'd go up there and find the dragon's home. Then, when Shayla couldn't fly away, she'd ask all the questions she'd stored up all winter.

Like why Shayla had summoned her into a raging snowstorm to save an injured wolf. She'd never spoken to a dragon before that awful night. Never known it was possible for anyone outside the royal family to have any contact at all with the magical creatures. But then, if the rumors back home were true, she had royal blood in her veins.

Krej, lord of the castle next to her home village, was first cousin to King Darcine. Krej had the same bright red hair as herself and many children in his villages. The hair was a lingering legacy from the lord's outland mother.

That was all in the past. She had escaped her abusive husband and her village. Now there was work to be done. Brevelan stepped forward and set about her morning chores with her usual energy. The song she sang lightened her mind as well as the weight of the work.

The work was for herself and her animals, not some duty imposed by an elder.

As she sang, her clearing filled with light and joy. This protected place was hers, and all who resided there responded to the security her songs offered them.

Just beyond where the stream crossed the road Jaylor saw the first obscure markings on the rocks at the side of the road.

YOU APPROACH THE BORDER, said the first sign.

The next mark a few feet beyond was less obvious to the eye. This one was written in ancient runes. The magic rather than the visual image leaped out at Jaylor.

THE KING'S MAGIC CAN NO LONGER PROTECT YOU.

Not exactly the king's magic. The Commune maintained the border, repelled possible invasion, and kept the overly curious inside. King Darcine had no real magic, nor had any king before him. This king had very little of anything left—health, personality, power. All he did have of value was a son. And no one in the capital had seen the prince for weeks at the time of Jaylor's departure.

He pushed beyond the sign. The air thickened and resisted his efforts. Jaylor stopped and looked back.

A faint shimmer in the air marked the spot where the last rune rested. Only magic could produce that kind of distortion. Only a magician could see it, penetrate it.

Ordinary folk couldn't pass that border. The Rovers had. The villagers must if they sought the witchwoman.

The wrongness of the situation bothered him. He should consult with Baamin, and soon. He wasn't supposed to ask for help on a quest. But it wasn't help he sought. He needed to warn the Commune. About the border and Rovers entering the kingdom. Warn them of dragons starving out villages and leading large numbers of people astray.

A few feet farther on, a path wandered off to the east and south. This must be the way to the home of the witchwoman. Kind of far out for her to serve the village. Her home would be in the foothills, possibly near the dragon's lair.

The path narrowed. Trees closed in, darkening the way. Once more he had the sense of another presence—behind him. Closer this time. A whiff of Tambootie in the air.

The Rovers? He stretched his heightened senses once more and encountered a void. Not just the absence of a presence, the absence of everything. Someone, armored, was sending Jaylor's awareness around the space he occupied.

A magician. In the pub he had encountered an old derelict who carried an image of himself as a vigorous man in his prime. A man with hair as red as Lord Krej's.

Three years before Jaylor had entered the University, Krej, the youngest son of the Lord of Faciar had been a journeyman magician. His father and brothers had been killed in a senseless hunting accident. A wild tusker had charged. Arrows went astray. Grief stricken, the new lord renounced his magic and took a bride. He had to have lost most, if not all of his magical powers on his wedding night.

The magician who followed Jaylor could not be Krej himself. Possibly a rogue hired by him, or a cousin from his mother's country? But why play with outlaw rogues when he'd been educated into the benefits, ethics, and strengths of traditional magic? Jaylor slipped off the path behind a tree. The rough bark was the same color as his dusty cloak. He merged with the tree. Even a master magician would find only a tree.

The reek of burned Tambootie preceded the nearing presence. Jaylor stilled his mind and his magic.

Just as Jaylor expected, it was the one-eyed man from the pub who emerged from around the bend in the path. Old Thorm, someone had called him. No longer drunk or derelict, he walked fully upright with hands extended before him. He sniffed the air carefully as he walked.

Rough bark scraped Jaylor's face as he pressed closer to the tree. With his mind, he sought the core of the tree, identified with it, made it part of himself.

His pursuer moved forward, still seeking by sense and by magic. He was abreast of Jaylor when he turned and faced him. Jaylor stopped breathing.

"You there, magician," One-eye hissed, "you can't hide from me. I can feel your magic."

Fear climbed Jaylor's back and brought moisture to his skin. His mind deliberately closed off the seeking words that were a spell in themselves. He thought nothing, moved nothing, was aware only of the smell of Tambootie and the essence of timboor that lingered in his mouth and groin.

The pursuer looked more closely. His head shifted right and left, above and below, seeking and sniffing.

Jaylor's sheltering tree dissolved before his eyes. His eyes locked with those of his pursuer.

"Whaour!" Some beast above him screamed.

One-eye jerked his eyes away from Jaylor, looking up in fear. His arms flew above his head in protection. Piercing turquoise shafts of glasslike light became speeding arrows aimed at his one good eye. They made contact and splintered into a thousand bright shards of brilliant color. Rainbows arced and danced on every beam of light through the tree branches.

"No! No!" One-eye backed down the path, his arms still over his head and face. "Leave me alone. Go away. Go away." He turned and ran back the way he had come. His shrieks of pain and terror marked his path. He left behind a lingering aura of evil.

Relief washed over Jaylor's entire body in waves of coolness. He looked up at the one small patch of visible sky. The blue-green color shimmered with a magic distortion. Squinting with his extended sight, he could just see the outline of a wing and a long, lashing tail.

The lilting, feminine voice came into his head unbidden. *You are safe for now. Hurry. They need you.*

Had he just seen and heard a dragon? Startled and bewildered, he grabbed a branch of his tree for support. He jumped back, amazed that the tree hadn't really dissolved. His hand came away with a clump of gray berries, dried and desiccated from the long winter, clenched in is fist.

Timboor. He'd used a Tambootie tree for shelter. Had the tree aided his magic sight or One-eye's? The reek he had sensed was Tambootie smoke, not the crisp sap he smelled now. He needed to stop and think about this. But the dragon had urged him forward. He pulled off another handful of the berries and stuffed them into his belt pouch.

Jaylor pushed on. He pondered the significance of the tree, of the man who'd followed him, and the dragon, and how they were all related to the magic that came to him with increasing ease. He hummed a strange little tune that visited him on the wind, the vibration of the music swelling in his chest and tingling through his body.

Song burst from him in joy. Nonsense words flowed through his mind as he tried to find their meaning. None came. He just sang with uplifting cheerfulness over a narrow escape, a good quest before him, a firm road to tread, and fresh air to breathe.

The song grew in him. He built a harmony to round it out. His strides lengthened, his mind cleared. This grand adventure was the best part of his training. He reaffirmed his determination to enjoy it.

The path rounded a bend to reveal a wide clearing bathed in glimmering sunlight. Near the center stood a neatly thatched cottage. Before the home stood a beautiful red-haired young woman. Her song lifted and swirled around and around her.

A robin perched on her shoulder, chirping his own version of the song, while a rabbit nibbled at her toes. Squirrels chased each other about the garden area in a joyful dance. A mouse peeped out from the thatch, its nose twitching in greeting.

Jaylor had found the witchwoman.

Chapter 6

Darville trotted into the undergrowth. Each step brought new and interesting smells to his active nose. He sorted through them with care and delight. Dominating all, was that of Brevelan, just as she dominated the existence of all the forest creatures. Underneath her human scent he detected the familiar traces of Mica, the goat, a pair of squirrels, the flustercock and his mates. Darville disregarded the odor left by anyone who shared the clearing with Brevelan. She would never forgive him if he killed any of her special friends.

He tested the air to right and left. Nothing new. He trotted farther, delighting in the spongy surface beneath his feet, the cool air on his tongue, and the sense of power in his frame.

A stream crossed the path. Exuberantly, he bounced into the chill water, rolling into an icy splash with a playful lunge. The cold couldn't penetrate his thick winter fur. His tongue lolled out in pure delight. He flexed his hind legs and bounded from the stream.

Instinctively, he shook water from his coat. The spray bounced back into his face. He wanted to share his joy in the shooting drops of water. Brevelan wasn't here. So the trees and ferns received the gift of his shaking. A little farther along Darville caught a new scent. Hare. He tasted and savored it. Just enough for a tasty meal, without any leftovers to distress Brevelan.

For a moment he wondered why the feelings of a woman should matter. They never had before. Brevelan's approval and goodwill were as essential to his being as was the dragon who flew the skies above. He'd never owed his life to a woman before. The least he could do was respect her wishes.

In the meantime he would take pleasure in the power of his body, the keenness of his senses, and the beauty of the day.

A short time later he licked the last morsel of hare from a bone just as a new sensation enveloped him.

Fear. The smell of it, taste of it, was thick in the air. It lapped at the pit of his belly.

Darville channeled all of his alerted senses into his search for the source of that mind-numbing fear. There. Into the wind, he found it. Brevelan was afraid. His muscles bunched and propelled him forward. Brevelan. He had to save her, just as she and the dragon had snatched him away from death last winter. Whatever threatened her would die. Shayla might help. But he no longer knew how to call her.

Darville raced along the path in the most direct route to the clearing, crashing through the undergrowth. His passage disturbed the homes of several creatures. He didn't care.

His breath came quick and sharp, his heart beat and beat, pumping blood to make him fast and strong. He had to protect Brevelan!

There at last was the clearing and Brevelan, his beloved.

She stood, hunted-still, staring at a man with a walking staff. Her fear beat around Darville in waves. It echoed and reverberated through his bones.

Darville could almost taste the hot blood from the man's throat as he cleared the last few strides. This man would die. Brevelan would be safe.

Instinctively, his front paws fought for traction while his hind legs bunched and coiled. Teeth bared, fur bristling, he leaped.

He hit a wall. Bounced. Fell. Pain. PAIN. Blackness.

A flying ball of fur crossed Jaylor's vision.

His arm came up, automatically, in a gesture of warding. The words of a spell rippled along his tongue.

"No!" the witchwoman screamed.

Time slowed. Jaylor could see only dripping fangs, sprouting from a gaping muzzle. Fangs meant for his throat. The wolf's body hit the height of its arc and kept coming toward him. He could see the anger, the hunger in the animal's eyes. And still it kept coming.

Jaylor looked into the golden, hate-filled eyes. He tasted the same hot blood, the same sense of urgency.

The wolf recoiled against Jaylor's armor and dropped to the ground. His huge golden body crumpled in the grass.

"No!" The witchwoman screamed again as she ran to the fallen beast. She knelt beside the wolf, hands gently probing the slack body.

"Get away. He's in pain. He'll bite anyone." Jaylor tried to pull her away from the head and lethal teeth. "He'll savage us both before he's fully conscious again."

"My Puppy would never bite me. Never."

"I don't know much about animals," he argued. Most of the last ten years he'd been isolated at the University. "But I do know wild animals can't be trusted, especially when they're in pain. Stay away from his teeth!"

She ignored him. Her hands caressed the wolf's fur and a soothing hum rose from her throat.

This beast must be very special to the woman. A companion. Or a familiar? One-eye's description came back to haunt him.

No. Women didn't have magic so they couldn't have a familiar, a focus for magic like his staff. This was probably just a pet raised by the woman from a pup. She'd called him "Puppy."

If that was the case, the wolf's health was important to her. The villagers had said, if they could be trusted to tell the truth, that he had to get past the witchwoman in order to find the dragon. Therefore, the woman's goodwill was important to Jaylor if he wanted to find out anything more about dragons.

"Let me see him. I think I just stunned him." Jaylor decided to try his few healing techniques.

"Get away. Haven't you hurt him enough?" Her despair stopped him just short of contact with the wolf's body. She probed at the front leg, which jutted at an awkward angle. The hum at the back of her throat intensified as she kneaded the thick fur.

Witchwomen had all kinds of tricks to make people believe they had magic. None of them really worked. His own mental probe revealed the source of pain.

"I can help him. Get around behind and hold his head. He might not bite you, but he will bite me," he grumbled. She didn't move. "Trust me, please. I know what I'm doing."

His eyes locked with hers. He looked away first.

"Do you?" Her tone froze any good feelings he'd been having. This woman was beautiful. She had an aura that invited confidence. But Jaylor wasn't tempted, not anymore. He'd seen her anger and despair when the wolf dropped to the ground.

"Do you have the brute strength to reset a dislocated shoulder?" He stepped back to allow her the distance she had deliberately set between them. "Your herbal potions and false chants won't do him any good. Magic won't help either. Not even the University healers can set bones that way."

She glared at him as if deeply insulted. Then, mutely, she dipped her face deep into the animal's fur, dangerously close to the mouth and huge teeth. Teeth that had so recently been aimed at Jaylor's throat. He pushed down his instinctive fear.

"You're a magician," she said flatly. "I should have known. The dreams were so detailed, I should have understood."

Stargods! What the *s'murghin* Tambootie did that mean?

Silently, the girl shifted behind her pet. Her small hands gathered the wolf's head onto her lap. The low hum came again.

Jaylor felt the soothing effect of her music. He was calm as he knelt beside the animal.

He shouldn't be. A wild wolf was unpredictable even in the best of spirits.

He rested his right hand gently on the wolf's injured shoulder. His mind sought the source of the damage.

When his fingers tingled, he knew he'd found the proper place. He applied pressure while his strong left hand encircled the paw.

Golden eyes opened and looked up into his own, with perfect trust and understanding.

Something in those eyes was familiar. They spoke to Jaylor in sentiments he was too nervous to understand.

"Careful now. He's awake and this is going to hurt." He pulled on the paw slightly, testing the wolf's reaction.

Nothing. The animal just continued to stare, patient and controlled. More controlled than Jaylor felt under the influence of that golden stare.

Jaylor swallowed, clamped his teeth shut, and pulled. He felt the strain across his shoulders first, then his chest. Breathe. Must remember to breathe. He pulled harder. His other hand pushed with greater intensity. Sweat dampened his shirt and trickled down his nose.

"Move!" Jaylor grunted. He was tempted to stop and rest. He didn't dare. The wolf was awake. Pain glazed the yellow eyes. If Jaylor relaxed, the animal would attack. Fear increased the pressure he applied to the joint.

"Move!" He grunted again. This time he visualized the bone sliding into place again, much as he had seen the cup fill with wine in the University cellars. With his thoughts came the sound of grating, like a rasp on stone. The ground beneath him seemed to vibrate with the force of his efforts and the rhythm of the girl's tune.

The joint snapped into place.

Jaylor sagged in relief. But he didn't let go of either the paw or the joint. He had to see the joint with his mind to make sure it was reset properly. He'd do it in a moment, when his shoulders and arms ceased quivering from the strain he'd put on them.

"You did it!" Awe tinged the girl's voice. Her fingers reached underneath his and dug into the thick fur. A different tune filled the clearing. "He'll need a bandage for a few days to make sure it doesn't slip out again."

Jaylor nodded, too spent to speak just yet. He wasn't sure how he knew, but he knew the woman spoke the truth.

He closed his eyes as he sank back onto his heels, his body and mind drained of energy. He'd used his magic once too often these last few days. Even with the nap yesterday and the drugged sleep last night, he could barely move his chest to breathe. His fingers reached for the timboor tucked into his pouch. He wasn't aware of the gray berry until it was halfway to his mouth.

Disgusted with himself, he shoved the magic fruit back

into the darkness of the leather pouch. He wouldn't use the drugging effect of timboor to rebuild his store of magic. Nor would he allow himself the luxury of artificial strength.

"I need to get him inside, near the fire." The woman's soft words penetrated Jaylor's tired mind.

Inside! The wolf probably weighed more than she did. *Stargods!* How was she supposed to get him inside? He'd have to help. It was only a few steps, though it looked a league across the clearing.

Wearily, he opened his eyes again. "I'll help you." His voice came out as a croak. A little ale, or even water would sure help him right now. He hadn't performed that much magic. This aching fatigue could be a kind of hangover from the timboor. He firmed his resolve to avoid the berries even as he felt his fingers inching toward the pouch.

"No. You rest. I've done this before." She smiled. The sun shone with her happiness. He closed his eyes against the glare and laid his head next to the panting chest of the wolf.

"Stupid." he told himself. "This beast is still in pain and could lash out." His gaze lingered on the yellow eyes. Wolf and man continued to stare at each other, measuring and evaluating strengths and weaknesses.

The girl returned in just a moment with a blanket. Gingerly, while Jaylor cradled the injury, they rolled the beast onto the blanket. She rested briefly before dragging her burden inside.

For the first time, Jaylor looked at her. Really looked at her. Her eyes were clear and sparkling blue, like the Great Bay in sunshine. Her skin was dusted with healthy freckles, already kissed by the sun at the equinox. A thick braid of University red hair hung down her back to below her waist.

It was rare to see hair that red outside the University. Rarer still on a woman. Not all magicians had true red hair, like hers. Jaylor's light brown locks only took on red lights in high summer when he spent most of his study hours outside. But it was more common to find red hair on a talented person than not.

Women had no talent, so they rarely if ever had red hair. He shuffled his numb body after her as she dragged the wolf toward the hut. "What is your name?" he finally asked. He didn't want to think of her as "The Witchwoman."

She was young for a witchwoman. Usually they were old and ugly, forgotten widows.

"Brevelan." The name floated over his tired consciousness like a soothing blanket.

"You are as beautiful as your name." Brevelan. Cool, calm meadows laced by quiet stream, sunshine and blue skies filled with rainbows. He reached for her hand and gathered it close against his chest. "I'm Jaylor." Peace. Sleep.

Brevelan placed a fresh bowl of water beside Puppy's sleeping body. She didn't want him moving any farther than necessary when he awoke. He would be thirsty from the herbs she had given him to ease the pain.

Jaylor, the magician, slept beside Puppy, next to the central hearth.

He could get to his own water when he awoke.

"Mrroww!" complained Mica. Jaylor slept in her place. Her back arched as she climbed onto his wide chest and settled in for a bath. Her multicolored fur already shone with cleanliness. Brevelan knew this was just a cat's way of testing a new sleeping place.

Cats had a way of probing a person's integrity. Mica seemed to trust this stranger. Brevelan wondered if she should. She didn't trust easily. If this man were indeed sent by her home village, she'd have to run again. But where? He stirred and mumbled something in his sleep. Mica braced herself against the movement then settled down as his big hand rubbed her soft fur.

Such strong hands. Strong enough to fix a wolf's dislocated shoulder as well as throw some nasty magic. His whole body looked as big and strong as his hands. Magicians had to be strong or they didn't last long at that University of theirs.

He wasn't bad looking either. Straight, clean lines to his nose and eyes. Beneath his untrimmed beard, his cheeks looked a little drawn, as if he hadn't been eating or sleeping properly. And that filthy, bedraggled hair and beard. Dusty brown now, but once washed and combed she was sure it would lighten up to a full head of auburn curls.

Some forgotten need in her wanted to smooth those unruly curls off his brow, feel the soft texture of his hair, ease some of the worry lines around his eyes.

"Forget it, Brevelan," she admonished herself. "He's a man. You won't get any tenderness or understanding out of the likes of him. So why try giving any?"

Would he never wake up? It was full dark, there was a thick soup of yampion root and beans ready for the eating. She was sure he'd need feeding when he finally did wake. Then she could ask him to go. Or sleep outside. Her own sleep would be much easier with him away from her bed. A bed that was more than wide enough for two.

"Well, Wolf, your mistress says there is a bathing pool upstream from here." Jaylor found himself addressing the pet in the same tone Brevelan used. He wondered if the girl had been alone so long she spoke to the animals just to hear her own voice.

The wolf turned his head to the right and whined. Jaylor followed his lead. Sure enough, they paced along a well-worn path beside the chuckling creek. Just beyond a slight curve in the path a fallen log and some well-placed stones created a small dam. Behind the blockage, the creek widened and deepened into a clear pool.

Jaylor tested the water with his hand. Still cool, but the frigid snow melt was warmed by an underground hot spring. He could shed his worn and dusty clothes for a real bath.

The wolf was not so cautious. He sprang from a low crouch directly into the center of the pool. For a moment his golden fur was lost in the splash of arching waves. Shimmering crystal drops caught the sunlight in a wonderful dance then fell back into their bed. The wolf opened his mouth in a grin. He whined again in a plea for company.

"I'm coming, Puppy," Jaylor answered the animal's plea. Right now the wolf appeared immature enough to deserve the name. Most of the time he was just "Wolf."

Quickly, Jaylor shed his tunic and trews, boots and loincloth. He dabbed his big toe in the cool water. He withdrew the cold toe then sank his entire foot into the pool.

Wolf whined again and paddled toward him. When he was knee-deep in the water he stopped and cocked his head toward Jaylor in question. Without waiting for an answer the wolf shook his fur clear of the drops that clung to the long guard hairs.

Jaylor couldn't retreat fast enough. Cold water sprayed over his naked body. Lumbird bumps rose on his arms and legs and the cold penetrated to his bones. Wolf looked as if he were ready to shake again. "At this rate, I might as well dive in." He resigned himself to the cold plunge.

The center of the pool was deep and clear, warmer than the shallows. The hot springs must concentrate here. He swam a few strokes before standing. He found he could just rest his toes in the mud and have his head break the surface of the water. But he had to keep his hands moving to maintain his balance. Air filled his lungs and he, too, shook his hair and beard free of excess water.

"You remind me of my misspent youth, Wolf." The beast was paddling around him in wide circles. 'My friends and I used to splash each other a lot on stolen afternoons along the river." That was the summer when Jaylor had been twelve and his companions ranged from eleven to fourteen. "There were four of us who used to slip away from our studies for afternoons of adventure. We had nothing in common except the urge to escape."

The many isolated islands in the delta of Coronnan River offered the perfect playground for adolescent boys.

"All four of us schemed together, but Roy and I usually ended up paired."

It had been a surprise to Jaylor, who had grown up along another smaller river in the north, to find any resident of Coronnan City who had never learned to swim. He thought all the population of a city totally surrounded by water and many lesser islets would have learned to master swimming early.

Roy had been so surrounded by adults—tutors, servants, guardians—he'd never been allowed to play in the water and thus had never learned.

Jaylor taught him to swim that summer and earned many a dunking in the years that followed.

"I met him in much the same manner I met you, too, Wolf," he mused as he began to swim. His muscles stretched with a new lightness as the water cleansed his skin and his mind.

"We both claimed the same island for an afternoon of

freedom," he continued his reminiscence. "He arrived by boat; I swam ashore about the same time. We challenged each other. I didn't know enough magic then to defend myself." He chuckled as he slowly made his way back to the bank and his clothes.

"That time I lost. But the next fist fight I won."

Wolf bounced out of the pool and sprayed everything around with water again. Jaylor didn't even bother to step away from the shower.

"Shall we explore the paths, my friend?" The beast grinned and cocked his head in a gesture so evocative of Roy that Jaylor had to look twice to make sure a human intelligence did not lurk behind those golden eyes.

Jaylor dressed hurriedly. Now that he was out of the water, the air was rapidly chilling his damp body. He needed to keep moving to get warm again.

Wolf took a few steps back the way they had come. Jaylor started in the other direction. The wolf spun in place and bounded after him.

The path was not well traveled past the pool. Jaylor had to push giant calubra ferns out of the way. Each time he touched one, the fronds shook and gave out the faintest wisp of fragrance. By summer the scent would be druggingly powerful, a legendary aphrodisiac.

Wolf bent his nose to the faint trail. It was now no wider than a hand's breadth. No human foot had trod this way in many days. Jaylor watched the animal as he sniffed and played with the scents in the air and on the ground. With a sharp yip he bounded off the trail.

Curious, Jaylor also stepped off the trail in the same direction. He met an invisible wall. His hands pushed at the barrier. Inside him, the magic he had gathered strove to counteract the magic that tried to flow through his limbs from the outside. He stepped back onto the path. His magic stopped fighting the exterior forces.

The border should have been like this. Jaylor squinted his eyes, allowing his magic to see what hindered his movements. There! A shimmery distortion, like looking at the bottom of the pool through several arm's lengths of water. He pushed at it again, allowing the magic forces within him to meet the wall.

Nothing happened. He pushed again, using more strength

and speaking the border release spell. His hand burned and pulsed, but the wall still did not give way.

He moved along the path a few more steps and tried again. If anything, the wall was stronger here.

Every few feet he pushed again, and again, until his hand was raw from the energy he'd expended.

"One more time. Then I'll circle back to the clearing again." He was getting tired. He needed rest and food to restore the magic in his body.

And not those meatless concoctions Brevelan served.

Using his eyes as well as both hands, Jaylor levered himself against the wall. It absorbed his strength then rebounded, pushing him back and back and farther back. He crashed through the underbrush, tumbling heels over head with the force of the thrust.

Brevelan stood next to his prone body.

"Did you have a nice bath?" she asked.

He was back in the clearing.

Chapter 7

"**D**ragon dung!" Baamin cursed. This was the third time a very simple spell had failed. He held his viewing glass to the light. There were no cracks, no flaws. Its smooth surface was perfect.

So why couldn't he make contact with any other magician? Several were waiting for his summons. They should be on the alert to answer through their own glasses.

He took a deep breath. In, three counts. Hold, three. Release, three. His mind was drawn out of his body and hovered just below the beckoning void of a deep magic trance. Magic flowed through him with velvet ease. Colors wavered and swirled in the glass.

At last!

He heard laughter, coarse and mocking. Alert to the spell going awry again, Baamin pushed the image closer to completion. Instead of the gaunt, lined face of the man he expected, a shaggy-headed monster with the body of a man looked back at him and sneered.

"With my head, and my heart, and the strength of my shoulders, I renounce this evil," Baamin recited the formula of the Stargods as he crossed himself. For good measure he completed the warding with the winged gesture of Simurgh.

"You didn't think I could do it, did you, Baamin?" The words floated about the room, followed by the image of Baamin's oldest enemy stepping out of the glass.

Baamin jerked back, throwing his armor in place as he sought answers to this abomination. This was the kind of prank he would expect of Jaylor. But how could a young man conjure up this manifestation of the red-haired beast/

man Baamin had fought during his trial with the Tambootie smoke? That nightmare existed only in the shadow world of Baamin's tortured dreams.

Eavesdropping on another's dreams was forbidden. To make doubly sure no one learned of his nightmares, Baamin had personally destroyed all records of his testing, all references to the beast, when he assumed leadership of the Commune.

His gnarled staff came to hand readily. He poked the vision, making certain the staff was as armored as he. Hard flesh and bone met the probe. The beast hadn't even bothered to cover his well-muscled body with clothing, other than a barely adequate loincloth. In Baamin's dreams, his nemesis had the decency to wear the same robes as Baamin did.

"Yes, Baamin, old friend. I'm real and I've come out of your dreams to haunt you." The mouth of the image worked but the words came from some other, indefinable direction. "I'm putting an end to the Commune." This time the image threw back his head and laughed long and loud. The gesture was familiar, belonging to a different man. Baamin was too befuddled by the presence of this monster to remember who.

"Every time you and your toadies throw the smallest spell, I'll be there to twist it round backward, sideways, or split it into good and evil twins. Dragon magic is finished, Old Baamin."

A knock on the door banished the image but not the voice. "Another time, Baamin. We'll finish this when I choose, and you'll not know ahead of time." The rolling laughter bounced around and around the room in decreasing spirals of sound until the glass absorbed it.

Rational thought deserted Baamin as he sat, stunned by the perversion. Had another magician read his dreams? Or had he gone insane and conjured up the beast again? The Commune had fought the monster back into another dimension after Baamin's adolescent testing with the Tambootie smoke had made him real.

Jaylor was the only other magician whose hallucinations had taken on three dimensions. But the red-haired beast had remained dormant at that time.

A second knock roused the senior magician from his stupor. He shook himself to mask the trembling that began deep inside him and radiated out to his hands and neck and knees. He couldn't allow anyone to suspect his own nightmares were interfering with his magic. Not yet, not until he had assured his supremacy over the Council as well as the Commune and University when Darcine passed on.

"Come," he called to the supplicant at his door. His voice broke. He was just tired. Perhaps he'd dreamed the beast/man. No magician in Coronnan could break apart one of Master Baamin's spells.

The door opened a crack. He could see one brown eye peering at him.

"Be you busy, master?" The voice was shy, hesitant about bothering a master magician.

"Not anymore. You disturbed my spell." Baamin growled. He reached for his flask and swallowed the last of the sugar water. Then he popped a mint into his mouth to hide the lack of alcohol smell. *Stargods,* he'd give a year of his life for a hearty swig of beta'arack, distilled from the monster treacle betas grown only in Rossemeyer. But he couldn't afford to befuddle any of his senses right now.

One of the kitchen boys crept into the room, wide-eyed and fearful. About ten or eleven years ago, the orphan, known only as "Boy," had been sent to the University from the poorhouse, one of many foundlings indentured each year. Boy was so late in developing that he couldn't be tested for magical talent. He was unusually slow at his lessons and undersized, but he worked hard and was willing to please, almost to a fault. He had his uses, especially when Baamin needed errands completed in secret.

"I needs to talk to someone, sir. Somethin' strange has been happening." An understatement to say the least.

Baamin sighed. The boy was proud of the trust Baamin seemingly had in him—trust only because the boy was too stupid to disobey. Now Boy came to the master with his troubles and triumphs, chattering freely when no one else in the University dared approach. It was Baamin's own fault.

"What sort of strange things? In the kitchen?" Probably the only normal portion of the University. Apprentice magicians were encouraged to experiment with fledgling powers anywhere but the kitchen. Cooking fires and carving knives were too dangerous for practice.

"Yes, sir. In the kitchen." The boy's eyes widened, deep dark eyes whose innocence wormed into Baamin's cynical heart.

Baamin nodded encouragement. This might be something he needed to know about. Boy had his uses.

"I'm used to the apprentices snitching deserts and such. 'Specially the brandied fruit when they can't get to the wine. Some even try the cooking wine."

Baamin allowed himself a small laugh. Apprentices only tried that trick once. Cooking wine was salted for a very good reason.

The boy grinned back. For a moment, with that lopsided smile, he almost looked intelligent.

"Happens all the time. Sweets mostly. This mornin', though, it was more than strange. Someone was magically carving big hunks of meat off the spit, while it was still cooking."

"Growing boys have big appetites. There have never been restrictions on how much they eat. Magic takes a lot out of a body. Probably some journeyman just finishing an experiment." But not many journeymen were left. All but the very newest were out on quest.

"That I know, sir. And I wouldn't question it, 'cept when the plate was full it disappeared, just like that." He snapped his fingers. His eyes looked straight into Baamin's once more, begging for belief.

"It what?" Baamin sat up straight. "Has someone learned Jaylor's trick?" Jaylor's talent hovered too close to rogue manipulation of the elements. If another student was developing this strange talent, Baamin needed to investigate and corral him.

With the decrease in the dragon nimbus, there wasn't as much magic in the air. Magicians trained in gathering magic could easily find rogue sources. The practice must be stopped until Baamin, the senior magician, had learned to direct and control those powers.

"That's what I thought, sir. Until the plate was returned to the scullery for washing. Only Jaylor does that. And he ain't here, hasn't been for moons."

And shouldn't be anywhere within magic range of the University either. *S'murgh* it, Baamin knew he shouldn't have allowed Jaylor out of his sight.

Baamin stared at his viewing glass. It was a big, master's glass, nearly as large as his hand. He could read the most obscure texts with it. Or contact someone anywhere in the kingdom when he was awake and alert. Jaylor's smaller glass couldn't provide enough power for a summons, let alone to transport food, unless. . . .

"There's somethin' else, sir." The boy peered at him from under his forelock. "Several days ago a wine cup showed up in the scullery while I was washing up after dinner. Didn't hardly notice it. Guess I just forgot who was here and who was out. Then a few minutes later one of your washbasins shows up. It had to be Jaylor. No one else cares how much work they make for me. They just leave cups and dishes all over. In their rooms, the library, class-rooms. Even in the stable, sir."

Warmed up, the boy might rattle on forever. Baamin had heard enough.

"I'm glad you came to me, Boy. I think one of the apprentices may have learned something from Jaylor and just taken his time perfecting it."

Baamin stared at his glass again. He dismissed the garrulous child quickly.

"More likely Jaylor knows more than you'll admit," Boy grumbled as he closed the door.

That was a possibility. And if Jaylor was transporting food and wine to some remote corner of the kingdom, was it because he was in trouble? Not if he was taking time to bathe.

What did it all mean? Those feats required more strength than Baamin had used in years.

"Tonight when the moon is full and can mask my spell, I'll call him." Baamin picked up the glass, fingering its lovely clearness. Its natural coolness calmed him "I've got to know what is happening out there. I'm not supposed to help on quest. Summoning isn't help. I'll just be monitoring his progress."

Meat! Brevelan could smell it. The contents of her stomach protested the odors. Her instincts for cleanliness forced her to hold it all back. She stumbled to the doorway. Where did that awful smell come from?

All the villagers knew she would not tolerate meat. They were wary enough of her not to violate this one rule of hers. Who would dare bring meat, cooked meat, to her clearing?

Darville emerged from the ferny undergrowth licking his chops with obvious relish. His golden fur glowed in the afternoon light.

Brevelan understood that the animal needed meat. It was part of his nature. But he couldn't cook it. Didn't need to.

Then her eyes caught sight of the broad back of the man. The magician. He was wiping his face with his sleeve.

"We don't need to tell her about the roast, Wolf. What she doesn't know won't hurt her. But a man needs a man's meal. All that mush and roots just can't fill an empty belly."

"They would fill your belly amply if you'd let them," Brevelan called to him across the clearing. "And what makes you think I wouldn't know about it? I feel the lives of every creature within the clearing, including yours." Sometimes. Many times she couldn't sense his presence, his emotions, nothing.

That man! He'd been here days and days, sleeping mostly, and eating up more of her supplies than she could consume in a moon or more. He claimed he needed shelter while he recouped his strength and power. In all that time she hadn't rested easily.

How could she, knowing he was so dangerously close? Most nights she lay awake waiting, wondering when he would demand what all men demanded.

When the darkness was so still she could hear her own heart beating, her bed yawned huge and empty. Lonely. She wasn't certain then that she really wanted to resist him.

She banished the image of the magician's long body stretched out, spilling over the ends of the double cot with his arm draped around her own slight form.

Puppy limped over to her side. He sat, as he always sat, leaning against her leg in affection, easing his weight off his injured leg. He looked up at her in a mute plea for attention. Her hand found his ears, scratched and tugged, automatically. He grasped her wrist in his teeth, then freed her hand so she could resume scratching.

"Your wolf needed food. I fed him. We didn't kill it either. It was already dead and cooked in the University kitchens," Jaylor defended himself. His stance was proud, unrepentant.

"A wolf might need meat. But you didn't have to indulge."

"No more work providing for two than one. That's one less meal you have to feed me from your stores."

"You could work at rebuilding my supply instead of sleeping so much."

"Now that I've had a decent meal, I might not need to sleep so much." He made to move into the cottage.

Brevelan blocked his way. "When you've cleaned the reek of dead flesh from your body and clothes, you can start turning the earth in my garden."

"Reek of dead flesh?" He stopped and looked at her as if he didn't comprehend her orders.

"Yes. Your body stinks of the meat. It will for a day or more. Perhaps it would be best if you made your bed outside." That way she wouldn't dream of him sharing hers. "The weather will be fair for a while."

"It's still glass cold at night."

"You've slept out when it was deep bay cold, as well as wet. You admitted as much just the other day."

"Yes, but then my body was strong, full of meat, not depleted by magic and a diet of gruel. I could tolerate the cold better then." He changed his expression to one of pleading innocence. His eyes opened wide. Their brown depths pulled at her heart.

Her resolve weakened.

He had recovered from his magic ordeal. He'd want more of her now, she reminded herself.

"Your body is full of meat. Your strength has been restored. You will sleep outside. And work for your keep." She finally broke eye contact. "Or perhaps it's time for you to leave. The way you came."

And how was that? No one but herself could enter or leave the clearing unless she opened the path. "I have no more hospitality for an uninvited guest."

"Uninvited?" His eyebrows rose in honest question. "If you didn't want me here, why did you open the path with your song? Why did you keep it closed when I sought to explore?"

"I didn't!" she gasped. "I was singing to keep the clearing inviolate."

"You sang, I harmonized, the path opened."

Aghast at the implication, she turned away from his probing eyes. "Gather your things and be gone."

"When the time is right."

"The time is always right for honesty. You seek the dragon. Then why do you stay here? I suspect you have no quest but me. Did someone in the village dare you, or bribe you, to seduce me?"

"Has any man from the village menaced you?" He sounded angry. At her or the villagers?

He was close now. Too close. She could feel the warmth of his body reach out to surround her.

With the warmth came the smell of meat. She backed away. "I refuse to be owned by any man." Her husband had tried. He died on their wedding night.

"You have no need to fear me, Brevelan," he whispered warmly. His eyes turned cold and blank. She couldn't read any of his emotions.

"All men are alike," she accused. Her husband had needed to inflict pain in order to feel lust. The men who had crowded outside their door on the wedding night seemed to think the two went together as well.

"I'm different. I'm a journeyman magician. Women are forbidden to me." He looked hurt.

"That means nothing. You are still a man."

"My powers mean everything to me. I'll not risk them by taking a woman before I have my master's cloak." He raked a hand through his hair, a gesture she was coming to know. "I'm just beginning to understand the nature of my power, Brevelan. It's stronger than I ever imagined. But I'll never have enough magic to heal the hurt that is deep inside you. Only a man can do that. I can't be fully a man until I finish my quest."

He stooped through the doorway and gathered his blanket and pack. He held them to his chest almost as a talisman. "Until your hurt is banished or I can cure it, I'll make my bed outside."

"Good," she replied. When he was gone, she grabbed the broom made of stiff straw. Furiously, she swept his bedding of soft grasses off the packed dirt near the hearth. Soon, no trace of his presence remained.

Brevelan looked about her snug home in relief. Once more it was fully hers. Once more it was empty.

"Puppy," she called. Her pet was across the clearing, watching Jaylor set up his camp. The single room seemed to grow bigger, emptier, lonelier. She needed the comfort of her familiar companion.

The wolf looked toward her, then back toward the man, in indecision.

"Come, Puppy," she coaxed. She had to make the man realize he could not steal the affection of her pet.

Slowly the wolf rose to his four feet. He looked at Jaylor with interest, then made his way back to Brevelan. He seemed to be telling her the man was his friend, but his loyalty would always lie with her.

Women! Jaylor was mighty grateful there were none to contend with at the University. It was bad enough the king's court and capital abounded with women. Women with their beautiful bodies and seductive laughs. Because those women were forbidden, he was always tempted. Brevelan was more than a mere temptation. Could her University red hair be a sign of some subtle magic that made her irresistible?

How was he to fulfill his quest when all he could think about was Brevelan? He'd watched her for over a week as she went about her daily routine. The gentle songs she sang, the sight of her tightly controlled braid of unusual hair, even the way she spoke to each of her animal friends as if they could understand her, captured his imagination.

Good thing she'd kicked him out of the hut. Another night of sleeping so close to her might have been the end of his control. And her cot was not a small bed meant for solitary slumber. It was wide, more than wide enough for two. If he followed his natural instinct to love this woman, his quest and his powers would be terminated. Had the Commune of Magicians planted her to test him?

He had to leave this place, get away from the allure of the woman. And soon. Once he completed his quest, he could bed every attractive woman in the kingdom with no ill consequences, red hair or not. But in order to achieve that end, he had to get Brevelan to lead him to the dragon.

He'd been trying for days to find a path, any path that would lead him up the mountain. So far every path led straight back to Brevelan's clearing and nowhere else. He couldn't even get back to the village!

The still-limping wolf followed him everywhere, unless Brevelan called him. Jaylor had hoped the beast would lead him on one of his many hunts. Wolf came and went through the invisible barrier without notice or ill effect. He just lunged forward and was off on a chase. When he returned he grinned in that jaunty way of his, as if laughing at Jaylor's inability to follow.

Jaylor laughed in memory of some of the wolf's antics in the bathing pool or chasing down a scent. His enjoyment of life was very reminiscent of Roy's. They had fallen into an easy companionship, too, just as Jaylor had done with the young scion of royalty during their boyhood. The wolf's presence reminded Jaylor sharply of how distant he and Roy had grown in the last two years.

Most of Jaylor's teenage energy went into defying the strictures of the University rather than pursuing old friendships outside the institution of learning. Since Baamin wouldn't promote him, Jaylor had determined to make the old man's life miserable. Roy had his own problems with family, tutors, guardians, and growing responsibilities.

Mica cautiously stepped onto his blanket. Her tiny paws kneaded the texture of the fabric. She looked up with round hazel eyes. "Mrrrow." She was asking him to sit so she could sleep in his lap.

"Not soft enough for you, Mica?" He scratched the cat's silky ears. He was used to the changing shape of her eyes. "These soft ferns are a better mattress than some beds I've made in the last two moons."

"Mrrow." The cat purred in almost verbal agreement. If any of the creatures in the clearing were sentient, Mica was.

"But my cot back at the University would be better than this."

The cat blinked. Her eyes changed shape again.

"Why don't I bring the cot here?" He could almost swear the cat had asked him that question. Brevelan seemed to understand all of her pets, as if she had thrown a spell to grant the beasts communication. So why couldn't he understand them, too?

Why couldn't he? Bring the cot, that is. He'd transported wine and wash water. Just today he'd brought a wonderful meal from the University kitchens. Why not his cot?

No, not *his* cot. Before leaving, he'd armored his room in such a way that it might be dangerous to tamper with from this distance. But the storeroom was full of cots, folded in the corner.

He rearranged the magic deep within him so that it looked like the overstuffed storeroom. With his mind he plucked a cot out of the magic. Then he reformed the image here in the clearing.

"MrrOW!" Mica protested and tried to climb his leg. Jaylor opened his eyes, startled at the cat's frantic actions. There before him lay a cot, unfolded and ready for his blanket.

"Silly cat. You asked for a softer bed." He set her down so he could spread his blanket. "While we're at it, Mica, why not another blanket, and a pillow? We might as well be comfortable." He chuckled as the two items appeared.

"Mrrrrrew," Mica agreed as she circled, testing the bed, then settled in for a nap.

A cool breeze broke into the clearing, ruffling Mica's colorful fur and raising the hair on Jaylor's arms. "It might rain tonight. If we're going to stay dry, I'll need to build a cover."

Mica opened one cat-eye. She had no more ideas and just wanted to be left alone.

"Magic or brute strength?" No reply from the cat.

"Brute strength. It takes less energy than magic." He scanned the few dead limbs in the immediate vicinity. "Or does it?" The meat and the bed had been easy, barely taxing his powers at all now that he was rested and well fed—and the aftereffects of the timboor had drained out of him. He hadn't worked any magic in several days, so his store of power was full. How much harder would it be to gather some branches for a lean-to?

Jaylor closed his eyes and folded some magic into a rude

shelter around three sides and over his bed. Nothing happened.

The spell needed more power. He lifted the cat long enough to slide under her and relax. Once more he formed the magic with an image of branches woven together around him. When he opened his eyes again, disappointment flooded him.

A soft chuckle brought his attention to the hut. Brevelan stood in the doorway. Her knowing smile mocked him. "I said you'd need to work for your keep. Letting your magic do it all isn't work."

Chapter 8

"**W**hat did you do to me?" Jaylor's voice quavered. "I did nothing." Brevelan backed away from him. His huge body stalked her across the clearing.

"If you did nothing, then where is my magic?" His hand reached toward her to stay her backward movement.

"It is still there." She eluded his grasp. The haven of her hut beckoned.

"No, it isn't. I tried a simple thing—twice. Nothing happened." There was panic in his eyes. "No wonder there are no women at the University. All I did was dream of you. I never saw or touched your body outside my imagination. And still you have robbed me of my powers." His hands shook. He placed them in his pockets to still the jittering.

"This clearing is mine." The ground beneath her feet tingled in response to her words.

"Yours? How? No woman owns anything."

"No. They are owned. But this place is mine. I control it. Everything in it obeys me." Except for the time when Jaylor had broken the magic barriers and found her.

Had she really invited him by singing a song to which he could harmonize?

"Not me. I obey only the guide within me that forms my magic. I don't even obey my master all the time. So how can I . . . Why am I . . . ?" His voice rose. He swallowed deeply. "Don't you understand I am nothing without my magic?"

"I understand that you are a man who would bend me to your will, rob me of myself."

"You robbed me of my magic. I see that as a fair trade." His hands darted from the protective pockets to capture her face. "If I can no longer work magic, there is nothing to keep me away from you."

Caught by the strength of his hands she could only stare into his eyes. There was anger there, bewilderment, even a little fear. He was as frightened as she!

A measure of control returned to Brevelan. He was as frightened as she!

"I've kissed girls before. At the king's court. I've kissed them senseless." His lips caught hers in a light teasing caress.

The sensation was pleasant, undemanding. A niggle of an emotion she couldn't describe fluttered in her stomach.

"Women sought me out. Experienced women, who liked the idea of a tall young man with the strength of a sledge steed for their lover." This time his lips held hers a little longer, enticing her with their gentleness.

The cold lump of pain deep inside her melted a little to be replaced with warmth.

Any semblance of control she had in his presence vanished.

"Please. . . ."

"Please what? Please do, or please don't?" His thumbs caressed her cheekbones.

His touch was light, tender, almost as if he cared for her. But he couldn't care for her if he had kissed so many other women.

"I always stopped at kisses before." He molded his lips to hers, seeking a response.

She felt her mouth soften. A quiver began at the base of her spine, a sensation so new, so lovely she didn't know if she liked it or feared it. "Why should I stop with just a kiss now?" He nuzzled her neck.

"Because your magic is intact." Even the weight of her pet wolf leaning against her in adoration could not match the fullness she felt at Jaylor's touch. She'd never known such tenderness, such wonderfulness.

"Why should I believe you? The spell didn't work."

"I did nothing to your magic."

"Then why didn't the spell work?" He withdrew enough to look at her while his hands continued to hold her face gently. She could escape if she wanted to.

If she wanted to.

"The clearing is mine. I don't know why. But when I first came here last summer, it called to me, sheltered me, obeyed me and no one else until you came. You are the only one who has found me against my will." She tried to explain the special attachment she had for this small home.

"Even the deadwood I would use to build a shelter obeys you? And what about the paths into the mountains? They all lead back here, nowhere else. That is magic, and women have no talent." His hands dropped as if burned by her skin. He began pacing, his hands combing his beard and untamed hair.

"Women are too worn out with bearing and raising men's brats to have any strength left over for magic. What talent I have has not been impaired by a man's interference."

Jaylor's mouth moved, but no words came forth. She could see in his eyes that her words troubled him.

"Interference. Strength. Yes. Yes, that is why magicians must avoid women until their powers are full and settled. Women drain their strength. Just as wifely duties drain a woman."

She waited while that idea sank into his brain.

"If your father had an undeveloped talent you could have inherited something from him." His eyes probed hers. "There is a way to know." He hesitated as if embarrassed. "I could look into your mind. I have followed other men's dreams before with just a touch." Again his hands reached for her face.

"No." She backed away from those wonderfully gentle, probing hands. "No." Panic tinged her voice. She forced mastery over her mind and trembling body.

See into her mind! Never. He might see what had driven her here to this remote clearing, so far away from her family and the husband she had killed.

The image of her husband stretched across their marriage bed, eyes bulging, tongue protruding, limbs rigid in death, flashed across her vision. The terror of that night visited her again. The terror and the relief. No one would look for the new bride early the next morning. She'd had nearly twelve hours to escape the prison of her marriage. Twelve hours to find the sanctuary of this clearing.

It had taken longer, closer to a full moon to walk the

length of the province. A moon's cycle in which she moved
closer and closer to the nameless thing that called her.
She'd known the calling since early childhood. Back then
she had thought it a yearning for peace and quiet, away
from the noisy family home. Now she knew it was the
empty clearing needing a new witchwoman.

But Jaylor must not see any of that. He would know
then that she was hunted, blamed for a man's death. By
law her life was forfeit. He must return her to her father's
village for judgment and punishment. She wouldn't think
what form that hideous punishment would take.

"To touch me that way is more intimate than if I allowed
you into my body." She stalled his forward movement.
Doubt clouded his eyes. She pressed her advantage. "You
can't dare to look into my mind."

Jaylor's hand dropped again in agreement. "You're right.
I can't take that chance."

"You still have your magic. But here in my clearing you
must use your hands to move things."

*My head aches with magic gone wrong. The glass is dark,
obscured by another. More of the Tambootie removes the
pain. I can see clearly again.*

The wolf! Injured. Good.

He would have died, except for the cursed dragon.

*He must die this time. Then I can get on with the rest of
my plans.*

*The witchwoman and her lover will seek the dragon, and
I will follow. Soon, very soon, all will be in place. I can set
right three hundred years of mismanagement by the inept,
so-called magicians!*

Brevelan paced in front of the door of her cottage. If
only Jaylor would hurry. He always headed for the bathing
pool first thing in the morning. So why was he dawdling
over his morning routine? At last he stretched and scratched,
ran his hands through his hair and beard then turned
toward the creek.

"Shayla?" Brevelan called to her dragon friend as soon
as Jaylor had disappeared among the ferns.

Hm? The dragon replied sleepily.

"What am I going to do with that man?" Brevelan had

never had a friend before, someone close enough to discuss this sort of thing. Shayla seemed to be the only one who could understand her dilemma.

Trust him. Came the succinct reply.

"Trust him? I don't even know why he is here." Partial answers and dragon riddles weren't enough this time. She wanted the truth, all of it and right now.

He is the only one who can save the Darville.

"I don't understand your obsession with a wolf. Why is he so important to you?"

He must be protected. That seemed to be enough explanation for the dragon. Brevelan could feel her friend sliding once more into drowsy oblivion.

"Every creature has a name." The cat had told Brevelan her true name. Every hare, squirrel, bird, goat, and chicken within the clearing had names for themselves. But the wolf was notably silent on the issue. Shayla had given him the name of a prince—Darville, from the city of dragons.

"You tell me nothing new. You are a very logical and practical creature. So why did you drag me out into that storm when you had not concerned yourself with any human for ten years?" Five breeding cycles Shayla had called the time. She had neither sought a mate nor concerned herself with people in all that time because the villagers had killed two of her litters. Why she stayed in Coronnan was a mystery.

Protect the golden wolf. The man is the only one who can save him.

"Why rescue the miserable beast? If you'd had him for supper, your life would have been simpler."

And Brevelan would have been even more lonely throughout the long winter months. Now that spring was in the air and Jaylor lingered, she didn't feel the empty ache quite so desperately.

Her thoughts stopped. Jaylor. She wasn't lonely with Jaylor nearby. She couldn't dwell on those impossible ideas. She had to press Shayla for information. "Why did you give the wolf a royal name? Is he the leader of his pack?"

What else should I call him?

"You could call him Wolf, or Puppy like I do, or any one of countless other names. You could name him Lord Krej or even call him Simurgh."

No! Shayla's roar of protest almost shattered Brevelan's mental ears. The roar continued, echoing in her head and around the foothills. *Never. Never consider the evil one. Do not even think of him.*

A wind rose and whirled about the clearing. It whipped the trees into a fury and drove all the small creatures toward shelter. A huge shadow passed overhead. Shayla was gone.

Brevelan stood her ground, not even bothering to subdue her swirling skirts. She might have known the ancient god of evil was at the heart of this puzzle. This wouldn't be the first time Brevelan had suspected his followers lurked within the kingdom. Even Lord Krej was rumored to have had dealings with a coven.

Three summers ago she had served at his castle for a banquet. All the girls from her village were bound to assist when extra servants were needed. Before the meal, while Brevelan spread fresh rushes on the floor, she had watched Krej in his Great Hall. He touched with fondness each of the six statues he kept there.

Most of the sculptures were of animals Brevelan had never seen before, did not know the names of. There was one huge cat, bigger than a pack steed, with teeth as long as a saber fern.

Krej talked to each of the statues. He sounded as though he were reminiscing about the capture of each. When he came to the cat she heard him say: "You led me quite a chase through that forest, special one. The trees hid you for a time. But you could not know they were all Tambootie and so they aided my search instead."

Then the cat blinked. Brevelan was sure of it because Krej cursed and waved his hands and the cat was still once more; captured in a prison of bronze.

"Behave, cat," Krej admonished the beast. "You have been granted the privilege of being sacrificed to Simurgh. You should be happy to serve the winged one."

This was worse than killing an animal for food! That at least had a purpose, sustained life in a way. Krej had imprisoned these beautiful creatures in stone and wood, metal and clay. Imprisoned their bright spirits for all time. She knew instinctively that each animal was still aware of that prison, not sleeping, not dead, but not alive either.

She had backed away, silently. By the time the banquet was served, Brevelan was at home, physically ill, unfit to be seen at the castle of one of the Twelve members of the Council of Provinces.

Wolf trotted up behind Jaylor. The beast had enjoyed splashing in the water almost as much as Jaylor had. Together they wandered the path back to the clearing in silent companionship.

"Whaoaar!" the dragon roared above them.

Strong trees bent with the wind of her passing. A mighty tail lashed across the sky. New leaves and old branches crashed to the ground around them.

Jaylor covered suddenly numbed ears with his hands. The sound of the dragon's anger echoed again and again through his mind.

Wolf merely stopped with one ear cocked as if listening. He showed no fear of the noise, and the unnatural wind did not so much as ruffle his fur.

When the dragon had passed overhead, her fury diminished, the wolf looked up to Jaylor as if to say, "Shall we go on home?" With his head tilted just so, his chin lifted and his golden eyes blinking up at Jaylor, Wolf looked so intelligent, almost as if a human soul resided within his body.

The Rovers had never found two of their missing men. Jaylor had the sudden urge to talk to Baamin. He needed to know more about dragon-dreams leading men astray. Dragons were the essence of magic. Could their illusions transform a man into a wild creature? And what of his friend back in Coronnan City? Jaylor desperately wanted reassurance that Roy had returned to the capital.

Stargods! *I need to end this farce soon. I can't tolerate any more delays. Time is running short. I have eliminated or bribed more than one old fool in the Commune. Some of the students have talent. But they are gone, dispersed, chasing wild lumbirds. Even this one, who has found the wolf is only pretending to do magic.*

I am the only one in Coronnan who can use the real power. Throwing dragon magic is child's play, a child size power.

Tomorrow I will finish the job. I must push the journey-man and the witchwoman to lead me to the dragon. The witchwoman is elusive. But I think I know her secret now. The wolf and the cat, even the rabbits and squirrels return to the clearing easily. Only people are kept out. There is a trick I must try.

First, I must take something for this headache. A little Tambootie ought to do the job. It will also prepare me for the task at hand.

Chapter 9

Jaylor fed another branch into the fire. His lean-to was in place. The physical labor had acted as a release for the questions that churned in his mind.

He clutched Mica to his chest for warmth against the chill of his purpose. She purred in rhythm with his agitated pulse. Was summoning a master while on quest in violation of the complex rules?

Jaylor moved his staff within easy reach of his hand. The plaited grain of the once smooth oak offered reassurance. In these uncertain times, he might need the stronger focus for his magic even though the moon was full.

When he'd cut the staff in the heart of the sacred grove, just before beginning his quest, the branch had called to him, claiming him as its owner. At the time, the wood had been straight and smooth. Every time he used this tool the grain bent and coiled, taking on a pattern similar to a loose braid. The more often he used the staff the stronger the communication between them grew. He needed to use the staff. The staff needed to be used by him.

He folded his long legs underneath him and sat facing the blaze. There was enough fuel to keep it burning for quite a while without attention. He extracted from his pack a small oblong of glass not much larger than Brevelan's tiny palm. This was his first viewer, given to him as an apprentice, much more portable than the slightly larger, brass-framed glass he had earned as a journeyman.

One of Brevelan's soothing songs drifted across the cool evening air. He allowed it to wrap his mind in comfort and relax his body.

Mica purred louder, harmonizing with the wordless tune.

She butted her head against his chin. He stroked the cat's unusual fur in rhythm with his breathing. Her warmth settled him.

Jaylor focused on the seething green center of a flame. The glass brought it closer, enlarged it until the fire filled his vision. Gradually, he drew the flame into his consciousness.

The part of him that was aware of the night—listening to Brevelan's song, chilling in the rustling wind, feeling the hard ground beneath his butt—separated from his magic. The rest of him hovered near the void and knew only the flame. He breathed deeper, deeper. The flame in the glass grew cool and distant. It jumped to the edge of the clearing. There it paused, hesitant to break the armor. Jaylor pushed it onward.

A tiny flicker of magic fire climbed hills, skimmed over the bay, seeking, always seeking. Through the forests and down the broad highway to the capital, it drew ever closer to a familiar mind. When it found the barrier of the mighty Coronnan River, it paused to gather strength, then jumped the channels twisting around the city and wound its way through the alleyways with growing urgency until it found the University and the one window that faced the courtyard. Light flowed from the window, drawing the tiny flame. Like seeking like.

It slid up the stone walls and glided through the opening to merge with a candle flame. Into Jaylor's glass came the image of Baamin. Like the journeyman, the senior magician held a glass, though his was much larger and rimmed with gold.

"Jaylor?" The old man murmured from his own trance.

"Sir," he replied. Had his master really been that old and worn two moons ago when Jaylor left him?

"Finally, I've gotten through to you!"

Surprise wound its way into Jaylor's consciousness. He thought he had done the summoning. "You have need of me, sir?"

"Trouble is brewing in Coronnan. Strange reports come to me from all quarters. What is happening in your sector?" The old man's image wavered in the glass. Jaylor strengthened his contact.

"Baamin, I have seen a dragon. Twice. Yet I do not believe I have finished my quest."

"Which dragon? Is it well? Are you alone or have you been followed. Have you encountered anything or anyone strange on your quest?" The magician's questions came out in an anxious rush.

Some of Baamin's emotions reached Jaylor through the spell. Jaylor's disquiet grew. Which strange event should he relate first? "I believe a rogue magician frequents the southern mountains. He disguises himself as a one-eyed drunk, but he looks upon himself as a younger red-haired man."

"We must beware of anyone in disguise, Jaylor. I, too, have encountered a rogue in a different guise." An impression of a shaggy-headed monster, very like a spotted saber cat but with bright red hair, superimposed upon Baamin's features then vanished before Jaylor was certain of what he had seen.

The lines of worry deepened on the old man's face.

"I encountered Rovers inside Coronnan. The border is nearly gone and no magician guards it," Jaylor continued.

"Dragon dung! Lord Krej swore to me, two days ago, that Journeyman Tomalin was stationed there. Have you seen the boy?"

"No. I have seen no one from the University." Jaylor sensed the summons diffusing. The spell wasn't weaker, just more spread out. As if someone were eavesdropping. He tightened his control of the flames and pressed on with his report. "I have found a great golden wolf that a dragon protects."

"Stargods guard us all! Jaylor, anything to do with the dragons is important. There are very few of them left. If a dragon protects a wolf, then the wolf is important."

"He was injured but is healing. He appears more intelligent than a beast should be."

"Stay with the wolf and the dragon. We need more information before you return to the capital." This time the magician's agitation nearly broke the contact.

Jaylor forced his mind back into the flame. It burned brighter, the image steadied. Wasn't Baamin doing anything to maintain this spell? Again he sensed that this conversation was not private. He had to phrase his next comments very carefully. "I am told the dragon saved the creature from some kind of trouble at the solstice." More than a moon before Jaylor began his journey.

"A number of the Rovers went missing about the same time. Could the soul of a missing man have been trapped within the wolf's body? Any missing man? Someone we know perhaps?"

Baamin's image drew away from the glass. The swirling colors in the border of the spell faded to blinding white. "If that is the case, after so many moons he will still think himself a wolf when the spell breaks. Beware, Jaylor. Beware of attack when you least expect it."

The danger was clear. Jaylor remembered the dripping fangs aimed at his throat. But how was he to break the spell? Baamin clearly expected him to. He didn't know who had thrown that particular piece of magic. Each magician left a trademark in the colored aura of his spells. That trademark made it possible to trace the path of the magic and then reverse it.

But Jaylor was useless at following traditional magic forms, and this didn't smell like a University spell.

"Sir, has my friend returned to the capital?"

"Your friend?" Baamin looked distracted and uneasy. "Oh, um, your friend, of course."

Jaylor breathed a little easier. Roy had been absent from Coronnan City for several weeks before Jaylor was sent on his quest. Not unusual. But always before, Roy had left a secret message for Jaylor regarding his destination and expected return. Just one small precaution against assassination.

"Sir, I need some books from the library on shape change spells if I am to finish this quest."

He could almost see the volume he needed. But it was an ancient tome, too fragile to leave the stasis spell placed on it for more than a few moments.

"Books are off limits on quest, my boy. You must continue alone." The old man looked more sad than querulous. "Befriend the dragon. Do whatever it asks. The dragon is our only hope. You must find a way to secure the border in your sector. I will work on the other points that have been breached."

The border breached at other points as well? What did

one say in the face of such a tragedy? Without the magic border, Coronnan would be open to attack from foreign armies as well as outlandish cultures. Chaos—or growth— would soon result. The people of Coronnan weren't ready for either.

"There is other news as well," Baamin continued. "Two ambassadors are on their way to Coronnan. The kingdom of Rossemeyer seeks to marry their princess to our prince. Refusal will be considered a declaration of war. Their enemy, SeLenicca, claims any alliance with Rossemeyer will require retribution from them."

"*Stargods!* How long before I can expect raiders on the border?" Both SeLenicca and Rossemeyer claimed the mountains southwest of here. No one controlled the passes and hidden valleys, except possibly the Rovers. Sudden blizzards sprang up at all times of the year. Armies from either country could cross the pass in two days—weather permitting—and simply walk across the dissolving border.

"By the dark of the next moon both armies will wish to remind us of our trade-treaty obligations. If the dragons would give me enough magic, I could summon a storm to detain the ambassadors and delay a decision. I fear you are on your own. You must seal the border and discover why the dragon protects the wolf before then."

"If you had enough magic? What is happening, sir?" Jaylor forced himself to maintain the spell. The questions raised occupied too much of his concentration.

"The rogue in disguise is perverting my spells. I can't maintain this summons much longer."

He wasn't doing much to hold it together as it was.

"Are you certain the man is a foreign rogue, sir?" Silly question. The Commune had too much control over their members for one to step outside the bounds of University training. Masters of dragon magic could combine and thereby increase their powers to overcome any individual magician. All of the rogues who couldn't or wouldn't gather dragon magic had sought more agreeable locations three hundred years ago, when the Commune established the border.

"A rogue of great power, Jaylor. I know not his origins. He or his accomplice stalks you even now, since you are so close to the last breeding female dragon."

"I don't think the one who stalks me is from some other country." Jaylor allowed an image of the one-eyed derelict to form on the glass. The image shifted and changed to a red-haired man in his prime, broad shouldered, lean of hip. He dared not risk giving the image a name or full details of his face. That could summon him into the spell, allow him to eavesdrop or, worse yet, interrupt the communication.

But the vivid color of his hair should give his identity away.

"Then his magic is of a nature totally alien to us. I know not its source, nor its potential." The image wavered. "Even now he pulls this spell away from me. I dare work no magic at all, for it just makes him stronger and me weaker." The sound of his voice faded. "Be careful, Jaylor. Be careful."

The spell dissolved from both ends.

Darville stirred. As usual, he was curled up on the hearth. From there he could open one eye and observe all of the hut, as well as the door. Not much passed his notice.

His body would not settle. The usual comfortable positions pulled his muscles wrong, twisted his bones. He stretched out, resting his head on his paws.

Something was wrong. He could sense it, feel it, taste it. He couldn't see as much in this position, but he felt better. Brevelan was fully in his sight. That was important.

He smelled disquiet in her. Something to do with the man. The man he now knew must be protected along with Brevelan. The dragon had told him so.

Perhaps he should be out there with the man. Then he could keep both his people under his eye. He yawned and stretched up to a sitting position. One hind foot twitched. He bent his head so he could scratch his ears. He didn't really itch. It was just something to do while he puzzled out his next move.

"What, Puppy?" Brevelan's voice washed over him with love.

His tail thumped. He knew it did and wondered why. It was as out of place as he was. Something was definitely wrong. He wasn't sure if it was outside himself or inside.

He just knew he had to move, had to seek the source of his upset.

"Out?" Brevelan asked. She rose and shook her head. There was love in her voice. He thumped his tail again and rose to all of his feet. He needed to be higher, to view things from a different position. He jumped up and placed his front paws on the wall beside the door.

His back stretched. He savored the tight pleasure of that stretch. Better. But still not right.

"Oh, all right." Her hand pulled the leather thong on the door and it swung outward. He slid through the narrow opening. His nose twitched.

Ahead was the scent of the man's fire. It burned hot and strange, but he sensed no danger. He smelled the rich warmth of the flusterhens, roosting for the night. The goat was there as well. He found Mica's scent mingled with the man's. That was fine. She would alert him to any danger.

His head swung from side to side as he trotted around the edge of the clearing. All was in order. Everyone who should be there was in place. No one who should not be there intruded.

Instinctively he lifted his outside leg and left his mark. The action seemed out of place as well. His scent was strong. No one threatened his territory. So why was he so restless? What was wrong?

The opening of the door brought a chill to Brevelan's shoulders. She should be used to the wolf's comings and goings by now. He wanted out at the strangest times.

How odd, she mused. She'd never had to housebreak him as she would a puppy or a feral animal. Darville knew not to soil her house.

When she opened the door, she saw the glow from Jaylor's fire. That banished her questions about the wolf and brought images of the man to mind. Images of his hands on her face, his mouth hot and seeking on her own. She should fear the man and the lust that drove him. Instead she wanted once more to experience the gentle warmth in her belly when his hands caressed her hair. She wasn't used to gentleness. If he'd beaten her, she could have resisted him.

She returned to her stool by the hearth with a sigh. The pot of herbs bubbling on the grate required a stir. It was something of her own invention to ease the birthing pains of the carpenter's wife. It would also dull the pain of severe injury. Puppy might need it again. Twice now he'd been injured. Twice she'd nursed him back to health.

He was just a wolf. What was so extraordinary about him?

She heard the wind stirring her thatch. A song rose to her lips in response. With the tune she secured her home and protected her clearing.

"Puppy!" she called the wolf from the doorway. It was time she slept. She didn't need the animal's restless wanderings to disturb her.

"Awroooo . . ." he howled mournfully in the distance. "Awroooo."

"Puppy!" Brevelan ran toward the sound. Jaylor's strong arm about her waist stayed her headlong plunge into the undergrowth. "Puppy, what's wrong?" she cried, struggling against the pinioning arm.

"Stay here." Jaylor commanded.

"He needs me," she insisted.

"Awroooo. . . ." Brevelan shuddered at the distress in the call.

"Stay here," Jaylor said again. He released her. "There's magic in the air, too much magic." He swung his staff above his head in an arc. An eerie glow filled the clearing. "I can find him by this light, but no intruder can use it to find us."

"Awroooo . . ." Darville was silhouetted against the dark trees. He stood facing the back path to the village, neck fur bristling, tail erect.

"We are being watched," Jaylor whispered. His arms redescribed the arc and the light vanished. "Get inside."

Brevelan resisted the pressure of his hand on her back. Darville's call was full of pain. He needed her.

"Go! I will see to the animal." He shoved her in the direction of the hut even as his long legs took him across the open space.

"Puppy," she called as Jaylor's hand came down on the wolf's neck.

The wail ended abruptly. Wolf and man turned and loped back to the hut together.

"Who is it?" she asked as Jaylor leaned heavily against the closed door. He seemed out of breath from his brief exertion.

"Which village do you hail from?" he returned.

She was silent.

"Don't bother." His eyes closed in weariness. "With that hair I can only guess that Krej's castle was very close to your home."

"How did you know?" She was too shocked to be defensive.

"Rumors of strange happenings, his neglect of his responsibilities. There's a rogue magician in this village. He obeys a man with hair as bright as Lord Krej's."

"You bring that man," she spat, "here?" She allowed her disgust for the man who had probably fathered her, as well as a half dozen other bastards, to color her voice.

"He'd have found you sooner or later. I am not his quest." Jaylor turned to peer out the door. "The clearing is armored. I don't know if it will hold against this rogue."

"Could Krej's rogue capture rare animals and imprison them as sculptures?" She needed to talk, to keep her mind occupied so she wouldn't remember how empty her home had felt until Jaylor once more filled the room.

"Who knows what powers a rogue can tap? Perhaps they seek to add a dragon to the collection. Or a golden wolf." He sank down to the floor, back still against the door. Fatigue rimmed his eyes. He'd been working magic again. Strong magic.

Silence surrounded them. Brevelan, too, sank to the floor. Her arms reached for her pet. She buried her face in his fur and clung to him. He filled her arms with warmth. But he wasn't Jaylor.

"Light the torches! Let's burn her out." Men's voices, angry, insulting, broke the silence.

Jaylor's head rose in alarm. Brevelan's chest tightened.

"If we kill the witch the path to the dragon will open," one of the fishermen yelled.

"We should 'a run the woman off last summer. Then there wouldn't be no dragon up there now," the barkeep sneered.

"I lost another cow this morning to the blasted dragon. I want that monster dead any way it takes to do it," screamed a farmer who had sought Brevelan's help when he'd nearly severed his foot with an ax. She'd saved the foot, but the man would limp for the rest of his life.

There were other comments from men she didn't know. But the one in command, that one chilled her bones.

"Let's smoke her out!" Old Thorm's voice, and yet it was stronger, better educated than the drunken troublemaker's.

"Witches can't fight a good fire."

She pulled Puppy closer, to still her shaking. She could face magic, or dragons, or even wild wolves. But fire? FIRE!

Jaylor's gaze darted about the hut, peering into the shadows. "Can you call Shayla?"

She wasn't sure whether she heard the words with her ears or her mind.

"Shayla?"

"She is the only thing he," Jaylor nodded toward the outside to indicate who he meant, "still fears."

"But they want to kill her!" She'd heard that much in the muffled sounds outside.

"Not when she flies. They want you to show them her lair. Call the dragon, Brevelan. You've got to call Shayla."

Chapter 10

Light and music flooded the bridge between the University and Palace Reveta Tristile. Baamin made his slow, observant way toward the banquet hall and the festivities being prepared for the arrival of two rival ambassadors. The emissaries from SeLenicca and Rossemeyer each sought to secure an exclusive alliance with Coronnan. The two kingdoms had been at each other's throats for generations. Coronnan traded with both.

Baamin wondered if he could convince his frail king that the pattern of the future that the magicians saw in the glass was the same pattern of entrapment represented by the two rival ambassadors.

Tonight the senior magician's responsibilities in matters magical weighed as heavily on his shoulders as the diplomatic chores.

Master Fraandalor, assigned to the court of Lord Krej, had just reported the discovery of Journeyman Tomalin's body on the shores of the Great Bay. Death by drowning, five leagues away from his post.

"My Lord Baamin." A minor courtier bowed low to the magician.

Baamin touched the man's bowed head briefly, then jerked away as if in surprise. "What have we here. Bruce? A flower? Why are you growing flowers in your ears?" He handed the posy to the smiling man.

"Flowers today, coins yesterday." Bruce lowered his eyes, unwilling to meet the magician's glance. His hands fluttered in front of him, almost seeking a warding gesture. "When you honor us with your presence, who knows what will be found in unlikely places?"

Tricks. Simple tricks that didn't even require magic. Still, the court expected this sort of thing.

And feared it.

"How fares the king?" Baamin prodded the sharp-eyed, sharp-nosed ferret of a man. Bruce was a notorious gossip. He was also master of the king's shoes and in a position to observe King Darcine in private.

Bruce of the Shoes shrugged, then leaned closer to whisper in Baamin's ear. "Good thing that foreign ambassador with the unpronounceable name sent a cask of beta'arack from Rossemeyer. Liquor perks him up like nothing else lately. A good strong dose of the stuff first thing in the morning works wonders on the king's spirits and constitution."

The liquor wasn't the only cause of the king's high spirits these days. Shayla was well and gravid. Therefore, Baamin knew, the king gained in strength. Today.

Baamin nodded sagely. They'd seen Darcine's spells of near manic strength before. But every day of good health was followed by longer and longer periods of depression and weakness.

If anything happened to the dragon or her dragonets . . .

Anxiously, Baamin looked around for signs of the forces that interfered with his magic and the dragons.

He straightened his shoulders and stretched to his full height, slight as it was. There were appearances to be kept up. While the king felt so well and strong, Baamin would attend banquets and balls day and night. There had been precious few celebrations in the last ten years.

"Ah, Baamin." Darcine waved for the magician to approach him.

Brightly gowned ladies and richly jeweled men filled the Great Hall with shrill laughter. All were masked for the event, except the king. Baamin sensed the tension in the posture and rapidly darting eyes of the nobility. They must know this gaiety was only temporary.

"Your Grace." Baamin bowed to his monarch.

As he straightened, he took the opportunity to carefully survey the tall figure of his friend. New tunic and trews of golden brocade, padded to disguise too thin limbs and slumping shoulders. A small replica of the Coraurlia, the glass dragon-crown, rested on his head. The token of his kingship contained hardly any heavy glass at all. Darcine's neck couldn't support the full weight of the crown.

The king didn't need to mask his face. His entire body was cloaked in the guise of health.

"You're late, my friend. But the night is still young. There is plenty of time to sample the delicacies the cook has provided." The usual feverish flush on King Darcine's face was now replaced with a more even and natural coloring.

Paint or healing?

"Have you seen aught of my cousin? Krej promised to attend this little gathering." King Darcine snagged a goblet of wine from a passing servant. "He is so very entertaining."

"Nay, Your Grace. Lord Krej has not privileged me with news of his activities." Baamin wanted to discount Jaylor's theories that the rogue magician operating in the south answered to Krej. The king's cousin, with his reputation as a fierce negotiator, was their only hope of avoiding war if the prince could not be found soon.

"We can enjoy ourselves without Krej. He does tell such outrageous stories though. When the ambassadors come, his wit will charm then into a favorable marriage settlement." The king made to move back to his guests.

"Your Grace, have you forgotten the most important element in the negotiations? Your son." He paused while the king turned back, his face and posture slumped under the strain of dealing with that matter.

Laughter rose and surged toward the entrance. Newcomers stood there waiting for all to acknowledge their presence before entering. Baamin peered toward the bubble of excitement. Too many people crowded too close to the masked lord and lady for him to see more than a swirl of bronze and ebony lamé fabric. Costly stuff.

"Perhaps this is your cousin, Your Grace, and his lady." Baamin gestured toward the brilliant figures.

"If not his lady, then another beautiful companion. Krej does have wonderful luck with women." Darcine winked knowingly. "Lady Rhodia is still recovering from her latest confinement. Yet another daughter. Very disappointing. I wonder who replaces her in my cousin's affections, and his bed, this time?"

"I don't think Lord Krej will keep her long enough for anyone to find out. Even your bold cousin won't risk another of Lady Rhodia's temper tantrums." The last time Lady Rhodia had caught Krej with a courtesan, she had nearly destroyed their costly suite in the royal palace as well as her rival's beautiful face.

Baamin turned away from the object of their discussion. He'd never liked Krej's arrogance, nor the look of disdain that always clouded his bay blue eyes. The soul within the man was as frigid as the depths of the Great Bay.

"Welcome, cousin." Darcine gestured toward the newcomer. In a complete departure from protocol, Darcine wandered away from his post on the dais toward Krej and the lady. The court flocked to them, currying favor and notice. Baamin held back, taking the opportunity to observe the entire banquet hall.

Every muscle in his body froze with fear. Icy sweat popped out on his brow and his back. In the center of the huge hall stood the monster of his nightmares, clothed in bronze lamé.

"What kind of joke is this?" he whispered.

Just then, Lord Krej lifted his masked face and stared directly at the Senior Magician, as if he had heard the frantic question. Beneath the mask of a spotted saber cat, Krej's eyes glinted with malice. Baamin mentally shook himself free of the dread that rooted him to the spot. There was a glamour about the masked figure. He needed to move closer and examine the nature of that magic distortion.

His private fears stopped him cold.

"Can you call Shayla?" Jaylor raised his voice. Brevelan clung to the wolf with fierce intensity. Her eyes were huge in the dim light from the hearth.

"Call Shayla?" she asked into the wolf's fur.

"Yes. Call the dragon," he pressed. His hand reached out to stroke her hair, to draw her attention to his words. He didn't need magic to see the terror on her face. The lightest touch and the source of her panic flooded through his fingers to his mind.

Fire. Hot. Smoke. No air. The heat. The pain.

Something in the girl's past brought on this terror. Something she dared not let him see.

Jaylor allowed his touch to become comforting. He stroked her cheek and cupped her chin gently. "Brevelan, trust me. There is no fire. We can get out of this if you'll just call the dragon. The rogue still fears her."

Tender warmth filled the gap between them. Jaylor wanted to wrap the girl in his arms and hold her. He was aware of her, but for once desire didn't overwhelm him. He needed more than physical union with her. Their one kiss had taught him that. If only the wolf were not between them, he would reach over and hold her tightly against his chest and treasure the completeness she offered.

"Bring the torches!" Old Thorm's voice carried on the evening breeze. "The thatch is damp, the smoke will drive her out."

"She's mine when she runs," the fisherman crowed.

"What gives you first right?" someone else challenged.

"Once we've had her, she won't be a witch anymore," Old Thorm chortled.

"What about the wolf?"

"I'll slit the devil dog's throat first, before he can protect his mistress, before he has the chance to drain the blood from another man's body."

Brevelan blanched. Jaylor pulled her, and the wolf she cradled, tight against his chest.

"I won't let them hurt you," he promised. Though how, he didn't know. There were at least ten of them. His magic wasn't designed to hurt people. That was the first law of the Commune.

His answer came from overhead. A roar that only a dragon throat could muster filled his mind and ears. Both he and Brevelan sagged in relief. Wolf looked up, his mouth open in a doggy grin.

Seek me, you impudent puppet of evil! The dragon's thoughts flooded the clearing. As if from a dizzying height, Jaylor saw the object of Shayla's wrath. He was disguised as a one-eyed beggar, dressed in rags. But Jaylor/Shayla knew him now, knew a powerful magician hid behind a glamour. Once revealed, this enemy could never again hide behind this flimsy disguise.

The vision pulled back, and Jaylor knew Shayla flew higher. Then, as she tucked her wings back and dove, the ground rushed up at him with frightening speed. Nine men hovered near the rogue—a vigorous, red-haired man in his prime. But dragon eyes weren't meant to focus on the details of human faces. Nine white blurs looked up. Only the fear in their eyes shone through.

Jaylor felt the roar of triumph pelt from the dragon's throat, and his own. The first flicker of flame erupted, with a roar dredged up from the roots of the mountains.

The hut shook and trembled with the rocking ground beneath it. Jaylor plummeted back into his own senses. He heard shouts and screams from the villagers outside. Through Shayla's eyes, but his own body, he could see them running from the fingers of flame licking their heels. One man rested while flames tickled another's backside. Then, before he could contemplate safety in another's pain, the first man felt the heat of Shayla's wrath again.

"Why does she just toy with them? She should flame them and be done with the menace." Jaylor spoke to thin air.

Brevelan opened her mouth to answer. Her voice cracked with a giggle that bordered on hysteria.

"Are you seeing this, too?" Wonder flooded his senses. For a moment they had all been linked into the mind of a dragon.

She nodded. Her eyes were still huge in the firelight.

"Shayla will never harm a man, even though these are the same ones who slaughtered her litters. Dragon pride compels her to honor the pact."

"The pact with Nimbulan—three hundred years ago?" Jaylor asked.

Brevelan shrugged her shoulders. "Shayla only said there was a pact, made with all of Coronnan. She can send dragon-dreams to lead the dangerous ones astray. But to her, our lives are sacred and must be preserved."

Superstition in the village had become perverted over the generations. That perversion now endangered all of Coronnan. Had it been directed by a single man—a lord with red hair?

"I'll get you yet, you monstrous beast from hell! My magic will defeat you." A loud voice boomed across the clearing in defiance.

Cleared of disguise, the educated accent and condescending drawl became very distinctive to Jaylor's ears.

Through Shayla's eyes once more they saw the faceless rogue at the edge of the clearing. Gone were the trappings of the one-eyed beggar. They watched him gather a ball of dark red and green magic energy in his hands. With a mighty effort of broad shoulders and strong arms, he hurled it toward the sky.

Shayla sent forth a magnificent burst of bright green dragon fire. Flames engulfed the magic ball, then shattered it into myriad starry sparks. The pinpoints of light drifted harmlessly to the ground.

Puny man. Shayla dismissed him with another lick of flame. The rogue disappeared into the sheltering trees. One last lashing of flames followed him away from the clearing.

"Thank you, Shayla." Jaylor formed the words in his head as he spoke. Brevelan's eyes were closed and he sensed her joining her gratitude to his.

We must settle this. Bring the golden wolf to my lair.

"Can't you just land in the clearing?" Brevelan asked.

The evil one may return. I am not safe on the ground. Bring the wolf to me. Close the path behind you.

"How will we find you? The mountain is huge, the trails difficult." Brevelan's voice shook.

Follow the path that only you can find. Blur your trail so he does not follow. Shayla's imagery disappeared from both their heads.

Jaylor looked to Brevelan and the wolf. She still clutched the animal to her. Wolf seemed perfectly happy there, his head nestling between her breasts.

If only she could learn to love Jaylor as much as she did this scruffy beast.

"Call your journeymen home, Baamin." King Darcine basked in his flower garden the morning after the ball. The spring sunshine flooded the bench he had chosen for this interview with his magician.

"Is that wise, Your Grace?" Baamin hedged.

"The dragons are protecting my son. They will return him when the time is right. I am well now and have the kingdom under control." The king closed his eyes as he turned his face to the source of the warmth. He looked like a contented cat napping in the sunshine. He'd gained a little weight this past week, lost a little of the gauntness.

"When did you learn that your son would be returned by the dragons?" Baamin mistrusted any predictions that didn't come from his own glass. A glass that had been dark and silent since the appearance of the beast-headed monster. The monster couldn't be the same rogue who plagued Jaylor's footsteps. No magician, no matter how powerful, could traverse such distances so quickly. Nimbulan had bewailed his inability to transport himself after he'd had to exile his own wife.

How much of the king's "control" was mere illusion created by the rogue?

Baamin's magic faded more each day. He could probably summon enough magic to throw a truth spell at the king. If he dared.

Long years of friendship and respect, as well as fear of the monster, stilled his desire to use magic.

"My cousin, Krej, told me in a dream last night. He assured me Darville is safe. The dragons need him for a while. We are not in a position to question the dragons." The king seemed once more a regal monarch instead of an ailing old man.

"How does Krej know so much about dragons? He is not the keeper of their lore."

"You forget, he carries the same royal blood in his veins as I do!"

"His mother is an outland princess, from SeLenicca with ties to Hanassa. Your mother, Your Grace, was a noble lady of Coronnan. The royal blood is purer in you." Baamin took a step away from his king. He didn't have to throw a truth spell to see an aura. But he did need space. The king's colors fluctuated and shimmered in and out of visibility. Darcine was not in control of his own emotions, let alone the kingdom. His health and resolve came from somewhere else.

"Does Lord Krej speak to you often in your dreams?"

"Lately he comes to me almost every night." The aura flared red with anger, then settled into a mild rainbow dominated by shades of green and red, the colors of Krej's crest.

"Lately?" Since dragon magic was on the wane and a rogue wandered Krej's province freely. "What about before?" Baamin prodded.

The king looked sharply at his magician. The aura flared

once more, this time with the yellow of uncertainty. Clearly he had not thought about this often. "Ever since Krej was a teenager at the University he has advised me through my dreams. Never often. Just when I really needed his wisdom."

"Your Grace, with the prince gone, your cousin Krej is the next heir. He is ambitious. Can you trust him so completely?" Baamin offered in his mild way. He had learned long ago it was not wise to be aggressive with Darcine. He tended to resent the trait in others when he had so little aggression in his own soul.

"Krej has only the welfare of the kingdom in his heart. He will do what is best. He tells me the truth."

"But perhaps not all of the truth."

"You defame a member of the royal family, magician." The king's back straightened indignantly. The aura faded, as if masked.

Or armored.

"I am sworn to defend the kingdom, Your Grace." Baamin swallowed deeply. Who had armored the king's aura? Was the monster eavesdropping on Baamin's very thoughts? "Our best defense now lies with your son. I cannot order my journeymen home until the prince is returned."

"You speak of defense. The border will do that. You need only obey your king." Darcine's meager strength seemed to wane a little as the sun slid behind a fluffy cloud.

"There are not enough dragons left to maintain the border."

"Explain," the king demanded.

"Shayla has bred. She is strong and healthy, so there is more magic this week than last. But she is the only breeding female left. There is just not enough magic left for us to hold the border inviolate. I have suspected this for a long time. But the change was so gradual that no one noticed until the border refused to stay in place." Sadness weighed his eyelids down to near closing.

So much good came from dragon magic, and not just the border. Now they would be left vulnerable to rogue magic as well as invading armies. Unless they took drastic diplomatic measures immediately. Was the marriage of Darville to the princess of Rossemeyer the answer?

That action would cause a war with SeLenicca. But if no

alliance was formed, Rossemeyer promised to invade. And if Coronnan stalled, the borders would be vulnerable to both countries.

"Lord Krej has said nothing of the border to me." Once more the king was alert and concerned. Just as he had been in his youth. "I cannot believe my cousin would not inform me of such a dire mishap."

"Rovers have been sighted at nearly all the border crossings."

"Rovers! Thieves and degenerates. Their women have no morals. The men will steal anything without compunction." Outrage radiated from the king. "Have they stolen any babies yet?" He half rose, as if to commence battle with these menaces out of history.

"Not yet." Baamin hid his concern at Darcine's agitation. The king wasn't strong enough to withstand such strong emotional upsets. "The few dragons left to us are doing what they can to defend against the Rovers with their dragon-dreams." But that could work against the kingdom if the Rovers decided to replace their lost men with babies born to Coronnan.

"Have the marketplaces watched. Rovers are adept at hiding. But their wares are unique. If you see some of their distinctive metalwork, then you know a Rover is lurking nearby."

"Their crafts are indeed distinctive, creative, and in many ways superior to ours. If we alert the populace to beware, perhaps we can learn something from these strange tribes."

"At what cost, magician?"

"The border was established for a reason, Your Grace. Perhaps those reasons were shortsighted. Have we really benefited from three hundred years of isolation?"

"'We trade with friends. We have avoided invasion. What more can we want?"

"Stimulation, creativity. Sometimes security leads to complacency. That has left us ill-prepared now that danger threatens." And the magic faded. They had no knowledge of the rogues who had been banished and might seek revenge.

"We still have armies. We can fight off any invasion."

"A very small number of troops who have grown soft

with easy living. They are more concerned with the color of their uniforms than with how to wield a sword."

Fashions hadn't changed; artisans still held to traditional forms, good in their way but lacking imagination. Even at the University there had been no exploration of new techniques, not even new medicines. The secret technology of the Stargods had revealed nothing new in the heavens for generations.

Young people lacked the stimulation to grow beyond their parents. Without that growth there was only stagnation, decay, and death. Now that he thought about it, Baamin saw all the symptoms clearly. He was as guilty of complacency as everyone else.

"Baamin, bring your journeymen home this very day. I would question them on the things they have seen. We must right the wrongs immediately, before our jealous neighbors steal our bounty." Darcine delivered his royal speech as if reciting instructions. "You will reestablish the border, or I will have to replace you at the University. Lord Krej has recommended someone."

Chapter 11

Brevelan couldn't delay much longer.

"It's time." Jaylor's words cut through Brevelan's tumbled thoughts. Dawn crept above the treetops. Birds greeted the sunlight with raucous song.

The sun was high enough for her to see the path up the mountain. "I must . . . I must . . ." She sought an excuse to remain. There was nothing left to do except leave. She had packed enough food for the two of them for three days. Their bedding was neatly rolled into Jaylor's pack. Her house and the clearing were in order.

"You can't stay, Brevelan. It's no longer safe. The villagers followed Old Thorm and broke through the clearing's magic. They found you once. Shayla won't stop them next time." His hand was gentle on her arm, urging her out of the hut.

"If I leave, nothing will be the same when I return," she protested.

"Already things change. A rogue magician has altered the path of all our futures. We must leave." This time Jaylor's tone was firmer.

"My animals. I must see to them." She hesitated as a lop-eared rabbit appeared among the ferns. Its nose wiggled in greeting.

"You have already told them to disperse. The clearing's magic can no longer shelter them."

He was right. She had sent each of her pets an image appropriate to its understanding. They must fend for themselves, take their chances in the wild, until she returned.

If she returned.

"Why must I go with you? Without you here the rogue will pass me by."

"You heard Old One-eye last night. He wants to kill Wolf as much as he wants to burn you alive." Jaylor allowed that thought to sink in. "Besides, Shayla said you are the only one who can find the path."

"Shayla." She started to smile at the mention of her friend. The usual warmth and closeness she felt with the dragon faded with the memory of flames flickering through the clearing last night. Deep inside she had felt not only her own relief and Shayla's battle lust but also the real terror of the villagers, her villagers. It was not unlike the sensation of pain and death she felt every time one of her animals lost its life to a predator. "She seems to be demanding a lot."

"She protects you and the wolf." Jaylor's tone was insistent.

"From stray rogue magicians? Why?" They had both been reluctant to discuss the strange attack on the clearing last night. She felt as if words would bring the men back with their torches.

"Think about it while we walk." He set his jaw firmly. Brevelan's stubbornness waned in the face of his determination.

"Come, Puppy." Brevelan called the wolf to her. Happily, he bounced to her side. As usual, he sat on her foot, leaning his weight into her. She ruffled his ears, cradled his large head in her hands, and briefly nuzzled him. "We have to go see Shayla now," she explained to him.

Her reluctance to leave the shelter of her clearing made her pack heavier. "I'm not sure he's healed enough to make this journey." Her words came out sharp and ill-tempered. Puppy's enthusiasm for the journey grated on her nerves.

Jaylor didn't reply as he stooped to lift his own pack to his shoulders. His long walking staff was already in his other hand. He fingered the interesting grain of the wood that ran down the length of the staff in a twisting plait.

"Maybe we should wait another day." She looked up at him with hope. The set of his jaw told her they couldn't.

"Mrrew?" Mica sat in the doorway. Her plaintive voice echoed around the hut that suddenly seemed empty, devoid of life.

"She's asking to go with us." Brevelan smiled for the first time. "She belongs here, more than I do. She was waiting for me when I found the clearing. Now she's demanding to leave with us."

"I can't keep her from following." Jaylor stared at the cat.

"Mrrow!" This time the cat's voice was emphatic, her eyes very round and humanlike.

"She won't be left behind." Brevelan looked from cat to man. There was a special bond there. Yet she didn't feel jealousy, not the way she did when Puppy showed a preference for the magician.

"Mrrow." Mica rubbed her face against Jaylor's leg. Her purr was loud, meant to gratify.

Jaylor bent to scratch her ears. Her fur rippled with different colors in different lights, as did slivers of mica. She was rightly named.

"It's a long trip, kitty. Maybe you'd better stay here."

"Niow!" Mica protested. This time she reached up with her claws to cling to his shirtsleeve. A quick scramble and she was perched on his shoulder.

"But, Mica . . ." Jaylor protested. He tried to dislodge the animal.

"It appears she is coming with us whether we like it or not." Brevelan smiled in earnest this time.

"How does it feel to be a cat's scratching post?" Brevelan giggled, just a little, at the sight of tiny Mica kneading Jaylor's broad shoulder.

Arching calubra ferns made a shaded aisle of the path. Their feet trod soundlessly on the thick bed of rose-lichen. The elusive scent of aromatic elf-leaves touched their nostrils and disappeared again, like fairies flitting past their senses.

Mica's twitching tail brushed a fragrant everblue tree that dipped long needles into their pathway. The pollen filled Brevelan's nose with its clean fragrance, banishing all other scents.

"Perhaps your cat would be happier in your arms," he muttered even as he smiled and reached to pet the now purring Mica.

"But your shoulders are so much broader and more

comfortable. She can see all around and not tire her tiny body."

Most of the last several hours they had endured the broken pathway in grim silence. Jaylor pushed the pace with an urgency Brevelan absorbed to lend speed to her own feet. She had used the time to memorize the landmarks of trees and rocks as she picked her way among them. As Shayla had said, there was a path visible, but only when she drew a song through her as if she were seeking a healing path through an ailing body.

"Jaylor, I have got to stop for a few moments," Brevelan protested. A steep incline loomed ahead of them. The stitch in her side needed time to unknot before she tackled the slope.

"Oh, all right." Jaylor paused beside a rock large enough to sit upon. Brevelan eased onto the worn surface. "We can't waste time though."

"Replenishing my body's reserves is not a waste of time." She stared at him until he, too, sat on the rock.

"Did Mica tell you she prefers my shoulders to yours?" he asked, eyebrows drawn together in puzzlement.

"Yes, she did." Brevelan had always listened to the animals. She'd been quite shocked as a small child to learn that others could not hear them.

"How? How do you hear them?" Jaylor seemed merely curious, not accusing as the man she'd called Father had been.

"It's not words." Only Shayla was verbal in her communications. "They look at me. I see into their eyes and feel what they need me to know." It was difficult to explain the sensation. She'd never found anyone willing to attempt an understanding. A tiny swell of affection for this strange man blossomed inside her. He'd invaded her life and made a place for himself there. Looking back toward her clearing, she tried imagining her home without him filling it. The image eluded her.

She touched her fingertips to her lips. The memory of his gently persuasive kisses brought a new flush to her face. He had been so tender with her. So unlike the man she had been forced to marry. Her husband had needed her terrified and in pain in order to become aroused.

"I've never heard of any magic that works like yours."

Jaylor headed back to the path with long strides. "When did this start?"

"I don't remember." Brevelan skipped a little to catch up with him. She had trailed behind him for long enough. "Maybe I should say I can't remember not being able to talk to animals." Animals didn't lie and cheat. Only people did that.

"My magic began like that. I just did it. No one taught me how." They walked side by side a moment in silence. "Most magicians can't do much at all until they are twelve or fourteen," he continued. "Even then they have to be taught to gather magic." He reached back to help her over a fallen log. Her fingers entwined with his so naturally she left them there.

"The first animal that called out to me in need was a sheep." She allowed her thoughts to drift back to her home. For once she didn't recoil from the pain. Jaylor's touch kept it at bay. "She was birthing and in trouble. It was late at night and the shepherd was asleep. I never questioned why I got out of a warm bed and trudged through the mud to help her." In her mind she relived the experience. She hadn't been much more than a toddler. "My da followed me and did the work. I was much too little."

"Was he very angry?" Jaylor stopped again. This time his hand touched her cheek solicitously.

"Only because he didn't understand." She tried to explain. Her mind knew that. Still, she felt the hurt of her da's rejection every time she worked her healing.

"My da did the same thing." Jaylor continued to stroke her cheek. "But I was lucky. We had a full-time priest in our village, not a circuit-cleric. He helped me gain entrance to the University early. At the University, everyone expects you to throw spells to steal apples or turn the letters upside down in a book." The memory of a smile tugged at his lips.

She felt that smile all the way to her toes. His hand dropped from her face to her arm and lingered.

"But my magic is different. I don't use traditional formulas. Other magicians can't follow or copy my spells. Nor can they join their magic with mine to amplify our powers." The smile disappeared to be replaced by a shrug of his shoulders. He started walking again at a furious pace.

"Once the masters realized that, they didn't encourage me much. They wanted me to give up and go home. One of them became so angry he suggested there must have been a rogue among my ancestors. There is no greater insult at the University."

"Why is one magician acceptable and another a rogue? As long as the result is for the good of Coronnan, I don't see the difference." She wanted to reach out and smooth the lines of tension from his brow.

"There are two kinds of magic." Jaylor closed his eyes as if trying to remember a lesson by rote. "The magic taught to me at the University is provided by the dragons. It's in the air and ground around us. We learn to still and prepare a special place within ourselves. It's almost as if we have an extra belly, put there for the sole purpose of gathering this magic. We then form it into proper spells and throw it out again."

He didn't have to tell her that women could not have that "extra belly."

They continued walking. As the path grew steeper, she became more thoughtful.

"I can't say I work my healing that way. I mean, I don't consciously gather it and then form it. It's just there." Brevelan searched his eyes for an explanation. Every time she tried to analyze her ability to heal, her mind went blank. She didn't know how she did it. People in pain or despair drew the healing from her.

"Traditional magic is bound to Coronnan and can only be worked for the benefit of the kingdom. The dragons see to that." He pushed aside one of the overhanging ferns. Once again the scent of elf-leaves whispered across their senses. "Magicians can combine and build stronger magic, but again only to make the kingdom safe. That is how the magic border was established and maintained. And how the rogues were exiled. A rogue works on his own, for his own benefit. I don't know where they find the magic. But each one must work as an individual. No one magician is stronger than the Commune and the ethics enforced by it."

"My magic works for the good of the kingdom."

"So does mine. But whoever hired Old One-eye wants something other than the best for Coronnan." He allowed the silence to fill the space between them.

"I'm not a member of the Commune, I can't 'gather' magic. Does that make me a rogue?"

Jaylor opened his eyes and looked deeply into hers. "I prefer the word 'solitary' as opposed to communal."

They stared at each other, and, slowly, she reached out to clasp his hand again. Stillness settled around them, isolating them from the sounds of birds and insects. Even Mica and Puppy seemed far away.

"My magic comes from deep within me. I don't have to follow exact formulas to keep it in line with everyone else's. If Old One-eye's magic forms inside him like that, then his only limitation is his own physical strength. I don't think he'll allow himself to be stopped by honor or integrity." Jaylor warned her.

"You face the same physical limits and you are much younger and stronger than he."

"But not as practiced. I've wasted most of the last twelve years trying to work the other kind of magic. I can do it. But it's harder for me."

This time Brevelan lifted her free hand to draw a finger along Jaylor's bearded cheek. The curling hair around his mouth tickled her palm, inviting a deeper caress. A contented sense of completeness filled her, gave her the courage to ask her next question. "Why is it so hard for you? If you have that extra belly, then you should be able to gather and throw magic."

A rough chuckle rumbled from his throat. "Traditional magic requires an inner peace and stillness. My insides are too restless to be still long enough to gather the proper amounts of magic."

She knew the feeling. There was always something more to do. Her body never wanted to be still. Until now. Standing here in the wilderness of the southern mountains, touching him, she felt as if everything in her life had a proper place. Her restlessness evaporated. "Perhaps we can join our magic, as we did to heal Puppy."

"That was no magic on my part," he protested vehemently. His eyes snapped open, but he didn't withdraw his hand.

"Wasn't it?"

"I merely pushed the bones back into place. You healed the muscles around them."

As if to prove his statement the wolf bounded back along the trail toward them. His step was strong and sure.

"Are you sure, Jaylor? Think back on it. How much of the effort you put into helping Puppy was brute strength and how much was magic sight?" She allowed her hand to drop just enough to clasp his.

"Oof!" The wolf jumped against Jaylor, muddy paws soiling his shirt. He dropped Brevelan's hand to fend off the animal. Puppy grinned in his special way and bounced back to the trail. "Your manners need a great deal of improvement, Wolf," Jaylor scolded him. He reached for Brevelan's hand once more.

Adventure! Darville raised his face to the sun and trotted along the path in front of his people. His instincts told him this journey was incredibly important. It was a return to a way of life that had been interrupted by his injury.

Already his nose felt keener. He was aware of much more than just the familiar scents back in Brevelan's clearing. His sight, too, was brighter. He was strong and eager for whatever the trail might bring.

A whiff of Tambootie drifted on the wind, an odor he associated with the dragon. Shayla had come last night, outlined in the moonlight, flaming Old One-eye. Just as she had that other time when Darville had fallen over the cliff. Only the enemy wasn't One-eye then. He was something else.

Deep in this throat Darville growled at the memory of the man responsible. The one-eyed man meant pain and changes Darville couldn't comprehend.

That man smelled of Tambootie. Shayla did, too, but the dragon smelled good. One-eye smelled evil.

There, on the wind, he caught again the elusive sent of Shayla. He savored it and proceeded forward, ahead of Jaylor and Brevelan. He'd go back soon and let them know the trail was safe.

He felt a need to stretch up again on his hind legs. This time he would linger against Jaylor's chest, make sure the man petted his ears instead of Brevelan's hand. Maybe he'd walk between them for a while, basking in their affection for him. He wasn't sure he approved of their affection for each other.

But first he would hunt.

Chapter 12

Jaylor's fingers suddenly felt empty and cold as Brevelan yanked her own hand free of his friendly grasp. She reached for her throat, her skin deathly pale.

"Aiyeeee!"

The shrill scream of a small animal broke the peace of a quiet mountain meadow. Delicate wildflowers swayed restlessly amidst the grass.

Jaylor looked to the source of the scream on their left. Wolf pounced and tore at the throat of a squirrel—his latest meal. He shrugged at the natural event. At least he would not have to worry about feeding the beast on the journey.

"No," Brevelan whispered through tight lips. She held her stomach and throat as if in deep pain, bent nearly double. Her face was drained of all color. She had pulled her hand free of his an instant before the scream.

"Brevelan!" Jaylor jumped to help her. "What ails you?" Tenderly, he cradled her against his side. He gave her what strength he could as he guided her to a rock where she could sit. His hands slipped against her cold, almost clammy skin. A shot of fear pierced his heart.

"Easy now. Rest a moment while I fetch some water."

"I must leave this place." She started to look over her shoulder toward the spot where Darville noisily ate his kill. Then she hastily averted her eyes.

"You're in no condition to move anywhere."

"It is the place that ails me."

"The animal Darville just killed." The truth dawned on him. "You felt it die, just as you felt an ewe's troubled labor when you were a tot." A chill knot formed in his stomach. "No wonder you couldn't stay with your own people. A village full of meat eaters would destroy you at every meal."

She nodded.

He was amazed she'd managed as long as she had.

"I soon learned to be elsewhere on slaughter days. It helps if I've never communicated with the animal, or if I'm not too close. Back home I couldn't separate myself from the herds. They needed me too often."

Jaylor helped her to stand. She leaned against him heavily as they walked away from the scene of the recent death. At the streambed he helped her onto the mossy bank.

"Drink. Then we'll be on our way. Wolf will catch up when he's ready." He looked back toward the animal just as the wolf looked up and grinned. "You don't have to enjoy it quite so much!" he called.

That grin. So like the young prince when he escaped his tutors and sought freedom among the apprentice magicians. Roy had enjoyed his pranks then, too, without a thought to the torment his guardians received at the king's hand for losing their prince.

Mica scampered back to the wolf. With an imperious paw she batted the wolf's muzzle away and grabbed her share of the meal.

"Not you, too, Mica. Don't you know you're hurting Brevelan?" Jaylor admonished the animals.

"Please, Jaylor. Let's just move on a little." Brevelan tugged at his sleeve. Her eyes were huge in her pale face. They were dark blue now, the color of the bay at sunset, almost black. He caught a fragment of her pain.

"Yes, of course." He eased her back onto the path. For a moment she leaned against him, gathering strength. His arms tightened around her slender body. She felt so good, nestled there against his shoulder. Tenderness filled him. He didn't want to move. But he had to.

"It is part of the nature of things for them to eat meat. I cannot begrudge them that. I can only ask them to keep their kill away from me." She took one slow step. Then another.

"Lean on me." He urged her forward. "We'll get you farther along before we have some fruit and another drink." He continued to hold her as they moved. She didn't pull away.

*   *   *

"How did Old Thorm break through our armor?" Brevelan's question disturbed Jaylor.

"I don't know." He rose from his crouched position before the campfire. Wolf had found this sheltered overhang for them long after the sun had set. The almost-cave was dry and vacant and should be a safe place to spend the night, safe from predators and conventional attack. But how did he protect them from a magic he couldn't understand?

"How are you feeling now?" He turned to face the girl. Her face was pale and her eyes shadowed. Still, she looked steadier than she had on the trail. Her sudden pain at the death of the squirrel bothered him. He knew he couldn't live with that kind of emotional pain day after day. No wonder she chose to live in isolation.

"Better," she said quietly.

"You felt that squirrel's death as sharply as a knife to your own throat." He shook his head at the memory. She had known the exact instant Wolf found his meal.

"I often do." This time he felt the sadness in her. She was throwing her own magic at him to help him understand. Jaylor was finding it more and more difficult to armor himself against her.

Uneasy, he cast the twig he had been chewing into the fire, then strode to the opening. He hated being so vulnerable. Aware that he was pacing restlessly from the fire to the cliff edge, he paused to think. Wolf matched him stride for stride.

"Did you know that squirrel?" He whirled to face her. The wolf whined at the abrupt movement. Strange that Brevelan put no blame on the animal as the source of today's pain. The bond between them was strong.

"No. But he was close. I had felt his presence. He was very happy to be out in the spring sunshine after a long cold winter. And Puppy was unusually triumphant." She smiled then, dotingly. Her love for the wolf swamped Jaylor. He felt a sudden surge of jealously that such a wonderful emotion was being wasted on a wild beast.

A breeze shifted the brush outside their shelter. Wolf shuddered against his leg. They both felt questing eyes out there, watching them from behind trees and shadows.

Jaylor sniffed the air outside the camp. The wolf mimicked him. They both tensed just before Jaylor's personal armor slid into place. There was something out there. Something magical.

Doubt filled him. He wanted to armor the camp. But if he could smell magic out there, then whoever, or whatever, watched them could sense his spell and be drawn to it, like iron to a lodestone.

"Can we protect ourselves from Old Thorm if he should come again tonight?" Brevelan's question left no doubt that she too sensed the magic presence out there.

The image of Old One-eye following on the trail to her clearing filled his mind. He'd been pressed against a Tambootie tree then, and the rogue magician had not seen him. Oh, he'd sensed where Jaylor had left the trail, but not where he hid. At the time, he'd thought it important to gather a handful of timboor berries.

He'd walked through the Rover camp, invisible to his captors while timboor filled his blood. He seemed to be made of magic for several hours after that. And was totally exhausted for days when the drug wore off.

"Maybe." Jaylor swung back to face her. The hope that filled her eyes gave him new purpose. "Have you ever eaten timboor?"

"The fruit of the Tambootie?" She wrapped her arms around herself and shrank away from him. Mica climbed into her lap and butted her head against the girl's chin, as if offering comfort. "It's poison." Brevelan's tone was evasive.

"I thought so, too. Now I'm not sure. Have you ever eaten of that tree?" He concentrated his gaze on her. There was no need to use magic to pull the information from her. It would come if he could just stare her down. He'd proved that often enough with his tutors. He was amazed how disconcerted people became under a long stare. They usually began to babble within moments.

"Once." She barely whispered as she buried her face into the cat's fur. Mica didn't protest the attention.

"Once," he repeated. "When?"

"When I was running away from home."

"Why did you eat it?" Wolf sat on Jaylor's foot and leaned heavily against his leg. His hand reached for the animal's ears.

Brevelan fussed with the cat and refused to look at him.

"Why, Brevelan? What induced you to eat a fruit you thought to be poison?"

Finally she looked him directly in the eye. He felt something akin to what she must feel when she communicated with animals. Her fear and desperation were as strong as his own when he was in the Rover camp.

"I was running for my life. I dared not stay on the roads, so I made my way through the forest. There was no one I trusted to help me. The animals gave me shelter."

Jaylor couldn't see the specific images she remembered. Her emotions became his own, though.

"Which animal gave you the knowledge about eating timboor?" The berries usually grew on higher branches, seeking the sun. Her helper couldn't be a ground feeder like the timid deer or rabbit.

"A gray bear." A smile touched her lips.

He felt her humor touch him as well.

"Most sane people would run from a gray bear."

"Especially a female protecting her young."

Jaylor grew colder from his core outward. Gray bears had a reputation for being particularly nasty, vicious even, when in the best of humor. A protective mother bear could rend a strong man limb from limb. Trees were no protection from the beasts. They could climb better than most cats.

"Next you'll be telling me she protected and fed you like her own cub." He stared at her, wanting to disbelieve. No one should be so powerful as to tame a gray bear. Or was it her gentleness that undermined overt strength? The power of this kind of magic awed him.

"What did the timboor do to you?"

She hesitated. Her eyes sought the dark corners of their shelter. When she looked back at him, he stretched out a hand to shield her from her own bewilderment.

"I could hear everything, the tiniest rustle among the ferns, the faintest bird song. I could even hear the tug and chomp of rabbits feeding." She looked away again when she mentioned the most silent of all animals. "The most astonishing sounds were the thoughts of the people I encountered. But I was safe then because I could tell if they recognized me, knew of those who pursued me."

Jaylor nodded in agreement. This sounded like his own experience. "Were your other senses affected: sight, smell?"

"Yes." There was more. He could tell from the way she refused to hold his eyes with her own.

"When you didn't want to be seen . . ." he prompted.

"How did you know?" She looked up, startled.

"The same thing happened to me," he reassured her. "I have some timboor in my pack. If we each take a berry, I don't think we could be found."

She nodded, then hid her face again in the cat's fur. "Puppy and Mica?"

"They are not creatures of magic. The berries will poison them." She looked up in dismay at his words. He felt a tug at his heart. He wanted, and needed, to put the sparkle of well-being back into her eyes. "I think our aura of invisibility will extend to those we love." He was the only one who needed to eat of the timboor. He realized at that moment that his love should surround Brevelan with protection for the rest of his days.

Why had she told him so much about her past? Brevelan had revealed more to this strange man in a few days than to anyone else in her entire life.

Too many people misunderstood her magic. They reacted with fear, or cruelty bred from fear. So she hid her innermost thoughts and feelings. Her family and acquaintances had known only as much about her as they could guess from her actions.

After the death of her husband, she knew she had to flee her home or be burned as a witch. She scooted away from the warmth of the flames.

Mica protested the movement.

Brevelan soothed her with a few distracted strokes. Her mind refused to move from the images she had dragged out of her memory.

Another woman accused of witchcraft. An old woman who had taught Brevelan much about the nature of plants, which healed and how, as well as which killed. Lord Krej sitting in judgment, not allowing the poor woman to speak any defense. Then the punishment. All in the district had been required to watch.

Death by fire. Clouds of oily black smoke.

Her mother whispering in her ear that this would be Brevelan's fate if Krej heard of her healing ability.

Heat, pain. No air.

Her breaths were sharp and difficult. Heat seared her throat with each gulp of air. And when it was all over and the ashes scattered across the bay, a triumphant Krej had taken four virgins back to his castle.

"Brevelan!" Jaylor's hand on her shoulder broke the images. "Brevelan, what happened? What did you see in the flames?" He shook her free of her memories with anxious hands.

"Nothing," she lied. The look in his eyes told her he knew it was not the truth. "I was just thinking."

"Or remembering," he stated flatly.

She refused to answer. Whatever she said, he would see the truth in her eyes.

Puppy wiggled closer to her. He pushed under her arm with his muzzle. She drew him close, along with the cat. She didn't question that these two animals tolerated each other's presence.

"Here. Eat this." Jaylor held out his hand. In his palm rested some dry berries that had once been deep red with yellow bands. Now they were dull gray.

"Will the essential oils still be there?" she questioned as she picked up one berry, about the size of her thumbnail.

"I think so. When I was given timboor, my captors had no access to fresh. They must have used dried."

She raised an eyebrow in question. It was safer to let him talk rather than question her past.

Jaylor recounted his experience with the Rover tribe while he petted each of the animals in turn.

"Modern magic texts proclaim everything about the Tambootie is evil. I can see how it might be abused. But evil? I wonder how much of our knowledge is carefully edited to avoid misuse rather than full understanding. I think I need to explore the effects of the berry more fully." His words floated over her.

She knew she would remember and understand what he said in the morning. For now she needed only to feel the smooth rhythm of his voice.

The fire came into sharp focus. In the heart of the flames she saw the wind stirring the treetops outside. Her body took on a new lightness, drifting upward and out into the forest. She was no longer a part of the cozy camp scene below her.

From her elevated position, she watched a man and a woman settle for the night. Their blankets were rough homespun. The dying fire grew pungent. The huge golden wolf crawled between them. A multicolored cat sought the wolf's back for warmth. In the darkness of night the silent thoughts of Brevelan drifted through the forest. Watching. Waiting.

Chapter 13

*They think to trick me with my own tricks. I needn't see
them to know where they are. My magic, the magic of
the Tambootie, guides me. Tonight I will spin my dreams
by my blessed Tambootie wood fire. I shall sleep safe and
warm, while they lie wakeful and wondering.*

*They shall have nothing—no king, no prince, no magic.
Tomorrow I will press them harder. Tomorrow I will find
the dragon. After I secure the monster, I shall kill the wolf
once and for all. And then all will be mine.*

And I shall have the dragon!

Warm, sweet-smelling hair tickled Jaylor's nose. He
breathed deeply of the lovely scent. Then he snuggled
closer to the source. A soft, feminine body filled his arms.
He could tell it was a woman by the curves that molded to
his hand.

A woman?

No! He sat up abruptly. A woman in his arms, before
dawn could only mean one thing. He'd lain with her and
lost his magic.

Sleep-befuddled panic engulfed him. Sweat, cold and
clammy, broke out on his back. His breaths came short and
sharp until the cold morning air chased the fog of sleep
from his mind.

Slowly his breathing returned to normal, and he thought
in logical patterns once more. The woman he'd held most
of the night was Brevelan. He had slept by her side in the
rough shelter of the almost-cave. He had dreamed of her,
but they had not lain together as a man and a woman.

The blasted wolf had seen to that. The beast had slept

between them most of the night; Mica curled up with him. Any lustful thoughts Jaylor might have had were successfully squashed by the fuzzy barrier represented by the animals. Jaylor wasn't sure when Wolf and Mica had wandered off to their own morning pursuits.

Cautiously, Jaylor worked a small spell. He lifted a few spare twigs into the embers of the fire and reignited them. His magic was intact!

He lay back down on the hard ground, grateful that his natural lusts had not overcome his good sense. His arm automatically stretched to bring Brevelan's sleeping body closer.

He pulled the rough blanket up to cover them both more fully. Her warmth relaxed him while her natural scent filled him with more energetic ideas.

It was morning and he was at his most susceptible. He really should move away from her—and soon. After watching her rise one morning in the hut, he had always made sure he was well on his way to the bathing pool before she slid from the protective warmth of her enticingly large bed. Her shift covered her entire body, but it was old and thin. The nearly sheer muslin couldn't hide the delectable shapes and shadows of her petite form.

Brevelan stirred in her sleep. She turned toward him, seeking his warmth in the chill morning air. Jaylor groaned. He had to move away . . . now!

"Mhmmm," she murmured. Her small hand slipped across his chest.

The gesture brought her breasts snug against his side. Excited tingles spread out from the point of contact. "Ah . . . good morning, Brevelan." Jaylor sought to rouse her before her innocent attentions drove him beyond control. Good thing they were both fully clothed.

"Mhmm. Cold." Her eyes remained closed.

"Let me build up the fire." He slid his arm from under her head reluctantly.

"Fire," She mumbled again. Then her eyes opened in panic. "Fire?" She sat up abruptly. The blankets fell away and she shivered.

"Wake up, Brevelan," he commanded. Instinct told him to go to her, hold her until the morning fogginess cleared her mind of the nightmare that haunted her. Disastrous idea. She was much too tempting with her soft, innocent beauty. Russet locks tumbled about her face. He needed to push them out of her eyes, caress her cheek, kiss her soft mouth. He also needed all of his magic, intact, to safely confront the dragon. He didn't know how much more magic he would need to shore up the border once they found Shayla.

Thoughts of their quest brought to mind the absent wolf and cat. He couldn't count on being alone with Brevelan long enough to fulfill what his body demanded.

"Where . . . where is Puppy? And Mica?" The panic had not quite left her voice as she scanned the shadows of the recess with troubled blue eyes.

"I don't know. They wandered off sometime in the night; probably to eat," he replied, keeping his back to her. It was best if he busied himself with feeding the fire. If he looked at her again, he would not be able to resist.

"How long ago?"

"I don't know. They were gone when I awoke." *And you were in my arms, where you belong.*

That thought startled him. She did belong with him. But she couldn't belong at his side night and day until he was a master magician.

"I'm going down to the creek for water." He stood as rapidly as his morning stiff body would allow. He stretched, easing his back. He turned to make sure Brevelan was awake and well. Another part of his body stretched and didn't ease. He took off for the creek at a near run.

"Mrrow." Mica greeted Brevelan.

"Did you have a good morning, Mica?" She watched the small cat sit next to the now glowing fire and wash her face.

Mica didn't deign to reply until she was finished with her face. "Mrrow."

Of course. Mica always had a good morning. It was her favorite time of day. The cat's emotions, which were almost words, pressed into Brevelan's chest with joyful energy.

Brevelan chuckled. This was her favorite time of day as well. With each new dawn came the chance to move her life forward, an opportunity to leave the troublesome past farther behind.

"Where is Puppy?" she asked the cat.

No reply. Either Mica didn't know or, more likely, didn't care. Mica reminded Brevelan that Darville could take care of himself.

"Are you sure about that?" Brevelan asked. There were times when the wolf acted as if he'd never lived in the wild before. He needed her help and companionship too often. He also needed her healing. Sometimes he seemed terribly clumsy for a wolf.

Mica blinked. Her yellow cat-eyes changed to rounded hazel-green. She blinked again and the cat was once more inside those strange eyes.

Brevelan tested the water in the small pot she had brought along. It was nearly bubbling, time to add the handful of grains. By the time Jaylor returned from the creek it should be ready.

A little tune came to her. She hummed it quietly. When it was set in her mind, she sang it a little louder. The notes sought out the dark shadows behind her, then swirled forward to reach across the forest. Contentment filled the recesses of the overhang.

Mica butted her head against Brevelan's knee. She scratched the cat's ears to keep her out of her lap. "I'm sorry there is no milk for you, Mica. We left Mistress Goat behind."

A loud purr was the cat's response. She didn't mind as long as her ears were rubbed just precisely there.

"Grrower!"

"What a nasty thing to say!" Brevelan sat straighter. She shivered at the intensity of the protest.

"Grrower!"

That wasn't Mica!

At the edge of the cliff Jaylor looked out at the scene he had not seen the night before. Morning mist clung to the valleys and ravines while the mountain peaks soared above to pierce a cloudless sky. Below, the forest stretched, seemingly forever. Vibrant greens and blues of early spring shimmered in the sunrise.

The last of the winter browns faded beneath the new growth. He picked out the bright and dark pattern of new growth on the everblues. Nestled here and there among them were the flat-topped Tambootie. This far up the mountain the trees of magic hadn't been destroyed by superstition and the need for more pasturage. The area was even too remote for the greedy copper miners who sought the veins of ore beneath the roots.

His body tingled as he caught a whiff of the pungent bark. Clean and crisp. A healthy smell, totally different from the reek of the evil associated with the Tambootie smoke.

Jaylor gasped a lungful of cold air. The beauty of Coronnan lay before him, as he had never seen it before.

Old-timers called this dragon weather: a little rain in the night, sunshine and beauty during the day.

The weight of his quest settled upon his shoulders. Baamin said the dragons were ill, needing a magic medicine to bring the nimbus up to strength. Were they merely ill, or were they being killed?

The embankment was steep and slippery from the rain. Saber ferns grew in profusion here, but they offered no handhold. He dug in his heels to keep from sliding headlong into the briskly flowing water of the creek. His boots stirred the damp earth. He smelled the cloying sweetness of crushed rose-lichen where his boots slipped in the mud. A nubby-berry bush snagged his leather shirt. These hazards were familiar.

He splashed a handful of cold water over his face, carefully at first. His ablutions became more lavish after the initial shock of the icy creek, restoring his natural assurance and good humor.

Wolf was not as cautious with the embankment or the cold water. He dashed down the bank to plunge into the water. He emerged with a gleeful grin on his face, water dripping from his coat.

Jaylor was reminded of the youthful prankster he had known several years ago. Roy's tutors had driven the boy to become more serious, pushing responsibility onto his young shoulders.

Jaylor hadn't seen much of his friend in the last two years. He didn't slip away from his duties to explore life in the city anymore.

Instead, he took to riding his steeds long and hard. Always, there was a cohort of soldiers to guard him.

No wonder he organized long hunts at every opportunity.

During a chase he could escape the suffocating presence of others and forget his responsibilities for a while.

Cold water splashed across Jaylor's leather trews. He stepped back, laughing. Wolf looked up, an entreating gleam in his eye. "Sorry, fellow. There isn't time today for a romp in the water. We have to find ourselves a dragon."

Wolf cocked his head, as if trying to understand. He splashed again, then bounded out of the water, spreading almost as much liquid in his path as he left in the creek. He shook a few of the clinging drops from his fur.

Jaylor could almost see the wolf's thoughts. He didn't feel right, so he took a step closer to Jaylor before shaking again.

In his haste to step away from the cascade Jaylor slipped in the mud. *"S'murgh it!"* he cursed as he landed on his backside. "You had to do that, you miserable beast."

Once again Wolf cocked his head in curiosity. The movement brought another small spray of water across Jaylor's shirt.

"Watch it, Wolf. You'd feel cold without all that fuzz. Spray me again and I'll shave you bald," he threatened with a laugh.

Jaylor anchored his awareness in the reality of his surroundings. There was the damp earth and fresh leaves of the growing trees. Birds were awake and chirping now. Below him the creek danced over rocks on its downhill journey. Above him was just the faintest trace of woodsmoke. Brevelan must have stoked the fire.

She would be cooking breakfast. Grains with a wild nutty flavor. If it were later in the season, he could gather some nubby-berries to sweeten their morning meal. Perhaps Brevelan would throw some dried fruit into the pot. A hot drink would taste good, too. Jaylor's mouth watered in anticipation. A proper meal would go a long way toward giving him the strength to confront a magic dragon.

"Come, Puppy. We need to get back to Brevelan." He started up the hill again.

"Grrrr," Wolf replied. His fur stood up on the back of his neck.

"Grrower!" Another animal answered, louder.

"Spotted saber cat," he whispered into the wind. The largest, meanest, hungriest wild beast in Coronnan. An adult male could grow as large as a gray bear. Its elongated front teeth equaled those of a wild tusker in length. And the beast sounded as though it stood in the opening of the cave where Brevelan was preparing breakfast!

"Come, Wolf. Now. Brevelan needs us," Jaylor urged.

"Grroowower," Wolf replied as he bounded toward the menace.

Waves of anger washed over Brevelan. Pressure built behind her neck and eyes, pressure to move. Her eyes glazed under the impact of the anger and outrage bombarding her senses. The pressure increased. Air inside her lungs fought with the weight of the atmosphere outside her body. The compulsion to move weighed heavily on her limbs. *Move.*

But where?

She was encased in a red cage of emotion. Walls of suffocating red marched closer and closer. She couldn't breathe. The walls threatened to wrap her in hot, airless, burning hatred. *Block it out.*

I must turn my mind away. She forced a separation from the red walls. Gradually her eyes focused. She sought the source of the emotional upheaval and wished she hadn't.

In the opening of the overhang, between her and escape, stood a spotted saber cat. The beast could be the twin or littermate of the only other one of its kind she had ever seen. The bronze statue that had blinked at her in Krej's hall. Its long teeth gleamed wetly in the early sunlight. Malevolence flashed deep within its eyes. That cat wanted nothing more than to use those huge teeth to rip her flesh open and taste her blood.

Chapter 14

Darkness dwelt within the cavern. The campfire glowed near the entrance. Behind it no shadow moved. Jaylor couldn't see Brevelan. Sweat clung to his brow and back. What if the cat had already killed her? Panic threatened to shatter him from the inside out.

The huge cat stood in the entrance to the overhang, its eerie roar echoing about the hillside. Jaylor took one silent step closer. Orange and gray fur gleamed in the early sunlight, temporarily blinding him with its brilliance.

"Grrower," the cat snarled again. Claws fully extended, one huge front paw reached up to strike at something in the shadows.

Each one of those claws was nearly as long as one of Jaylor's fingers.

One more step and he would be able to see if the cat's intended prey was Brevelan. A tiny pebble rolled under his boot. It struck another, larger stone. The sound drew the cat's eyes, eyes that were slitted with malice. The huge body remained between Jaylor and the cavern interior.

He crouched to ease his rapid breathing. He had to get Brevelan out of the way.

"Grrower." Once more the cat turned his attention toward the shadowy movement in the dark recess.

A rock that just fit Jaylor's palm came to his hand. Without bothering to stand straight again, he flung the stone. It bounced off the largest gray spot just behind the cat's ribs.

"Yeehowl!" The beast protested as it moved sideways and deeper into the recess.

"S'murgh!" Jaylor cursed.

Another growl filled the overhang. Wolf stood beside

him, fur on end, ears upright. He too was ready to do battle.

Wolf bared his fangs and approached the cat. *We must save Brevelan.* His growls came close to words, their meaning clear in Jaylor's mind. Yellow wolf eyes narrowed to glittering slits.

There wasn't time to puzzle out that moment of coherent communication. The cat slunk beyond the campfire toward Brevelan's hiding place. Where was she anyway?

"We need a weapon, Wolf." His pack and staff were between the cat and Brevelan. He needed the staff as a focus for a blast of magic fire.

Jaylor gathered the magic necessary for the spell. Which spell? He'd never used magic for offense, only as armor for defense. "I'll think of something." His mind drifted away from his body, watched himself from afar.

Breathe in slowly, he told the body he was watching. *Feel the magic essence roll and form into a tangible shape. An arrow of light and energy. Like lightning.*

Breathe out. Let the magic grow in power. Say the words and watch the spell emerge from the body.

Nothing happened. He gulped back the panic. Once more he hadn't been able to throw the proper spell. He could hear his teachers grumbling, the other apprentices laughing at his clumsiness.

Maybe he had said the wrong spell. He rolled the words back across his visual memory. No, the words were right, the spell was proper. So what went wrong?

"Grrower!" The cat spat again as it took another step forward.

Movement caught his eye. Up there, on the small ledge at the back. Brevelan crouched, knees under her chin, Mica clutched to her breast. Even from the opening he could see her shaking. Some of her distress spilled out to him. For a moment he was shaken by the intensity.

Without thinking, Jaylor brought his staff to his hand with an image. "I won't let it hurt you," he declared. The words cleared his mind even as his body sent forth the first shot of red and blue flame.

A pitiful little bolt of fire, it barely reached the cat's thick fur. Its tail twitched in annoyance at the tiny pinprick against its flank.

"We'll have to do better this time," he muttered to no one in particular. He calmed his pounding heartbeat and evened his ragged breathing. That was supposed to be the simple part. Still, his mind echoed with the fear that was palpitating against the walls.

He had to forget the deeply ingrained limitations and restrictions on magic as taught at the University. The Commune, working in concert could use magic as a weapon—for the good of the kingdom. Individuals couldn't throw those spells alone. But that was traditional magic. He was Jaylor, the solitary. If One-eye could use personal magic for his own greed, then surely Jaylor could summon enough to save a life.

Breathe in three, out three. In, one, two, three. Out, one, two, three. Again, two, three.

His vision cleared as he shifted his feet to a better position. Sound ceased, and time slowed. The rock walls glowed with silver light. He isolated the cat from its surroundings. The sun and fog of its fur filled his mind. He raised his staff with one hand, then grasped it with the other. His mind focused on the twisting grain of the wood, long fingers of magic braided along its fibers.

With a mighty effort he sent forth chains of fire. They pulsed, then merged into one huge ball. The dark recesses were filled with heat and light as bright as noon in the clearing.

"Yeeowl!" The cat looked him in the eyes, startled.

Jaylor held its gaze. He allowed his eyes to tell the beast he was serious this time. Another burst of his signature blue and red flame braided along the staff.

The cat jumped back toward the cave entrance to avoid the magic fire.

"Grrow." It spat one last comment before turning and bounding past Jaylor and away through the forest.

"Arrooff," Wolf howled in triumph. He chased the beast away from the entrance, baying in triumph, his fur still stiff and teeth bared.

"You can come down now, Brevelan." Jaylor turned to her once he was sure the cat was gone. Brevelan didn't move. Mica began squirming away from her clenched hands now that the danger was gone.

Wolf trotted to a spot just beneath the ledge and whined.

"You're safe now, Brevelan." Jaylor coaxed. He reached up a hand to help her down.

Mica used it to reach the ground. Brevelan maintained her fearful crouch, eyes fixed, body trembling.

"Brevelan!" Jaylor spoke as sharply as he dared. "That cat may come back. We have to leave. Now!"

She whimpered slightly. At least she was responding.

"Come now, take my hand. I won't let anything hurt you." He reached up his hand again.

She didn't move. "*S'murgh* it, Brevelan. You have to come down. Now." This time he grabbed her arm and shook her.

Finally she looked at him. "I felt its need to kill. For a moment I needed to kill."

"I have failed, Your Grace." Baamin bowed his head before King Darcine in the royal family's private solar. He was careful to add a touch of humility to the carriage of his shoulders. It wouldn't do for the king to see how happy he was that he had failed.

"You dare to come to me, your mission incomplete?" The king's eyes narrowed in speculation. For a moment Baamin was reminded of the younger Darcine, strong and eager for battle.

"I am sorry, Your Grace. The magic has failed me. I tried to reach my journeymen. Something, or someone, interfered. The kingdom's magic has faded beyond my ability to gather it."

"Impossible." The king pulled himself up to his full height. It was a stance he had not assumed much in the past few years. His subjects had almost forgotten how imposing he could be when necessary.

"Nothing is impossible, Your Grace." Baamin straightened too. The top of his head barely reached the king's nose. He had to rely on his bearing and bulk to claim the respect due his position as Senior Magician, Chancellor of the University, and adviser to the king.

"Dragon magic is woven into the very fiber of this kingdom. It cannot fail. I am stronger, therefore the magic must be strong."

"Shayla has mated. You are stronger because she carries young. But she is the only breeding female dragon left. The nimbus of dragons is pitifully small, Your Grace. All the others in my records are too old, or dead, or they have left," Baamin argued.

"Left? Dragons can't leave Coronnan. They are bound to us." Darcine's shoulders caved in a little. He seemed to lose the strength to hold them back.

"The bonds of magic and Tambootie are not enough to hold the creatures when they are driven out by superstition and slaughter. Uneducated villagers have stopped planting the Tambootie. They no longer tithe their livestock to the dragons. Indeed, many have killed dragons rather than worship them. Shayla's last two litters were slaughtered in the nest. We are lucky she stayed. You are alive today only because she mated again."

"When did this outrage occur? And why was I not told? There is no greater crime in this kingdom than murdering a dragon and I was not told!" Grief and anger gripped Darcine's features. "Those responsible must be punished."

"The first time, I learned of it even as the lung disease gripped you. We feared for your life, Your Grace." Baamin swallowed deeply. He searched his king's face for signs of the weakness that had gripped him ever since.

"And the second time?"

"Shayla bred again, as soon as she could, so we . . . I felt it best to let you heal without that knowledge. The next litter was killed as well."

"That would have been two years later, when my heart failed." Deep sadness drained the straightness from his shoulders. "Was there no one who would lift a finger against the murderers?"

Baamin rested a comforting hand against Darcine's back. "The healers said the news of the second tragedy would kill you for certain."

"Where were the lords when this slaughter took place? Surely they would seek out and destroy anyone who dared harm the nimbus?" Darcine found his padded chair with shaking knees.

Baamin thought about assisting his king to the chair. In spite of his new vigor, Darcine's body was still painfully thin, and so frail he looked as if the slight breeze from the open window would crumble him to dust. Baamin decided he'd done too much assisting in the past. They had all, counselors and lords alike, allowed the king to become weak and uninvolved over the years. At the time it had seemed logical to ease his burdens as his health failed. Darville had been around then, young and strong, eager to take responsibility onto his broad shoulders.

Now Darville was missing. They could no longer rely on him. That left Krej, the king's cousin, as the logical person to consult. But it was that lord's tenants who had laid the traps for Shayla's mates and her brood.

"Your lords have become lax in their duties. You have not taken the time to keep track of them." Baamin hated to say it, but it might be the only way to force the king to take some responsibility for his inattention.

"Darville will see to it . . ." The command died on the king's lips. "My son is missing."

"You must use your strength, now, while you have it, to delegate authority to those you can trust—those you know have the best interests of Coronnan in their hearts."

"I shall handle this myself, Baamin. I dare not trust even you with this chore. Call the lords. I will meet them this evening.

"I can't."

"What?" Darcine roared with some of his lost power.

"I don't have enough magic to summon them. You must send messengers." Baamin assumed an attitude of defeat.

He must have time to convince Darcine to give the Commune authority over the lords.

"Messengers will take time. Three days at least."

"It is necessary. What little magic I can summon drains away as fast as I gather it. Something, or someone, is interfering with the very fiber of magic."

"Then send the messengers within the hour. You may commandeer the fastest steeds in my stable."

Three days. Was it long enough to find a way around the fading magic? Though his soul recoiled from it, Baamin knew he must seek out a source of rogue magic. It was the only way to counter the actions of a foreign rogue and find out who employed him.

"You didn't kill the cat." Brevelan's weak voice sounded more a question than a statement. She cleared her throat and tried again.

"You could have killed it. But you didn't." That was better.

"I didn't have to," Jaylor replied. His voice was a little strained. After all, he was carrying her, and uphill at that.

She felt strange moving over the terrain without the physical effort of her own limbs. Strange in a very nice way. She couldn't remember being carried since she had learned to walk.

She shivered again in memory of why Jaylor found it necessary to carry her. The cat's mind had been so filled with hatred that it had refused the touch of her empathy.

Jaylor's arms tightened and chased away her chill of emptiness. For a few moments she soaked up the nice feeling of his comfort, his care. Then she leaned back just enough to see his face when she spoke. "Why did you spare the beast? Most men would have killed it anyway, just to prove they could. Then they would excuse the slaughter by saying they had to, to make sure it couldn't come back."

She watched a gamut of emotions cross his face before he settled into a smile.

"There was no need." He held her eyes with his own for a moment.

She felt his gaze warm her all the way through to the cold, empty place in her belly. It seemed only natural for her to rest her head once more on his shoulder.

Jaylor adjusted his hold to grasp her more securely. "Besides, you were shaken enough by the encounter. If I had killed something that large and close, you would've been useless for the rest of the day."

He was deliberately containing some very strong emotions. She could tell by the tremor in the pulse of his neck. She snuggled just a little closer. The beat of his heart echoed against her ear. Her own heart beat in the same rhythm.

"I've never before encountered an animal who refused the touch of my mind."

"I wondered about that. A gray bear is bigger, and just as mean. But one sheltered you. Why not the cat?"

She clung a little tighter as she recounted the story of the cat in Krej's great hall. "I think it might be the same cat."

"If so, it would associate Krej's cruelty with all people. No wonder it fought your magic."

The ground was becoming rough, strewn with loose pebbles and larger rocks. Behind them, Puppy whined. He trotted closer, brushing his body against Jaylor's leg.

"We'll stop in a moment. There's a fairly level boulder top just ahead."

Something akin to disappointment washed over Brevelan. As soon as they reached that broken boulder he would set her down. The wonderful security of his arms would be withdrawn.

"Here we are." All too soon she felt him lowering her to the stone surface, not so much a boulder as a ledge jutting out from the hillside beside the path.

Puppy didn't wait for him to step away before he butted his head between them. He licked Brevelan's face and whined again.

"I'm fine, Puppy," she reassured the wolf. As Jaylor straightened, she continued clinging to his neck with one hand. Puppy's wiggling body pushed farther into her lap. Mica chose that moment to scamper onto her outstretched legs. For a moment all four friends were caught in one hug. Brevelan wanted to cry with relief and happiness.

"I think we should find something to eat," she said to mask the depth of the emotion she felt. "Too bad we left the packs and our breakfast in the cave."

"No problem." Jaylor's grin was infectious. She found herself matching it.

Her back tingled where his hand still rested. She felt a tremor course through his body to her own.

The packs appeared beside her and his staff, more gnarled than before, came to his hand. With another blink of his eyes the campfire and breakfast pot appeared.

"Doesn't that tire you?" She looked up concerned.

"Not nearly as much as going without food," Jaylor replied.

Chapter 15

Baamin leaned all of his bulk into the ancient door. Oak panels, aged to the stiffness of iron, creaked open slowly, held back as much by disuse as by the spell that had sealed them for so many years. Three centuries of dust assaulted his nose. Minute particles tickled and irritated until he sneezed loudly. The cloud swirled faster.

"Dragon bones!" he cursed, and sneezed again.

At one time the corridor running past this room had led to a tunnel connecting the University with the Palace Reveta Tristile. Many generations ago, a spring flood had damaged the tunnel. Repairs had been deemed too costly, and this long hallway and its rooms had been abandoned, nearly forgotten.

"What is this room, master?" the kitchen boy asked. His eyes grew huge with wonder.

Baamin sneezed before he could reply. Some of the dust and mold had settled, but not all. A large swirl of it still filled his nose with another itch. He held his breath to stop the next sneeze.

"You know the value of books, Boy?" he finally managed to choke past the gathering tickle.

"Yes, master. Books are the storage place of knowledge. Without knowledge we are no better than the animals." The boy recited dutifully. His eyes held enough intelligence that he just might understand the words he quoted, in spite of his teacher's reports on his limitations.

"Very true. Unfortunately, some of my predecessors decided knowledge of some subjects is dangerous." Baamin shook his head in dismay. So many of the precious books were in a terrible state of decay, despite the spell that had sealed the room for so long.

His search for the room had lasted five years. He wasted another three in breaking the protective seal. Now he had found the key, apparently just in time. He didn't like secrets. Abandoned and forgotten books bothered him.

Lords secretly employing rogue magicians bothered him more.

"How can any knowledge be dangerous, master? The teachers insist that we must learn all we can to make us stronger." The lad gently ran a finger along the spine of a large tome. His hand came away grimy, leaving the gold letters of the title glittering in the dim light of their lantern.

"Has your history tutor told you of the Great Wars of Disruption?"

The dark-eyed boy nodded.

"When the rogue magicians refused to join the Commune, they were cast out of Coronnan." With good reason. The selfish interests of the rogues were responsible for prolonging the war.

Baamin continued, "Indeed, many could not join the Commune because their magic would not link up with other magicians. The kind of magic they performed was banned. And their books were burned."

"Someone hid these books to save them from the fire?" Fear tinged the boy's eyes.

"Yes, they did. I don't know who. It could have been a rogue who hoped to come back some day—the records say many magicians thought the Commune could not last. More likely it was one of our own who loved books for themselves rather than hating them because of their content." Baamin would have done the same thing.

He sighed in anguish as he plucked a small book from its shelf. The dust that covered it was all that held it together. Leather binding and vellum pages crumbled in his hands.

The protective spell had not done its job properly. It had kept intruders out but not stopped the ravages of time. It was evidence of the haste in which the spell had been constructed. Baamin suspected the book burners had turned rabid. Whoever secreted these books away would have had little time and a great deal of fear hindering him.

"Why do we need these books now, master?" The boy

was puzzled. His eyes wandered over the vast number of the volumes; his hands remained carefully at his sides.

"Because the magic is changing. The Commune is no longer strong," Baamin sighed. So much good came from the Commune. If only the King and Council looked more to the Commune for guidance rather than for power and communication. Maybe the Commune was a little rigid in its traditionalism, but the wars of lord against lord, prompted by power-hungry magicians, had ended. The kingdom was at peace. "We need this rogue magic to negate a growing threat to the kingdom." Baamin needed rogue magic to summon his magicians back to the University before the lords gathered. The boy didn't need to know that. His only purpose was to carefully clean the books and note their titles.

Baamin must also keep this room a secret. He had no doubt the boy would keep his mouth shut. He had already proven his ability this last week. No one else at the University knew of Jaylor's antics with the wine cups and the sliced meat. Then, too, there was the matter of the cot and blankets missing from the storage room.

What would Jaylor's next stunt be? Very likely he would borrow a larger viewing glass or maybe a book of spells from the library. Or possibly a book from this very room?

Baamin shook his head, partly in dismay, partly in amazement. How had he reared a rogue magician in these very halls without noticing? All the evidence was there, in the very early manifestation of power, in the wine cups and wildly distorted spells. Maybe it was a good thing the tutors had thought young Jaylor merely inept at throwing magic. If they had realized he was a rogue at work, they would have banished him long ago.

'Twas Jaylor who had discovered the rogue inciting dragon murder in Lord Krej's province. 'Twas Jaylor who had been the first of the journeymen to see a dragon. Perhaps he would learn the importance of the wolf the dragon protected, too.

Baamin almost hoped not. He needed to know what prompted the dragon before anyone else did. He needed knowledge and information to deal with the unexpected and unexplained. He began searching through the books in earnest.

* * *

Closer and closer they lead me. I must push them to move faster. Soon they will pass the place where I removed Darville from my path. And shall again. It is as close to Shayla as I have come on my own.

On the first dragon hunt, blind luck led us to follow a man in dragon-thrall. The next time, the old witchwoman was tricked into showing the way. I had to kill the old crone. Then the dragon changed her lair, relaid the path. She became smart, as smart as Maman. Almost, I lost the desire to pursue. But the Tambootie gave me the will to persevere.

My patience has been rewarded. I set everything else in place. Now, the girl will lead me. Once beyond this cliff top, nothing can keep me from my dragon.

At last, all the years of planning, the murder of my father and older brothers, the destruction of the nimbus, and Darville's enchantment, are coming to fruition.

No one in the kingdom will resist me. I will no longer have to steal my Tambootie. Dragons will bring it to me.

Brevelan's path up the mountain narrowed as it curved around a steep cliffside. An ancient landslide had left a wild scree above the narrow ledge they traversed. Occasional tufts of grass clung to the thin soil, telling Brevelan the age of the slide.

Below them, a sheer cliff dropped to a cluster of trees and a swift stream. In the rarefied air, Brevelan could see the details of the scene very clearly. She felt a moment of disorientation as she looked over the edge. The height was dizzying. Puppy whined and pressed closer to Brevelan. His body trembled against her. She reached to give him the comfort he craved.

"What's his problem?" Jaylor turned back from the steep path to check on his companions.

"This place bothers him." Brevelan crouched down to wrap her arms completely around the distressed wolf.

"Why?"

She sensed the man's armor falling into place. He was nearly as wary as the wolf. There was a presence behind them again. She felt it the moment she stopped concentrating on her footing. The spotted saber cat or Old Thorm?

She didn't like the thought of either one creeping up behind them.

"I don't know," Brevelan replied. She crooned a soothing tune to the wolf. They needed to continue on, put more
distance between themselves and whatever matched their
movements. The follower had also stopped but had not
turned away.

"Mrrow?" Mica added her own questions to the conversation. The fur on her back stood upright. Her tail swished
in agitation.

Brevelan saw Jaylor wince as the little cat dug her claws
into his shoulder. He batted the offending claws lightly. In
response Mica butted her head into his shoulder. Her fur
smoothed a little.

"Has Wolf ever been here before?" Jaylor peered around
the ridge they were climbing. They were very high now.
Shayla's lair couldn't be far.

Cautiously, Brevelan looked around, without releasing
her gentling hand on Puppy. Her gaze was drawn to the
valley below. It seemed familiar. She looked closer.

The height distorted her vision and balance. She knew
the terrifying urge to throw herself into the warm air rising
from the valley floor. She closed her eyes as she backed
up, attempting to break the almost familiar need to launch
into flight.

Behind her squeezed eyelids she saw a winter storm
threatening the gray sky and the crumpled body of a golden
wolf at the foot of the ancient landslide. She remembered
feeling panic, followed by the overwhelming need to save
that wolf. She needed help.

"The last time I saw this place was through Shayla's
eyes." She gulped in an effort to return to her own body,
her own emotions. "Darville was below, injured, and she
couldn't get to him to help him." She opened her eyes
again and looked at Jaylor. Just as Puppy was drawing support from her, she needed the magician's calming presence
to relate the rest of the story.

"That was the first time Shayla spoke to me. She needed
my help. At her prodding, I was compelled to follow her
lead and take Darville back to my hut." She relived the
moment when another mind had invaded her own. She was

used to animals calling to her in their time of need. But never before had an empathic link been so verbal, so intelligent and overwhelming.

Always before, and since, she'd had the choice to refuse the animal. But not that one time.

Not until she had dragged the wolf on a blanket, through the growing blizzard to the safety and warmth of her own hearth, had Shayla released her from the compulsion.

"And the dragon checked on him daily, told you his name? Are you certain Darville is the name she gave him?" Jaylor touched her shoulder. His brown eyes widened. Worry creased his brow as confusion clouded his emotions.

Brevelan nodded. "I've never understood why she protected him so fiercely. It would have been easier for her to make a meal of him. I'm glad she didn't." She hugged Puppy close again. "The winter was long and lonely. He kept me busy, kept me company. Shayla was someone to talk to when I craved the sound of words. They are my family now."

"And you never questioned the name Shayla gave the wolf?" He paced back and forth in front of her, dangerously close to the edge of the cliff. He seemed oblivious to the crumbling rocks in his agitation.

"Yes, I questioned Shayla," Brevelan defended herself. "The only answer I received was, 'That is his name.' "

Jaylor stopped his pacing abruptly. "Darville is his name," he echoed her words. "*Darville* is his name. *Stargods!* It can't be. It just can't be." He rubbed his hand across his eyes then looked more closely at the wolf.

"What can't be, Jaylor?" Brevelan held tighter to her pet, filling her hands with his long fur.

"Why didn't you tell me this before? I could have consulted Baamin and found out for sure." He fumbled in the packs. Clothing and provisions went flying as he sought some object of dire importance.

"Found out what, Jaylor?" Brevelan refolded his spare shirt and gathered her packets of grain and dried fruit.

"You don't know?" He sat back on his heels and stared at her openmouthed.

"Know what?" she demanded, exasperated at his thick male understanding.

"When I left Coronnan City a few weeks after the solstice, Prince Darville had been missing almost a full moon.

We were friends. When I asked to see him, to say good-bye, I was told he was in a monastery contemplating an unfortunate dalliance with a lady. The Darville I grew up with never regretted any of his encounters with ladies. The Darville I knew had no time for quiet contemplation and far too much energy for cloistered celibacy."

"So?"

"So, I believe the tale was a cover-up. The king and my master are close friends. They are hiding the fact that Darville is missing."

"Are you suggesting that this animal is our prince? Don't be ridiculous."

"Dragons and the royal family are connected by tradition, honor, and blood. Shayla is bound by instinct and magic to protect those with royal blood. Do you have any other explanation for her ties to a scruffy golden wolf named Darville?"

Jaylor's words chilled her.

"Are you telling me that my wolf is part of the royal family?" Disbelief and understanding warred within her.

"He is not just a wolf. Look at him. Really look at him. Do you see the intelligence in his eyes?" He held an oblong of glass between her and the wolf. "Look through the glass and tell me he is just a wolf!"

Brevelan clung to Puppy's thick fur. He smelled of dog, and fresh air, and the plants he had brushed along the way. His tongue panted in the slight breeze, radiating heat. He swallowed, then licked her cheek in affection.

Darville had become a part of her life, a very important part. She had told him things she would not confide to another human, shared her home, her food, her love with a beast. She refused to believe he was anything other than wolf.

And yet . . . ? There were times when he seemed so very intelligent, listening to her with comprehension in his eyes. And there was Shayla's almost reverent protection of him.

When she thought about the situation, it seemed very likely indeed that her pet was more than he appeared to be.

"How?" she asked. If Jaylor's words were too unbeliev-able, she would reject them and not allow him to take Darville away from her.

"I don't know. I can only presume Old One-eye is behind

this. The prince has been missing since just before the winter solstice. I believe I was sent to find a dragon in hopes the dragon would know something of the prince's location."

"Instead you found a witchwoman with a wolf for a familiar. A wolf with a princely name and a dragon guardian," she breathed. It could be true, it was all so logical. And yet . . . and yet her heart did not want to release the wolf who had been her constant companion for months. Tears gathered in her eyes.

She remembered the saber cat trapped in bronze. Its anguish had made her ill at the time. Did the wolf at her side know he was trapped inside an alien body? Would he remember and carry the hatred as the cat did?

If Darville was indeed a man, then he must be restored to his true form, and soon. But when that happened, he would cease to be her companion, her confidant, her friend. She hadn't been able to trust any man in a long time. Would she allow herself to continue trusting *him?*

The answers lay with Shayla. Blindly, Brevelan began walking again. Up the narrow pathway.

"I won't believe you are truly a man and not a wolf until I see it with my own eyes. Until then we belong together. Come with me, Puppy."

Darville lay down on the path, muzzle on his paws, and whined. His eyes pleaded with her.

"It's obvious he won't pass this spot." Jaylor looked around for a solution. "We've got to get moving. Our follower is getting closer."

"Come, Puppy," she coaxed, catching some of his urgency. She, too, felt the threat. It was like a snake climbing her back, tightening its coils around her neck.

Darville whined pitifully, scooting farther away from the cliffside.

"Come with me." She put every ounce of command available into her voice. Darville's golden eyes widened then closed, effectively severing the channel of communication.

"He's not going to come willingly," Jaylor huffed. "Here, take Mica. I'll carry Darville." He handed the cat to Brevelan.

"Isn't he too heavy for you?" Brevelan cradled Mica close to her chest.

"I'm big enough to manage, for a short while anyway." The wolf was bigger and heavier than most of his kind. "He should be fine once we pass the ridge." He stooped to gather Darville.

A few small rocks bounced off the cliff, almost striking Darville's head. The wolf backed up again, his paws scrabbling on the stony path.

Brevelan and Jaylor both looked up toward the source of the disturbance. They could see nothing unusual.

"You probably don't remember the summer you were sixteen, Roy, but I carried you home the night of the midsummer fair." Jaylor bent to persuade the reluctant member of their company. "Even if you weren't a wolf right now, you wouldn't remember that night. We'd both had too much to drink and one too many fistfights with the local bullies."

Darville cocked one ear as he listened to the soothing cadence of Jaylor's voice. This time he didn't protest when strong arms gathered him up. "You wouldn't allow me to use your real name because you didn't want to be different from the others in our gang. So I called you 'Roy,' short for Royal." He scooped up the wolf, arms around his legs so he couldn't break free. "Now let's get out of here before the entire cliff gives way."

Following his words a larger stream of dirt and rocks broke free. Brevelan scanned the cliff once more. A flicker of movement caught her eye. Something was up there, disturbing the precarious balance of the hillside.

Brevelan ducked under the veil of dirt that lingered after the initial shock. "Quickly, get around the corner!" she called to Jaylor.

He bent into a sprint to follow her. The heavy burden in his arms slowed his progress. Another rock struck Jaylor's shoulder, bounced, and landed on Darville's back. The wolf yelped and wriggled, desperately seeking escape.

Jaylor stumbled on the loose rocks and went down on one knee. Puppy twisted free and ran up the path toward the unknown.

Beneath the roar of the rockfall came the hideous, maniac laughter of a man she knew. Not Old Thorm, or a foreign rogue magician. But her father—Lord Krej.

Chapter 16

"Jaylor!" Brevelan ducked beneath the barrage of cascading rock. Above her, the distinctive roar of a rockfall grew louder, closer.

Another rock struck Jaylor on the back. His eyes glazed in a disorientation. Stunned and bewildered by the blow, he seemed incapable of making the lifesaving decision to move.

All thoughts of Darville and his true nature fled from Brevelan. The man she loved was in danger.

Brevelan grabbed Jaylor's arm and heaved him upright by shear force of will. He stumbled and lurched along beside her, too dazed to choose a direction.

"Come on," she ordered through gritted teeth. "You have to move. Now."

The roar grew louder yet. She had to get him out of there quickly. Upward she propelled him, in the wake of the howling wolf.

Jaylor wiped blood that dripped into his eyes from a cut on his forehead and stared around him. A rock as large as Brevelan's clenched fist bounced off his boot. The new pain seemed to jolt him back to reality.

"*S'murgh* it." He stopped and looked around. "This isn't a natural avalanche. We've got to catch up to the wolf before One-eye finds him!" He reached his hands backward and his staff sprang to him. A single wave of his tool and a dome of shimmering blue and red light protected them from the increasing flow of soil and debris from the hillside.

Together they dashed along what was left of the path.

"Mica? Where is Mica?" Brevelan turned back to search

for the cat. In all this dust and turmoil Mica's coloring would be impossible to discern.

"Forget the cat. We have to protect Darville." Jaylor spun her back toward their path.

"I can't. She's my friend," she shouted over the roar of the collapsing scree. Half the mountain seemed to be raining down on them. Her heart lurched to think of Mica buried underneath all that weight. Desperate to find her pet, Brevelan yanked her arm free of Jaylor's grasp and dashed back toward the spot where they had stopped with Darville.

"Look with your heart, not your eyes," Jaylor commanded right behind her. "You've got about five heartbeats before the whole hillside goes."

"There!" A flutter of her heart directed her gaze toward glistening movement in the dust. Brevelan dove toward the spot. Dust filled her eyes and choked her. "Mica," she squeaked. "Come, Mica."

Jaylor's arms locked around her waist. Her body flew backward, not forward.

"Mrew," Mica pleaded for release.

"You can't save her, Brevelan," Jaylor pulled her backward. "I can't hold back the rockfall with magic anymore."

"I can't not save her. Please, let me go to her," she wept, still reaching.

"I can't let you hurt yourself to save a cat."

Brevelan went limp in his arms. His grip slackened. She lunged out of his grasp toward the tiny bit of overhang that still protected Mica from the rocks.

A tree crashed beside her, not three arm's lengths away. The mighty trunk bounced and rolled, caught a moment on the lip of the path then careened on down the steep slope.

Brevelan's fingers closed on a handful of dirty fur just as Jaylor hauled her backward once more.

Again the wolf has escaped me. We are too near the dragon. Shayla's aura grants him luck. Not much longer.

The magician must die. Torture? Drowning? Something deliciously hideous will occur to me. Perhaps he will become an ivory statue in my collection. I've never had a human before.

Yes. Yes. New statues. The wolf is already gold. He only

needs gilding. I shall make the girl watch and know the horror of their undeath. Then it will be her turn to die. Her death will infuse me with power.

The cat can escape. She is useless.

"Stupid, fool woman. You could have been killed." Jaylor shook Brevelan, forcing his fear into her. Without thinking, he clutched her tightly against his chest. His arms enfolded her and the filthy cat in a cocoon of safety and love.

"*Stargods,* Brevelan, what would I do without you?" he whispered, awestruck at the implication.

Her eyes lost their sparkle. Something haunted her expressionless face, but no empathic emotions radiated from her. Jaylor looked more closely at Brevelan.

He felt as empty as she looked. Surely they could find something more than a blue cloak for him and a secluded clearing for her!

"I can take Mica again." He reached for the little cat hiding her head in the crook of Brevelan's arm and shivering.

"No." A spark of emotion lit Brevelan's eyes again. She clutched Mica tighter as she pulled out of his reach.

"Fine. You carry her, or let her walk by herself." *Stargods!* He'd been carrying one or another of his companions the entire journey. He felt like a nanny, not a magician within moments of completing his master's quest.

There was nothing left to do but trudge on up this endless mountain in search of a mythological dragon. Stubbornly he set one foot in front of the other. He'd find that dragon if it killed him, and he'd drag the others with him whether they liked it or not.

It was the resolution they both wanted. Wasn't it?

"Arroof!" Darville barked and bounded forward.

"Darville!" Brevelan called.

In two leaps the wolf was around a bend and out of sight.

The cloud came back into Brevelan's eyes. "Come back, Darville!" Her whisper was plaintive, almost desperate. "Come back to me."

The only reply was another sharp bark.

"You've got to catch him, Jaylor. It's not safe for him to be separated from us." She clutched his sleeve anxiously.

Her touch spread warmth up his arm. He wanted to grasp

it and hold her close until her eyes sparked with enthusiasm again.

"Please, Jaylor. You've got to catch him," she implored.

"Yes." Briefly he clasped her hand then set off in pursuit. "You can hide in that clump of bushes until we come back for you."

His shoulders were tight from carrying first Brevelan and then Darville. She was so small, so special, he'd hardly noticed her weight. Darville, on the other hand, had been heavier than Jaylor thought possible. He knew the beast was big for a wolf, but he'd weighed as much as a man.

Darville is a man. He only appears to be a wolf, Jaylor reminded himself.

"Arroo, arroo, arroo, roo roo." Darville's concentrated bay announced his excitement.

Energy surged through Jaylor's limbs, his heart pounded faster. The wolf would only howl like that if he encountered another being.

"Darville!" he called.

"Darville!" Brevelan echoed just behind.

He turned to prevent her from rushing forward. A few tendrils of bright red hair sprang from her once neat braid. Her eyes looked as huge as the Great Bay and sparked with an intense glow of protectiveness.

"Wait." Jaylor stopped long enough to halt her headlong dash around the next bend. A large everblue with needles as long as his hand obscured his view. Beyond it a Tambootie soared, blocking the sun. In its shadow anything could lurk unseen.

He swallowed deeply to clear his mind of the wonderful vision of Brevelan. Her lips pursed in determination, and there was a light of battle in her eyes. As she hurried, her breasts strained the fabric of her bodice while her skirt was kilted up to allow her legs freedom. Would she ever dash to his rescue in such an immodest manner?

"Wait, Brevelan."

"But. . . ."

"Let me see what awaits us first." He didn't pause for an answer, or another protest.

Tambootie! Hot and sharp. A wave of pure magic assaulted him as he rounded the bend. He walked into a palpitating miasma of the stuff. His eyes watered, his skin tingled. Power invaded his entire body. All of a sudden his tongue was too big for his mouth and seemed to fill his ears as well. Even his hair itched.

Memories surged through him with each straining heartbeat.

He was back in that stone room filled with cloying smoke. Ogres and snakes assaulted him and dispersed with a word. His pulse pounded, then stuttered. He fought to draw air into his belabored lungs.

Sharp mountain breezes stung him back to reality. This time there were no walls to close in on him. He was out in fresh air with companions to help, if he needed them. He thought he was prepared for whatever the smoke could make him see. The reality in front of him was no match for delusion.

Shayla dipped her head in greeting.

"Master," the kitchen boy peeked over a pile of books, "I think I've found somethin'." He sat cross-legged on the cold stone floor of the hidden room.

Baamin looked across the waist-high stacks of discarded volumes piled between them. Not all of the books in the sealed room were as fragile as the first one he had touched. Many, especially those hidden behind the first layer, were in pristine condition. Evidence of the power of the original spell despite the haste of its construction. The outer row were mostly history chronicles, familiar and of no particular value. Behind them were books he had never seen.

"What, Boy? What have you found?" He breathed in a mouthful of mold and began to cough again, even as he reached across the lopsided stack to grasp whatever the boy held. The cold and dust crept into his old body, making his movement stiff and awkward.

"An old book, sir. Real old. I don't even recognize the writin', sir." He held up his treasure, open to the title page.

The strange script wiggled across the page like so many snakes. Words and images started to form in Baamin's mind but would not take hold. This was definitely a book of magic, very old magic. He doubted he could make writing confuse a reader like that. His discomforts were forgotten in his growing excitement.

Out of habit, Baamin calmed his mind and stilled his

body, as if gathering magic. When he opened his eyes the letters held their place and formed words.

> ### PRIVATE JOURNAL OF NIMBULAN:
> ### MAGICIAN TO THE KINGS
> ### FATHER OF DRAGONS
> ### VICTIM OF THE WARS OF DISRUPTION

The last line was written in the same but an older and shakier hand, in a different ink. It appeared to be almost a postscript.

"Nimbulan!" Baamin breathed his excitement outward this time.

"Founder of the University. He's the greatest magician known." The boy's eyes widened in wonder. "Do you think his journal will tell you how to summon your magicians?"

Baamin felt much the same sense of awe. Nimbulan was remembered with reverence. His ideas and experiments had led to the development of the Commune. Without him the border would never have become reality. Coronnan would have been consumed by civil war and left as easy pickings for greedy neighbors.

"If he doesn't tell us in his journal, perhaps he will mention a book that will." As he took the slender volume from the boy, he allowed his hands to caress the smooth leather of the binding.

Nimbulan was mighty in the annals of magic, not just for his achievements but for his loyalty and compassion as well. He was a man whom all his successors tried to emulate.

Baamin felt humble in the face of such greatness. He'd never be able to wrestle the kingdom through this current crisis. How could he possibly hope to live up to the legacy of such a magnificent predecessor?

"I'll take this to my private chambers, Boy. Keep looking." He stumbled to the door, consumed by his need to read the journal without interruption.

"Sir?" The boy disturbed his train of thought.

"Yes?" he replied absently.

"What if I find something else?" There was hope as well as a tinge of bewilderment in his voice.

"Then bring it to me. But do so quietly. We don't want anyone else to suspect the existence of this room." The boy would obey. He wasn't intelligent enough to do anything else.

Shayla defied Jaylor's attempts to describe her. Beautiful beyond words. All colors. And yet no color. Light reflected back and around the viewer. She was as translucent as an opal yet as glistening as a diamond.

The dragon dipped her steedlike muzzle to his level. He felt speared by the large multicolored eyes that scanned him, one at a time. Above the eyes, a ridge tapered up into a wicked horn, as long as his arm. That horn was repeated in spines parading down her long neck and back.

With majestic dignity, the huge dragon propped her short forelegs on a fallen log, resting her weight on her powerful haunches. From each foot sprouted a set of long colorless claws, matching the spines in shape and texture.

Behind her, a thick tail tapered to a sharp arrowhead point. It looked as lethal as its counterpart. Her wings, too, could be considered weapons. At the end of each rainbowed vein lay a wicked hook. Jaylor revised his preconception of her size. Two sledge steeds together would match her width. Two more would be needed to fill the height of this magnificent dragon.

But her best defense was her shimmering opalescence. In flight she would be invisible.

Jaylor should have felt intimidated by her. Instead, he was filled with a glowing sense of affection. The great eye that scrutinized every bit of him—inside as well as out?— held only curiosity, no malice or greed. And, thankfully, no hunger.

You may touch, Shayla responded to his unspoken desire. The words were as clear in his mind as if the immense creature had spoken.

He reached a tentative hand to her velvet-soft muzzle. When he would have pulled his hand back she butted into his outstretched palm, just as any tame steed would nuzzle for attention or treats. The smooth fur that covered her body invited an extended caress. He reached around to her cheek bulge and scratched.

Ahh! He felt her sigh of delight.

"Awroof," Darville begged for his share of attention. He stood with his front paws on the same log as the dragon.

He seemed taller, closer to his true height as a man. But he still held the form of a wolf. Jaylor gave the wolf his requested scratch while keeping his other hand on the dragon. Now that he was touching her, communicating with her, he couldn't bear to lose contact.

"Oh, my!" Brevelan gasped.

Jaylor turned to look at her and smiled. He extended his hand, inviting her to share the wonderful experience of tactile contact with Shayla. His arm came around her shoulders quite naturally. For a moment the image of family flooded him. He shrugged it off, but it returned.

You did well. You all came. Shayla rotated her eyes to see both of them at once.

"We were followed," Jaylor explained.

I know. He used timboor to hear your footsteps. We must hurry. The dragon indulged in one last caress and then reared up and turned. Her movements were graceful and precise. None of her dangerous claws, or wing hooks, or sharp tail spines touched her guests. Instead the massive tail seemed to encircle them and guide them toward an opening in the cliff.

You must remove Darville's enchantment now.

"Me?" Jaylor stopped and clasped his hands behind his back in uncertainty. "You're the magic dragon. I'll need your help."

Only you can save him from degenerating into a wild beast.

"I can't do it alone."

The air is full of magic. For a brief time I can give you more. It must be enough.

They have found her! I can feel it. The core of magic has expanded to include them.

They seek to reverse my spell. But they can't. They never will. It is a special spell, a secret. When the magician tries to unravel the magic around the wolf they will both be forever frozen in undeath.

I will rejoice with Simurgh to add them to my collection.

Chapter 17

Baamin lit a small oil lamp in the dim recess of his inner study. The day had suddenly gone dark. Chill dampness promised rain. He shrugged off the sudden iciness climbing his spine and returned to the fascinating book on his desk.

As much as he would have liked to dwell on the early life of the great Nimbulan, there wasn't time now. He had to skip large sections of the magician's private journal.

He paused and read a paragraph here and there. The painful Great Wars of Disruption were retold in heart-wrenching detail. Each contender for the throne, in that long ago civil war, had brought to his cause a different magician. When armies failed, sorcerers fought. Many died.

The words recounting each death tore at Baamin three hundred years later. He knew what it was like to lose a friend and compatriot. As long-lived as magicians tended to be, very few of his contemporaries still survived. He remembered the agonizing sense of loss at each death and felt again the reduction in magic caused by their passing.

Dragon magic needed numbers of men working together. It grew and expanded like a living being under the careful cultivation of the Commune. A strong Commune was the direct result of a strong nimbus of dragons. And there were so few dragons or magicians left! The fate of the kingdom hinged on the dragons.

Now Baamin faced the need for strong magic and a strong king without the means to provide either.

Darcine might appear to be reviving. But Baamin suspected it was only temporary and dependent on Shayla's gravid condition. The last two times Shayla had bred, the normally indecisive king had undergone similar periods of renewed strength and determination. Each time the baby dragons had been slaughtered, King Darcine had fallen gravely ill. If anything should happen to the dragon or her litter this time, the king would not survive.

A sentence caught Baamin's eye.

The pattern has become clear. Lord. . . .

The name was smudged and unreadable. Perhaps Nimbulan had deliberately obscured the name to avoid calling its owner and thus giving him power.

Lord . . . has been gathering an alliance among the other lords for many years. He has carefully arranged marriages for his numerous children into the homes of his strongest enemies. Through these children he has formed a network for coercion and extortion. Few noble families dare contest his bid for power.

Was history repeating itself? Krej had at least seven legitimate children and untold numbers of bastards. Even those too young for marriage had been betrothed in rites as binding as a wedding. Nearly every noble family was allied to him in some way. His network was in place.

And there was a rogue magician within the boundaries of Krej's province.

Baamin longed for proof that Krej had hired the rogue to work mischief among the dragons.

Krej's right to the throne was strong. If Darcine should die before Darville was found, there was no one else strong enough to hold this country together.

Was that Krej's plan, too? Had he arranged the slaughter of the dragons to weaken the king and make his own leadership seem essential to the welfare of Coronnan? It seemed logical until you considered young Darville. He was a prince of character and wisdom, in spite of his high spirits and preference for long, solitary, and dangerous hunts.

Where was the boy?

Shayla protected a golden wolf in the southern mountains. What was the connection?

Baamin turned several more pages. This history was compelling in its parallels to modern times. But he needed information about magic, not politics.

I must break the habits of a lifetime. No more can I dip deep within myself for the source of my magic. Now I must take the time to locate an outside source, gather it, change

*it, and throw it back out. Inefficient as this method seems, it
is necessary.*

*Magic was so much easier when I could close my eyes
and find the power beneath my feet. With my own magic,
the words of a spell were changed by that power into deeds.
It seemed I need only open my eyes again and find the
deed accomplished.*

*I only wish my beloved Myrilandel could share in this
new force. Alas, women and children no longer have the
ability to work with us. Since we must banish the old form
of magic, we must also exclude them from the joys of this
new force and the intimate ties of those who join together
with it.*

"So I must delve deep within myself for the source of
personal magic," Baamin mused. "Not so different from
dipping into the reserves of magic I have gathered."

He closed his eyes. Nothing came to mind. What should
he try? Something simple to begin with. Perhaps Jaylor's
old trick. From memory he recited the words that would
form the image of a cup filled with cool wine. At first he
saw it in the cellar. Then he put the cup on his desk.

The crash of broken crockery startled him out of his
reverie. On the floor, beside him, lay a broken wine cup;
one just like those reserved for students. He had brought
the cup through the sealed doors and into his study! Only
the cup had slipped to the floor and crashed. He had forgotten the slope of the reading surface.

"I'm as bad as the apprentices!" Baamin's eyes watered
from his near hysterical mirth. "Imagine me, Senior Magician and University Chancellor back among the rawest of
students."

Never, in her dreams or in her conversations with Shayla,
had Brevelan imagined a dragon could be so wonderful.
She had seen vague images of the dragon and her consorts,
but never this full, splendid view of power and iridescent
light.

A bubble of joy replaced the weight of dread in her
midsection. She wanted to laugh and sing with her companions. Shayla's magic already encircled them, bound them
all together. Brevelan need only enrich the bonds with her
own magic song.

The weight of Jaylor's arm about her shoulders made the circle of her love complete. Together they strode into the cool depths of the cave Shayla called home.

The entrance was just large enough for the dragon to spread her wings in preparation for flight. Deeper into the mountain it opened into a massive room, dry and cool. In one corner was a nest of dried leaves and everblue needles, with some feathers and bits of raw wool for softness.

Brevelan refused to think about where those bits came from. The bowl of the nest was wide and sheltered from the wind. Perfect for Shayla's brood.

"When will the babies come?" she asked timidly.

Winter Solstice. The dragon yawned. *Before long I will not be able to fly.*

"How will you eat?" Jaylor asked as he poked among the piles of loose rock that had been cleared from the center of the cave.

The fathers will share.

"Fathers?" he asked.

Brevelan smiled. Her magician had not been privy to the images of the mating flight. He had no way of knowing Shayla's preference for multiple fathers for her litter.

"Fathers," Brevelan answered. " 'The more fathers, the larger and stronger the litter,' " she quoted.

His mouth lifted in a long lazy smile. The line of his thoughts was clear.

Sit, my friends. Shayla curled her tail around her haunches. Once more she dipped her elegant neck so that her eyes were level with Jaylor and Brevelan. In the dim light of the cave interior the irises appeared quite red, slashed by a long, horizontal pupil. Deep inside the dark slash were all of the colors reflected by Shayla's soft iridescent fur.

Brevelan stared lovingly at the dragon, entranced by the penetrating gaze of her hostess. Shayla seemed to read her soul, strip it bare, and judge her mettle. Brevelan quivered a little as she adjusted her body and mind to that friendly but intimidating stare. Jaylor mimicked the gesture.

Drained by the dragon's scrutiny, Brevelan accepted the invitation to sit. A pile of leaves, without feathers and fur, near a large rock looked made for her. She sank into it, grateful for this small comfort. Her light pack made a wonderful pillow for her head against the rock. The minor injuries inflicted by the rockfall hadn't bothered her until she thought about resting. Now stiff muscles and aching bruises surged to the surface. She eased herself into a more comfortable position.

As usual, Puppy sat, leaning his weight against her. His head tipped and rubbed her shoulder. Mica scampered into her lap and commenced an overdue bath.

Brevelan accepted as natural that Jaylor chose to pace rather than sit. While his mind worked, his body needed to keep moving. His restless energy brought to mind why they were here and the dangers that awaited them.

There is not much time. The evil one comes.

Inside Brevelan's head appeared the image of the one-eyed derelict. A second image appeared of the spotted saber cat's head perched atop the powerful body of a man. Brevelan didn't need Shayla's mental pictures. She would know her enemy anywhere, in any disguise, by his insane laughter.

"Why can't you just change Darville back to his normal form?" Jaylor stopped prowling long enough to address Shayla directly. As tall as he was, head and shoulders above Brevelan, he barely reached Shayla's shoulder. Above him towered the dragon's long neck and graceful head. "For that matter, why did you allow it to happen in the first place?"

Brevelan pulled the wolf closer, cherishing the last few moments of their companionship. Once the spell was thrown from him, he would be a prince and no longer her familiar.

By the vows that were taken many years ago, I grant him protection. The same vows limited my powers.

"What?" Now Jaylor sat, suddenly and not altogether gracefully, on a nearby rock. "Isn't that why we came? So you could transform him?"

I make the magic for you to gather. I do not force it to bend to my will as mortals do.

"I'm not very good at gathering magic. I work better with my own brand." Once more he put his hands behind his back.

For this you will need both my magic and your own. I shall guide you.

"For this I need to know how it was done. I can't reverse an unknown spell."

Was that truly panic in his eyes? Brevelan sent a small amount of courage toward him.

"For this spell, you need only watch a master and weep that you will never be able to do it yourself." A new voice announced from the cave entrance.

Brevelan didn't need to face her enemy to know he was disguised in the second image Shayla had sent her. The bronze and gray fur of the spotted saber cat head gleamed in the sunlight at the entrance to the cave. Oiled human muscles rippled along the magician's strong arms and bare torso. His sturdy legs anchored his barely clothed body in a broad stance.

On another man, a man less evil, his naked splendor could have been compelling. Brevelan nearly gagged with fear and remembered pain. The last naked man she had seen had tried to rape her on their marriage bed.

A stream of red and blue flame erupted from Jaylor's staff, aimed at the intruder. The plait of fire sped toward its target almost faster than the eye could follow. An arrow point formed at the end of the magic spear. The monster's eyes narrowed and he waved his own staff—straight grained with lumps at irregular intervals down its length—in a wide arc.

Jaylor stood frozen in place, arm still raised, staff in hand. His red and blue arrow melted to mist.

Darville growled and gathered his hind legs beneath him for a lunge. Saliva dripped from his fangs in his eagerness to taste the magician's blood.

Thorm raised his staff again.

Brevelan leaped in front of her pet. She had to protect Darville from any further hurt at the hands of this monster.

Darville swung around Brevelan and lunged for the enemy's throat. A reddish haze spread over and around Thorm as he laughed once more. A wall of magic stopped Darville's lunge. He tore at it with teeth and claws.

Jaylor broke free of his paralysis. A second braid of fire erupted from his staff and met the same fate as the first. His intended victim only laughed, that taunting, high-pitched laugh he'd heard at the rockfall.

"I penetrated your style of magic long ago, University man." Thorm sneered. He made it sound as if the hallowed institution of learning were merely a refuse pile, its students so much dirt and offal. "I can stop any spell you throw. Dragon magic is useless against a true magician!" he crowed.

Jaylor stepped toward Thorm, staff raised, and stopped, frozen in place again. A hazy green bell pulsed and swallowed him.

"NO!" Brevelan screamed. The force of Jaylor's mental pain at the paralysis nearly knocked her from her feet. She launched herself toward him to break through the magic. "Stop him, Shayla. Stop him before he hurts someone." Another pain assaulted her. From behind her she felt a crippling agony in her legs and arms. Shayla! Her beautiful, wonderful dragon was hurt.

Instinctively, she sent forth all of her strength and courage to support the dragon. Another wave of despair rocked her. She matched it with a high piercing note of healing song.

"Shayla!" The music echoed and reverberated back to her. "Fight for your life, Shayla!" The notes died in the vast emptiness of the cave. There was no mind or soul there to receive her healing.

Chapter 18

Brevelan turned to look for Shayla with her eyes when she could no longer find the dragon in the place within her heart.

Her movement must have attracted Thorm's attention. The air crackled with energy. She could smell it, taste it, almost wade through the thick wall. A haze of green magic enveloped her, just as it had Jaylor.

The confines of that nasty bell of red and green shimmering lights held her body frozen. Trapped with her was the reek of Tambootie smoke.

"Jaylor!" she called. The words echoed within her mind, for no sound erupted from her body. She called again with her magic, pouring as much emotion as she had left into her cry.

Just a faint tickle of responding fury reached her through the spell. Jaylor lived!

"Puppy?" If the wolf were still free, perhaps he could divert the magician's attention long enough for Jaylor's magic to release them.

The wolf's response was stronger, but still masked. She forced her eyes to move to her right where she had last seen him.

Teeth bared, neck fur on end, he was crouched to spring for Thorm's throat. She could hear his deep, menacing growl, muffled by yet another magic barrier.

"Think you can wreak revenge on me, Wolf?" Thorm sneered with Krej's voice. "You'll have to be faster and stronger than that." He laughed. The irritating waves of his cackles echoed around and around the cave.

Brevelan sought Shayla again. Her mind reached nothing.

Her eyes found only a dim outline of the magnificent body.
The dragon, too, was captured in the web of magic, unable
to move. But unlike the others, her mind was as frozen as
her body. Horror gripped Brevelan. She tried again and
again to find a glimmer of the dragon, in her mind or in
her heart.

Nothing.

Something within her died. She went limp, no longer resisting the magic. The disguised rogue was too strong. He
held their defeat within the sweep of his knobby staff.

A forceful personality intruded on her despair. Mica
clawed her way into her awareness. *Stay with us, Sister!*
The command came along with a large dose of courage
and strength.

What was this? Mica, her sweet little kitty, was supporting her, Brevelan, with words and empathy. The cat had
never spoken to her before. But then, she hadn't needed
to. The bonds of communication were strong enough without words.

With the cat's help, Brevelan reinforced her emotional tie
to Jaylor and Darville. The channels opened, their thoughts
mingled. Together they must fight the source of the magic,
drain it, and then break free.

"Oh, what a splendid addition you will make to my collection," Thorm gloated. His hands ran lovingly over Shayla's flank, his caress almost that of a lover.

Brevelan swallowed her revulsion. How could they allow
him to touch Shayla with his slimy hands and filthy mind?

"You do remember my collection, pretty one," he stated
rather than asked of Brevelan. "You are from Krej's village, aren't you?" He looked up from his fondling of Shayla's front horn.

Brevelan couldn't respond, even if she'd wanted to.

"With hair like that," he reached through the haze to lift
a bright lock off her cheek, "I would almost think you one
of his get." His eyes widened.

"Of course! You're his oldest daughter." He laughed,
nearly hysterical with his own humor. Cruelly he pulled the
strand of hair just before releasing it. "Pretty as you are, I
can't spare the time to take you. Next time, sweetheart.
Next time." He blew a kiss through the confining haze.

The lascivious caress left a wet imprint on her cheek. She longed to wipe her skin free of the rogue's touch.

Jaylor's jealous rage pounded against his bell. The haze thickened and grew, feeding on the energy of his emotions.

"You're the one the villagers want to burn for witchcraft. Seems you murdered your husband on your wedding night." Thorm looked directly at Jaylor now, fueling the younger man's anger and the magic that confined him.

"Didn't she tell you about that, boy? She wouldn't want to broadcast her past to those gullible fisher-folk. They might decide to burn her, too. But you, you're her lover. Surely she would confide in you."

The blast of emotion from both Darville and Jaylor shook the red-haired monster. He shivered once, but his mask did not slip. Then he turned his attention from Brevelan to the wolf and the magician. "I can see you both have strong feelings for the chit. Perhaps I shall tell the elders of the village where to find her. You would be forced to watch her burn, before they fed you to the fish in the center of the Bay."

His eyes narrowed in evil speculation. "You know, of course, they blame her for the rainy summer that caused their crops to rot in the fields last year. They also think she is responsible for the very hard winter that took the lives of all the old ones and some babies, too."

Not the babies! A huge emptiness settled inside Brevelan. Babies she had helped bring into this world were gone before they'd had a chance to live.

Tears of pain and grief worked their way through the magic. They slid down her cheeks and dropped to her breast. But she couldn't feel the moisture, only the pain of death for infants who had become a part of her as she brought them to life.

"May all the foul spirits of Simurgh's hell and beyond take you!" Jaylor cursed as loud as his mind could scream. "How could you betray your king and cousin, the kingdom, and the Commune with this abomination?"

"Still spouting ethics, boy? You of all people should have no qualm about ethics. Where do you think I found this wonderful creature to do my bidding?" The monster gestured to his naked torso and mask. "I read your thoughts, boy. Thoughts you stole from Old Baamin's dreams. I'm surprised you didn't recognize me sooner," he taunted.

"I recognize only your corruption." Desperately Jaylor sought contact with Brevelan and Darville.

Jaylor railed against his own ineffectiveness and the rogue's audacity. His accusations against Brevelan were just too preposterous to contemplate. Brevelan couldn't murder anyone. Least of all her husband on her wedding night! And this monster had accused Jaylor of being her lover and still having the strength of magic to throw those braids of flame. If the situation weren't so serious, he'd laugh himself silly.

"The day progresses, and I do want to be out of this cave before moonrise." The rogue shrugged his naked shoulders in dismissal of his prisoners as he returned his attention to Shayla.

Jaylor carefully watched each gesture the man made. Whatever happened, Jaylor would need to undo it later.

"Watch all you want, University man," Thorm laughed. "Your false magic won't be able to negate my powers. If I allow you to live long enough to try your puny spell, that is."

Could the man read his mind? If so, Jaylor had to bury, very deeply, all thought of his rogue powers. Thorm mustn't know that Jaylor might be able to counteract any spell that was thrown.

"What substance best suits a life-sized sculpture of a dragon?" Thorm mused rhetorically. "My gray bear is pewter, and the spotted saber cat was bronze. But then I had to let the cat go as bait for Darville." He whirled to face his captives. "Nice touch that, turning the prince into a wolf. It suits his personality."

Jaylor felt Darville's growl echo through his body. Was it possible some sentience was returning to the prince now that he was confronting his enchanter? Jaylor hoped so. The wolf's cooperation would make escape and the spell reversal easier.

"But for a dragon," Thorm continued his gleeful monologue, "I think glass would be proper." He snapped his fingers in delight. "Yes, glass. You can see through dragons as well as the best glass, and only those of Lord Krej's rank deserve that wondrous substance. Glass, smooth, clear, and yet it reflects light in a myriad of colors. Wonderful glass." He almost sang it.

As the words took on a lilting quality, the air became heavier, filled with the stench of rotten Tambootie. Magic filled the confines of the cave. Clear and colored eddies swirled around the silent figures, over the piles of rock, and through the carefully constructed nest. Waves and waves of thick magic combined, pulled apart, and flowed with the rhythm of the spell-driving music.

A blue vortex grew and swirled into a tower of wind. Lightning flashed within the artificial tornado. It grew taller and broader, filling more and more of the cave. Then it moved around the perimeter of the cave in one huge circle.

A second vortex of green sprang up and circled the cave in a tighter circumference. Green combined with the blue and they twisted faster. Red, yellow, and purples joined in turn. With each new color the violent storm of whirling magic flew faster, higher, wider.

The magic wind sucked leaves and bits of fur from the nest into its central vacuum. Small pebbles lifted and darted about with more and more debris. Faster and faster yet, the eerie winds circled the cave.

Magic engulfed the figure of the dragon. Shayla's hide took on the color of the Bay in sunlight as the first unnatural storm swirled around her. Then she absorbed each color in turn until all the colors of the spectrum glowed together. All colors became no color. Blinding, piercing opalescent glass.

Jaylor watched in awe as the spell matched the chanting words in intensity and speed. Everything in the cave was sucked into the magic, even the existing magic. The green in the haze engulfing Jaylor thinned. His eyes cleared and he saw the same thinning around Brevelan and Darville. He tried to move his hand. His finger twitched, barely.

Concentrate, fool! he admonished himself. *Use the Tambootie in the air to shatter this immobility just as I used the timboor in my blood to remove myself from the Rover camp.*

His eyelids closed with effort. He turned his thoughts inward, gathering strength. A coil of stored dragon magic was ready for release. He pushed it aside and sought a different source. It was hiding where he had put it when he banished all thoughts of rogue magic.

Jaylor drew the thin line of magic upward to his eyes. His mouth wouldn't move enough to speak the words, so he created them in the front of his mind, for his imagination to read. The line sped from his eyes to the imagined letters, wrapped around them and then shot, like a barbed arrow, straight for the enemy's heart.

Darville couldn't move. Panic filled his body. He tried to growl in response to what he could not understand. The deep rumble vibrated in his chest, but he couldn't hear it as he should. This curious fog surrounded him, blocking his view of Brevelan and Jaylor. The evil one remained in his sight.

His ears heard the other noises about him with their usual keenness. His nose worked, too. He associated the curious smoky smell with the evil one. He growled again.

The faintest of sounds reached his ears. His fur bristled again, the way it should. Brevelan looked closer than just a moment ago, clearer. Jaylor, too.

"Glass! My pretty dragon is made of glass," the evil one chanted.

His words penetrated all of Darville's senses. He understood every sound the cat-headed man uttered. Anger and revulsion filled his suddenly cold body.

Even as he understood the entire scene, the rest of his senses dimmed. He felt as if his ears and nose were filled, like the times he had a winter cold. And his suddenly bald limbs ached. His back and thighs felt as if he had ridden his steed far too long.

Curious, Darville allowed his blurry eyes to look upon his body, to find the problem.

Vertigo engulfed him. He was a man. A naked man. He felt his skin hen-bump in response to the cold and his embarrassment at having been caught in the presence of strangers without his clothes. And not just any strangers.

The ball of multicolored fur that he presumed was a cat grew and uncoiled into the most beautiful woman he had ever seen. She, too, was naked except for the enveloping wave of hair that shimmered to her hips and below. As the woman turned, light reflected off the lustrous curtain, now blond, then brunette, with a touch of red and deep sable brown.

She lifted her arms in joy. From her lips sprang a clear and sweet song. The most glorious song of freedom he had ever heard.

All too soon the woman shrank back into her cat persona. Just as he had shrunk to the size of a wolf on that fateful afternoon.

His past engulfed him in a wave. He saw again his betrayal on the ridge · . . . .

The spotted saber cat tracks he followed disappeared in the rocky scree. Snowflakes drifted lazily into the crevices of the path. He turned to speak to his cousin and hunting companion. Krej was nowhere in sight. Darville drew his sword. Waning winter light made the weapon appear black and dull.

The snow increased in intensity. Through the heavy veil of flakes stalked the saber cat. Coming toward him.

He shifted his feet for better defensive balance. The uneven ground tilted his balance. The cat came closer.

No, it wasn't a saber cat at all, but a man with the cat's head. Had Krej killed the creature already? If so, why was Krej wearing only a loin cloth in freezing weather?

A slight shift of wind cleared the snow away for a moment. The man who stalked him wasn't a man at all, but some kind of monster with a beast's head.

"Krej, save yourself!" he called to his cousin. "I am, Darville, I am saving myself," the beast spoke with Krej's voice. "With your death I am only one heartbeat away from the throne. Soon, very soon, I shall rule and my magic will grant me supremacy over all kingdoms!"

Fury filled Darville's eyes. Krej, his own cousin, had betrayed him. He had to kill the man before the snow froze them both.

Magic flame hit him in the chest, robbing him of breath. He thought it was his own anger.

As he had been taught in countless arms classes, he separated his mind from his body. He needed all of his wits, cool and alert, to divert the next blast of magic.

He succeeded in catching a ball of green flame with his sword. It bounced off the polished steel and hit a rock as

big as a dog. The stone shattered. Dust and gravel filled
the air.

Momentarily blinded, Darville didn't see the next blast.
It struck his head, blinding him, shattering his control. His
balance failed. The air around him shuddered and parted.

He was falling, falling into nothing. Cold vanished from
his aching body. Fur covered him. His nose told him he
had fallen into a snowdrift deep within the forest. . . .

Part of Darville rejoiced that the enchantment was broken. He was no longer a wolf, but a man once more. Even
then, he mourned the loss of his keen wolf vision and sense
of smell.

Then, just as suddenly, blackness swamped his awareness.
But he was warm again. His fur coat was back. The stinking
smoke filled his nose and he growled.

Chapter 19

A shriek beyond physical hearing tore a great rent in the air surrounding Baamin. The gaping difference in air pressure made the hair on his arms and neck stand up. Even his three-day-old beard bristled and cracked. His wine cup shattered in midair.

What was wrong? The air smelled different. Something was missing.

The magic was gone!

"Where is it?" He sniffed fruitlessly for a faint whiff of the ever-present—so easily ignored—spicy aroma of magic, something akin to Tambootie but not quite. His eyes widened as he sought every corner of his study for some clue to what was happening.

No magic anywhere. He couldn't smell it, taste it, feel it. And he certainly couldn't gather it. The only other time that had happened was when a dragon died.

"Shayla!" he whispered into the blankness. "What has happened?" Panic engulfed him. His breath came in short quick pants. He felt dizzy and heavy. "SHAYLA!" he wailed.

Darkness tried to enclose his vision even as the back of his neck threatened to separate from his body.

"Darcine?" he whispered.

By feel alone, he groped his way to his desk. He must run to the palace. He must summon the Commune.

He must contact Jaylor. The journeyman was near the dragon. He would know what transpired.

Where was his glass? He needed the glass and a candle to call Jaylor. Where the *s'murghing* Tambootie was his glass! The desktop was empty. He couldn't find the glass, his most precious tool. Sweat dripped into his eyes, darkness encroached. He had to find the glass.

It slid into his hand, summoned by his thoughts and rogue powers he didn't realize he had tapped.

His vision cleared instantly.

With shaking fingers, he struck the flame rock with a rough metal rod. A spark leaped from the rock to the wick. It wavered, nearly died, then caught. His breathing calmed.

Baamin held the glass in front of the candle with still trembling fingers and began his spell. For a moment nothing happened. Then he remembered again to seek his magic in a different place. Now that he knew where to look, it was there, waiting, full of life and ready to spring forth at his calling.

He reduced the aching pace of his lungs. Air swept deeply into his body. He held it the required three heartbeats and released it on the same count. Tension flowed from his muscles as the air escaped. His eyes focused on the leaping green flame, found its hot core, and sent it on its journey.

In his mind Baamin saw the tiny flame skip across the river boundary of Coronnan City, over the tilled fields, southward beyond the Great Bay. At a tiny hamlet in the foothills the tiny flame paused, seeking direction. Then upward it climbed into the mountains. Baamin followed.

He saw a hut, burned and abandoned. Forest creatures cowered at the edges of a clearing, equally forlorn and abandoned. The flame moved on.

Upward, ever upward, Baamin followed the seeking green morsel of magic. Finally it lingered on a small plateau. It hovered a moment, then recoiled in a straight shot back into Baamin's eyes.

The beast-headed monster twisted his torso into an impossible angle. He reached out and caught Jaylor's magic arrow between two fingers. Playfully he lifted the weapon to his lips and blew on it. The blue and red magic withered and died.

"You'll have to work harder than that, University man. I saw your attack coming. Your impudence just earned you a longer, slower death. My coven will delight in your screams. We'll have an orgy at your feet as Simurgh rips your soul from your body."

Brevelan's hope sank to the cave floor along with the attack.

"Well, my pretty little witch, I'm finished here." Thorm reached through the bell of magic to tug at Brevelan's hair one more time.

From any other man the gesture might have seemed affectionate. She knew that no such emotion ever entered this man's breast.

"Under other circumstances, I might consider training you to be my successor." The rogue magician quirked one eyebrow. "But circumstances dictate differently. As soon as I have settled my glass dragon in her new home, I'll be back to finish with you and the University man." He laughed. There was a weakness in his mirth—fatigue. He had worked some very strong magic in the past half hour.

Brevelan watched Thorm marshal his energies once more. With a mighty upward heave of his shoulders and arms, he commanded the glass figure that had once been Shayla to levitate an arm's length above the floor of the cave. The dragon had been reduced in size to little more than an extremely large sledge steed.

Thorm hovered the statue briefly, then gestured for it to follow him. He exited with a salute to the entrapped companions. The statue followed, drifting on a pillow of air.

A flash of muted colors streaked across Brevelan's limited vision.

"Yeowwll!" Mica screeched as she landed on Thorm's bare shoulder. Her fully extended claws and teeth drew blood.

"Aiyee!" Thorm hunched and whirled, trying to dislodge the cat from his back. He lost control of the statue.

Tons of clear glass dropped to the ground, rocked and titled. On the edge of one hind leg and tail the sculpture that had once been Shayla teetered and threatened to crash.

Pain washed back into Brevelan from the rogue magician. His spotted saber cat features blurred and faded for just a moment. His familiar face and hair as red as her own burst through the disguise.

Recognition tore at Brevelan's consciousness.

"Enough!" Thorm shook his arm, flinging Mica to the ground. With the same gesture he righted the statue with a magic tether. His feline mask reasserted firm control over his appearance.

"Mica!" Brevelan's scream echoed around the cave, bounced against the walls, and crashed back to the bells of magic isolation.

No response. The little cat lay limp where she had fallen.

"The same fate awaits you, little witch," Thorm—and yet not Thorm—sneered. "I'll be back for you and your lover. Only your deaths won't be as quick." With one last hate-filled glare, the beast-headed monster stalked out of the cave, his glass prize in tow.

Brevelan's anguish slammed into the green and red hazes. Now that Thorm was no longer present to maintain the magic, they shattered under the violence of her revulsion and grief.

Brevelan ran across the cave. Her hand brushed against Mica, checking for damage. Mica breathed in a painful wheeze, but there were no broken bones. She scooped up the cat and moved onto Darville. With a heart full of love, she gathered the quaking wolf and the little cat into her arms. A soothing melody sprang from her heart to theirs as she rocked gently in time with her song.

Slowly the animals' pain and confusion drained into her. She absorbed it, contained it, then dispersed it outward. Mica stirred and snuggled deeper into Brevelan's lap. She butted her head against Brevelan's hand, urging her to examine the wolf more carefully.

Brevelan's fingers sought deep into Darville's fur for hurt, while she searched his eyes for understanding.

"To be a man, trapped in this other body. Do you know of your entrapment, Darville, or has he taken away your mind?" A confusion of emotions disrupted the flow of her magic. She paused in her litany of grief to rub her face in his fur. Her tears dampened his neck.

"Brevelan." Jaylor's hand touched her shoulder.

She gathered its warmth and strength so she could pour more of herself into the wolf.

"Brevelan." Jaylor's voice was stronger, more demanding. "Dear heart, let me take care of this."

The endearment passed over her understanding. She heard only the insistent tone. Jaylor could take care of the problem. "What? How?" she stammered.

"I saw what happened. Thorm didn't have enough magic to transform Shayla and maintain Darville as a wolf while keeping us trapped as well. He had to pull some magic away from Darville to complete his spell." He looked about the cave, as if searching for clues. "I think I can break the enchantment."

Relief flooded through her.

"Please, Brevelan, step away. I need a clear field to work." His hands pulled her up and away from the wolf.

Golden eyes marked her movements with questions. The wolf clearly didn't understand what was happening, had happened, to him. But Brevelan knew that during the time the magic was pulled away from him he had suffered through the entire experience again.

Jaylor stepped between her and Darville. She moved aside to watch. He glared at her. For some reason he didn't want her to know how he did it.

She glared back. Darville had been her constant companion since last winter. She had nursed him through injury and illness. He had comforted her in her loneliness and despair. They both needed to be a part of this transformation.

"This won't be pretty," Jaylor warned even as he began the deep breathing she knew was the beginning of his spells.

"Not very much in this life is."

His eyes pleaded with her to step behind him again. She refused.

"Then make yourself useful. Get my cloak out of my pack." Even as he spoke, his breathing deepened further.

She fetched the cloak. When she returned to his side, his attention was beyond her, turned deeply within himself.

The staff snapped into his hand. He angled it so that it pointed at the wolf's heart. Darville looked up. Expectantly?

A low hum issued from the twisted wooden fibers of the staff. It echoed the tune Thorm had chanted while he danced magic around the cave. Jaylor, too, began to hum. His hands trembled on the staff. He gripped it tighter to control his focus. The staff shook and jerked away from Darville.

Jaylor fought the staff back to his target. It jerked away again just as braided lights of red and blue, green and yellow, with a strand of purple down the center, sprang from the tip. Magic light encircled the bewildered animal in a loose spiral. The magic widened to include Jaylor and Brevelan. Shock waves rippled through the magician. Jaylor broke off the spell before it went any farther awry. Pain clamped around his chest.

It was a good thing this was a solitary spell rather than a traditional one. He had ended it with a thought rather than a lengthy recitation of formulae.

"He laid a trap in the spell," he whispered. "The staff knew it and refused to direct the magic where I aimed it."

Brevelan sent him strength. He stood straighter, but not to his full height. His eyes squinted with the effort to keep them open.

"But now that I've found the trap, I can go around it." He began his work again. Magic plaited around the staff in vivid colors. It sprang backward through Jaylor, around the cave and over to Darville, twisting in the opposite direction from before. A single arrow of multicolored magic pierced the wolf's thick fur. Darville took on the colored glow as the power grew and brightened. He shed his fur, grew longer, paler. His legs and arms straightened. His head reared up and his eyes became aware.

The magic retreated from Darville and surrounded Jaylor. For a moment the magician donned a mantle of golden fur, shot with the red and brown of his own coloring. Then the hair broke free and fell from him in a shower of pinpoint lights.

Jaylor sagged. His skin took on the tinge of gray exhaustion. Each breath rattled in his chest.

Instinctively Brevelan reached her arms to hold him up. He clutched the cloak she held against his chest. "If I could sit a moment. I'm so cold," he whispered. She eased him onto a boulder. When his breathing slowed, she turned her attention to Darville.

Quickly she assessed the long clean limbs and golden hair of a tall man, crouched on the ground. One long foot lifted to scratch his ear in a parody of a wolf's gesture. He looked puzzled that the foot didn't fit, his back didn't twist, his head hung too high.

Only then was Brevelan aware that Darville, her prince, was naked. She turned her eyes away even as she held the cloak out to him. Jaylor had known this would happen. That was why he had asked for the cloak, why he had tried to block her vision.

"You'll need this, Your Grace." She held out the garment. He didn't take it.

"Darville!" He looked up at her. Understanding began to glimmer in his eyes. Still he crouched on the ground, looking as if he wanted to wag a tail that was no longer there.

"I was afraid this might happen," Jaylor said.

Brevelan looked at him as she spread the woolen cloak over Darville's now shivering form.

"He's been a wolf for many moons. It's going to take some time for him to remember what it means to be fully human." Jaylor's voice gained a little strength. The pulse in his neck still beat in irregular tattoo.

"Will he remember the time he spent as a . . . as . . . under my care?" Heat crept up her face. During that time she'd had no need for modesty. Darville had been just another animal. Why should she hide her body from him?

"I don't know."

She turned from her embarrassment to practical matters. "We need to find a place to camp for tonight. I know you are both exhausted, and Mica still hurts, but Old Thorm will come back. Soon. We must hide from his wrath until we are all rested and stronger."

"We have to go after that man," Darville croaked. He stretched his legs and stood slowly. She could see discomfort cross his face as he adjusted to his new posture.

"We'd waste more time than we'd save," she asserted, then looked away. She'd forgotten who he was. One didn't address the prince of the realm in that tone. She should have shown him more respect. That was hard to remember when she had been coaxing and ordering him around for moons.

"She's right," Jaylor groaned. His eyes were shadowed and his skin still had that gray tinge. "I have to rest, to eat. There is no more magic in me and not enough strength to gather more." He sniffed the air and frowned. "If there's any magic left."

Darville surveyed the cave. His eyes sought every crevice, assessing it as if it were a military encampment. "Very well." He strode to the entrance. His back was straight now, his step firm. "We might as well stay here. It's sheltered. There's wood for a fire and a spring at the back of the cave."

"What about . . . what about our enemy?" She couldn't bring herself to name him.

"I doubt he'll be back for several days. He's wounded, thanks to Mica. He's fatigued from throwing too much magic, and he must continue the spell to transport Shayla. We're safe here for tonight." Jaylor yawned and seemed to shrink within himself.

"I'll scout the perimeter," Darville announced. At the cave entrance he started to lift his left leg, just as the other Darville, the wolf, would have done to mark the edge of the camp. Face flaming, he stood straighter. "I don't suppose you have an extra pair of trews in your pack, old friend?"

Baamin guided his seeking flame back up the mountain. Slowly, warily, it crept toward the cave entrance. He pushed beyond aching eyes and throbbing head to make the flame go where he sent it.

He met no resistance at the cave mouth this time. The weakened spark of green flame hovered and tried to retreat again. Apprehension grew in the old magician's breast. Never before had a spell fought him like this. Drawing on his newly found reserves of magic, he forced the tiny flicker of light to move onward, deep into the mountain.

There, finally, it found its like, another fire maintained but shielded by a magician's stare.

"Jaylor, at last!" Baamin breathed a sigh of relief. "What is happening? Where is Shayla?"

"Baamin?" The boy's startlement relieved the older magician's subtle fears. They were back to their normal relationship of master and journeyman. Last time they had talked, Jaylor had been in control of the magic as well as the interview, a man fully grown and worthy of his master's cloak.

"Who else would call in this manner?" Baamin almost chuckled. But his errand was too vital to linger in polite conversation. "Answer me. I fear that time is of the essence. Where is Shayla?"

"Gone, sir."

"Gone! She can't leave. She is tied to this kingdom by instinct and by magic."

"Perhaps I should say stolen and enthralled. The rogue transformed her into glass."

The image of a giant crystal, reflecting back the light of a hundred moons flooded Baamin's mind. "How? Why?" He stammered.

"To gain a kingdom."

"And the wolf?" Defeat dragged at his shoulders. With Shayla enchanted so, too, would the king be. If the golden wolf were indeed the missing prince, as Baamin had suspected all along, he had to be restored and returned to Coronnan City. Now.

"Nearly his old self, sir."

The boy didn't elaborate. No image of the wolf or his restored form came through the flame. Something was wrong.

"There was a man beneath the glamour of golden fur, wasn't there?"

Jaylor nodded wearily.

"Can you do anything about him?"

"I did."

The image of Darville riding through the woods on a spirited steed flashed across Baamin's mind's eye. Darville as he had been last autumn, before his disappearance.

"Wonderful, boy. Wonderful." For the first time in weeks, Baamin knew relief. "We need him in Coronnan City immediately."

"Weeks of travel at best, sir. And, sir, there are . . . um complications." Jaylor stalled.

"What am I to tell the Council of Provinces and the king?" If the king were still alive.

"As little as possible. We follow the rogue at dawn."

"To what purpose?" The candle flame leaped higher. An ember of hope glimmered from Jaylor's end of the summons.

"To rescue a glass dragon." Jaylor hadn't used that flippant tone since he'd broken the spell on the wine cellar door and replaced it with one even the masters couldn't reverse. His inebriated, taunting laugh had haunted them for weeks. "Are you drunk, journeyman?" Baamin forced sternness into his voice.

"No, sir." His reply was slightly subdued. "Just fatigued beyond caring."

A sense of the great magic the boy had worked that day washed over Baamin. He understood. He gulped. If Jaylor had truly fought Krej's rogue that hard and then found enough strength to restore the prince, his magical prowess was greater than anyone had believed possible. He was a master already, without the talisman of the cloak.

Baamin was talking to a stronger magician than the entire Commune combined. He needed more information.

Chapter 20

Fatigue pulled Jaylor's eyes closed. The campfire Brevelan had built at the rear of the cave gave him enough warmth to still his trembling muscles. His stomach was pleasantly filled with one of her rooty stews. Already the nutrition had begun to replenish his body. An herbal tea soothed his body's aches. Mica purred gently in his lap. He should be able to sleep.

Yet the image of Lord Krej's face slipping through the mask of the beast-headed monster disturbed him almost as much as his own exhaustion. He had to put a stop to the man's treachery. But who would believe him? To accuse a member of the Council of Provinces, without physical evidence, invited trouble. The evidence of his eyes and ears while ensorcelled by a rogue magician was no proof a mundane man could accept.

His mind tumbled and spun with the day's events and the conversation on the other side of the fire.

"I feel as if I know you." Darville nursed a cup of the same herbal tea.

"You do," Brevelan's soft lilting voice replied in even tones. Yet Jaylor could hear the tension behind her words.

"No. I'd remember you if I did. You're too beautiful to forget." The prince's voice became lilting in flirtation.

Jaylor knew how the patterns of Darville's speech changed when he spoke to women—whether he wanted the woman or not. It was his nature to flirt with all of them, old or young, beautiful or plain.

Jealousy gnawed at Jaylor's innards like a hunger.

"Why were you in the wild mountains with Krej last

winter?" Jaylor found himself interrupting their quiet conversation.

"He wanted to hunt a spotted saber cat." Darville replied. "I needed to get away. It seemed like the ideal recreation." His eyes never left Brevelan. He reached to touch a tiny curl at her temple but stopped short of touching her.

Mica ceased purring. Her head lifted, ears back, eyes narrowing suspiciously. She watched the prince through rounded pupils. She knew what was happening, even if Brevelan did not. Jaylor willed the cat to distract her mistress.

"We encountered a saber on our journey here," Brevelan said. Subtly she shifted away from Darville.

Jaylor breathed a little easier. As much as he liked his royal friend, enjoyed his company, he didn't trust him around women. Their teenage escapades were more legend than truth. Still, Darville had never been forced to curb his natural curiosity and hunger for women as Jaylor had.

"Perhaps it was the same saber cat. Krej said it had escaped from his nets and he'd tracked it this far." Darville gave up watching Brevelan.

"The only saber reported within the kingdom in the last generation was the sculpted one in Krej's hall."

Darville looked from Jaylor to Brevelan and back again in obvious question.

Brevelan turned her gaze away from both of them. "Krej, or his magician, captures rare animals and changes them into precious metals. Didn't you hear him say his spotted saber cat was bronze, but he had to let it go?" Now her eyes sought Jaylor's, seeking confirmation.

"I wasn't paying much attention. I was too busy fighting his magic." But he had heard other, more disturbing things.

"That makes sense," Darville mused. "I saw the saber cat. We were tracking it. Then Krej disappeared and that monster attacked me with magic." His voice rose in anger.

"Krej led you into a trap," Jaylor asserted. "You are all that stands between him and the throne."

"My father . . . ?"

"Your father is ailing. He has never been strong. Your disappearance and supposed death could very well kill him. He may be dead already."

"And this traitor of a cousin," Darville spat the word, "has been hiding his pet rogue for years. That is the only way he could hope to defeat me. A conventional attack by a warrior would not have succeeded." He stood up and began to pace.

His borrowed trews were too short and too loose. He looked less than majestic as he prowled the perimeter of their camp. "What will happen to the kingdom now that Shayla has been enchanted?" He whirled to face Jaylor directly.

"I don't know."

"Can the Commune of Magicians maintain the border without the dragons?"

"Doubtful. It was breaking down weeks ago when I passed through it."

The prince paced again. "We have neighbors who envy our peace and need our resources. As soon as they discover the open border, we are vulnerable to invasion." He sat again, not on a rock, but on the ground, crouched. His head tilted and one foot came up to scratch. But his body no longer twisted in that manner.

His face and neck flamed in embarrassment.

"What am I, magician, a man, or a wolf?"

"You are a man now. You were a wolf for many moons. Some of those instincts linger. It may take a few weeks to forget." Jaylor looked into the fire, hoping to find some solutions in its green flames.

"I can't wait that long!"

"There is nothing more I can do. You alone must overcome those . . . memories." What else could he call them?

"But I don't remember being a wolf, other than those last few minutes before you restored me."

"Nevertheless, you were a wolf. Brevelan cared for you in that guise all winter."

"Brevelan?" He turned toward her, eyes wide. He started to lean against her leg, as he used to. "Brevelan. I do know you. You wouldn't let me hunt near you." He reached for her hand. His long fingers stroked the palm.

"Aye" she whispered in reply. But she didn't try to pull her hand away.

"Will you care for me again? Will you come with me to

Coronnan City? I need you to guide me until I am fully
me again." Darville kissed the back of her hand, as he
would the hand of any court lady.

"No," Jaylor found himself answering instead. "I need
her with me. I have to restore Shayla. She will be one very
angry dragon when she comes out of the spell. Brevelan is
the only one she trusts. Only Brevelan can keep Shayla
from flaming the entire kingdom in revenge for the actions
of your cousin." Mica butted her head against his hand
in agreement.

"Then I must go with you, too. Without Shayla the male
dragons will desert the kingdom. They must honor their
bonds to me and stay." As he had many times in past
months, Darville curved his jaws around Brevelan's delicate
wrist in wolf greeting.

*I have my beautiful dragon. She is crystal and light. Sun-
shine will refract from her into a million rainbows. The false
Stargods could not produce a miracle so beautiful as my
dragon.*

*Only Simurgh has the power to change my dragon into
glass.*

*I have used all of my Tambootie. I must have more to get
me back to the capital before the Council knows I have
been gone.*

*The illusion of my visage on the body of young Lord
Marnak cannot last much longer. If the boy wishes to con-
summate his marriage to my Rejiia, he will follow my orders
and retire from court. Disaster will follow if his pockmarked
face emerges through my illusion.*

*These mountains are full of my trees of magic. In the
village there is one who owes me his soul. He will face the
dangers and gather the leaves willingly.*

*With a fresh supply, this headache will leave me once and
for all. I will have the strength to finish what has been or-
dained by Simurgh. I have my dragon.*

So, now she knew for sure. Krej, her natural father,
hadn't hired a rogue magician. *He* was the rogue. She'd
know his evil laugh anywhere. Brevelan pondered yesterday's events while she busied herself with preparations for
the journey back down the mountain.

Jaylor already suspected her true parentage. Had he seen through the monster mask as well?

If he hadn't, she dare not speak that truth. Jaylor might believe her, but no one else would. She was Krej's bastard, accused of witchcraft, and a runaway from justice. To accuse a member of the Council of rogue magic promised dire consequences for herself.

She must keep her own counsel.

Did Jaylor remember Krej's comments? He had given no indication that he had heard the magician accuse them of being lovers. If he had heard, he hadn't acted upon it. Most men she knew would have taken Krej's assumption as permission from a father to proceed.

She shook her head and roused herself from her thoughts. The day beckoned with a myriad of tasks.

Brevelan watched Darville draw lines in the dirt. His stick described the great arc of the bay. At its apex he inscribed a small circle, Coronnan City. Radiating outward from the capital, the boundaries of the twelve provinces took form. Then he added the mountains that nearly encircled the kingdom. At the southeastern corner he marked a large X.

"Crude, but accurate enough for our purposes." Jaylor examined the drawing. The sparkle in his eyes denoted the return of his good humor. He was still a little pale, and tight lines formed beside his mouth. But his muscles were firm, and his feet made restless patterns on the cave floor.

"Can you do better?" Darville stood from his crouch beside the map to his full height. He was defensive, yet easy with his old friend.

"Only with magic," Jaylor admitted. "And that I would rather conserve right now."

Brevelan watched the two men stare at each other, measuring and assessing. She was reminded of two dominant hunting dogs in the village kennels. Rivals as well as work mates. Rivals for what?

Jaylor's eyes caught her own and lingered. Darville too sought to capture her gaze. She raised her chin and stared out the cave entrance defiantly. She would not be the center of their contest. As soon as Shayla was restored, Brevelan would return to the privacy of her clearing. And the loneliness.

"Once the rogue gets out of the mountains, he can put his burden on a sledge." Darville avoided naming the nature of that burden. All three of them shivered. "He shouldn't be hard to track in these hills. We've lost part of a day. But we travel light, and we don't need to guard our backs."

"On the contrary, Darville." Jaylor added a few details to the map. "In the mountains he need only levitate the dragon. She's heavy, but then so is a wine cup to an apprentice. For a magician so practiced and grown so strong, his travel through here," he pointed to the southern mountains on the map, "will be easy. We have a better chance of catching him closer to other people, where he must travel surreptitiously." He surveyed the map which was now more complete, a few lines redrawn to make it more accurate.

"Which pass will he take out of here?" Darville crouched again to examine their handiwork.

"This one." Brevelan found herself pointing outside the cave toward a valley between two lines of peaks. She didn't need a map. She could follow Shayla without one, she realized. A faint glimmer of the dragon had reawakened in the back of her heart.

"Not likely," Darville contradicted. "This one is wider, easier." He pointed to a different valley.

"This one is more familiar and direct. It is where he left you to die, knowing no one would try to help an injured wolf when they sought a missing prince," Brevelan asserted.

"No one but you." Darville's gaze softened as he searched her eyes.

"I'm an outcast from my people because I do such things. Thorm couldn't know I was near enough for Shayla to call." She had to remember not to refer to the rogue by his true name.

"There is a lot this rogue doesn't know," Jaylor interrupted. "But he is so arrogant he won't admit there is anything about magic he can't master. That is our true advantage. He thinks my magic traditional and therefore damaged with the loss of Shayla. He will travel openly in the mountains because he thinks he frightened us into believing he is all-powerful."

"He's not all-powerful. He had to fight us to complete

his spells," Brevelan added. She raised her eyes to the tall magician, who moved restlessly back and forth near the cave opening.

A raindrop landed on the rocks outside. It was fat and heavy, the prelude to more to come. A damp breeze found its way into the cave.

"Thorm had to draw magic away from Darville to finish his work with Shayla," Jaylor mused as he paced. "So we know his powers, great as they are, have limits."

"If we tax his strength every step of the way, perhaps he will have to drop the spell a little to deal with us." Darville's enthusiasm for the upcoming battle speeded up his own steps around the cave.

"First we have to find him. Let's go." Jaylor gathered his pack and staff.

"It's raining." Brevelan draped her thin, homespun cloak about her shoulders. They both looked at Darville in his borrowed, ill-fitting trews and cloak.

"I can't stop the rain. Only dragons are supposed to have power over the weather," Jaylor said.

"Without the dragons, the rains will be as heavy as they are in SeLenicca—so heavy they damage food crops. Only trees thrive in that amount of rain," Darville reminded them. "Spring will be delayed, crops will fail." Some of his eagerness faded.

"And people will die," Brevelan said.

"I can't change the weather, but I can provide for us." Jaylor set down his pack. He grabbed his staff with both hands.

Brevelan felt the change in the energy pulsating from Jaylor's body. A ball of sparkling lights flew into the cave. Then a small puff of wind brought a new pack, filled with journey foods, and deposited it tidily at her feet. From its top spilled a new cloak, similar to Jaylor's, but smaller, to fit her shorter height. She dipped her hands into the folds of thick wool and snuggled it against her face. It smelled new and fresh and clean. She felt warmer already.

Beside her bundle, another appeared. More food and clothes for Darville. "Raiding the University stores again?" he asked Jaylor. A smile tugged at his lips. Had Jaylor done this often to supply their boyhood pranks?

"They were intended for the use and comfort of students.

I'm still a student, technically." Jaylor shrugged as he reclaimed his own cloak from his prince. "Get changed. We need to move."

"Just who is in command here?" Darville whirled to face the magician. Brevelan held her breath, unsure of her own reaction to this minor skirmish for authority.

She braced herself for the onslaught of strong emotions that always accompanied this kind of confrontation. She was so prepared she barely felt the slight whoosh that hit her.

"I am," Jaylor replied. "We are dealing with magic, not armies and soldiers. I am the better equipped to decide our strategy."

He had tight control over his emotions. Darville bared his teeth and growled deeply. The hair on the back of his head began to bristle. She sent him enough peace of mind to ease her own tensions.

"And I am your prince, possibly king already!"

"You are still partly wolf, and I can make you one again if you push me." There was no malice in Jaylor's voice, only authority.

"Would you really?" Darville laughed at the obvious absurdity.

"If necessary." Jaylor smiled too.

"And I will make you both rabbits if we don't begin this quest," Brevelan replied. She looked back at them from the entrance. "Are you coming, boys?"

As they passed in front of her, Brevelan tugged at Jaylor's sleeve. "Jaylor, if it is this easy for you to transport food and clothing across the kingdom, what will prevent Thorm from sending Shayla to his castle by the same method?"

"I don't know. Unless she is still alive within the glass and transport will kill her."

Chapter 21

The sensation of being followed crawled up Jaylor's back like a swarm of hungry wood ticks. He shrugged his shoulders underneath his pack.

"Mrreww," Mica protested sleepily from her customary perch.

"Oh, hush, Mica." He reached up to scratch between her ears. She rubbed her head against his palm, and he felt her concern.

"Who follows us, Mica, when we know our enemy is ahead?" he whispered to the cat even as he checked Brevelan's position in front of him. Darville strode beside her. Jaylor could see in the unevenness of each step that the prince was having trouble matching his impatient stride to her short legs. The need to range ahead, then circle behind haunted Darville.

"What's wrong?" Brevelan swung around to face Jaylor.

Darville stopped, too. His hand reached for a sword that, under normal circumstances, should swing at his hip. At the same time his lips pulled back in a snarl. His nose twitched, testing the air.

"Mica thinks we're being followed." Jaylor continued to stroke the cat's ears.

"Are we?" Brevelan's eyes searched about her. She too was stretching her senses.

"I think so."

"Into the bushes." Darville pushed them off the path into the low shrubbery.

Around the smaller plants that verged on the path, taller, straighter trees cast sheltering shadows. Jaylor looked at each trunk until he realized he was searching for the distinctive mottled bark of the Tambootie. It was early spring, with little chance of finding any timboor to help hide them. On this, the uphill side of the path the trees were all long-needled everblues. Their pungent resin filled his nose and mouth with a healthy clean scent.

Across the path, on the downhill slope, nestled a clump of the trees he sought. His senses were so filled with ever-blue, he couldn't smell the Tambootie, nor could he see the bark in the deep shadows. However, the unmistakable flat tops of the trees lower down the hill were clearly visible.

"Stay down," Darville hissed at him.

Jaylor wasn't aware that he had half stood. He crouched down again. Tight muscles in his thighs and back reminded him of yesterday's exertions. Darville was as comfortable sitting on his haunches as he had been the day before—when he was still a wolf.

The hiss of Brevelan's deep, in-drawn breath alerted him to the presence of their followers. He desperately needed to ask what she felt from the intruders. Darville's glare warned him that absolute silence was essential.

"There's another dragon tree." One voice drifted to them from around a curve in the path.

"Ain't we got enough *s'murghin'* leaves for the master?" A second, gruffer voice responded. The timbre of the voice triggered a sour taste in Jaylor's mouth. Why?

"Master said two baskets full. Then meet him where the creek joins the river that flows to the bay."

Brevelan's eyes went wide. Shock stilled her features. She knew something.

From somewhere deep inside him, Jaylor found a thin line of magic. He strung it out in an umbilical to Brevelan.

The meeting place, it's close to the village, on the back path to my clearing. Her thoughts came to him clearly. But she held something back, as if she sensed his magical eavesdropping.

What, my sweet? What disturbs you? he prodded.

The barkeep.

The gruff-voiced man. The rancid taste of steed-piss ale. The man approaching them had been among the villagers who tried to burn Brevelan's home. He would acknowledge only one master—his legal lord, Krej.

The other man is a steward at Krej's castle. He, too, may be a magician. Brevelan's thoughts found him on their own.

"That one." The two men came into view. The steward pointed to a healthy tree, not quite as tall as its neighbors. The barkeep set down his two oversized baskets. One was full, nestled into the other, empty one. "Don't look big enough to climb to the top," the barkeep grumbled.

"You don't have to go to the top to get the new leaf shoots."

"Your master specified top leaves only."

"Because dragons eat from the top. That's the only part of the tree they can reach while they fly. I'm sure a dragon would nibble any part of a Tambootie tree it could get to. Just fill the basket so we can move on."

"Can't understand why," the barkeep whined as he stooped to separate the baskets. "Ain't good for nothin'. Can't even eat 'em. Almost as poison as the fruit. Poison to every livin' thing except *s'murghin'* dragons."

Almost as poison as timboor? Jaylor pondered the statement. He could eat timboor, so could Brevelan. He'd bet Darville couldn't, nor the barkeep or Krej's steward. But the master himself, Krej, Lord of Faciar, cousin to the king, and rogue magician, probably could. What was his use for the leaves of the same tree? And was this the evidence he sought to convict the rogue in the eyes of the Council?

"Just get to work. And stop grumbling," the steward ordered. "When Krej is king, you won't question his orders."

Darville growled. He reached for the absent sword even as he leaped onto the path to challenge the two men.

Mistake. Once again the wolf instincts to defend had taken over. Jaylor couldn't take a chance. If either of the men should recognize their prince, and escape, Krej would know that Darville was restored. That piece of information had to be kept secret for as long as possible.

Jaylor's magic caught up with Darville in mid-leap. From one eye-blink to the next, a bundle of clothes landed on the path as the angry prince grew shorter, hairier, meaner, and even more angry. Once more he was a menacing wolf determined to rip out the throats of his adversaries.

*   *   *

The shock of landing on all fours sent ripples of pain
along Darville's back. The unnatural jarring did not disturb
the momentum of his quest. The two men needed to die.
He needed to do the deed. His eyes narrowed. From deep
in his belly came the sound of blood lust. He leaped again
before the men could react.

The first man, the one he'd never seen before, was his
target. Familiarity with the other man made him divert his
attack. But they were both evil. They both would die.

His weight carried both himself and the man to the
ground. Triumph pounded through him as his mouth watered. Saliva dripped from his teeth. He could taste the hot
blood even before he sank his fangs into the quivering, pale
flesh of the hairless man.

This man would die easily. Then he would kill the other.
Screams erupted around him. He paid no heed.

Louder they came. And louder again. They were the
screams of the man beneath him. He shouldn't be able
to make a sound with his throat ripped and his blood in
Darville's mouth.

A cry of distress penetrated his need to kill. The distress
grew and became his own. Brevelan called him.

The death of this man would kill Brevelan as well.

Brevelan.

His other self.

He sat back on his haunches. The man rolled away and
scrabbled up the slope. The other man was gone. His frantic cries echoed through the valley below as he slipped on
the rough path.

"The witchwoman! The witchwoman lives. She has sent
the wolf to kill us all."

Darville forgot the men and his need to kill. Brevelan
was calling him.

He had defended Brevelan and sent the men fleeing. To
show just how pleased he was with himself, he scooted
downhill a few paces in mock pursuit. He stopped and
bayed at his retreating quarry. The exercise burned some
of the extra energy pounding through him. Then he bounded
back to Brevelan's side, tail thumping.

Her foot invited him to sit on it. So he did. Her arm was
within easy reach. He greeted her by taking her wrist, ever

so gently, into his open mouth, even as he leaned his full weight into her.

Brevelan.

This was where he belonged.

Tears sprang to Brevelan's eyes. Darville's love and sense of belonging washed over her. She welcomed the familiarity of his wolfish greeting. She needed the warm contact of his body pressed against hers. For a few moments longer she cherished the bond that held him close.

"He is a man, Brevelan," Jaylor gently reminded her. "And a prince."

"I know." She choked out the words. A huge lump formed in her throat. Her body ached for the wolf to continue leaning into her. It was not to be.

"Step away, Brevelan. I need to change him back."

"I know." This time she couldn't watch. She pulled her long braid over her shoulder and played with the bark fastening. The tendrils of escaping hair took her concentration. She loosed them, ran her fingers through the long strands. Deftly she rebraided the distinctive red hair.

No matter where she went, its rare color stood out, identified her with Krej. She would always be known as a witch-woman, whether she had magic or not, just because of her hair.

"When you have finished, give me your knife." she commanded Jaylor.

"Why?" He sounded startled.

"I wish to cut off this braid. It's cumbersome, dirty. If we are to travel the length and breadth of the kingdom in search of Shayla, I do not wish to be burdened." She turned to stare at Jaylor, commanding him with her eyes.

"No," he returned flatly. Darville looked from one to the other, waiting for the magic that did not come.

"It is my hair, my choice."

"No." Jaylor took a step toward her.

She wanted to back away from his advance. His eyes held her in place. She remembered the thin coil of magic he had used to connect them. But once he had read her thoughts, once she had known the pattern of his mind in hers, she had returned the magic and spoken to him without words.

Something special bound her to him, just as she was bound to Darville.

She couldn't allow that to happen. She was destined to live her life alone. If she allowed herself to depend on these two men for comfort, companionship . . . love. . . .

"Give me your knife." She stiffened her resolve.

"Brevelan." He reached out an empty hand in entreaty. "Your hair is beautiful." His words were soft. She strained to hear them.

"Beautiful?"

"You are beautiful, unique, special. Please leave it."

Of its own volition her hand came up to touch his fingertips. It was like touching his mind again. As their hands joined, they were connected by that same something that had allowed her to send him words without speaking. A swirl of bright red and blue and copper magic encased them. She stepped into the circle of his arms. His lips touched the top of her hair.

The magic spun faster, tighter. He lifted her chin with one hand as the other held her against his broad chest. She raised up on tiptoe to be closer to him. Their lips touched. Jaylor deepened the kiss, merged with her, became one being with one mind, one idea, one goal.

Gently, Jaylor raised his head. A finger traced her lips. Wonder filled them both.

The magic died. As fast as it had sprung up, it faded. Deep inside herself, Brevelan felt the emptiness of its absence. She looked into Jaylor's eyes and saw the same emotions. He looked deflated. She felt lonelier than ever.

"You will not cut your hair." Darville's deep voice penetrated her abstraction. He was once more a man and naked.

"Get dressed," Jaylor responded. He shook himself free of the lingering spell. She looked for the telltale signs of fatigue. They were absent. Jaylor didn't even look hungry.

"Those men got away. They'll talk. Our enemy will move faster, change his plans. We need to follow quickly." Darville moved briskly, efficiently, once more a prince and a soldier.

"I'll regather the scattered leaves." Jaylor made no move. Rather, he stood facing his old friend, spine rigid, eyes defiant.

"No. We haven't time," Darville decided.

"They were important to Krej's minions. I will find out why."

"No," Brevelan gasped. She stepped between the two tall men. "You mustn't. Tambootie is too dangerous!" She reached to touch his chest, to implore him not to experiment.

Darville took her other hand.

She gasped for air. Their jealousy was suffocating her.

"You seem to have lost weight, master magician."

Baamin looked a long way up to the man who broke the taboo and spoke to the Senior Magician before being addressed. Maarklin, the exceedingly tall magician to the court of Nunio, looked down his even longer nose toward Baamin. He still wore his blue master's cloak over his unadorned fire green robes. His height and natural bearing added elegance to the simplest garments. During their days as apprentices they had called the tallest of the class "Scrawny."

They'd called Baamin "Toad knees" then. No more. Now they called him "Master."

"The strain of the times," he replied with a dismissive wave of his hand. There were reasons for his decrease in girth. Like a sudden revulsion for the taste of meat. Traditional magic required a magician to restore his body with animal protein. This rogue magic thrived on breads and roots. Meat now made him sluggish. But Scrawny didn't need to know that.

"Unusual summons, sir," commented Fraandalor, the member of the Commune posted to the court of Krej in Faciar. He too was tall, but slightly stooped, as if his blue cloak and shimmery gray robes were too heavy for his shoulders. Years ago he'd been known as "Slippy," like the sea snakes that washed up on the shores of the Great Bay every summer. Sea snakes provided a sweet nutritious meat when prepared properly. But the cook had to be careful lest careless cooking left a natural poison in the meal.

Baamin reminded himself that Slippy could very well have been corrupted by his lord's greed for power. Or by the temptations of rogue magic. Was Slippy the man wandering the southern mountains in the guise of Baamin's nightmares? Impossible. He couldn't have performed magic in Shayla's cave two days ago and be back in Coronnan City today.

"Unusual circumstances." Baamin perspired heavily under his formal court robes, blue cloak and trews, long gold tunic and fine cambric shirt that hung on his reducing belly. Responsibility and new powers lay uneasily on his shoulders.

"Gentlemen, please take your places." He waved them to the thirty-nine chairs placed around the formal table, made especially for the Commune of Magicians almost three hundred years ago. It was round, as tradition dictated, forged by dragon fire of solid black glass—perhaps the most valuable item in the entire kingdom.

Except for Shayla, Baamin thought. *A glass dragon is much more valuable.*

"Did you say something, sir?" The magician to his left raised a puzzled eyebrow.

"Just arranging my thoughts." Baamin took his own place farthest from the sealed door. The room was as round as the table, devoid of windows or decorative hangings. The only contents were the huge glass table and stone chairs. It was kept comfortably warm through a system of vents from the kitchen fires. Even so the perspiration turned cold on Baamin's back as he assumed his role as leader.

"A most inconvenient summons," Slippy reiterated.

"Most inconvenient circumstances." Baamin glared at the questioner. "Gentlemen, the king is gravely ill. He barely draws breath, his body does not move."

"That shouldn't make much difference," Scrawny snorted. "He hasn't done anything in years. By the time the kingdom realizes he's dead, we will have a smooth transition of power to Darville."

"There are . . . ah . . . complications." Baamin coughed.

All attention centered on him. His personal armor slid into place just before he felt their probes into his mind. Probes that were forbidden by traditional ethics. His armor was strong, fueled by his new inner powers. He easily absorbed the probes and turned them back to the senders.

The lines of magic honed into arrows of poison and sped back whence they came.

Seven of the twelve reared back in pain. Astonished at Baamin's individual power, they put all of their remaining magic back into their own armor. The slim traces of magic that had been in the room disappeared. The other five magicians slumped slightly from the attack, then straightened in respect. Their armor remained solid.

The five undoubtedly held rogue power. But did they know it? Had they practiced with it? Were they in league with other rogues?

"We are still a Commune," Baamin asserted. "And if we don't work together for a common good, the kingdom is in danger of collapsing."

"There isn't enough magic left," one of the seven protested. He was gray with fatigue from maintaining the little protection he could summon.

"Perhaps, perhaps not. But if we work together, we can overcome the problem without resorting to the jealousy and civil war that disrupted us once before. We may have to attract new dragons to the kingdom." The noise of their questions and protests assaulted his ears as painfully, but less dangerously, than their magic. Baamin reasserted his power over them without magic.

"I said together!" His voice boomed around the room.

Silence.

"Shayla has been kidnapped and transformed into a glass statue by a rogue."

The silence became deeper, more profound.

"I have forces in the field seeking her location. We are the best-educated men in the kingdom. I need you here, searching for a solution to the divisions that threaten the Council." He speared each one with his gaze. The Commune had been built on interdependence, trust, and common goals. The Commune must continue with or without a king. With or without a dragon.

Chapter 22

Desperately, Baamin swam up through the folds of sleep. He had to awaken. He had to end these repetitive dreams.

Blackness closed over him, dragging him deeper into the world of his worst nightmares.

His own naked body pranced around and around a giant cave. His fuzzy sun and fog face sprouted long, long, longer teeth. Powerful muscles rippled beneath his sweating skin. A tune poured forth from his soul. Each note conveyed magic into the most massive spell of his life.

His magic swirled around an amorphous form of crystal. Awe struck him nearly dumb. A dragon transformed into precious glass shimmered before him. He'd never seen a dragon before. Might never see one again.

At last the song died on his lips, and he fought for reality again.

Dawn glowed on the horizon outside his window. He sat up, panting for breath. Exhaustion still dragged at his muscles. Yet he feared to sleep again. If he closed his eyes, he would dream.

The same dream that had haunted him time and time again for the last four nights.

Was it all a dream, or had he actually transported himself to the southern mountains and wreaked havoc on the kingdom by kidnapping a glass dragon?

Darville sniffed the air for danger. The smell of smoke was old and wet. It permeated the clearing even now, some four or five days after the villagers had torched Brevelan's hut, probably only hours after she had left it. His nose felt clogged. Then he remembered he was human again. His wolf senses were dulled.

"Let me scout around," he whispered.

Jaylor nodded in reply as he quietly set down his basket of salvaged Tambootie leaves.

Darville watched Brevelan's eyes fill with tears while her chin jutted forward. *Stargods!* but she was brave. Even though his memories of the moons he had lived here were dim, he knew this woman, knew all of her moods, her strengths, as well as her vulnerability. For her he vowed revenge. The prancing rogue and his *s'murghing* minions would pay for this destruction.

He scouted the perimeter of the clearing with care. No snapping twig or scuffling undergrowth betrayed presence. Every few steps he sniffed and tasted the air.

Maybe his senses were dulled. But he knew what danger should taste like. That combined with the soldier's skills he'd been taught since childhood should serve him well. But he'd feel a lot safer if his familiar sword hung from his belt, or if he could really smell again.

The clearing and its environs were empty. Had been for several days. He missed the rabbits and squirrels, the goat, and the nest of mice in the thatch. Only the partially destroyed hut and hints of memories remained.

Three-quarters of the way around the clearing his boots scuffed against something soft. Underneath a network of debris, he found the soft brown fur of a lop-eared rabbit. He recognized the small scar across the dead buck's nose. This had been one of Brevelan's pets. It had been trampled by heavy boots.

Darville's anger ran cold through the veins. The creature had probably returned to the clearing seeking shelter from the strangers who invaded this place, only to be caught in the melee.

Saying a silent farewell, he recovered the rabbit with dead leaves and ferns. At least he could spare Brevelan the knowledge of this one small loss.

"They're gone. The area is completely empty," he informed his companions upon his return. "The thatch is gone, and part of one wall, but the hearth is undamaged."

"We'll stay the night," Brevelan decided for them. "I'll gather kindling. You two get to work on a roof of some kind."

Darville looked at Jaylor. A spark of animation hit his friend's eyes.

"Yes, Mother," they replied to her stiff back as she marched into her ruined home.

"Remember to wash when you're finished," she called back over her shoulder. "Little boys need to bathe every evening," she scolded them. A false note tinged her levity.

"Think she'll feed us real food if we behave?" Darville thought greedily of a thick haunch of venison. But he doubted he'd be able to eat rabbit again.

"Depends on how you define real." Jaylor avoided his eyes.

Darville felt his old friend's laughter. "I mean some meat. Roots and gruel can't fill an empty belly after a day's hard work."

"They will fill you if you let them." Jaylor finally looked at him.

This time Darville looked away. His belly felt slack. It protested constantly. He knew Jaylor had felt the same hungers many times in the last two days. Yet he had accepted Brevelan's meatless diet. "I don't think I can continue to work hard and walk all day without meat," he replied sheepishly.

"I could change you back into a wolf for a few hours, let you hunt." Jaylor's face looked bland, except for a tiny twitch at the corner of his mouth. The same twitch that had been a signal for a new mischief when they were children.

"Would it be for only a few hours?" Darville was skeptical. He knew his friend's penchant for practical jokes.

Once, when Jaylor was thirteen and he fifteen, their gang of wild and restless friends found sport in tormenting a stray dog. Sickened by the cur's pitiful squeals of pain and confusion, Darville had flung himself into the midst of the cruelty, fists flying. Jaylor wasn't far behind. When fighting the older and more numerous boys proved futile, Jaylor had used his waning strength to throw a spell. Each of the bullies sprouted a dog's tail.

And the tails were tied together with bits of devil's vine. A particularly thorny, choking, and pernicious weed.

Confused, the bullies had chased each other in circles, trying to unite their bonds, pricking their fingers, and unable to remove the thorns or the knots.

The stray dog had bounded free.

That memory reassured Darville. Jaylor wouldn't leave him in wolf form for long. And then he wouldn't have to eat another stew of roots and herbs.

"It's a deal. Do you want me to save you some of the kill?"

Jaylor's face fell. Darville felt chagrined. He'd used the wrong words.

Kill.

Brevelan could never forget that each bite of meat had once been a life.

"I guess not." Darville tried to smile. "After we fix the roof, we can take a dip in the pond."

"You splash too much," Jaylor replied, his own sense of humor returning.

"Only when you dunk me."

"Who, me?"

Darville slapped him roughly on the shoulder. "Of course, you. You've been doing it since we were babes in short britches. You never could resist rubbing it in that you were bigger than I."

"Younger, too."

"Not as smart."

"Stronger and more stubborn."

"That's for sure." They continued to wrestle as they crossed the clearing and began working on the thatch.

"It's too dangerous," Brevelan affirmed to Jaylor.

Jaylor tried to ignore her.

"I agree." Darville faced him, hands on hips, shoulders back and chin thrust out. "We haven't time for you to experiment. Old Thorm, or whoever that rogue might be, is probably already out of the mountains."

Brevelan and the prince were joining forces against Jaylor's determination. He wasn't sure he could fight both of them. Darville was strong enough to knock him senseless. Brevelan had the power to persuade him of anything. Anything at all.

"Mbrrt!" Mica confirmed her own opinion of Jaylor's

seeming foolishness. She paced in front of the warm hearth, round hazel eyes glowing, back arching.

"Not you, too, Mica?" Jaylor protested to the anxious cat. Her soft presence had always seemed supportive. Some of his determination slipped away when he raised his eyes from the basket full of Tambootie leaves.

The herbage had begun to wilt over the day and the night since it had been abandoned by Krej's steward and the barkeep. Still, the scent from the essential oils permeated Brevelan's partially repaired hut. A vacancy lingered behind his ears and his heart beat irregularly whenever he closed his eyes.

"This is too important to ignore. Krej and his pet rogue use the leaves in some way to increase magic powers. I have to understand how this works if I'm going to undo that very complicated, very powerful spell." Verbalizing helped define his motives. It also made sense of the floor that kept tilting toward the repaired roof.

"I'm sure he doesn't eat the poison. And even if he does, he'll wait until he's safely back at the castle." Brevelan grabbed a dented pot full of water and placed it over the flames to bring it to a simmer. The sputtering green flames lighted her face, highlighting her delicate features. The red of her hair took on a coppery glow, an elemental color firmly rooted in the soil of Coronnan.

Jaylor wanted to reach out and touch her gently, to reassure her and let her know he loved her. His fingers itched to bury themselves in her thick hair, separate each beautiful strand into a copper veil. The leaves called to him, begged him to forget the color that was grounded in the soil. Why not fly with the colors radiating from the wonderful leaves.

His hands continued to grip the basket on the floor in front of him.

"This is something I have to do." He returned his gaze to his study of the leaves. If only he could look into them, delve their secrets the way he looked into a spell book with his glass.

"I'm sure Krej uses an infusion. It's safer, easier to control the dosage." Brevelan continued her preparations for that procedure.

"Maybe he makes a salve of them and rubs it on his

skin." Darville dipped his hands into the basket, then quickly withdrew them as if burned.

Jaylor ignored them. He sought the thin shard of glass in his pack. It was wrapped in a special oiled cloth, several layers thick. When he withdrew it, he felt for a telltale vibration out of habit. The glass was cold and lifeless. No one was summoning him.

With a special vision, used by all magicians when holding a glass, he sought the secrets of the leaves. Their image jumped at him, larger than life. He adjusted his hold on the glass, concentrating on the variegated green and white center vein of a particularly fat leaf that had not yet wilted. He forced his mind to look at the leaf as if it were just another spell cloaked in obscure language in a forgotten book.

"An infusion of sun-dried leaves is the logical answer. How could one man eat that many leaves? But it would take several basketsful to prepare a year's supply for an infusion," Brevelan chattered on.

Jaylor ignored her.

Mica climbed into his lap. She butted her head against his hand. He nearly dropped the glass.

Jaylor pushed the cat away. She protested and climbed back. Her almost human stare dared him to push her away again.

"Consult Baamin at the University. Maybe he knows what to do with Tambootie," Darville suggested.

Jaylor barely heard him. The continued comments of his friends no longer held import. There were only himself and the leaves of Tambootie enclosed within the walls of the hut.

A drop of thick oil on the spine of the leaf shimmered with green and gold, red and blue, purple and orange. All the colors that glowed through Shayla's fur were in that drop of all color/no color liquid. He touched the drop with his fingertip. It clung. He licked it off.

Sweet/bitter/cold/hot/bland/spicy.

All the flavors of the world burst forth on the tip of his tongue. He tasted all the colors, saw all the flavors. His soul expanded to find more colors, more tastes, new sensations.

Jaylor licked the spine of the leaf where he could see

more drops. They exploded into his system, filling him with wisdom and knowledge.

Life was suddenly reduced to a simple equation.

Magic became natural and easy.

He licked the leaf again, chewed its green and white tip, needed more.

His mind soared upward, outward. His soul chose a different direction.

Dimly he knew he licked and chewed a second leaf, a purple one this time, then a third solid green and a fourth mottled pink and green. They gave him the power to merge his mind and body and soul. He chose to drift separately.

"Is he . . ." Brevelan gulped back her fear. "Is he dead?" Fiery green ice sped through her rapidly numbing body. *Jaylor!* Her mind screamed. *Come back to me.*

Darville hunched over Jaylor's slumped form. He felt for life-sign at his friend's neck. He shook his head in puzzlement, then pushed his shaggy golden hair back out of his eyes and tried again. "I can't tell." He shook his head again, this time in despair.

"Let me." She shouldered him aside. Panic nearly choked her. Jaylor had eaten several leaves, perhaps six or seven, before she and Darville had noticed. They had pulled him away from the lethal basket of leaves, but not in time.

"Jaylor," she whispered.

Still no response.

Her mind called again in protest. *Come back to me!*

A faint vibration responded to her call, not from his body but from the void, above and beyond reality.

"Jaylor!" she demanded of the vibration.

It hummed and threatened to drift away, uninterested in her plea.

"Don't you dare leave me." She firmed her grasp on that thin thread of life.

It drifted no farther away but did not return. When they had hidden in the bushes beside the path, Jaylor had used a thin umbilical of magic to touch her mind. Traces of that silver thread still trailed away from the faint vibration.

She searched her own soul for the other end of the fragile magic cord. It was buried deep, behind the tiny throbbing bit that was her connection with Shayla. Her end was copper,

Shayla's was as transparent as glass. Color didn't matter. She had to splice or weave all the magic strands together.

I rode through the day and night for four days. Eight journey steeds died beneath me. I pressed them too hard with compulsions. They failed me. If only those fools hadn't lost the Tambootie, I could have flown to Coronnan City on the winds.

My magic is stretched too thin. My head aches. There are spots before my eyes. I had to abandon Shayla to my servants. They will transport her to the great hall by sledge. I must be in control of the Council before my agents lead the enemy army over the border. Coronnan will win the battle with them, but only if I am the one to lead our troops to victory. That is the arrangement made with Simeon of SeLenicca many moons ago.

I didn't have the strength to project my image onto Marnak's body, nor through Scrawny's glass. The Council must not act without my "presence."

I must have my Tambootie to keep up this pace. Coronnan needs me even if the Council of Provinces doesn't know it yet.

Chapter 23

"**Y**ou and your cosseted Commune have failed, Baamin." Krej glowered at the magician who sat in the Council for the ailing king.

"In what way, Lord?" Baamin stalled. The Twelve—the lords of the Council—sat in a round room, larger and more luxuriously furnished than the one used by the Commune. The twelve windows boasted colored glass in the pattern of each lord's device. Their elaborately carved chairs bore the same designs. The thirteenth chair was specially carved with dragon heads curving over the top, dragon claws at the end of each arm and leg. It was empty now, reserved for the king.

Behind each lord and slightly to the right sat his magician. For three centuries, master magicians had been posted to the twelve courts as advisers and links to the king and Commune. For those same three centuries the magicians had owed first allegiance to the Commune, the combined body of all master magicians, rather than to any one lord—or king.

No one lord could gather power over another through his magician.

The system had been devised by the lords.

Now Krej was throwing doubt on the value of the Commune.

After the nightmares of the last week or more, Baamin questioned his own value within the Commune.

According to Jaylor, Krej had arranged the destruction of the dragon nimbus and therefore robbed the kingdom of Communal magic that could overpower any single rogue.

But how to prove it, when Baamin doubted Krej's guilt himself.

If the Commune was tightly knit, as protective of its individual members as they were of the whole, the Twelve were even more so. Krej's treason would have to be proved by concrete evidence, not magical observation.

"The western border is all but gone." Krej looked into the eyes of each lord in turn. "Raiders are infiltrating. I have pleas for help from six villages that have been sacked, burned, their men killed, and their women raped and kidnapped. Children wander hungry and homeless—vulnerable to the Rovers who also prowl our lands. Word of these tragedies will reach our jealous neighbors soon. They will mass their armies and attack, then they will take our unprotected resources rather than paying dearly for them. What do we have left to fight them with?"

Baamin felt a compulsion spell behind Krej's words as well as his magnetic gaze. Who dared throw such a spell? Outward magic was forbidden in Council. By law and tradition, a magician was allowed to communicate with his lord through magic but could throw no other spells.

Who had grown so strong that he defied this most valued of prohibitions?

"We have an army." Andrall, Lord of Nunio, Scrawny's affiliate lord, argued at the prodding of his magician. "We've kept them trained for just such an emergency.

"They've gone soft, fighting imaginary enemies," Krej returned. "And who is to lead them? King Darcine," he sneered the title, "is near death. His son is missing. Off dallying with his latest mistress, I presume."

"Don't you know where Darville secludes himself?" Baamin asked desperately. He tried to throw a truth spell over this domineering lord. The spell bounced back, neutralized and harmless.

Krej was armored. That spell was legal in Council, but it was usually thrown by a magician to include himself and his lord. Baamin couldn't detect the source of the spell.

"How should I know where our feckless prince has wandered?" Krej stood and began pacing the room with calculated and controlled steps.

"Gentlemen," he addressed the room, "the kingdom is

in crisis. Our protective border is disintegrating, our enemies are massing for attack. Rossemeyer on our southeastern border is demanding marriage to our prince or they will declare war. SeLenicca, to the west, claims such a marriage will be an act of war against them. And where are our beloved king and his son to sort out this nonsense? Darcine lies dying and Darville was last seen out hunting several moons ago. Neither is in a position to guide us. Even the Commune, which has protected us so long, has become ineffectual."

There were murmurs of anxious agreement around the room. No one questioned Krej's source of information. Baamin felt the five still strong magicians "nudge" their lords with reassurance. They were men he thought he could trust, men who had been close friends for many years.

The other magicians tried persuasion, without success. If they had powers beyond traditional magic, they didn't yet trust them enough to call upon them. These magicians were younger than himself. He knew them as masters but not as men. Could he trust them enough to teach them rogue magic?

"I have summoned Prince Darville home from his monastic retreat," Baamin stalled. He kept his shoulders straight, his face impassive. It would not do for Krej to penetrate his own armor and learn the extent of his magic as well as his doubts and fears. He couldn't forget that Krej's face had been beneath the mask of his nightmares at the ball.

"And how long will his return take? There are no monasteries within a week's hard ride." Krej answered his own question. "Gentlemen. We don't have that long. We need to take action now! We must show ourselves as strong enough to repulse all our enemies. Enemies that have been trying to penetrate our border for generations."

Krej's pacing ceased. He stood directly behind the king's chair, a copy of the throne in the Great Hall. His position and posture effectively assumed control and eliminated Baamin from view by the other Council members. His handsome body and the high back of the throne stood between the magician and the rest of the room.

"In the absence of the king, we, the Council of Provinces, have the power to act for him," Andrall interjected. "We can raise and provision an army, order the magicians to summon the dragons, if necessary." His voice calmed much of the turbulent emotion in the room. Scrawny was prompting him.

Wasn't he? The "nudge" didn't feel right, didn't carry Scrawny's signature. Baamin peered around Krej to get a better view of his colleague. Andrall's magician was staring at Krej as if enthralled. Slippy was actually prompting the Lord of Nunio. Law specifically forbade a magician to advise any but his own lord. And why was Krej's magician prompting the one lord likely to stand up to Krej?

"What dragons?" Krej thundered. His voice echoed about the room in ominous thunder rolls. All were stunned into quiet.

"Have any of you ever seen a dragon?" Silence greeted that question. "What good is a creature of myth? Where is the magic they are supposed to give us? We must act now, elect a leader." Himself no doubt. "And send what is left of the army to fight the raiders. Let that be their training ground for the conflict to come with the trained troops and mercenaries our neighbors can summon."

"Our king still lives," Andrall reminded them. "We don't need to elect a leader. As long as we are in accord, we can function for him."

"Read your history, Lord Andrall," Krej sneered. "Do you know what happens when you try to run a war by committee?"

Several men in the room shuddered, including Baamin. *Stargods!* Krej was right. The last time that had happened, Coronnan had dissolved into fifty years of civil war.

"In view of the circumstances," Lord Wendray from the border city of Sambol stood and addressed the assembled Council of Provinces, "very shortly I will be in dire need of an army. The raiders grow stronger every hour. Even now I should be home organizing defenses. Gentlemen, I am a merchant, governing a merchant city on the western border, not a warrior. Give me an army to defend the vulnerable western reaches. But give me an army led by a capable general." He leaned heavily on his pudgy fists.

"There are several capable generals in our army," Lord Andrall argued.

"But none of them has ever seen real combat," Krej

countered. "For that matter, no one within the kingdom has ever seen combat." He stood behind Scrawny for a moment.

Baamin watched their auras merge and grow. Scrawny! His oldest friend, the magician he trusted most, was in league with Krej. The joined aura of red and green magic expanded to include five lords and their magicians. All five men were linked to Krej by marriage or betrothal to one of his children. All five were weak, malleable men. None of their magicians—three of them old friends who had demonstrated rogue abilities—resisted the illegal magic persuasion.

Couldn't any of the other magicians see the magic? Why weren't they fighting it?

"You are the youngest, most fit and best educated of all of us." Lord Marnak, whose son was to marry Krej's fourteen-year-old daughter next moon, spoke in an enthralled monotone.

Hastily, Baamin summoned his own magic in a counter spell. Illegal though it might be, he had to break Krej's command over the Council.

Power rippled through his body. He massed it, allowed it to strengthen, then threw it at the buzzing aura of red and green haze. The power erupted from his mind in a silver-blue dart. He aimed it at Krej's heart. The illegal aura buckled a fraction under the assault. Krej closed his eyes in concentration. The red and green haze reformed around the shattered pieces of Baamin's magic.

Deep within the inviolate aura, Krej smiled. His eyes narrowed, evilly. Baamin didn't have to hear his mocking laughter to know who had won this minor skirmish.

"Lord Krej is the best qualified to lead us out of this entanglement. He is the strongest and the closest relative to the king," Marnak mumbled on. "We must make him regent."

"I disagree!" Andrall stood in protest. The aura rippled around him but did not cover him. Who was Protecting the Lord of Nunjo if not his own magician?

"You have been outvoted Andrall," Krej drawled. "I am now regent of Coronnan and I command you to be quiet while I make plans for our defense."

* * *

"You must rest, Brevelan." Darville's hands gently pressed her shoulders back against the thin pallet on her cot.

She shook her head in denial. "I can't." The words came out a croak. She swallowed deeply and spoke again. "If I let go, even for an instant, I will lose him."

As if in response to Darville's urging her to rest, her control over the thin copper and silver tendril of magic that held Jaylor to this reality came nearer to shredding. For three days she had maintained the contact. She had pulled on it, spliced it, rewoven it dozens of times, and still he resisted her tether.

A deep sadness threatened to engulf her. Could she continue to live without Jaylor? Yes, she could survive. But did she want to?

She'd known him less than a moon, and already his presence was as natural to her as breathing. She couldn't let him slip away.

She concentrated on splicing the bond that held them together. The scent of Tambootie floated through the hut.

"At what cost?" Darville sounded as cranky and impatient as she felt.

"How can you ask that?" she demanded. It had been so much easier when Darville was her favorite puppy. Now he was a man, a handsome man who filled the hut with his vibrant presence as much or more than Jaylor ever did.

They had cleared the hut of every trace of the cursed Tambootie leaves as soon as Jaylor's inert body failed to respond. But the drug was in his system. Removing it from the hut resulted in no change.

Then she had tried coaxing him back with more Tambootie. Still no change.

"He's my friend, too." Darville looked chastened. "For many years he was my only friend." He wandered to the open doorway where a thin shaft of sunlight tried to penetrate the interior. In the five days since Shayla's transformation, this was the first letup in the rain. "I learned early that the people at court befriended me because I represented power, glamour. Standing next to me made them feel bigger than they really were. Except Jaylor. And a few of the town boys who knew me only as Roy and not as a prince." He took a deep breath.

Brevelan felt his gentle memories. She had no energy left to strengthen his feeling of quiet nostalgia. She lay back upon the bed.

"It was easy for me to slip away from tutors and guardians. They were more interested in their own positions than in me. That's how I met Jaylor. He had slipped out, too. He likes being outdoors. He claims he can't think or study behind stone walls," he chuckled. "But when we were together, neither of us did much studying." His grin lifted with remembered mischief.

Brevelan drew Darville's emotions into herself. Carefully she allowed her body to relax while she wrapped Darville's pleasant reverie around her contact with Jaylor. Maybe this trip through childhood memories would encourage his spirit to return.

"We were constantly in trouble. No one had ever allowed either of us to play before. We gave each other that ability."

"I'm happy you found one true friend. It's important to someone in a position of power. Jaylor will always be someone you can trust."

"Because he loves me and not my position. He has his magic. That's stronger than any temporal power I could grant him."

They were quiet a moment. Brevelan used the time to check her tie to Jaylor. It was stronger and so was the Tambootie smell. She relaxed a little more, easing the tired strain on her neck and back.

"But it was you who rescued me, nurtured me, taught me to trust again." He whirled to face her. "I can't lose you, too!"

"His spirit has not drifted farther away. I must believe he means to return to us. When he can." She tried to let Darville feel her concern for both of them. It was a weak attempt. Too much of her energy was still channeled into her fragile contact with Jaylor.

"We need him to restore Shayla." Darville sounded defeated. "I sense the male dragons want to leave the kingdom if she and the litter she carries aren't returned soon." Despair tinged his posture as well as his voice.

"How are you linked to them?" Was it similar to her own awareness of Shayla, a link she held even now entwined and braided with her contact to Jaylor?

"They, the entire nimbus, are just there, somewhere in the back of my head, or my heart. I don't know which. I do know where each one is, when they mate, when they have disputes." His excitement turned to a deep sigh. "When they die."

Brevelan looked deeper into herself. Only Shayla was there. Her mates were missing.

"And your father?" she prompted.

"For three hundred years, there has been a special . . ." he reached for the right words. "A special link between a king and his dragons. The royals are aware from birth, but only the anointed and consecrated king is bound so tightly his very life is affected by the health of nimbus. I've never had the 'why' explained."

They both shivered. Shayla was encased in glass. What had that done to the king?

They had no way of knowing what was transpiring in Coronnan City. Jaylor had had no contact with Baamin since the night in Shayla's cave.

"So that's why your father has always been sickly," she stated flatly.

"Ten and twelve years ago several villages, not just the one here, went dragon hunting," Darville explained. "I was twelve the first time. Too young to lead the Council."

Mica came in from her scout of the clearing. She butted her head into Darville's ankle. He stooped to pick her up. With the purring cat on his shoulder, he continued his narrative. His words took on the cadence of the cat's purr. The rhythm drifted over Brevelan like a soothing song.

"Over the centuries, people have forgotten the wondrous things dragons did for the kingdom during the Great Wars of Disruption. Nimbulan lured the dragons to Coronnan— they were mostly very young dragons seeking nests of their own. I don't know how he gained their loyalty, but they went into battle for him, found a lord worthy of the crown, ended the long years of civil war."

"Why kill them? I really can't understand why our people went so far out of their way to murder such wondrous creatures."

"Not everyone can see the beauty, the majesty, the magic in our dragons. They have forgotten why we owe the dragons a debt of gratitude. Some know only that they raid cow

pastures and scoop boatloads of fish out of the bay. The
original pact with the dragons guaranteed them hunting
rights and tithes of livestock. In normal years there is more
than enough for both people and dragons. But in bad years,
when people are living on the edge, just barely surviving,
they look for a cause. Some found the dragons' natural
feeding habits a good reason for their own failure." They
both shivered at the implications.

The magic umbilical tugged from Jaylor's end. Some portion of him was aware of the conversation. He had something to add.

"Jaylor thinks Lord Krej deliberately impoverished his
province to foster that notion. The Equinox Pylons have
gone undecorated for over a dozen years." She felt lighter,
less tired. Jaylor wasn't actively trying to escape his ties to
Coronnan. He was interested. He would return.

But when?

Darville whirled about, his shaggy blond mane flying in
agitation. "Krej can't undermine the welfare of his own
people! He took oaths when he assumed the lordship."

"Men can break oaths, can never mean to keep them
even when swearing." Like a husband who vows to cherish
a new wife and then abuses her.

"I have to remember my 'wonderful' cousin is really a
traitor, capable of anything. Last year, when Jaylor was
engrossed in his exams, I was very lonely. Krej became a
constant companion. I thought he was a friend, too." He
sighed. Mica butted her head against his chin in sympathy.

Brevelan felt his loneliness. It became her own. She
reached a tentative hand to touch his cheek. The contact
sent tingles through her body. She was reminded of the
times Jaylor had kissed her. She needn't fear a man's touch,
only certain men's. She spread her hand to cup his face.
He leaned into the caress and kissed her palm.

"We'll work it out, Brevelan. But you must rest, even if
you don't sleep." Gently he guided her shoulders back onto
the bed. A deep warmth and contentment engulfed her.

She closed her eyes for just a second. The thin strands
of copper, silver, and glass that held Jaylor to Coronnan
dissolved.

Chapter 24

Quiet drifting. Light and shadow. Heat from the sun, cool from the moon. He slid upward until the colors and patterns of Coronnan melted together. A copper thread dangled from his hand.

He caught a purple updraft, found a dragon playing there. He grabbed hold of a silvery green wing and allowed the creature to guide him through the pink air.

Upward they soared. Blue wind rushed past them. The yellow-red-green-yellow sun came closer. Their speed slowed as they reached the ultimate height. They hovered a moment, cherishing the wild sense of life pumping through each of them. Their hearts beat as one, and the wind harmonized by thundering past them in an interesting counter rhythm.

Below, the green land divided itself into puzzle pieces with bluish-silver lines of magic. The lines resembled the fragile cord, sometimes copper, sometimes silver, bonding him to the body he had abandoned an eon ago. A few white cloud puffs obscured any other borders, the ones established by men but recognized by no one else. The magic border that should surround this insignificant patch of green had faded to nothing.

Sharply downward they plunged, so fast their breath was pushed back into their throats. Sharp cold air became a wall. They pushed it aside with the blink of an eye. A steep cliff of black granite rushed to greet them. At the last moment they flattened wings and pulled up to soar again over the top. Flushed and exhilarated, they leveled off.

Together they surveyed the snowcapped mountains. Their

bellies were numb. The game lurking in shadowed ravines offered no interest or relief. But a Tambootie tree needed cropping. Compulsively they snatched at the top layer of new leaves as they skimmed past, away from the sheltering mountains.

Over level ground again, a different dragon flew under them. He switched from the green wing to the blue back. A moment's unsteadiness. Then he found a new pulse and he merged his identity with the older dragon.

This dragon flew more intricate patterns. They dipped and soared, played with the wind, spun and reversed in a tail's length.

A city squatted like an ugly beetle on the islands of the Bay delta, enmeshed in an intricate web of bluish-silver magic.

They spied on puny creatures below as they went about incomprehensible tasks. Some battled, some coupled, some slept.

Many men met in a closed room.

Time rolled forward and back, sometimes quickly, sometimes drifting as lazily as he.

A familiar man, cloaked in a dirty aura, met two others by a chattering stream in southern forests, just below the clearing where six magic lines converged. They felt anger in one man, fear radiated from the others. Beside them stood Shayla, encased in magical glass. Sparkles of sunlight on her covering blinded them.

Or was it their tears?

He and all of the dragons shuddered. Heat built deep within them. Flame touched their tongues and needed release. He dropped the slender thread that bound him to his other life, his other love. Strands of copper drifted away from him. *She* would not approve of their actions.

Another dive. Terror filled the faces of the men. They should turn back. Men are not for killing.

No! Turn back!

What matter? *That one* had ensorcelled Shayla and the litter she carried. *That one* had endangered all. That one deserved to die by dragon fire.

He felt the contempt of the angry man who didn't fear a flaming dragon anymore. Bits of an angry soul reflected from the glass that was Shayla. The two were intertwined. Kill the man and they would kill Shayla.

"Noooooo!" he screamed.

"Master?" The kitchen boy poked his head around the corner of Baamin's quarters.

"Yes?" he replied wearily. The boy moved closer. He seemed taller, more defined than just a few days ago. Adolescence must finally be catching up with him.

"Master, you haven't eaten in two days." Worry creased the boy's brow.

Baamin felt a small surge of gratitude before his worry and fatigue filled him again. No one else cared what happened to him. Krej had taken over the Council and the magicians. Since then no one had consulted him about anything. So he sat, alone, in the dark of his study with only his books and his nightmares for company. He brooded, he plotted and schemed.

And reached no conclusion.

He didn't trust Krej, Lord of Faciar, Regent of Coronnan. Yet, what else could they have done but elect him regent?

Stargods! There was no one else to lead this kingdom against its enemies. No one until Darville returned. Dragons only knew when that would be!

"I'm not hungry."

"You need food to replenish your magic." The boy placed a plate of soft cheese and bread on the desk, next to Baamin's elbow. The flowing sleeves of Baamin's robe spilled over a text, he didn't remember which one.

"What good is magic? Krej is solving our problems with armies and spears." And doing it very well, with energy and organization. Coronnan hadn't seen the like for more than ten generations.

"Armies destroy much more than just other armies. Nimbulan said so." The boy stared at the arc he drew on the stone floor with his bare toes.

Interest flowed through Baamin's veins again. "You read the journal?" How was that possible? The boy was so stupid no one had bothered giving him a name!

"Bits, sir." He still refused to look up.

"How many bits?" Baamin reached to lift the boy's chin so he could see his eyes, see if intelligence glimmered there.

"Enough." There was a brief flash from the large brown eyes, then they were lowered again.

"Enough to learn the principles of old magic?" Baamin slid a little truth spell over the boy. At first it began to glow with the green fire of truth, then abruptly died.

Armor would bounce the spell back. This one just ended, as if absorbed and nullified.

Brevelan awoke from her nap feeling empty, deprived, and utterly alone. Frantically she search for the slender thread binding her to Jaylor. Shredded fragments of copper dangled uselessly from her soul. All traces of silver and crystal were gone.

Jaylor was gone. While she slept, his spirit had slipped away.

She bent her will to the magic thread, trying desperately to repair it, to build a new one. Anything to bring him back! The silver hid from her. There wasn't enough magic within her, within all of Coronnan to find it. She was alone.

Never again would she listen for his steps as he explored her clearing. Mica would have to find a new shoulder to ride on. Brevelan could go back to preparing small, sparse meals for herself alone.

She would be without her faithful wolf familiar, too. Darville needed to return to his own life in the capital. Tears rolled down her cheeks. Tears of guilt and heartbreak. She didn't try to hide them from the golden-haired man who whittled by the fire.

Darville came to her then. Crouched beside the bed, he pushed a stray tendril of hair away from her face. She leaned into his hand. His gentle caress cupped her face. Strength and comfort flowed between them. Since that first storm last winter, Darville had been with her constantly. In her loneliness she had hugged him close many times.

Now it was his turn to hold her.

"What are we going to do now?" she whispered into his shoulder.

"Whsst, little one. When you are rested, we must go to the capital and find Baamin. He'll know how to help Shayla, if anyone can." He stroked her hair.

They both looked at the extra cot by the hearth where Jaylor's body lay. It was just an empty shell. Their friend was no longer there to give it life and animation.

Jaylor was gone! The emptiness washed over her, pulling her into cold despair.

Darville hugged her closer, sheltering her from the pain, making it his own. She yearned for his warmth. For a moment she allowed herself to sink into his embrace, to savor the feel of his arms encircling her. His lips brushed her hair and his beard tangled with it. She could almost pretend he was Jaylor. Then his scent filled her.

He smelled of trees freshened by a spring rain. He had picked a few wildflowers, and their pollen lingered. Mica had been in his lap. His hair was damp, as it had been so often after a playful splash in the pool when he was a golden wolf. She savored the comfortable familiarity of him. Her fingers reached and tangled with his thick, uncombed golden hair. When she tried to pull away, he held her tighter.

"Let me hold you, little one." He sat beside her, cradling her against his chest.

She needed to be this close. His heartbeat filled her mind. Her pulse quickened to match his rhythm. Their hearts entwined and beat as one. She felt her being merging with his. Wordless communication soothed them both, brought them to understanding. Her arms encircled his waist. This was Darville, not so different from the companion she had cherished for all those many moons.

Darville kissed her cheek and eyes. How many times had his wolfish tongue caressed her? He couldn't hurt her then. How could he hurt her now? She need not fear this man who was so much a part of her. But they were still two separate beings. She needed to join with him, to find the wholeness that Jaylor had taken with him.

Her mouth found Darville's lean, bearded cheek. He turned his head to capture her lips. Such a warm, undemanding kiss. Her heart swelled with tenderness. Her breasts were too small to contain her emotion. They tightened.

She deepened the kiss, demanding more of him, and herself. Her body nestled against the firm wall of his chest. His kisses fanned over her face, down to her neck. His tongue found the most sensitive delicate hollow, his hands sent flame through them both. His desire became hers. Her need filled him and grew stronger.

Heat built deep within her, expanded, surrounded him, and flowed back. Heat and need. There was so much they needed to share, to say to each other with voices and bodies.

There was a tug at her shoulder. She shrugged out of her kirtle and shift. The heat continued to build even as cool evening air washed over her sensitive skin. An ache built with the heat.

The roughness of his shirt teased her taut nipples. Impatiently she pulled the garment up over his head. His skin covered sleek muscles that rippled and molded under her touch. Their bodies melted together as if they had always belonged together. They needed to join their bodies to complete what their souls had already begun.

Colors burst forth. Bright splashes of copper and gold. Darts of the colors of their lives spread out across the heavens, into the void where only dragons and souls existed.

Passion and need rose and soared within them, pulling them higher, faster, ever farther. A distant blue blended with their elements and drew others into the vortex until they were all colors, no colors, swirling in the wind created by dragon flight, soaring with dragon ease on the currents above and around them.

They flew with dragons. A braided shaft of red and blue separated from the nimbus and twined around them, joining their union. It plaited and blended their copper and gold within its unique twists of blue and red, binding each part into a whole.

Time drifted in lazy circles. Brevelan did not, could not fight it. She was complete. The lonely emptiness that had driven her was filled to overflowing. Her need was temporarily sated. With a deep sigh of contentment she closed her eyes and slept, wrapped in warmth and love.

Morning light crept through cracks in the walls of the hut. Brevelan lazily opened her eyes. It was late. She needed to be up and about. There were chores to be done.

The double cot was crowded as usual. When the nights were cold, Darville and Mica joined her. Often several squirrels and mice, a rabbit or three, and sometimes even the bright yellow and gray jay bird, who scolded her so frequently, cuddled close to keep her cozy. A better arrangement than sharing a narrow pallet with three blanket-greedy sisters.

She shifted a little, surprised at just how crowded the bed was this morning. A heavy arm, sprinkled with golden hair, rested across her waist. A leg encircled hers.

Awareness burst upon her. The arm belonged to Darville. He was no longer a wolf, but a man. A strong, and wonderfully gentle man at that. She touched the fine swirls of hair on his chest. With her toes she caressed the leg and felt a responding movement from behind her.

She stilled her body and mind, as she did when secreting herself in the forest. Darville was not the only person in bed with her.

Cautiously she peeked over his broad shoulder, toward the cot by the hearth.

It was empty!

"Jaylor?" she called softly, with her mind as well as her voice.

"Hmmhph?" he murmured from behind her.

"Jaylor!"

"What?" he replied, a little more awake.

"What!" Darville responded.

Her eyes met Darville's, then they both looked to the other side of the bed, toward the wall, where their friend lay, relaxed and grinning, and as naked as they.

"Good morning," he greeted them.

Chapter 25

Jaylor examined the hut with new eyes. He leaned against the open door, surveying his surroundings. The circle of stones forming the hearth was the same as he last remembered, and yet not. When he looked at familiar objects straight on, they were covered with distorting mist. But a sideways glance revealed sharp outlines, clearer than he had ever experienced before. Sort of the way he had to tackle a difficult spell-unraveling.

He turned his attention to a reexamination of the objects he knew so very well. The oversized cot against the far wall definitely looked different. His experiences there colored his perceptions. The blankets had been straightened, just barely. The imprint of three tightly woven bodies still remained, while the smaller cot he had spirited from the University storerooms stood empty and barren.

He grinned. Life, as well as the air around him, had taken on a new clarity. He could almost see through solid objects in the familiar/odd room. Brevelan was more transparent than anything else. Perhaps her empathic abilities made her so easy to read. Or was it the intimate entwining they had experienced while he was in the Tambootie-induced coma?

She was embarrassed, puzzled, pleased, and appalled, all at the same time. He grinned again, felt his body stretch all over, including his manhood, and didn't bother to suppress the feeling.

Yesterday he had flown with dragons. Today he knew more about magic, and himself, than ever before. He was willing to bet even old Nimbulan didn't know what Jaylor knew now. Yesterday he had feared the power Brevelan had over his mind and body. Today knowledge had wiped away the fear.

But before he could explore that thought, turn it into action, there was a rogue to tend to.

For the safety of the kingdom and the well-being of the beloved dragons, Krej had to be removed from power—temporal and magical. Jaylor's Tambootie-induced vision of Krej screaming at his servants beside the glass statue of Shayla had ended all doubt of the rogue's true identity. Sooner or later the all-powerful lord would slip and expose his magical abilities. Jaylor intended to be present with other reliable witnesses when that happened.

"Someone comes." Brevelan raised her head from the pot of stewing grains she stirred. She refused to meet his eyes, or Darville's, for that matter. Her head remained lowered as she hastily exited. In a few moments, her thoughts would either open or close the path for the visitor.

"How does she know that?" the prince asked. He had been pacing the room, anxious for their simple meal to be finished so they could continue their pursuit of his cousin.

Restless energy had infused the prince since their early rising. Jaylor felt it pulsating against his own aura. He resisted the urge to pace alongside his friend.

"This clearing is in a focus of magic." He eased a soothing timbre into his voice. "It attunes itself to each of its tenants in turn."

Darville responded to the tiny spell of his voice and settled on the rickety three-legged stool beside the hearth.

"Don't manipulate me with your magic!" he demanded even as he fought the lethargy Jaylor imposed upon him.

Surprised he would notice, Jaylor drew back the slight control. He shouldn't be surprised. Last night Darville had been as active a participant as he and Brevelan. Henceforth the three were linked in a way he hadn't yet explored.

He continued with his tale. Darville needed to know what was involved with Brevelan and the clearing. His future might depend on that information.

"For three hundred years this small glade has protected, sheltered, and fed special witchwomen." Jaylor posted himself near the crack in the door to observe Brevelan's return, with or without company. "I believe Myrilandel was the first."

"Who?" Darville was only mildly interested. His arms and legs still twitched but his mind was calmer.

"Nimbulan's wife. He had to exile her, along with the other rogues, when he established dragon magic. But he provided for her and their children. That is why the cot is oversized, so he would have a place to sleep when he visited. That is why the hut wouldn't burn completely, only the thatch that has been renewed since he threw the protective spells."

"Explain this 'focus' of magic. Can it be used against Krej?" Darville asked. "I thought dragons were the source of magic, and they are dwindling. With Shayla's enchantment there shouldn't be much of anything left."

"For conventional magic. Nimbulan was what we call a rogue, or a solitary, long before he tapped the power of the dragons and the Tambootie, which could make magic communal. Ask yourself, what was his source of power? How did he entice the first dragons and enslave them to this kingdom and your royal line!"

"Maevra is near to birthing. You must come now. She needs you." A strange voice came from the edge of the trees.

"Yes, of course. Just let me gather my things," Brevelan replied.

"She can't go alone." Darville whispered. "Krej may have sent these women to entice her to a witch-burning."

The prince's anxiety wound through Jaylor, becoming his own.

"You can't be seen there. Krej's spies will report your restoration. They don't trust me either."

The door latch rattled in warning.

"I'll be but a minute." Brevelan eased through a narrow opening. It was pushed wider by her golden wolf. She raised her eyes in surprise.

From behind the door, Jaylor put his finger to his lips to signal silence. He held Darville's discarded clothes close against his chest.

"They'll expect him to be by your side," he mouthed. She nodded her acceptance. A smile tugged at the corners of her mouth. "You just wanted him to hunt for himself so you could have more breakfast." An infectious giggle threatened to erupt from her.

He smiled back at her. She was once more comfortable

in his presence. The sun poked through the cloud cover and dispersed the rain. Jaylor's vision cleared.

Darville guarded the door of the carpenter's home. He blinked his eyes in the sunlight and stretched out across the doorway. Occasionally a person or two wandered past. They were curious. New pups always brought out the others. They had to inspect and sniff to make sure the newcomers were worthy of the pack.

He eyed them suspiciously. When one ventured too close he growled, low and deep so they would know he guarded the ones inside. Brevelan was with the woman.

His other-man-self knew Brevelan, his mate, needed protection. But she wasn't whelping. It was the other woman. Her cries of pain and the smell of her fear unsettled him.

Darville couldn't see Jaylor, secreted in the woods. But that was all right, as long as his scent was near.

His nose wiggled as he sorted the scents of each of the passersby. Some he knew. Some he didn't. There was no malice among the women, just curiosity. Only one man smelled of evil. He also smelled of rotten fish.

Then there was the man across the common. He had stationed himself in the opening of the cave. Every so often he drank from the long container in his hand. The container that men called a mug smelled of the foul water they drank in that cave. The man had no smell.

That warned Darville. He cocked his ears, allowed his neck ruff to stand in alertness. Men disguised their smell when they stalked prey. If the man-with-no-scent hunted Brevelan, he would have to get past one very protective wolf. And Jaylor, too.

A flicker of movement off to one side told where Jaylor hid. Darville crept forward a paw's length and growled again. The movement should signal to Jaylor that the man at the cave was trouble.

A thin wail of a human pup pierced the air. All movement in the village stopped. Darville sensed each person listening, leaning closer to the carpenter's home. The wail repeated, stronger this time. The pup lived. The carpenter emerged from the cave. He pushed the scentless man aside in his hurry. Darville let him pass into his home. He had no right to stop him now that the whelping was finished.

*   *   *

"A girl!" Disappointment hovered on the edge of the carpenter's voice.

"The child lives. She is healthy. And your wife will grow strong again to bear another," Brevelan reprimanded him. The birth was finally over. She and Darville and Jaylor could now get on with their journey. She hated to take the time away from their quest, but she was compelled to assist Maevra. Whether these people admitted it or not, this village needed her as much as she needed them.

The new father inspected the tiny scrap of life she held before him.

"You said it was a boy." He didn't reach to hold his daughter.

"I said the child was large enough and strong enough to be male." The child was also determined. She just might become the next witchwoman for this village.

Maevra roused from her exhaustion. "She's hungry, just like her father. Give her to me." She reached out for the now squalling infant.

Brevelan returned the babe to her mother. She wanted out of this dim, confining house. The dark emotions of the father, her own fatigue, and the smells of birthing threatened to choke her.

She needed Darville and Jaylor to dispel her loneliness again.

"We were promised a boy," the carpenter sulked. "Old Thorm said you might substitute a changeling so you could keep the boy for yourself. Yourself and that meddling magician!" His tone turned menacing. A growl from the doorway stopped his words.

"Only the Stargods can promise the gender of a child. Take up your complaint with them," Brevelan spat back at him. She edged closer to the door and Darville's protection.

"You take the name of our gods in vain!" Clearly the man was drunk. Or under a spell. Otherwise he'd never dare risk the ill will of a witchwoman.

She looked to Maevra and the now nursing child. Once the man returned to normal, he wouldn't harm his wife and daughter. His malice was all directed toward Brevelan.

"I'll demand no fee for midwifing a live and healthy child, since the result displeases you." Brevelan allowed her disgust for the man to wash over him. Maybe if he saw himself as she saw him, he could shrug off whatever compelled him. He stepped toward her. Darville bared his teeth.

"Get out, witch." Fear palpitated around him. "Get out and take the *s'murghin'* familiar with you. No decent priest should tolerate you and your kind. You won't be welcome back." His arm pointed to the door, uncompromising. Darville stepped closer. His teeth dripped, the hair on his neck stood straight up.

"No, Darville," she commanded. The carpenter appeared a little startled at the princely name. "His blood isn't worth your time." She gripped the animal's fur and tugged him backward. "If I were indeed in league with the source of evil, I would curse you, and curse this village." She held in check the power she felt rising within her.

"This time I'll only leave a reminder with the men who condemn me."

From the doorway, the freedom and safety of the woods enticed her. Jaylor hovered there. He would hear and understand her need for the words that spilled from her lips.

"Until you forgive me in your heart, as well as with words, until you know for truth that I wish you and yours only health and happiness, and until you can come to your wife with gratitude for the gift of the child she has given you, you will not be able to bed any woman." The words came from someone else, somewhere else. She didn't really wish this village ill. Still the words flowed. "And no child will be conceived in this village until all the men here feel the same."

The carpenter blanched and looked as though he would faint. Brevelan ignored him and marched out of his house.

Moments later, from the shelter of the trees, beyond the sight of the village, Brevelan hugged each of her friends in turn.

"Remind me not to make either of you angry at me," Darville said with a chuckle.

"That was some curse you laid, Brevelan," Jaylor agreed as he handed Darville his clothes. Hen-bumps covered his back in the cool spring air as he bent to pull up his leather trews.

His legs were long and well muscled, straight now but

still bristling with fine golden hair. His buttocks were tight . . . Brevelan spun to face in the other direction, embarrassed by her train of thought as well as her hungry appraisal of his body.

"I didn't intend to curse them." She studied the pile of packs and Mica washing a neat paw on top of them.

"And you didn't, Brevelan." Jaylor's hand was gentle and warm on her shoulder. "You held back the full blast of your anger. I felt little power behind your words."

She leaned her cheek against his caress, gathering comfort from him.

"Not much anyway," Darville muttered.

"I'm willing to bet that every man for miles around is going to spend the better part of the next nine months trying to prove you wrong. Some will even go so far as to drag their women beyond the village so the child will not be conceived within its limits." They all chuckled at that.

"But there was power," Brevelan murmured. She glanced over her shoulder to make sure Darville was clothed before confiding in them both. Since last night she had been thinking of the three of them as one person, bound together by duty, quest, and love. She needed both of them to unravel the mess she had caused.

"What do you mean?" Jaylor's eyebrows raised.

"As my anger grew I could feel a tingling drawing up from the ground below. It filled me to overflowing. I had to release it. The word came from the power, not from me."

"Stargods!" both men exclaimed.

"Sounds like old Nimbulan chose this place for his exiled wife with reason." Jaylor began pacing, hands out as if testing the warmth, or the power, of the ground he walked.

"Nimbulan?"

Briefly he explained the history of her clearing.

"So that is why the clearing called me. It chose me as its next witchwoman." This truth troubled her. As a child she had feared her magic, almost as much as her da had. Gradually she had come to accept it as a part of her. But if her magic came from the clearing and not herself, she could never master it, never come to peace with it.

"Partly." Jaylor reached out for her again. She dodged his hand. This was something she had to understand and control on her own.

"Brevelan." This time it was Darville who captured her shoulders. "Listen to him."

"The clearing chose you because your magic is strong."

Had he been reading her mind? Of course he had. After last night they had all three been communicating more with thoughts than words.

"Your magic is your own. It was with you at birth. You came by it naturally. The clearing needs someone as strong as you. It doesn't give you magic, it gives you the peace to explore and grow. Witchwomen of your caliber need the clearing for protection. Otherwise, you would have to face the prejudice and malice of villagers like these every day."

"It's not their prejudice. They liked me and were learning to trust me until Old Thorm told them differently."

"Krej. Old Thorm is just one of his many disguises."

"Let's move." Darville thrust Mica onto Jaylor's shoulder as he organized the packs. "If that's the case, they'll follow soon with torches and stones. We've got to be halfway to the capital before dawn." He gathered Brevelan close in a brief hug of reassurance. "While Maevra was birthing, the barkeep was watching me. He had no smell."

"Krej must have given him magic armor. As well as instructions to sow distrust in the village."

Chills ran up Brevelan's spine. How could her own sire, blood of her blood, flesh of her flesh, hate her so much?

"No, he's just incapable of caring for anything other than his power. It's as addicting as the Tambootie," Jaylor confided as he, too, hugged her close.

She gathered them both to her side. "It will be a long journey." She sought the eyes of both men. "We will be together constantly. I want you both to know I will tolerate no jealousy." She tried to keep her voice stern, but the love she felt for them, and from them, lifted her mouth into a smile. "I will be owned by no man."

"Neither of us will do anything without your consent, Brevelan." Jaylor looked to Darville for confirmation. The prince nodded his agreement.

She loved them both, would cherish them both while she could. "I know that," she replied. "And when this business is finished, we will each go to our separate destinies."

They nodded in solemn agreement even as they pulled her closer.

Chapter 26

Baamin watched the rain wash the window shutters with a steady stream of cold water. The cobblestone courtyard of the University was totally deserted. Not so the market square. Everyone had a task, either preparing themselves or acquiring equipment and stores for the growing army. Increasingly heavy rains had to be ignored. Armies couldn't wait for the elements.

The shouts and clangs of mock battles deafened observers on the nearest mainland from dawn to dusk. Those not so occupied sought refuge from their numbing fear of invasion in prayer or charms. In living memory nothing had so threatened the peace of their mundane lives as the news of border raids that penetrated ever deeper into the provinces.

Coronnan was going to war. Troops had been mustered from every station of life in all twelve provinces. No one was exempt. Training took place near the capital, and then massed troops marched somewhere to the west.

Baamin sighed heavily. He was Senior Magician and king's councillor. But no one had told him the location of army headquarters. He knew, of course. But he wasn't supposed to know. He had been abandoned along with the king he had served well for so many years.

No one else bothered to remember the king who lingered near death. Lord Krej was their leader now. He infused the populace with the energy and knowledge to save them all. Something the magicians hadn't been able to do when crisis struck.

Baamin's own self-doubts heightened his lonely depression. Was he responsible for the terrible disasters that threatened his homeland? Or had he only dreamed those terrible moments in Shayla's cave?

"Aah . . . aah . . . aahchoo!" Seven students dived to protect feeble candle flames from the blast of the sneeze erupting from the eighth apprentice.

Inside the University, the few remaining apprentices shivered and sniffled in the damp classrooms. Fuel had been rationed for Lord Krej's grand defense of the kingdom.

"How are we supposed to learn a summons if you blow out our candles!" one frowning boy complained as he wiped rheumy eyes with the back of his sleeve. Greasy tallow candles gave off a lot of oily smoke and a weak flame. Spells became misdirected in the clouds of ugly smoke. The good beeswax tapers had all been confiscated by Lord Krej and his generals.

Apprentices, too, had been commandeered into the army. There was no magic left for them to work. Therefore the University had no right to reserve boys from service to their country. Of the thirty apprentices entrusted to Baamin a few weeks ago, only eight showed any rogue potential. He had lied and lied and lied again about the boys' ill health and weak constitutions so the recruiting officers would overlook them.

"Now, boys," Baamin soothed his irritable charges. "We'll try it one more time. Find a core of magic deep within you." He paused long enough to allow them to do this. "Close your eyes and keep a strong image of your receiver in your mind. Now send the magic through the flame into the glass and onto your partner."

Only the sound of an occasional raspy breath broke the silence of the room. Baamin's gaze wandered to the newest apprentice, sitting in the corner, away from the other boys and their contaminating colds. His concentration was absolute. The rest of the boys might not have existed. His candle burned steady, bright and clear, unlike the other boys', magnified by the glass he held in front of it.

The kitchen boy. Who would have thought the stupid drudge, who possessed only a charming smile and a willingness to please, would turn out to be the most adept rogue magician of the lot?

Baamin didn't know how else to explain this newest phenomenon. The boy couldn't gather magic. So he had been barred from the classrooms years ago. He could, however, drag up enormous quantities of the stuff from some other unknown source. They really should give him a name. "Boy" just didn't seem to describe him anymore.

"Did anyone ever give you a name?" he asked under his breath.

The boy shook his head. He was concentrating on sending the flame through his precious shard of glass across the room to his study partner.

Across the room, one of the boys sitting in a circle sat up in surprise. The summons had reached him. No one else was having the same success.

"Would you like a name?" Baamin prodded.

The boy nodded again as he prepared to receive his partner's attempt.

"What name?" This was why the boy was considered stupid. He was incapable of carrying on a conversation.

"Only when I'm concentrating on something else," he replied to Baamin's thoughts.

"What?" The senior magician had to sit, hurriedly. The boy was thought-reading, without a trace of a magic umbilical and while learning a new spell! This was unheard of.

"Nimbulan could do it." The boy sat back in his chair as his partner once more tried to direct enough magic to send his flame through the glass and across the room.

"Did you read that in his journal, too?" Baamin felt moisture on his brow. The room was frigid and he was perspiring. What was he going to do with the boy?

"You're going to train me. That's what you're going to do with me."

"Stargods!" Baamin kept his mind closed. The boy looked up, puzzled.

"You shut me out."

"It's impolite to read another's thoughts without an express invitation."

"How else am I supposed to know what's happening around me?"

"How long have you had this . . . er . . . talent?"

"Don't you have it, too?"

Baamin's head threatened to separate from his body. All

the blood rushed to his stomach and tried to turn that beleaguered organ upside down. The hot moisture on his brow turned icy.

"Lesson is over," he announced to the boys. "Pick new partners and practice going from one room to the next. We'll meet again after supper." The boys rushed from the room, eager for food and replenishment. Baamin snagged one collar before its owner could escape.

"Pick a name for yourself." His tone commanded the boy to obey without hesitation. He didn't try a compulsion spell; it wouldn't work. Like the truth spell, the boy would just absorb it, dissect it for any new knowledge, and likely turn it back on the throwing magician.

"Like what?" The boy's eyes opened wide, revealing dark brown windows that begged him to open his mind again.

The senior magician resolutely kept it closed. He knew too many secrets to allow this untried boy unrestrained access to them. But then the boy had probably been private to state secrets for years.

"Anything you like. You seem to have no family to please, and no traditions to fall back on. Choose something that describes yourself, or what you would like to be." He tried to resume the friendly father figure image that invited trust.

"I want to be like Nimbulan, or like you, sir." The eyes begged entrance again.

Baamin was falling deeper and deeper into those eyes. At the last moment he stepped away from the boy, shaking his head clear, his thoughts firmly shuttered. How much had this boy learned from people who didn't know of his telepathy?

"Quite a bit, sir. That's why I can do magic. I've been practicing what the boys think about when they study."

Stargods! He'd found a way into his mind anyway.

"And just where did you find the magic to practice with? You were tested several times, and you can't gather magic."

"Why gather and store it? There's a never-ending supply at your feet."

"At my feet?"

"Yes, sir. In the ground, there's bluish-silver lines. They look kind'da like the dragon wing tips. Can't you see 'em, sir?"

Baamin shook his head in dismay. He couldn't see them yet, but before the boys had finished supper he'd find a way.

And where had Boy seen a dragon to know what the lines looked like?

"I don't think you should call yourself 'Nimbulan' or 'Baamin,' Boy. People would think you were giving yourself airs above your station in life." An inkling of a plan took shape in Baamin's tired brain.

"But I won't always be a kitchen drudge, or an apprentice."

"No, not always. But for now it's important that everyone else sees you as a kitchen drudge, perhaps in the palace where you could hear the court and army gossip." Again the boy's eyes widened. He saw what Baamin wanted.

"A name's important. I'll think about it while I'm listening to the regent's cook and steward."

"Lord Krej leaves for his own castle next week."

"I'll practice the summons spell tonight. I'll need you as a partner so I can find your special vibration anywhere."

"Uh . . . Boy, have you ever read a man's dreams?"

"Only once, sir. Too boring and confusing." He shrugged his shoulders in a timeless gesture of dismissal.

"Do you think you could tell if a man's dreams originate within himself or are imposed upon him?"

"Never tried."

"Forget I asked." Baamin shooed the boy toward his dinner. He couldn't take the chance of anyone reading his current nightmares.

"Halfway to the capital by dawn?" Jaylor snorted sarcastically. Dusk was crawling across the countryside and they were barely two hours' walk from the village. Rain plagued every step.

Buckets of intense downpour flooded creeks already swollen with spring run-off. Hard-packed roads and newly plowed fields took on the cloying texture of the mile-wide mud flats in the Great Bay. Every step Jaylor took became an effort.

Rain such as this could only be the *Stargods* mourning the loss of their beloved dragons.

If he was tired, wet, and chilled from the ceaseless plodding, how did Brevelan feel?

"A figure of speech. We need to hurry. Who knows how much damage Krej has done already." Darville reached again for the missing sword at his hip. "Come on. We can't fly like dragons. We've got to reach Krej's castle between here and the capital as soon as possible." He lengthened his stride to emphasize his need.

"I think we'd best find shelter for the night," Jaylor voiced his own opinion. "We'll make better time in the morning when we're rested and fed."

Darville stopped short. Their eyes met each other's in defiance, over the top of Brevelan's head.

She shivered and they both reached an arm to draw her close. They shivered with her, feeling everything she felt.

The men's eyes met again in challenge. The rain dripped into silence, surrounding them with a wet curtain. The three of them might have been the only creatures alive.

"If you'd both loosen your hold a bit, I might be able to breathe." Brevelan pushed at both their chests.

Jaylor felt the heat from her hand. He wanted to take the time to absorb it, cherish it. Instead he eased his grip on her shoulder. He noticed Darville did the same.

"You're feverish, dear heart." The cause of the heat in her hand disturbed him. His own body flushed in sympathy. "We'd best find shelter." Even Darville, with his one-track, lumbird mind, should see the sense in that.

"Last summer, a charcoal burner gave me directions and a meal. He moved back to the village and died last winter." Her eyes closed in momentary pain. Jaylor knew she had felt the man's death, probably nursed his last illness.

"Perhaps his hut is still standing. I'm not sure I could find it again from this direction." Brevelan shivered again. This time her arms encircled both men to bring them close again, as if she needed the heat of their bodies to chase away the chill of the rain as well as the chill of death.

Her sense of loss passed quickly. But not before it engulfed Jaylor and, from the look of him, Darville, too. They were becoming too sensitive to her uncontrolled emotions.

"We'll more likely find leaning walls and a collapsed

roof," Darville grumbled as he kissed the top of her head. His lips lingered a moment. Jaylor felt their cherishing warmth almost as soon as Brevelan did. He clamped down on his instinctive jealousy. The three of them were too closely linked. They all knew/felt what the others did.

"I'll scout ahead." Darville broke the empathic link. "If I were a charcoal burner, I'd want my hut sheltered from the weather, close to the burner but protected from a chance flame." He scanned the woods around them. "Over that way." He dropped his pack and moved off in an easy lope. Even in man form, his stride resembled that of a golden wolf.

Jaylor snuggled Brevelan close against him within the folds of his cloak. His chin rested on top of her head so that her breath fanned his chest. "He won't be long," he reassured her.

"He will probably find the place by smell." Her tone was light, almost a giggle.

Smiling, he, too, kissed her hair. "There seems to be some advantage to changing him back and forth. He's a wolf with a man's intelligence and a man with the keen senses of a wolf."

"And what of you? What have you retained from your flight with the dragons?" She looked up into his eyes.

"I don't crave meat if that is what bothers you." Instead he craved the Tambootie, just as the dragons did. The giant winged creatures required the herbage as part of their balanced diet. It also gave them invisibility. He didn't need it for health or protection, yet he still felt compelled to eat it.

Jaylor allowed Brevelan to probe and absorb his emotions. "What I remember is a tremendous sense of wonder. They are such magnificent creatures, yet so sad. Without Shayla, their need for Tambootie is all that keeps them in Coronnan. Their anger at Krej may be strong enough to break that one chain. If they can find Tambootie elsewhere, even a different variety that doesn't make them invisible, they'll leave, taking their gatherable magic with them."

Some of the sadness engulfed them both. They gulped back sobs together.

"We have to save Shayla." Brevelan stepped away from the embrace. Her determination surrounded her like an aura.

"We have to get you warm and dry," Darville broke into their private thoughts. He grabbed his own pack and Brevelan's as well. "The hut still has a roof and a stash of dry firewood. There's a stream nearby for clean water." He marched off, leaving the others to follow.

A fresh torrent of rain strengthened the existing downpour, sending icy runnels down Jaylor's neck. "That's all we need, more water!" he called after his friends and lovers.

Love. It was their love, for each other and theirs for him, that had brought him back from the ecstatic flight with dragons. Only an emotion so powerful could break his addiction to the herb that fed the dragons and created their magic. But would it last? Would their love be enough to fill the aching emptiness left behind when the evil herbage wore off?

No wonder Tambootie was considered the essence of evil. Even now he hungered for it, wondered if he could work any magic at all without it.

The raiders have gone too far. I paid them to harass the farmers and steal a few cows. Instead they have burned everything in their path.

The merchant city of Sambol on the border is in danger. No traders have dared pass through the region because of the raiders.

Simurgh take them all! I only needed an excuse to raise the army and discredit the Commune. I don't need a full-scale war and a disruption of trade.

All my generals and lords keep running to their priests and shrines to pray for guidance and deliverance. Stargods, indeed! We must rely on ingenuity, perseverance, and cunning, not on feeble prayers to nonexistent deliverers. Simurgh helps only those who fight for themselves and for him. If my head didn't ache so badly, I could convince them with a snap of my fingers.

Chapter 27

Baamin crept softly around the islands of Coronnan City. The cloying mist of midnight saturated and chilled his plain brown cloak. His boots made soft squishing sounds in the mud. Only this late were the streets free of milling crowds, soldiers, and priests. He needed privacy to trace out and memorize each of the elusive silvery-blue lines Boy had brought to his attention.

His path took him across a series of city bridges east to west, the same direction as the sun.

The line he was following wavered and fled from beneath his feet. He paused and squinted. It eluded him.

"Stargods, help me," he pleaded. This wasn't the first time he had lost track of the power. His body cried for sleep. The blankness of fatigue covered his mind. And yet the need to know more gnawed at his soul.

He hadn't been this tired since his apprentice days, learning to gather magic and throw it back out again. No wonder Jaylor wielded this rogue magic with ease. He was big, with powerful shoulders and a horrendous appetite. He could probably lift a sledge steed without magic.

Out of long habit, Baamin reached within himself for some magic to guide him and to restore his aching muscles. The well was empty. He hadn't even tried to gather any magic in several days. Deliberately he stepped back onto the silver-blue line, at least where it had been the last time he could see one. From the depths of Coronnan he pulled some magic into his tired body. He allowed it to feed and restore him, more so than a meal and a nap could.

Had he done this in his dreams and traveled to the far corners of Coronnan, wreaking havoc? He'd always been taught that the very essence of rogue magic was evil. The idea surfaced that his untapped rogue talent had finally eaten away at his University-trained ethics.

He tried to banish the idea and failed. If only Lord Krej were not a constant reminder of how the greed for power corrupted.

Krej had to have lost his magic talents when he left the University fifteen years ago. But his addiction to power could have developed during his magical training. Since assuming the Lordship of Faciar, he must have nurtured the insatiable need to the point of seeking out a rogue to do his dirty work.

Baamin could never accept Jaylor's assumption that Krej was the rogue himself. The lord's presence in the capital while the rogue was operating in the southern mountains was too well documented.

If Krej were deposed or killed, would the rogue return whence he came and leave Coronnan in peace?

Sounds from one of the small cottages sent Baamin slinking into the shadows. "*S'murghin'* hound!" A disgruntled voice drifted across this quiet corner of the city. A door opened. Another muffled curse and the thud of a foot catching the cur in the ribs. "Stay out all night. I'll not disturb my sleep just so's you can pant after that bitch in heat." The door slammed.

The dog wuffled and snorted through his nose. Baamin continued to press his back against a cold stone wall, willing invisibility.

The dog found him anyway. He sniffed at the magician's feet and hands, lifted his leg, and sauntered off. Baamin watched him go before slipping out of his hiding place back onto the path of magic he thought he had been following. It was the same route the dog had taken.

A silver glint off to his left winked at him. He whirled to catch a better glimpse of it. The lovely trail wandered back the way he had come, west to east, the path of the moon.

He stepped onto the line and squinted his eyes. The old, old planetary magic filled him, climbing through his tingling feet and legs into his hungry belly. It rested there a moment and then climbed higher into his sight.

Blue, silver, white, palest green, the colors burst through

him. An entire web of power lay at his feet. He continued his tracing, following wherever the web led him, along the path of the invisible moon. He no longer needed the cloud-shrouded orb to guide his steps.

Now that he knew how to look for the web of power, he found the old magic had a luminescence of its own. How had he missed it all these years?

Because he hadn't looked. Nimbulan had gone out of his way to eliminate all knowledge of the old magic when he discovered the power generated by the dragons. There was too much danger from magicians using magic for their own gain rather than for the good of the kingdom.

Only when the Commune could combine their magic against all others had magic become "safe."

Krej had found a way to break the Commune. If there was no magic to gather, they couldn't combine against him. Doubts gnawed at him again. Suppose Lord Krej had only capitalized on the work of another traitor?

Baamin would never know unless he mastered rogue magic and understood his own soul better. So he continued his cold lonely march around the city, weaving in and out of old alleys, through small houses and shops.

The city sat in the middle of a vast network of power. Its ancient location commanded more than the head of the Bay. It commanded the beginning and the end of the magic. No wonder the University had been situated here. Those buildings were older, much older than the central keep of Palace Reveta Tristile, which boasted a fair number of secret passages and subterranean tunnels. More secrets might yet be hidden within the ancient halls and cellars of the University, like Nimbulan's library.

The courtyard between the University and the palace contained an outpouring of blue, so tightly wound together it appeared as a large column coming straight up from the center of the world. Here was where the kings were consecrated. Here was where the nimbus of dragons confirmed a man's right to rule the kingdom and themselves.

He'd never seen an entire nimbus of dragons gathered for such a ritual. He'd never seen a single live dragon—unless his dreams were more memory than imagination. There hadn't been a need in the past ten generations for a dragon to consecrate a new king. The crown had passed easily from father to son in smooth order since the end of the Great Wars of Disruption. Was that why the dragons had begun slipping away from Coronnan? Because they weren't needed anymore?

But they were needed. Now more than ever. They needed to confirm Darville as rightful ruler and provide enough traditional magic to oust the usurping Krej. To control a rogue.

Baamin envied Jaylor, who had touched Shayla, talked to her, seen her fly. He just hoped the boy had had time to give her that tiny vial of medicine. Just two drops of the ensorcelled water would increase her litters and speed the maturation of her young to insure a healthy nimbus once and for all.

Jaylor had to find Shayla and break the magic hold over her.

Until then, Baamin would make use of whatever magic he could find. It was his duty to protect the kingdom and its rightful rulers any way he could.

Even if he discovered himself to be the villain of the piece.

If only he could see a dragon, he could happily die.

They are lost again. Such a simple trick. They are too stupid to learn that I am in control and will remain so. The journeyman is stronger than I thought. But he'll never break the spell—even if he is smart enough to realize just how important the wolf is.

My spies tell me all. They can do nothing less. The wolf is still a wolf. I am in control of Council and Commune.

I don't need the crown—though that token would be nice—for I have power. As long as I have my Tambootie, I need nothing more.

The weakling Darcine will soon die. Without Darville the Council will have no choice but to follow me.

"*S'murgh* it!" Darville cursed behind the hand he used to wipe rain from his face. "The charcoal burner's hut." Three days of plowing through rain and mud and they were right back where they'd started. Three days of wandering in circles, sleeping under hedges and getting wetter and more miserable by the minute.

At least Brevelan wasn't really sick. The last time they were at this hut she had merely been suffering from exhaustion, physical and emotional.

"Jaylor," he grabbed his friend's arm. "You've got to do something. Krej has enchanted the pathway."

"Like what?" Jaylor blinked back at him. He looked too innocent. Darville knew that look from their childhood years. Underneath the wide-eyed gullibility a plan was forming.

"You could summon up some of your legendary magic and break the enchantment." They didn't have time for these games.

"You could be less lumbird-brained and blaze a new path," Brevelan accused.

"The existing pathway is most direct, easier walking, and level!" he asserted.

"The path is enchanted to draw travelers away from the capital." Jaylor studied the twisted wood of his staff. His eyes squinted along its length back the way they had come. He was using some kind of magic to discern the nature of the problem. "I expect it's part of Krej's defense. If we can't find Coronnan City, invading armies can't either."

"So, do something. You're the one who broke his other spell."

"First we're going to get dry and have a meal," Brevelan insisted. She turned and began trudging through the gray trees toward the gray shadow that was the hut. The rain was gray, too, as was the mud beneath their feet. Even their clothes and faces looked gray.

Coronnan was losing its vibrant colors. The life of his kingdom was draining away in the incessant rain. Darville had to get back to the capital before Krej destroyed everything.

"We don't have time," Darville returned.

"Don't argue with her." Jaylor grabbed his arm.

Darville shook off the restraint, anger and frustration feeding his normal restless impatience.

"Haven't you yet learned that she's the strongest of us all?" Jaylor reclaimed the sleeve. His powerful fingers threatened to rend the cloth.

Darville stared at the restraining hand. Jaylor stared at his staff. Brevelan stared at them both.

"I suppose we should take one more night to dry out before we try again." Darville surrendered to their superior advice. "There's a farm about another hour further along."

"The farmer is one of Krej's spies." Jaylor pointed his long staff at Darville's chest. "Do you really want to be a wolf again tonight? You make a very handsome pet."

"Don't start that, Jaylor. I have very little patience left. Why don't you call someone at that University of yours and find out what's happening in my capital?"

"I can't waste my magic on a summons if I'm going to break another of Krej's spells in the morning."

"You're stalling! Why?" Darville accused. He reached once again for the sword that should hang at his hip. He felt empty, off balance without the weapon.

"I'm conserving my magic for important spells."

"And what's more important than getting me back to the capital?"

Just then Mica chose to slash his shoulder with her claws. Pain jolted him back to the reality of their circumstances. The little cat arched her back and hissed at both of them. Her claws continued to dig into his flesh, through several layers of heavy cloth.

Stop it!

Darville wasn't sure if the cat or Brevelan shouted in his ear. The voice that halted his next verbal assault sounded like both of them combined.

"Stop this childish bickering," Brevelan commanded. Her delicately shaped hands rested on her hips, her lower lip quivered. Her eyes, slitted just like the cat's, held him captive. Beside him he felt Jaylor also squirm under her gaze. Perhaps he was right. Perhaps Brevelan was the strongest of them all.

Silence settled over them. Mica broke her defensive stance by cleaning her front paws while still atop his shoulder. Darville felt just a little weak-kneed when Brevelan finally looked away. He stiffened his spine to correct for the weakness.

"Now," Brevelan took command once more, "we need more dry wood and clean water."

Darville stomped off the path in search of any bit of old wood hidden beneath something that would have kept off the worst of the rains. He needed to move quickly and strongly to shake off the lingering effects of Brevelan's control. A control that came from her own strength and his love for her, not from any magic.

He kicked himself for allowing her that much power over him. As prince of the realm, he had to learn to be independent of outside influences. A strong king listened to his advisers, weighed the merit of their words, and then made his own decisions. Something his father had never learned.

And he, Darville, would never, ever, be as weak as his father.

But Brevelan had been right. He and Jaylor, and Brevelan, too, couldn't afford any petty bickering. But *he* should have been the one to make that decision. *He* should have noticed the enchanted pathway would not only lead travelers astray but disrupt their unity as well.

It was classic military strategy. He'd learned it from ancient textbooks before he was ten.

Divert. Disrupt. Demoralize. Destroy.

This was a lesson he would remember when the time came to rescue Shayla. Krej was proving to be a sound strategist. Darville would just have to be smarter.

"Master?" Boy poked his head into Baamin's study as dawn crept across his windowsill.

"Yes, Boy?" He propped one eye open from his brief doze at his desk. He had spent another long night tracing lines of magic power. The hours of extremely hard work were taking their toll on his aging body. He'd had to have several robes altered to fit his decreasing girth.

But when he finally slept, he slept soundly and dreamlessly.

"I heard somethin' in the palace last night."

Baamin sat up straighter. If the boy risked coming to his study, even at this very early hour, the news must have import.

"Lord Krej, he's expecting some 'bassadors."

"Ambassadors," Baamin automatically corrected the boy. "Speak properly, Boy." He spoke more curtly than he'd intended. With a great show, he unscrewed the cap from his flask and took a swig. Would Boy read his thoughts again and know the restorative in the metal bottle was only sugar water?

"Ambassadors, sir. From Rosie Mire. Something about an alliance."

"Rossemeyer?" Rossemeyer, a poor desert kingdom with an abundance of nomadic mercenaries, the treacle beta, and not much else. The warriors they bred preferred real wars instead of training exercises to keep up their legendary strength. They were coming to enforce their ultimatum. Darville as bridegroom to their beloved princess, or war.

Which natural resource did Rossemeyer covet—black fire rock, gemstones, the lush flood plains of Coronnan River? Perhaps they knew Prince Darville was missing and the entire charade of alliance was an excuse for invasion.

Then again, Rossemeyer could be searching for an abundant supply of the Tambootie.

Baamin didn't know why he thought of the aromatic wood as a natural resource. Once the idea took root, he began to see it as the answer to many questions.

Chapter 28

Jaylor sighted along his staff. He pointed it straight down the main north-south road. Or rather, he pointed it where the road should be. Due north. But the road appeared to be coming from the northeast. The edges of the road wavered with more than just the distortion of rain on mud.

He changed position, aiming the staff and his concentration along the new sighting. *Stargods!* The road shifted, too. Now it appeared to be more to the northwest.

"Where is the road now?" he asked of Brevelan and Darville who stood directly behind him, far enough away not to interfere with his concentration.

"Looks like it runs due west, straight into the Bay," Darville replied. "But it shouldn't."

"No, it shouldn't. Which means we are fighting a delusion. A very strong delusion." Frustration gnawed at Jaylor's concentration. With all this strange magic bouncing around him, he couldn't think or see straight.

"If we followed the sun, rather than the road?" Brevelan's voice was tentative.

He gathered her hand into his own to reassure her, and himself. "The time has come to start breaking down some of Krej's spells. By the time we reach his castle, I want his magic in tatters. The more energy he spends repairing what I have torn apart, the less he'll have to throw at us."

She gulped and nodded. He did the same and knew that Darville mimicked their actions.

"What about those blue lines of power you described?" Darville asked. He, too, was squinting, trying to see where they should be going. "Can you tap into them, or use them as a guide?"

"Lines of power," Jaylor mused. "The dragons showed me lines of power, running through Coronnan, like so many irrigation ditches, emanating from the very depths of this world." His vision focused backward to his flight with the dragons.

Blue-silver webs encasing the world far below him. Tambootie trees seeking them out. Veins of copper ore filling the hollow paths of burned out power.

When he'd come out of the Tambootie-induced vision of dragons, he hadn't been able to focus his eyes if he looked at something head on. Only when he inspected individual items from the side could he maintain a clear view.

The trap in Darville's transformation spell had been laid for a direct attack. Breaking the spell had required a round-about route. Jaylor turned his body due west. He looked sideways at the road running north, moving only his eyes.

There! The thoroughfare ran true to form with no evidence of magic glamour distorting the edges.

"The Tambootie has caused Krej to approach everything sideways," he announced.

"So?" Darville cocked his head in a very wolfish way. Jaylor grinned at his friend.

"So all I have to do is decide which direction he faced when he threw the spell. Then I face opposite to unravel it." Jaylor nearly danced in front of his friends. Impulsively, triumphantly, he gathered them in a massive hug. His warmth and joy spilled over to include them all. "I know his secret now!"

"Mrrew," Mica informed him that he was a little late of coming to this knowledge. She poked her head out of the folds of Brevelan's cape. "Mbbbrrrt!" *Beware the tricky magician.*

"Of course, Mica. We should have known Krej would never do anything directly." Brevelan scratched behind the cat's ears. "You daren't take any more Tambootie, Jaylor. Can you reverse his spell without it?"

"If I let the web beneath my feet power the spell . . ." His thoughts tumbled out of order. "Lines of power run straight. Tambootie twists."

Jaylor sought the blue-silver lines. His eyes squinted nearly shut. Colors blended together, grass and sky, trees and road. A bright spring flower faded to nothing in the kaleidoscope he created with his vision.

He isolated the traces of yellow and banished them from his sight. Red, too, he eliminated. Shades of purple and brown were easy. The greens were prevalent. They took more concentration. But finally they, too, fled from the swirl of colors.

Only the blue was left. A strand of the single color danced about, twined, and braided back on itself. Elusive, lovely, powerful. It strung itself forward and back, into a delicate tracery of magical lines. Some ran up the trees into the sky. Some danced around his feet. But one line. One long, straight, and thick line ran directly beneath his feet, from south to north.

He needed to make his spell twist though he drew power from a straight line. Six paces back, the road bent unnaturally around no natural barrier. He looked closer at the bend. Two power lines joined at an oblique angle. If he traced one line into the junction and the other line out, he almost saw a curve. The original road builders had left the junction clear. Remnants of an ancient Equinox Pylon lay crumbling there.

He moved back and stepped directly onto the joint.

"Just twist the magic around and get us out of here," Darville grumbled. "We aren't getting any drier standing around waiting for the road to straighten itself out."

"Easier said than done, my prince. But I'll see what I can do." Jaylor turned to face east. Krej's castle lay to the west. His Great Hall filled with unnatural statues gave him inspiration.

The road bounced within his vision again. He ignored it, seeing only the true direction of the blue lines. Slowly he drew power through his feet, up his legs to his belly and chest, then out along his outstretched arm and staff. The road aligned with his vision. "Got it!"

Slowly, he pulled more magic up further into his heart. It resisted, humming a discordant note. He pulled harder. The magic fled from his body, leaving a sour sound in his ears.

"Tricky bastard! He should have faced west, so he didn't." He shook his head to clear it of the lingering noise.

"Give me a moment to clear my head." He faced west. Brevelan's small hand touched Jaylor's shoulder. He leaned his cheek against it. Warmth and reassurance filled him.

He clasped Brevelan's trembling hand with his own.

The magic vibrated in answer.

"Hum something, Brevelan," he suggested. Excitement filled him once more. "Something sweet and lyrical." The exact opposite of the jarring notes that lingered in Krej's magic.

A soothing little tune came from her throat. The magic within him sang it back.

"Sing with her, Darville," he commanded with strength and new courage.

"What!"

"Don't argue, just hum, the same thing she sings." His heart beat in counterpoint. He lifted his own voice and wove a deep harmony to their higher tones. Each musical line blended and twisted around the corner. He had his curve of music around the straight line of power.

The magic filled him, spread through all their limbs, climbed to new heights. The three of them were one being, sharing thoughts, emotions, power. One body vibrated with pulsing magic. They took off and soared together once more. He leveled his staff along the line of blue—right where the road should be, while his body looked toward the Great Bay.

Blue. Silver. Green. Red. Purple. Copper. More blue. The colors of Coronnan braided themselves along the staff and shot forth in a line, straight and true.

The road found its direction, wavered and shimmered, then settled along its original route.

"I believe we have a journey to make, my friends." Jaylor smiled as he lowered the staff and took his first step on the road to Castle Krej. He kept Brevelan's hand tucked into the crook of his elbow. Darville's hand rested on his shoulder. None of them was willing to break the unity they had found while flying with the dragons.

Mica purred. The soaking rain gave way to broken shafts of sunlight.

They are coming closer. I can feel their presence. The journeyman is more clever than I thought. He has broken one spell. There are many more traps along the way. I shall twist and twist again the magic that will delay him. He'll never break through my defenses. No man can defeat me. I have accomplished too much.

If only this headache would go away. The pain throbs constantly, demands my attention when I need all my concentration to maintain my spells and save the bumbling army from their own mistakes. I can't allow the minor inconvenience of a lost battle to destroy my schedule of conquest.

A little more Tambootie. I must have a little more to ease the pain, increase my concentration, strengthen my spells.

Baamin stood outside the door to the king's study, uneasy, undecided. Only it wasn't the king's anymore. Krej's ambition had gone too far. The Lord Regent's inflated conceit needed to be curtailed before he managed to destroy Coronnan and the Commune with it. But was Baamin, Senior Magician, the man to stop the king's cousin?

He couldn't delay any longer. Someone had to take action and he seemed to be the only one capable of seeing what needed to be done.

With a flourish of his staff and a flash of harmless blue powder, he stepped through the doorway, into the king's study.

"The border city of Sambol has fallen," Baamin announced.

"What!" Krej shouted, half rising from the thronelike chair behind the desk.

"The border city of Sambol fell to a series of attacks by a well-organized army, disguised as raiders," he repeated. "Raiders who carried purses of gold drageens from the mint in your province of Faciar." The news wasn't pleasant. Krej's surprise at the news was. "How did they obtain uncirculated coins that only you could have provided, Lord Regent?"

"Sambol can't have fallen. I had messages from Lord Wendray last night. He assured me that his troops had beaten back the men who breached his walls." Krej waved his hand in dismissal, totally ignoring the implied accusation that he had paid the raiders to attack Sambol. "How did you get in here, old man? I gave orders banning you from my presence."

"I'm a magician. I have my ways." Baamin shrugged. He was enjoying Krej's discomfort. Krej had spent his boyhood either in his mother's isolated care or in the University. So he'd never learned about the existence of the myriad secret tunnels that ran through and beneath Palace Reveta Tristile. But Baamin knew them and could enter nearly any room in the palace. He'd explored them numerous times when he and Darcine were young.

"The dragons have deserted the kingdom. There is no more magic to make you a magician," Krej asserted. The Lord Regent settled back into his chair but continued staring at Baamin as if he were vermin.

"Are you sure about that?" Baamin refused to move from his place just inside the door. He allowed his eyes to squint just a little. There was the faintest trace of a silver-blue web at his feet. It faded into nothing where Krej sat.

Either Krej couldn't find the lines, didn't know they were a power source, or he'd been unable to move the desk and chair to a stronger location.

"I'm very sure, Baamin." Krej, too, was squinting now. What did he see—the lines or Baamin's aura? Swiftly, Baamin drew in his thoughts and energies. His mission would be for naught if Krej saw either the vial of deadly powder in Baamin's pocket or his intent to use it. If Baamin found the courage to kill Krej tonight, problems would surely follow. If he allowed Krej to live, the red-haired lord would continue to wreak havoc on them all.

A knock on the door behind him did not disrupt the locked gazes of the two men.

"I . . . ah . . . brung yer . . . ah . . . wine, sor." A slurred, juvenile voice stammered shyly.

The kitchen boy slid between Baamin and the doorjamb. He seemed shorter, younger, more ragged, and more stupid than he had just last night. His shoulders were slumped in a posture of humility and defeat. In the classroom he stood straight and proud. The master resisted the urge to examine his pupil for signs of magic disguise.

"Put down the tray." Krej barely registered the boy's presence.

Boy did as he was told with a clatter, and more than a few drops of wine splattered across the desk and Krej himself. A quick picture of Krej gasping for air, his face purple, tongue swollen, life fading, flashed into Baamin's mind. He nearly gagged at the thought of a man dying in such a horrible manner, by his poisonous hand.

Still, the deed needed to be done. He was resolved. The only way to save the kingdom from Krej's manipulations was to eliminate Krej.

"Clumsy oaf! Who had the audacity to send such a stupid, filthy, miserable idiot to serve me?" The Lord Regent pushed away the boy's attempts to mop the spill. Each swipe of Boy's less-than-clean cloth resulted in more wine spreading across the documents on the desk and Lord Krej.

"Go. Now, before you do any more damage," Krej bellowed as he cuffed the boy's ear.

Boy ducked quickly. Almost too quickly, as if he had seen the blow coming before it was sent.

Baamin saw a document disappear into Boy's filthy, oversized tunic. His only acknowledgment of the theft was to close his eyes slowly as Boy scuttled past him out the door.

Baamin breathed deeply and recaptured Krej's attention. "If you doubt my information, then send a messenger on your fastest steeds to intercept the wounded rider Wendray dispatched before dawn. The city has fallen. What's left of the defending army is in well-organized retreat." Baamin paused to allow the news to penetrate.

He fingered the vial in his pocket. If he started murmuring the proper spell now as he stood over the line of power, the magic would be at its most potent as he slipped the powder into Krej's wine.

"Or perhaps messages would travel more quickly if you allow your pet rogue to summon Master Haskell who's stationed there. He knows as much or more than your own spies," Baamin goaded as he took two steps toward the desk and the glass of wine. The words of the death spell were firmly fixed in his mind. He need only utter them.

"Your imagination runs wild, old man," Krej sneered. "Leave me." He drank deeply of the wine, pointedly offering Baamin none. "Go pester someone more gullible with your dangerous maundering." The regent's eyes narrowed as he once more scanned the senior magician. "You belong in a monastery with the rest of the failed magicians who become false priests of the mythical *Stargods*. Priests are the only people willing to put up with you." He waved a hand in dismissal.

"Check your sources again, Lord Krej." Baamin damped his temper and his forward movements at the slur against the official religion of the Three Kingdoms. "You might also make sure you have taken into account all that I know about you and about the king's dragons."

The information to convict Krej was at hand. Baamin need only find all the bits and pieces and present them to the Council. Forfeiture, humiliation, and death were the penalty for treason. Horrible, painful death.

"You haven't heard the last of me, my lord." With a smile, Baamin threw a handful of green powder that exploded into blue fire. The poison remained firmly in his pocket.

Tricks and sleight of hand.

But Krej's temporary flash-blindness gave Baamin the opportunity to disappear quite dramatically.

And left the Lord Regent alive and well, for now. Considering the death that awaited a treasonous lord, Baamin wasn't doing Krej a favor by allowing him to live tonight.

"Simurgh take your dragons and your magic. I am the only one who can save this country from three centuries of mismanagement. Not you, not your dragons, and certainly not some ancient legends about saving angels descending from the stars to wipe out a nonexistent plague." Krej's words echoed down the halls.

"You'll learn, Lord Krej," Baamin muttered from his hidden alcove. "You'll live and learn not to question legends and certainly not to tamper with the Senior Magician!" He touched the vial again. "I couldn't bring myself to kill another man tonight. I don't think I ever could." Perhaps his nightmares were only the product of his overactive imagination. Now he knew deep in his soul he could never kill another man, never transform him into anything less than a man.

The road curved west to avoid a rampaging stream. Jaylor considered the obstacle carefully. It was too wide and fast to ford. They must follow the road and hope for a bridge.

Darville threw a rock into the frothing water. "Is there any place in the kingdom that is dry?" He looked up to the heavy clouds. The rain washed some of the travel dirt from his face and beard.

"It's possible this bad weather is caused by a lack of dragons." Jaylor slumped. He was tired. They were all tired. They'd been on the road for more than a week and had traveled only a little over two leagues.

"Do you hear voices?" Brevelan reached a hand in front of her, testing it, weighing it for emotions carried on the wind.

"I don't remember a village in this vicinity on my journey south." Jaylor pointed his staff along the road, focusing on its vibrations.

Darville took several cautious steps. "I don't think we should be seen." He sniffed the air. The hair on the back of his neck stiffened. He bared his teeth. "Into the bushes." He dragged Brevelan with him, expecting Jaylor to follow.

"That won't be necessary." A strange voice spoke behind them.

As one, they whirled to face the hidden speaker. "Zolltarn!" Jaylor cried in alarm. He stepped in front of Brevelan, putting a barrier between her and the stranger.

The Rover looked older than he had a few weeks ago. But the wings of silver slashing through his blacker-than-black-hair and the whipcord lean strength of him were the same. Though worn and threadbare, his garish red shirt, his trews and boots as black as his hair, were carefully mended and clean. Around his lean waist was wrapped a brilliant sash of purple.

Brevelan peeked around Jaylor's broad back for a better look at the man's face. Jaylor felt her curiosity but sensed no fear.

"Ah! my young magician friend." Zolltarn narrowed his eyes as if assessing Jaylor and his companions. His wary stance belied the amiable voice.

"I haven't time to linger in your camp, Zolltarn." Jaylor was equally on guard.

"Perhaps your friend would be willing to aid us as you could not?" The Rover's black eyes scanned Darville.

"My friend is needed elsewhere as well." A new hardness

came into Jaylor's voice. He clutched his staff tighter, prepared to aim a paralyzing spell at the Rover.

"What kind of aid should I give to people exiled from Coronnan?" Darville sounded wary. As he should.

"You don't want to know, Roy." There was a time when they would have laughed at the kind of aid needed by the Rovers. Since they had shared Brevelan's bed, assisting Zolltarn in rebuilding his clan seemed betrayal.

"But he is young and strong. My tribe could benefit greatly from his services." Zolltarn smiled with a wicked leer. "And I am sure he would draw great pleasure from the duty."

"Does he mean what I think he means?" Darville asked.

"He does." Jaylor didn't need to share his friend's thoughts to know he had guessed Zolltarn's purpose. "Not this time, Zolltarn. We must be on our way."

"When we reach the capital, we will find you, maybe continue this discussion." The Rover stepped closer.

"You go to the capital?" Brevelan sounded apprehensive.

"We were invited by the new Lord Regent. He needs many men. We need to search for one of our own who was stolen from us."

"You won't like Krej's idea of duty, Zolltarn." Darville finally spoke. "He needs men for an army to fight raiders and invaders on the western border. Some of those he asks you to fight might be your own kin. You won't be allowed to search for anyone, least of all one of your own who is lost."

Alarm spread across the older man's face. "Then perhaps we will find a different road to follow." He placed one friendly hand on Jaylor's shoulder; with the other he firmly grasped the staff. "Can we at least offer you a night's hospitality?"

"Zolltarn?" Brevelan dared address the man. He turned to her, releasing his grasp on Jaylor's shoulder but not on the staff.

"You have questions, little beauty?"

She blushed under his admiring appraisal.

"Why are you being so kind? Legends of your people tell us to be wary of your thieving."

The Rover threw back his head in laughter. The movement caused his arm to jerk at the staff. Jaylor held tight.

"Ah, little beauty, your legends were created by old women to frighten children. We are merely passing each other in journey. Though I could use the men," his eyebrows lifted in a knowing leer. "I have found they will serve me better if they come to me willingly."

"You won't find many willing in Coronnan. We have been taught to avoid you, lest you steal our goods, our children, and our souls." Darville tried to step between Zolltarn and Jaylor.

Seven other Rovers jumped from concealment in the woods. Darville still pushed forward. The others grappled him. He swung his fist and connected with one jaw before being wrestled to the ground. Arms and legs flying, he brought his opponents down with him

The blood lust of his youth swelled through Jaylor's body. He and his gang of town boys had learned to fight in the streets and alleys of Coronnan City. They could hold their own with the dirtiest fighters in the capital.

He flung one knotted fist upward to connect with Zolltarn's perpetual grin. His staff blocked a kick from behind.

A third Rover caught Jaylor with a blow to his middle. He doubled over and turned around, one booted foot kicking out behind, into the center of Zolltarn's chest.

Brevelan screamed behind him. His blood froze. She didn't have the clearing to protect her. How would she fight off strong men?

New fury impelled him into the fray. He swung his staff right and left, knocking Rovers aside. One after another they fell with bruises and breaks as he fought his way to Brevelan's side. Only one man remained between him and his beloved. He brought the staff down on the man's head. The bold young Rover with broken teeth and a malicious smile slumped to the ground as the twisted wood broke into three ragged pieces.

"Enough!" Zolltarn cried to his men. "The magician has broken his staff, we have no need to steal it." The Rovers melted into the woods, carrying their wounded with them.

Chapter 29

"**M**y staff!" Jaylor yelled as he took off after the retreating Rovers. "You *s'murghin'* bastards broke my staff!"

Dense woods closed around him within a few steps of the path. Heavy underbrush tangled every footstep. Thick vines reached out from low hanging tree limbs and encircled his ankles. He was flat on his face in the middle of a saber fern.

Desperately he hacked at the vine with his knife. The pithy plant oozed a corrosive sap that dulled and discolored the blade.

"Give it up, Jaylor." Darville limped over to his prostrate friend. "We'll never catch them now. They melted into the shadows like so many ghosts."

"They broke my staff, Roy." Jaylor resorted to the adolescent name for the prince.

"I know, Jay. I know and I'm sorry."

"The staff was my only hope of reversing Krej's spell on Shayla."

Disappointed silence hovered over them.

"We'll cut you another staff, Jaylor." Brevelan picked her way through the overgrown ferns and downed trees to his side.

"That won't help much. I have to be matched to the staff. The wood grain has to be used to my brand of magic to channel it, focus it. The more I use it, the stronger becomes the partnership. We just don't have enough time to break in a new one."

"Could we mend the old one?" Darville suggested.

"The fibers would be too weak."

"Then we'll have to find another way." Brevelan reached out a hand to help him up.

He just stared at her.

"There is no other way." He cradled the broken pieces of wood against his chest.

"We just can't walk through there." Brevelan stared at the jumble of cottages nestled together. The back of each cottage, hut, and prosperous farmhouse faced away from the looming fortress. Sheets of rain set up a further barrier between Castle Krej and the village, between herself and the people who lived here.

Each step became heavier and more reluctant than the last.

"This is the most direct way to the castle . . . and Shayla," Darville complained about her slower pace. He tried to take her arm and urge her forward.

Brevelan recoiled from his touch. "You don't understand," she nearly sobbed, retreating into the haven of Jaylor's shoulder. His arm encircled her, but she felt no strength, no support from him.

She knew these two men so well she expected to feel every emotion they felt as soon as they did. Now they were closed off, consulting each other over the top of her head.

They had been on the road for weeks. Every meal, bed, and thought had been shared equally. They had no secrets from each other. Except this.

"I can't let them see me! And Jaylor doesn't have a staff to grant us invisibility." This time she stepped away from them both, backward, the way they had come.

"Brevelan, my sweet, no one who knows you could believe you killed that man," Jaylor reassured her. "Even Krej didn't really believe it when he taunted you in Shayla's cave. He was only trying to feed your fearful memories to negate your magic." He reached for her hand.

She stood firm. "But I did kill him." She lifted her face to the rain. The water couldn't wash away her memories of that awful night. . . .

In the bridal chamber, the village women had bathed Brevelan. Combed her hair until it shone. Fussed over the fresh bedding and finally slipped a clean shift of fine linen and embroidery over Brevelan's head. They had winked and remarked on that fineness and how the new husband would appreciate it—for a few moments anyway. And what a shame to leave the garment on the bride since it would only be torn away so quickly.

They had left, giggling. But a few had looked back over their shoulders with a trace of concern. This was considered a good marriage. Brevelan was young and healthy. The bridegroom was as old as her da but prosperous and had sired several sons on each of his first three wives.

Brevelan shuddered with a chill born of more than the evening dampness. Before the exquisite coverlet could warm her, *he* came in.

He was drunk, of course, as were his ribald companions. Good-naturedly he blocked the doorway with his squat body. Barred from their fun, the other men, and a few women, shouted their displeasure.

Brevelan didn't have to understand the exact words, or her husband's crude reply, to know they expected to watch the proceedings. It was a part of close-knit village life for the celebration of a wedding ceremony to extend to the bedroom. They all wanted to make sure the groom was capable of siring any child the bride produced months down the road.

The blood drained from her face and hands. Her trembling become more violent as her husband shoved the door closed and barred it. The pounding on the mismatched slats of wood became louder. He slid Brevelan's carved wooden clothes chest in front of it. The intruder's entrance would be delayed, should they manage to break though the buckling wood.

"We'd best hurry or they'll think they have a right to be part of this." His smile showed no mirth or joy.

She couldn't reply.

His good woolen tunic fell atop the chest. The straw mattress shifted under his weight and his boots landed on the floor with a thud that echoed through her mind with menacing force. The mattress shifted again as he stood long enough to shed his trews. Only his knee-length shirt covered his bulging need for her.

She shrank away to the far edge of the bed.

"Come here, wife," he demanded. His eyes narrowed to slits.

She couldn't obey, though she'd vowed to before the priest and village. Instead she pulled the covers higher.

"Don't play shy with me." He climbed closer on his knees, braced with one heavy hand. The other yanked the blanket from her grasp. There was the sound of rending cloth as the embroidered edge tore through her fingers.

Someone outside the door laughed at the sound. So did her husband.

"We all know there's no such thing as a virgin in this village. Lord Krej makes sure of that." Spittle foamed at one corner of his mouth. His excitement mounted. He grabbed her breasts and squeezed until she cried out in pain. "If his brat isn't already growing inside you, mine will be soon enough."

That shocked her. Hadn't he heard the rumors? Didn't he know Lord Krej was probably her father? Their lord might be cruel and lustful, but he wasn't so evil as to rape his own daughter!

"Doesn't matter whose brat." He belched. The foul smell of too much ale combined with too much meat in his body assaulted her. She wanted to retch. "One of his bastards brings favors to the family. I could use a few favors." This time his mouth came down on her in a punishing, open-mouthed kiss.

She gagged.

He laughed. Then he hit her, backhanded across the face. Once, twice, then a third time for good measure. With each blow his hand tightened until it was a fist that connected with her eye. Her lip split, too. She tasted the copper of blood and fear. She tried to push him away.

"No. Please, no," she begged.

"Got to teach you who'll be master in my house," he laughed and belched again. "Can't have you thinkin' you know anything but what I tell you."

Without another word he captured her small useless fists in his free hand. His grip was as punishing as his kiss. His leer traced every inch of her barely shrouded body. Once again he crushed her mouth.

She could feel bruises forming. The small pain in her face and hands built and traveled to her shoulders. Her chest and stomach cramped in fear. Instinctively she drew her knees up in protection.

Still forcing her hands above her head, he used his weight to wedge her legs down and apart.

He was heavy. She couldn't breathe, couldn't think. Her pain and fear mounted and spread. She sensed her emotions swelling into an empathic cloud that formed outside her body, filled the room, and echoed from floor to ceiling. A scream escaped her lips as her fear magnified itself again. The listeners laughed. Her husband shuddered, breath burst from his mouth in a soundless explosion. He collapsed across her.

Her imprisoned hands didn't respond to the sudden slackness of his once too-tight grip. His inert weight across her body hindered any movement. When she finally levered away, her vision was transfixed by his protruding, staring eyes, the spittle and blood on his lips, the ugly black blotches on his face.

Deep within her the healing instinct demanded she reach out and dissolve the blockage to his brain. Her fear of him overrode that instinct. He was dead already. She could do many things to help him, if he still lived. But no pulse fluttered against her tentative touch, no breath stirred his graying beard.

The sounds of the people waiting at the door retreated. They must have believed the deed done and so lost interest.

Brevelan was alone with the man her radiating emotions had killed. . . .

"Is that why you ran, little one?" Darville chuckled as he enveloped her in one of his possessive and protective hugs.

Even Jaylor was smiling.

"You didn't kill the man. He killed himself." Jaylor added his own strong arm to the embrace. Mica was there, too, butting her wet, bedraggled head against Brevelan's chin.

"You're wrong, both of you." There was still one thing Brevelan needed clarified. "Part of my healing talent is to take a person's fear and pain into myself and give them back the strength to fight their ailment." She swallowed hard and looked away. "On that night," her voice dropped in shame, "I couldn't take away his need for anger. I felt it and it terrified me. Instead of giving him peace and gentleness, I gave him fear—agonizing, paralyzing terror. I was like Jaylor's glass. I took my small emotions and made them bigger. So big his mind couldn't handle it and forced his body to die."

"Perhaps," Jaylor mused. "More likely there was a weakness in his body that would have killed him the next time he felt any violent emotion. He sounds like a man who couldn't live without anger and couldn't live with it."

"Remember the spotted saber cat, Brevelan," Darville interjected. "It refused all contact with your mind. That man was so filled with anger and hate he wouldn't have accepted your gentling even if you could have broken down his barriers."

Love from all of them poured over her.

Brevelan stood straighter and stronger for that love. She hadn't realized how strong was their bond. While she thought she had only relived that fateful night in her mind, they had shared the entire experience. Just as they had shared the magic when they broke Krej's diverting spell. Just as they had shared the flight of dragons the night Jaylor had returned to them.

Baamin continued to mull over the alliance the kingdom of Rossemeyer wanted with Coronnan. The promise of trade and mutual military aid hinged on the marriage of their princess, Rossemikka, to Prince Darville.

He read again the document Boy had purloined from Krej's desk. Though couched in pleasantries, the language of the missive clearly outlined the consequences if the alliance failed.

How would the Lord Regent respond to this offer and the impending arrival of two ambassadors? He didn't have a prince to exchange for the much needed armies. He had only a golden wolf wandering the kingdom with a journeyman magician and a witchwoman of uncertain power.

But Baamin had access to the prince. If Darville ever arrived back at the capital.

"Boy?" He summoned the boy's image through his glass and his candle. He was so easy to find, even across the miles, as if Boy's mind were tuned especially to Baamin's thoughts.

"Call me Yaakke, sir." The boy's image was clearer than most master magicians'.

"Yaakke?" Son of Yaacob, the usurper. Now why would Boy choose that name? And who did he plan to supplant?

"That is the name I have chosen, sir." Behind the boy were the noises of Castle Krej's busy kitchen.

"We'll explore that later, B . . . Yaakke. Have you seen my journeyman yet?"

Yaakke closed his eyes briefly before responding. "They approached this village, sir, then turned back."

"Keep track of them. I need to speak to Jaylor as soon as you can contact him. And see if you can keep them out of trouble." He'd given up trying to summon Jaylor himself. His journeyman had either ignored the spell or cut him off. What was he hiding? Or was Krej's rogue interfering and interrupting the communication?

So his beloved Brevelan was like his glass, Jaylor thought. She magnified magic. What if, instead of using his glass on a flame, he summoned Old Baamin by holding her hand and staring into her eyes? She'd have to sing to amplify the natural resonance of the land. He was impatient to experiment.

The rain drizzled down his forehead to drop from the tip of his nose. This was neither the time, nor the place, to play with new magic techniques. He needed to be warm and dry, comfortable, before he tried something so outrageously new.

He'd have enough problems when he finally encountered Krej. Without a staff, he'd need every bit of concentration and familiarity with the spells before he freed a dragon from a glass prison. He'd kept his senses alerted to every tree he passed, hoping against hope to find a new staff. So far nothing had called to him.

"I think we'd best find a place to hole up until dark." Darville scanned the dreary village once more.

"There's an inn several miles north." Brevelan pointed the way. "The landlord caters to traveling merchants. Krej likes the luxuries strangers bring to his market. He doesn't like to house and feed them. Nor does he like his villagers talking to outsiders. We might get the idea that other lords are not so harsh or demanding. No one will question the presence of strangers at the inn."

"Are they all legitimate merchants, or does Krej trade

with magicians and mercenaries from afar, as well?" Darville stared murderously back at the castle.

"There have been rumors of covens and sacrifices to pagan gods for years. They started with Lady Janessa, Krej's mother." Jaylor thought back to his early years at the University when court gossip couldn't say anything good about the foreign wife of King Darcine's uncle.

"That's one lady I don't care to meet again." Darville turned away from the lair of their enemy. "Her eyes are eerie, uncanny—always fully dilated. She looks at people like a slippy eel devouring a nomad Bay crawler."

They trudged along the wide path. The mud, churned by the huge feet of sledge steeds, made walking difficult. Twice they were forced off the track by swearing farmers prodding their beasts with loads of produce in the direction of the inn.

"Darville," Jaylor spoke quietly to his friend. "We are on Krej's home territory. He must not see you." He sympathized with the prince's distaste for the coming transformation.

The broken pieces of his staff were in his pack. Fortunately he'd thrown this spell often enough not to need the focus the wood provided.

"Everyone here will gladly spy for Lord Krej," Brevelan added. "Some say they owe their souls as well as their livelihood to him. He'd know of your presence and our purpose within moments.

"I know, I know," Darville groused. He turned his back as he shed his cloak and warm tunic. "Try and keep my clothes out of the mud." He handed his outer garments to Brevelan, his pack to Jaylor. His fingers lingered on Mica's wet fur as he set her down on the path.

"Be gentle with me when we share a meal this time, Mica." He rubbed the side of his nose where she was in the habit of swatting him away from his kill. "At least I'll be warm and less likely to feel the rain."

He shrugged his shoulders in preparation for the spell that would hit him square in the back if Jaylor used the staff. Without the focus, the magic engulfed him in a cloud. He didn't even flinch as his form shifted into that of an oversized golden wolf.

Chapter 30

The inn smelled wrong. Too many strangers here. Darville couldn't sort their scents. He sensed fear and greed. Illness, too, but he didn't know which smell belonged to which person.

He paced beside Brevelan, keeping her between himself and Jaylor, pressing closer to her with each step. His neck bristled with disquiet. A growl boiled just below his throat, not quite ready to emerge. He was prepared for anyone, anything that might attack her.

Thwack! A water jug shattered on the beaten ground beside the well. A woman stood hunted still, her silent stare jerked between them and her broken jug. Then she ran back toward the inn. Brevelan took a step toward the woman. Darville followed, keeping his place between Brevelan and the inn.

He showed his teeth and allowed the growl to travel up his throat. The woman had smelled of fear and betrayal. He could almost taste her emotions on his tongue.

"Mama?" Brevelan sounded strangled. Jaylor held her close. Darville growled again.

"Go away." The woman looked over her shoulder from the doorway of the inn. "Go quickly. You killed him. The Stargods have cursed us because his death went unpunished. The elders will burn you." She bent her head and turned to flee. "Only when you are dead will this rain stop and crops grow." This time she looked Brevelan in the eye.

There was sadness dwelling in her as well as a burning anger.

"Don't be ridiculous." Jaylor pushed Brevelan behind

him. "The entire kingdom is cursed with too much rain, not enough sunlight. It's part of a natural weather cycle."

His words were brave, his actions wary. Darville growled again.

"They will burn you." The woman stepped away from them.

"Why are you here, Mama? The wife of the headman should be at home." Brevelan reached a hand to stay the woman's retreat.

"Because you killed a man and went unpunished, there is no bread, no crops, nothing to feed my family. I'm here to earn a bit of bread so the babies won't cry all night and the men will have enough strength to wrestle some kind of crop from the ground." Her bitterness poured out of her. Brevelan stepped back from it.

A tear trickled across Brevelan's cheek. Darville pushed his head against her leg, offering her comfort.

"Yikiiii!" A stone hit Darville's flank. It was weakly thrown and dropped without damage. But it hurt. He spun in his tracks looking for his attacker. No stone must be allowed to penetrate his guard and reach Brevelan.

Angry men streamed out of the inn. They were all around them now. Some with stones. Some with torches.

Brevelan was frightened. Jaylor was, too. They were all in danger. Darville kept his guard.

"The witch and her lover have returned to taunt us with our misery. She's bastard born, no get of mine. See how she consorts with familiars." A man at the front of the pack shouted.

"Da, please listen and understand!" Brevelan pleaded.

The crowd moved closer.

"Kill them! Burn them all. It's the only way to stop this cursed rain." Another man waved his torch, beckoning the others forward.

Darville sprang at the man. His teeth sank into the arm that carried a torch. Another man kicked him. He bit that one on the leg.

Shouts and kicks from every direction. His teeth sank into flesh here and there, front and back. He tasted blood and knew satisfaction.

Part of him knew that Jaylor struck out with fists and the pieces of his staff, even as he backed away from the crowd. They both worked to keep the angry men away from Brevelan.

Then a chance stone struck her. Blood trickled from her temple. Jaylor caught her. Darville spun to find the throat of her attacker. Brevelan was down and he had to rip out the man's throat.

A torch followed the stone. He smelled burning cloth. "Back, Puppy, back." Jaylor's words penetrated his battle-maddened mind. He knew they had to retreat.

Still he fought the people who pressed him. There were fewer now. He lusted for the blood of one of them, any one of them.

Suddenly he was flung backward. A flash of light blinded him. He landed with a thud on his side and knew only blackness.

Jaylor ran with the unconscious Brevelan over his shoulder. The backlash from the magic nearly blinded him. He wasn't aware that he'd thrown the spell. It must have emerged from the depths of his need to protect Brevelan and Darville.

When his eyes cleared, he saw the wolf collapse under a stony attack. His breath nearly stopped until the wolf staggered to his feet and followed him.

From somewhere he found enough strength and magic to drop a barrier between the angry men and himself and his companions. He'd been thinking about throwing magic since the first attack but hadn't had time to think a defense through.

His steps grew heavier, the path dim. Sweat poured into his eyes and fear clouded his judgment. Then he was into the woods and beneath a dense cover of brush.

Darville limped in a few moments later. He lay panting where he dropped.

Brevelan stirred a little and moaned. Blood still trickled from the darkening spot on her temple. Jaylor touched the spot as gingerly as he could. She moaned again and dropped back into the darkness that held her mind.

Helplessly he held her close against his chest. His stomach turned cold when he touched her pale face. She was so still! He was almost too tired to search for her mind or her aura. Somewhere he found enough magic to examine her more closely. She lived, but her mind had retreated from the raw emotions of the villagers. She was hurt more within herself than without.

And he was untouched. Guilt cramped his gut. His personal armor had protected him. It had risen so fast, so instinctively, he was barely aware of its presence; he hadn't thought to extend it to her and Darville. His thoughts had been only to fight, and anger at the cruel superstition that moved strangers to attack an innocent woman.

Darville's ear pricked at a rustling nearby. The hair on his back and neck stood up in warning. No sound issued from his throat as he prepared to spring at any intruder.

The noise stopped. Jaylor reached for the pieces of his staff again even as he extended his personal armor to include his companions. His favorite tool might be useless for magic, but it had proved an effective club.

"Journeyman?" A small voice whispered from the bushes to their left. "Journeyman, Master Baamin sent me to help."

Jaylor relaxed his grip a little as he recognized the kitchen boy who so cheerfully washed the wine cups.

Darville remained alert.

The boy emerged from his cover, a leading rein in each hand. Behind him two steeds plodded. They were handsome beasts, well fed and curried. Jaylor couldn't say the boy was equally well cared for. He was skinny, ragged, and dirty, but older and taller than when he'd last seen him. Boy stood straighter with more confidence, too.

"Here, sir. It's the best steed I could steal from Krej's stables."

Jaylor squinted at the ragged lad huddled before him. Why had Baamin sent this boy? Wasn't there anyone else at the University more intelligent, more reliable?

"I'll take the wolf across my saddle. We'll follow quick as we can." The boy urged the mounts forward.

Jaylor tried to capture the boy's eyes with his own and failed. Boy looked everywhere but directly at him. Mostly his gaze hugged the ground.

"The wolf will be fine." He reached to scratch the ears of the exhausted Darville. The wolf returned his gesture with a weak lick across his hand. He was tired and sore but recovering. "It's the lady I'm concerned about. The steed must carry us both swiftly. There's a monastery in the inland hills, several hours from here. Do you know it?" Few were aware of the existence of that retreat. The inhabitants were mostly older magicians who no longer had the strength to gather magic and throw spells. They spent their days mapping the heavens for an omen of the Star-gods return and painting wonderful images of miracles. These respected elders had one of the best healers in the kingdom at their disposal.

Jaylor pulled Brevelan's limp form closer. A large purple swelling was already appearing on the side of her face. No rain penetrated his thick copse to wash her pale face clean of the blood and mud of their attack.

"I don't know the place. But I can follow. May I hold her while you mount, sir? You've got to leave quickly. The steed will be missed and they'll chase you." Finally, the boy looked up. His dark eyes were wide and innocent. They begged Jaylor for understanding and. . . . He didn't know what the boy wanted from him.

Jaylor shook his head clear of the need to open his soul to those eyes. Even if this was the kitchen boy, Jaylor had learned too much to entrust his secrets to anyone.

"No." Distrust filled him. The boy had arrived too soon, before the fight was truly begun. He couldn't possibly have run all the way from the castle in the amount of time the inn patrons took to gather and launch their assault.

The boy had to have stolen the two mounts and headed for the inn about the time Jaylor was throwing his transformation spell onto Darville. Before any of them knew trouble was brewing.

Instead of speaking further, Jaylor lay Brevelan across the steed's back. With one hand he steadied her inert body and tangled the other in the coarse mane of the fidgeting beast. He vaulted up. Once settled, he shifted Brevelan to cradle her against his chest.

"The wolf is not damaged. He can run beside us to the monastery."

"My master, Baamin, bade me to watch out for you three. I'll follow with the wolf." Grim determination stretched across the boy's face as well as . . . disappointment?

Jaylor wasn't sure what to make of the boy. Better to

keep him in sight than risk his spreading mischief else-where. They still had a long ride to safety.

"Very well. Follow as best you can."

The first of the wounded from the battle of Sambol limped into the capital. Of one mind, they headed for the market square beneath the walls of Palace Reveta Tristile. Shocked and benumbed citizenry followed in their wake.

As the crowd grew, so did their anger and bewilderment. Lord Krej had promised victory. They had put their trust in the man who promised safety and protection.

Emotions ran high, surging ahead of the exhausted soldiers to the gates of the palace. Shouts awakened the dozing guards. Pounding fists on the closed gates alarmed the Council.

Baamin inched his way through the crowd. Everywhere there were cries and wails of anguish as news of death and mayhem followed in the wake of the retreating army.

Most of the capital citizenry ignored the magician's progress toward the palace walls. They were too caught up in their own misery to notice anything. The rest of the people were either openly hostile or avoided contact with him with disdain. They recognized his blue robes if not his face.

Baamin nearly wept at the disrepute fallen on magicians as much as at the anguish of the people around him. There had been a time when he could prowl the market and no one looked twice at his magician's robes. Magicians were commonplace in the capital. University-trained healers and priests were sought after frequently.

He forced his way toward a stricken soldier who stood swaying, barely standing with the support of a plain walking staff. A bloody bandage wrapped his head, another barely covered a gaping wound along one arm. Gently Baamin touched the man, lending him strength as he sought a rudimentary healing spell.

"Get away from him, ye murderin' sorcerer!" An unkempt woman pushed Baamin away from the man he sought to help.

"Keep your treacherous 'ands to yerself, sorcerer!" another woman spat at him.

"We'll take care of our own. If it weren't for the pampered magicians, we wouldn't be in this war. My Johnny wouldn't be dead!"

"Kill the magicians and stop the war!"

Baamin backed away, doing his best to fade into the crowd. Fortunately they were so caught up in the press toward the palace that the malcontents didn't have time to carry through any threats to his person.

At a shop entrance he discarded the blue robe, and was clad in only a simple shirt and trews—like everyone else. Only then did he press forward through the crowd.

He stopped short before a dry fountain. It had been twenty, possibly thirty years since he had wandered through the capital city alone. As soon as he had received his master's cloak he had been assigned to a court. After ten years he had returned to the University to teach and do research. Most of his time in those days was taken up with his duties. There were servants to run into the market for him, deliver messages, and so forth. Excursions outside the University walls were limited to trips into the countryside with his students.

And in the last fifteen years, since becoming Senior Magician and adviser to the king, he rarely left the University except to go to court. Those trips were usually in the company of soldiers, servants, courtiers, scribes, and other hangers on.

Baamin had not truly come in contact with the people of Coronnan since his journeyman days.

Carefully he watched the people around him. Those who continued to go about their daily business had no use for magic. Those who bewailed the losses in the battle sought their own, unlicensed healers and priests—not those who were University trained and magicians of the Commune first.

In the last thirty years, magic had been confined to the realm of politics.

No wonder the people sneered at him, avoided him, made the sign of protection against evil behind his back. Magicians, like politicians, had become dirty and evil in their minds.

And Krej exploited those fears in his public attempt to discredit and strip the Commune and the University of talent and authority.

But Krej's promises had backfired. Distraught women pelted the formal balcony with sewage and rotten vegetables. With new resolve, Baamin faced the protected window where royals were accustomed to appear before their people.

Krej emerged from behind drawn shutters. The disgusting missiles ceased to reach as far as the balcony. The Lord Regent looked weary, strained. He licked his lips frequently, as if thirsting for something unattainable. Finally, Krej lifted a benevolent hand to silence the jeering crowd.

Baamin, ever sensitive to the presence of magic, nearly recoiled from the soothing power emanating from that hand. No, not directly from that hand, from someone hidden behind the shutters, or possibly standing at a further distance. Anger boiled up in him. Never in the history of Coronnan had magic been allowed to sway the will of the people—at least not since the Great Wars of Disruption.

Now Krej was authorizing illegal magic openly, because he thought there was no one to notice or counter the spell. Baamin fought the urge to throw his own spell over the crowd. That action would put him on the same level of deceit as Krej. He couldn't live with himself if he sank to such a level. And in that moment he had proved to himself that he had not been the prancing rogue who stole the last dragon from the kingdom.

He raised his own hands. For the first time in his life he was grateful for his short stature. Krej could not see the raised arms above the crowd.

A tiny silver-blue spiderweb appeared between his fingers. Baamin concentrated all his will into maintaining the filaments of magic light.

Like any good spiderweb, the magic became sticky, attracting flies. Krej's spell was the fly lured and trapped into the web.

The angry noise of the crowd rose to a new crescendo. No longer lulled and persuaded by Krej's magic, they pelted the Lord Regent anew with filth and rotting garbage.

Krej raised both hands and the spell increased. Baamin continued to draw power into his hands. His arms ached with the strain of holding them up under the onslaught of new magic. Still he trapped Krej's power.

This couldn't be the Lord Regent! Yaakke was still at Castle Krej reporting on the regent's activities. Who, then, wore the mask and glamour of the king's cousin? And who maintained that glamour? Pieces of Jaylor's puzzle began to fall into place.

"People of Coronnan!" image-Krej addressed the crowd. His voice boomed over the populace. The people shouted angry curses back. "Listen to me. We have won a great victory."

"Lies! All lies. Our wounded say different," an angry tradesman shouted back.

"Count the dead. They are more than the living!" cried a woman with a black shawl of mourning over her hair.

A rotten apple smashed into image-Krej's chest. It splattered against the plush nap of his overtunic. His outline wavered, revealing a slimmer, shorter man than the Lord Regent. The bloody mess of a spoiled egg followed the apple. It missed the target as magic armor finally surrounded image-Krej. More proof that the man on the balcony had no control over the magic flying into Baamin's trap.

Stones appeared among the flying missiles. An overripe pear penetrated image-Krej's armor, followed by a jagged piece of paving.

Image-Krej retreated to the safety of the room behind him as guards moved out into the crowd. With cudgels and staffs they pushed the crowd back from the palace courtyard, back from the market square, almost into the surging Coronnan River.

At last Baamin lowered his trembling arms. His knees sagged. He barely had the strength to stand, but he forced himself to melt back with the crowd rather than be discovered by the guards.

No more would he allow magicians to be merely politicians, isolated from the people, oblivious to their needs. Magic needed to be for the good of the general populace and not just the lords and leaders.

"You can't bring her in here!" a stooped old man with wispy gray hair and beard whispered to Jaylor from the safety of the monastery gate. "No woman may pass through that door."

"I'm a journeyman on quest. I demand a healer for myself and my companions in order to complete my quest. It is my right." Jaylor pushed the gate with his booted foot a little harder than he meant. It flung out of the old man's grasp to crash against the stone walls of the outer court.

"There hasn't been a woman inside these walls for three hundred years. Just her presence could disrupt the entire flow of magic among the brothers."

"*S'murghing* nonsense." Jaylor stomped into the courtyard, surveying the place. Darville, followed by Boy and the horses, stayed close on Jaylor's heels. Like a castle, the monastic retreat was built with tall crenellated outer walls, a courtyard with stables and kitchens, carpenter shop and smithy housed in sheds around the yard, backs against the defensive walls. The heart of the monastery was the stone tower in the center, right next to the impressive chapel. Both edifices butted up against the eastern wall.

The guest hall to the far right stirred with more activity than the main building. Three men, coarsely dressed in homespun, sat on stools before the entrance. Their boots were new and clean. Stacks of armor and weapons surrounded them. A grizzled, gap-toothed man dunked a soiled rag in a bucket of grease, then applied it to a sword. A very long and sharp sword.

"Lord Krej is gathering mercenaries," the gatekeeper continued to whisper. "They have stopped here to rest and gather new supplies."

Rude male voices erupted from within the guest hall in bawdy song. The smell of stale beer, urine, and unwashed bodies followed the obscene lyrics out the window.

"Show us to a room away from the dormitory. We'd rather not disturb them." Jaylor stepped forward again.

A fold of his cloak drooped to reveal more of Brevelan's face and head. The gatekeeper gasped at the sight of her University red hair.

Jaylor could almost read the man's thoughts. Hair that bright indicated a rare and special magical talent in males. What, then, was this woman capable of?

"In Masters' Hall there are many empty quarters." There were hardly any masters left to inhabit the spacious suites.

"Fine. The wolf will stay with me. The boy must return to his duties with the horses." Jaylor beckoned Darville forward.

A servant ran out from the stable to catch the steeds.

He ran an admiring hand along the neck of Jaylor's mount as he looked to the old man for confirmation that these magnificent steeds would really be entrusted to such as he. The boy yanked the reins away from him.

"I'll keep watch for your return," he called to Jaylor as he vaulted into his saddle. With the clatter of shod hooves against stone, Boy disappeared through the center gate.

Jaylor mounted an outside staircase that led to the isolated third story of the main building. No soldier poked his head outside the guest hall into the gathering darkness. Only the three cleaning armor were in a position to see him, or the burden he carried, and they appeared too involved in their work to notice.

Darville's nose brushed his leg with each step, unwilling to be separated from Jaylor and Brevelan.

With the scuttling gatekeeper in the lead they slipped down a dark corridor toward the wing reserved for masters.

They stopped before a massive doorway. The portal was sealed by magic. The old man touched the lock with his staff. The door remained firmly closed.

Jaylor heaved against the resistant wood with his shoulder and a muttered spell. The door sprang open.

"How did you do that? You're only a journeyman!" The old man gasped in wonderment.

"This has been a long quest." He buried his face in Brevelan's hair. "Too long and dangerous a quest."

"I'll send the healer." The old man backed away in awe.

"Puppy?" Brevelan roused from her stupor.

"He is safe," Jaylor assured her.

But he didn't hold her any closer, didn't caress her hair. Her first waking thought had been for Darville.

Chapter 31

A warmly furred, wet muzzle pushed at Brevelan's hand. She scratched his ears.

"Yes, Puppy, I know it's time to get up," she murmured. Her eyes were so heavy it couldn't possibly be morning yet. She lifted reluctant eyelids. Pain slashed through her head from the light of a single candle. Memory followed the pain with equal ferocity. She and Darville weren't back in her safe clearing anymore.

"Where are we?" She curled into a tight ball, burying her painful head in her arms.

No verbal answer, only Darville nudging her. She opened her right eye, the one that didn't hurt as much as the other. Threadbare tapestries, which had once been rich, covered the walls of a very large room. A real candle lit the space beside the bed, while a gentle fire in a fireplace, not a central hearth, added warmth as well as cheery light. Sturdy shutters covered long narrow windows barring the cold and rain from these opulent furnishings.

Cautiously she stretched to explore the bed where she rested. It was too wide and comfortable. More than wide enough to accommodate herself and two others who had grown used to sleeping rough, drawing warmth from each other. They'd never get used to these luxurious surroundings designed for the wealthy and privileged who lived in the capital. Was she in the palace?

Somehow she doubted that. Darville was still a wolf and Jaylor was not present. She suspected they had been brought to the University. But everything was bigger, richer than Jaylor had described his meager journeyman's quarters.

"Are you all right?" She petted Darville with questing fingers. She sought injuries, despite the growing pain in her head with each movement, each thought.

For answer, she received a sloppy kiss across her hand and cheek. He took her wrist gently into his mouth in loving greeting. She returned the gesture with a scratch behind his ears. The wolf took her response as permission to climb into the high bed with her. Once beside her he urged her into quiet repose again. Mica roused from a sleeping ball at her feet and scooted to her other side.

As if they were back in her own clearing she nestled between them, drawing comfort from their nearness and protective concern. She was no longer embarrassed that her beloved wolf was really her cherished prince. Jaylor must return soon and restore him to his natural form. Then all would be well. Jaylor would see to that.

She fell into a light doze.

A sound roused her. Men's voices spoke softly on the other side of the door. Her fingers curled into Darville's fur. Her mind groped for the identity of the men. A familiar step on the floor of the outer room. Then the door was pushed open a crack.

"Dear heart, I've brought the healer. He'll take away your pain." Jaylor smoothed her brow with the gentlest of hands.

Deep inside herself she found a small soothing tune. She tried to hum it, but her head hurt too much. Jaylor's hand continued to caress her forehead. She allowed his love to fill her and chase out the other, hurtful memory of men with stones and torches, the painful rejection by her mother and her da.

The tune followed his love into her mind.

"The swelling has stopped. But the bruise is painful." Jaylor informed the other man.

Brevelan peered at the small man who wore the robes of a master magician. Jaylor, still in his travel clothes of trews and tunic over a homespun shirt, appeared so much more wholesome and masculine than the little man who scuttled like a beetle toward her. She cringed away from his barely washed hand. Dirt and something that smelled of blood clung to his broken fingernails.

She clung to Jaylor's hand. The bond between them healed her more than the potions and powders the healer pulled from a pouch at his overfed waist ever could.

The smell of meat on an unwashed body assaulted her senses when the healer reached to touch her wound. She felt the death of the animal the man had eaten for his supper. Had he killed it himself?

Then the man's own emotions engulfed her, pressing her back into the bed like the walls of a dungeon. Precious air became scarce. She didn't need to hear his thoughts to know his intent.

Desperately she tugged at Jaylor's hand until he looked directly into her eyes. She had to communicate to him the man's evil intent.

"Grrrowwwwl." Darville's teeth threatened the man's approach. He must have understood her silent communication.

Jaylor's eyes finally locked with hers. She fed him as much information as she could through her own. His deep brown eyes widened in surprise, then slitted in thought.

"You may return to your master." Jaylor didn't look at the healer.

"The lady is in pain. It is my duty to ease it as best I can." The healer's voice was squeakily high, almost effeminate.

"She is not used to strangers. Your presence will hinder any healing," Jaylor asserted. Brevelan continued to cling to him.

"Nonsense. I'll bathe the wound in this salve and give her a dose of this powder in a cup of wine. Red wine, I think, 'tis rich and will restore her blood faster." The man continued to fuss with his pouch near the candle.

Red wine to mask flavors not intended for healing! "No." Brevelan found her voice stronger than she thought. "Your true master bade you to use witchbane and adderroot."

The man gasped. He stepped away from the proximity of the bed as his hands crossed at the wrist and flapped away any evil. "What witchcraft is this?" His voice sounded strangled.

"It's true, then. You serve a different master than the *Stargods* and the elder of this monastery!" Jaylor rose to tower over the man. The breadth of his shoulders shielded

Brevelan from the little man, but not from the emotions of hate that beat back and forth between them.

Once more she sank into the oblivion of black sleep.

The thick book landed with a thud on top of the growing pile at Jaylor's elbow. "Useless," he muttered and reached for yet another tome.

"Not useless, just not containing what you sought." The Elder Librarian straightened the pile of books that threatened to topple. He caressed each volume as if it were a beloved child.

"Precisely." Jaylor flung another of the volumes at the library wall. It struck the neat rows of other books and brought them to the floor with it. Elder Librarian dashed— as fast as his years allowed—to rescue the abused books. "How do I find a counterspell to a spell created by a man with complete disdain for traditional magic?" Jaylor muttered to himself. "A spell that will work without a staff."

The noise created by the fall didn't ease the growing sense of time wasted. "I'm supposed to be more stubborn than smart, if you believe my master. So why can't I find some answers by sheer perseverance?" He looked to the old man. All the members of this community were older than time. Worn out old men with no other place in Coronnan. He shuddered when he remembered the time one of his teachers had suggested Jaylor, along with his poorly aimed spells, remove himself from the hallowed halls of the University to this very monastery.

"Perhaps, because you are smarter than your master thought, you will find the answer with your mind or your heart before your impatience wins." Only a very old man could have the patience of this librarian. " 'Tis not the nature of the spell you must unravel that troubles you. You know that answer already, but not until the other problem leaves your mind clear."

Jaylor looked the man over with new insight. He'd been using his magic vision so much lately he hardly realized what he was doing. There was a small web of power just beneath his feet, feeding his enhanced vision. The librarian's aura showed worry and fortitude and patience.

And there was no smell of meat about him.

"You've given up eating meat," Jaylor stated flatly.

"I've lost my taste for it." The elder shrugged.

"Since when?" Suddenly he needed to know the answer, as if trusting this man depended upon it.

"Since there was no magic left to gather." The old magician's eyes avoided his.

"Most people of Coronnan don't gather magic and they still eat meat."

"True."

"Brevelan forced me to lose my taste for meat. I find my magic different, but stronger, since then." He clued the old man to speak of his own change. He had noticed the elder choosing his place to stand in the room, right over another power spot.

"It occurred to me that there must be another source of magic, older than man himself, used by the magicians we now call rogues." Elder Librarian raised his eyes and allowed them to meet Jaylor's for the first time since the journeyman entered the library. "Traditional magic has only been available for three hundred years."

Jaylor felt the older man's probe, turned it aside, and sent one of his own. It, in turn, was pushed back toward him. This was no failed magician put out to pasture! But for whom did he use his power?

"Adderroot is a poison I know of. Which is witchbane?" Jaylor decided to test this man for reaction. If he showed suspicion at the combination, then he knew of the healer's attempt to poison Brevelan.

"Witchbane?" The librarian moved to one of the long lines of his beloved books. "Witchbane? I've heard the name but not in a very long time." He rummaged behind a few books and withdrew a very old one. "This might tell us." He blew dust from the spine and cover reverently.

"The healer sent by the gatekeeper tried to give some to Brevelan last night." Suddenly Jaylor had to trust the old man who counted books as dearer friends than his fellow elders.

"Oh, dear!" Elder Librarian paled. "I suspected our enemy had placed spies within our midst. I had no idea it was someone so highly respected."

"Or so trusted by all. Isn't he the same healer who was consulted when the king's heart fluttered and nearly failed a few years ago?" Suddenly Krej's master plan fell into place. "Has he been slowly killing the king?"

"Possibly," Elder Librarian whispered, as if afraid to utter such treason. "I thought the destruction of the dragon nimbus was responsible."

So this old man was aware of the loss of the dragons, too.

"But only Darcine's health is in question. His son is hale and hearty, strong and determined." Jaylor began pacing, making sure his steps stayed close to the lines of power he sensed beneath the stone floors.

"Darville was never consecrated. His tie is not as tight to the dragons."

Jaylor began talking to himself, straightening his thoughts with each word. "The bond is tight enough for one dragon to risk everything to protect him." He stopped by the window. In spite of the chill rain outside he had opened the shutters earlier. As always, the confines of a building destroyed his ability to think creatively. He leaned out to look down onto the massive courtyard. Cool rain pelted his face and cleared the fog from his thought processes more than mere words could.

"But that, too, was part of his plan. Our enemy had no hope of finding and snaring the last dragon without the prince. That was why he lured him into the mountains, then tried to kill him. It was a trap for the dragon!" He paced to the next window and threw those shutters open also.

"A trap delayed by the intervention of a witchwoman." His words came out loud enough for the old man to hear. Silence pulsated between them as they thought, trying to find the logic in one so warped as Krej.

"Where does her magic come from?" Elder Librarian's eyes looked innocent. His questions seemed to be just to satisfy the insatiable curiosity of a man dedicated to books and knowledge.

"She believes Krej to be her true father. You noted the hair color. Krej's mother is from another land. Who knows what kind of magic talent, or lack of ethics, she passed on to her son?"

"Krej! It can't be. Why, Brevelan must be at least eighteen, maybe older. If Krej were truly her father . . . he was barely sixteen himself, just a new journeyman when she was born. I knew him then. His powers increased until the day he left the University at twenty. He was married within the moon. Since then he could have no magic!"

Jaylor couldn't help grinning. "Sex and magic have very little to do with each other." He knew that for certain, now.

If anything, his powers had increased, or was that the Tambootie he still craved.

"We have not yet found witchbane in the book." Elder Librarian looked away first.

Jaylor grinned at his embarrassment. Magic, old and new, he could discuss with this respected elder, sex he couldn't. "No, we haven't found a reference to witchbane."

Jaylor tried to comb his hair with his fingers. It was neatly tied back into a courtly queue. He scraped his jaw with his hand instead. That, too, felt strange without the beard he'd grown used to. Now he was groomed as a magician should be. Even before he was bathed, shaved, and combed to look like a master magician, he felt that he was a master. He just didn't have a cloak to prove it.

And there wasn't much of a Commune left to grant him that honor.

"But what you really need is a book on unraveling spells when you don't know how they've been thrown." Elder Librarian climbed up a sliding ladder searching for a different volume. Like a bay crawler he pulled himself along the shelves sideways.

"I know who threw it and how he did it. But there are pieces of his soul wrapped up in the spell."

"An evil soul within the spell?" The old man gasped as he stumbled to the chair opposite Jaylor. Elder Librarian breathed deeply, searched the shadowed corners for answers, and finally looked back to Jaylor. "There is a book in my quarters. A very old book that was forbidden three hundred years ago. No book should be destroyed, so, when I stumbled across it, I hid it rather than cast it into a fire. I will fetch it for you. But you will not like the information contained there."

"Why not?" Jaylor probed the man. The spell shattered when it hit armor.

"During the Great Wars of Disruption, such spells were common. They hold traps of great magnitude for other magicians. The only way to break the spell is to die."

Chapter 32

Elder Librarian was not entirely correct, Jaylor mused as he carefully closed the ancient book and set it aside. He didn't have to die in order to break Krej's enchantment of Shayla. If, and that was a very big if, he could capture the pieces of Krej's soul entwined in the spell and encase them with his own ephemeral spirit, then he might survive. But his own soul would be doomed to wander with Krej's throughout the firmament or writhe in hell for all eternity. It all depended on just how nasty Krej really was and if he had allowed any of his good qualities to form the spell.

Was Shayla's freedom and the safety of the kingdom worth the cost?

Without a staff the question was moot.

He shook his head and paced the outer room of the suite he and his companions occupied. Mica sat in the middle of the hearth rug bathing an already immaculate paw. Brevelan and Darville slept in the inner chamber. He should join them. The moon had set hours ago. The night was far advanced.

This was a decision only he could make, and his resolve still wavered.

Brevelan and Darville had helped him before when he broke the spell of diversion on the road. He couldn't allow them to help him again at the risk of their lives and their souls. Mica purred her agreement.

"I've found a way around Krej's traps twice," he quietly told the darkness in the corners of the room. "I've got to try. For Darville and Coronnan, I've got to try."

Darville stirred in his sleep as Jaylor quietly rustled among the packs. At the first indication of his friend's wakefulness, he stilled his hand on the three pieces of his staff, now tied into a bundle like so much kindling. Regret for the lost tool—an extension of himself clouded his vision.

"What keeps you awake old friend?" Darville whispered. Brevelan slept soundly on.

"I must finish my quest," Jaylor replied tersely.

"Let me find my trews and boots." Darville yawned as he too searched the packs.

"No, Roy. I have other chores for you." Jaylor stared directly into Darville's sleepy eyes.

The golden-brown pools glimmered in the reflected light of a shielded candle. He didn't blink as Jaylor wove his next words deeply into the prince's thoughts.

"Brevelan will need witchbane from the healers' quarters. She must throw it in Krej's face, make sure he breathes it. Or she can mix it with his wine, but he must drink the full cup. It will negate his powers. But she must be careful how she handles the drug. Not one single drop must touch her skin.

"You, Darville, must face the Council with a sword on your hip to defend against assassins. Elder Librarian will see you transformed back into a prince if I do not return. And if I fail, Darville, you will protect Brevelan. As long as I know she is safe, I am free to risk everything."

The words washed over Darville's furred back. He understood each and every sentence. He would follow the directions until each command was completed.

Darville scouted the crowded courtyard of the monastery. Mercenaries sat in the weak sunshine, mending and polishing their gear. Few, if any, of them paid heed to a scruffy golden dog or a multicolored cat on the prowl. Darville knew that Brevelan was hiding somewhere near the piles of war materials. It was dangerous for her to be seen by any of the foreign men. She had her task and Darville had his. As soon as they were all certain the healer was entrenched with a mug of ale and a long tale to tell a bawdy crew, the companions moved.

The healer's scent was strong in his rooms. Darville found the things he had touched, learned the individual scents, minus the healer's. Somewhere in these two rooms was the potion Brevelan needed. He searched his memory for the scent the man had carried when Brevelan was hurt.

Mica leaped onto a sturdy table. Her nose was as busy as his own. He nudged open the lower cupboards. While his nose worked, his ears were alert. No sound of steps outside the door. Darville was sure he would smell the approach of the healer before he heard him, so distinctive and strong was his odor.

There was nothing of interest in the cupboards, nothing that reminded him of the first time he had seen the healer.

A jar rocked on the table as Mica sought the shelves. Darville growled a warning to her. They didn't have much time. She had to be careful. She hissed her arrogant response.

He sought the boxes under the bed.

"Meroower?" Mica questioned him.

He bounded closer, nose questing. She had found what they sought, wrapped in leather and tied with rawhide.

"Grriipe," he yipped instructions.

Carefully the little cat grasped the bundle in her mouth. It was too big.

Footsteps echoed in the hall. Someone was coming!

Darville whined as quietly as he could. The cat spat at him.

The person stopped with a hand on the latch, lifted it.

They froze.

The door began to open. Then the latch dropped. The person moved away, as if he had changed his mind.

Impatiently Mica batted the bundle to the table with her paw. She followed in a graceful leap. Darville stood against the table, happy to stretch his back. The bundle fit easily in his mouth.

From her position on the table Mica swatted the latch until it opened. Then they both slipped out and away. Brevelan should be back in their rooms by now with the weapon she was to steal from the watchtower.

They have evaded me. The staff is broken and useless but still they find magic to counter my plots. They must have been helped. But who? Who would dare defy me?

Baamin. The old meddler must have found a way. He is dangerous, not as weak as I thought.

I'm not sure I have time to neutralize him.

The Council comes.

I will inform them of the battles my armies have won. No one will dare question my information. If I say the battle was won, then we won.

They will be forced to see that only I can save Coronnan. Only I can be their king. The University must be terminated. Only I can control the magic.

I'll need more Tambootie.

Night had come round again. Alone, wrapped in his nearly invisible dark cloak, Jaylor studied the village behind him and the castle above him on the hill. It was a huge castle. One of the oldest in the kingdom, dating back to before the Great Wars of Disruption, possibly even to the time of the Stargods. It stood on a strong defensive point overlooking the bay on one side, the capital valley on the other.

From the crenellated outer wall, a single sentry commanded a full view of the narrow but fertile valley. The back of the citadel was dug into a cliff. Five tall towers soared upward, imitating the sheer, unscalable walls of the cliff face. As tall as those towers reached; the rock barrier behind was higher—so high no enemy could scale downward or drop into the stronghold and live. Neither could they approach unseen.

There, displayed in the grand hall, protected by Tambootie wood paneling, he hoped to find and free a glass dragon.

If he was strong enough.

If he knew how.

If he could manipulate any magic without the aid of his staff.

Once again he saw in his mind the clouds of colored magic, heard Krej's chanting voice, close to the music his daughter used as a channel, but not quite. Jaylor had always used his staff to control the raw power he drew upon. His magic was tightly focused. Krej's was just as powerful in final effect but spread over a broader surface.

It was the difference between a widely spread drizzle and a short intense squall. They both dumped the same amount of rain with entirely different intensity. Great bursts of energy opposing a slow, smooth dispersion. Would his magic be strong enough to blast through Krej's before his strength was gone?

He rubbed his hands along the short pieces of his staff. Zolltarn had set out to steal or destroy it, probably on Krej's orders. They had succeeded.

"It was only a focus, not a part of the magic," he reminded himself. Still, he felt naked without the length of twisted wood.

But the staff was gone and he was alone. Jaylor had only himself to count on, or blame, for this night's work.

The small gate by the kitchen midden was easy to find, since he knew where to look. Elder Librarian had done his work well in providing the original building plans for the castle.

The sky was black; no moon showed through the clouds during this bleak hour after midnight. The cooks and drudges would all be asleep. He must work his magic and leave before they arose for their morning baking.

He slid through the dark halls, one hand on the cold stone walls, counting his steps, memorizing his path. The great hall was at the top of a narrow stair. A tapestry to his left was the entrance to the banquet hall, formerly a soldiers barracks. Opposite that opening was a thick, locked door.

The lock snapped under his mental probe. The door to the wine cellar at the University had been harder to open. Krej must not fear intrusion. The lock was merely for show.

The smell of the Tambootie wood paneling assaulted Jaylor's senses. It filled his head and made the constant craving for the leaves of the tree deepen. But there was no change in the amount of magic he controlled.

Cautiously he moved toward the menacing figures on display. He recognized the great tusker and gray bear from Brevelan's descriptions. There was an empty pedestal that must have held the spotted saber cat—the one Krej had released to entice Darville into the mountains. Other figures loomed about him, but he didn't take the time to investigate.

And there, in the center, rearing up on hind legs, wings half unfurled, was Shayla. Starlight from a dozen open windows glistened through the glass dragon. She shimmered as if alive, just waiting to pounce on her prey.

Jaylor swallowed. His quest was nearly ended. He just had to break this one last spell!

He turned away from Shayla so that he saw her only by sliding his eyes far to the left. The bundle of his staff in both upraised hands, he counted his breaths. In—one, two, three. Hold—one, two, three. Out—one, two, three. In again, hold it three. Out for three counts. His heartbeat matched his breathing. His mind and body stilled and prepared.

Blue lines of power slipped before his vision. He found one that pulsed in tune with his heart and lungs. It flowed through him with ease.

Vibrations of magic trembled in his hands and along the pieces of wood. He aimed the jagged ends of them at the glass sculpture slightly behind and to his left. Silver-blue webs encircled his fingers and reached out to every corner of the room until they found the glass dragon.

The magic encircling Shayla hummed and wavered. The dragon blinked in surprise. She fought the spells woven around her.

Jaylor pushed more power through his body. He felt himself rising to the heavens with the magic that was all around him.

The humming grew louder, shriller. His ears hurt, his mind reeled as his heart beat faster and faster until it would no longer be contained within his frail body. Shayla fought him, fought all the magic. Her eyes grew larger, her mouth tried to open.

With one last, mighty shriek Jaylor crashed to the ground and Shayla froze.

"Jaylor!" Brevelan wrapped her arms around the staggering magician. Dawn crept through the windows as she led him to the nearest chair. "Where have you been for two days and nights?" Her fingers checked his pulse as she pushed aside his soggy cloak.

His breathing was ragged and his heart irregular. Exhaustion left his skin gray and tight.

"I failed. I'm sorry." Tears flowed down his cheeks in the dried path of others that had been shed earlier.

"Shayla. You've been to Krej's castle, alone?" Darville marched into the sitting room from the sleeping chamber.

He hadn't slept anymore than Brevelan had these past two nights.

Brevelan eased a lock of hair off Jaylor's forehead, checking for fever. His eyes were too bright, his pulse too rapid. "You need food and rest," she commanded as she beckoned Darville to help their companion into bed.

"I'll not sleep. If I do, I'll dream of Shayla, trapped within the glass forever. She tried so hard to be free it nearly broke my heart." Jaylor dropped his head into his hands, his body racked with sobs.

"What went wrong?" Darville began to pace along the same path he had nearly worn into the hearth carpet since Jaylor's midnight departure. His boots trampled a garden of faded woven flowers.

"Nothing, everything. I couldn't use my staff. There were traps in the magic, more traps than I'd planned for."

Jaylor didn't resist Brevelan's attempts at comfort. He was too preoccupied to notice the tune she hummed. She forced strength and peace through her fingers into his scalp as she massaged his temples and brow.

"We've overcome his traps before." Darville stopped his pacing.

"Not like this one. Trapping Shayla in glass was probably the greatest piece of magic ever thrown. Breaking that spell would be even greater. I'm not even a master yet, how could I be so arrogant as to think I could accomplish anything close to Krej's power?"

"Stop that, Jaylor!" Brevelan ordered. "You're tired and temporarily defeated. But you've already accomplished great things. You'll break the spell. You just need more time and a little help." She drew him up to stand beside her. "Now off to bed while I fix a hot meal. When you've slept, we'll try something new." She couldn't allow him to see the worry she felt for him. He'd never been this self-doubting. Many ailments of the spirit she could heal. This one was deeply rooted, feeding itself with memories of every failure from his youth.

"You don't understand, beloved. If I don't manage to break the spell, Shayla will die, the nimbus will be broken, and Coronnan will be at the mercy of Krej and all the outland kingdoms. If I do manage to break the spell, I'll die. I'm not sure my mind will allow that."

"Would some Tambootie help?" Darville looked hopeful. Jaylor stopped to think a moment.

Brevelan hid her fear. The last time he had eaten of the Tambootie his mind had been lost, nearly forever. What would a repeat dosage do?

"I don't think so. Krej seems to have found a way to feed his powers with the drug. I just separate from my body when I use it."

Good. He had dismissed the dangerous idea. "A new staff, then?" Darville prompted. Jaylor just shook his head and wandered toward the sleeping room.

"A new staff, indeed." Brevelan glared at Darville. "A magician's focus is highly personal. Not just any piece of wood will do."

"I was only trying to help."

"You did. We'll mend the old staff while he sleeps."

"Mend the wood? You can't do that."

"I think I can, with a little help." The tune was already forming in her head. After all, a broken staff couldn't be so much different from a broken bone or the dislocated shoulder of a golden wolf.

Chapter 33

*S*tupid, stupid, STUPID! Ambassadors all the way from *Rossemeyer to offer an alliance and now they want to withdraw. Can't they see how much I need their armies, their wealth? With their support I could win the war in a week and conquer all of my enemies in a moon.*

But they insist the alliance is dependent on our prince marrying their princess. News that Darville is missing caused them to retreat into private counsel. They wouldn't even consider marrying the chit to me. Of course, I'd have to eliminate the current wife. About time anyway. The only brats she can whelp are girls and I need sons.

Seems the King of Rossemeyer has moral reservations against such a move. S'murghing fools. Why be squeamish about breaking marriage vows of fealty and honor taken before the Stargods—gods that no longer exist—when an entire kingdom, nay empire, is at stake!

I'll take some Tambootie. Then I will be strong enough to convince the drooling imbeciles of the rightness of my course. Perhaps I should feed the ambassadors some Tambootie as well.

From his outpost in a fisherman's hut, Baamin closely monitored the activities in Krej's castle. Yaakke had placed a piece of glass near a candlestick in Krej's chosen meeting place. Through his own glass and a hearth fire Baamin "saw" the family solar above the banquet hall. Seven of the Twelve sat on benches, chairs and window sills, wherever there was a place to rest their ample bottoms. Some were weary from a long journey. Others were fearful of

Krej. One, Lord Andrall, was downright worried about the course of the war.

The border city of Sambol had fallen to SeLenicca three days ago. Krej's army had been routed. The enemy was marching up the Coronnan River unhindered.

Clearly, Queen Miranda of SeLenicca and her consort, King Simeon, would not allow the proposed marriage alliance with Rossemeyer to take place.

"We do not have the resources to fight the square beards." Andrall's weariness showed in the planes of his face. "There is no prince to receive the ambassadors from Rossemeyer. They are leaving at dawn. How long before their army joins that of SeLenicca? They both want our copper and our gold, not to mention our crop lands and protected fishing."

"You must find a way to call the dragons, Lord Regent!" Lord Jonnias urged. "If only one dragon flew over the enemy encampment, they would run back to their own lands in cowardly fear."

"There are no dragons left, fool!" Krej nearly screamed. That is why King Darcine is so near death."

Apparently only Baamin knew that Darcine had indeed died yesterday morning at dawn. The messenger bearing those dire tidings would arrive at the castle within hours. If Darville were not present when the news reached the Council, they would be forced to name a new king.

Krej was the only candidate.

Unless there was a live dragon present. Shayla could refuse to consecrate Krej as king. She could choose Darville as the next ruler.

Not even the Council of Provinces could argue with a dragon.

Baamin closed his observations of Krej's castle. He had to summon Jaylor. They were nearly out of time.

Lights winked from the arrow-slit windows of Krej's forbidding castle. It loomed over the valley, massive, black, unapproachable in its cliffside isolation. The sun hovered a hand's width above the great expanse of the bay. A gloomy twilight hovered in the sheltered valley below the home of the Lord of Faciar, Regent of Coronnan.

Darville tugged the coarse woolen peasant's hood closer

about his face. The sword strapped to his back made it impossible to humbly slump his shoulders in imitation of the other men around him. Still, it was surprisingly easy to blend in with the crowd of villagers trooping into the castle to prepare for the evening's festivities.

He almost wished for his familiar wolf form and senses. His tall human body just couldn't hear and smell as well. He had to be more alert than ever. Grief for his father had to be pushed aside until a later time.

A sensation of being watched prickled along his spine. He bent over from the waist, back still straight, to catch a runaway apple. Using his position, he looked about. No one seemed overly curious. He straightened up cautiously.

He noticed Jaylor's eyes dart anxiously about as he bent to heft a bulky sack to his shoulder. There was a weariness in his stance, as if he carried a burden heavier than the sack and the mended staff secreted within it. If his posture were merely an act to blend in with the peasants, Darville would applaud Jaylor. But it wasn't. The magician had been depressed for days. When the summons came from Baamin, his mood had become worse.

Darville couldn't read Brevelan's feelings at all. Sometimes she seemed to have absorbed Jaylor's onerous worries. Other times she was bright and cheerful. Right now, she just kept her face buried in the basket of cabbages she carried. Earlier, Darville had combed a great deal of flour through her hair to mask its bright color. Now it was tightly braided and coiled at the nape of her neck, like that of any respectable matron.

The length of her slender neck tantalized him. He suppressed the need for her that filled him day and night. Not until this adventure was finished could he indulge in the luxury of thinking of Brevelan as his own. When he ruled the kingdom, then and only then could he make Brevelan his queen.

Torches flared at the kitchen entry. A guard, in Krej's colors of green and dark red, scanned each face. Doubtless the Lord Regent had passed orders to watch for the trio.

Darville only hoped Krej still believed him to be a wolf so the guards would not be on the lookout for a tall blond prince as well as an equally tall magician and their delicate witchwoman companion.

The guard grabbed Jaylor's shoulder, spinning him to face the light. Darville's breath caught in his throat.

Before his eyes Jaylor's shoulders drooped, his profile blurred and shifted. Fascinated, Darville watched the spell of delusion transform his friend from youthful magician to stooped and wizened old man who needed the suddenly visible twisted staff of wood to support his body.

The guard shrugged and allowed him to pass. Darville let loose the air he'd trapped in his lungs. Several more people passed through the inspection point without question. Brevelan was next.

A heavy hand came down on her shoulder. She looked up with frightened eyes, like a startled doe. Her face was very pale in the torch light. The guard fingered a tendril of hair that had escaped the thick coil. His words dropped to a whisper.

Darville saw the heat rise in her face. He kept his eyes on the guard while his free hand sought the dagger at his belt.

Killing the guard would only draw more attention to himself. He slid the long knife back into its sheath. He had to control his emotions.

Even as he berated himself he watched Brevelan's eyes turn cold. She raked the man's body with her gaze and it was obvious he came up lacking. This time the guard's face turned red. He dropped his hand and allowed her to pass.

Once again Darville breathed deeply in relief. Just a few more people and he, too, would be into the castle.

The guard stopped another woman. She seemed more receptive to his proposition. They lingered in the doorway blocking the passage of the other peasant helpers.

"Hey! What's the hold up?" Darville heard himself shout in the rough estimation of a peasant accent. "We've got work to do. Let's get this *s'murghin'* inspection over with. Lord Krej don't like his dinner bein' late!"

"Yeah. Don't want the lord angry with us for your dallying!" Another man called.

"Stop pesterin' our women and get on wi' yer job."

"Stop yer yammerin'." The guard cursed the mob surrounding him. Embarrassed he passed them all through with only a brief glance at their faces.

Sometimes the best way to avoid detection was to call attention to oneself.

The kitchen was hot. An entire side of beef roasted in the giant fireplace on the central wall. Darville sniffed deeply of the belly-warming aroma. Game birds turned on smaller spits at side hearths. Long tables down the center of the huge room were crowded with men and women chopping vegetables, sifting flour into cavernous bowls, and doing all the other noisy, busy work necessary to preparing a banquet. Small boys darted about fetching supplies while smaller girls swept up discarded peelings and other residue.

Heat and savory smells washed over the prince. The noise of a hundred people filled his head. It was like coming home. The kitchen in his own palace was much the same. As a small, lonely boy he had sought refuge there when his parents and tutors were too busy to entertain him.

There was always at least one cook or drudge willing to let him taste and experiment.

Before the nostalgia could blind him, he sought his companions in the throng. Jaylor was already edging toward the staircase leading to the upper floors. Brevelan had just deposited her cabbages near the scrub sink. As she straightened, her face lost all color. Her eyes began to roll in faint. He was beside her before the others noticed her odd behavior.

Meat. The smell alone would make her ill. The sight of it roasting, plus the churning emotions and frantic activity of all these people, had caused her to seek refuge in unconsciousness.

He grasped her around the waist just as her knees buckled. "Not here, love." Again he used the rough syntax of the people around him.

A woman with a huge chopping knife glared at him.

"Like as not it's her first child, eh?" The woman opened her mouth in a near toothless grin. He tried to smile back at her. "Well, get her out of here. We don't need another body underfoot," the woman commanded.

Darville didn't argue. The woman was too occupied with her turnips to notice he led the wilted Brevelan toward the interior of the castle rather than back outside into the fresh night air.

"The main hall is there." Brevelan pointed to the archway to their left. "That is where the banquet will take place." She peeked through the draperies masking the servants' staircase from the huge central room.

Pain throbbed behind her eyes, the pain of Jaylor's coming ordeal and the press of too many people. She gulped back the flood of emotions. If only there were a tiny tune somewhere in her soul that she could summon to counteract the rising panic within her.

But there were no tunes left in her. Grief for Jaylor overwhelmed all else.

Jaylor seemed calm since reaching a decision that freed his emotions from fear. The wild mood swings he had suffered since he'd failed to transform Shayla the first time were gone. But, she sensed, he was shutting her out of his mind as well as his feelings.

Darville, on the other hand, was fairly bouncing with excitement, despite his suppressed grief for his father. He tried to hide it from her, but she knew him too well. When this night was over, Darville would be king, duly consecrated by a dragon.

"I'll need a place to hide until the assembly is gathered and you are prepared to . . . to do what ever it is you're going to do," Darville said. His eyes scanned the hall with a soldier's eye to strategy.

"Take Mica." Brevelan pulled the dozing cat out of Jaylor's pocket. "She'll find you a place." Briefly she nuzzled the cat's head. Mica's eyes opened round and hazel, and for once she didn't shift to a vertical amber slit as she looked into Brevelan's heart. Understanding passed between them.

"I guess this pesky cat can be of some use," Darville growled, though his voice held the same tone as a puppy's whine for attention. He pulled Brevelan close and kissed her hard. "For luck," he whispered for her ears alone. One gentle finger caressed her cheek.

"You have the witchbane?" Jaylor interrupted.

"Right here." Darville patted his breast pocket. "I won't hesitate to throw it at Krej at the first sign of magic." He looked once more into the hall and slipped through the draperies.

Alone with Jaylor, Brevelan turned her attention to the next task.

"I can smell the Tambootie paneling." Jaylor's nostrils pinched in distaste.

"All of the walls in this room are covered with the wood, even the floor and ceiling. Krej used to keep a Tambootie wood fire burning in the hearth, until it made the servants so ill they couldn't continue their duties." She had to breathe through her mouth to keep the acrid odors away.

The staircase landing seemed to grow smaller as Jaylor's magic filled it. Brevelan touched his arm and felt much of what he saw.

The animals were still there. A gray bear, a wild tusker as large as a hut, a snow-white stag with fifteen points on his rack and several others she could not name. The spotted saber cat was gone, she hoped never to return. No animal, no matter how ferocious, deserved the living death of Krej's sculpture cages.

In the center of the room on a low, wide dais stood Shayla. All of her intense beauty was captured in the glass. Each transparent hair of her fine fur was crystallized to reflect back the light of a thousand torches. Along her spine, horns, and wing ridges a rainbow of colors swirled, daring the eye to look anywhere but at her.

Brevelan tugged at Jaylor's arm. "Shayla said that dragons eat of the Tambootie to become the source of magic, yet they have none of their own! Krej eats Tambootie like a dragon. How can he throw magic and be a source as well?"

"That I don't know. Unless his body reacts with the Tambootie differently. When he is near, I can sense no gatherable magic anywhere near him." He shook his head, puzzled. "There is no time to worry about that now. I must find the strongest point to stand. There are precious few lines of power running through. this castle."

"No one is in the room." She felt all the emotions in the castle, but they were behind her and above her. "No one except Krej can stand to be in this room for more than a few minutes."

"Where is he right now?"

"Above." His emotions were easiest to separate from the others. "He is very upset about something." Too upset. She had to block him out before his anger became her own.

"Good. Maybe he'll be so preoccupied he won't notice

us." Jaylor pulled her tight against his chest and kissed her with fierce passion. "For luck," he grinned.

Deep in his eyes she saw another sentiment. The kiss was for farewell.

Chapter 34

A myriad of servants scurried among the trestle tables below the dais. Plain white cloths covered the boards; pewter platters and plain iron knives marked each place. The head table, on the dais, where Krej and his special guests would sit, was covered with the finest white damask and set with plates of gold and cutlery of fabulously expensive and incredibly rare steel, forged in secret half a world away.

Spring flowers sweetened the rushes underfoot and tasteful arrangements of greens and dried plants adorned baskets about the room. A grouping of three such tall baskets shielded a tiny alcove where Darville crouched unseen, with the pesky cat, Mica.

He shifted his weight for the umpteenth time. Mica hissed at him to be still. He felt like swatting her. His legs and back ached from the unnatural position. Mica was perfectly content to curl her small body into a tight ball and doze until action was needed.

But the image of Mica transformed into a lovely nude woman, with hair as bright and multicolored as the cat's shimmered before Darville's mind. Had he dreamed the true nature of the cat or had he really seen her in Shayla's cave? He shook his head clear of the image.

He couldn't nap and he couldn't dwell on dreams. He needed to stay alert. He half-wished for his wolf form. The four-legged creature would be much more comfortable hunkered down in this cold corner.

He shifted again just to spite the cat. This time his purloined sword clanked against the stone wall at his back.

A servitor in green and red tunic and trews whirled to

seek the source of the noise. Darville froze, hardly daring to breathe. The blacker than black hair with wings of silver at the servant's temples looked familiar.

The man scanned the room with wary eyes. They rested on Darville's hiding place then moved on. So did his hands. One moment the table was fully set. The next, two of the knives were missing.

Zolltarn the Rover! Of course. Darville knew he'd seen the man before. Like as not, more than two of the metal knives would be missing before the guests were seated.

Darville tried to blend in with the stones at his back. It didn't work. As soon as the other servitors were gone from the room, Zolltarn began searching the flower arrangements.

Silently Darville stood and eased his dagger from his sheath. When the Rover was close enough, he dragged the thief back into the shielded alcove.

"A sound and your throat is slit," he hissed. His right arm encircled the man's chest. His left held the wicked dagger across the bobbing apple in the middle of Zolltarn's throat.

"Probably not, companion to the magician and the little beauty with red hair." Zolltarn almost chuckled, as much as any man in such a position could chuckle.

Darville raised an eyebrow but kept silence.

"A knife in a throat is a messy way to die and you have not the time or patience to clean up."

Mica hissed her agreement.

"A knife in the back is just as easy and cleaner. So answer my queries instead." Darville swallowed deeply. Though trained for combat since early childhood, this was the first time he had held a man's life in his hands.

"I can but try. Krej pays well for information. Can you pay more?"

"You payment will be your life if you answer truly. How much does Krej know about me and my companions?"

The man laughed, but not loudly. It was an evil kind of sound. That made it easier to prick the stretched skin of the Rover's neck. Zolltarn stopped abruptly as a tiny drop of blood oozed from the cut. Darville swallowed deeply again at the sight of the blood he had inflicted.

"The Lord Regent asked if I had stolen a wooden staff

from the magician and his lady who were traveling with a great golden wolf."

"And if you saw such people in your journeys, did you steal the staff?"

"Ay, yes, we did. A shattered piece of wood is as good as stolen. I report everything to Lord Krej when he pays. But I did not know then that his description of you meant a real wolf. He would give much to know the wolf now walks on two legs instead of four."

Darville breathed a little easier. He didn't release the pressure on the man's neck. "What will buy your silence?"

"The promise of your seed for my people after this night's adventure. Your sons would be kings."

"My sons will be kings anyway. I do not waste my seed on temporary alliances." At least not since he'd met Brevelan. She was the only woman he wanted now.

"There is a boy, Yaakke, in the kitchens. He could grow to be very powerful if guided by me." The man's voice becoming seductively smooth. Fortunately, Darville had spent enough time with Jaylor and Brevelan to resist this attempt at compulsion.

"I am not like my cousin. I do not trade in lives. If the boy wishes to go, he may. It is his decision, not mine."

"Then I do not know what to ask for. You do not look as if you could pay more than Lord Krej. After all, he is Lord Regent with the wealth of a kingdom at his disposal."

Anger burned deep within Darville's gut. Mica hissed again. It sounded like she was commanding him to kill the evil Rover. He was very tempted. But the man might be useful yet.

"I can tell you where my cousin keeps his prettiest baubles. It will take you most of the night to break the seal on the lock."

"I am a Rover. I can smell such hiding places."

"Not in this castle, home to a rogue magician." The Rover made a hasty (if halfhearted) gesture against evil at that comment. His eyes went wide, but there was no struggle to wiggle free of the very sharp dagger at this throat. "In a moon or more of searching you might find it. Do you have that kind of patience?" Darville felt more than a little satisfaction at the visible signs of the Rover's fear.

Zolltarn started to shrug, but the knife blade scraped his neck once more. Another drop of blood oozed from a cut. "Tell me and you have my silence."

Baamin pushed aside intruding servitors and guards with a regal gesture of his staff. He allowed his armor to glow in his signature colors of yellow and green. No man tried to interfere with him twice.

A tap of his staff against the wide double doors to the banquet hall gained him entrance to the private feast. Eerily silent wind preceded him down the center of the room.

Shocked silence followed.

"What are you doing here?" Krej half rose from his thronelike chair in the center of the dais. His voice sounded unnatural in the increasingly heavy hush.

The senior magician stopped his progress toward the high table. All around him the noble men and women of the kingdom gasped at Krej's impropriety. One should never be this rude in public, and certainly not in front of foreigners. The ambassadors from Rossemeyer made frowns of disapproval toward their host.

Baamin suppressed a small smile. He needed the support of all these people. Very shortly he would ask the nobles to turn against the man they had elected regent. But that was only a small portion of his duties tonight.

If Jaylor failed, then he, Baamin, Senior Magician, had to follow through with Shayla's rescue.

"It is my right to sit at Council," Baamin stated simply.

"The Commune is broken. You have no more rights, old man, just as you have no more magic." Krej sneered.

He must be very certain of his position to risk such a public display. It was time to upset some of his security.

"Are you sure about that?" Baamin raised his right hand. It held a ball of unnatural red fire. He pointed at the ball with his left hand. One finger wiggled. The ball raised and bounced about the room. It landed in the headdress of one highborn lady but did not ignite it. The red flames split into a myriad of stars cloaking the lady in flattering sparkles of blue, red, and gold.

"Oh, how lovely." She caught a few of the cold sparks in her hand and blew them to her husband, like a lover's kiss sent across the room. As each morsel of light landed in the man's palm it spread and grew into a delicate flower.

More smiles and exclamations of pleasure.

"I have arranged my own entertainment for tonight." Krej reseated himself. "Pay him no mind, gentlemen." He spoke more casually to the ambassadors at the high table. "An old man, feeble in the brain."

"So feeble I can not do this anymore," Baamin taunted as he brought forth thunder and lightning. This time the crowds cowered in anticipation of rain. It came, but Baamin evaporated it before it could drench the guests. It did, however, douse some of the torches. Select portions of the hall plunged into darkness. Shadows crept outward in imitation of uncertainty and evil. One small and insignificant drudge nodded to him from one of those shadows.

Tricks and sleight of hand to alter the mood of the assembled guests. Baamin had to make them vulnerable to his suggestion when he denounced Krej.

"Enough of this play, Baamin. You were not invited because the kingdom has no more use for you or the Commune. My armies are now our source of protection. Return to your University and pack your belongings. Three mornings hence, my soldiers will take possession of the buildings as barracks and storage and training ground." Krej dismissed him with a wave of his hand.

"I think not, my Lord Krej. By morning our rightful ruler will command the army." The time had come to finish this game. He could sense Jaylor's readiness. He need only be sure Krej's attention was fully engaged.

"I am the rightful ruler of Coronnan. Need I explain to you once more that during this last, and most likely final, illness of our king and in the absence of his heir I have been elected regent?" Krej's face was heated, growing nearly as red as his hair.

"But I am missing no longer, cousin." Darville stepped from his hiding place. His strong left hand rested on the hilt of his sword. His other hand lingered near a pocket as he moved close to the dais. Though not richly made, his clothes were respectable, and the prince's very regal bearing left no doubt as to his identity.

The ambassadors shifted uneasily. They looked from

their host to the newcomer, unsure of where to place their allegiance.

"You might as well be." Krej was standing now. "You've been away for several moons with no explanation, no regard for the welfare of Coronnan. You've allowed your father's health to fail through your unconcern. And now that I have things under control, you've decided to return." His hand waved to the guards who lined the walls. They began to move slowly forward.

"You should know precisely where I was, cousin. For 'twas you who lured me away, and you who allowed a rogue magician to entrap me into the guise of a golden wolf." Baamin and Jaylor had agreed beforehand that they could not accuse Krej of rogue magic without visible proof. Hopefully Krej would supply that proof before the night was over.

Noble guests looked carefully around for signs of any rogue. Some made the cross of the Stargods, others crossed their wrists and flapped their hands in an older gesture against evil. Three cowering women did both. Baamin could hardly think over the babble of frightened whispers. That suited him fine. The prince was handling the situation quite nicely.

"The last time I saw you, Lord Krej, I was ensorcelled in the guise of a golden wolf, familiar to a witchwoman, who just happens to be your illegitimate daughter." Stunned and superstitious silence met that announcement.

Baamin silently applauded the young prince for linking his recent captor with Krej. The witchwoman probably kept the enchanted wolf in hiding on her father's orders.

At that moment a small bundle of multicolored fur chose to race and bound through the great hall. Baamin recognized the cat from Yaakke's report. He called her Mica. A suitable name considering her nearly iridescent fur.

Mica made a show of circling Darville's legs, while yowling her displeasure over something. The prince ignored her.

"Get that cat out of here!" Krej jerked back from the edge of the table just as Mica leaped from the dais to the table. She spat at him with incredible disdain but did not linger near the Lord Regent. Instead she sauntered to the ambassador, sniffed his hand, licked it and began to purr so loud Baamin could hear it half a room away.

"This cat," the ambassador's face lit with a mighty grin, "where did she come from?" He stroked her fur with lingering affection.

Krej continued to lean away from the cat's presence. "It's just a cat. There are numerous ones about to catch mice." Not likely, judging from Krej's dislike, or fear, of this one.

"The cat came with me," Darville interrupted.

"She is near duplicate of our princess's pet, such unusual fur. The cat was much beloved but disappeared some time ago. Princess Rossemikka has mourned the loss ever since." The ambassador's attention was now on the prince.

Baamin continued to watch Krej for signs of trickery. "A gift of this cat to the Princess Rossemikka would be a suitable token for one who seeks alliance," the second ambassador suggested.

"NO!" Krej bellowed, but not at this suggestion. His eyes narrowed to angry slits, his face paled to the color of the table cover. "He can't. I won't let him rob me of my treasure!" The Lord Regent jerked to his feet unsteadily. "Guards, into the great hall. Kill the intruders!"

Hastily, Baamin threw a magic barrier across the archway. No one must interfere with Jaylor.

But Darville was faster. His right hand flung something into Krej's face. "Poison! The prince has poisoned me," the Lord Regent screamed in pain. He clawed at his face with desperate hands. His breath rattled and gasped.

"Go to Jaylor, quickly!" Darville commanded Baamin as he drew his sword. "I'll hold off the guards as long as I can." Already the prince's sword slashed and grappled with the soldiers seeking to defend their lord.

"Is Shayla still alive?" Jaylor whispered.

Brevelan nodded. "Just barely."

Jaylor began deep breathing in preparation for the ordeal before him. From Brevelan's raspy tone he guessed his time was limited. Shayla's imprisonment would kill the dragon very soon. Her freedom would see his own death.

He was resigned to it now, after days of worry and depression. There was a lightness in his mind and body. His life, and death, had a purpose.

The magic beneath his feet vibrated through his being in rhythm with his respiration. He nurtured the flow for sev-

eral counts until he felt full to exploding with raw power.
He raised the mended staff over his head until the magic
pulsed within it too. With luck, Brevelan's splice would last
through this one last spell.

He didn't want the magic and the power raw. It needed
to be refined and fine-tuned to imitate Krej's original spell.
In his mind Jaylor relived the scene in Shayla's cave.

Once again he saw the beast-headed rogue capering to
his own chanted spell. He had used the chant very much
as Brevelan, his daughter, used her music.

The magic vibrated again, in time with the remembered
chant.

There had been words, too. Words describing the desired
result of the spell. Jaylor didn't like words. They tended to
be imprecise, ambiguous, compared to the very vivid pictures he created in his mind. But this spell had been created
with words, so it must end with words.

> "Precious dragon from glass.
> Precious glass from sand."

The magic hummed louder within him. He felt the pressure of people at his back, anger, fear, and the clash of
steel. He didn't care. Nothing mattered but the power of
the music inside him.

> "Ordinary sand from the sea.
> Nurturing sea from creator air."

Brevelan sang the tune beside him. It filled him to overflowing. The staff glowed. With great effort he contained
the magic within him. The spell was not yet complete.

> "Blessed wind from air.
> Purifying air for freedom.
> Freedom for dragon made of glass,
> sand,
> seA,
> aIR,
> WIND!"

With the final words he pictured that glorious flight with the dragons playing with the wind, soaring above Coronnan in an exquisite cherishing of the ultimate freedom. There were no chains to the ground, no compulsions to eat of the Tambootie, no restrictions, and no pain.

Colors burst forth from his staff in a glowing storm, red and blue and copper in a braided shaft arrowed toward the back corner of the room, bounced and fled straight into the heart of the dragon, green and red and the elemental copper flowing in a hazy halo about the sculpture. Blue and red balls bounced about the room, landing on each of the other sculptures, himself and Brevelan. All the colors of Coronnan split into a bright haze that filled the huge hall. Then they wove back into braids of magic that twined with each of the sculptures.

The sound of wild gusts of air pushed the magic into the directed targets.

Bits of copper broke loose from the braids of bright colors. The element sought and surrounded tiny morsels of emerald and dark ruby encased in the glass.

Krej's life spirit contained in the spell faded and fled to the far reaches of the hall.

Freed from the restrictive traps, Jaylor's magic burst loose. Just barely, he kept it within his control.

His overworked lungs and heart stuttered. And still he drew more power up from the bowels of the planet, fed more and yet more magic into the spell.

The magic of Coronnan pulsed through his veins, tore through his body mercilessly. With a mighty effort he turned the staff to the dragon's tail. It twitched. With the tiny movement, glass broke and tinkled to the floor. That small amount of freedom generated a greater swipe of the mighty tail.

Farther and farther up the dragon's spine the glass fractured, splintered, shattered. With each release, Shayla's tail slashed farther and farther. It beat at the glass on her hind legs and belly. It flogged the metals encasing the other animals nearest her. Those, too, began to shatter. Then her front legs shook free of the ensorcellment.

Jaylor heaved his staff forward to Shayla's broad chest and neck.

He was the power, the *Power* was Jaylor. He mastered the *Power* and was mastered by it. Nothing existed except the *Power*.

He saw the dragon as she had been; he was with her, in her, her mate and herself all at the same time. Through her eyes he saw himself and the quaking Brevelan, who touched the dragon's mind. He saw Darville fighting for his life with a purloined sword against three hefty guards, and Baamin's feeble attempts to contain the fight and their enemy Krej as they all spilled into the Great Hall. He felt Shayla's pain and loneliness, cherished the freedom that was creeping up her back and neck.

With a mighty twist, the last shower of glass cascaded from her head and horn.

"Grrooowerrrrrrrrrrrrrrrr!" Shayla roared, once more herself. The other animals echoed the triumph of Jaylor's magic over their enchantment.

Jaylor slumped to the floor, deflated at the separation from Shayla's and Brevelan's mind.

The magic ceased to flow. Jaylor ceased to breathe.

Chapter 35

"**S**eize him! Seize him you fools," Krej ordered his burly guards.

Three men advanced on Darville, swords drawn and at the ready. The prince moved to stand between them and the doorway to the Great Hall. He had to give Jaylor and Baamin time.

Slash and parry, duck and dive under the man's guard. He pushed all of his concentration, anger, and strength into maintaining his position. He'd fought three men on the training field. Three bored soldiers who were afraid to be too aggressive with a prince.

These three men in red and green surcoats were well trained and eager to please a ruthless lord. They pushed Darville back, closer and closer to the door. One man distracted him with a flourish of fancy blade work.

Darville answered him stroke for stroke. A second man slipped in under his guard. Blood trickled down Darville's arm. His mind registered the fact that he was wounded. His body had yet to feel it.

He clenched his free hand into a fist and slammed it into the face of the man with the flourishing sword. He staggered backward into the arms of the third man. That left only one to deal with.

Then the cut began to burn and so did his mind. With renewed fury and bared teeth Darville slashed and lunged until the bigger man and his partner were pinned against one of the long tables. The third man seemed to be out cold on the floor.

A woman screamed and overturned her chair as she backed away from the fight. Servitors and nobles alike ran or scurried into dark corners for protection. Strong men cowered and weak women stared at the blood on his arm and the blood on the throat of the guard in fascination. The other guards hesitated in a semicircle around him. Darville didn't know what kept them back. Had Baamin thrown some kind of armor? A little late if he had.

"Swear your loyalty to me!" he commanded the man pinned beneath his sword. "I am your prince, soon to be your king. Swear your loyalty or die."

The guard gulped loudly. The sword point scratched his throat as the words worked their way up. "I swear," he croaked.

"And you, all of you as well will swear." Darville swung around to face the crowd. A few of the nobles were already on their knees murmuring the words of fealty.

"Forget this puny princeling. I am your rightful lord!" Krej screeched, half blinded by the witchbane.

No one answered him. Hands covering his face, the Lord Regent turned and ran toward the Great Hall.

Darville saw the move and lunged to capture his cousin in a cruel grip. "Call off your men, Krej!" he commanded.

Krej continued to hold one hand over his eyes but said nothing. Darville realized his cousin's magic was neutralized, or he would never have been able to touch the man. The witchbane had worked.

"Very good, your grace," one of the ambassadors applauded with voice and hands.

"We believed your people weak. You have just proven yourself a warrior worthy of our princess," the other ambassador bowed low. He still cradled Mica in his arms. The traitorous cat looked all too content to stay with him.

"Look at him, you traitors!" Krej bellowed. "Look at how he bares his teeth and his hair stands up, just like a wolf. He is still part wolf and can never be trusted. Is this the man you wish to be your ruler?" With a mighty jerk, Krej pulled away from Darville and lunged once more for the tapestry that masked access to the Great Hall and Shayla.

Darville bounded after him, sword at the ready. The entire crowed followed.

The woven drapery tore down the middle and slipped to the ground in limp folds.

No one noticed a weary royal messenger, spurs clanking on the stone floor, limp into the banquet hall.

"SHAYLA!" Brevelan commanded with voice and mind. The great dragon head swung back and forth in anger, mouth agape, sparks dripping from her teeth. Her gaze pinned Krej and Darville to the wall near the entrance.

He must pay for his evil. Shayla's voice once more filled Brevelan, after weeks of absence. Even with the anger, Brevelan felt a little more complete now that her dragon was with her.

"Not here, not now, and not by you." She fought for control.

I am the one wronged.

"But restored."

My young?

Brevelan pushed her awareness to the tiny life forms within Shayla. Eleven of them, where before there had been twelve. Sadness at the one lump of inanimate flesh filled them both. But the others were fully formed and nearer readiness than they should be.

It is too soon! Shayla wailed with a spittle of flame from her gaping muzzle. *They will be born out of cycle.*

Brevelan sought to contain the fire. "They will live. And so must you. Kill my father now and this crowd will gladly watch you die. Your brood with you."

Another morsel of flame ripped toward the growing crowd huddled against the interior wall.

"No, Shayla. If you kill my father, you kill me as well." Brevelan knew it in her heart. She was tied by blood and magic to the one man in the entire kingdom she wished she could disown. Blood of her blood, flesh of her flesh. She would feel his death, share his pain more fully than any but Mama. If the death of an unknown squirrel in the meadow pained her, Krej's death in the same room as she would kill her.

"Grrrooowerrrrrr!" Shayla belched forth one more burst of defiant fire. She whirled about the room, seeking escape. Her tail lashed back and forth, sweeping a pathway. Yet it kept free of the recumbent form of Jaylor, her deliverer. The one time she came close to his body she almost curled her tail around him in a protective coil.

The magician loves you. The words came to Brevelan with typical dragon abruptness. Then there was only silence.

Darville sagged with Shayla's silence. There was a momentary hole where his heart used to be. He pulled Brevelan tight against him to fill the void. The world righted for him again.

As long as Brevelan was at his side, he was complete. He was in command.

"A live dragon, ensorcelled in your own Great Hall, Lord Regent?" Darville almost spat his question. He whirled to face his cousin, pointing his sword at Krej's throat. He wished he could murder the rogue magician on the spot and get away with it.

"You are in no position to question anything, wolf-man." Krej eyed him levelly. Though shorter and older than himself, Krej was still a commanding presence.

"Rogue magic was outlawed three hundred years ago for precisely these reasons," Baamin reminded them all. "Magic cannot be allowed if it is used for the sake of greed and power. It must be controlled by the Commune and used solely for the good of the kingdom."

"The statues were present in my hall, yes. But you will never prove that I am a magician, nor that I did anything more than accept great art from a stranger. No one in his right mind will want to prove anything else," Krej reiterated. "I was the only one capable of organizing a fragmented kingdom. I brought forth the army. I defended our borders. Even as we speak, Lord Wendray is retaking the border city of Sambol." He paused long enough to look his fellow councilors in the eye. "You will all stand with me because I am the most able to continue to rule."

Shayla roared her disapproval of that. Her wings flapped and she prepared to exit, but her tail still encircled Jaylor's body.

Darville wondered if he should go to his friend, see if he still lived. Why else would the dragon protect him, as she had protected Darville last winter?

But Darville couldn't afford to remove his attention from the Council members just yet. Krej was so very sure of himself, so very compelling in his belief that he was in the right. How could the Council disagree?

"And what happens when the war is over or when my father dies?" Darville forced himself to think like a king, plan for the years to come and not just for the moment's need and the grief he continually thrust aside. His spine took on the formal posture and regal bearing he had been taught as a child. It came naturally now despite his longing to bare his teeth and growl his frustration.

He hardly noticed when Brevelan turned away from him, skirts kilted to her knees as she ran to Jaylor's side. She would be back when he needed her. Of that he was sure.

"We will address that issue after the war or when Darcine finally dies. He should be recovering now that Shayla is flying." Krej gestured his dismissal of the matter.

"We will address that issue now, since you created the war." Darville's mouth lifted in an involuntarily growl. He needed to sink his teeth into Krej's neck and taste the hot blood. He needed to kill!

With great effort he mastered his bestial urges.

"My lords," a tired voice whispered. A man in the royal livery looked to both Darville and Krej, not knowing who should receive the message. "My lords," he spoke a little louder to the entire company. "King Darcine is dead. He passed into the dimensions beyond at dawn yesterday."

Silence descended over the room with a crash. Then a hubbub of questioning voices arose like a roar. The noise was no louder than Shayla's own cry of mourning. She let forth one mighty blast of dragon fire against the outside wall. Wood and stone exploded outward. The stench of burning Tambootie engulfed the room.

Heavily, clumsily, Shayla lumbered toward the gateway she had made. Her wings flapped in the limited space, gathering speed.

The wind created by her laboring pinions pushed Darville back into the crowd. He reached out a protective arm toward the dragon. Only Jaylor, still lying on the floor in the boneless heap where he had collapsed, and Brevelan kneeling at his side, remained in the center of the room.

With one last mighty sweep of wings and tail, Shayla bellowed forth her anger and launched herself into the dark

night. The other animals shook free of the last traces of
magic and followed her.

"Shayla, come back to me," Brevelan whispered through
her tears.

Not while the evil one lives. He has killed my king.

Darville gave the assembly a moment to think about the
awesome sight of a dragon in their midst.

"My father is dead. I am the next legal heir," Darville
announced to one and all.

If only life were that simple, Baamin wailed to himself.
"The king is dead," he bowed his head in a moment of
grief for his old friend. "There are two claimants to the
throne, Darville as prince and Krej as duly elected Lord
Regent. Shayla has flown away without naming her enemy
and without consecrating the next king. She has gone and
has taken her mates with her." He faced the crowd and
allowed the gravity of the situation to sink into their minds.

"Who now decides how we should be governed? Council
and Commune must come to an agreement." The old magician was suddenly weary and doubtful of the outcome of
that agreement.

"Without dragons, there can be no legal magic and therefore no Commune," Krej reminded them all.

Baamin has witnessed the tremendous power working
through Jaylor, tonight. Boy—Yaakke, as he preferred to
be called—possessed power as well. With a few more like
them he could play watchdog over individual magicians to
keep them ethical and controlled. The Commune could still
serve a purpose.

But the throne was in contention. Baamin's Commune
would support Darville, give him the edge to control the
Twelve.

"I've lost ten farms, two dozen people, and more, to the
raids across the border in the last few weeks," one lord
spoke up at last. "I have to support Lord Krej as regent if
not king. He's shown what he can do for this kingdom.
Darville's young yet. Untried and still showing signs of his
ordeal with wolves."

Lord Andrall from the extreme north stepped forward
to stand beside Darville. "What has Krej done for this
country? The army is routed, the battles have all been lost.

He's lied to us repeatedly. And how does he know what is happening on the field of battle if he isn't using magic?" Andrall swung his gaze back to the regent with malice. "I've never trusted you, Krej. I didn't vote for your regency. Now I stand by my lawful prince. I think once we've heard his adventures, we'll all agree he's had enough experience to launch the next campaign against our enemies."

Baamin looked about in distress. This was what he feared most. The Great Wars of Disruption had begun under similar circumstances. He had to reconvene the Commune immediately.

"While the king was so ill, it was our right to elect a regent. The dragon didn't approve Darville as king. How do we know he's not the 'evil one' she mentioned? I stand by Lord Krej." Lord Jonnias moved to stand beside the regent.

One by one the lords moved to the side of their chosen commander. Against the wall their ladies separated equally. Baamin felt powerless. This was one time he could use no magic. Decisions like these had to be made freely; if made under magic compulsion they would break apart eventually.

Finally Kevinrosse, the chief ambassador from Rossemeyer, moved forward. "We came to seek alliance with Coronnan. Our offer was for marriage between Prince Darville and our beloved Princess, Rossemikka. Lord Krej tried to offer himself in the marriage. We found that dishonorable in that he is already wed." He continued to caress the small cat he carried in his arms. "If he is willing to behave with such disregard for morality in the matter of an alliance, we believe he will do so in every other matter." He swallowed and looked around at the divided company. "Therefore, Rossemeyer extends the offer of marriage, alliance, armies, and wealth to Prince Darville."

"Mere promises from a poor kingdom that has always been our enemy. Promises that our neighbor SeLenicca have vowed will lead to war. Which war do we choose? In either case, Coronnan needs a strong leader, experienced in battle." Krej dismissed the ambassador with complete contempt.

"Then we will war among ourselves as much as with our enemies," Baamin muttered. He felt utterly defeated. The kingdom he had dedicated his life to preserving was divided. But he had seen a dragon this night. He had heard some of her words. There was nothing left to live for.

"Jaylor?" Brevelan whispered. She knelt beside him, ignoring the arguments of the politicians behind her. Jaylor's eyes remained closed. Gingerly she felt for a pulse at his neck. At first she despaired of finding any flutter of life.

But her healing sense pulled outward, demanding to be used. He must be alive. He must. She hadn't felt his death, only his pain and the utter blankness of his retreat from that pain.

She flattened her palm against his chest. Energy pulsed through her into his heart. Push, retreat, push and retreat again, forcing Jaylor's organ of life to pump blood. Push and retreat.

One beat of response. Barely.

His lungs shuddered and strained for air. She gave it to him.

She sought his mind, fearing it had flown away with the dragon, as it had once before. No, it was there, deep within, hiding from the pain. Best to leave it there a while.

A lilting tune of peace and love came into her head. She sang it to him with crooning care. The notes rose in a haunting cry for her lover to return to her. Her song soared and filled the room with her love for the dying magician.

"The clearing will be so empty without you, dear heart," she finally whispered through her tears. "I will be so empty without you."

A little life stirred under her hand. The tune came out louder, stronger. She wept with the poignancy of her music and relief that he was fighting to join her once more. His heart stammered in its rhythm, caught her song and found its proper cadence. She felt her own heart join his in the battle to retain life.

With a tremendous shudder his lungs fought the paralysis of his pain. She took some of the pain away, allowed it to dissipate in her stronger body. Air left her lungs and filled his body and left him again and filled her until he was breathing in the natural course.

His eyes struggled open, glazed with pain. She tried to take it away, but it was too powerful. Her body and mind recoiled from the task. She had to protect the new life within her as well as his.

"Shayla?" Jaylor croaked past parched lips and tortured lungs.

"She is safe," Brevelan reassured him. Her own lungs were beginning to ache with the force of maintaining his life.

"There is no magic left within me. I used it all up. There is nothing left of me." His sadness nearly overwhelmed her. But with it was resignation as well.

"Your magic will come back." It had to. She knew he would never be complete without it.

"No. There is only so much a man can do. This night I used a lifetime of power. There is no more." His eyes closed. The blackness nearly swept over her, too.

"Jaylor!" she called. "Jaylor, come back." Her mind screamed for him, but he was hiding from the pain of loss as well as the pain the magic had ripped through his body.

"Brevelan." Darville stooped beside her. "Brevelan, it is important you hear what I have to say."

She looked up. Tears blurred her eyes. She blinked them back. There was time yet to think of Jaylor. He needed rest more than her healing touch.

"Yes, Your Grace, I'm listening." She had to remember now to address him as her prince and not her friend or her puppy.

"These men," he pointed to the richly dressed one who carried Mica and his equally resplendent companion, "have offered an alliance. They want me to marry their princess."

Her heart felt stabbed. Darville marry? It would be the end of their companionship, the end of the love that had sustained them through so many weeks of hardship. She clutched Jaylor's cold hand along with Darville's, reforging the bond.

"I told them I cannot. My heart is already committed to you."

She sagged with relief. Still she clung to them both, as she had since Jaylor had invaded her clearing.

"The Council is divided. To reunite them I think it wise for me to marry Lord Krej's oldest daughter." He didn't give her time to feel pain over that. "Though born out of wedlock, you are Krej's daughter. Royal blood runs strong through you. You have spoken with dragons, that is proof of your birth."

Jaylor's hand twitched in hers. His eyes opened and he stared directly into her soul. Mica hissed and leaped from the ambassador's arms and into her lap. Her purr spoke volumes.

Brevelan's decision was made. "I could never be your princess, Darville." A tremendous ache surround her heart. Though she loved him, they could not be together. "I can never live in a city, can never preside over a table filled with meat. The numbers of people your princess would need to see everyday would cripple me with their uncontrolled emotions."

She sought his eyes for understanding. He, too, was filled with the pain of the separation that must come. "I love you dearly, but Jaylor needs me, and I love him, too. You need someone stronger, better educated, lovelier than I."

"But it is you I love. You are more than just my princess, Brevelan. I need you, as much or more now than I did when you rescued a wounded wolf from a killer storm. Coronnan needs your sensitivity and compassion. Only you can guide me as I rule them," Darville argued.

"You need a woman bred to politics, educated and sophisticated, who can share your life in the capital. I cannot. Now if Master Baamin will order a litter, I will return to the monastery with Jaylor. He needs me." *But I love you. I love you both.*

"Jaylor, did you give the dragon the vial of medicine before she was enchanted?" Baamin asked urgently from directly behind Darville. There was no answer, only a few labored breaths.

Almost reverently the old magician removed his own blue cloak with white stars on the collar and spread it over Jaylor.

Brevelan continued to hold Darville's gaze with the love they no longer had the right to express.

"Master, is everything gonna be all right now that the dragons're gone?" A filthy boy tugged at Baamin's robes in anxious query.

Brevelan watched the urchin rather than be tempted by Darville's pleas.

"Yes, Yaakke. We will work to make everything right. We know our enemy; we can find a way to defeat him."

"What about him?" He pointed a grubby hand toward Jaylor. "Will he be all right, master?"

Brevelan longed to take the child and dunk him into the nearest bathing pool. But she didn't have the time or energy to spare. Jaylor continued to breathe by force of her will alone.

"The best healers in Coronnan will be summoned to make sure Jaylor gets well," Baamin reassured the boy. "But he has wielded a great deal of power this night at tremendous cost to himself. He needs time to rest and solitude to meditate."

"No other healers will be necessary, Master Baamin." Brevelan stood to face the senior magician and the gathered assembly. "As soon as we are both rested, I will take Jaylor back to the clearing. The clearing Nimbulan created to protect Myrilandel and their children and generations of dragon guardians who followed them. Jaylor and I must be there when the dragons come home."

Epilogue

*T*hey think they have defeated me. I still have a few surprises up my sleeve. They shall not deprive me of my treasures or of the power. The Tambootie has made me one with Simurgh. We will not be denied.

It will take a little time and much planning, but the fools will learn. Somewhere there is an antidote to witchbane. Perhaps I shall take a little retreat and find the answer in an ancient book dedicated to Simurgh. A book whose pages are pressed from the Tambootie. Then I shall start again. Maman will help, she is the high priestess of Simurgh.

I cannot allow another weakling to rule Coronnan. Only I can wield the power concealed within her depths.

Only I can have a glass dragon for a pet.

THE
PERFECT
PRINCESS

This book is dedicated to
Tim,
my almost perfect prince
of a husband.

And in memory of Trinket,
the Siamese kitten,
who wandered into our house one day
and graciously agreed
to share it with us for
the next twelve years.

Prologue

Four massive plow steeds nodded their long heads, almost asleep in their traces. Coils of steamy breath drifted from their nostrils in the predawn chill. An enclosed litter with plain black draperies was balanced across the four broad backs. The beasts shifted under the burden placed into the litter. Last evening's spring drizzle continued in fits and starts, and their giant, unshod hooves made little sound on the still damp courtyard paving stones.

From the exterior courtyard, the black stone walls of Castle Krej appeared wrapped in gloomy silence. 'Twas inside that the storm raged.

Senior Magician Baamin listened to the protracted arguments with his extended senses and shook his head dispiritedly. The old man gently tucked a warm blue cloak around the prostrate form sheltered within the litter. Only then did he try to say farewell to Jaylor, the only journeyman magician who had survived the quest to find an invisible dragon.

But at what cost? And for how long?

The hastily constructed litter swayed. Meager torchlight cast wavering, elongated shadows—like so many ghosts released by the magic Jaylor no longer possessed—around his once strong body.

"Go in peace, my boy," Baamin whispered. The young man lay unmoving, unresponsive. Only an occasional shallow breath indicated he still lived.

A tear touched Baamin's old eyes. "So much promise wasted on a single spell. But what a magnificent spell, my boy." He shuddered in memory of the massive amount of magic that had bounced around the Great Hall of Castle Krej a few candle-lengths ago.

"You have made me proud to name you magician. If I had ever had a son, I would hope he would be as strong and honorable as you."

A small hand touched his shoulder. Sympathy and understanding radiated from the slender young woman at his side. He marveled that she could spare so much emotion from her empathic contact with the young man who meant a great deal to both of them. But Brevelan had grown beyond empathy. She had the ability to mutate emotions, ailments, and thoughts and turn them to healing.

A rare creature out of legends.

Why was so much talent wasted on a woman who would never be allowed to enter the University for training?

"I will heal him." Brevelan wiped the tears from Baamin's eyes. His sadness lifted a little. Just a little.

She touched Jaylor's chest to make certain he still breathed. The faintest glimmer of coppery light passed from her hand into Jaylor's body. He stirred and groaned within his coma.

"If anyone can heal him, 'tis you." Baamin clutched his own shoulder where the witchwoman had touched him. Had that bizarre light passed into him as well? "Take him back to your mountain clearing where you can keep him safe. I'll send Yaakke with you. His boisterous spirits should keep you both from brooding, and his magic will keep you in contact with me at the University. I shall throw a summons your way at each full moon." Baamin signaled to his youngest apprentice to join them. Subdued for once, the dark-eyed adolescent moved between the heads of the lead steeds.

From the depths of his robes Baamin withdrew a large rectangle of precious glass, framed in gold. He tucked it into the blue cloak that covered Jaylor's shoulders. "Here's a master's glass, Jaylor, to go with the master's cloak. Tonight you have surpassed your quest and earned these symbols of your accomplishments. I doubt any other master magician in all our history could have worked that spell and survived."

The old man allowed his sad burdens to settle on his shoulder. He needed to go back to the Great Hall of the damaged castle. The irate lords, the confused young man who should be king, and treacherous royal relatives just might listen to Baamin's counsel. If they didn't, the kingdom of Coronnan seemed certain to splinter into rampaging chaos.

Before the magician could move toward the broad entryway, Prince Darville pelted down the steps from the keep, waving an arm above his head to keep the litter in place a few moments more. "Brevelan, wait!" he called.

Brevelan turned her wide blue eyes toward Baamin in near panic. "Help me make Darville understand," she pleaded.

"Don't go, Brevelan." Darville nearly skidded on the rain-slick paving. He came to an abrupt halt within a finger's length of the small woman with witch-red hair.

"I have to take Jaylor back to my clearing." She turned away from the prince, hiding her face.

Baamin stepped back one pace to observe them. Their love for each other was so obvious, touches of her coppery aura entwined with the prince's golden afterimage. Baamin ached for their necessary separation.

Women were a mystery the old man wasn't sure he wished to understand. Love and sex wasted too much energy. Energy that Baamin needed to devote to magic and diplomacy. He remembered, fleetingly, the one woman who had claimed his love. After one night together she had deserted him rather than spend her life as the lonely and forgotten mistress of a magician.

"The best healers in the kingdom, in the entire world, are trained at our University," Darville asserted. "Come back to the capital with me, Brevelan. We'll care for Jaylor together." The prince cupped her delicately-boned face in one of his large, warrior's hands.

"You have a kingdom to rule, Darville," Baamin reminded him. "Your Council is divided. Your cousin seeks to usurp your rightful throne by fair means or foul. You cannot spare the time or energy to heal your friend."

"I will heal Jaylor." Brevelan straightened to her full height, seeming to stretch upward and outward with power.

Baamin had never seen anything like it in a female. Where did the girl get the magic to give her that kind of an aura? *Stargods!* Women didn't have magic!

Correction, women didn't have traditional magic. Since Shayla, the last breeding female dragon and source of magic, had flown away, all that was left in Coronnan was the solitary magic thrown by rogues. Without limitations and controls, solitary magic had been outlawed in Coronnan hundreds of years ago.

"Please stay, Brevelan," Darville pleaded. His hands began to shake with the strength of his emotions. "I need you. I can't think straight without you. Your love was all that kept me from sinking permanently into the feral instincts of a wolf body. You have to stay with me." Darville's mane of blond hair glistened damply in the combined light of dawn and dying torches. His queue had come undone hours ago. His wild tangles added a sense of untamable vigor to the planes and angles of his too-thin face.

"You have the ability to heal yourself, Darville. Jaylor won't survive without me."

"Then come to the capital at least. I need you near me."

Baamin had never seen his prince so insecure, so vulnerable. Those moons of ensorcellment in the guise of a wolf had taken a heavy toll on Darville's mind as well as on his body. These were weaknesses the prince had best hide from the Council and Lord Krej. That greedy cousin wouldn't relinquish his regency powers easily.

"All the minds and emotions of the throngs that dwell in your city would kill me, Darville. You know that better than anyone. Let me go in peace. Please."

Darville's hand dropped to his side. His fist clenched tightly. A muscle in his jaw jumped. Then he bowed his head in acquiescence. "Go quickly, then. Before I lose my courage and command you back."

Baamin nodded to his apprentice, Yaakke. The boy tugged on the harness of the left leader steed. The litter swayed and lurched as the beasts began their plodding journey. Jaylor groaned from the depths of the blankets. Brevelan turned her back on Prince Darville as she reached a loving hand to soothe the ailing magician.

"I love you, Brevelan," Darville whispered.

"I love you both," she whispered back.

Neither of them seemed to notice Brevelan's cat, Mica, who crept from the shadows and parked herself on Darville's foot.

"Merrow," she begged for attention from the prince. He

didn't respond. "Merrower!" This time the cat rubbed her head insistently against Darville's leg.

Baamin stared at the creature, eyes wide with questions. He swore the cat had spoken out loud, first in reassurance, then in petulant tones.

Before he could puzzle out just how telepathic the cat was, the raging arguments inside the castle spilled into the courtyard. Twelve lords, their magician advisers, and their retainers aimed for the desolate prince. Darville picked up the cat and cradled her in his arms. He stroked her fur in rhythm with her calming purr.

"Your Grace." Lord Jonnias puffed out his round belly to emphasize his importance. "We will not countenance Lord Krej's arrest for treason without further proof of his misdeed."

"Further proof? He transformed me into a wolf with illegal rogue magic and left me for dead. Is that not enough?" Darville's upper lip lifted in a growling sneer.

"By your own testimony, you did not see your cousin, Darville. You said Lord Krej had fallen behind in the hunt. The foreign rogue who actually threw the spell was disguised as a naked man with the head of a spotted saber cat."

"A *red-haired* spotted saber cat," Baamin clarified. He'd seen the beast-headed man a few times himself. "Hair as red as Lord Krej's."

"I was never on that hunt, *Prince* Darville," Krej sneered the title. "I don't know who was masquerading with my face, but I was with my wife, attending the birth of my youngest daughter. No one, not even a rogue magician can be in two places at once."

"Jaylor saw Krej and his minions transporting Shayla, our beloved dragon, here. Our *last* dragon. We watched Krej ensorcell her into a glass sculpture." Darville ignored his cousin and advanced on the strutting Jonnias. The pompous little man withdrew two steps for every one his prince advanced.

"Excuse me, Your Grace, but we cannot accept as evidence what your friend saw while in a magic trance, nor what you saw while still ensorcelled yourself." Lord Andrall cleared his throat and looked at the paving stones rather than face his prince.

"Then why did we find that same glass sculpture here, in Krej's Great Hall?" Darville growled menacingly, teeth bared. In the uncertain light his nose seemed longer, his untrimmed beard took on the aspect of whiskers. And that mane of hair! Did any wolf in the wild with its ruff bristled look more dangerous than Darville at this moment?

The cat leaped from his arms and circled warily, clinging to the shadows.

"I'm sure there is a benign explanation." Jonnias couldn't resist inserting one more comment. "Lord Krej is renowned for his art collection and his generosity."

"Every last piece of sculpture in that collection was a living animal captured in stone or metal by magic," Baamin reminded them all. "How did you come by such unique pieces of art, Lord Krej?"

"At a great deal of expense, Master Baamin. Expense lost to a careless spell that released all of the animals, not just the dragon. And now my home has been extensively damaged in the bargain." He turned a malicious eye on the Senior Magician. "You really should train your journeymen better."

"You won't gain my sympathy with your sad tale, Krej," Darville growled at his cousin. "We lost the dragons because of you. Without the dragons we can't maintain the magic border. Rovers have already infiltrated. Our enemies are invading from the west, and you complain about some stones and mortar!"

All eyes turned toward the charred hole in the western wall of the keep. Awe struck them silent a moment as they recalled the vision of Shayla breaking free of her sculptured glass prison. 'Twas her fiery green breath that had blasted the great hole in the otherwise impregnable wall. 'Twas the all color/no color spines of her wings that had widened the opening for her to fly away from Coronnan forever.

"Without the dragons we don't have traditional magic. We don't have any defenses, and we don't have our king. When you ensorcelled Shayla, you killed my father!" Darville howled and launched his body across the space that separated him from the assembled lords. His hands encircled Krej's neck.

A torch fell and sputtered on the damp stones. Shadows rose and wavered. Colors and forms lost definition.

Feral snarls erupted from the prince's throat. He rolled on the ground with his victim, not releasing his stranglehold. Krej choked; his face grew red and mottled as his feet scrabbled on the wet ground for purchase.

Magical golden light haloed the combatants. Light that shone on the yellow fur of a huge wolf. Men screamed in primal fear.

Was Darville a man or a wolf? Baamin couldn't tell anymore.

"Release him, Darville," Baamin ordered, trying desperately to break through whatever mind haze held the prince. He fought his way to the center of the milling men, avoiding the flailing limbs and snapping teeth of attacker and defender.

A silvery-blue line of magic wandered beneath Baamin's feet. He anchored himself to the surging power and rolled a fistful of magic into a barrier between Darville's hands and Krej's vulnerable throat. He was about to throw the barrier when the golden light around Darville surged defensively toward the ball of magic.

"*Stargods!*" Baamin breathed shallowly through his teeth. "The boy's been infected with magic." Instead of throwing the magic, Baamin wrapped it around his hand, like an armored glove. He reached between the two men to separate them.

Darville jerked back and away from his touch as if burned. He lay on the ground, twitching. Spittle foamed at his mouth as his upper lip continued to curl back from elongated fangs.

"Get a healer," Lord Andrall called to a hovering retainer.

"No!" Baamin countermanded. "No magic must be thrown, even to heal." He knelt beside the now fully human young man. Anxiously, he drew all vestiges of magic back into himself. He held one hand over the prince's heaving chest. Red sparks bounced into Baamin's palm. Magic sparks. No natural fire on Coronnan burned any color but green.

"What's wrong? Why did he revert to his wolf form?" A cowering lord ventured to peer into Darville's pain-contorted face.

"Who threw the spell to transform him?" Jonnias looked

about nervously, as if expecting himself to be the next victim.

" 'Twas no new spell." Baamin continued his examination of the prince. "I've read of this. When a mundane is the victim of too much magic, his blood becomes infected. Like a disease. The emotional stresses of this night further weakened him. Exposure to any magic at all, even that of a healer, will only make it worse."

"Can it be cured?" Lord Andrall peered over Baamin's shoulder.

"In time."

"Can he rule?"

"When he is cured."

"What will we do until then? The king is dead. The prince is almost dead."

"We have a regent," Jonnias reminded them. "Lord Krej led us quite nicely for many moons during the boy's absence. He is an able general, as well as a diplomat. I don't see why he shouldn't continue. With the Council's guidance, of course."

"Krej is a rogue magician!" Baamin protested. "We wouldn't be in this mess without his treasonous manipulation of temporal and magical power."

"That has yet to be proved, Baamin," Krej choked a response, rubbing his injured throat. Bright finger marks were already bruising.

"A compromise?" Lord Andrall inserted himself between Baamin and Krej. "This witchbane drug you spoke of earlier. How effective is it?"

"The ancient sources claim it will neutralize a man's magic instantly. Given in the proper dosage, the effect lasts about eight days." A heavy dosage had been thrown at Krej at the beginning of the night's adventures. No wonder he hadn't armored himself against Darville's attack.

"Then, if Lord Krej agrees to take a dose of witchbane every week, he can't continue his magical plans, if he had any magic to begin with." Lord Andrall glared at each of the Council members present, daring them to contradict him.

Jonnias was the only one brave enough to question the man whose diplomatic skills had soothed many a problem in the Council of Provinces. "What if Lord Krej is falsely accused and is actually a mundane? The drug could kill an innocent man."

"Witchbane has no effect on mundanes," Baamin asserted. "And it causes only brief pain to magicians." He hated the thought of Krej being placed into power again. But what choice did they have? Until Darville shook off the effects of magic infection or Krej was proved guilty of treason, there was no other man of royal blood left in Coronnan.

And there were no more dragons to choose a new king.

Sadly, Baamin agreed to the compromise. His eyes turned once more to the ugly breach in the stone walls of the keep. "I have seen a dragon!" he whispered to the wind. "The last dragon anyone is likely to see for some time to come. I cannot guess how this kingdom will survive without a dragon. But I can live, or die, with no regrets, for I have seen a dragon!"

Chapter 1

*D*ragons have hunted my people for a millennium. Our existence is bane to them. For when the populace realizes the power we wield, they transfer worship from dragons to us. To the covens.

Only the perseverance of our Nine has protected us from the depredations of the greedy dragons. All of the other covens have passed into oblivion.

Now the dragons are gone. We should send out our tentacles of power unhindered. We need to found new covens and spread our dominion through the three kingdoms, and then the world.

But Maman has left us, passing from this plane of existence into a new dimension of power. The coven is bereft. Without her central focus, the eight-pointed star has stalled, will fragment. We will lose all that we gained when the dragons departed.

A new center for the star must be found among the remaining eight. I have the potential to ascend to the focus. But I must have more power to triumph over seven. Another seeks the same.

I have a plan. Even now my power expands into the other territory, if I can recruit the new ninth, then no one will dare contest my move to the focus.

The Princess Rossemikka is the key. The treaty between Rossemeyer and Coronnan is just the beginning. I will force my princess to marry Prince Darville in spite of my rival's interference and his attempts to claim her body.

A cold autumn wind rushed along the river from the Great Bay, warning of the rain squall to follow. The tall man lingering in the shadow of University Bridge retreated into the deep hood of his cloak, pleased to see that others in this busy marketplace also hid their faces. Except for his height and the breadth of his shoulders, he should blend into this black-clad crowd.

Since the war with SeLenicca began last spring, black had become the dominant color in Coronnan City. Not for fashion. Not for practicality or elegance. For mourning.

The man slouched purposefully. The curve of his back lessened his height and added the illusion of breadth. With luck, no one would notice anything unusual about him as he crossed the bridge to the University of Magicians.

One last time he checked the fringe of the market crowd for the ever-present Council guards. The fugitive had crossed and recrossed six bridges among the islands of the capital city. He had wandered and slunk through as many crowded squares to end his flight from the palace within sight of his starting place. Now he examined the market square on the little island nestled between the palace and the University for remnants of pursuit. The man-at-arms who had followed him from the gates of Palace Reveta Tristile should be thoroughly lost in the wynds and alleys of Coronnan City.

Three men with short swords on their belts stopped and hovered near the blacksmith's booth. None were the man who had followed him so diligently. But they watched the University Bridge as if they knew who would try to escape across it.

They had to capture the man before he traversed the bridge. Council guards and royal armies were not tolerated at the University of Magicians.

He needed a diversion.

"Meow?" A brindled brown cat stropped his ankles.

"Not now, Mica," he hissed at his pet. She was probably the most conspicuous cat in the entire capital. Her brown/black/gold/bronze fur was unique. Everyone in the kingdom knew where Mica belonged and the name of her master. So he'd left her behind. And now she had found him.

If only she could transform herself into the beautiful woman of his vision in the dragon lair five moons ago. Now that would be a diversion!

In his mind's eye he saw again the long-legged young

woman with multicolored hair flowing past her hips. She raised her arms in a glorious song of freedom. Her words whispered through his mind, haunting him with a poignant message he could almost understand. Then the magic had all gone awry and the woman had vanished back into the cat body. This same cat who followed him everywhere.

"Hey, you there!" One of the three guards advanced toward the bridge.

The man retreated farther into the shadows beside the arched supports, ducking his head so the folds of his cloak became a mask. He shifted his balance onto the balls of his feet, ready to run. Mica slunk away quietly.

Heavy boots splashed through a nearby puddle, spraying him with blobs of mud. A stripling lad with wispy hair and feet too big for his body ducked and dodged as he ran through the crowd, around the ancient Rover woman who read palms, past the bridge entrance, a loaf of bread barely hidden under his ragged shirt.

"Stop! In the name of the Council, stop where you stand!" Two guards followed the boy, a lot less careful of whom they pushed aside and how roughly. A fat baker waddled in their wake. The Rover woman stuck out her foot and tripped the baker.

The tall man peeked out from his hiding place. He hoped the boy escaped. Judging by his physical condition, he needed the bread more than the fat baker. Too many people in Coronnan needed bread they couldn't afford. The combination of war and crop failure was eating away at the kingdom's vitality. Conditions must have worsened if the boy risked theft practically beneath the palace walls.

A crashing splash brought shouts of anger and dismay. The escaping lad had pulled the linchpin on the far side of the bridge, collapsing the span into the rushing river with the two guards on it. Merchants and customers alike, but not the Rover woman, hurried to haul the Council's men out of the water.

The river wasn't deep right there, as the fugitive knew from experience. He didn't spare the men any remorse. They probably needed the bath. Two down, one to go. Then he could complete his mission in the University.

The one remaining guard shouted orders as he trudged toward the collapsed bridge, knocking over an awning that sheltered a pile of baskets in his clumsy frustration. Other patrons of the market, led by the ancient woman in Rover black with bright purple accents, howled and shoved each other. Confusion reigned.

Altogether, a typical day at the market.

No one barred the path anymore.

The tall man slipped silently onto the bridge. A tiny brindled brown cat clung to the shadows at his side.

The hair on the back of his neck prickled as if he were being watched. He checked over his shoulder. The movement dislodged the hood of his cloak. For one brief instant his face and head of distinctive blond hair were exposed to the feeble sunlight. Even though he'd restrained his mane in a fashionable queue, the bright color, combined with his height and the presence of the cat were dead giveaways to his identity. Hastily he adjusted the folds of thick oiled wool.

With renewed purpose, he took the last two steps toward the end of the bridge, confident of his safety and success now that he'd escaped the Council guards. The future lay in the information he must impart to Baamin, Senior Magician and Chief Adviser to the Crown.

"Excuse me, Your Grace." A heavy hand landed on the man's shoulder. "The Council requires your presence. Immediately. The flagship of Rossemeyer has been spotted at the head of the Great Bay."

"S'murgh it!" Prince Darville cursed. "Inform the Twelve Lords of the Council of Provinces that I must consult with my adviser before I can join them. The marriage treaty carried by the ambassador from Rossemeyer is too important for me to judge alone." He couldn't tell the guard his real excuse for seeking out the Senior Magician when he'd been forbidden contact with the University. That was too private, too essential.

"I'm sorry, sir. I was told to bring you back to the Council Chamber without delay and without any magicians." The soldier looked as if he wished to give in to his prince's demands, but was afraid to ignore the order the Council had given him.

"Then come with me while I consult with Lord Baamin. I will return with you to the Council shortly." Darville began to step off the bridge. The young guard couldn't be more than eighteen and was probably as green as the hills. He'd never question royal authority.

"Come with you . . . in there?" The man-at-arms stared in terror at the walls of the University. His jaw flapped in protest, but no words emerged. His feet remained firmly rooted where he stood on the bridge.

"Yes, in there. Where else am I to find the Senior Magician?" Darville had never understood the superstitious fear of magic that ran rampant among the populace. He'd grown up with a fledgling magician as his best friend. He'd fallen in love with a woman who wielded magic as easily as she sang a lullaby.

Pain stabbed his heart. The child Brevelan carried in her womb belonged to Jaylor, his best friend. She'd chosen the father of her child, ill and weak though he was, over the lawful ruler of the realm.

He pushed the pain of those thoughts away. He had to think of Coronnan and the future; not his private regrets.

"What is your name, young man? I'd like to be able to address my escort and bodyguard by name." Darville draped a comradely arm around the soldier's shoulders and headed for the open gate of the University.

"I'm called Fred, sir. But I need to warn you, Sir Holmes is leading a full squad of men to search for you." He hung back, resisting the friendship offered by his prince.

"I have no doubt that Sir Holmes will lead that squad on quite a wild lumbird chase. He's in on my plan to consult with Master Baamin." Darville dragged the boy off the bridge into the courtyard.

"Yes, sir." Fred stopped short at the entryway. "I can't go in there, sir." He touched head, heart, and both shoulders in approved *Stargod* ritual, warding against evil. Then, surreptitiously, he crossed his wrists and made a second, much older, flapping gesture.

"Come now, Fred. Master Baamin is a friend of mine, as well as a valuable and wise old man. He won't hurt you."

"But they're magicians, Your Grace! They'll steal your soul and eat your heart for dinner."

The boy's absolute horror both stunned and tickled Darville. Superstition was one thing. This dread was quite another. He needed to turn the boy's fears into a joke.

"I assure you, Fred, the magicians of Coronnan do not

steal souls and eat men's hearts. They are men themselves and oath-bound to serve all people." He fought back a smile.

Fred did not look reassured.

"Magicians are our healers. Our priests are magicians. We owe our communications and much of our defenses to the University. They deserve our respect and courtesy, an occasional virgin, and maybe the first fruits of the season, but not our souls. You wouldn't be a virgin by any chance, would you?"

"I'll wait here for you, sir." Fred tried to back up onto the bridge again. "I wouldn't go in there unless a dragon was chasing me, Your Grace."

"Then you are a virgin!" Darville teased.

Fred ignored that comment.

"Look, Fred, unless I go in there now, there aren't likely to be any dragons in Coronnan ever again."

Fred didn't say anything to that.

"If I had just one dragon to name me king, I could bring the seceding provinces back into the alliance. I'd end the divisions in Coronnan so we were no longer weak and vulnerable to the invasions from SeLenicca." Darville pinned Fred to the wall with his gaze. "My mission to Lord Baamin might very well bring back our dragons!" He had to impart some of the urgency of his quest to the boy.

"And I wouldn't have to make a marriage treaty with Rossemeyer, our former enemy, nor learn that princess' unpronounceable name," Darville added under his breath.

Mica circled and recircled their feet in a complicated pattern. A compulsion to walk through the gate *together* rose from her purring circles. Fred's eyes widened in fear. He searched around for an avenue of escape.

"Uh . . . sir, I don't think those guards coming toward us are going to let you through the gate of the University." Fred fingered the hilt of the sword that hung awkwardly at his hip.

"They won't cross the bridge," Darville reassured the boy.

"But the magicians behind them will." Color drained from Fred's face, leaving red splotches high on his cheeks.

"Simurgh take them all!" Darville cursed. All five of the magicians marching behind the rank of ten Council guards were assigned to the courts of lords loyal to Lord Krej.

Darville had no doubt any of those five master magicians

wouldn't hesitate to throw a spell that would make Darville seem to revert to his wolf form just because he was near the University gates.

Suddenly those gates seemed to shimmer and thrust him back toward the bridge. The magicians had armored the door against intrusion. He had to get out of here. Now.

"I think I know a way out, Your Grace." Fred made the feeble warding gesture again, then tugged on Darville's sleeve, indicating that he should come along.

Darville followed the young man's gaze. The University walls seemed to grow straight up from the river. No escape there. But across the courtyard lay a second bridge, one that led into the heart of the city. Darville scooped Mica into the inside pocket of his cloak and took off at a run, Fred close on his heels.

The heavily armed guards pounded after them while the five magicians remained in the courtyard, arms crossed, too proud to be seen running in pursuit of an errant prince.

At the far side of the bridge, Darville skidded to a halt. Fred slid down the last arched planks of the span and fetched up right beside him. One guard had made it as far as the bridge, the others were just a bit slower.

With a mighty yank, Darville pulled the linchpin of the bridge, just as the young thief had done earlier.

"Yoowll!" The guard on the bridge fought to cling to the railings. He scrambled for a purchase for his feet. They slipped again and again on the rain-dampened planks. He was sliding into the muddy, surging river, even as his fellows grasped his flailing arms to help him back up onto solid ground.

"Quick, down this alley before they go around and catch you, sir." Fred led the way between the backs of two sprawling workshops with overhanging dwellings above.

"You just got promoted to sergeant, Fred."

"Begging your pardon, sir, but you can't promote me. I'm a Council guard."

"Then I'm transferring you to the Palace guards as a sergeant." Darville dived behind a dustbin as heavy footsteps entered the narrow alley behind him.

"What are you going to pay me with? Most of the Palace guards are being paid by the Council and owe their loyalty there, instead of to you. Though they don't much like working for Lord Krej." Fred crawled over a wall into yet another alley; this one barely wide enough to admit them single file. The confines of the river islands didn't allow for much room between buildings.

"I still have some funds—rentes from the city—even though the lords are withholding their tithe to the king until I'm crowned." Darville stopped for breath and looked around. He hadn't been in this part of the city since he and Jaylor had been boys. "There's a path off to the left that will work us back toward Market Isle. We can get into the palace from there." He led the way.

"I've got a widowed mother and three sisters claiming my pay." Fred paused to make sure they weren't being followed.

"I said I'd pay you."

"Just making sure. I mean, what's a man to do when he's got family depending on him and the price of bread goes up every day? Some of the troops have wives and children to think of."

Silence lay heavy between the two men for a moment. "I'll accept the transfer," Fred offered. "Rather do honest work for you than spying for the Council anyway. Once they know for sure where their pay's comin' from, some others might follow me."

Darville wanted to laugh. He hadn't had this much fun since he was sixteen. Eluding his tutors and governors was a full-time occupation then. Circumventing the selfish ends of the Council seemed to be taking the place of those childish pranks.

Darville leaped over a pile of garbage with a lithe spring, reminiscent of his misspent youth. His landing was a little awkward and he growled a curse.

"Good. Don't be obvious about recruiting. The time might come when I'll need the element of surprise. As of this moment you are my personal bodyguard. Move your things into the alcove beside my apartment. Where I go, you go."

"Yes, sir." Fred snapped upright to full attention. "I promise to serve you faithfully to the exclusion of all others. Even if you turn back into a golden wolf and rip out my throat."

Chapter 2

"**P**rincess Rossemikka! What have you done?"

Rosie opened one eye and glared at her governess Janataea and the silent maid hovering in the doorway. Her vision rapidly shifted from clearly gray-toned to an onslaught of confusing colors. To mask her momentary disorientation, she concentrated on how her fingers flew through her thread game. The length of colored embroidery silk never tangled and knotted in her intricate pattern.

If only she could weave the threads through one more series of movements, she might understand how the circles of life and fate had brought her to this instant in time.

"Rosie, this . . . this is a disgrace," Janataea wailed.

Rosie didn't think so. She had taken the tangle of threads in Janataea's embroidery box and organized them. Just because she had chosen to arrange the skeins in a star pattern on the floor instead of in the box, it shouldn't bother her governess.

"You know what this is, don't you? This is an eight-pointed star, a cabalistic sign that is forbidden." Janataea's voice grew strident.

Rosie didn't know what made an eight-pointed star different from a five or six. She didn't know anything that hadn't occurred to her or been told to her in the past two years. Her life and memory were empty prior to that awful night of dust storm and rage.

Anger born of frustration tore at her reason. She wadded her cat's cradle into a mass and flung it in the general direction of Janataea.

Rosie's fingers arched and flexed. She stretched and

yawned, slowly and deliberately, as she turned her back on Janataea and the maid behind her.

"Rosie!"

Janataea's vexation couldn't touch Rosie.

She continued her vigil in the window seat where she preferred to sit out the lonely hours. A streak of autumn sunshine warmed the spot.

Janataea's hand stroked Rosie's hair, just behind her ears. The princess leaned into the caress.

"Hmmm." She shut her eyes. Almost. A narrow slit allowed her to continue to observe her governess.

"Come now, Rosie. I didn't mean to upset you." Janataea's fingers massaged the sensitive spots behind Rosie's ears. "Choose a dress so we can join your brother and your uncle at the court. Then there will be a nice banquet. With fish."

"I like fish." Rosie started to drift off into another nap. She hated making decisions. Janataea always chose her gowns for her, unless another servant was in the room. Then the elaborate protocol of the court demanded the governess defer to the princess. For the temptation of fish she just might accept the role assigned to her by a fate she couldn't comprehend. "Very well, the brown velvet with gold trim." Barely a decision. When forced, she always chose that gown.

"That gown suits you best of all. The golden brown is so like your own hair." The governess gave the bold white streak in Rosie's waist-length mane one last caress.

"A witch's mark," the castle servants whispered.

The story that flew through the castle like dust on the wind said that Rosie's Uncle Rumbellesth, regent of Rossemeyer, had locked her in a tower room as punishment for running away. That same night, Rosie's pet cat had turned up missing. Rosie had howled and screamed, torn her hands trying to claw her way to freedom, and driven the entire castle nearly mad with her violent protests.

Exhaustion had claimed her at dawn.

Everyone within the environs of the castle had walked cautiously and spoken in whispers for many hours. At last, Regent Rumbellesth had summoned his willful niece. She faced him in the grand audience chamber a changed woman, quiet and docile, with no memory of her life up to that moment.

The streak of white hair was a constant reminder of the emptiness that taunted her. Uncle Rumbellesth proclaimed that the once defiant princess had been branded as a result of exorcising her demons.

The whispers continued. Princess Rossemikka had been marked by a witch.

Rosie held her arms out from her sides so that Janataea and the nervous maid could clothe her. Not a word passed between them. Rosie rarely spoke unless directly addressed.

As the heavy cloth folded around her slim body, Rosie ran her hands down the soft nap of the velvet. Just like silky fur.

"Your uncle has requested that you sit at his left tonight. Please remember to use your knife and fork when you eat the fish," Janataea instructed her charge as she adjusted the high-waisted gown just under Rosie's firm breasts.

The bodice was barely wide enough to cover her nipples, but it was less revealing than most of the gowns worn by the women at court. In Rossemeyer the display of an ample bosom proclaimed a proud ability to bear and nurse children.

The skirt drifted from bust to floor in straight lines. Her hair was bound up and hidden beneath an intricate cap and snood of gold lacework from SeLenicca. No hint of a woman's hair or ankle could be revealed in Rossemeyer, lest they incite a man's lust.

The maid was dismissed before Rosie spoke again.

"Isn't Mama dining with us?" A stir of unease penetrated Rosie's mind. Verbal assaults were limited when the Queen Dowager joined the family at table. Otherwise, "Uncle Rumbelly" and Rosie's brother Rossemanuel argued continuously all night.

"Queen Sousyam is ill again. She hasn't been truly well since you demanded the impossible in exchange for your consent to marry Lord Jhorge."

"My uncle's son is a pimple-faced, squeaky-voiced, viper. His hands feel like snakes on my skin." Rosie practically hissed her dislike of her cousin.

"Then it's a good thing the boy withdrew his offer."

Janataea circled the princess three times, widdershins, as she inspected her grooming. Not once did her long skirt even brush the eight-pointed star on the floor.

"If Uncle Rumbelly has a new candidate for my hand, I won't sit at the banquet, even if I don't get any fish."

"I don't know what the Lord Regent has planned." Janataea clasped Rosie's hand in her own and led her from the luxurious suite.

"I can't go until I have washed my hands and face," Rosie said, drawing back.

"Very well, but hurry."

Half a candle-length later, Rosie paused behind the draperies covering the doorway to the family salon behind the banquet hall. She watched the quiet room for several moments before entering.

Rossemanuel sat at a narrow table. Sheaves of parchment littered every available surface. His hasty writing kept pushing a bottle of ink precariously close to the edge of the table.

He stopped writing a moment. A quill pen made from the long flight feathers of a Kahmsin eagle dangled from his fingers. The pen dripped ink onto the document in front of him.

"Rossemanuel, cease your endless writing. No one ever reads your reports anyway." Lord Rumbellesth's temper was at the growling stage. He'd quaffed at least three tankards of beta'arack. Distilled from the monster treacle beta, the liquor was one of two exports from Rossemeyer. Valiant mercenary regiments were the other.

Manuel looked up at his uncle, biting his lower lip in thought. Then his eyes glazed over and he returned to his writing.

The Lord Regent shrugged his sloping shoulders and poured himself another tankard. His distended belly marred the straight fall of wide pleats from shoulder to toe of his traditional, black sand-colored robes. The vast amount of fabric issued to clothe his otherwise spare frame was a symbol of his power and wealth. But none of those advantages could cure the growth that ate away at his innards. Only increasing doses of beta'arack could temporarily numb the pain, a little.

"Eavesdropping again, Princess?" Rumbellesth threw the

draperies aside so quickly the supporting rod nearly broke from its brackets.

Rosie narrowed her eyes to look more closely at her uncle's puffy skin and mottled red nose. His hair was thinning on top, streaked with gray where it fell to his collar in limp, greasy strands.

She wrinkled her nose in disgust at the Lord Regent's lack of fastidiousness. How did he tolerate all of that body dirt accumulating hour after hour, day after day? Even in a land noted for its lack of water, there were other ways of cleansing the body. Her feet began an unplanned retreat from the room.

"Don't go yet, Sis," Rossemanuel protested.

Rosie smiled at her favorite brother. He was younger than she by two years, but taller, with the same brindled brown hair and greenish-hazel eyes. She embraced the boy who was always gentle in his teasing. In less than a year he would achieve his sixteenth birthday and his anxiously awaited crown.

He would take control of Rossemeyer away from their increasingly erratic uncle.

As Manuel resumed his chair, Rosie moved the ink bottle to a more stable position and set the dripping quill into it. She automatically began straightening the parchments into neat piles.

"Leave your endless fussing while I address you," Rumbellesth roared.

Rosie's hands continued their work as she looked over her shoulder toward the regent. He sighed in exasperation.

"Your brother has convinced me to tell you privately, before the gathering of the court, that I have found you a husband." Uncle Rumbelly swilled another huge mouthful of his potent drink.

"Niow!" Rosie protested. Her fingers curled inward until her long nails dug into the table wood.

"Yes, Princess," her uncle sneered. " 'Tis your duty to marry. 'Tis my duty to provide you with a husband. And you will do us the courtesy of not rearranging the tableware before you consent to pick at your food."

"Tell me it isn't true, Manuel." She reached for her brother in desperation. "You know how strangers frighten me. They want to touch me, to trap me in a cage! They ask questions about. . . ." She reached a tentative finger to the streak of white hair above her right temple.

"Don't, Rosie. Don't frighten yourself. Prince Darville is not a cruel man. I met him once. A few years ago. We had a grand time hunting together. He has a marvelous sense of humor. You'll love him."

Rosie didn't think so.

"Think of Rossemeyer, Princess," Uncle Rumbelly advanced toward her, shaking a bony finger in her face. "We haven't had a decent war to bring in ready cash in many years. Prince Darville needs this alliance," Uncle Rumbelly boasted. "Coronnan is on the brink of civil war and our old enemy SeLenicca is massing for invasion to our west. This is a grand opportunity to strike a major blow at SeLenicca and reestablish our country as an empire."

"I won't do it, Uncle." Rosie stood straight and defiant, just as she was told she used to.

"You will or I'll have you burned as a witch. You and that spawn of Simurgh governess of yours. How about if your mother joins you on the pyre as well?"

War wasn't hell. It was piles and piles of detail work! Prince Darville suppressed a groan. Sir Holmes stood in the doorway clutching a bundle of rolled parchments larger than the ones carried by the last three clerks.

Moonlight glimmered through the diamond panes of the mullioned windows of the prince's tower room. Crenellated battlements neatly divided the silver orb in two. Almost time for Baamin to initiate a summons to Brevelan.

"Don't seem right to me." Fred lounged in the window-seat, cleaning his fingernails with a knifepoint. "Council's acting like a bunch of spoiled bullies. You slip through their guard once and they pass a law forbidding any contact between you and the University in general, Lord Baamin specifically," the new bodyguard grumbled.

Darville yanked the brown velvet restraint from his queue. Grateful for the release, he flipped his head back and forth, an indulgence he rarely allowed himself in the presence of others. Fred's fear of Darville's wolf persona nagged at the prince. And yet the young guard continued his faithful loyalty, in spite of his fears.

"The Council believes they are protecting His Grace,"

Sir Holmes corrected Fred. He knew his prince too well and didn't retreat from the feral mannerisms.

Sometimes Darville believed his enemies on the Council fostered the superstitious fear of his magic infection so they wouldn't have to relinquish any of the power they had gained. A healthy prince might demand to be crowned king.

"I've got to get back to the University tonight!" Darville pounded his desk with a clenched fist. A hand's breadth now lay between the bottom of the fat moon and the highest castle wall. Some things didn't wait for any man, prince or no.

"Do something with those reports, Holmes. Watch my back, Fred. I'm going to try slipping past the ogre across the hall." Darville reached for the sleeping cat who occupied the corner of his desk. His long fingers scratched her brown and gold head.

Mica twitched an ear, half opened one eye, and surveyed the prince. The eye appeared round at first, then shifted to the natural vertical slit of her species. She obviously thought her time would be better spent asleep. She allowed her heavy lid to close. Darville scratched the cat's ear again to encourage her to come completely awake. Mica returned her head to the nest of her paws and ignored him.

"That might not be wise tonight, sir." Holmes assumed a rigid pose between Darville and the doorway. "These documents are from the front. Lord Wendray's messenger must return before dawn. I fear SeLenicca is massing troops for another battle."

"Twenty minutes. All I need is twenty minutes with Master Baamin." The guard across the hall, who stood a head taller than Darville, wouldn't accept the excuse of the privy again so soon. Less than an hour had lapsed since the last time.

One of the sentries on the battlements stood beneath the glowing moon. His head and shoulders were outlined in silver. Darville could delay no longer.

"I'm sorry, Your Grace. The Council of Provinces insists they review your reply before it is sent." Holmes shifted his feet slightly. He now completely blocked Darville's exit.

Stargods! The Council was growing bolder. There had been a time when the Twelve consulted him on every move instead of troubling his ailing father. He had to reestablish that relationship and prove that the magic infection had left him completely before they would crown him king— the first among equals on the Council. Managing the mountains of detail work was only a part of his plan to appease the Council and prove his worth.

"How long will it take me to read those blasted reports." Nine of them in the bundle. An hour for each. Then another hour to formulate an answer. At that rate the reply wouldn't leave the castle until mid-morning. "I've just spent hours rewriting the treaty with Rossemeyer." Something his hovering staff seemed incapable of doing. "My mind is more tired than my body."

Darville stretched his back and rubbed his eyes. There was a trapdoor leading to a secret passage beneath the massive desk. If he asked for help in shifting the desk, the exit would no longer be secret. The time might come when he needed that advantage.

Holmes looked at the bundle he carried in both arms. His expression was bleak. "Lord Wendray thinks we need to convince Rossemeyer we do not need their troops. Such a show might prevent an invasion from Rossemeyer at a later time."

Darville groaned again. This time out loud. Wendray was right. Rossemeyer's ambassador was less and less careful to gloss over the questionable clauses of the treaty.

Mica roused from her nap. Without bothering to bathe her face, she wandered across the desk and butted her head against Darville's chin. *Delay no more. Baamin begins his summoning spell now.* Her message seemed as clear to him as the thoughts Brevelan conveyed directly into his mind when she was near.

"Summarize the reports for me. I'll be back within the hour." In one smooth movement, the prince rose and scooped the cat onto his shoulder. Fred assumed his post one pace behind and to Darville's right, giving the prince a clear field for his dominant left arm to wield a sword.

"Your Grace, these reports really are most important. Your marriage to Princess Rossemikka could be jeopardized by further losses on the western border," Holmes protested.

Mica chose that moment to dig her claws into Darville's padded tunic. He batted the offending paws. Lately she chose references to the impending marriage as a cue to sink her claws into his skin.

"Please, Your Grace, just a few moments to look at the most urgent report," Holmes pleaded.

Darville had waited too long already. Frustration and anger rose in him like a storm tide. His upper lip lifted in a feral snarl. The hair on the back of his neck seemed to stiffen and stand. "You are supposed to be on my side, Holmes." The power of the wolf fired his blood.

Holmes pressed his back against the massive wooden door. His mouth worked in silent protest while his eyes stared in unblinking fear. "With my head and heart and the strength of my shoulders, I renounce evil and magic." Holmes dropped the charts as he hastily crossed himself in the warding gesture of the Stargods.

Mica's claws dug deep into Darville's shoulder again, bringing him back to the current reality. He finger-combed his hair in an attempt to remove the wolf image. Holmes gulped and sidled back into the anteroom. Fred gasped and put two more paces between himself and the prince.

"Magic isn't evil," Darville announced to both of them. "But magicians can be corrupt and black of soul." Like his cousin, Lord Krej. "I will be back shortly."

"If you must, Your Grace." Holmes stooped to gather up the scattered rolls of parchment.

Darville sighed. He'd offended and frightened valuable men.

"No, Your Grace. You may not keep your appointment with Baamin." A new voice from the doorway caused Darville to pause. Mica hissed at the newcomer, brown fur stiff, back arched.

"Lord Marnak, by what authority do you interfere with your lawful ruler?" Darville assumed his most haughty posture. Mica hissed again.

"For your own protection, the Council insists on monitoring your movements. We cannot afford any further magical contamination of the royal family." Lord Marnak the Younger bowed slightly but remained firmly in place, blocking Darville's exit.

Fred's hand shifted to the hilt of his sword. Darville gestured for him to keep the weapon sheathed.

"The order from the Council is to soothe their own

superstitious fears rather than for my protection," Darville asserted, even as he took a step toward Marnak. This sniveling weakling was one of four, nongoverning lords hastily appointed to fill the vacant seats left by seceding provinces.

The elaborate interdependency of the twelve provinces, with the monarch as the key, had been set up three hundred years ago to prevent secession and civil war. Now those relationships were breaking apart, and Marnak owed his elevated position at court to the Council and not to his prince.

"Perhaps the order came from your father-in-law, Lord Krej, and not from the Council as a whole." Darville pressed on, testing the slighter man's desire for a fight.

A look of unease came into Marnak's eyes. His gaze shifted to the side, to the floor, anywhere but directly at Darville.

"What's the matter, Marnak? Afraid to think for yourself?" Darville saw the punch coming and ducked under it. A swift jab with his elbow into Marnak's kidneys sent the young lord sprawling on the floor. Now Darville could honestly say he'd escaped Council supervision to avoid an attack by a member of that august body.

The prince launched himself into a sprint for cover. Fred closed and barred the door behind him.

Darville's soft, indoor shoes whispered across the stone paving with little traction. Behind him, he heard the heavy footfalls of pursuit. The ogre hadn't wasted any time. He knew who issued his weekly pay—the Council and not the denuded treasury of the crown.

Darville dove into an unlit corridor and hugged the shadows. Senses stretched, he paused to catch his breath. Not for the first time he longed for the sharp hearing and keen night vision he had enjoyed when trapped in a wolf's body.

"Nothing down this hallway, Corporal," Fred spoke with determined authority to the following ogre. "His Grace must have gone down the east corridor."

Darville blessed his new friend's quick thinking. But he couldn't count on further help. Until the conspiracy to crown the prince grew beyond a few guards loyal to more than their salary and Sir Holmes, he'd have to resort to subterfuge to move about as he needed.

He eased down the corridor, counting his steps. His legs

were longer than they had been the last time he sought the hidden doorway. He adjusted his stride to match the paces of a gangling thirteen-year-old. His fingertips memorized the bumps and crevices of the bare stone wall.

Forty-seven steps. He caressed an imperfection in the mortar. Under pressure the imperfection grew into a crack just as three men turned into his corridor. More pressure yielded the loud scrape of stone on stone. The crack still wasn't wide enough to admit his adult body.

"S'murgh it!" he cursed. With renewed determination he pushed harder on the stone wall. The barrier shifted slightly. Dust and bits of broken stone cascaded onto his head.

Chapter 3

Brevelan's eyes opened within her trance. She searched the confines of her hut, seeking the ripple that had disturbed her concentration. Jaylor lay in exhausted sleep upon their wide cot. Yaakke, Baamin's apprentice and her link to the University, sat across the open hearth from her, also in trance. All seemed normal, as normal as could be without the presence of Darville and Mica.

The magic that normally lay hidden deep within her soul rested near the surface of her reality, as Baamin had taught her. In this condition she was ready for the summons that had come through Jaylor's glass every full moon since last spring.

Thus attuned, she sensed the harmonic vibrations of all magic within her sphere of power, including Jaylor's unused staff that was currently barring the door to the hut. Perhaps it was Yaakke's lack of control over his own trance that had disturbed her.

In time, with training, she would be able to initiate her own summons, at any phase of the moon. Yaakke could throw the spell sometimes, when he bothered to concentrate and the moon was full to aid him. Jaylor could talk her through the procedure, when he wanted.

Since his ordeal last spring, when he'd lost his magic and damaged his heart in the process, he avoided all mention of magic. His staff was losing its potency from lack of use. The once twisted and plaited grain of the wood was gradually straightening, except at the two places where Brevelan had spliced the wood, much as she would a broken bone. Those two joins were as strong and twisted as ever.

Brevelan's eyes focused and then blurred. Tangible real-

ity faded in and out. One moment she could see the outlines of each familiar person and object clearly. The next
those details faded and shimmered with auras.

Since childhood, she had been reading the colored layers
of light surrounding all living things without knowing it.
Jaylor's colors were red and blue, the same signature colors
as his magic, radiating out from his reclining body in tight
layers. The layers were deeper and the colors truer now
than they had been five moons ago. His heart was healing,
but not enough to support the great magic that had ripped
through it.

Yaakke's aura splashed around him in every bright hue
the human eye could fathom. The untamed blobs of color
shifted and changed with each breath until they filled whatever space surrounded the boy.

Brevelan had no idea what colors she emitted. The gift
of seeing one's own aura was very rare.

The glass in her hand thrummed with life. Light flashed
from the fire through the glass. Baamin's face, old and wrinkled, aging almost before her eyes, followed the burst of
green and yellow. The rope of entwined colors, so similar to
the Senior Magician's aura, looped around Brevelan and
Yaakke, binding them into the spell. Then it circled the room,
armoring it against eavesdroppers. Yet it avoided the recumbent form on the bed and a dark corner near the
roof tree.

Was Jaylor setting up unconscious armor against involvement in Baamin's magic?

Brevelan hadn't time to consider.

"Has Shayla made contact with you, Brevelan?" Baamin
asked without preamble.

"Nothing specific, just a general awareness of her life."
Brevelan sighed with regret. The loss of her dragon friend
had left her lonelier than she had expected.

"Darville has been trying to contact me for three days.
Every time the Council and their magicians have stopped
him. I fear his message has something to do with the
dragon." Baamin shook his head in dismay. "Jaylor must
return to assist me. The master magicians have diverted
their loyalty from the Commune and Coronnan to their
individual lords. The Council of Provinces ended yesterday's session fragmented. Krej's faction has forbidden all

contact between palace and University. The Council, as a whole, can decide nothing."

"My husband is not well enough to travel." Brevelan couldn't take Jaylor out of the protective clearing. Not yet. Not while his spirit ailed and his body still mended.

"I could send him to the capital," Yaakke announced brightly.

"How, son?" Baamin's face looked puzzled.

"With a blink of the eye, sir. Same way I bring meat from the University kitchens." His adolescent face colored. "Ooops, sorry, Brevelan."

She frowned at the boy. He knew very well she never allowed meat within the boundary of her clearing. She felt the death of all living creatures. Sometimes the physical pain was so great her magic closed down for several hours, or even days.

"No, no, 'tis too dangerous to transport a living person, Boy . . . I mean Yaakke. No one has ever accomplished such a feat and had his charge live through it," Baamin intervened.

Brevelan sensed his alarm and nearly rejoiced in it. As long as Baamin was hesitant, Yaakke would not risk such a transport.

She hoped.

"If I sent a litter and steeds, could Jaylor travel?" Baamin seemed desperate.

The ripple in Brevelan's concentration returned. She had the acute sensation that someone was listening, someone who had no right.

"Jaylor can barely walk the length and breadth of the clearing. He could not survive the journey," she protested fiercely. Yaakke looked at her strangely. They both knew that Jaylor was stronger than she indicated. She returned the boy's look with a glare, praying he would not reveal her prevarication.

"What do you need Jaylor for?" Yaakke asked instead.

Brevelan breathed a sigh of relief. "Perhaps Yaakke could return to you."

"I need Jaylor. Only he knows enough of this rogue magic to ferret out the true loyalties of both the Council and the Commune. Without the controls of dragon magic, every member of the Commune is a law unto himself. I have no power or authority over them anymore," Baamin's voice faded into a mere whisper. "Twice this week I have intervened in magic duels. Last week a lord was severely wounded by the magician of a rival lord. This must stop. I need help."

Brevelan grieved with him for the loss of a unified Commune and Council. Without Shayla—or any dragon— Darville could not be consecrated king. A unanimous Council could authorize a coronation. That was an unlikely event, considering Lord Krej's rival ambitions.

Brevelan again searched the place in her heart where Shayla should be, as she fruitlessly did, many times each day. The invisible dragon lived. The faintest of glimmers brightened Brevelan's being. But she didn't know where Shayla laired and she couldn't discover if the eleven dragonets had whelped yet.

The black vacant spot near the roof tree of the hut spread outward and down. There was a presence within that blackness. A presence that Baamin's magic should have armored them against.

The child within Brevelan's womb kicked in recognition of that presence. Alarm spread through her veins. Her heart pounded in her ears. She began to hum. Her song lifted to the roof tree, cleansing the hut of alien minds. Her soul lifted with the song, rising out of her body. It spread upward, outward, until she filled the clearing. Her mind sniffed for the intruder. It was gone.

Below, her baby cried out. Its unformed mind sought wildly for the comfort of her ever-present thoughts. The cries stopped abruptly. Comforted by someone else? Jaylor perhaps?

Brevelan sent a tendril of copper-colored magic backward to tether herself to her own body and the baby. When her empathic contact with her child was once more firmly established, she allowed her soul to rise higher, above the trees. She sang a spell to reinforce the boundaries of her home. Her inner vision sought farther, up the mountainside to Shayla's empty lair, down the course of the creek to the village, outward to the nearby border of Coronnan.

Nothing.

Whatever had disturbed her was gone, fled before an identity could be recognized by any but the baby.

* * *

I have them now. I have found the new ninth. A twist here and a lie there and she will be made to see the truth of Simurgh.

Old Baamin wants Jaylor in the capital. I want Brevelan in the capital. But not yet. Not until I have everything in place and the coven is ripe to accede to my power.

If only I had time for the baby to grow into his true calling. But I will have to make do with the mother. She can be manipulated and controlled through the baby.

Darville fumbled along a small ledge just inside the tunnel as the door swung closed on its pivot. No light penetrated the stone walls to relieve the subterranean blackness. There should be a bit of fire stone and a candle hidden here from his last exploration of this ancient and forgotten escape hole.

Gone! What did he expect in eleven years time, that no one else in the entire *s'murghing* castle knew of his childhood playground?

"I'll have to take the chance of traversing the passage in the dark," he muttered under his breath. He'd done it before, on a dare from Jaylor, twice landing on his face from hurrying too fast over the paving stones. Unseen ghosts and mindless evil had pursued him in imagination then. He was older now and knew that ghosts had no power, and evil was always channeled by a mind. He took a deep breath for courage and stepped forward.

He felt for breaks in the stone paving with his soft-soled shoes. Running his fingers along the wall, he pushed himself deeper into the blackness, following a gradual curve downward. Over and over he reminded himself that the starbursts of light before his eyes were mere illusions. There was no light, no other life in the tunnel.

Something furry brushed his leg. He leaped aside, his pulse racing.

"Meow?"

"Mica! How did you get in here?"

"Miower," the cat replied. Moving a pace ahead, she spoke again.

Darville stepped closer to her. "Make sure you stay out from underfoot, Mica, and we'll get through this together."

"Meow." *Of course.*

Very quickly the narrow passage opened into a larger one. The light here seemed more gray than black. They had reached the primary tunnel where it ran below the river bedrock, connecting castle and University. A torch glowed at each end.

Darville headed for the University end at a run. He was probably too late to join Baamin in his summons, but he might be able to pass a message along to Brevelan at the tail end of the communication. If anyone could save Shayla, Brevelan could.

After many moons of silence, the dragon had reawakened her ties to the last member of the royal family in a desperate plea. Darville hadn't just dreamed Shayla's distress. He'd lived it with her.

One more bend and the corridors of the University should be in view. Darville picked up speed. Mica scampered behind him at a slightly slower pace.

Footsteps. There were footsteps behind him. The Council's guards must have used the main access to this passage off the wine cellar. Darville didn't pause long enough to listen to his pursuers.

He looked ahead. The light was brighter, his goal nearly in sight. He focused on the single torch reflecting off iron bars.

Iron bars meant the gate was closed.

What gate? There hadn't been a gate there when the tunnel was reopened last summer. He slid to a halt, his fists grasping the solid iron shafts. He shook the barrier in his frustration. A wolflike howl of rage rose in his throat.

So close. He'd come so close to speaking to Brevelan. The dragons would remain lost for a while longer.

"There is to be no further contact between you and the University, Cousin." The oily voice of Lord Krej pulled Darville back to his senses.

"Do you fear Lord Baamin so much you can't allow him to advise me, as the Senior Magician has always advised the monarch of Coronnan?"

"You aren't the monarch yet. And 'tis the Council of Provinces which has given the order," Krej said calmly. "To protect you from a recurrence of your illness." He dangled a long brass key tauntingly from his fingers.

"At your insistence." Darville eyed his cousin's companions rather than the key. Weak and sniveling, Marnak was no threat; the man-at-arms beside him might be. Both sported long blades on their belts.

Where was Fred?

"You have bought the Council, allied them to you by threat and by marriages to your daughters, Krej. The rest you have subverted with your rogue powers." Darville inched his dagger out of its sheath.

"Your fanciful tales of my participation in your ordeal with magic are just more evidence of your mental unfitness." Krej moved to pocket the key.

"Niow," Mica protested as she launched herself toward Krej, claws extended, murder in her eyes. The regent raised his crossed arms to protect his face from her wicked claws and gnashing teeth. A fiery glow surrounded the cat, sealing her to her prey with magical armor.

Darville didn't wait for a formal engagement of blades. With a quick twist of his wrist, his ceremonial dagger sent Marnak's longer blade flying. He swung around to face the man-at-arms. In the same motion he kicked backward into the young lord's gut.

The guard glanced quickly toward Krej for permission to engage his prince in battle. But the regent was occupied with one very angry cat and a magic that isolated them from mundane interference.

"Never take your eyes off your opponent," Darville reminded the guard as he slipped under the lowered tip of the sword. The narrow blade of Darville's knife nicked the man's throat. The sword clattered to the stone floor in surrender.

"Forget the *s'murghing* prince, you fool," Krej choked as the glowing armor broke down and he flung the cat free of his arms. "You're supposed to be protecting me!"

Mica scampered away, the bright brass key dangling from her mouth.

"Another time, Lord Krej," Darville barely saluted his cousin. "We'll have this out, another time, I promise. Right now I have an appointment."

Mica presented him with her trophy. The lock was new and well oiled, it opened at just a touch of the key. Darville kicked the gate shut behind him and hastily relocked it. Then he pelted down the corridor to the main tower with all the speed his athletic legs could muster, the key safely in his pocket.

"Magic!" Marnak grunted as he clutched his belly and tried to stand. "The prince worked magic, Father."

"Nonsense. 'Twas the cat's magic. The cat was a witch's familiar before she adopted Darville. Now she works her evil ways on him. We must separate them."

Krej's words made Darville pause on the first step. Would his cousin and once trusted ally really deprive him of Mica, his only friend? He couldn't afford the time to think about that now.

The moon was just reaching the height of its nightlong arc when Darville burst into the Senior Magician's private sanctuary.

"Prince Darville, talk to her, please. They must come to the capital." Baamin pleaded as Darville barged into the tower room.

"Brevelan?" He looked carefully at the piece of glass held upright in a special gold frame. All he could see was the stack of books on the other side, their titles magnified by the glass. "Is she there."

"She was a moment ago." Baamin peered closer. "Yaakke, where is Brevelan?" Anxiety tinged the old man's voice. "She shouldn't be able to leave the spell until I release her."

There was a moment of silence while Baamin cocked his head as if listening. Darville couldn't hear anything. He started pacing the room. "Tell her that Shayla is in a cave with lots of water around and she's hurt. I think it's a wing. She can't fly. She needs us!"

Baamin passed the message to whoever was on the other side of that glass.

Mica nosed open the door. Her purr filled Darville's heart while Baamin consulted the glass again, now speaking, now listening. Darville scooped up the insistent cat.

Instead of letting her perch on his shoulder, he cradled her warm body against his chest. Stroking her silky fur soothed him. He fell into the rhythm of her rumbling music. His eyes glazed, and he lost focus.

The face and voice of Brevelan appeared clearly in the glass.

"Break the summons, Baamin. We have been observed."
Lines of worry folded around her eyes.

Darville's heart swelled with joy and pain at the sight of
her. He loved her so much! She could have been the perfect
princess for him.

But no, Brevelan had chosen Jaylor. She had her reasons.
He knew them, understood them. Deep inside he wept for
the loss of her.

Mica's purr stopped. The image of Brevelan disappeared
as quickly as it had come. The cat butted her head against
Darville's chin seeking the same comfort he did.

"Brevelan, who has the power to invade this spell?" Baamin asked.

There was no answer.

Baamin whirled to confront Darville. "Did Krej take the
witchbane this week?"

"I watched him swallow it yesterday," the prince affirmed. Lord Krej went along with the treatment in his
usual half-joking manner. He had convinced all but a few
skeptics on the Council and Darville that he, Krej, was the
victim of the prince's malice rather than the perpetrator of
dire magical plans against the kingdom.

"There is no antidote to witchbane and no one else in
this kingdom has exhibited enough power to invade one of
my spells." Baamin scratched his chin in thought.

"Could Krej have hired a foreign rogue?"

"If so, we must find him before he corrupts or masters
us all."

Chapter 4

Janataea's voice roused Princess Rossemikka from her
nap. "The time has come, Princess. You must put on
your cloak and go down to the ship."

Rosie picked up her ball of thread and began to untangle
her last cat's cradle.

"Come, Rosie," Janataea coaxed.

Rosie unwound herself from her curled sleeping position,
still puzzling the knot in the center of her work. She should
resist Janataea's orders. There was something wrong with
the command. One look at the older woman's eyes dimmed
her flicker of perception. Compelled by an overwhelming
need to obey Janataea, Rosie dismounted the seat with a
small jump.

The deeply rooted compulsion sent her to stand one pace
in front of her governess. One pace. No more. No less.

Janataea draped a cloak of oiled wool over Rosie's shoulders, then lifted the girl's thick braid to the outside. The
governess' hands were soothing as they stroked the plait
smooth and coiled it into a concealing head covering. Rosie
leaned into the caress. "Hmmm." Her throat vibrated
with pleasure.

Outside the castle, a fresh breeze touched Rosie's face.
She lifted her head and sniffed the bright morning air. Salt.
The wind was coming from the sea. A storm would crash
upon the shores of Rossemeyer's protective cliffs by sunset.
The two river valleys would receive the blessed rain. On
the high plateaus where everyone lived, nobles and peasants alike, the wind would howl and fling sand with punishing force.

Little if any rain would relieve the dry desert air. But

the people of Rossemeyer would huddle within their dwellings and wait for the storm to pass.

Every ship in the harbor would be well out to sea by the time the storm ripped into the harbor with murderous waves. Rosie would be on one of those ships.

"I don't want to go," Rosie protested Janataea's guiding hand. She turned and tried to slip through the governess' grasp.

"Of course you want to go, Your Highness. You sail to meet your new husband." Janataea was insistent.

"I have no need of a husband. Men frighten me. I won't go."

"You will or we'll both be burned as witches. You heard your uncle. Think about me if not yourself, Princess Rossemikka," Janataea hissed with anger. "Think about your mother!"

Rosie blinked at her governess. "Why isn't my mother here to see me off?" Rosie ignored Janataea's words and tried to slip past her again. She twisted her body into impossible thinness. But her governess was used to her ways.

"Queen Sousyam is not well. You know she has not been herself since the night your cat disappeared and you lost your memory." Janataea made it sound as if Mama's health was Rosie's fault. "You must not disturb her rest."

This time Janataea's grip on Rosie's arm almost lifted her from the ground. She was propelled forward with a force Rosie couldn't comprehend.

An honor guard of heavily armed warriors awaited them at the gate to the outer courtyard.

Rosie narrowed her eyes against the sunlight, blinking to adjust her vision from the darkness of the castle. The first lord in line offered Rosie his arm to escort her outside. Rosie pulled away from him with a spitting hiss. Only Janataea and Manuel were allowed to touch her. She would delight in a hug from Mama. But Queen Sousyam never tried.

"Be polite, Your Highness," Janataea corrected her. "Lord Aahmend-Rosse has earned the right, by his prowess on the field of battle, to escort you aboard."

Rosie obeyed the compulsion of her governess' voice, shuddering only slightly under the man's touch.

"Rossemikka!" Manuel called out from the doorway. His pounding footsteps followed rapidly.

Rosie resisted the tug of Aahmend-Rosse's arm and turned to receive a hug from her brother.

"I hate it that you have to sacrifice yourself like this, Sis," Manuel panted. "But there is no other way. Uncle Rumbelly has mismanaged everything. I'll be able to claim my crown in another six moons. You can come home to visit then, often and for however long you want to stay." He clasped his sister tightly.

She accepted his touch where others repelled her. Manuel alone had fought to help her regain many of the memories she had lost.

"Prince Darville is vulnerable," Janataea hissed. "You must marry him before he has a chance to organize his forces and confirm loyalties. His dragons might come back at any time. You must marry him before he has the opportunity to close his borders again with dragon magic. For the good of Rossemeyer, we must leave now."

"You're right that the Prince of Coronnan needs us. But he might lose his civil war, even with our troops. You could be in grave danger, Rosie. I want you to be very careful and come home at the first hint of trouble." Manuel clung to Rosie with a fierce possessiveness.

"You are not yet King of Rossemeyer and cannot offer sanctuary to your sister once she's married," a gruffer male voice reminded them.

"Uncle Rumbelly," Manuel hissed. His inflection made the name a curse.

"I am still regent and I decree that once married she will be a foreign queen and no longer welcome on our soil." Their guardian staggered into the courtyard.

Rosie couldn't tell if he stumbled from pain or from drink. How did Rumbellesth, with his sloth and illness, command the respect and loyalty of the disciplined warriors who stood guard on the castle walls? Rossemeyer, by tradition, produced only whipcord lean, strong, and fierce survivors. War and conquest were everything in their desert culture. Yet still Rumbellesth governed.

Hypocrisy ruled everywhere. Rosie expected her betrothed to be the same. Repulsion rose in her throat. She clung to Manuel and the safety of the familiar.

"The tide will not wait." Janataea urged her charge forward.

Rosie's hand lingered in her brother's. She continued to look at him with fond regret, even as she was led to the docks and the ship that would carry her to her destiny.

Brevelan paced the boundaries of her clearing, following the path of the sun, as she did every morning and every evening. The child within her stirred uneasily. He had been restless, upsetting her stomach since she had returned her consciousness to her body last night. Her baby didn't like being left alone. How would he react when the time came for him to separate from her body at birth?

She strode faster, working her way through the trees surrounding her clearing. The baby moved in agreement with her increased pace. She was seeking the path of last night's intruder. He was seeking . . . seeking what? Whom?

Someone, other than herself, had been in communication with the unborn child while she had vacated her body last night. But who?

"Brevelan," Jaylor called to her from the garden. "Where are you, Brevelan?" He seemed to enjoy grubbing about in the dirt since his magic had deserted him. The work had brought his heart almost back to normal—for a mundane. But a magician needed more.

Brevelan was happy for the help, but concerned that gardening was Jaylor's only exercise, mental or physical. Perhaps if he started throwing a few small spells, his heart would completely heal and his magic would return in full.

He had been such a big and vital man last spring. Now he seemed almost shrunken, weak of will as well as of body. There was a time when she had feared him, and wished him reduced in size and dominance. Watching his feeble attempts to regain his health tore at her heart.

She wasn't sure he was quite as helpless as he seemed. Daily, his aura increased in vitality and size. Perhaps he had heard his child's silent questing for her last night and reached out with his mind and his magic to soothe the baby.

A warm spot in her heart began to glow. If Jaylor was reaching out to the baby, then his path to healing had just become easier. More than that, she wanted the bond between father and son to be strong, even before birth.

"Coming, love." She closed her eyes and shifted the clearing around her so she emerged from the wooded boundary right beside her husband. "Now what is it you need so desperately?" She smiled at him with new contentment.

Jaylor looked startled to see her so close. He hid his face as he bent to apply his shovel to a good-sized tuber plant. "Should I dig all of these roots now and place them in storage, or just enough for today?"

"Don't hide from my magic, Jaylor." Brevelan reached a hand to lift his chin. He jerked away, as if afraid to look in her eyes. " 'Twas you who taught me not to fear magic. 'Twas you who gave me the freedom of mind to use my magic as it was intended to be used. To protect me and mine."

"I can't . . . you wouldn't understand." Lately, most of their conversations ended this way.

"You forget what I am, Jaylor. Your pain is my pain, your loss is mine. I know what you feel as no one else can. And so does our son."

Finally he raised his head to look at her. "You've given me more than any man had a right to ask of you. Without you I'd be dead now. Sometimes I almost wish you had let me die. I'm not fully a man without my magic."

"You are my husband, the father of my child. Isn't that enough?"

"I haven't been much of a husband since the wedding—for which I was barely conscious, if I remember it at all. And don't forget the possibility that I am not the child's father. There were three of us in that bed when I awoke from the Tambootie overdose."

"It matters not whose seed started this baby. You will be his father. You will shape his life and teach him to be a man."

"How, when I'm not truly a man?"

"Aren't you?" A glint of mischief sparkled through Brevelan. "Yaakke has gone to the village. He won't be back for hours. We are alone, as we haven't been alone since you . . . since you took ill." She reached for his hand and kissed his palm. The child within her didn't stir in recognition of the contact.

She pressed the shaking hand next to her cheek. Something tight within her unfolded. Just this brief touch flooded her being with light and joy. She stepped closer to feel the warmth of his body. He smelled of sunshine, of rich loam, and clean sweat from hard, honest work.

Jaylor didn't draw away. "There was a time I could read your thoughts without trying," he said wistfully.

"You are reading them now." His hand had turned to cup her face with tenderness. Her tongue darted out to touch his palm intimately. "Come back to the hut."

"No. I've spent too much time in that bed these last five moons. I want you out here in the fresh air, with the scent of newly turned soil and everblue sap on the breeze, with the warmth of the sun on our bare backs."

"There's a lovely bed of moss and a shelter of calubra ferns down by the bathing pool."

He dropped the shovel and followed her.

A weapon. I have a weapon to keep my rival in his proper place within the eight-pointed star. The meek little princess brings a dowry of ten thousand troops. They won't allow my rival any temporal power. He will resist and drain himself of magic in the process.

Maman's death was premature. We had no time to plan for her passing. She named no successor.

Didn't she know we would fight to move into her place? Yes, she knew. She made certain we would fight. Only the strongest will succeed. That is what she intended, for the strongest to become the focus.

I am the strongest. The dragons will never return once I am at the center of the star.

"Before you execute my timid little cat," Darville stated evenly, glowering at each of the twelve lords in the circular room, "define the word witch." Only Krej held his glance. All of the others looked away in embarrassment.

Darville was confident they wouldn't find his purring friend where she hid beneath his chair. The gentle rumble erupting from her throat was so low, only he could hear it. After the scene in the University tunnel last night, he was certain that Mica was singing an invisibility spell.

Hers wasn't the only spell in the room. A master magician sat behind and slightly to the right of each lord, except Darville. Some of them, at least, were probably throwing armoring spells around themselves and their lords. Why did they feel they needed the protection? They were all working toward the same end. Weren't they?

"Your Grace." Lord Andrall cleared his throat. "I was always taught that a magician throws magic for the good of the country, and a witch spins magic for her own personal interests and no other."

"The way I saw the incident Lord Krej has described to you, if there was any magic worked, it was done on my behalf." Darville speared Lord Krej with his gaze. "That means my cat is a magician and not a witch. Judgment of her actions is therefore subject to the Commune and not the Council." Darville stood to dismiss the meeting. He wasn't yet allowed to sit on the empty dragon throne or wear the Coraurlia, the glass dragon crown that sat in the center of the round table, but he meant to reestablish the same dignity and authority granted to the king.

Before the war with SeLenicca, leather armchairs and rich stained glass lent an aura of calm dignity to the room. Now the strain evident on the men's faces and their tense posture dominated the atmosphere. Conducting a war without one clear leader, while governing a country facing famine, was taking its toll on all of them. No decision was ever allowed to stand without endless modifications.

Four of the twelve provinces had already withdrawn from Coronnan and sided with the enemy SeLennica because of the lack of leadership. Apparently, King Simeon's flirtation with magic seemed safer than living with a fragmented governing Council.

Stargods! He'd wasted enough time with his infection and dithering over details. He had to cut through the selfish arguing of these men. Appeasement never accomplished anything.

"Your Grace?" Lord Andrall requested his attention in a tone of voice so meek it seemed an apology. "We seek to protect you. Your ordeal last winter placed a great strain on all of us. When we hear reports of your . . . ah . . . strange behavior," his glance slid to Marnak, "well, Your Highness, we fear that association with any magic will cause you to revert."

Darville stared at his longtime champion. Andrall and his province of Nunio had always, always, been loyal to Darville's family; they were related on the distaff line. The lord of the northernmost province refused to meet his glance.

"Baamin has stated time and time again that my blood is clean of magic. The only way I can revert now is if a spell is deliberately thrown for that purpose. The Senior Magician could also protect me from such a spell, if he were allowed his lawful place in this Council as my adviser."

"But he is a magician, Your Grace, out to protect his own kind. Of course he will say what he thinks we want to hear rather than the truth," Jonnias parroted a longstanding justification.

"Or perhaps you want me to be vulnerable to such a spell from your own magicians." Darville leaned forward as if to accuse Jonnias of such heinous behavior. "A rogue who I believe sits among us and commands the loyalty of some of you when it rightfully belongs to me, could also cause me to revert. Is that what you want?"

"Never!" Jonnias sat back, puffing out his fat belly and turning up his nose at such an accusation.

"Why not banish Lord Krej from the Council and leave me and mine alone?" Darville lifted a casual eyebrow. Only the most rigid self-control kept his voice normal.

"Lord Krej has been punished enough without proof that he is indeed the rogue magician of your imagining," Marnak the Younger defended his father-in-law. Marnak the Elder remained silently neutral.

"How has Lord Krej been punished? He is still Lord of Faciar. He still sits in this Council. He ordered *my* paymaster to withhold funds from my troops, then when he paid them again, half the drageen owed to them, he told them the coins came from his pocket and they owed him their loyalty, when in truth the money came from my treasury. He commands armies who are more interested in fighting me than our enemies. Tell me how he has been punished for changing me into a wolf and depriving Coronnan of her best protection—the dragon nimbus." Darville looked each lord and magician in the eye. *"Tell me!"*

"Lord Krej is forced to take the witchbane," someone whispered.

Darville growled his disagreement in very human tones. He deliberately kept his teeth covered. Still, eleven men reared back in their chairs, anxious to put as much space between themselves and his supposed wolf temperament as possible. He caught a glimpse of a snide smile on the face of the twelfth man, Lord Krej.

"This is why we must separate you from all contact with magic, Prince Darville." Lord Krej's contempt for him was clearly visible to all now. "You'll never be allowed to wear the Coraurlia while you lack control of your beastly instincts."

" 'Tis proximity to you, the cause of my 'beastly instincts,' that makes me lose control, Krej."

"Then perhaps I should withdraw to Faciar and run the war from there with my true followers," Krej challenged. "Many trust my proven leadership over your untried royal blood, in spite of your accusations of rogue magic, and no matter the source of their pay." The expression on his face appeared suitably humble for the benefit of the Council.

"You won't escape the witchbane so easily, Krej. Nor will you divide the Council further. You will remain in Coronnan City where you can be watched. Just stay out of my way and out of my personal life." Darville stalked to the door of the chamber.

"A king has no personal life," Krej called after him. "And the malevolence of your pet is the concern of the Council and of all of your citizens."

"Then I demand the presence of Senior Magician Baamin to root out the souce of truly malevolent magic as well as treason. Neither of which come from my cat."

"Impossible, Your Grace," Jonnias half-rose from his chair. "We can't risk magic contamination."

"If proximity to a magician is the source of your fears, why haven't you banished your own magicians? Have any of you considered that possibility? Well, I have. Sergeant!" he called to Fred. "Have the magicians removed from Council. They are all barred from this chamber until further notice."

Twelve men-at-arms marched into the room, each carrying a vial of witchbane. Twelve magicians left in a huff, gathering their formal robes close against them, lest they be contaminated by their mundane lords. Lords shouted and raised their fists. Chairs overturned. Chaos reigned. But only Darville pounded on the table with the hilt of his dagger. "Enough!" he shouted. "This session of Council is dissolved."

Lord Krej continued to smile and narrow his eyes, as if he knew that Darville had fallen into a trap of his own making.

Chapter 5

From her perch on the first spar above the deck, Rosie
watched the pod of mandelphs sporting in the wake of
the ship. A ray of sunshine caressed her cheek. The summer
was waning toward autumn. Her eyes drooped at the
loss of the sun's heat.

"Your Highness, would you do me the honor of returning
to the deck?" Kevin-Rosse, the ambassador to Coronnan
looked up to her chosen seat and swallowed
nervously.

A flicker of memory from somewhere hinted that Kevin-
Rosse was afraid of heights. Good. Perhaps he'd leave her
alone. As the entire crew and entourage were supposed to.
Janataea had declared Rosie's solitude inviolate.

Rosie turned her attention back to her current elaborate
cat's cradle where it lay nearly forgotten in her lap.

The ambassador apparently overcame his fears and
stepped up on a crate next to the mast to bring him closer
to her height. Rosie edged farther out on the spar.

"Please, Your Highness, I need to talk to you."

Rosie looked up and contemplated the crow's nest.
Kevin-Rosse's gaze lurched upward in the same direction.
He paled visibly and came no closer. Rosie didn't want to
talk to Kevin-Rosse. His words always left her feeling guilty
and uncomfortable.

"I'll talk to her, you bumbling idiot!" Janataea nearly
pushed Kevin-Rosse off the crate. She gestured for a gawking
sailor to pile up more crates to form a crude staircase.
Then, holding onto the mast with one hand and the ambassador's
shoulder with the other, she proceeded to climb to
Rosie's perch.

Rosie glared at Janataea only briefly before peering upward again. Unfortunately, her governess was between her and the mast, the easiest way up.

"Tell me what secrets cloud your eyes, Princess?" Janataea retrieved a hairbrush from her pocket and indicated she would gladly brush Rosie's hair.

"Why do those fish follow the ship? They seem to want to play with us." Rosie continued looking at the fish rather than at Janataea. If she looked at her governess, she would have to reveal every thought in her head.

"Legend claims the Stargods banished the priests of the old religion to the sea." Janataea settled into a sitting position next to Rosie. She waved the brush tauntingly. "The mandelphs are the descendants of the workers of old magic, trying desperately to return to the land so they may worship their god properly. They seek to play with us to lure us into allowing them to climb aboard."

"A sad legend." Rosie wanted to ask why the priests and their magic had been banished. She didn't dare. That would lead Janataea to probe deeper into her thoughts.

Janataea sucked in her breath. "Speak to me, Princess, or I will throw this brush into the sea."

Rosie ignored her. She loved to have her hair brushed. But right now, keeping her thoughts her own, no matter how trivial, seemed more important.

"You have allowed your hair to escape your snood. 'Tis indecent. Speak to me of your thoughts or I will leave you to the not-so-gentle attentions of every man on board this ship!" Janataea stood up, perfectly balanced on the spar. She seemed larger, more dominant than usual.

Rosie shrank back to avoid the coming compulsion to obey. "I am told that in Coronnan the women cover their breasts, but allow their hair to fall free," she excused herself.

"And they are a dying race because the women cannot nurse their children when they need to. False modesty is beneath you, Princess. Cover your hair and tell me what troubles your mind." Janataea spun a new spell with the lilting cadence of her words. Her pale blond hair was caught demurely beneath a silver head covering, almost the same color as the locks it restrained. Her breasts were full and round, spilling above the deep neckline of her gown.

In Rossemeyer, Janataea was considered the ultimate in feminine grace and beauty.

Rosie dropped her eyes to her own chest. She was eighteen, fully matured, and her breasts were small and pointed, barely feminine at all. Maybe Prince Darville wouldn't like her lack of endowments. Then she could return to the safe familiarity of her window seat in the castle.

But no, Darville needed Rossemeyer's armies. He would marry Rosie, whether he liked her or not.

Rosie felt herself weakening under Janataea's will. She looked to the land that was looming off to her right. The closer they came to Coronnan, the stronger she felt. She was soon to be the wife of the Prince of Coronnan. One day she would be queen. Keeping her thoughts private seemed imperative.

Janataea's words grew into a song, weaving around Rosie with insidious tendrils of will-sapping lethargy.

"Tell me your thoughts. Tell me what instructions the ambassador gave you. Tell me how you will ensure Rossemeyer's domination over your new country."

"I am to seek out the one who defies my husband," Rosie found herself reciting in a monotone. "I am to kill him because he will ally with SeLenicca."

"Krej!" Janataea hissed in alarm. "The Lord Regent believes King Simeon of SeLenicca will honor such a treaty. More fool he," she muttered almost to herself.

"Then I am to poison the leader of the magicians. The Commune of Magicians must never again be allowed to advise my husband against Rossemeyer."

"Oh, my," Janataea giggled. "Marvelous idea. I wonder why I didn't think of that? Hee, hee," she tittered in growing laughter. "Such wonderful fun to bring old Baamin to his just deserts. Krej has been trying to do that for years without success. But you and I will succeed. Won't we, my little princess? First we will make him grovel. Hee hee, ho, haw haw!"

To Rosie's dismay, her dignified governess laughed long and loud. She laughed so hard she had to grasp the mast for support. Her breasts escaped the confines Of her gown entirely, bouncing with the rhythm of her laughter. The riotous sound of her laughter rose to the peaks of the mountains on their left. It swelled and spilled across the waves to the distant blur of land on the right. It filled Rosie's head with growing unease.

One for the table. Six for the root cellar. Jaylor drove his shovel deep into the ground, seeking yet another yampion plant. The blade bit into the dirt and held.

Sweat ran in rivulets from his back and brow. The sun was hot for this late in the year. Perhaps the good weather would hold until all of Coronnan's harvest was in.

Stargods, but they needed a good harvest after a winter of unrelenting rain that rotted stored foods and bred new diseases, followed by the incredibly cold spring and wet summer. Many villages would barely have enough food to last through the coming winter as it was.

He drove the shovel deeper. A shiver of something . . . something powerful and special rippled up the handle of the shovel. Jaylor stopped his toil and waited for his heart to miss a beat. His pulse skittered in recognition of the rippling energy. He had hit a line of magic power, a ley line according to an ancient tome he'd read last spring. If his magic was gone, he shouldn't feel the tingle all the way to his hair.

On the distant wind, a peal of laughter echoed around the mountains. Jaylor raised his head to listen. It was a sound that didn't belong there. Out of long habit he squinted his eyes to focus on the silvery-blue line of power gripping his shovel. He shifted his body until he was comfortable drawing the magic into himself through the twisted wooden handle of the shovel. A thought and a word channeled the magic to ears and eyes.

Aided by magic, his FarSight extended through the forest, over the hills and beyond the horizon. An easy spell that cost only concentration and maybe a headache and temporarily blurred vision afterward.

A ship was sailing through the Great Bay below him. A foreign ship. Two women perched on a spar. One of them was laughing uncontrollably.

Then Jaylor remembered that he no longer had any magic, nor would his heart support the massive power surges through his body. He had used up a lifetime of magic, and then some, in his massive spell to break Shayla free from

Krej's prison of glass. His awareness of the ship and the laughter vanished.

But he had just worked an elemental spell. His body tingled with excitement and a niggle of power. His heart continued to beat strong and steady.

His magic was returning!

Carefully, oh so carefully, he visualized the silvery-blue ley line again. Nothing.

He shifted his body and squinted the way he had learned to find magic.

Nothing.

Disappointment flooded through him. Just like his apprentice days when he had been the last to learn the techniques of gathering magic.

But this wasn't dragon magic, and he wasn't gathering it. He was drawing on primary powers comprised of the four elements—kardia, air, fire, and water.

The line had been directly beneath his feet a moment ago. It should still be there. Power didn't move, only man's perception of it shifted.

He tried again. Slowly, carefully he gripped the shovel as he would his staff.

A glimmer of power tingled in his feet, rose to his knees, hovered there. He routed the energy upward, avoiding his vulnerable heart.

Brevelan's voice raised in song across the clearing. The power rose in his body as her voice ascended in pitch.

S'murgh it! The magic responded to his wife's song but not to his talent. Jaylor damped his attempt to find the magic. He didn't want to do it if he had to be helped.

Then he looked at the shovel again. Really looked at it. The familiar handle had been replaced with his cast-off staff. He examined the spiral grain. It was straighter now than last time he'd looked at it.

He recreated in his mind the day, not yet a year gone by, when he had cut this staff from an oak tree where mistletoe grew thick. . . .

He ran his hands along the straight limb he trimmed from the tallest oak tree on Sacred Isle. Its rough bark fell away from his knife. The tip of the branch broke off precisely where he wanted. When he handled this primary tool of a magician he felt taller, more competent.

Until he returned to the student wing of the University.

The other journeymen, all younger than Jaylor and possessed of their staves for many moons, taunted him with his inept choice. "Only Jaylor the bumbler would pick a straight staff," claimed Robinar, the acknowledged leader.

"Don't you know that a magician's staff is supposed to be twisted and gnarled?" the youngest of the journeymen reminded him.

"A magician's staff is an extension of his personality. A straight staff means a boring magician with no skill," chimed in another young man.

Jaylor allowed their words to roll over him. His anger simmered just below the surface. He'd never been very adept at magic. But he knew he'd cut the right staff. This piece of wood fitted him. It felt *right* in his hands.

Tomorrow they would all separate. Their master's quests would take them to the twelve provinces of Coronnan. Just once, just this once, Jaylor needed to prove himself in their eyes.

He planted the staff in front of him and gripped it tightly as he closed his eyes. With a deep breath, he dropped into the lightest of trances. In his mind he was in the wine cellar, a place none of them had ever visited but each knew intimately through magic.

First one cup, then another and another filled with the richest of wines. Seven cups for seven journeymen.

His fellow students stopped laughing when they found themselves balancing the brimming cups. And not the rough pottery mugs reserved for students. These were Baamin's own glass cups. Precious glass reserved for only the highest ranking officials in Coronnan.

"Laugh at me again when you can perform such a spell!" Jaylor raised his cup in toast. "To seven new master magicians."

His companions raised their cups in silence, their eyes fixed upon Jaylor's staff.

The once straight grain of the wood had begun to twist. . . .

By the end of Jaylor's quest, the staff had become more plaited and gnarled than any of the staves carried by his class of journeymen. Each spell he threw had shaped the tool to become a true reflection of the character of his magic.

Jaylor was the only one of the seven to live long enough to achieve master status. Krej had seen to that.

Now he was so weak, his wife had to lend him magic for the simplest of spells. Why bother trying?

Chapter 6

"**H**ere, kitty, kitty, kitty," Darville coaxed. He rubbed his fingers together as if he held a tidbit. His back bent into a very undignified crouch on the docks.

"Your Grace, surely you can assume a less . . . ah . . . um . . . a straighter pose while awaiting the ceremonial barge. What if your new bride should see you with your bum in the air?" Sir Holmes moved to stand between Darville and the crowd that lingered on the dock with them.

"The barge will sail when the Guild of Bay Pilots decrees and not one heartbeat sooner," Darville grunted. "Come, Mica. Come, my pretty kitty."

"Niow." Mica turned her back on Darville and scooted farther under the jumble of dockside cables and crates. She made it clear that she wanted nothing to do with barges and docks or anything that touched the unpredictable tides and mudflats of the Great Bay.

"Come, Mica!" This time Darville tried a direct command. Mica pressed herself farther into her hiding place.

"Your Grace, we don't have time to wait on the whims of your cat," Sir Holmes reminded him of his duties. "The ambassador is already displeased that the Princess Royale must enter Coronnan by way of Syllim Island like any other immigrant. We can't afford to be late. Such an insult could negate the treaty before it is ratified."

"Tell that to the *s'murghing* pilots. They hold the key to the maze of currents." Darville straightened from his doubled-over position and dusted off his knees. "Mica probably isn't a very good sailor. She can meet the princess later. What is the girl's name again? Something unpronounceable."

"Rossemikka. Ross-eh-mick-a, sir. All of the royales carry the honorific 'Rosse' as part of their name. Officials of the government add it to the end of their names when they take office. I'm told by the ambassador's valet that the family calls her Rosie."

"Rosie, huh? Are there roses in the bouquet I'm to present her?" Darville adjusted his gold brocade tunic to fit smoothly over his chest and shoulders. The *s'murghing* court garment hadn't been designed for crouching and stretching to grab an errant cat.

"I believe most of the flowers on the ceremonial barge are roses, Your Grace." Sir Holmes sighed and looked longingly back to the palace. "Or magic simulations thereof. The long wet winter and spring destroyed a goodly number of plants."

"The bad weather destroyed more than roses. What are the latest figures on the harvest?"

"I didn't bring them with me, sir. I thought it impolite for us to conduct business during this all-important meeting." Holmes assumed his most officious pose. He wasn't very convincing.

"Not looking forward to the hours of speeches and polite entertainment, Holmes?"

The aide shook his head. "I'd rather be on the front lines of battle, sir. Life at court is too complicated for my tastes."

"I've had to sit through this sort of thing with a smile plastered on my face all my life."

"Your Grace." Holmes looked around him to make sure there were no eavesdroppers. His face turned red. "Rumor has it that the women of Rossemeyer cover their hair and their ankles, but not their breasts! Sir, how does one keep from staring?"

Darville smiled at the image of the half-naked women of Rossemeyer. His entire body smiled at remembered pleasures he hadn't thought much about since his illness. Since Brevelan.

His smile faded.

"I imagine that once you get used to something, the forbidden is enticing and the revealed becomes unexciting. As for the dreary entertainment, my tutor in court protocol suggested I imagine every person in the room, except myself, stark naked. No padding. No disguises. How much prancing and posturing do you imagine the esteemed members of our Council would do in such a situation?"

Just then Lord Jonnias strode past them. His richly brocaded, wine-colored tunic and knee-length trews couldn't conceal his scrawny neck above his very round paunch and his sticklike legs below. For this excursion no one wore the cumbersome floor-length robes that were *de rigueur* at court.

"Pompous busybody."

Darville wasn't sure if Holmes had actually whispered that comment or if they had both thought it at the same moment.

"Sir Holmes, there is a faded white rose in the spray decorating the gangway. How dare you use anything less than a perfect flower for our new princess!" Jonnias fumed.

"Imagine a featherless lumbird squawking for attention," Darville whispered. "Think of that while the officials drone on with speech after speech that says nothing but how important the speaker thinks he is. You'll have no problem keeping a smile on your face." He slapped his aide on the back.

"If you say so, sir." Holmes made a mighty effort to appear somber, as he jumped to correct the flowers in the offending spray. "But I don't think I'll ever get used to seeing a woman's naked breasts in public."

"I doubt I will either," Darville mused as he again remembered past pleasures.

At last the Admiral of the Guild of Bay Pilots emerged from within the hangings of the ceremonial barge.

"Your Grace, my lords. We will sail in three minutes," he intoned, then disappeared again.

"We'd best board the barge, Holmes. Cousin Krej is looking murderous."

"Does he ever look less than murderous?" Holmes quipped, still unable to control his giggles.

"Not since his wife moved to the capital to be closer to him. Any guesses about the name of the mistress he dismissed to make room for Lady Rhodia in his wing of the palace?"

Holmes smiled and nodded knowingly. "Chances are she left the capital as soon as Lady Rhodia's baggage train was sighted. I wouldn't want to be the victim of that lady's temper tantrums," Holmes whispered behind his hand.

The last time Krej's wife had caught the lord with another woman, Lady Rhodia had nearly destroyed their apartments within the palace. Early in their marriage she'd earned the nickname Rhomerra, the legendary harpy messenger of Simurgh, the evil winged god of ancient times.

Darville scanned the crowd of nobles and officials gathered for this august occasion. "Where is Senior Magician Baamin?"

"Um . . . he . . . um was not invited, Your Grace."

Darville's mood darkened. He should have known the Council would interfere with his specific request for his adviser to be present.

"There will be no magicians on the barge, cousin." Unseen, Krej had come up behind Darville. "Out of respect for Rossemeyer, where magic has no place at court, the Council of Provinces has asked all of the Commune to withdraw from the festivities."

The Lord of Faciar appeared as regal as any king today, his glowing-green and deep-red tunic was rich with gold embroidery that highlighted his ruddy hair and fair complexion. He stood nearly as tall as Darville, as broad across the shoulders, but thicker in the hips and thighs. Not yet forty, Krej was in his prime. A powerful lord and warrior, able administrator and leader.

"If no magicians are allowed, then you must excuse yourself, Lord Krej." Darville glared at his cousin.

"You dare insult me!"

"I seek to eliminate your hypocrisy!"

The royal rivals continued to glare at each other.

"Your Grace, my lord, the time has come to depart," Sir Holmes reminded them in embarrassed tones.

Darville breathed a sigh of mixed relief and trepidation. Which was worse, sparring with Krej, the endless waiting, or actually having to meet the Perfect Princess from Rossemeyer?

A brightly uniformed captain released the boarding ramp. His scarlet tunic stretched tightly across shoulders broadened by a youth spent at the oars of the barges that plied the mysterious currents of Coronnan River. The

representative of the Guild of Bay Pilots graciously allowed
the royal party aboard his vessel. Even a king could not
board a vessel without such an invitation.

The Bay Pilots were proud of their duties, ranking themselves with the magicians in keeping the kingdom safe from
invasion. No one else dared navigate the random changes
of the river channels through the mudflats to the bay
proper.

Darville placed one foot on the ramp, only to discover his
cousin already there. "A bit presumptuous, Krej. I believe I
am the ranking royal in this farce today." Darville assumed
his mask of bored sarcasm. Otherwise he might just shove
his ceremonial dagger deep into Krej's ribs.

"A position you do not deserve. I am regent. I should
be first aboard."

"Correction. You were regent when you thought you had
safely confined me in the body of a wolf. I am restored
now, body and mind, through no action or wish of yours."
Darville glared with mistrust and dislike.

Stargods! Why did he allow Krej to goad him into hot
replies that did nothing to improve his relations with the
Council?

Angry with life and himself, Darville shouldered Krej
aside and mounted the ramp. He kept his spine stiff and
unyielding, his chin high, and his emotions deeply buried.

Rosie watched the bright yellow banners of the Coron-
nian royal barge as the vessel followed a zigzag approach to
the island. She clung to the safety of a deck chair beneath a
canopy on her own ship. Janataea sat beside her, cooling
her smiling face with a lace fan.

The island wasn't the forbidding chunk of rock Rosie
had been led to believe, but a series of smaller islands connected by massive bridges. Nearly as large as a sizable
town, the outpost of Coronnan supported a bustling population atop those bridges. Jetties trained the river currents
between the lesser islands so that the rest of the shore built
up silted mudflats nearly a mile wide.

One large stone building dominated the inside curve of
the half-moon group of islands. All travelers and cargo
must pass through that building to gain access to Coronnan.

Only Coronnite barges plied the shallow channels between the island and the capital city.

" 'Tis an insult, Highness. They deliberately keep us waiting to make us appear vulnerable." Ambassador Kevin-Rosse paced the deck beside Rosie's seat in growing fury. The planes of his gaunt face appeared sharper than usual, his cheeks more pinched, and his thin mouth was pressed so tightly together it appeared nearly lipless.

"Not surprising, since Rossemeyer has pushed the marriage and the treaty from the beginning. We stand to gain as much as Coronnan from the alliance," Janataea reminded the tall man. She had sobered since her laughing fit this morning, but a strange flippancy lingered in the governess' manner.

Rosie watched both of her guardians closely, trying to determine her own attitude from theirs. She didn't mind waiting, as long as the sunshine slipped beneath her sheltering awning. The warmth was more intense here in the lowlands north of Rossemeyer, the winter was slower in coming. She liked that idea. Cold darkness only made her sleepy.

"I give them five minutes. Then we withdraw!" Kevin-Rosse stalked over to the captain of the ship.

Good. Then Rosie could return to her familiar home and safe routine. She wouldn't have to allow strangers—a strange husband in particular—to touch her, force her to make conversation, demand things of her.

"Withdraw now and Darville will make peace with SeLenicca!" Janataea screamed at the ambassador's back. Panic flushed the woman's face.

"Why do you fear such an alliance, Janataea?" Rosie asked. Her governess was wise and learned. But this was the first time she had exhibited any passion for politics.

"SeLenicca cannot be trusted. Time and again they have sought to conquer Rossemeyer. When that fails, they resort to assassination of our royals. Your own father fell victim to one of their poisoned arrows. Some believe it best to maintain a balance rather than have any one kingdom dominate the other two. 'Tis best for Rossemeyer to keep SeLenicca weak and isolated."

"We hate SeLenicca, but we are not at war. Why?"

Rosie wasn't sure where the questions came from. Usually she was curious about *things,* like the shape of the shadow behind the wardrobe, never *ideas.* The breeze blowing in from the shore seemed to carry the question.

Kevin-Rosse's glowering presence cut off an answer. "Never utter those treasonous ideas of balance and peace, woman," he hissed at Janataea. His long body bent nearly double to bring his face within inches of the governess'. "SeLenicca must never be allowed to gain enough strength to threaten us again." Bright red splotches appeared on his cheeks and his breathing became harsh and uneven.

"We're lucky our ancient enemy has no unwed princess to offer Darville." Janataea baited the ambassador. "He might prefer alliance with them." Janataea's wide-eyed innocence didn't seem to appease Kevin-Rosse.

"Silence, woman. Remember your place. You are not noble and your position in Princess Rossemikka's household is tenuous. I cannot foresee the future Queen of Coronnan clinging to her childhood governess." Kevin-Rosse stood to his full height, straightening the wide pleats of his brocaded robe. Once more he was in command of all that lay within his field of sight.

"Don't count on it, Lord Ambassador. I shall retain my position of authority long after I see you dead."

"Your Highness, the barge appears to be docking. We must meet your groom." Kevin-Rosse bowed low to Rosie, offering his arm in escort.

Rosie pressed as far away from him as her deck chair would allow. A hiss of warning gathered behind her teeth. "I don't want to."

"Rosie, behave!" Janataea sounded exasperated.

Rosie looked at her hands clasped in her lap. She had to obey. But she didn't have to let that man touch her.

Gingerly, she stretched her body upward on the side of the chair opposite the ambassador. His arm was still presented for her convenience. She ignored it while she smoothed her gown. "I must wash my hands and face."

"She's absolutely lovely, Your Grace," Sir Holmes breathed into Darville's ear.

Across the wide expanse of the customs building, Darville watched his bride and her entourage disembark from the huge ship. Lovely wasn't grand enough to describe the girl. She was a vision, his vision, of the most beautiful woman in the world. The naked woman he had seen in Shayla's cave must have been a dragon-dream of portent. For the first time he looked upon this arranged marriage as something personally desirable.

"Rossemikka," Darville whispered. The air seemed to shimmer around her hair, covered in a golden net, and her iridescent gown. As promised, the neckline of her gown dipped deep into her cleavage. The heart-shaped curve of the bodice just barely circled the tips of her breasts, promising a wider view should she make any sudden movements.

Perhaps this was the dragon-dream and his earlier vision the reality.

"Give her the flowers, sir." Holmes prodded Darville's back.

"Your Highness." Darville bowed low in awe. Close up, he could see the rippling gold in her brown hair beneath the lace veil, the same color as his cat, Mica. He didn't care that the white streak across her temple separated her from his dream vision of her.

Boldly, he held out the fragrant bouquet. He retained his hold on the stems long enough for his fingers to seek her delicate hand as he transferred his token. The girl jerked her hand away from any contact with him. She buried her face in the flowers and refused to look at him.

"You are more beautiful than all of the flowers in my realm, Princess Rossemikka."

Rosie lifted her head finally. But her eyes raised no higher than Darville's collarbone. Her nose wrinkled, not in disgust, but more in a gesture of curiosity. She sniffed daintily.

"You smell of magic, Prince Darville. Are you a sorcerer like King Simeon of SeLenicca?"

Chapter 7

Darville paced the circumference of the Council Chamber, knotting and unclenching his fists in time with his anxious thoughts. His mid-region demanded food, then twisted in rejection of the idea. This had been a most distressing day.

The retreating sun set ablaze the colored glass in the western windows. He stared at the light, absorbing the fiery greens and bay-blues. Starbursts of those colors blinded him to all else.

Only then did the vision of Princess Rossemikka leave him. He'd been so happy, so prepared to love her, once he'd realized she was the woman of his dragon-dream. Only to have her throw the entire Council into turmoil with those few words.

Asking Darville if he were a sorcerer, indeed. How did she know that was the one sentence that would undermine the fragile relationship between himself and the Council of Provinces? The chit couldn't have said anything worse if she'd been coached by Lord Krej himself!

He'd never marry her now. How could he trust her? The much needed troops from Rossemeyer were gone forever.

His relationship with the Council was in shambles.

Enough. Darville was Crown Prince, rightfully king. The time had come to steer the course of his own future before Krej and his puppets had a chance to take advantage of Princess Rossemikka's near fatal words.

"My lords." Darville nodded curtly to each of the lords as they entered the chamber. Behind each lord, strode a cocky magician.

"Where is Senior Magician Baamin?" the prince demanded. He clenched his teeth against the cramp in his gut. What was he doing standing here, talking, preparing to "discuss" the kingdom's problems. He needed to be out, urging his steed to a frantic pace, or running, or swimming. Anything physical, rather than this polite talk.

"Your Grace, must we remind you that we have forbidden contact between yourself and the University?" Lord Jonnias puffed up his chest and squawked his oft repeated arguments. "If a foreign princess can smell the magic on you when you've had no contact with magicians for over a week, when you insulted all of these worthy gentlemen by forcing them out of Council with witchbane, then the spells are in danger of overtaking you again."

"What the princess smelled was the Tambootie that haunts my cousin. He was directly behind me at the time." Enough politeness. Darville whirled to face his rival, an accusing finger pointed at Krej's handsome face.

"I am under the influence of witchbane. Even if I were a magician, what use could I make of Tambootie?" Krej protested. His eyes were open wide with a look of incredulity. Who would guess at the evil the man had plotted last year?

"Then I overrule the Council. Each of you, mere governors of the provinces, has a magician adviser. I am your king, therefore, I demand the same right. I have chosen Lord Baamin as my adviser."

"You are not king!" Krej growled. He was hovering behind the dragon throne as if he intended to sit there himself. Still wearing his formal tunic, Krej looked as if he belonged in that chair of chairs. All he lacked was the glass dragon Coraurlia perched atop his red hair.

Red hair. The inherited evidence of magic talent. Brevelan had Krej's bright red locks. Jaylor's hair and beard were dark auburn, lightening with red highlights when he was exposed to the sun. Baamin's now white head had once been blond with red lights. There was no trace of red in Rossemikka's hair—only that odd white streak across her temple.

Darville sniffed. There was so much Tambootie essence in the chamber from the presence of the magicians, he couldn't tell if any still clung to his cousin or not.

He longed for the time when the addictive herbage was

banned throughout the kingdom. Only dragons should be able to feed on that tree.

"Sir Holmes, escort Senior Magician Baamin to the Council Chamber immediately." Darville shouted his order out the door as he strode to the other side of the throne.

"Your Grace!" the Council gasped as one.

"Since the Princess Rossemikka holds me in so little regard as to belittle me in public at our first meeting, I declare her an unfit candidate to be my queen. The treaty is null and void."

"You can't do that! We, the Council, signed the treaty. You must comply or Rossemeyer will invade. We will be fighting a war on two fronts," Lord Andrall reminded him.

"I am already fighting a war on two fronts, my lords. Have any of you even taken the time to read the treaty?" Darville threw the offensive document into the center of the table. No one reached for it.

"Section three, clause four, paragraph two," Darville quoted. " 'The Regent of Rossemeyer will station at least one member of his family with each battalion.' Clause five, last paragraph: 'In the event Rossemeyer finds itself at war, Regent Rumbellesth reserves the right to call his troops back to defend their homeland, without notice.' That means he can declare war on us at any time and already have troops in place—troops our armies have come to trust. *And* he will have a member of his family ready and able to usurp the throne as well."

Darville circled the room once more, anxious, restless, angry. He'd taken the time to change to a mud-brown field tunic. Now he needed to be out in the field. "Read it, my lords. Read the *s'murghing* document and then tell me the treaty is to our advantage." He pounded his fists on the table.

No one dared look at him. Not even Lord Krej.

"Moments ago I was informed that the city of Sambol, which guards our western border, has fallen to King Simeon's army once again. Our crops were damaged by the long winter and too wet spring. There will not be enough food this winter to feed both the people and an army. And while I battle these devastating problems, you," he pointed an authoritative finger across the table at each and every one of the Twelve, "you restrict my every move, refuse to pay your tithes, post spies and guards, and deny me access to my most trusted adviser." And then there was his traitorous stomach that cramped in rhythm with Shayla's labor.

Dead silence reigned. Every man in the room sat in guilty awareness.

"No more!" Darville shouted his disdain for the men. "Wars and kingdoms cannot be run by committee."

"Now just a moment, Prince Darville." Krej's face was turning as red as the maroon of his tunic. "You have no right to override the Council. We are a ruling body of equals, our provinces are interdependent. None of us has more power or resources than another. Our monarch is a neutral arbitrator with a tie-breaking vote. A leader, but not a dictator."

"The army mustering below this window gives me the right to overrule your shortsighted decisions. An army of five battalions loyal to me, paid by me out of my income from the city." He paused for breath while he allowed that information to sink in.

"During all those months that I did all of the data work of the Council and little else . . ." Darville gestured to the stack of bookkeeping records by his chair, "I discovered that all of you have neglected to pay your tithes for many years—even when my father was alive and duly crowned. Therefore, I declare all of you in arrears and your titles forfeit by right of the compact of Nimbulan. All of you signed that compact when you inherited your titles. This Council is dissolved as of this moment. *My* troops and a fully loyal Palace Guard will arrange my coronation and I will proceed with ruling this country as it should be! From the front. I ride within the hour."

He stalked to the doorway, paused, and turned back to face the silent men. "You may regain your positions of authority when you join me at the front with a full complement of troops and supplies."

"Guards, seize him!" Krej screamed.

"Why, Krej? What reason could you possibly have to prevent me from defending our country from invasion, pillage, and rapine?" Darville thrust men and chairs aside as he lunged toward his cousin.

The massive throne fell backward. The crash of dense wood on denser stone riveted the attention of all in the

room. Only Krej's drawn sword was between the two rivals
for the throne.

They both stared at the quivering sword. Deathly quiet
hung around them and the menace of a naked weapon,
drawn in anger in Council. No one looked away from the
sword as the sound of heavily booted feet marched into
the room.

Fred led a squad of armed men into the chamber. They
ringed the room, fingering their weapons. But they looked
to Darville for direction. He gestured for them to stand at
the ready, their weapons still sheathed.

"You cannot endanger yourself on the field of battle,
Your Grace." Krej's tone was anything but meek or submissive. Instead he glared into Darville's eyes, daring him
to disagree. Daring him to draw his own sword and fight
out their grievances.

"Since time began, the Kings of Coronnan have led our
armies to victory. I will follow in the footsteps of my esteemed ancestors. Interfere at your own risk, Krej." Darville took up the challenge.

"A compromise, Your Grace?" Lord Andrall pushed his
way between the rivals. "You may choose your own advisers and we will crown you king on the day you marry the
Princess Rossemikka."

Darville yanked his gaze away from Krej. He had to
think. The Council had backed down, offered what he
really wanted, once he'd asserted his natural authority. But
could he still marry the princess? She had betrayed him.
Just as Krej had.

A prince could trust no one. No one but himself. Knowing that, he was forewarned and forearmed.

"I will not have a queen whose first interest lies with
Rossemeyer. Nor will I have a wife who dresses like a trollop, exposing herself to all eyes."

"Speak with her, please, Your Grace," Andrall pleaded.
"Get to know her a little. Inform her of our customs."

"She accused me of being as murderous as King
Simeon."

"She asked if you were a sorcerer. King Simeon is the
only known monarch capable of magic," Andrall added.

"Though how he throws magic in SeLenicca when no

one else can remains a mystery," Krej said, still holding his sword.

"I intend to find that out. If we are ever to control magic again, we, the mundanes, must understand it as well or better than our magicians." Darville allowed his shoulders to relax a little.

"Just speak with her, Prince Darville. Perhaps she was told to say those words to throw us into this very turmoil. Perhaps she didn't know how her accusation would upset the Council. 'Twould be typical of Rossemeyer's tactics." Andrall continued pleading his case.

"After I consult with Senior Magician Baamin, in my private study, I will consider speaking with the princess." Darville righted the throne and solemnly sat in it. "My lords, we have lost a battle. 'Tis time to mobilize relief forces and plan a new strategy."

My rival has not nearly the control I was led to believe. The meeting between Darville and Rossemikka was a disaster, just as I planned. But I compelled her to say those damning words. I controlled her from the beginning. Not my rival.

Kings and regents are all fools if they think they have real power. They will all look to me once I let them know I manipulate one and all.

But first, I must bring the new ninth to the capital. Temporal power means nothing if our rituals are incomplete. I can wait no longer to bring Brevelan into the coven.

Jaylor carefully wiped Brevelan's fevered brow. She was so tiny and so pale, her fragility tugged at his heart even more than her strength did.

One of the field rabbits nudged her ear from the other side of the bed, offering his own slight comfort. At her feet a greenbird twittered in sympathy. In his agony, Jaylor couldn't appreciate the love these creatures held for his wife.

"Don't you dare die on me, Brevelan!" he ordered through the knot in his throat.

"So fierce, my husband? What happened to the weak shell of a man who doubts his own recovery?" Her last words were muffled by a rising groan. She clutched her rounded belly as if to contain the pain.

"Shouldn't you have one of the women with you? I know nothing of midwifery and little of healing." Jaylor dipped the cloth in the basin of cool water. No fever flushed Brevelan's skin, but she radiated heat in waves from her discomfort. The hut was sweltering. Jaylor was chilled to the bone.

The illness had come on her suddenly, while they went about their daily chores. One moment Brevelan had been singing to her flusterhens. The next she was writhing on the ground in pain. Jaylor had scooped her up, cradling her against his heart. Panic had frozen his mind.

Only Yaakke's prodding had given Jaylor sense enough to bring Brevelan inside and dispatch the boy to the creek for fresh water.

"A midwife could not help me. Shayla is in labor three moons early and therefore so am I." She groaned again, rolling to her side on the wide cot.

"Shayla! Brevelan, are you in contact with Shayla?"

"She never left me." Brevelan spoke through gritted teeth.

"Do you know where she is? We must bring her home to Coronnan."

"She is in labor as we speak. She could not fly back, even if she were willing." The pain eased and Brevelan lay on her back, panting with exhaustion.

" 'Tis you I must save, beloved. What can I do to help?"

"We must find a way to sever my tie to Shayla. I have not the strength or the will to do it myself."

"Perhaps the child is ready to come after all. Perhaps his growth was accelerated, like the baby dragons, by all of the magic that was thrown near the time of his conception." Jaylor felt a moment of hope. As much as he feared the birth, dreaded discovering he might not be the child's father, he was excited by a new life. If dragon-dreams were to be believed, then this was just the first of many children who would fill this clearing with laughter.

"The babe is not yet ready. Trust me, Jaylor. Our son must wait his turn. 'Tis merely my magic responding to Shayla. The bond must be severed."

"But how? I have no magic left in me. Even if I did, I'm not certain I have the stamina to throw the simplest of spells." Jaylor hung his head. The nightmare of his magic filling Krej's great hall visited him again and again. The terror, the pain, the exultation of the greatest spell in modern times was too much for a single man to live with.

Guilt threatened to wash away the little niggles of power he had been nursing lately. What if his next spell really killed him, as his last one almost did? He was just beginning to find reasons to live again. Reasons like Brevelan and the baby.

"I have to try the spell, Brevelan."

"You can't," she whispered in fear. "A spell of that magnitude would kill you. I couldn't live if you died."

"You and the babe mean more to me than my life, Brevelan. I have to try!"

"Find another magician. Guide him, but don't risk yourself." Her voice was growing weaker.

Jaylor dribbled a little of the water into her mouth. She lay quiet a moment, waiting out another pain.

"Yaakke can summon Baamin. If the three of us link through the glass. . . ."

"Baamin cannot find Shayla. He has tried often in the last six moons. I think we must bring my father into the spell. He is closer to the dragon throne than I. His bond to Shayla should be strong, if he would only search for it."

"No! How could you think about allowing Krej to work magic again? I won't permit his presence anywhere near you."

Brevelan sighed deep and long. "Then I will die and the babe with me."

The Princess of Rossemeyer stood framed in the doorway to Darville's study. The candlelight caught in her golden hairnet and shimmered around her brocade gown. At least this gown of hazel-green was more demurely cut than the one she had worn earlier. But she still revealed much more of her bosom than Darville believed proper.

"I am told I owe Your Majesty an apology." Her voice was husky, as if she had been crying, and she refused to meet Darville's eyes.

Her hands fluttered restlessly, seeking something to occupy them.

"In Coronnan I am addressed as 'Your Grace.' " Since she wasn't looking at him, Darville allowed himself the luxury of drinking in her beauty. The sight of her only brought depression. She was the woman in his dragon-dream, yet he could never trust her, never love her.

He didn't stand to greet her as court manners demanded. Mica purred in his lap beneath his desk. Some of the weight in his gut dissipated with her quiet rumbling. His hand dropped to pet her silken fur.

"Your Grace, I apologize for my unwitting remark earlier." Those constantly moving hands found a mote of dust on a globe and brushed it away.

"If you didn't know my Council holds little regard for magicians, especially lords who are also magicians, then the apology is accepted, the insult forgotten." He forced the words out. This was what Baamin had advised. Do whatever was necessary to keep the girl close and under observation. He didn't have to marry her immediately. There was still time to evaluate her and the treaty.

In other words, stall.

"So easy, Your Grace? I expected punishment." Her gaze flew upward in startlement.

Her hands were suddenly, unnaturally, stilled.

"Are you often punished, Rossemikka?" Sympathy for the young woman sneaked into Darville, an emotion he didn't want to feel.

"My . . . my uncle does not approve of me." The princess took a step toward him. Her slippered feet seemed to snuggle into the woven carpet that surrounded the desk. She searched the room for something, then finally looked directly at Darville.

He was amazed to see the hazel-green eyes flip from a slitted pupil to round as she stepped into the brighter light of the candelabra on his desk. Darville glanced down at Mica, willing her to look up at him. He had to see if the girl's eyes were an illusion, or the exact opposite of his pet's.

Mica purred a little louder, arched her back into one of her massive stretches, then peeked above the rim of the desk to see who had joined them. "Merow?" Her little nose quivered in excitement.

"Is that a cat, Your Grace?" Rossemikka's voice cracked in fear. She stiffened in the center of the carpet. Her balance shifted forward onto her toes, as if prepared for flight.

Her subtle shift in posture sent the light glinting on the

streak of white hair at her temple. This couldn't be the woman of his dragon-dream. The woman in Shayla's cave hadn't had that blatant streak in her hair.

Legend claimed such a mark to be a witch's brand. Long, long ago, before the Stargods came, witchwomen were said to be marked by the rigors of their initiation into the coven.

Mica twitched her tail once before leaping to the center of the desk. "Mmbbbrrt!" she chirped and rattled her teeth, as she did while hunting. Her back claws raked Darville's thigh in her haste to meet the princess.

"Keep it away from me!" Rossemikka backed toward the door. Her slitted eyes, wide with terror, never left the cat.

"There is nothing to fear from Mica." Darville was bewildered by the woman's reaction. "My pet is merely curious."

"Keep it away!" she cried. Her arms came up to shield her face as Mica crouched for another leap.

"Calm yourself, Princess. Mica is merely curious. As you should be. I'm told this cat is a twin to the one you lost."

"My little cat was not so vicious."

"Mica? Vicious?" Curious she was, a nuisance at times, and a loving companion. But Mica vicious?

"NO!" the princess screamed and ducked faster than Darville's eyes could follow as the cat launched toward her. Rossemikka scrambled for the doorway. Mica landed clumsily on the flagstones beyond the carpet. She lay there a moment, stunned by the shock of her landing.

Without another word, Rossemikka fled the private study of the king. Darville was hot on her heels. He barely noticed Mica scuttling into the shadows to nurse her wounded pride and jarred body.

Chapter 8

Brevelan stared at the roof tree of her hut. For the moment it was in focus. Quite an ordinary beam of wood, except for its age. The hut had been here, nearly intact for over three hundred years. It had sheltered many generations of witchwomen. The villagers claimed the hut and the clearing had been empty for a dozen or more years before Brevelan had claimed it, a little over a year ago.

When Brevelan had needed a place to hide from her witch-hunting home village and family, the clearing had called to her, drawing her ever south until she had stumbled across the threshold. Frightened and confused, she had remained hidden for several months until the villagers had needed a healer.

Now she needed help and healing. The child was draining all of her strength. There was nothing left of her to fight the magic that chained her to an invisible dragon.

A new pain clawed at her belly and her back. The room swam out of focus. A scream started in the back of her throat and died there. She hadn't the energy to push it out.

For the blink of an eye Brevelan saw all of the auras around every object and being within sight.

Jaylor was all blues and reds, with hints of crystal and copper. He was weighing his staff in his hands, as if judging the temper of the wood. His colors spread out and included his favorite tool.

"Jaylor, you mustn't try to sever the bond to Shayla," she whispered. The pain receded, leaving her limp and sweating. "Your heart won't support the magic."

"You can't hold on much longer, Brevelan. I have to do this for you or die trying," Jaylor insisted.

Brevelan fought the next wave of pain, rose with it, rode it to its crest, then tumbled back down to the reality of the hard bed in a small, smoky hut. It would be such bliss to just let go. Allow the blackness on the edges of her vision to take over, sink into the oblivion that beckoned her.

"I love you, Brevelan," Jaylor whispered, as he lay one end of the staff across her heart, linking them together. He took one deep breath, held it for the required three counts, and released it.

Instantly, Brevelan felt the calm separation from reality induced by the first stage of his trance. Another deep breath and blue and red lines began to pulse around him, along the staff and through her body.

"Don't risk it, Jaylor," she pleaded, uncertain if her voice was loud enough to be heard.

A third deep breath and the magic Jaylor projected braided and folded back along the staff. Brevelan's own breathing deepened, slowed. The confines of the hut disappeared. They were floating in the void between the planes of existence. Blue and red mists supported them in a sea of colored lifelines. Time warped and became meaningless. The awful pain and weakness were left behind, part of another body, another life.

"Look for crystal." Were those her words or their thoughts? When Jaylor's spirit had been lost in a Tambootie overdose, she had tethered him to reality with a strand of copper life from her own heart.

"There are too many colors, all braided together!" Fear made Jaylor's voice acid sharp in the swirls of magic. The sounds echoed, becoming dull and hollow with each succeeding reverberation. They filled her head, yet left a vacancy.

Brevelan couldn't see her husband through the clouds of her mind. She needed to reach out and touch him, reassure him before his fear of failure broke the spell.

The magical nature of the void revealed the patterns of Jaylor's life, but not his physical body. One layer of his aura, a blue halo around his heart, was incomplete.

The next contraction racked a body. Her body, and yet

not hers. She felt no pain, yet was acutely aware of it and unable to continue her telepathic communication with Jaylor. This wasn't working. Exposed to magic, as they were, the labor intensified. Shayla was too close.

"Colors define and describe," Brevelan gasped.

"Copper for you," Jaylor panted, as if out of breath or short of blood. "Red and blue for me. Red and green for your father. Who is gold?"

"Gold?" A golden wolf danced across her mind's eye. A golden prince who was lover and best friend. A child with golden hair stood beside her, eldest of six, in a dragon-dream.

"Darville," she sighed. Or perhaps the child. "Follow him to Shayla."

Jaylor picked his way through the pulsing stands of life. At last he touched crystal entwined with gold and copper, but not blue and red.

The body he left behind doubled over, a fist clenched over his heart. The staff fell from his nerveless left hand.

The void took on form and solidity. Brevelan fell back into the bed with a whoosh and a new wave of pain.

"I am so sorry, my dearest love. I've failed you again." Jaylor hung his head in guilt and regret. His fingers clenched and opened against his chest as the pain eased with the passing of the magic. "We need help."

"Why, Baamin?" Darville asked. "Why did the princess exhibit such terror in the presence of my cat? Her fear of Mica seemed to provoke the attack." Darville stroked and soothed Mica where she lay limply across his chest and shoulder. She nuzzled his jaw in weak appreciation of his love and attention. He sensed that her awkward landing on the hard stone floor was still troubling her.

Darville's stomach rumbled and cramped. How much longer could Shayla's labor last? He needed the soothing contact with Mica to keep his stomach under control as much as she needed him.

With each pain rode an awareness of another entity also in pain. He prayed that she was safe, protected by the male dragons. Was he, Darville, safe if anything happened to Shayla during this vulnerable time?

He couldn't forget that his father, as consecrated king,

had been so closely tied to the dragons that Shayla's ensorcellment had killed him.

"Stop pacing. I can't think while you prowl this room like a caged wolf," Baamin grumbled from his chair beside the king's massive desk. It was a comfortable armchair, soft and firm in the right places. A low stool cradled the old man's feet in front of him.

He kicked at it aimlessly.

Darville squinted at Baamin. The old man's green and yellow robe hung on him in pathetic wrinkles, his body almost shrinking before the prince's eyes. He'd been old for as long as Darville could remember. Now he seemed more ancient than anyone had a right to be. The loss of the dragons and traditional magic weighed heavily on the Senior Magician's formerly strong shoulders.

Baamin took a long swallow from his legendary flask, winced and cursed as he refitted the cap.

His temper hadn't improved much either.

"An apt description," Darville growled and continued to prowl his study. "I've been accused of being more wolf than prince a little too frequently of late." Even his sympathy for Old Baamin couldn't take the sting out of that particular insult.

Once more a full moon hung above the battlements. An entire cycle had passed since Darville had traversed the tunnels to share in Baamin's summons to Brevelan.

The prince drew thick brocaded draperies across the window to block out the silvery glow. The noise of the sliding rings on their rod was loud and abrasive in the quiet room.

"You have always demonstrated that characteristic restlessness, Brat. Your need to be out-of-doors, free from the constraints of court rules and strict guardians, riding fast with the wind in your face, a fierce hunter. . . . Your own personality shaped Lord Krej's transformation spell. Even if you had never spent those four or five moons as a wolf, you would be called one." The old man pulled out his flask once more and took a long swig of cordial followed by a mint to cover any telltale odor. The recipe for that soothing liquid was Baamin's treasured secret.

"Your father was more like a stag, proud and silent, easily startled." Baamin capped the flask and secreted it again in one of his numerous pockets. "I am rather like a frog, ugly and knock-kneed, loud and offensive."

Darville snorted a laugh at the old man's attempted humor. "Better an offensive frog than a poisonous eel or arrogant flustercock that is more voice than substance, like some members of your Commune of Magicians I could name."

"Too many of your Council of Provinces are more squawk than thought; easily led. A strong king can control and use them to advantage. An evil regent could easily destroy the entire kingdom because of them."

"Tell me your thoughts, Baamin. Why would the princess become hysterical at the sight of a cat? Especially a cat who is supposed to be a duplicate of her own beloved pet?" Darville stopped his pacing long enough to look directly into Baamin's tired eyes.

"Perhaps Mica is the cat, Rosse, who vanished from a locked tower room over two years ago. She has demonstrated some magic." Baamin reached up a trembling hand to scratch the cat's ears. Mica leaned into the caress and purred a little louder.

"I don't think she is Rosse." Darville finally sat in his own chair, a smaller, more comfortable version of the dragon throne in the Council Chamber. He'd demanded it be brought out of storage shortly after his meeting this evening. For the first time in his life, he realized how well his frame fit the height and depth of the demi-throne.

"Why couldn't she be Rosse?" Baamin's shaggy white eyebrows lifted in curiosity.

"Did I ever tell you what happened in Shayla's cave while the beast-headed man, who I still believe was Krej, threw the spell that changed the dragon into a glass sculpture?"

"A little of it. I heard most of the story from Brevelan."

"Brevelan didn't see what I saw." Darville sorted through the images in his head.

"There was so much magic ebbing and flowing, Krej couldn't maintain the shape-change spell on me. I took back my own form for a few moments. At the same time, this cat grew into the most beautiful woman I have ever seen. She rose up like a goddess, hair streaming to her hips. She lifted her arms and her voice in a glorious song."

He paused in his recollections a moment, stroking the purring cat. "Then she collapsed back into Mica's body."

There, the words were out, the confused images in his mind took firm hold and became reality. "I think I returned to the wolf form at the same time, so I've never been totally certain of what I saw. Yet the image has haunted me."

"A woman trapped inside the cat's body, just as you were trapped in the guise of a wolf?" Baamin's expressive eyebrows crashed downward until they formed a solid line across his brow.

"Rossemikka looks to be the twin of the woman I saw ensorcelled. Except for the streak of white hair at her temple. The princess bears a witch's brand. Mica does not."

"Let me see her. Have you noticed the names, Darville? Princess Rosse-mikka owned a cat named Rosse, the cat's twin is Mica—Mikka is not so far off in pronunciation." Baamin brought Mica into his own lap. Her purring stopped as she squeaked a protest at the move.

From the deep folds of a hidden pocket, Baamin produced a round of glass. This wasn't the large master's glass in a gold frame he had used for the summoning spell. It looked more like Jaylor's journeyman glass. A more useful tool to carry in a pocket than the larger one the Senior Magician was entitled to.

Baamin peered through the magnification of the lens. His free hand stroked Mica's back in long gestures that outlined her bone structure from nose to tail.

"Hmm . . . very interesting." He paused in his examination to look for inspiration in the ceiling. "What are you, Mica?" Baamin mused as he examined the cat.

"Does she tell you?" Darville remembered the times of near telepathic communication with the creature. Brevelan was empathic with animals and people. She had named the cat based on her emotional communication with her. Could Mica have "told" Brevelan a version of her own name?

"There is something very uncatlike about her, but it is well cloaked. Where is the Princess Rossemikka, Darville?"

"In her suite, with the doors locked and her dragon of a governess standing guard."

"The blonde with the . . . um . . ." The old man cupped his hands in front of his chest depicting the magnitude of Janataea. He blushed more heartily than a man his age should have.

Darville chuckled for the first time in many, many hours.

"I have seen a true dragon and lived to tell about it," Baamin stated proudly. "One overprotective governess shouldn't trouble an old man like me. Though she'd be a lot easier to handle if she were a man." Baamin gathered his voluminous robes about him and stood. For all of the strain and fatigue that showed in his eyes and his greatly reduced body, Baamin's shoulders were unbowed.

"Are you well, Baamin?" Darville couldn't imagine life in Coronnan City without this most trusted of wise men. But then he hadn't been able to imagine life without the dragons, or his future without Brevelan not so long ago.

"I'm old and tired, Darville. But the news that Shayla is back in contact with you takes several years off me."

" 'Tis a contact I'm not appreciating at the moment. Her labor is most uncomfortable, though I'm only getting echoes of her contractions, rather than real pains. How do women stand it?"

"I must find Yaakke. He will work the summons. There must be a way to channel and focus magic from one person, through another, the way I use my staff." Jaylor pushed authority and decision into his voice. Much more than he felt. Brevelan was weaker. Dangerously so.

If only there were a little dragon magic, they could link and increase the power of the spell.

But the solution to Brevelan's problem might forever end the possibility of dragon magic in Coronnan.

"Very good, young man. You'll make a proper, thinking magician yet." Krej sneered behind Jaylor.

Jaylor whirled to see the red-haired lord leaning negligently against the doorjamb. Yaakke stood silently behind Krej. The boy lifted his shoulders in an apologetic shrug.

Brevelan needs him, Yaakke explained in Jaylor's thoughts. *I know I'm not supposed to transport people, Master.* Yaakke backed away from the hut as if he expected to be beaten for his audacity.

Jaylor forced himself to remember the boy had been a nameless kitchen drudge not so long ago. He'd never known any form of correction other than punishment. Considered retarded because of his slow physical development, he hadn't been allowed an education or the right to a true name. Only when the dragon magic faded and Yaakke's rogue powers were unmasked did his intelligence, and his uncontrolled talent, become evident.

You could have killed a member of the Council of Provinces! Jaylor sent back telepathically. Only when the words left his mind did he realize his throat was closed in awe of the boy's success at a spell that had defied magicians since time began.

"Nice trick, Jaylor." Krej moved into the hut, inspecting corners and crevices as if expecting filth. "Transporting me out of an important meeting without my consent. We've been trying to perfect that spell since time began without success. How'd you do it?" An aura of menace pulsed around him. Fury blazed from his eyes.

"Your daughter needs your help."

"My daughter? She's acknowledging me, is she? Who's to say I will accept yet another bastard brat as being my own? Tell me how you did it, Jaylor."

"I've seen your presence linked with hers through magic. You are the only person alive who can save her and her child." Jaylor saw a glimmer of fear in Krej's eyes and something else, too. Was it respect? He wasn't sure this prideful rogue would help if he knew the elusive spell was thrown by a mere boy, an untrained apprentice.

"If you've enough magic to transport a living being across half of Coronnan, then perform whatever spell she needs yourself."

"My magic was . . . damaged releasing Shayla from your glass imprisonment."

"For that disservice I refuse to assist," Krej snarled. "Don't you realize how much this kingdom has benefited from the loss of dragon protection! New ideas and trade, economic growth, creativity . . ."

"I see invasion on the horizon," Jaylor returned heatedly. "I see outlaws pillaging and raping, because the magic border dissolved before we had a chance to open it through negotiation. Crime is running rampant in the streets because the magicians don't have the combined power to predict and intervene."

"Master! My lord, please," Yaakke intervened. "While you argue, Brevelan lies dying." He crossed the small room to hold Brevelan's limp hand. "Help her." He gulped back a sob. "Please."

"Lord Krej." Jaylor forced himself to use the honorific. "If we accomplish what needs to be done to save your daughter—my wife—our baby—then Coronnan's tie to the dragons will be severed forever. You will have accomplished what you set out to do."

"You heard the dragon the night as she flew away. She and her consorts will never return as long as I hold power. I intend to remain in power a very long time. Give me another reason to help two peasants with a difficult birth. There isn't enough food in the kingdom for those that live. Why add another mouth to feed?"

Images flooded Jaylor's mind from Yaakke. The boy's search for Krej had found the lord in the middle of a magic ritual with seven other faceless rogues. The aura of magic around them all was strong and complete.

"Save my wife and child and the kingdom will never know from me that you are truly a rogue magician in league with a coven of Simurgh, or that you have found an antidote to the witchbane. In the eyes of the world you will remain as mundane as you claim to be."

Krej stared at Jaylor, mouth slightly agape in surprise. Malevolence filled his eyes. "Word of my contact with the coven must never leave your mouth. On pain of never-ending death at the hands of Simurgh."

"I swear."

"Swear by Simurgh!"

"I swear by the Stargods, or none at all. And your coven must not harm the kingdom."

"Very well. An oath on those you believe in is better than no oath at all," Krej acknowledged. "You might not believe this, but my plans are for the good of Coronnan." He turned his back and stripped off his rich tunic. The cream-colored cambric shirt he wore beneath the velvet and brocade was sheer and clean.

Yaakke's tears stopped, but he continued to hold Brevelan's hand with reverence. "She's the only one who treated me like a real person. Everyone else sees me as a witless kitchen drudge. You have to save her, my lord, Master. You have to save her."

"My daughter, huh? I thought she was mine the first time I saw her. She'd make a better heir than any of the brats my wife produces on a regular basis. At least she inherited some magical talent." Krej pushed the sleeves of his shirt above his elbows and strode to the fire. "Must you live in this hovel?"

The hut had never looked ruder, poorer, smaller.

"Don't forget your grandson," Jaylor reminded him. "Your first grandchild."

"I wasn't much older than she is now when she was conceived." Krej looked down on the wilted form on the bed. "Her mother was my first bedmate, not the best, but memorable because she was the first. I'll need a glass." He turned back to Jaylor with brisk authority. Jaylor produced his master's glass from a place of honor on the shelf above his bed. Possession of such a fine piece of rare, clear glass was the achievement of a lifetime.

He'd never used it.

"They made you master?"

"They didn't know I'd live." Reluctantly, Jaylor handed his treasure to the man who had been his archenemy.

"I'll need some Tambootie."

"Why?"

"To counteract the witchbane Darville douses me with on a weekly basis."

"Here, sir." Yaakke produced two fat leaves of the tree of magic out of thin air.

"Have you taught the boy how to transport people? We would pay much to learn that spell."

"My name is Yaakke," he asserted.

"Yaakke? Son of Yaacob, the usurper. A bit audacious, *Boy*." Krej sniffed and turned his back on Yaakke. "Brevelan, give me your hand."

"No!" Jaylor shouldered his way between his wife and her father. "I cannot allow you to touch her."

"You ask my help, then dictate the terms of the spell?"

"I protect my wife from a man who has tried to kill her more than once."

"Then how do you propose I save her life? If I can't touch her, my magic can't reach her."

"I will be your staff. Focus your magic through me."

"Magic warps and reshapes wood. Look at your own staff to see how much. You risk your life to save the chit. Is she worth it?"

"Yes!"

Chapter 9

Where was Janataea? Uncle Rumbelly was going to be very angry when he heard how Rosie had disgraced herself with the prince.

Rosie hugged the shadows in one of the corners of her spacious apartment. The little space between the big bed and the wardrobe looked snug enough to hide her from whoever the Lord Regent of Rossemeyer sent to punish her. She slid to a sitting position, her back to the wall.

Rosie didn't like the smell of the room she had been given. It was too clean, the hangings and furniture smelled of soap. There was no dust to collect the scent of those who passed through the room. How could she hide in a room that wouldn't mask her scent?

And she was alone. Utterly alone. Janataea was the only one she knew in this long, long wing isolated from the rest of the huge palace. Kevin-Rosse was quartered across the city, on an entirely different island, in the embassy.

That was another thing she didn't like, the islands. Hundreds of them connected by slender, untrustworthy bridges. The city was nothing but islands surrounded by water. Deep water. Shallow water. Muddy water. Clean water. All of it moving very rapidly toward the Great Bay.

Rosie shuddered and ducked her head against her knees.

Janataea had promised to be back in a matter of an hour, long before Rosie finished her interview with Prince Darville. But her time with the prince had been cut short.

"H-hsss-ch," she hissed to herself. "I mistrust him. Him and his witchcat."

What was she to do? Janataea would tell her.

But Janataea was gone on an errand. Gone for hours now. Janataea had broken a promise.

"I can't trust anyone but myself!" she wailed. "And sometimes I can't trust myself. Why did I say those ill-timed words to the prince when we hadn't even been introduced?"

A light knock on the door sent Rosie scuttling deeper into the shadows. She crouched, ready to launch herself into either flight or an attack.

The knock came again. Louder, longer. "Your Highness?" a strange male voice asked. A gentle voice. Reassuring, trustworthy. "Are you there, Princess Rossemikka?"

"Who . . . who is it?" she stammered from her hiding place.

"Senior Magician Baamin, Your Highness. I have a message from Prince Darville. May I come in?"

Baamin, the magician from the University whom she was supposed to seek out and poison. Kevin-Rosse promised dire punishment if she did not.

The magician sounded so meek and gentle he could not be a threat to Rossemeyer. She didn't dare trust him. He was a magician and therefore incapable of telling the truth.

In Rossemeyer, magicians were solitary scholars who sought the mysteries of the universe. They were known to lie, cheat, steal, and even kidnap and murder to serve their quest. But this was Coronnan, where the magicians were trained in a university, posted to the lords as advisers. Coronnan's magicians were supposed to be trusted.

"I do not wish to speak of the prince." She found herself standing. Her muscles relaxed from their panic. She didn't know why.

"Then we won't speak of him." A pause while Rosie searched the room again for some sign of Janataea's hovering presence. "This door is thick. Talking through it strains an old man's voice. May I come in?"

"Do you need permission to enter any room?" She quivered in fear.

A low chuckle drifted to her perked ears. "When entering the presence of a lady, a gentleman always asks permission."

Rosie decided to trust his politeness. "Then you may enter."

"Through a locked door?"

"You are a magician."

"That is true." The bar across the inside of the door lifted easily and the lock turned by unseen hands.

Rosie gasped as the massive panels of hard oak swung open on silent hinges. She wanted to protect herself with one of the gestures she'd seen used whenever a magician passed. But she didn't know the rituals, didn't know if they worked.

Framed in the doorway was a man about her own height, with a round face and a twinkle in his blue eyes beneath massive white eyebrows. His robe was the same color as his eyes and was much too big for him. He almost tripped over the hem on his first step forward.

Baamin looked up and down the corridor, then hitched the middle folds of his cumbersome garment higher through his belt of golden rope. He strode confidently toward her, only to trip again on an uneven tendril of fabric.

"Dragon dung! Oh, excuse my language, Princess. I haven't had time to commission a new garment." He fussed with the blue wool again to hide his blush.

His embarrassment warmed Rosie's heart. How could a man with such an inviting smile and humorous eyes be evil?

Unless all of his actions were a charade designed to lull her suspicions.

The smell of beta'arack permeated the man's skin and clothes. A smell almost welcome in its familiarity.

"Have you come to punish me for . . . for . . . the scenes I made today?" Rosie hung her head, not wanting this endearing old man to be the one to lock her in the tower. Maybe that was not deemed punishment here. Maybe she would be thrown into the churning river.

"No, Princess. We do not punish people here for being afraid."

Rosie sensed the coils of compulsion traversing the gap between herself and the old man. Her head reared up in instant fear. She retreated from the magic toward her hiding place against the wall.

"I have come to find the root of your terror and see if we can banish it." The compulsion vanished. "Perhaps you ran from the cat because you do not know what wonderful companions they can be." His voice invited her to confide in him. He reached a trembling, age-spotted hand to her in friendship.

Rosie shook her head in denial.

"Perhaps we should sit. This old body tires easily these days." He dragged a light, armless chair from the corner and set it at an angle to the padded chair beside the fireplace. "I may not sit until you do. 'Tis court protocol."

Rosie edged toward the chair, uncertain if she should trust him or flee. The door had been left politely ajar. She could run. But where? She chose to sit, curling her legs beneath her.

"Now tell me, Your Highness, what do you like about our fair country so far?" His tone was fatherly, inviting her to be candid.

"Nothing."

"Oh, dear, dear me. That is very unfortunate. Are we so much different from your home in Rossemeyer?" Baamin reached across the narrow gap separating their chairs to pat her hand.

Rosie started to withdraw from his touch, as she would with any stranger. Then, at the last moment, she allowed her hand to remain in her lap. He covered it with his warm, dry palm. His skin was calloused and cracked with age, but his touch was gentle, ever so gentle and reassuring.

"Everything smells wet. The river is too big and too close." Rosie wrinkled her nose.

"I understand Rossemeyer is very dry." He reached into his robes and withdrew a flask that smelled of the familiar distillation of the treacle beta from Rossemeyer. He offered her a sip. Rosie shook her head. He took a long swallow and continued, "Your few rivers are narrow and irrigate only small areas, I hear. Rain falls but once or twice a year on the plateaus."

Rosie shrugged instead of commenting.

"Once the winter rains begin here, they won't stop until next summer. Damp does terrible things to an old body. I don't like the wet either, Your Highness." Another swig from the flask, and he put it away. If she could gain access to that flask, she could insert the poison Kevin-Rosse had given her. But did she really want to?

"Your gown is lovely, Princess." His words took on a lulling quality. "The color is very like your eyes. The chair's upholstery is a shade darker, as if it were made for you. Sitting there, you look very like a queen. Do you want to be our queen?" He fumbled in his pockets and withdrew a small square of glass.

As he peered more closely at her dress and the chair, his eyes were enlarged. Rosie could see the rheumy fatigue in them.

"What is that glass?" A glimmer of curiosity sparked through of Rosie's misery.

"An aid, my dear. These old eyes don't see very well anymore. With it, I can see the details of your gown much better. Such a wonderful color on you."

"I don't much care what I wear. But I did choose this fabric. I like the feel of it." Rosie ran her free hand along the nap of the brocade.

"An excellent choice." Baamin straightened in his chair and looked at her levelly.

Rosie did her best to push herself back into the recesses of the soft pads of her chair. She knew that look. This pleasant old man was going to tell her something she wouldn't like.

"Princess, you were expecting punishment. Will you tell me why?"

She looked away from him, into the brightness of the fire. Punishment was expected, endured, not spoken of or protested. Yet . . . yet she didn't want to be thrown in the river, or shut into a lightless tower room, or deprived of food.

"My uncle disapproves of everything I do."

"Your Uncle Rumbellesth, the Regent of Rossemeyer?"

She nodded. "He says I am defiant. Only an abomination would dare do the things I do."

"And what do you do that he believes so awful?"

"I . . . I . . . um . . . Master Baamin, I don't know. I don't remember doing any of the things he proclaims illegal!" she wailed.

He disappeared! In the middle of the opening ritual he vanished from the coven's protected shrine.

We have sought that spell for countless generations. Al-

ways we have failed. Every ritual breaks down, or the subject dies.

My rival performed that little feat just to make my bid for power seem trivial. He did it to seek the focus himself. He will claim the succession by right of birth. I cannot allow that. She was my mother as well as his. I will dissolve the coven before I allow him to take Maman's place. I will destroy him and form a new eight-pointed star.

Then I will take control of Coronnan, and Rossemeyer, and SeLenicca. No more will my people be exiled. No more will we be a fragmented race.

If I must take Tambootie to succeed, I will. I am powerful enough to control the addiction. My rival believes he has mastered the weed. I know he has not.

"I was prepared to die when I unraveled your spell, Krej. Even hoped I would, because I could imagine nothing greater in my lifetime than saving the dragon nimbus of Coronnan. Indeed, I was almost disappointed when I woke up." Jaylor gulped back the emotion that thickened his throat.

"Brevelan saved me. I'm told her song of healing was the most beautiful music ever heard in our kingdom. That's what she has given me. More than life, more than magic. Your daughter has shown me the beauty of life, the beauty of her spirit. I must do everything in my power to save her and the child she carries."

"A bit maudlin, Jaylor." Krej sniffed in disdain. "However, you will make a better staff than any mere piece of wood because you won't resist the flow. You might even help shape it. Let's get to work."

Jaylor peered closer at the red-haired lord. If he didn't know the man so well, he might just think Krej was touched with emotion, too.

That thought vanished with the change of expression on Krej's face as he nibbled on the succulent leaves Yaakke had given him. His bites were small, as if he were only consuming the leaves as a necessary prelude to working magic. But his eyes took on the light of a fanatic, eagerly anticipating the heights to which the drug would take him. The second leaf disappeared into Krej's mouth in one eager gulp.

"I need more. There weren't enough essential oils to combat the witchbane." His pupils dilated and began to glaze.

Yaakke squinted at Krej in the way Baamin had taught all of his students to focus magic sight. "Your aura nearly fills this room. You've had enough," the boy pronounced. "Any more and you won't be able to concentrate. You might kill Brevelan."

"You dare contradict me? Me!" Krej roared. He lifted his hand to strike the boy.

Yaakke stood firm.

"Are you feeding magic, or are you feeding your craving?" Jaylor asked. "I followed you into a Tambootie trance once. I know the needs the drug induces."

Krej glared at him.

Jaylor stared back.

At last they both looked at the now unconscious form on the bed. "The boy must leave. His magic might interfere."

Jaylor nodded to Yaakke. "Go to the other side of the bathing pool."

Yaakke pleaded with his eyes to stay.

"You heard him. We can't take a chance on your uncontrolled magic breaking into the spell and destroying it prematurely."

The door closed silently behind the boy's tear-streaked face.

"What do I look for?" Krej asked in a normal tone of voice. There was only a hint of strain in his shoulders.

"Once in the void, seek out a crystal umbilical. It should be entwined with Brevelan's copper life force."

"One cannot cut crystal with a knife." Krej placed a firm grip on Jaylor's shoulder.

"You can snap it with a quick thrust." Jaylor linked his fingers with Brevelan's limp ones. She was cold and weak. They had to hurry.

"A clean sever could be mended with fire at a later date. I won't allow that." Krej focused the gold-rimmed piece of glass on the flames in the hearth. "The umbilical must be smashed into several pieces."

Jaylor sighed in resignation. "So be it."

One breath. A second deeper one. As they exhaled a third time, they melded into a trance.

Krej's magic pulsed through Jaylor's blood. A bubble of blood-red and fire-green magic worked its way from the point where the two men were joined, down his chest, into his heart. It paused there a second, blocked by damaged pathways. A little extra push from Krej and the bubble pushed through and dissolved the scar tissue, seeking direction, then sped outward along Jaylor's arm to his fingertips and into Brevelan.

She spasmed. A second bubble followed the first, enlarging the pathway through Jaylor's healed heart. It passed easily into Brevelan. She twitched again, less violently, accepting the magic more readily.

A third and a fourth bubble flowed in rapid succession. Jaylor was on fire, inside and out, as the alien magic fought with his own. He forced his mind clear. He couldn't allow himself to think, or to direct the spell. He was only a staff, only a focus.

Krej's aura grew and filled the room, overlapping everything else. From his vantage point outside his body, Jaylor saw his own aura seek to overcome Krej's in intensity, then subside in subservience. Brevelan's yellow and orange and copper colors were fading rapidly to gray.

The magic flowed more smoothly. The bubbles swirled through Jaylor. They spread to all of his arteries and back again. There was pain, and yet no pain. He willed himself out of his body, observing this odd feeling.

Red and green bubbles danced before his eyes. They joined in long chains and wound around and around the three linked figures in the room. The last vestiges of reality faded. The void beckoned.

The chain of signature-colored cords, pulsing with life, extended from each of them, joining with others in the void.

"Crystal umbilical," Krej repeated.

"Separate the crystal before you break it," Jaylor reminded him.

"There are two plaited together. One is copper, one is crystal, but they take color and texture from each other. Soon they will be indistinguishable."

Krej directed Jaylor's hand to the bound cords. His fingers moved with a puppet's lack of volition and inserted themselves between two whorls. His arm tugged gently until one loop separated. Which was it, crystal or copper?

"Smash it!"

His fist came up to obey.

"Which is it?"

"It doesn't matter. Smash it!"

Chapter 10

"**S**mash the cord, Jaylor. Do it now, before it bleeds all of Brevelan's life force away!" Krej commanded.

Jaylor resisted the puppetlike manipulation of his fist. Which loop of the umbilical belonged to Brevelan, and which to Shayla? He couldn't be sure; they both looked the same. Neither was totally copper or crystal, but a blend of both.

"Color defines and describes." Brevelan's words came back to him.

The separate loop under his fist was dull, fading from bright metal to lifeless clay. Deep in the twining mass of colored cords pulses another one, the same color, but glowing with brightness and vitality.

Brevelan was dying in her premature labor. Shayla was birthing her healthy brood on time. The withering umbilical at hand had to belong to Brevelan. He must grab and separate the bright one.

"Obey me, Jaylor. Smash the cord." Krej's words drifted through the swirls of magic. With them came the compulsion to raise a fist and slam it down onto the copper umbilical of life.

Inch by inch, Jaylor's fist came up. He resisted, fought Brevelan's father with all of his will. Sweat broke out on the body he had left behind. Black stars clouded his vision, both real and magic.

His hand was at the apex of its upward arc, prepared to drop with incredible force. Forcing control back into his muscles, Jaylor managed to open his fist. But he couldn't stop the forceful downward plunge of his arm.

At the last second he diverted the momentum. He was

tangled in the plait of colored cords. The blue and red one of his own life felt hot from his resistance. Krej's maroon and green colors were slick with ill intent. The gold one, representing Darville's loving bond to both Brevelan and Jaylor, was cool and distant.

Jaylor slid his hand deeper into the colors until his fingers closed around a tube of cold glass. The cord pulsed against his palm.

"Forgive me, Shayla," he whispered. With one last effort of self-will he yanked on the cord until it was totally separate from the mass. Then he allowed Krej's deadly wish to take over once more. His fist smashed the bright crystal once. Twice. A third time. Slivers of crystal danced in the glow of magic.

And still his fist came down as a hammer, breaking even the slivers into smaller pieces. Again and again he pounded the glass. His hand was raw and bleeding. Yet Krej continued to use him to pummel the dragon with years of hatred and frustration.

"Cease, Father! You're killing the dragon," Brevelan screamed.

Where did my rival go? I cannot find him anywhere. Always, his mind has been as close to me as a thought. Now he is gone. Armored.

This mischief must stop before the coven pushes him to the focus, leaving me behind.

I must follow the trail of his foul-tasting Tambootie, even if it takes me through the void. Our kind are not welcome there. There are traps laid by the spirits of our ancestors. They wish to keep us with them. I am not yet ready to join Simurgh.

Reality surged back around Jaylor with a jolt. He was in the hut again. He slumped over the bed, exhausted. Both hands rested on the edge of the mattress where Brevelan had lain in agony only moments before.

"Stupid bitch," Krej cursed. "You broke the spell!"

"You went too far. You were trying to kill Shayla or me—you didn't care which—not just separate us." Brevelan hung on her father's upraised hand.

"Brevelan, are you all right?" Jaylor reached a weary

hand to his beloved. She was standing, neither strong nor hale, but standing nevertheless. Her face was still paler than moonlight.

They had saved her. And the baby?

"You've done what you came for, Lord Krej." Brevelan stared at the magician. Her posture mimicked her father's perfectly. She had inherited more than just her red hair from the man. "Go, now, before I use some of your own brand of magic on you. Would you rather face the Council of Provinces as a flustercock, or," she grinned in a manner that made Jaylor shudder. "Or would you rather be impotent?"

"Not even a thank you, for saving your life?" Krej shook himself free of her grasp as if she soiled him.

"You would have killed her had I not fought your murderous impulse," Jaylor accused. "Get out. Now."

"I cannot return on my own. Teach me the spell and I will gladly leave you—forever." Krej stood firm. The fog of the magic spell was clearing from his eyes. But lines of fatigue radiated into his temple.

"Yaakke!" Jaylor called. The boy poked his head inside the door so quickly he had to have been listening, or even watching. "Find refreshment for his lordship and find out where he wants me to transport him. When I have rested, I will perform the spell."

His apprentice nodded and winked. A big smile spread across his face. At least he understood that the source of the spell was to remain secret.

But how long would he play the game at Jaylor's bidding?

A clump of heather quivered in the morning breeze. Darville tightened his grip on the reins and clamped his thighs tighter around the mettlesome steed who decided the movement was a good excuse to assert his will. The strong stallion tried to rear, and when that failed, he fought the bit and controlling reins with nervous dances. A lesser man would have been thrown.

This was what he needed, Darville reminded himself. A strong war-steed willing to give him a hard ride. The troop of men and officers at his back were soldiers on patrol instead of huntsmen. But the principle was the same, a wild ride through countryside in search of a quarry. Human quarry instead of beast this time.

Raiders had been sighted two days' ride to the northwest of the capital. Too close. They must be routed out before the capital itself was endangered.

In keeping with his pronouncements to the Council, Darville had taken charge of this expedition. If only his mind were on the task instead of on Baamin's report, he might just enjoy this battle of wills with the steed.

The old man couldn't decide if Princess Rossemikka and Mica were one person split by magic into two bodies, or two people, each in the wrong body. A third possibility existed. One or the other was a powerful witch controlling the actions of her twin.

The heather moved again, almost unnaturally. Darville touched the tiny pewter dragon dangling from his right ear. Baamin had fashioned the talisman for him last night. Through the medium of the metal, the magician could armor Darville with protective spells.

Snooty Princess Rossemikka probably wouldn't like his dragon any better than his cat.

"Just over that ridge, Your Grace, there should be a village. We can water the steeds while we question the folk for signs of strangers." A middle-aged knight pointed toward a line of foothills. The leader of this century of men looked tired. His comfortable life of privilege, with the occasional ritual of military training, had been thrown into upheaval by this war.

"If the village still stands, then they haven't seen any outsiders," Darville reminded the man, the closest thing to a veteran in his army. "The steeds drank at the last stream, and the one before that. We'd best push on until we find evidence of where the raiders were, then follow their trail."

Sometimes I think I am the only man in the kingdom with a grasp of tactics. What could he expect after three hundred years of peace enforced by the magic border? That he would have troops and reserves standing ready to fight any and all corners without additional training? All of Coronnan had become too dependent upon that border.

"The villagers may still have seen something," the knight protested.

"Send two men who can be trusted not to get drunk in

the local pub to question them. The rest of us will ride farther north." Buoyant resolve lifted Darville's spirits. "There are caves in those hills. Excellent hiding places for raiders. Let's root them out." Darville spurred his eager steed forward, leaving the others to follow or be disgraced.

Sir Holmes, who had been at the rear of the century, was the only one keeping pace with him. Fred had been to his left, but was now falling behind. If these men had been trained by Rossemeyer, there would be no question of their ability to keep up, or complete their assigned task.

He'd have no troops from Rossemeyer if he didn't find out the truth about their princess . . . soon. The key to the princess was Mica; that seemed obvious. Darville wondered if his cat was safe in Baamin's care while he roamed the countryside. Mica was vulnerable to both the whims of the Council and the princess' venom.

"Your Grace." A winded officer, about Darville's own age, drew alongside his galloping steed. "You must not endanger yourself so. Please stay closer to your troops."

"Then have your men keep up with me!" Once more, Darville dug in his heels. His face stung with the force of the wind. The air whipped past him with the cold bite of autumn. For the first time in nearly five moons, he felt strong and clean. His mind cleared and sought a path as straight as his steed's.

He knew what he had to do. By the time he proved himself in the field with this expedition, the dark of the moon would be upon them. That was the time to find the truth about Mica and the princess.

Baamin claimed the spell was too risky without further investigation. But not knowing might prove even more dangerous.

"Aiyeee!" A helmeted man appeared out of a clump of heather, whirling his broadsword above his head.

Darville's steed screamed and reared, pawing the air with angry ferocity. The raider lunged. His huge blade aimed directly for the steed's exposed belly.

Yanking fiercely on the reins, Darville swung his mount aside. His own blade was unsheathed and sweeping toward the head of his attacker before either had time to think. The sword missed by a hair's breadth.

Another raider appeared behind the first. A dozen more

behind him. A quick glance over his shoulder confirmed Darville's suspicion that his men were in disarray. Useless yells of panic surged through the air.

He whirled his blade above his head in an age-old signal to rally round him. None seemed to see or understand.

"*S'murghing* amateurs," he cursed under his breath as he swung at a lunging raider. His sword bit deep and tasted blood. Red spurts erupted from where the man's arm had been. Shock kept the raider on his feet, gasping, flailing to find his missing limb.

"Aiyeee!" Another raider jumped in front of him, grabbing for the steed's reins.

Darville yanked his mind back to the present crisis. That raider fell with a great slashing wound to his belly.

Parry. Thrust. Rear. He maneuvered frantically to stay asteed and alive. Cavalry had the advantage over foot. Unless the mounted men were thrown into disarray by surprise and heavy losses early in the fray.

He tried again to rally his men into some kind of formation.

Off to his left, the knight who had wanted to stop at the village fell with a lance through his body. Silently, be slithered to the ground to be pounded by the hooves of his own mount. Other bodies littered the ground. The heather soaked up their blood as if quenching a drought. The smell of blood and dust, death and pain rose around the troop. The noise deafened his senses.

"Dragon dung! A century of cavalry against a dozen raiders and we're losing." Darville impaled a hook-nosed man. Two teeth showed through his death grimace.

"Form up!" Darville deliberately reared his steed so his men could find him in the melee.

The young knight who had cautioned him slashed through the throng to take his position to Darville's right and slightly behind. Holmes was at his left shoulder. Fred, in a too large helmet, fought his way to Darville's rear. Other men won control of their steeds as they found previously practiced positions.

Raiders surged around the flanks of the wedge of cavalry. There were more of them now. Perhaps three dozen in all.

Darville dug in his spurs, brought his sword up over his head and forward. He leaned over his steed's neck, his sword pointing ahead. Behind him, his men followed suit as they raced through the throng of attackers. The raiders laughed and jeered at the rapid retreat.

"After them! Don't let the prince escape!" cried a huge fair-haired man sporting a square beard in the style of a SeLenese nobleman.

Darville dared a glance at this apparent leader. His chain mail looked new, and his helmet shone in the fall sunshine. He was no outlaw dependent on the spoils of pillaged villagers.

The troop's path took them uphill. At the crest of the ridge, Darville wheeled the formation around to face his enemy once more. Without a word of command he charged back into the jeering outlaws. His men followed eagerly, their weapons at the ready.

"I want the leader alive!" Darville commanded as his sword bit into the gut of a man who dared stand in his way.

Fred and Holmes raced toward the man with the distinctive square beard. The enemy's sword swooped and sliced into Fred's mount. As the boy jumped free of the falling steed, Holmes removed the head of the foreign nobleman with one vicious blow.

Chapter 11

Brevelan stretched her arms over her head in a luxurious welcome to the bright morning sunshine. Birds greeted her. The morning mist dissipated under her gaze. Life was beautiful once more. Her back muscles arched in relief after the long weeks spent in bed recovering her strength. The baby stretched, too. His head pressed against her ribs while a foot planted itself firmly upon her bladder.

After the hours of pain and weakness, she appreciated that small, but very normal discomfort. She looked down at her swelling belly. Every day the child seemed to grow faster. Her gown strained over the bulk of the baby, where before the ordeal of premature labor it had draped loosely.

"Good morning, love." Jaylor's arms sneaked around Brevelan's middle as he nuzzled her neck in greeting.

"And a beautiful morning it is." She turned in his embrace to receive a more intimate kiss. A piece of her mind sought Yaakke's presence to make sure of their privacy. They were safe. The boy was down at the bathing pool, splashing in youthful abandon.

"How do you feel?" Concern touched Jaylor's brow as he ran his hands over her body.

"Very well. Remarkably well. I think I could climb the mountain today." She couldn't help smiling. Her body and her mind were throbbing with vibrant health.

"You mustn't overdo until we know for sure you are truly recovered. It has only been a fortnight. I'd be less concerned if we were nearer the University. Surely among all those magicians there will be one who could help you in another crisis. I'll not trust Krej again, especially with your life." He pulled her tightly against his body, reminding them both of how close they had come to being permanently separated by death.

Brevelan shuddered in premonition. "Then perhaps we should go to Coronnan City."

"The journey is too long. A week or more of fast walking, if there are no delays. It will be too hard on you." His hands lingered on her as if he needed constant touch to reassure himself of her well-being.

"But I feel like running and jumping, working and playing with boundless joy. At the very least, I am going to clean the flusterhen coop today."

Jaylor lay his head back and roared his laughter. "You did that yesterday—while you were supposed to be still abed, recovering."

"Yaakke could send us to Coronnan City." They both sobered at that thought.

" 'Tis too chancy." Jaylor shook his head and clung to her, lest she try the journey on her own.

"He did it twice that night without undue fatigue."

"I think I need to chat with the boy. He stretches himself too far, too fast. One day his magic will backlash on him."

"Lord Krej was ready to pay dearly for the secret of the spell. I felt him seeking a way to force you to tell him," Brevelan said. She ran her fingers through Jaylor's auburn curls. Today his mind was clear and strong; no trace of Krej's malevolence tainted his thoughts. And his heart beat in a regular rhythm without any trace of damage or blockage.

The image of Krej's magic dissolving the blockages had been real. Jaylor was now healed.

"If Krej finds out that Yaakke threw that spell, he'll risk anything for access to the boy." Jaylor denied her suggestion once more.

"My father has beguiled the Council into believing he has only the best interests of Coronnan at heart. Perhaps Yaakke could serve as bait for a trap. If the lords saw how desperate Krej is to further his own ends, his magic would be exposed, but not by you."

"Yaakke is too vulnerable. His sense of morality is too unformed. I'd rather not risk him."

"I'll not have you risk yourself."

"Don't worry, love. I know Krej. He'll never be able to corrupt me."

A cloud drifted across the sun. Brevelan felt the chill of darkness encroach on her soul.

Rosie listened to Janataea's quiet, even breathing. She could count on her governess being asleep for at least another hour. When Janataea awoke in time to dress for dinner, she would have a headache. Blame for her ailment would fall on Rosie, followed by suitable punishment. Usually several hours locked in the wardrobe after dinner. The routine had been followed nearly every day since their arrival in Coronnan.

At least dinner would be a quiet affair. Prince Darville had refused to see Rosie since that awful night when his cat attacked her. There was no doubt in Rosie's mind that the evil beast had been trying to kill her. His Grace had sent a message that he would be reviewing his troops in the field. Most likely that was an excuse to avoid another embarrassing meeting with her.

She couldn't use an appointment with the prince as an excuse to avoid Janataea's increasingly foul moods. Rosie didn't ride and she wouldn't read, though she'd been taught the rudiments. She was running out of places to be that were outside the suite when Janataea awoke.

"Tell my governess that I am invited to share a glass of wine with Senior Magician Baamin." Rosie dismissed the tiring woman with a wave of her hand.

Though it was true the old magician had invited her to visit him anytime, he had not specifically asked her to come today. Janataea approved of Rosie meeting Baamin. She had been instructed to kill the Senior Magician, Chancellor of the University, and adviser to the crown. Rosie doubted she would bother following those orders.

Sometimes, when the pain was too much for the beta'arack Baamin swallowed in increasing doses, the old man's temper was as vile as Janataea's or Uncle Rumbelly's. But he never directed his anger and frustration toward Rosie. Some lord named Krej and a dragon called Shayla were the victim of Baamin's acid tongue.

Rosie wished she could use words as effectively as the

elderly magician. Quite frankly, she liked Old Baamin. She would visit him today and take her time getting there.

Everyone would understand if she became lost in the dark passageway that led from the palace, underneath the river, to the University.

Endless nooks and crannies within the palace corridors invited exploration. Over the past fortnight, Rosie had discovered many of them. The corridor she followed ended at a blank wall. Backtracking a little bit, though, revealed a concealed doorway and access to a tunnel. Rosie loved the tunnels.

She ran her sensitive fingertips over the stone wall to her left. A drop of water splashed on her face from above at the same time she was trying to avoid a shallow puddle at her feet. The perpetual dampness within the long spiral staircase was a nuisance. But the smells that lingered in the stale air were so interesting and the tunnels harbored the most unusual shadows.

She wound her way deeper down the stairs than she had ever been before. The dark silence suited her.

A mouse scurried toward her from the opposite end of the long curving tunnel. It stopped short within a few feet of her. Whiskers and nose bounced up and down. The mouse looked behind, as if deciding which direction was safer. Barely an instant later, it dashed past Rosie and into a crack between two of the wall stones.

Curious. Tiny creatures were supposed to run from her. There must be someone or something coming this way. She hoped it wasn't the cat. Rosie would willingly face Janataea's increasingly unpredictable moods rather than that cat.

Every time she came within a few yards of the multicolored creature, Rosie felt sick to her stomach or dizzy, or both. Frantically, she searched the tunnel for a means of escape. The mouse's crack was too small for her human body.

The scrape of leather on stone sounded in the distance. A shoe or a boot. The footfall came again to her ears. Heavy and slow. A man's tread, moving with care over the slippery dampness.

The flicker of a torch on the walls reflected a huge shadow of a man just around the next curve of the tunnel.

Her nose twitched and her tongue tasted the air. The smell of male sweat and horse and . . . something too elusive for her to grasp quickly, masked the man's identity.

Rosie froze in indecision. She didn't have permission to explore the palace and its secret passages. But she hadn't been told to stay in her apartment either. Should she run and invite pursuit and punishment, or stay and accept whatever reprimand the man chose?

Before she could decide, the shadow moved forward, wavered in the uncertain light, and consolidated into the figure of a tall slim man. His golden hair hung free about his shoulders. Several days' growth of beard shadowed his cheeks and jaw. He wore black leather riding clothes and a long sword at his hip. The torch he carried in his right hand was fresh and burned brightly.

"Your Grace," she whispered, as she dropped a curtsy. The cat wasn't with Prince Darville. She breathed easier.

"Princess Rossemikka? What are you doing down here?" His voice was curt, but not angry.

Rosie shrugged. "Exploring. I was bored." She didn't dare look directly into his eyes. As she rose from her curtsy she made sure she took a step backward.

"Then we do share at least one interest. I spent my childhood memorizing these passages. But you travel without a light?" He held his torch higher to illumine more of the tunnel.

"I didn't think to bring one." She put two more steps between them. Moisture filmed her upper lip and her back.

"Are you one of those rare individuals who can see in the dark?" Darville sounded envious.

How was she to explain that she didn't exactly see in the dark? Her perception was more a matter of knowing where she was and what her next step should be. All of her senses guided her, not just sight. Rather than put the complicated thought into words, she lifted one shoulder in the age-old gesture of indecision and moved farther away from him.

Her nose twitched again in the tunnel's shifting currents of air. She smelled blood on the prince. Old blood, not fresh. And fear gone stale. Rosie wanted to run from him and the coiled tension in his muscles.

"Why do you fear me?" His free hand jerked out to grasp her arm, as if sensing her need for flight.

Rosie shrugged again and swallowed a scream.

"You seem to fear many things." Darville's hand turned gentle, but still restrained her.

"There are many things I do not understand." She looked behind her, seeking a way out. "Until I do, I'm . . . I prefer to watch from a distance." Rosie tugged her arm a little. Politeness had been drilled into her for so long she feared offending her betrothed almost as much as she dreaded remaining in his presence.

"Wise advice, Princess. We would all profit from watching and listening rather than jumping to raw conclusions. My Council should be so cautious. And so must I." A smile touched his lips. But his eyes were too weary to echo the sentiment.

"I was told you were patrolling the hills with the army. Have you been gone all of these last five days?"

"I've just returned."

"Alone?"

His smile spread further. "We stable the steeds on the mainland. I came across by boat to the end of this tunnel, rather than walk through the city across the bridges." The smile vanished. "There are times when even a king must be alone with his thoughts. When he must make a decision without benefit of council."

"Then I will not intrude, Your Grace." Rosie ducked her head and tried to back away. He retained his grip on her arm.

"Please stay. I need to see someone fresh and beautiful and innocent. You're the only one I know in the city who answers that description." His sadness radiated from him in almost tangible waves. "And call me Darville. If we are to be married, we might as well enjoy the privilege of first names. I understand your family calls you Rosie?"

"I must return, Your Gr . . . Darville. My governess does not like me to be out of her sight for too long." She struggled against his grip.

"A young woman needs a chaperone. But I hope when you are my queen, Mistress Janataea will not continue to govern all of your actions."

What did his expression imply? He was both fierce and disgusted. She hoped he would not vent his emotions on her.

"Janataea is very devoted to me. I cannot dismiss her." True enough. Rosie couldn't dismiss her guardian; only Uncle Rumbelly could do that. But she would certainly like to. Especially when Janataea came back from one of her secret outings in the middle of the night. For a long time Rosie had suspected her governess of having an affair with her uncle, or even with Kevin-Rosse. Now she wasn't so certain. Janataea's disdain for men seemed too genuine to allow a sexual liaison.

"I'll consider retaining her for our children." Darville smiled down at her as he took a step along the corridor. His grip on her arm remained.

"Release me. Please." Rosie gulped.

"Release my hand or release you from our betrothal?" He stopped walking to turn his glittering eyes on her.

"Both."

"Explain." His hand fell away. Flickering torchlight made his golden eyes fierce and feral.

She was reminded of a wolf. Then she remembered the elusive scent on him. Death. Darville had recently killed something. Or someone.

"I'm afraid of you. I'm afraid of marriage. Uncle Rumbelly made all the arrangements before he told me. I don't know you, or your country."

Darville's face lost all expression. "Ignorance breeds fear," he muttered. At a cross corridor he paused, then moved on past it. "I'll show you back to your apartment."

Rosie didn't ask what was down the ignored tunnel. Her curiosity pulled her. Next time. She'd explore that one tomorrow. If he allowed her to stay in Coronnan.

"This next corridor leads to the royal suite. We'll move in there after the wedding. And off to our left is the staircase that will take you to your present bedchamber." His tone was cold and impersonal.

"You still insist on marrying me?"

No answer.

They began to climb the narrow stone steps.

"Do all of the bedrooms have secret exits?" Rosie was surprised she hadn't found this one. But then, she hadn't had the opportunity to explore her own suite, not with Janataea keeping watch on her.

"No. Only the family chambers are important enough to need an extra way out. This is the oldest part of the palace—the keep. It was built almost a thousand years ago, before Coronnan was consolidated into one kingdom. In those days, war and pestilence raged. My ancestors built a fortress in the center of the largest island. The river was a natural moat." His manner lightened, as if he had made an important decision.

"But the palace is so big now. It covers almost the entire island." The time he spoke of was incomprehensible to Rosie. And so was the prince. She had expected him to hit her for invading his tunnels. Instead he was giving her a history lesson.

"There have been a few years of peace," Darville smiled. "My family expanded the palace, and rebuilt sections that were destroyed during the last war. Palace Reveta Tristile—the palace of a sad rebuilding. Everyone lost a great deal during that war."

And he was the last of his line. He needed her to provide children. He needed the armies that were her dowry. She was trapped.

"Who else knows about these tunnels?" Rosie looked forward and back apprehensively.

"Frightened of invasion? I assure you, Rosie, these tunnels are part of our defense in case of invasion."

"No. Not invasion." Though Kevin-Rosse and Uncle Rumbelly would give much to know a secret way into the castle. If they invaded and assassinated Darville, she would be released from the marriage.

Or killed with him.

"I just do not want strangers wandering into my bedroom." She took the last step to a landing which ended in a wooden door.

"There is more to fear from those we think trustworthy. Their betrayal hurts more than invasion." His mouth took on a new grimness. "Watch from the shadows, Rosie. Watch and know your true enemy before you act."

Was he talking to her or to himself?

"The upper entrances of the tunnels are cunningly hidden and mostly forgotten. You are the only person I have ever encountered down here, Rosie. The river entrance is well concealed and requires an expert boatman to negotiate the currents. You needn't fear strangers." His voice was gentle, but his touch remained firm, almost possessive.

Rosie shied back.

Without another word, Darville pushed against the wooden panels. The door slid sideways into a recess in the stone. Before them was the brocaded curtain that decorated the back of the wardrobe cupboard. With the wooden door in place, one would never suspect the wall behind the massive piece of furniture was not solid stone.

Next time Janataea locked her into this dark wardrobe, she had an escape route.

Chapter 12

"**E**xplain the procedure to me once more." Jaylor clamped down on his impatience. He was well again. Truly well. His heart had miraculously healed while Krej's magic burst through the blockages. Now he was anxious to expand his magic and explore new techniques.

" 'Tis so simple, Master, I don't know how I do it. I just do it," Yaakke protested. He held out his empty palm. A flusterchick appeared in the boy's hand. The baby bird pecked angrily at his fingers.

"Pretend I'm a senile old man who has forgotten everything." For the first time, Jaylor had a glimmering of understanding for his own tutors. How many times had he failed to explain to them how he performed a spell? And each failure resulted in keeping Jaylor from advancing with his classmates.

"As senile as Old Baamin?" Yaakke grinned widely.

Jaylor nodded his agreement. "Master Baamin was born senile. Now talk me through the spell, as if you were telling my master." He placed a comforting hand on the boy's shoulder. "Send the chick back. I'll observe your magic every step of the way."

They both took the three ritual breaths that sent them into a light trance. Jaylor waded through the colored mists that radiated from Yaakke to find a core of magic. Yaakke blinked and the chick vanished.

There was a lone rabbit at the edge of the clearing, hiding under one of the saber ferns that marked the beginning of the forest. Jaylor decided to copy the boy's spell. Yaakke maintained a guiding influence within the trance. They found the animal's aura and observed it for several heartbeats. Then Jaylor murmured the transport spell, grabbing the rabbit with his mind.

Jaylor's muscles twitched and shook. Blackness encroached on his vision. He breathed slower to steady the spell. Then he reformed the wiggling creature at his feet.

Two rabbits sat in front of him, identical in coloring.

The more timid one to his left scampered away for the security of the ferns. The remaining one was bolder. It jumped to Jaylor's crossed legs and bit him. Then it hopped to a clump of grass and began its next meal.

"I didn't have time to find your thoughts!" Jaylor protested. "The rabbit split into two halves of the same whole. We have to find it and put it back before Brevelan finds out." Life wouldn't be easy for either of them if Brevelan discovered something wrong with one of her creatures.

"It should have worked." Yaakke shook his head in dismay. "I was right beside you the whole way."

Yaakke looked at Jaylor strangely, his head cocked to one side.

Jaylor calmed his frantic pulse, forcing his aching muscles to cease their trembling. Magic had never been so difficult. He would have to gain more strength before trying the next spell. A few moments of calm meditation.

There was supposed to be a silvery-blue ley line filled with magic power directly beneath his rump. The magic should have surged through his body and completed the spell properly, with only a little guidance from his mind. He was too tired to seek a solution to the double rabbit right now.

"But it's so simple!" Yaakke placed a steadying hand on Jaylor's knee.

"If the spell is so simple, why did Lord Krej offer me a knighthood and three estates for it?" He threw off the boy's gesture of comfort, more angry at himself than at Yaakke. The meditation hadn't worked.

"How come Lord Krej could work magic with only two Tambootie leaves? That's not the antidote to witchbane," Yaakke said, changing the subject.

"You're right." Jaylor hadn't thought about that. The ancient textbook that had given him the formula for witchbane specifically mentioned that Tambootie enhanced whatever was present in the body: magic, disease, health, drugs.

"I vowed not to tell anyone Krej is working magic again. That night I was too worried about Brevelan to notice how much Tambootie he ingested—barely enough to feed his addiction, not enough to fuel his magic."

"The magic was in him before I brought him to the clearing. That's how I found him. Lord Krej's magic is very distinctive. I'd smell it anywhere."

"I have to get to the capital right away. The antidote must be discovered and neutralized. I also have to keep Krej from making any more mischief like he did last spring. Explain the spell again, Yaakke, so I can send myself." Decisive energy pulsed through him again, his momentary weakness and the rabbits forgotten.

"I can't."

"Think, Yaakke. Think about it very hard. This is important."

"But you can't send yourself. You can only transport other things. Just like you do the wine cups from the University cellars. You're better at that than anyone. Even me."

"Then why hasn't Lord Krej figured it out? He said a living subject always dies or is maimed when transported. And I split that rabbit. Why can't we make it work?"

"Did you imagine the rabbit about five heartbeats younger than it really was at the tail end of the spell?"

"Younger? Time. Are you moving them through time, then?"

Yaakke shrugged. "I guess so. That's what Nimbulan's great-grandfather surmised in his journal. I found it in the forgotten library at the University—the one that was hidden in the cellars and sealed at the end of the war."

"And when you don't know where someone is, you can locate them by smelling their magic."

"Sort of. I guess it's like when you and Brevelan said you're connected by colored umb . . . ubil . . . whatever. Everyone is different."

Excitement danced around Jaylor like a firefly, lighting this idea, then the next and the next. His imagination soared with the dragons.

Dragons.

"We could bring Shayla back!"

"I already tried. I couldn't find her. I guess 'cause I can't gather dragon magic."

"Then we have to try harder. Walk me through the spell again." Before his third breath, Jaylor was back in the void. His mind sought a presence. A greenbird this time. At the touch of his mind, the bird flew from its perch in fright. He caught the bird on the wing and brought it to his hand, perched as it had been on the branch, seconds before.

"Twuweep?" the bird squawked in puzzlement.

Jaylor's eyes snapped opened. He'd done it!

"Twuweep!" The bird took off again, frightened by Jaylor's convulsing arm muscles.

"Master, are you all right? Master!" Yaakke screamed.

Blackness encroached on the edges of Jaylor's vision. His legs began to twitch as uncontrollably as his arm. Heavy saliva collected in his mouth, seeking escape.

"Breathe, Master. You've got to breathe," Yaakke implored as he pumped on Jaylor's chest. "Breathe in, one, two, three. Breathe out, one, two, three." The boy was near tears forcing air into Jaylor's lungs.

The preliminary effects of the void calmed Jaylor's frozen mind. Breathe in, one, two, three. Breathe out, one, two, three. His muscles settled into a pattern of mild shaking.

"Don't tell Brevelan about this, Yaakke."

"Playing with magic that you don't understand is too risky, Darville." Baamin upbraided his monarch with all the many years of his experience in dealing with adolescents at the University.

"How are we to understand how this particular magic works if we don't take a few risks?" Darville tried not to feel like one of the Senior Magician's erring apprentices.

"You are the only legitimate heir to the throne. Please allow someone else to take the chances. If we lose you, we lose the kingdom." Baamin moved closer to the massive desk that stood between them in the king's study.

"There seem to be plenty of claimants for my position. Lord Krej would be delighted if I died or was maimed in this enterprise." Darville braced his legs against the rear wall and his rump against the desk. With the strength of his long thighs he shoved. The desk didn't budge.

"Would the kingdom be delighted with Lord Krej as their king?"

Darville looked sharply over his shoulder to his short adviser. The old man seemed to have lost even more weight in the last week. At least Baamin had had the sense to have his robes altered to fit his diminished frame. Concern for his old friend made Darville pause in his exertions.

"To quote a very wise man: 'The fear bred by ignorance is more crippling than the wounds earned in gaining knowledge.'" Darville pushed again. The massive desk that had served the kings of Coronnan for many generations seemed bolted to the floor.

"I said that in reference to politics, not magic." Baamin moved around the desk to face Darville.

"Of late in Coronnan, magic and politics are so intertwined there is no separation." He put his feet back on the floor.

"Then allow me to force this first confrontation between the princess and your cat."

"At the moment, I think you are more valuable to the kingdom than I am. Besides, how would you explain your presence in the lady's chamber if caught? Your reputation would be ruined, Master Baamin." Darville chuckled under his breath. Magicians were notorious for their ignorance of women. In the old days, when there was still dragon magic to be gathered, magicians were forbidden knowledge of women until after they had achieved master's status. Most magicians couldn't be bothered to expend their precious energies on women even then.

"And I suppose your reputation would survive intact?" Baamin raised one eyebrow in that irritatingly superior way of his.

"Mine would be enhanced for the higher class of partner! Yours would be in tatters."

"I have not always been old, young man. Nor have I always been celibate." Baamin attempted to look down his nose, a difficult feat considering the differences in their heights.

"Your mother hatched you fully grown, complete with

education and white hair. Just ask any of your apprentices,"
Darville teased. He put his feet back up against the wall
for another try at the desk.

"And some men never grow up. Just look at you and
Jaylor." Baamin reached under the desktop and pressed
something just as Darville pushed against the wall. The
prince slid across the top slab of wood and toppled onto
the hard floor as the desk swung aside on a pivot. A gaping
hole in the stone floor lay where the most solid portion of
the desk had been. The top rung of a ladder showed just
below the edge.

"How'd you do that?" Darville stared at the escape hole
in amazement.

"The mere touch of a lever. Your father and I explored
the tunnels when he was a very young king. I believe he
called upon his betrothed, your mother, in much the same
manner as you plan to visit Princess Rossemikka. Your parents' wedding had to be put forward by several moons."

"My father never did anything adventurous," Darville
protested. The late King Darcine had been a loving father,
devoted husband, and a total idiot when it came to politics.
He was incapable of making a decision and allowed the
Council to rule without interference. Now that Darville was
trying to assert authority, the same Council was fighting
him for control of every decision. Even when they lacked
a decision, the Council would not agree to one proffered
by Darville.

"Like me, your father wasn't born old and weak-willed.
We had our bold moments, just as you and Jaylor had
yours. That is why I didn't stop your childhood pranks. I
could have, you know." Baamin extended a hand to assist
Darville to his feet.

"You knew about our friendship?" Darville and Jaylor
had always considered that portion of their young lives
quite secret.

"I am Senior Magician, Roy." He invoked Jaylor's nickname for the royal son who wished for anonymity. "As
well as Chancellor of the University. Very little occurs on
University Island or Palace Isle that I don't know about."

"Even the time Jaylor taught me to swim at Sacred
Isle?"

"That was your first meeting, was it not?"

Darville nodded.

"You were thirteen and Jaylor eleven. Who do you think made it possible for you to steal a boat and for Jaylor to slip away from his lessons?"

"And the time he carried me home from festival dead drunk?"

Baamin shook his head in mild dismay. "I didn't find out about that until you awoke the next morning with the worst hangover in history. I arranged for the healer to dose you against the whore's pox in his vile remedy for your more obvious symptoms. I do hope you have learned to be a little more . . . ah . . . discreet in your liaisons." One bushy white eyebrow raised in rebuke.

Darville looked away in sadness. He and Jaylor had shared much as teenagers. But never the women. Jaylor took his magic too seriously to risk losing it by bedding a woman.

Until Brevelan.

The bond among the three of them was so strong that there had been no jealousy, no need for discussion. Just a natural need to be complete. All three of them.

But in the end, Brevelan had chosen Jaylor as her mate. She, with her special brand of magic, must have known that the child she carried was fathered by Jaylor's seed and not Darville's. He could not imagine Brevelan choosing any man but the father of her child.

"I haven't been with a woman since Brevelan and Jaylor married."

"I haven't been with a woman since I was elected Senior Magician. I allowed myself one last wild night before assuming responsibility for the Commune." Baamin paused a moment, lost in memory. "I often wondered what became of that dark-eyed beauty. I never saw her again."

Baamin gestured to the gaping desk, breaking the somber mood. "Who's first, you or me?"

Dwelling on the past would gain nothing for either of them. Darville needed a princess as his wife and mother to his children. Rossemikka came with impeccable breeding and an admirable dowry of ten thousand trained troops to cut off the menace of SeLenicca. But before he could marry her, he had to discover the secret that existed between the woman and his cat.

"I go alone. You need to stay here and make sure the members of the Council believe I am with you. They will not take kindly to this escapade."

"No, they will not. They fear anything to do with magic these days, even their own magician advisers. I think the Commune is allowed to post those advisers only because the University of Magicians produces the best educated men in the three kingdoms. The time may soon come when all magic is outlawed. Then only outlaws will throw magic."

"Come, Mica." Darville lifted the steeping cat from her latest nest on the windowsill. She snuggled contentedly into his arms and purred loudly. Darville stroked her silken fur with fondness. This might be the last time he held his favorite companion in this guise. He wanted to cherish the moment.

Baamin lit a small candle lantern from the sconce on the wall and handed it to Darville. "Be careful, Your Grace. If anything untoward occurs, you have only to touch the dragon earring and picture me in your mind. I will find a way to come to your rescue."

Chapter 13

My rival reeks of Tambootie once more. His trail should have been easy to follow. Yet I couldn't face the void. Not alone, without guidance or an anchor to this reality.

I thought my rival had broken his addiction. And yet, on the very night he disappears in the elusive transport spell, he returns with the drug heavy on him. The oils permeate his skin, his clothing, his breath.

Is that the secret? We have fostered superstition against the trees so the simple mundanes would fell them, eliminate them from the face of this planet. The trees are the source of the dragons' magic. Without the trees, the dragons are just another menace to be hunted and slaughtered.

I believe we have made a grave mistake. I will experiment with the herb. Perhaps the Tambootie will give me the courage to face the void. If I am correct, we must change our tactics and salvage what we can of the once great forests of Tambootie.

But first I must check on the princess. There is a great deal of magic in the air tonight. She must be safe from all spells. Rossemikka is much more important than just an alliance between the desert warriors of Rossemeyer and the bumbling traders of lush Coronnan. She is the future.

Jaylor drew a shaky breath into his tired lungs and looked around. He was in the scullery of the University. Yaakke had placed him in the one place in the capital that the boy knew best and which was likely to be deserted at this time of day.

Long shudders coursed through Jaylor's body and he shook his head to orient himself. His abrupt passage from the tree-scented clearing to this stone room offended his logic, as well as his nose. For several heartbeats there had been nothing. Worse than the magic void, worse than the nightmare of his rite of passage in a windowless room filled with Tambootie smoke.

But he had survived.

No wonder the key to transport lay in time. The shock of the void was so great that a soul needed to be existing in some other dimension at the same time in order to re-root itself at the end of the trip.

He took another deep breath to steady himself. His cured heart beat strong and in a regular rhythm. He just hoped his magic was as sound as his heartbeat after Krej's magic had poured through him. He had a task to complete before Brevelan was sent to him. She and Yaakke needed to know for sure that the spell worked, and that she could survive the journey with the baby intact. A summons would be ideal but might prove too draining on Yaakke's magic.

Jaylor took a third deep breath and pictured in his mind the locked wine cellar of the University. The private reserve contained the best wines from three kingdoms. Apprentices were invited to imbibe at will—as long as they could bring the cups of wine to their quarters magically. By the time they mastered the complicated spells, they were ready for promotion to journeyman.

Jaylor was unusually adept at this particular spell. He'd mastered it easily his first week at the University. But he hadn't used the traditional method of levitating the cup along the myriad corridors to his room. Instead, he'd used rogue magic to instantly transport the wine to his hand.

No one had recognized his triumph as legitimate and Jaylor couldn't explain how he had accomplished the unheard-of feat. Yaakke wasn't so different from himself after all.

With the wine cup firmly in his mind, Jaylor emblazoned a message into the crockery. "SAFE AND WHOLE" burned into the pottery. Then he filled the cup with the finest of red wines. A new shudder rippled along his legs and arms. The muscles cramped and twitched. His mouth watered at the thought of rich fruity wine. That would restore his confidence and his strength. So he filled a second

Chapter 14

" 'Twas over two years ago . . ." Mikka's voice drifted off in memory.

Oh! She had spent a glorious three days in the mountains, dressed in her brother's old clothes, voluminous trews and a tunic that nearly reached her knees. Under the tutelage of Erda, an old Rover woman, Mikka pushed her muscles and her wits to the limit as she learned to identify dozens of plants and their healing properties, as well as to survive in the high desert. The exercises of mind and body felt good after the restrictions imposed upon her by Uncle Rumbelly.

This wasn't the first time she'd slipped away from supervision for a lesson in the healing arts. An hour here, an afternoon there. She was never absent long enough for anyone to miss her.

However, there were some lessons that couldn't be learned during those stolen hours in the back of Erda's colorfully draped market stall.

On her last afternoon of luxurious freedom, Mikka ran down a hill to show Erda her latest discovery, a rare blossom consisting of long pink filaments that could be fermented into a poultice to clean out infected wounds. Her enthusiasm overtook her feet and she stumbled and rolled to the edge of their primitive camp.

She fetched up against the boots of the frowning captain of the guard. Erda was bound and gagged. The grimly silent man threw Mikka onto the back of his own steed. He didn't dare bind the hands of a royale, but his speed and handling kept her from throwing herself off the horse. They raced back to the castle in record time. The

cup for himself. The first was sent back to Yaakke. The other he brought to the scullery.

His hands curved around the cup lovingly. He opened his eyes to taste the favored drink.

There were two cups. One in each hand. One pure vinegar, the other unfermented fruit juice!

His spell had split again.

Darville stepped into the boxlike remains of the desk. The ladder held his weight. The darkness of the tunnels beckoned him.

He found his way to the main passage easily. The cross tunnel to the princess' chamber was only a few paces along to his right. His small light illuminated a circle around him, isolating him from the rest of the tunnel, from reality, from himself.

This might as well be the magic void Jaylor talked about when he entered a trance. For Darville, the eeriness of the tunnels became an alien territory, a journey through the void to a magic answer.

He met no resistance at the top of the staircase. The few gowns hanging in the wardrobe didn't hamper his passage. Cautiously, he blew out his candle before he opened the doors of the wardrobe a crack.

Silent darkness greeted him. The moon was in its most remote phase. No light penetrated the heavily curtained window. By feel alone, he found the massive bedpost that reached nearly to the ceiling. As if guided, his free hand found the opening in the draperies that shielded the sleeper from drafts and prying eyes.

Mica roused in his arms. She squeaked a quiet inquiry. Then she shivered in his grasp. Darville sensed the alertness in her body and imagined her ears perked and nose twitching. Before she could jump and awaken Rossemikka, he placed the cat on top of the mound of covers that must be the princess.

Instantly the enclosed bed space was filled with a magical glow of wondrous blue light. Waves of light and magic nearly forced Darville to close his eyes and back away. He fought the impulse. Whatever the outcome, he had to know what happened tonight.

The cat grew. The woman shrank. They surged back and forth. The white streak in Rosie's hair gleamed brighter, jumped from her body to Mica's and back again, highlighting, merging and separating, merging again, then with a snap the light was gone.

"You may light the lantern again, beloved," a sweet, melodious voice rose from the bed. It was Rossemikka, and yet not. She sounded huskier, more sure of herself, and much more sensuous.

"Rosie?" Darville's voice cracked as it hadn't done since he was twelve.

"Mikka, Rossemikka to be more precise. Rosse is my cat. Please light the lantern so I may see you properly."

The soft feminine voice sounded sweeter than his favorite ballad. Unexplained dampness on his palms made the simple act of striking fire stone clumsy, adolescent. Darville blushed at his ineptness, and thanked the Stargods for a few more moments of darkness in which to recover.

"Rosie, Mica. Mikka, Rosse. Please explain," he pleaded. At last, the wick caught a spark and he raised it to reveal the woman who had haunted his dreams since that day in Shayla's lair.

Rippling strands of hair flowed down the naked body of Princess Rossemikka. Gold and brown of harvest mixed with just a hint of the bright red of autumn leaves in sunshine. No brand of white at her temple marred the silken mane that covered her body, almost adequately.

On the bed, nestled into the pillow, was a sleeping cat. Her fur was the same wondrous mix of color, except for one white ear and eye.

"It's a long story, Darville. Do you have the time?" Mikka reached a familiar hand to caress his arm.

"Until dawn. Baamin says this transformation is only temporary. The two of you must embrace willingly for the spell to be reversed permanently." A lump formed in his throat. He'd found her, his perfect princess, but only for a few hours. Come morning, the cat would once more be in control of the woman's body.

They both knew that Rosie would not willingly embrace Mica for any reason, even a restoration of nature's balance.

Mikka looked at the cat for a long moment. When she

returned her attention to Darville, tears made her eyes overbright. "You must know the truth. Then you will be able to end this wickedness. And I beg of you, Darville, terminate this evil spell, even if you must use force. Even if you must kill one or both of us. Promise me."

Darville caught her emotional pain. The tragedy reminded him of his own experience. Lord Krej, disguised as the half-naked, beast-headed man, had left him to die in the forgotten, often reviled body of a wolf. His memories left him mute.

"Swear to me, Darville, that you will do whatever must be done to restore the balance of souls. If you don't, I fear the coven plans to use us as pawns. Their plans grow bigger with each season. I believe they want to wrest political power away from legitimate governments. And they will use us to do it." Her hand gripped his arm in desperation.

"I swear, by all that binds me to my destiny as King of Coronnan, that I will restore the balance of souls."

"Then I will tell you how it came about, so that you can understand. . . ."

Stargods only knew if her teacher would survive the dungeons, where the other guards would take her.

"Never has there been such a scandal in this family!" Lord Rumbellesth bellowed from his thronelike chair.

Mikka faced her raging uncle without a word, head high and chin thrust forward in affirmation of the rightness of her actions.

"No daughter of mine will ever debase herself with foreign lore and peasant herbs and remedies."

Uncle Rumbelly grimaced in pain and swilled a huge mouthful of beta'arack.

"Since I am certainly no daughter of yours, then I shall continue to prepare myself for my life as Princess Royale of Rossemeyer." Disgust for her mother's brother overcame her dignified silence. "I choose to set an example for our people. We must have healers of our own and not be dependent upon foreign magicians."

Just then, two guards led a badly bruised and humiliated Erda into the audience hall. Mikka sped to the side of her longtime friend and teacher. A heavily armed courtier grabbed her around the waist and hauled her back to face her uncle.

"If word of your disgraceful behavior leaks out, your chances of a successful marriage are ruined," Uncle Rumbelly spat.

"Listen to your uncle, dear. He knows best," Dowager Queen Sousyam echoed her brother's sentiments.

"If he," Mikka indicated her loathsome uncle, "were to produce a candidate worth marrying, I might have reason to listen to him." She refused to dwell on her current predicament. This wasn't the first time she'd been hauled before Uncle Rumbelly for discipline. Nor would this be the last, even if she married one of his sniveling princelings.

"You are a princess and must set an example for your ladies. How can you do that dressed as a boy, exposing your limbs, and with dirt all over you?" Rumbelly reminded them all of her inappropriate behavior.

Queen Sousyam shuddered delicately and wrung her hands.

"What is exposed? My hair and ankles are covered!" Mikka protested.

As the mother of three children, Queen Sousyam was

entitled to fully expose her skinny, jiggling breasts. Mikka's gowns were cut a little higher, as befitted a virgin, but still low enough to display her potential.

"My brother's cast-off clothes cover more of me than the gown you wear, Mother. These trews are so full, you can't possibly discern the shape of my legs."

"How dare you mention your anatomy in such a blatant manner?" Rumbelly took another swig of his liquor.

The Queen Dowager looked close to fainting.

Mikka's mother was a mouse, without a thought of her own. Tradition had been pounded into her since . . . oh, forever. Well, Mikka was not going to bow to tradition. It was up to her to stand up for the rights of herself and her brothers in the face of their power-hungry uncle. Why, Uncle Rumbelly wasn't even a royale. Just the younger brother of the Queen Dowager.

"Mayhap it is time to set a new kind of example for the women of Rossemeyer." Mikka turned to confront the gathered courtiers, rather than her uncle. "We are a land of warriors. Our mercenaries bring much needed gold and trade to our impoverished shores. But *he* restricts our campaigns to 'safe' little wars because we lack healers of our own for battlefield injuries and illness, and we dare not trust foreign healers who might be our enemy in the last war or the next." Mikka's face flushed with exhilaration. Rossemeyer needed change and she intended to provide the impetus. At sixteen she was considered an adult, ready to face the challenges of her life alone.

"Our soldiers are as tired as I am of the humdrum mercenary wars imposed on us by you, Uncle. Rossemeyer should conquer empires. Now we barely conquer boredom."

"Go to your room, Princess Rossemikka," Lord Rumbellesth commanded.

The quiet calm of his voice only hinted at the roaring anger underneath his words.

"When I am assured of Erda's freedom and well-being."

"You defend a Rover?"

"I care for a friend."

"Never name one of those loathsome thieves as friends!" Rumbellesth's face became splotched with high color. He reached for his ever-present cup of distilled spirits. "You will retire now."

"Release Erda," Mikka called to the guards holding the old woman upright. The men looked first at her, then to the regent. After a moment's hesitation, they obeyed her.

For a moment it looked as if Uncle Rumbelly would explode. Mikka had purposely defied him in little ways for years—showing up late for audiences with prospective husbands, walking in the gardens without the protection of her governess, and pointedly refusing all drink except water when Rumbelly was noticeably drunk. Her open disregard for his orders looked to be the absolute end of his patience.

"I have had enough of your disrespect. You need a husband to bed you and tame your unnatural inclinations. Name your husband." Rumbellesth glared at Mikka through slitted eyes.

Mikka felt the cold menace in that gaze. She knew she was in trouble, yet she persevered. "Guarantee Erda's freedom and well-being."

Rumbellesth waved a hand at the Rover woman. The older of the two guards released Erda's bonds and placed a polite hand under her elbow as he escorted her back out the side door. The ancient woman glanced over her shoulder toward Mikka as she was led away. Her blacker than black eyes seemed to warn her. Warn her of what?

"She is safe. Now name your husband." Rumbellesth took another swig of beta'arack. A little of the yellowish liquid dribbled from the corner of his mouth.

"I find all of the prospects lacking." Mikka stared at the offensive drops of liquor.

"You have been paraded before a dozen eligible young men. Choose one, tonight, for you shall be wed on the morrow."

"No." Mikka suddenly felt cold. This time her uncle meant to marry her off without delay.

"Then I must choose for you. So sayeth the law," he pronounced to the assembled diners. "At the fourth hour after dawn you will be escorted to the chapel where you will be joined in perpetual wedlock to Lord Jhorge, my son."

Clammy-handed, sour-breathed Jhorge! A year younger

than herself and still dependent on his father for the smallest decisions.

"Never. I'll never marry that mealymouthed, whitetailed hare."

"Oh, Mikka," her mother wailed and twisted her heavy rings around and around her bony fingers. "What will it take to make you see reason? You must marry. Name any price, just so you marry Lord Jhorge."

Any price? She could ask for the kingdom's wealth and her uncle would be honor bound to grant it. Instead, she requested the impossible.

"I ask the privilege of *Singing* to my own babes."

"Singing? The Princess wishes to *Sing?* First witch's remedies and now *Songs!*" Lords and servitors alike murmured in awe as they made the flapping gesture against evil.

Witches *Sang* their evil spells. Therefore, all women were forbidden to make music with their voices or other instruments in Rossemeyer.

"Guards, remove the princess to the south tower." Rumbellesth lowered his gaze from the soldiers standing at the door. His pale gray eyes seemed to bore directly into her private thoughts.

The south tower.

A dark and grim cell where she would be forgotten, unfed, unloved.

Mikka fought the trembling of her chin.

The south tower.

Prisoners died there.

"Your governess will be sent to see to your needs. You shall have no books, no companions, and the meanest of foodstuffs. And you will not leave that tower until you agree to marry. You, Princess Rossemikka, need a strong hand to tame your impulses and teach you to be a proper woman."

A heavy hand gripped her arm with cruel strength. She felt bruises forming under the iron fingers.

"What shall I do?" she whispered to deaf ears.

She whispered her question again to the impatient Janataea hours later.

"I don't know, my princess. Your uncle has promised to replace me as your tutor and guardian before we break our fast at dawn." The tall spinster, who had been with Mikka since her coming of womanhood, prowled the single room allotted to them. "The Lord Regent has pronounced me unfit to be a royal governess. I have allowed you to slip away to learn forbidden things once too often." Janataea picked up a sampler of crude embroidery. "I see Lord Rumbelly has decided to allow you some needlework to occupy your hands while imprisoned."

"That's my punishment. I have to learn proper women's activities in order to entice a husband. As if any man would be interested in anything but my title and marriage portion." Her brother faced the same problems in choosing a wife. At least Rossemanuel could wait another two years until he was old enough to assume the throne without a regent. Then he could choose his own queen.

A harsh yowl broke their contemplative silence. The screech of cat claws scratching at the locked door sent shivers up Mikka's spine. The annoyed guard, posted outside, opened the door just wide enough for Mikka's pet cat, Rosse, to enter. Then the portal was locked and barred up.

With tears in her eyes, Mikka picked up her closest companion. The small cat grumbled and mewed her protest at having to search the castle for her mistress. Mikka soothed the variegated brown fur with gentle strokes.

"It is not fair. I won't waste away into a stupid mouse like my mother," Mikka proclaimed to the silent walls of her prison.

"There is a fine line drawn between a strong woman and a . . . and the kind of women who are outlawed in this kingdom." Janataea did not look at Mikka as she made this pronouncement.

"What kind of woman is that?" Mikka didn't look up from the cat.

"A long time ago, the legends say, there were women warriors who fought alongside the men. They were strong and beautiful. Ideal companions to our fierce mercenaries. In battle, these women surrounded their men with protective spells. Their *Songs* of magic were said to send opposing armies into madly disorganized retreat. But the leader of the women's brigade loved only women and refused to take any man to her bed. She seduced the queen." Janataea refused to look at Mikka.

"Another woman might prove a better lover than some of the rabbit kits my uncle wants me to wed."

"That kind of woman is not considered a suitable subject for an innocent princess to discuss." Janataea finally turned to face her young charge. "Some say that long-ago queen, Safflon by name, was a powerful witch. She refused her husband access to her bed until he acknowledged their only child, Jaylene, as his heir. When he refused, the queen and her lover brought a plague on the entire country. The female warriors were executed, en masse, in their barracks. Queen Safflon was with them. They were all witches." While the news of the ancient massacre penetrated Mikka's thoughts, Janataea fingered the folds of her gown, which always concealed numerous pockets.

"How awful." Mikka clutched Rosse tight against her breast, as if the cat could protect her from a similar fate. The pet scrambled to her customary place on the princess' shoulder and began her bath.

"Since all of the women warriors worked witchcraft in protecting the armies, I presume my ancestors also condemned all witches. Is that why women are forbidden to *Sing*?"

Janataea nodded silently. "However," the governess continued the lesson, "every few years rumors spread through Rossemeyer that some witches escaped. A race of women warriors is said to exist far to the west of here. Jaylene was exiled after her mother's death. She may have set up a court somewhere with the survivors."

Mikka found the story horrible and fascinating at the same time. She could see a similar fascination in her governess' expression and posture.

Janataea was tall and strong. Her arm and back muscles were well developed, though she never seemed to exercise. Mikka had watched her pick up the royal brothers with ease, one under each arm, when they were ten and twelve. No small weight for a big man. And Janataea disliked men intensely.

Could it be that this favored governess was really one of the legendary female warriors? Mikka's imagination ran wild with possibilities.

"If I could escape," Mikka thought out loud, "I could

seek out these women and enlist them to my cause. If I returned with an army at my back, I could supplant Uncle Rumbelly." Childish dreams at best. Escape was out of the question.

Mikka's prison was one level below the top watch platform of the tallest tower in the castle. There was a sheer drop to the bottom of a rocky cliff from the single, arrow-slit window. The guard outside the door was well armed and loyal to her uncle, even if Mikka could open the massive planks of wood.

"A foolish notion, Mikka." Janataea began to pace the circumference of the room, widdershins—opposite the path of the sun. Little furniture impeded her progress. There was only a cot for sleeping and a single stool for sitting. Not even a hearth interrupted the smooth lines of the walls.

"I know. I was only wishing." Mikka sank onto the cot. She wasn't willing to give in to despair yet. But her hopes were fading fast. Rosse butted her head against Mikka's chin and purred her sympathy. The princess reached a loving hand to her pet.

At least she had Rosse to keep her company. No one in the castle was willing to suffer the cat's temper tantrums if they were separated for long. That was why Mikka had given the cat part of her own name. As long as Rosse was with her, Mikka felt . . . well, she just felt better.

"There is no evidence such a nation of women warriors truly exists." Janataea was staring at Mikka in an odd way after her third circuit of the room. "Yet there may be a way for you to escape."

"How?" Mikka looked up with excitement, as well as a little trepidation.

"There is magic in your family," Janataea stated flatly.

"Magic, bah," Mikka dismissed the subject. "Leave the incantations and prayers to feeble old men and priests. Strong men and knowledgeable healers are the answers to Rossemeyer's problems."

"Then why did you ask to *Sing?*"

"Because *Singing* is the one thing they could not give me."

"On your mother's side, the magic is strong," Janataea continued. "Lord Rumbellesth started training as a magician when he was very young. But he gave it up because his power didn't come fast enough, or full enough. He enjoys a different kind of power now."

"He enjoys making other people miserable. But that won't help me escape."

"Still, there is magic in your family. You carry the potential in your body, either for yourself or your offspring." Janataea had narrowed her restless pacing and was examining the princess with a critical eye.

"Tell me what you are plotting," Mikka urged.

"Your bond with the cat is very strong. She is almost a part of you." Now Janataea was dipping into the folds of her skirt pocket for a little leather bag she always carried. "The cat has the freedom of the castle. You do not."

"So?"

"So you and the cat will exchange places."

"I can't very well go creeping about the castle on all fours, expecting people to believe I'm a cat," Mikka snorted.

"You could if your soul was in the cat's body, and Rosse's less rebellious personality was in yours."

Stunning possibilities rolled over Mikka. As a cat, she could prowl the castle, spy on anyone. She could even leave the grounds, go into Erda's market stall unescorted. And if she could go that far, she could leave Rossemeyer's desert plateaus altogether. Perhaps she could travel west, across the mountains to find a nation of women warriors who would welcome her strength and intelligence, instead of reviling her.

"Let me think about it."

"Do not take too long in the thinking. The dark of the moon is only days away. That will be the best time to make the exchange."

Three days later, after a diet of stale bread and water, and no exercise for mind or body, Mikka knew she had to take drastic measures to escape.

"How?" she asked Janataea, without preamble on the evening of the dark of the moon.

"First you must fully relax, my princess," Janataea crooned. "Lie down on the cot with Rosse on your chest." Her words took on a lilting quality, unlike anything Mikka had heard emerge from a female throat.

Mikka obeyed. Rosse curled her tiny brown body into a ball for a nap. Her one white eye and ear were barely slitted to observe the ceremony.

Janataea pulled nine candles from her pockets. She placed eight of them around the bed where Mikka lay. The ninth she held over the princess' recumbent form. With a pass of the hand, the candles flared to life. Another wave of the hand and the ninth hovered in the air above Mikka's forehead without support.

"Now, Rossemikka, breathe slowly, ever so slowly. In, two, three. Hold, two, three. Out, two, three. Hold, two, three. Again. In, hold, out, hold." Over and over again the *Song* guided Mikka's breathing until the unnatural rhythm took on new importance and her body knew no other sequence.

Breathing became a dance, slow, stately, magical.

With each breath Mikka's muscles relaxed a little more. Her mind drifted, separated from her body, and observed.

"Think of the cat. You are Mikka, she is Rosse. Together you are Rossemikka. You are one being. Woman-cat. Cat-woman," Janataea intoned.

Mikka's other self watched as the two images on the narrow cot merged into one blurry lump of variegated brown and gold. The image took on the iridescent glow of Rosse's gorgeous fur, instead of Mikka's own dull brown.

"Bring the cat into yourself. Take yourself into the cat."

The images blurred further, separated, and blurred again.

"Keep the cat within you." Janataea sprinkled a little powder from her pouch over the entire length of princess and cat. The candles flared high. "Step away from the cat. Take her body away from her." The governess clapped her hands three times, spun in place three times, widdershins again, and repeated the clap as she sang the instructions.

Waves and waves of sound rolled around and around the circular room. The mysterious powder erupted into cold flame, unnatural red flame that turned hair and fur to burnished gold. Janataea's magic fire flashed and bounced from girl to ceiling, to floor and back again. Mikka's consciousness was yanked downward with unimaginable force.

And the deed was done. Mikka blinked her cat's eyes at the distorted images around her.

"From time to time you will remember who you are."

Janataea's voice sounded strange and distant. Her words didn't quite make sense, but Mikka understood them. "As time goes by, your memories will dim and you will truly become a cat. You may never again be a princess, unless both you and Rosse are embraced and willing." Janataea smiled as she caressed the hair of the reclining princess.

At dawn, a tiny brindled brown cat slipped from the castle while a brown-haired princess with a single white streak at her right temple slept.

A long time later, the little cat found a clearing that called to her, comforted her, and protected her in the mountains west and north of Rossemeyer.

Chapter 15

LIFE bursting with colorful emotions. DEATH with all its pain and sorrow. Grief, joy, love, hate, vengeance, lust, hunger, replete.

All the emotions of thousands of capital inhabitants burst upon Brevelan before she fully emerged from the void. The baby moved restlessly within her womb. She wasn't sure if the child was as uncomfortable as she amid the onslaught of emotions, or if he sought closer contact with the life all around them.

Her feet touched the stone floor. She drew one deep breath through her mouth and held it until she opened her eyes. Even without the passage of air through her nose, she was aware of the cooking odors that permeated this portion of the building. Many animals had died to feed the population within these walls. At least she hadn't known any of the creatures, hadn't treated their small ailments. Their deaths weighed upon her, but not heavily.

Life bloomed too vibrantly within her to dwell on death outside herself.

"Jaylor?" Brevelan sought her husband.

"Here." His voice was weak and shaky. Had the transport affected his heart in some adverse manner?

"What's wrong?" She touched his mind with comfort. The empathy twisted to despair and bounced back. He was heavily armored.

There was enough light seeping into the room from the kitchen hearth to discern his shaking figure sprawled in the corner beside long shelves of cleaning supplies. Two wine cups sat on the floor in front of him. They appeared to be full.

She knelt beside her husband and reached a tentative hand to encircle his fists, clenched upon his knees. Her touch was repulsed before she made contact. His armor extended through his entire body, not just his mind.

"Are you ill? Did the spell harm you?" She peered closely at his face. Lines of sorrow were etched from his mouth to his chin, from his eyes to his brow. His eyes would have told her the entire story—if he had raised them from the wine cups.

"Let Yaakke know you are safe, then we must find Baamin," he murmured around his clenched jaw, still not looking at her.

"Not until you tell me what is wrong!" She forced her hand under his armor, as only she could do, to run an exploratory finger down his face. No fever. Some small physical pains, nothing worrisome. Just this tremendous sadness and . . . and fear.

"I don't know what's wrong." Still his voice didn't rise above a whisper, nor would he look at her. She thought she saw a drop of blood at the corner of his mouth, but couldn't be sure in the dim light.

"I am a healer, Jaylor. I snatched you away from Death's greedy maw when you poured your life into your magic to save Shayla. But I can't help you if you don't tell me what's wrong."

"Don't try, Brevelan. 'Twould kill me thrice over if you were harmed by my malady. Promise me you will not heal me with magic. Promise me!" Finally he looked up. A dark twisted shadow clouded his eyes.

"If I promise to restrain my natural healing instincts, will you promise to seek another healer?"

He swallowed in indecision.

"I cannot risk anyone's life and magic."

"Then I cannot promise."

"Brevelan, you must. Don't you see that your life is much more important than mine?"

"No, I don't. Without you my life is nothing."

"And the babe? Think, Brevelan. Darville is the heir to the dragon throne. Lord Krej is next in the bloodline. Krej is your father. If Darville sired your baby, then he has an undisputed claim to be king someday. In these uncertain times, you dare not risk yourself or the baby in any way!"

The drop of dark moisture became a slow trickle down his chin. His words were slightly slurred, as if his tongue were swollen, or badly bitten.

"Your son's claim will be disputed. I was born out of wedlock. This child was conceived before we wed. We will discuss this further after we have found and consulted with Master Baamin." She rose from her crouch, not daring to look at him. Could the child ever fill the emptiness Jaylor's absence evoked in her?

Over a year ago she had fled from all people, family and strangers, seeking a solitary life with only the forest creatures for companionship. She had been happy in her protected clearing with a pet wolf the dragon had named Darville, with the cat, Mica, who had taken possession of the clearing before her, a few flusterhens, and a goat.

Then Jaylor had burst into her clearing and her life. She could not go back to the clearing alone. Even if she had to tolerate all of the thousands of people here in the city and their rampant emotions, she would stay with Jaylor, heal him, cherish him, give him the children he deserved.

"Where will we find Baamin at this hour?" She kept her back to Jaylor, lest he sense the direction of her thoughts. He could follow her thoughts without magic, as she could his, as they both could Darville's.

"In his study, or his chamber. Possibly the library."

She felt her husband approach and knew he reached a hand to touch her, then dropped it before contact could be made and her healing invoked.

"You needn't fear touching me, Jaylor." Not so long ago she had feared his nearness. Now she needed constant doses of it. "Seek Baamin with your magic."

"I can't."

"You have magic. I can see it in your aura. A small spell will help keep your heart strong, now that the blockage is dissolved."

"I don't dare."

"You've resisted healing for over five moons. When will you accept the fact that your last spell didn't kill you or your magic?"

"You don't understand!"

Just then their packs and Jaylor's staff clattered to the floor. Yaakke had sent them as soon as he was rested from

the two transport spells—not that the boy ever seemed to
need rest from any exertion. The staff rolled across the
stones to Jaylor's feet, like iron to a lodestone. But it wasn't
a smooth motion. The wood jerked and paused as if lopsided and topheavy.

Brevelan stooped to peer at the focus for Jaylor's magic.
The wood grain was twisted and braided once more, as if
Jaylor had been using it frequently. There was an odd pattern to the coils now. Two braids marched down the length
of the staff, one twisting right, away from the other left-
handed plait. She couldn't think what would cause such an
odd twist and split in the staff's reflection of the magic
that passed through it. Couldn't think of an answer and
dreaded knowing.

"I seem to have bitten my tongue quite badly. Can you
locate Baamin with your mind? He should be able to stop
the bleeding." Jaylor ignored the staff resting on his foot.

Brevelan handed the tool to him. She raised an eyebrow
in question, not quite daring to ask what had caused the
odd pattern in the wood. Jaylor turned his back to heft the
packs to his shoulder. His lack of an answer told her more
than she wanted to know.

"Master Baamin is not in the University."

*The Tambootie is wonderful! Why have I never seen its
potential before? It allows me to see so much more clearly,
both forward and backward in time.*

*With no effort at all, I can see bumbling old Baamin
shielding his wayward princeling from my gaze. His magic
is strong, but not stronger than mine. Darville is visiting a
lady's chamber as I would expect from a man with the dis-
cretion of a mongrel around a bitch in heat.*

*A wisp of a thought and my vision rolls to the princess.
She sleeps quietly. But not alone. If anyone has allowed
that evil cat to creep into her room, I shall kill them, most
unpleasantly. I must hurry to her side. She cannot be compromised before the wedding.*

"Did I hurt you when I swatted your muzzle?" Mikka
ran a hand down Darville's straight nose. Her fingernails
were long and slightly curved. "You were quite selfish when
you were a wolf."

"I don't remember that life at all." Darville continued to stare at her, being very careful to keep his eyes above her neck.

Mikka was suddenly aware that her only covering was her hip-length hair. She'd spent nearly three years wearing nothing but cat fur. Her transformation back to womanhood hadn't registered until now. A lifetime ago, she would have been embarrassed to be seen by a man. But this was no ordinary man. This was Darville. He understood her ordeal and why she had sought escape in a cat's body. No other man would.

"When Jaylor was changing me back and forth from wolf to man, I retained more of my experiences," Darville continued. "But the moons before that are a complete blank." His hand traced the line of her head to rest just above her ear and scratch. Mikka leaned into the familiar, affectionate caress.

"Why did you do that?" she asked. The caress was too intimate for an unmarried woman and a man.

"I always scratch your ears when I must think . . . I mean . . . when you . . . when I. . . ."

They both looked to the cat sleeping on the bed pillow.

"Move, Rosse." Darville lifted the contented cat to the foot of the bed.

"This is my place." Mikka scooted against the headboard and leaned against the pillow. "And this is your place." She patted the pillow beside her to indicate Darville should stay next to her.

"My valet complains every morning when he has to brush cat hair off the pillows." He chuckled as he settled into position. His right arm draped naturally around Mikka. "How much do you remember of your ensorcelled life?"

"Almost everything. More than Janataea predicted. I don't think she realized the magic in me was so strong." Out of long habit she curled her body into his circling touch, rubbing the top of her head against his chin.

"Your magic was certainly very uncatlike six weeks ago when you broke the lock in the tunnels." He pulled her closer yet, as if expecting his cat to crawl into his lap and purr. "If only we knew what Janataea really wants," he mused while he stroked her hair the length of her back.

"I think she had planned the spell for a long time. Could

it have something to do with the land of women warriors? Was she hoping I would find them for her?"

Darville glanced at the sleeping cat at the foot of the wide bed. "She is a very powerful witch. If she wanted to find that mythical place, she would have done it on her own. No. From what I have seen of your governess, I believe her motives have something to do with control. She has power over Rosie. I've seen her put destructive words into the poor girl's mouth. She'd never be able to compel you to that extent, Mikka. My Mikka." He brushed his lips across the top of her hair with quiet affection.

"I don't want to go back to being a cat, my love." She wrapped her arms around his chest and clung to him.

"I don't want you to go back. I like you much better as a beautiful woman. But what can we do? Baamin said this transformation is only temporary. At dawn you will revert."

"You must find a way to save me, Darville."

"Now that I have found you, I will move heaven and Kardia to keep you. But I have no magic. Baamin is too old and skittish to tamper with someone else's spells. Jaylor has lost his magic. You will have to give me the answers, beloved."

"I have no answers, only my love for you." She looked up into his face and saw an answering emotion. He pulled her across his lap, holding her tightly against his chest. She caressed his face, lingering near his mouth. Their lips met, fiercely possessive, demanding.

"Where would Baamin be, if not in his chamber? There are only a few hours until dawn." Jaylor wasn't aware that he had spoken aloud until his words echoed slightly in the long corridor leading to the master's wing.

The luxurious apartments had been mostly empty for several years. During the long decline of dragon magic, fewer and fewer men attended the University. Fewer graduated to master's status. Now that the dragons were gone, the entire structure of the Commune was in upheaval. Jaylor sensed no one in any of the chambers now, nor could he smell any armor blocking his senses.

Many of the older magicians who were uncomfortable with the changing nature of their spells had retired to the monasteries. The remaining masters were posted to the twelve courts as advisers and sources of instant communication with each other and the capital.

"Could Baamin be in the palace? With Darville?" Brevelan asked.

Jaylor wanted desperately to gather her into the circle of his arm, to draw comfort and healing from her touch. But he didn't dare. Two of the last three spells he had thrown had split dangerously. Two rabbits, one vicious, the other more timid than usual. Two wine cups, one pure vinegar, the other fresh fruit juice.

His third spell, transporting the greenbird, had worked. But he'd been incapacitated afterward with a seizure so strong he'd lost control of every muscle in his body.

He'd had a seizure with the two bad spells. Milder, shorter. Just before completing the spell, his knees had begun to shake and his vision blur. Control came back to him almost as soon as the spell was complete.

Maybe he could seek Baamin with his mind. That wasn't really a spell, just a reaching beyond normal senses. He barely needed to establish the first level of trance for such a simple feat.

One deep breath and his mind soared free from his body. A second deep breath and awareness surrounded him.

Jaylor identified the occupants of each of the rooms in the University. He chose an empty one at the end of the hall that would suit him and Brevelan nicely for the duration of their stay in the capital. He already knew that Baamin's quarters were empty. As was the library. His thoughts drifted above the stone walls of the University. As if a bird perched on the steeply pitched slate roof, he surveyed the surrounding islands of the city, seeking a familiar mind.

Over there, on Palace Isle. Or was it Sacred Isle. A single bonfire and the movement of several armored minds caught his attention.

"Jaylor! Jaylor, what is wrong?" Brevelan tugged anxiously at him.

He plummeted abruptly back into his body. Disoriented by the sudden downward whoosh of his thoughts, Jaylor could not control the trembling in his hands and knees.

"Baamin is in the palace. You will have to summon him.

I can't do it, Brevelan. Tell him to come quickly. Someone is performing a ritual on Sacred Isle." He leaned heavily against her supporting shoulder.

"Probably just some novice priests practicing for the solstice." Brevelan led him down the corridor to the empty suite in the corner.

"At this hour of the morning? The solstice is almost two moons hence." He wanted to say more, to describe the jerky movements of seven or eight nude dancers around a single bonfire. But he hadn't the strength of body or of will. "Light a candle. Use my glass. Summon Baamin back to the University."

"That will not be necessary." A new voice halted their progress. At the end of the dark corridor floated the face of Lord Krej. For the blink of an eye his features blurred and softened with feminine touches, then hardened back into the forbidding countenance of Brevelan's father. He seemed to drift toward them in the dim light, disembodied, until Jaylor's vision cleared enough to see the outline of his black woolen cloak that covered him from chin to floor.

"You could join the ritual on Sacred Isle, become one of the elite with power beyond reckoning," Krej coaxed.

"At what cost?" Brevelan chanted as she moved in front of Jaylor, shielding him from Krej's compulsion with her armoring song.

"We have no need of your bribes, Lord Krej." Could his father-in-law heal this terrible warp in his magic? Jaylor fought the temptation to seek an end, any end, to this terrible weakness that either split his spells or spasmed his body. Concentrating on his words kept the involuntary muscle spasms at bay. But it took all of his energy. Another offer might prove too tempting to resist.

"How did you get here?" Krej spoke sharply. "Have you traveled over a thousand miles from your mountain retreat in two weeks' time, risking my unborn grandson? Or did you use the transport spell?"

"That is none of your business." Brevelan stood as tall and straight as her tiny form would allow. One hand rested on the bulge of her belly, rubbing the baby lightly in small circles. "Move aside."

Krej obeyed. Jaylor couldn't be sure if he reacted to Brevelan's compulsion or stood aside for his own reasons.

"I will have the spell from you. You can't hide that kind of magic long."

"Discover its source by yourself, as we did," Jaylor spat. His muscles were obeying his thoughts again. He wanted to reach out with his hand and detain Krej while he questioned him more closely. How did he get into the University? What was the nature of the magic he wielded, in spite of the witchbane?

"Don't play innocent with me! Where did you find the spell to transport living beings?" A whiff of raw Tambootie drifted from his body.

"In the most obvious and unlikely places," Jaylor quipped. He and Brevelan were almost even with the door they sought. A few more steps and they would be within the armored privacy of the master's suite.

Krej's addiction to Tambootie disturbed Jaylor. Need for the drug would make the lord unpredictable, violent even, in his quest for more and more of the sensation of soaring with dragons.

Jaylor had been there. The temptation to merge his body, mind, and magic with the Tambootie grew to enormous proportions. For a long moment the urge to eat the drug was more than he could continue resisting.

Krej's hand drifted out from the folds of the all concealing cloak. His elegantly long fingers held a sprig of Tambootie.

Jaylor's hand reached involuntarily for the leaves.

"Begone!" Brevelan screamed at her father.

The cloaked figure vanished. Jaylor collapsed onto the stone floor, too weak to follow Krej; too shaken by the overpowering need to move any farther under his own power.

Chapter 16

*D*awn brings an end to our ritual. The Tambootie smoke
drifts away. My mind comes back to Coronnan and my
duties. I must check on the princess. I have left her too long.
Too often.

*But the rituals require my presence. We have not all been
joined together 'round the same fire in many moons. So we
meet again and again, storing up our spells and tightening
the bonds that keep the coven alive. I am satiated with magic
and sex.*

*The power of the coven allowed me to send my rival's
image to encounter Jaylor and Brevelan. They were the
source of the disturbance in the magic field tonight. I will
have that spell from them. Then the coven can meet and
dance our rituals 'round a Tambootie fire anytime we need
to—or want to.*

*Until then, I must stay close to the princess. Our long
years of planning will come to naught if Darville suspects
the truth. He must marry Rosie, as she is, and produce a
child. A child who will rule the three kingdoms. A child
whose every move is determined by me.*

The soft gray light of predawn filtered under the heavy
curtains of Rosie's room. There was not so much a lightening of the darkness, as a shift in the quality of the light.
Darville watched the outlines of furniture emerge.

His arm tightened about the woman who lay in his arms.
She stirred. He pressed his damp cheek against her soft
hair, lest she sees his tears upon awakening.

If she did awake. In just moments Mikka would cease to
be, and the cat who slept at his feet would emerge as Rosie.

"I can't watch. I'm sorry, but I can't watch." He closed his eyes in regret.

"Shush, beloved. We will still be together. And I trust you to find an end to this dilemma." Mikka lifted her face to look at him. She traced the line of his jaw with her eyes and a long fingernail, as if memorizing every inch of him. "It's not so bad being a cat." The corners of her mouth lifted in an almost smile. "No responsibilities. No one notices when you enter and leave a room. People talk in front of you, as if you couldn't hear or understand them."

"Don't try to make it better, Mikka. I will find a way out for you, and quickly, because I don't think I can bear to live without you."

"I knew this past night would happen the moment Brevelan dragged that icy, sodden blanket through the door of her home with the bedraggled, scruffy excuse for a wolf collapsed upon it. I knew even then, when you were a wolf and I still a cat, that we belonged together, forever."

They hugged again, clinging to the last moments of the darkness. "But until then, I shall be your spy. The Council does not like you and your new authoritative ways. I shall listen to their plans and report back to you."

"How, Mikka? How can you tell me what is happening?" Darville looked closely at her beautiful face, her wide, intelligent hazel eyes, her pug nose and even teeth. He kissed each feature.

But even now he was noticing a change. Her round eyes were beginning to slit into a vertical pupil.

"With magic. Brevelan will kni-ooww."

Darville closed his eyes so he couldn't see her shift back into her familiar cat form. Her lovely hair would shorten from a beguiling curtain to a concealing coat. Her ears would lengthen and point. Whiskers would sprout from her face.

He couldn't watch.

And he couldn't be caught here, in the bed of the princess, before the date for the wedding had been set. Last night he had almost hoped he would be caught, so he could force the marriage on a compromised Rosie.

Now he needed to stall the wedding, even more than Rosie wanted him to. He just could not, would not, marry Rosie. Mikka would be his only bride.

When the woman in his arms transformed into a small bundle of fur, and the cat at the end of the bed grew into a woman, Darville slid through the bed hangings nearest the wardrobe.

"Meww?" Mica pricked her ears. Small sounds of someone moving through the outer chamber reached them.

Silently, he gathered his discarded clothing and lantern. Mica hopped down beside him. She urged him into the wardrobe with a shove of her damp nose against his bare calf. He paused long enough to scratch behind her ear, then slipped into the massive piece of furniture.

"Princess Rossemikka, time to get up," Janataea cooed.

The heavy cabinet door closed on Darville's naked rump just as he heard the outer door open and the governess enter the room.

Yaakke blinked his eyes in astonishment. When he had searched for a place to set himself down, he had sniffed for the greatest concentration of magic. He'd tried time and again to visualize the old familiar scullery and transport himself there, but never succeeded in moving himself more than a few inches above the ground. So, instead of seeking a specific place, he just sniffed for magic around the capital and sent himself there.

"There" should have been the University. Where else should one find magic, other than the training ground for all respectable magicians.

But no. "There" proved to be the central clearing of the Sacred Grove on Sacred Isle.

The apprentice magician drew in a deep lungful of air to replenish himself after the transport. Great racking coughs sent him to his knees.

Tambootie smoke, thick and sour, hung like a healer's pall of herb smoke ignited over the bed of a plague victim.

Someone had worked a great deal of magic here mere hours ago, on the night of the dark of the moon.

Yaakke shivered in the dawn chill. He couldn't think of any spells that were stronger at the dark of the moon rather than at the full. Unless Lord Krej had joined some evil friends here. He wasn't convinced that the witchbane did any good at all in neutralizing that man's magic.

The sun rose off to Yaakke's left, sending streaks of light

through the early morning mist. Droplets of moisture glistened and danced about the grove like a myriad of fairies. Yaakke refrained from crossing himself or flapping his crossed wrists in the ancient gesture of warding.

What danger to him were the wee motes of light? He, Yaakke, the kitchen boy who was judged too stupid to even have a name, had just completed the greatest magic spell in the history of Coronnan! Even old Nimbulan, the man who had made a pact with the dragons, three hundred years ago, hadn't known how to transport himself.

Exultation made him giddy as he pranced with the fairy lights. He circled the great clearing once, twice. Heel—toe—kick, step, step, turn. Kick—kick—clap. The old, old rhythm of the solstice celebration drummed in his head. He sang the words that seemed so much nonsense, but which he knew to be an incantation in the oldest of languages.

On his third circuit, exhaustion and laboring lungs brought him to a halt beneath the largest of the sacred oaks. Above his head he espied a dangling limb, broken off by some winter storm and stripped of bark and leaves during the course of the summer. The branch appeared to be just the proper length for a magician's staff.

Yaakke's eyes widened in glee. His master's staff. Of course. The staff was being provided for him by the Stargods in recognition of his greatest feat of magic.

With renewed energy he hoisted himself up to the first massive limb. Above him the lesser branches appeared to form almost a staircase leading him to the dangling piece he sought. Up, ever upward he climbed until he was face-to-face with his treasure.

A wave of uneasy awe made his hand hesitate. What if the staff were intended for someone else and he had merely stumbled upon it prematurely.

Never! There were no more journeyman candidates at the University. The staff was meant for him. He reached out and closed his hand around the smooth straight grain. The wood vibrated and tingled in recognition of his touch. Ever so subtly, it molded to his grasp.

Yaakke channeled a thought down the staff. A magic cloud of red, green, blue, purple, yellow, and every color imaginable in between, blossomed from the end of his focus. A casual step from the security of the tree brought him onto the cloud. Another thought and he fell clumsily, arms flailing wildly until his right arm, with the staff still clutched tightly in that hand, caught on a lower branch. He dangled awkwardly above the beckoning grove, sore and embarrassed.

"Thank you, Stargods, for the rescue!" he whispered to the appropriate powers.

Silence greeted him. More than just the silence of the forest. It was the utter absence of sound known only to the privileged few who attained a direct encounter with the Stargods.

The magnitude of his actions hit his head and shoulders. Fatigue weighed him down. He wouldn't admit any degree of tiredness in front of Brevelan, but here, in the face of the Stargods, who knew everything, he succumbed to the total lack of energy. In the past twelve hours he had performed more great magic than most masters achieved in a lifetime.

He needed sleep and food.

He needed to climb down.

"Now I will go out into this world and do great deeds to save my people from destruction, just as You saved us from a plague a thousand years ago," he promised, as he fumbled for hand- and footholds.

But first a nap. Then he had to get off the island. No bridges gave access to Sacred Isle and he was much too tired for another transport just yet.

Rosie stretched and yawned. For the first time in weeks she felt truly refreshed and comfortable. Her night's rest had been filled with wonderful dreams of warmth and security. If only she could remember the details.

"How did you sleep, my princess?" Janataea cooed from the window where she threw open the draperies with sharp thrusts. A serving maid hovered at the door with a basin of hot water for washing. The maid was different from the woman who had served her yesterday. She seemed to be absorbing every detail of the room with avid curiosity.

Janataea pursed her lips in disapproval of the maid's scrutiny. The governess had evicted more than one of the constantly changing servants who gossiped too long and too frequently about the women from Rossemeyer. Janataea liked her privacy.

"I slept very well, Janataea." Rosie stretched again and realized she was naked. She didn't remember taking off her sleeping shift, now a rumpled mass up by the pillow, nor did she remember scooting to the foot of the bed. Her nose wrinkled as she tried to figure out why she might have done such a thing.

Strange odors came to her. Someone had been in her room last night! Fearfully, she searched the room for other signs of intrusion. The wardrobe door was firmly closed. A maid always slept in the anteroom to discourage entry from the hallway.

Who could have been in this room. She sniffed more carefully. Male. Sweating, rutting male!

Anger raised the hair on the back of her neck. How dare he? For it could only be Darville who had come to her through the secret tunnels. Did he think he could compromise her into an early marriage?

Not if she had anything to say about it.

"Prince Darville awaits you in the small solar, Your Highness. He has ordered smoked fish for your breakfast," Janataea commented, as she sorted through the gowns in the wardrobe.

"No." Rosie drew the sleeping shift over her head before accepting the wash water from the maid. Normally she would have ordered her from the room while she bathed and dressed. Not today. Today she wanted the woman to gossip.

"No? You don't want smoked fish for breakfast? Perhaps you would prefer a freshly broiled river trout." Janataea continued to search for the perfect gown.

Rosie narrowed her eyes to look carefully at her governess. Janataea looked more energetic than usual. Her skin glowed with sensual awareness. She looked younger than the thirty-two years she claimed. But she'd been thirty-two two years ago as well.

"I mean, no, I will not break my fast with the prince."

Janataea turned and scowled at Rosie. Rosie returned her stare with determination.

"This is not the time for pranks, Princess Rossemikka. Need I remind you of your position, your duty!"

"I have decided to marry no man. I shall join the convent of the Stargods. There I need not fear the touch of any man."

"Oh, my," the maid gasped.

"Get out!" Janataea screamed at the shaking servant. "And not a word of this to anyone. If I hear any gossip I'll know whose ears to lop off."

The maid ran from the room without bothering to close the outer door. Her wooden clogs banged on the stone floor, marking her progress to the back stairway that led to the kitchen.

"What brought this on, Rosie?" Janataea spoke in her most soothing voice.

Her words took on a singsong quality that Rosie recognized as the beginning of a spell. Soon, very soon, she would be compelled to obey her governess, unless she did something right now.

"Darville tried to sneak in here last night with his cat."

"He wouldn't dare," Janataea hissed.

"He dared. I'll not marry him."

"I'll see that he destroys the cat."

Something twisted inside Rosie. She didn't know why she should be distressed at the demise of a creature she feared and hated.

"I'll still not marry him. My mind is made up. I shall join the convent before this day is out."

"Then I'll make sure you marry before noon." Janataea stormed out of the room. This time the outer door slammed behind her and the lock turned.

Rosie smiled. She dressed quickly in her warmest green woolen gown and rust colored cloak, then opened the wardrobe and drew aside the brocaded covering. Janataea would never lock her in this room again.

Chapter 17

"**S**he's gone, Baamin," Darville paced beside his adviser, adjusting his long stride to the old man's shorter legs. He burned with the need to run, throw something, swing a sword, or just smash his fist into one of the massive walls of the University. From his shoulder, Mica growled her agreement with his mood.

"Calm yourself, Your grace; I'm certain your princess will return as soon as her temper has worn thin," Baamin soothed. "There has been a new development here at the University that will take precedence over your concern for the Princess Rossemikka."

"Not bloody likely." The stone floors of the inner reaches of the University corridors echoed under Darville's sturdy riding boots. He'd been about to mount a search party for Rosie when Baamin had claimed his presence. Now he stomped through the master's wing instead of riding a fleet steed through the markets and lanes of the capital.

"You know as well as I do, Baamin, that if word of the princess' disappearance reaches Kevin-Rosse, the treaty will evaporate and we'll face a new invasion across the southern passes."

"What if I offered Brevelan's help in finding your runaway princess, eh?" A grin spread across the wizened features of the elderly magician. "And maybe even Jaylor's help, too?"

"Jaylor has his magic back? So soon, and strong enough to work through a summons?" Darville stopped his progress down the hall long enough to grab Baamin's sleeves in eager anticipation. He didn't dare think about Brevelan.

"Better than that, Your Grace. They are here, and Jaylor has his magic back, with a few complications." Baamin nodded and grinned as Darville slapped his back in eager camaraderie.

Moments later they were in the master's suite at the end of the long hallway. Heavily carved furniture and thickly padded upholstery lent the room an air of decadent luxury, a legacy of the last inhabitant, not of Brevelan's simpler tastes. Rich tapestries kept out the drafts and damp of thick stone walls, while bright rugs cushioned Darville's step.

Brevelan knelt by the cheerful green fire crackling in the fireplace. Darville remembered the song of blending that touched her lips as she stirred a concoction on the hearth. Through a half opened doorway, he glimpsed a rumpled bed.

The entire scene was too reminiscent of the last time Darville had shared a room with Jaylor and Brevelan. It had been in the guest hall of the remote monastery, a day's journey from Castle Krej.

Brevelan's poignant song of love that had brought Jaylor back from the dead still rang in Darville's ears. She would never sing like that for him. But she might sing as beautiful a song of magic that would restore the true Rossemikka to him forever.

"Darville!" Brevelan jumped up from her place by the fire. She ran the few steps to the doorway and flung her arms about him in joyous reunion. "I daren't call you 'Puppy' anymore. You are much too well groomed to ever be mistaken for my pet wolf." She reached to ruffle his hair behind his ears, as she was wont to when he was truly a wolf.

"If only you knew how many people want to consign that role to me permanently," he groaned and laughed in the same breath. He reached out to hold her tight, stroke her hair, indulge in the sensuous scent of herbs that clung to her. But she didn't fit against his body as snugly as she had when they had parted last spring. A quivering movement in her belly reminded him that she carried another man's child.

"You look well," he said matter-of-factly, holding her at arm's length. Her eyes clouded in puzzlement.

"Merow!" Mica chirped from his shoulder. The cat

scrambled to launch herself across the gap to Brevelan's arms, claws digging into Darville's shoulder through the padding.

"Mica, my sweet," Brevelan cooed as she caught the cat in mid-leap. "Oh, how I have missed you."

"Mi-i-oow." Mica had missed Brevelan as well.

"Where is Jaylor?" Darville took a step back from the loving caresses shared by the two women he loved.

"In the library, with books piled eight-deep all around him." Brevelan raised pain-filled eyes to him. "He is greatly troubled." Like the last night Jaylor had spent in a library of magic and learned that in order to free Shayla he would have to risk his life and his soul.

"Is he devising a new plan to save Coronnan?" Darville started toward the wide windows that overlooked a courtyard. The library was across the way, four stories high with more books on more subjects than any known library in the world. Some of those books were rumored to have been left by the Stargods. If the answer to Jaylor's problem lay in a book, that book was in the University library.

Darville decided to hasten over there to greet his oldest friend. Perhaps if he put some distance between himself and Brevelan, he'd feel less uncomfortable. Somehow he felt guilty for having betrayed his love for Brevelan by sleeping with Mikka last night. At the same time, he knew remorse for betraying Mikka by still being in love with Brevelan.

"Jaylor acted as a staff for Krej during a major spell." Baamin spoke in awed tones. "His magic is strong, but it splits into two faces, good and evil."

"With Krej!" Darville whirled to face Baamin, accusations and denunciations halfway to his lips before he saw Brevelan's pain-filled face.

" 'Twas the only way to save my life, Darville," she reprimanded. "My bond with Shayla was never totally broken, just hidden. The night her babies were born I went into premature labor. My father was the only person who could sever the bond."

"Couldn't Jaylor, or that apprentice boy, what's his name?" Darville asked, still not willing to accept Krej as Brevelan's savior.

"Jaylor tried, and his heart failed. Yaakke has no royal

blood to connect him to Shayla. Only my cursed father could find the bond and separate us in time." Brevelan stood straight and defiant against Darville's anger.

"Then we have lost the dragons forever." Darville stared out the window, seeing nothing.

"You are still bound to the dragons, Darville. If one magician could sever a tie with a dragon, why couldn't another magician trace a similar bond?" Baamin asked.

"But who is strong enough? Is Jaylor's heart truly strong enough to risk such a mighty spell? I won't ask Brevelan to risk bonding with Shayla again, until the baby comes. Will you undertake the spell, Baamin?" Darville pressed his adviser.

"I have a plan," Baamin stated gleefully, as he rubbed his hands together in anticipation.

Both Darville and Brevelan stared at the Senior Magician.

"Jaylor found a binding spell in one of my texts. A spell written in Rover language, with symbolism that defies modern translations. If we could consult one of their women of power, she might unravel Jaylor's problem."

Darville lifted Mica from Brevelan's arms. He petted her back and ears, nuzzling her delicate face with his own. "And what of the missing princess? I need to find Rosie more than I need the dragon nimbus right now."

Rosie looked around her in dismay. Where was she? There were so many new sights and sounds and smells, she couldn't sort them out, couldn't find a reference point.

Not that she knew where she wanted to go in the first place. The vague notion of entering a convent as a means of escaping marriage to Darville had seemed an excellent notion when she was within the familiar walls of the palace. Now she faced the reality that she didn't know how to locate a convent and wasn't sure what a convent really was.

No one had discussed religion with her since she had lost her memory. She knew there were priests and nuns and monks dedicated to preserving the images of the Stargods and to healing. The priest-healers were also magicians. But what did the nuns do besides remain cloistered and virginal?

Rosie's winding path took her through a market square. Dozens of people in rough clothing jostled her as they sought goods and services at the various booths. No one seemed to notice her.

They were all too busy with their own lives.

The smell of meat rolls, freshly baked, reminded Rosie that she had escaped without breakfast. She followed the scent to a booth where a slight man in an enormous white apron was arranging trays of the savory treat. Behind him, a stout woman in a very small apron kneaded dough. Flour dusted her face and arms all the way to her elbows. The man was scrupulously clean.

Customers selected pastries and paid for them with coins. Rosie watched the transactions carefully. She'd been told about money. Uncle Rumbelly complained constantly about the cost of her clothing, how there was never enough money left over to buy what he needed. But how did one come by money?

Why did those little circles of metal have value?

She had no idea. Rather than show her ignorance by asking such a question, she moved on. Her stomach growled in protest. Almost, she turned back to beg the baker for some food. Pride wouldn't let her.

The palace market square led to a bridge. Timidly, she crossed to the next island, wary of the surging power of the water beneath the planking. This island seemed to be filled with the homes of the people who worked the market square. She smelled the location of a candy kitchen, heard the blacksmith, spotted the bright colors on the sign of the weaver, and nearly stumbled over the wares of the toy-maker. More people bustled in and out and around these places, but no one sold their wares on this island. All of the goods were being transported to the market.

She moved on to another island, and another. Every square inch of land was used for houses or markets or industry. The crowds grew thinner and more suspicious of her as she moved away from the large central islands. With each wary look and twitch of skirts out of her path she was aware that she was a stranger here.

Across the expanse of the river delta she thought she saw large fields ripe with grain. Men in wide hats and

women with skirts kilted above their knees worked with
scythe and rake at a frantic pace, all the while watching
the dark clouds on the horizon.

Where did all these people come from? Her isolated life
among the royales had kept her removed from the populace. She began to wonder if Rossemeyer's mighty armies
would be enough to conquer these people. But she also
understood why her uncle wanted to gain possession of this
moist, rich land. The high desert plateau that comprised
most of Rossemeyer could never support all the people
who lived there. Food was imported in large amounts. And
the only commodities Rossemeyer produced in abundance
for trade were the treacle beta and fierce mercenary warriors.

Yet another market sprang up in front of her. She was
very far from Palace Isle now. Activity around these booths
had wound down to a more leisurely pace. People didn't
seem to be using coins for their purchases. From the
shadow of a corner hut Rosie watched a woman trade a
flusterhen for a length of cloth. A man exchanged a finely
worked leather belt for some tools. Others merely bar-
gained with words.

Only the old woman at the opposite corner seemed to
demand the little round pieces of metal. For each coin she
would take her client's hand and study the palm. Then she
would make a pronouncement. More coins elicited a
lengthier statement.

Rosie wished she could hear what the ancient crone was
saying. She was hungry enough to be willing to hold a
man's hand for the few coins necessary to purchase a meal.
She stepped out of the shadows to better hear the woman's words.

"You look hungry, little lady," a man's voice hissed in
her ear. "Hungry enough to eat a flusterhen raw. I know
where you can get some dinner." A large hand closed on
Rosie's shoulder. Fat fingers clutched her with surprising
fierceness.

Rosie looked up into the stranger's florid face, bordered
with an oddly trimmed beard. Curiosity warred with her
need to avoid his touch.

"There's fresh-caught fish and boiled yampion root just
across on the next island. I've got a boat to take you there,

a nice big boat that won't rock or tumble you into the river," the man coaxed.

Rosie's stomach growled in response to the vision of the meal this man could offer her.

As she opened her mouth to agree to go with him, new scents assaulted her nose. She smelled the sour ale on his breath and the pungent sweat of a liar. Enough to make her reconsider. Then she caught the acrid stench on his clothes. It was the same kind of odor she'd discovered on her sheets this morning. A man with the need on him.

Where is she? I must find my princess before Simeon kidnaps her. He wants to put aside his queen and marry Rossemikka. But he can't annul his marriage to Queen Miranda. She is the lawful heir to SeLenicca. He is merely her consort.

Simeon's ambitions grow too high and too fast. I don't care that his grandmother was the first wife of Rossemikka's father. All magicians were dealt a severe blow when good Queen Safflon was first exiled for witchcraft with her daughter Jaylene. Then, when she defended herself and her followers with a conjured plague, she was publicly tortured and executed.

Poor Jaylene died heartbroken and impoverished when her father married Sousyam, the deceitful mouse, and sired Rossemikka and her brothers. Jaylene's son, Simeon, was still an infant. Maman raised Simeon as one of her own, alongside my rival and myself.

But Simeon must wait. He is not destined to rule the three kingdoms. Maman decided that, the coven agreed. The child Rosie produces and the child Miranda now carries will wed. And their children will rule the three kingdoms with the coven as their advisers. And I shall rule the coven.

Simeon thinks to change the ruling of the coven by abducting Rosie back to SeLenicca. He doesn't know what forces will fly out of control.

SeLenicca was barren of magic until Simeon married Miranda. His magic must be artificially induced. Perhaps he uses the scrubby, less potent variety of Tambootie that grows there. In such an environment Rosie will revert to her natural form. Then there will be two cats and no princess.

Chapter 18

"**I**f Baamin needs an old Rover woman to cure Jaylor, then we will find him one," Brevelan whispered to Mica. She stroked the cat who hid in a produce basket slung on her arm. "We both know the Rovers cannot be trusted. But we must brave their curses to cure Jaylor of his warped and twisted magic."

The cat purred her agreement.

Warped and twisted magic. Just like Brevelan's father. Was this the legacy of using Krej to sever her bond with Shayla?

Mica nudged Brevelan's hand, distracting her from those depressing thoughts onto different ones, just as depressing.

Her meeting with Darville this morning had been strained. Though the bond of communication and empathy still existed, something now stood between them. Something like resentment? Or was it embarrassment?

She scratched Mica's cheek and ear, drawing comfort from her familiar presence. Mica was still Mica. And yet . . . ?

Mica belonged with Darville now, if this cat could truly be said to belong to anyone.

Darville had taken command of his kingdom and the Council. His personality colored everything in the palace. He had also proved himself on the field of battle. The people of Rossemeyer would welcome him as husband to their princess. His life had spread far beyond the comforting limits of Brevelan's clearing.

The baby kicked and stretched. The loneliness of Brevelan's circling thoughts receded.

"Baamin says there is a small market square three islands

north and two west from University Island. Sometimes Rovers bring their wares for trade. They aren't supposed to be in Coronnan at all, but the magic that kept them out is gone. And Rovers . . . rove. That's bred into their nature. Only very strong magic will keep them out, or curb their thieving instincts."

From the depths of the basket, Mica agreed. Brevelan drew a checkered cloth over the top of the basket. What cat, other than a witch's familiar, would consent to be carried in a basket?

A few steps beyond the gate brought Brevelan to the first bridge. It looked sturdy and well traveled. She put one cautious foot on the wooden planks. Waves of distrust and fear assailed her. She wanted to run away, put as much distance between herself and this river crossing as possible.

Brevelan looked sharply all around her. There was no sense of an individual as the source of the violent emotions. She touched the wooden railing as she placed her right foot firmly on the bridge. The emotions rose again. She lifted her hand from the railing. The emotions eased.

The bridge didn't sway and didn't threaten to crumble. Beneath the walkway, the waters of Coronnan River gushed in a joyous race to the Great Bay. She tested the bridge again with one foot.

It must be the stone foundation of the bridge that retained the fear of the people who had erected it.

Three hundred years ago, the country had been in the grip of the Great War of Disruption. Lord fought lord. Magicians sought ever more powerful spells to aid their own battles and those of the lords. Families divided. Chaos reigned.

The last remaining member of the royal family had slowly gathered together an army and a city. The river became their greatest defense. All of the bridges in the ancient city were replaced during that time. Each span was designed so that a single defender could pull a linchpin. The bridge would then collapse behind, cutting off any pursuer.

It was this sense of overriding fear that permeated the bridges, even though most of the original parts had been replaced time and again.

Brevelan sought the release device with sensitive fingertips. From the strength of the emotions embedded in the wood, she expected the defense mechanism to be clean and well oiled.

Rust and grime flaked off on her fingers. The bridge had been neglected for many generations. Quite possibly, no one could pull the linchpin now.

She moved on to the next bridge, and the next, forgetting the press of the populace and their unarmored emotions. In the inner city all but a few of the bridges showed the same degree of neglect. Gradually, as she worked her way toward the lesser markets, she noticed that about half of the release mechanisms had been replaced. Recently.

As Brevelan approached the last bridge she needed to cross, she spotted a man in a small boat moored to the supporting arches. He wore a bright red tunic with gold braid on his sleeves and a jaunty boatman's cap. His legs were encased in sturdy trews that hung loosely about his ankles.

The boatman stared at her. His eyes narrowed in suspicion. Brevelan felt his wariness, as well as his arrogance.

"Goodman, what brings you out on the river on a day when the current is swift and treacherous?" she asked, probing his mind to no avail.

"Goodman!" Outrage poured from his mind as well as his soul. "How dare you demean me as a mere tradesman. I am a ranking member of the Guild of Bay Pilots." His self-assurance was almost strong enough to convince Brevelan of his superiority.

"Forgive me, good . . . sir." Brevelan ducked her head in an accepted posture of subservience, which he obviously expected. "I've never met one of your Guild. I didn't recognize your uniform." From beneath her lowered lashes she scanned the bridge and the man's boat.

Tools and oddments of rusty metal littered the bottom of the boat. The linchpin on this bridge was very new.

"Every citizen of Coronnan City knows the Bay Pilots and owes them proper respect. Who are you that you do not recognize the families who have kept the sea pirates and invaders away from our shores for centuries?" Even as he spoke, the man was scrambling to intercept Brevelan's passage across the bridge.

"I've just come from the country with my husband, good sir." Mica chose that moment to wake. The noises coming from her throat were more growl than purr. "The villages aren't safe anymore. There're outlaws and evil magicians at every turn. We fled to the city for safety," she prevaricated.

"As well you should, goodwoman." The pilot preened. "The Guild will keep the city safe, in spite of the interference of the Council and the magicians. We'd all be better off if we threw the whole lot to Sorcerer Simeon and his horde of evildoers, and left the running of the city to those of us that live and work here."

Mica poked her nose out from under the covering cloth and sniffed the air around them.

"Prince Darville will lead our men to victory," Brevelan asserted while she probed the pilot's emotions. She could learn nothing from him. The habit of secrecy was so deeply ingrained in the man, he allowed no thought or emotion to escape.

"If our prince is still alive," the pilot snorted. "The Council's got him hidden so's he won't try to be king and take power away from the arrogant bastards. Get rid of 'em, one and all, I say."

"And does the rest of the Guild agree with you?"

The man's eyes narrowed again, suspicion clouding them. "Why do you want to know, goodwoman? Why do you keep me here with your questions when I have work to do? Are you a spy, or mayhap a witch? I see red hair beneath your scarf. Only witches and magicians have red hair." He took a step closer to her, his fists clenched as if he might strike her.

Brevelan clasped her abdomen in instinctive protection of the baby. Mica growled within the basket.

"Never!" Brevelan stood as tall and straight as she could. "Are you a spy? You, who tamper with the bridges. You are the one who keeps me here with your arrogant posturing. Move aside." She put the full force of her magic into her glaring eyes.

The man returned her stare a moment, then took one step back. "The Guild will want to know about you. Can't have foreign spies and witches learning about our defenses. You'll come with me, woman, and answer to the Guild."

"What right has the Guild to detain innocent citizens?" Brevelan stood her ground.

"The Guild of Bay Pilots is . . . is the Guild!" The pilot

suddenly looked confused, as if he'd never had to understand why Guild orders must be obeyed. "You'll just have to come with me!"

Brevelan ducked under the man's reaching grasp. She ran across the bridge as fast as the bulk of her belly and the hindering basket would allow. The pilot ambled after her, confident his superior position in life would allow him to catch her. He was halfway across when Brevelan reached for the linchpin. He halted abruptly in his tracks.

Brevelan moved her hand away from the shiny new mechanism the man had just installed. He took a step closer. She reached again for the release that would topple him into the angry river.

"I can't swim, goodwoman."

"My quest is honest. Outlaws and raiders stalk honest women in the villages. I don't trust you."

"Yes, goodwoman." He took a cautious step backward.

Brevelan dropped her hand to her side. Slowly, the pilot returned to the riverbank where his boat was secured, glaring menace and retribution with each step. When he was safely ashore, she loosened the linchpin. It slid easily within its housing.

"Don't do that!" The pilot stared at her, aghast.

"Can I trust you to leave me alone?" The wooden planks on the bridge groaned as she played with the linchpin.

"I am a Guildman. My word is trusted." Trusted, not trustworthy. The Guildman crossed himself in the manner of the Stargods. When he dropped his right hand from the gesture, he let it rest crossed over his left. A flicker of either hand would invoke the much older ward against Simurgh.

Brevelan backed away from him. She knew she shouldn't trust him. What few emotions he allowed to escape fluctuated wildly.

With a low groan of wood pushing against wood, the bridge shuddered and collapsed, one plank at a time. The Guildman held up the linchpin on his side of the river. "This is the only bridge onto Last Isle. You'll not be leaving 'afore I come back with my captain, witch," he hissed, as he climbed back into his boat.

Now what? Brevelan stood in indecision and near panic. Her fingers itched to throw a spell at the man. He would look very nice as a strutting flustercock. Not today. She had a Rover woman to find before the Guild caught up with her. Then she'd worry about getting back to the University.

The image of a fat rodent appeared in her mind. Mica wanted to chase the self-important river-rat into a pile of refuse where he belonged.

"Next time," Brevelan promised the cat.

"What do you mean, Brevelan went in search of a Rover woman?" Jaylor yelled for any and all to hear. The fact that Darville was within a pace of him, and he sat in the middle of the library where quiet reigned didn't affect the volume of his protest.

"Since when have I had any control over Brevelan?" Darville asked quietly. "I'm still her favorite 'puppy.' " He slumped against the doorjamb.

Jaylor knew that pose, knew the worry behind Roy's eyes and the coiled tension in his back and thighs. He'd seen it too many times over the years.

"How long has she been gone, Roy?" Jaylor thrust aside the tome of magic to grab his notes. If he had to find his wife and a Rover woman, he wanted the aid of the simple binding spell he'd spent a night and a day puzzling over.

"Too long. She left before noon and the sun is now about an hour to setting. Even Old Baamin is getting anxious, and he sent her out. Oh, and she took Mica with her."

"Does that signify something?" Jaylor stared again at Darville's posture. The prince was definitely in a high state of agitation.

"Mica signifies a great deal. You haven't seen some of the tricks she has pulled recently. There are people in my capital who would dearly love to drown that pesky cat and anyone who tries to protect her."

"There seems to be something you are not telling me, Darville."

"Some things I don't even tell Baamin. But if you will find three women for me, I'll let you in on all my secrets.

"Only three women, Roy? Are you losing your touch or becoming more conservative in your old age?"

"Neither. I have fallen in love."

"Last spring you were in love with Brevelan."

"I still am, in a way. But she is your wife now, the mother of your child. I can't intrude on that relationship."

"What if the child is yours?"

They'd never had any secrets from each other. Right from the start the two boys had been brutally honest with each other. Lies ended with black eyes and swollen jaws when they were found out.

"Impossible. She married you."

"She rescued me. You know her compulsion to heal. The child didn't affect her decision."

"She rescued me, too, at one time. But she refused to marry me. I can only presume she chose the father of her child."

"How could she tell?"

"Women know."

"Does your new woman know that you love her? Do you know you really love her?"

"I am hopelessly, irrevocably . . . passionately in love with Mikka."

"Mica?"

"Mikka. There's a difference. Now, help me find them. I've searched most of the capital with a troop of trusted cavalry. But my citizens don't trust anyone in uniform."

Chapter 19

Brambleberries! The last small ones of the season drooped on the vines. Yaakke plucked a handful and thrust them into his dry mouth. The sourness started a flood of saliva. His stomach growled. The berries barely filled the gnawing emptiness that was the aftermath of too many spells thrown too quickly.

Stargods! he was hungry. He hadn't felt this empty since his early days as a kitchen drudge and his meals were whatever scraps he could steal before the other servants found them. More than once he'd had to fight for the meager pickings and ended up bruised and supperless.

That's when he began listening to other people's thoughts—to protect himself. He'd been listening for as long as he could remember, without knowing he was doing it.

But he now knew that not just anyone could listen to another's most intimate conversations with themselves. Nor was it polite to invade their privacy. Brevelan kept hammering at him to respect other people and remember his manners.

No one had respected him or remembered their manners around him until he'd revealed his rogue powers! From birth until after his thirteenth or fourteenth birthday he had been "Boy," a foundling too stupid to learn anything more than scrubbing pots. Too insignificant to even have a name. His past and his true age were lost in poorhouse records.

Just because he couldn't gather dragon magic.

Oh, well, he sighed, as he grabbed another handful of berries. Brevelan had a point. He didn't want strangers learning all of his secrets, so he shouldn't try to learn theirs. But there were times when it was ever so convenient to know what other people expected of him.

Yaakke scanned several of the small, uninhabited mounds of sand and snake grass that appeared and disappeared each season in the huge river. A dozen of them dotted the watery landscape between here and the mainland. Aits, the locals called these temporary islands. City dwellers ran bets as to which ones would survive the winter floods. City boys made daring games of swimming around them.

Six aits between here and the next true island. Yaakke didn't think he could make it that far without a meal.

He set a new path around the brambles. His feet plodded to a sandy cove on the north side of Sacred Isle. A five-foot cliff, held up by massive tree roots, sheltered the cove from prying eyes.

Resting on the quarter-moon beach and tied to one of those exposed roots was a rowboat.

Instantly, Yaakke stilled his body and his mind. His personal armor snapped into place. Who could be on Sacred Isle? Priests came here to prepare for festivals. The equinox was weeks past.

Journeymen magicians came here in search of a staff. He clutched his own new tool protectively to his chest. There were no journeymen left at the University. And only five apprentices, other than himself.

Who else? He sought for a memory, any memory that might tell him who had left the boat.

Guild Pilots roamed the waterways and islands at will. But this boat was plain and small. The oarlocks showed signs of wear, and paint was flaking from the sunbleached seats. No respectable pilot would be caught dead in so neglected a boat.

Who, then?

His mind drifted back to the spell that had brought him here. He'd sniffed for a strong concentration of magic. He'd landed on Sacred Isle, in the middle of the most blessed grove, with the remains of a Tambootie wood fire at his feet.

Tambootie was increasingly rare and most people still considered it the embodiment of evil. He remembered Lord Krej eating two fat Tambootie leaves. Krej had been deeply involved in a rogue ritual when Yaakke had found him. A Tambootie wood fire had burned at the center of that ritual.

Yaakke slipped back to the Sacred Grove. Dozens of bare footprints scuffled the area around the fire. A witch dance!

Panic swelled his tongue inside his mouth. The recently uncontrolled saliva dried. Even with his wild and unexplained magic, until he'd eaten heartily and slept several hours, he'd be no match against the evil of a full coven. He dared not bring food from the University kitchens to help overcome his weakness. A witch would be able to smell the magic. But would a witch be able to tell who stole the boat?

Probably. If the witch were still on the island. He sent out a quick mental probe, not really magic, just "listening." The dart of consciousness spun outward in ever widening circles. He found two deer, five squirrels, one lizard, eight field mice—no nine, one was still abirthing. Birds of all description sang through his mind. Then, finally, he touched a dream. A human was dreaming of a huge bonfire of Tambootie with naked figures dancing around it. Four men, four women.

A sniggle of guilt coiled inside Yaakke for eavesdropping on the witch's dream. He pushed it aside. This was important, and interesting. Inside the dream the naked figures coupled and danced, taunted and coupled again with new partners, not always of the opposite sex.

A second dream overlapped the original vision. The same dream from a different viewpoint.

Uh-oh. Had he stumbled upon two witches?

The two dreams wove a seductive web into Yaakke's mind, enticing him to slumber and join with their memories. Each time two witches joined, a surge of magical energy erupted from the grove. Residue from the spells thrown by the coven during those surges was the magic Yaakke had followed during his transport across half of Coronnan.

Yaakke's adolescent body reacted to the erotic dream with intense interest. He listened to the witch's thoughts and followed the images to the thicket where the dreamers slept off the night's activities and the drugging effect of the Tambootie. Sheltered within the burned-out trunk of an immense oak slept a middle-aged man with a square-cut beard and close-cropped hair. He was half draped over the body of a voluptuous, auburn-haired woman. They were both naked.

A foreigner. Citizens of Coronnan City were clean shaven and wore their long hair neatly restrained in a queue.

This stranger didn't seem affected by the cool river mist. Not with the woman clasped so tightly against him. Maybe they were both strangers from a colder clime. Red hair on a woman was unusual. He'd know her if he ever saw her again.

Even as he watched and "listened," Yaakke observed the dreamer's body rouse while his mind continued to sleep. Witch or no, this man wouldn't be aware of Yaakke's presence or of the boat's absence for several hours yet.

Rowing across the turbulent river would be tiring. But not nearly as much as transporting himself to another island. Yaakke caressed his new staff, wondering how much easier magic would be with the tool. Maybe he should try bringing food to refuel his body.

The witch and his lady mumbled and squirmed in their sleep. Yaakke silently withdrew from the thicket, embarrassed by their intimate display. Theft seemed more ethical than watching these two perform, or starving to death on this island of blessings and profanity.

The baby squirmed and bounced within Brevelan's belly. This walk across the city had taken too long. Her feet were swelling and her eyes were tired from her careful scrutiny of so many strangers. Both she and the baby needed food and water.

Mica's humming purr ceased abruptly.

Cautiously, Brevelan peered around her to see what had disrupted the cat's pleasant reverie.

A market square spread out in front of her. It looked like any other village market: one baker, one horse-trader, one carpenter/fix-it, one barkeep, and not much else.

Except there was an old woman sitting on a stool at the extreme corner of the square, as close to an exit as she could perch and still be part of the market. She wore a plain black skirt and kirtle, like any matronly tradeswoman.

But her blouse was bright purple, her kerchief was red banded in black, and the hem of her skirt was pieced with strips of red and purple, yellow and green. In front of her was spread an assortment of mended cooking tools and gaudy, tooled silver jewelry. Her costume proclaimed her a Rover. The palm reading she performed for a succession of men, young and old, confirmed her identity.

Brevelan checked the cat's reaction. Mica's face poked out from beneath the checkered cloth. Her nose twitched and her eyes grew big. But she wasn't watching the Rover woman.

All of Mica's attention was directed across the square on a girl, and the man who urged her to follow him. The cat's hissing growl grew louder.

The baby lurched again, just as he had that time an alien presence had soothed him when Brevelan's spirit left her body. Was he reacting to that same presence?

Everyone, including the Rover palm reader now, watched the well-dressed girl and the man with the foreign-looking beard and close-cropped hair, who had a firm grip on her arm. No one paid any attention to Brevelan or her cat.

"Is that Darville's errant princess?" Brevelan whispered to Mica. Who else would dare wear a gown of such costly fabric and daring cut at the bosom into this remote corner of the capital?

Brevelan moved closer.

So did the Rover woman.

"You dare accost one who is pledged to a convent!" Rossemikka proclaimed loudly. Everyone in the market could hear her words. Words that were calculated to require the locals to protect her.

Then her manner changed abruptly. Her eyes slitted and her body looked softer, rounder, more voluptuous. Her lips pouted and she leaned closer to the man who was trying to maneuver her into an alley.

"Of course, there are some men who thrill at the chance to defy the Stargods. The risk of being outlawed by every priest in the land heightens the adventure." Her voice was both enticement and challenge.

A snarl rose from the throats of several of the locals, men and women alike. Respect for the institutions of the Stargods ran high among the populace of the city.

Mica's tune choked briefly. Brevelan suppressed her own laughter. The girl was cunning, no doubt about it. No man within hearing distance would dare touch her now. Indeed, the barkeep was fingering a cudgel with hands itching to bash a head or two.

"Shut your mouth and come with me, woman! Come quietly or you won't get any dinner," the foreigner hissed. His eyes shifted uneasily about the square, while his grip on Rossemikka's arm never loosened.

"Merowerrrr!" Mica challenged the man as she stood up in the basket. Her back arched and the fur along her spine stiffened.

"Hush, Mica! Get down. We don't want to attract attention." Brevelan tried to hold the cat back.

"Merowerrrr!" Mica squirmed out of Brevelan's grasp and leaped from the basket. Her claws were fully extended. Her eyes glowed a murderous red.

"A witch! A witch and her familiar claim the girl," the barkeep shouted and pointed at Brevelan with the cudgel.

Half the crowd turned their attention toward Brevelan. A heavy boot lifted to kick at the leaping cat.

"Why is that bridge down?" Darville wondered out loud. Another distraction. Rosie had been missing almost an entire day, Brevelan and Mica nearly as long. Yet he couldn't neglect his city, and a collapsed bridge in this sector indicated something terribly wrong.

"Dragons only know," Jaylor replied as he bent his back and shoulders into his oar stroke.

Darville searched both banks of Coronnan River for a clue. The pilings that secured the planks on each bank were intact. A board dragging against a piling in the water on the Marner Isle side caught his eye. The current caught the wood, swirled around the piling, then released it as unseen forces pushed the water on course toward the bay.

"Pull over to that piling," Darville commanded his friend.

"Wrong direction. We want Last Isle. Our women are still lost," Jaylor protested.

"This might be important. If the bridge has been down for long, Brevelan and Mica couldn't get across to Last Isle."

"If the bridge has been down that long, you would have heard the locals' complaints."

"Don't bet on that. The Council has been going out of its way to make sure I hear nothing of what happens outside the palace. My spies are good but not infallible."

Without that bridge, the residents of Last Isle would be stranded. Very few of the capital's citizens kept boats for transportation these days. Maintenance and moorage were too expensive for the common folk. Boats for defense and escape had been unnecessary for three hundred years.

Darville grabbed hold of the loose plank as Jaylor maneuvered the boat closer to the steep embankment. The hull scraped on more planks and handrails. Darville hauled on the rope holding the loose plank. More boards rose from the river. Beneath them, dipping deep into the river, the bridge seemed almost intact. Someone had collapsed the bridge from the Marner Isle side.

Why? There was no other bridge to this most remote of the city's islands. Whoever had pulled the linchpin had trapped everyone on Last Isle. But how long ago had this happened? The wooden plank was totally soaked from the river's surging current. Not waterlogged.

"I think we need to make haste, Jaylor. Brevelan could be in trouble."

"Take the oars a minute." Jaylor thrust the sweeps into Darville's hands without waiting for a reply. "Hold her still. I need to touch the plank. Maybe I can read who has passed across it."

With the ease of long practice, Darville helped his friend into position. He watched the water and the boat with only half his attention.

Jaylor's body went totally still as soon as his hand touched the wood. His eyes closed as his breathing deepened. For a moment, the late afternoon sunshine almost glowed through the magician's body.

Impatiently, Darville fought a swirl in the current. When his attention fully returned to Jaylor, every muscle in his friend's body twitched out of control.

"Jaylor! Come out of your trance," he commanded with a frightened wobble in his voice. Somehow, he hadn't quite believed Brevelan's report of how Jaylor's magic had warped. If every spell, even this simple one, sent him into convulsions, his magic was totally unreliable.

Jaylor didn't respond to the verbal command. Under his grasp, the plank shattered into a thousand pieces. Sharp splinters pierced Jaylor's hand. Blood welled up from several wounds, dripping down the hand and arm that jumped with increasing spasms.

"Jaylor!" Darville released one oar long enough to shake Jaylor's shoulder. No response.

The river surged again, stole the loose oar, and swung the boat around. The current grabbed the streamlined little craft and eagerly propelled it toward the sea.

Chapter 20

The Cat! Darville's CAT. The evil little beast stalked across the market square toward Rosie. That must mean the prince was nearby.

Rosie froze in her tracks. Her abductor yanked on her arm to draw her away from the crowd. She couldn't respond. Her heels dug into the dirt of their path.

Air knifed into Rosie's lungs. Once trapped inside her, she couldn't release it. Her head lightened and threatened to disengage from her neck. White spots crackled before her eyes.

Like magic, the cat stopped her attack on Rosie in midleap. Hissing and spitting her annoyance, the creature dropped to the ground but came no closer.

The drunken man's hand tightened around Rosie's upper arm. "Quickly, we can escape that vicious cat this way," he urged. He took two more steps toward the alley, forcing her to follow. She stumbled and threw her weight back, away from him, not certain who to fear most, the man or the cat. Still he dragged her farther away from the protection of the crowd in the market square.

She raked his arm and wrist with her long fingernails and drew blood.

"*S'murghing* harpy!" he snarled. In retaliation he clamped both of her hands in one crushing fist.

"You're hurting me!" Rosie screamed, as she bent her knees and dropped to the ground, heedless of her gown. Janataea was going to be very angry when she mended the dirty rips.

He yanked hard on her arms. Her shoulders wanted to separate from her arms. She fought the pain, fought the man. All the while, the cat spat and cried as she paced an arc in front of Rosie.

Her mind raced to Janataea, the governess who had intervened with Uncle Rumbelly sometimes when she was troubled back home. She would be no help today. Rosie had run away. This was her punishment.

Something snapped in the back of Rosie's mind. Today she wouldn't calmly accept her fate. Baamin had told her punishment was not a normal path in life.

In desperation, she sought the faces of the crowd for help. The old woman who had been reading palms for coins appeared beside her.

"Help me!" she called to the old woman, taking a chance, her only chance.

The crowd moved closer, murmuring curses in all directions.

"You have only to wish to come with me." The old woman's voice was surprisingly crisp and young, yet seemed to contain the wisdom of the ages.

Rosie's eyes riveted on the woman and her garishly colored clothing. The crowd seemed to drop behind the woman. Their movements slowed to unreality. Their angry protests fell to murmuring.

No·one but the old woman was close enough to rescue her from square-beard.

"If you really want to come with me, nothing will stop you. No one will impede you." The woman spoke again in the same tones Janataea used when she put a compulsion on Rosie.

"I want . . . I want. . . ." What did she really want? She wanted to be safe, on familiar ground, with familiar people who smelled the same, day after day. Could the old woman give her that?

"Enough!" Darville's voice arrested the entire market square. Water dripped from his unrestrained hair and his wet clothing outlined and clung to his powerful muscles. Strong scents of the river masked all other traces of the tall figure moving through the crowd. If he smelled of the river, then he must intend to drown her for her disobedience.

Darville merely glared at Rosie as he stalked through the crowd. He paused a moment to touch the shoulder of a small, insignificant-looking woman who carried a basket, then pushed forward to confront square-beard, who still had not released Rosie's arm.

"Release the Princess Rossemikka," he commanded in a tone that would tolerate no disobedience.

"What right you got to deprive me o' my doxie?" The decisive man suddenly dissolved into a slurring drunkard with a country accent that didn't fit the other voices in the market. His square-cut beard and short hair were also out of place.

"I said, release the princess, foreigner." The last word became an insult as the prince reached for the dagger at his hip.

"Foreigner!"

"Stranger?"

The crowd's whisperings surged louder, angrier, yet still they held back, as if barricaded from the focus of the action.

"Do not interfere!" the old woman warned as she tried to elbow Darville aside. "By her own wish, the girl belongs to me!"

Rosie continued to search the eyes of the old woman for help. The punishments Janataea meted out were nothing compared to the fate she knew awaited her at Darville's hands. Drowning in the river! Almost any fate was preferable to that.

"Do you know who I am?" Darville glared at the individuals in the crowd who dared defy him.

"Doesn't make much difference, unless you're a priest," the barkeep with his cudgel remarked. "The girl's pledged to a convent. Said so herself. That means no man takes her away from this island. She goes alone, or she goes with a priest." He slapped the end of his club into his upraised palm in a menacing rhythm, as if testing its weight.

"She is betrothed to me unless she has managed to find a priest and make other vows since sunrise." Darville looked as if he hated making explanations.

"I never agreed to the betrothal," Rosie spoke to the barkeep. He seemed to be the only one truly listening to her. "My uncle signed all the papers without even asking me. Darville, here, insists. . . ."

"Darville!" The crowd gasped, inching forward to see

their prince closer, or tear him limb from limb. Rosie couldn't be sure which.

"And I will take her back to Rossemeyer." Squarebeard, suddenly sober, reasserted his grip on Rosie's arm. She tried to yank it back, ignoring the increased pressure on her muscles and bones. "I have been sent by the royal government to retrieve the princess."

"Not unless you aim to get to Rossemeyer by way of King Simeon's court in SeLenicca." A dark-eyed youth stood behind the drunk. He held a long staff across the alley retreat.

More protests from the crowd.

"Enough!" Darville shouted over the noise. "The princess will return to Palace Isle with me. We will sort out this mess there."

"No. I'd rather face King Simeon's magicians than marry you." Rosie knew the crowd was on her side. She tried to squeeze closer to the barkeep for protection. But the small woman with the basket stood in her way.

"Just be quiet, Princess Rossemikka. For once in your life, keep your likes and dislikes to yourself, or, so help me, I will drown you in the river myself!" Darville glared at her.

Rosie had no doubt he meant every word of it.

Outside the mental armor Brevelan had thrown around herself and Mica, the emotions of the market crowd pressed with increasing urgency. Mica paced the edge of the wide barrier yowling her displeasure.

I must protect her. He must not contaminate her, Mica told Brevelan. The cat's anxious pacing also spoke of her need to break through and claw at the eyes of the man who held Princess Rossemikka with such volatile possessiveness.

Brevelan edged closer to Darville in case she had to extend her armor to protect him. She didn't know how she would help the girl while keeping Mica away from squarebeard.

A wall of impenetrable magic stopped her in her tracks. Eyes wide with alarm, she searched the crowd with every sense available to her for the source of the spell.

No one. Nowhere could she smell magic. Again and

again she searched for this new threat. Then she counted the people around her with her own special empathy.

The Rover woman was missing. Was she truly missing, or just so heavily armored that no one could see her?

Brevelan searched again with that knowledge. There was a hole in the crowd that her senses slid around or over, but never through. She refocused her eyes. The hole began to shimmer with shifting light and undulating magic. Mica stalked from Brevelan's side into that other armor, and back again.

The Rover woman must be there. But why would her armor admit Mica, a cat with potentially dangerous emotions running rampant?

Garlic, tons of it, comprised the main ingredient in the magic of armor.

Brevelan edged around the wall of magic and found herself on the other side of Darville. *Stargods!* The Rover was throwing her armor around Rosie and the knot of verbal combatants, as well as herself.

"Meww?" Mica questioned Brevelan's unease. She was content with the presence of the Rover woman.

Brevelan looked a little closer, trying to penetrate the redolent miasma. Her tongue flicked out to taste it. With the flavor embedded in her tongue, her ears opened to hear a strange incantation from the center of the protected bubble. The Rover woman's magic was triggered by *Song* and by herbs, just as Brevelan's was.

"That smell makes me hungry enough to eat one of your meatless stews," Yaakke remarked behind Brevelan. He and a staff that was already beginning to twist blocked the foreigner's exit into the alley.

"How did you get here?" Brevelan asked. Too many strange emotions flooding her system left her only mildly startled at the boy's appearance.

His hunger radiated from him, engulfing her. Her stomach growled in sympathy. The baby kicked and squirmed in protest. He, too, was as hungry as the apprentice.

"Same way you and Jaylor got to the University." Yaakke shrugged and winked.

Then Brevelan looked at the boy, really looked at him. His eyes were blank with fatigue and his cheeks hollow, as

if he hadn't eaten in weeks. The first time she had seen
Jaylor, he'd been in the same condition.

"We've got to get out of here. All of us." Brevelan didn't
realize she had spoken until she heard the words.

"How?" Darville asked her without taking his eyes or
his dagger away from the square-bearded foreigner. "The
bridge is down and Jaylor's on the next island with our
boat. The currents swept us away from every landing. I had
to swim the last channel."

"I can tell Brevelan how to transport us," Yaakke volun-
teered. At least he hadn't offered to throw the spells himself. As exhausted as he was, such a stunt would end in
disaster.

"No!" Darville protested. "Brevelan can't endanger herself or the baby by working any more magic than
necessary."

The baby kicked in agreement.

A pair of blacker than black eyes peered out from behind
the garlic armor. "What you thinking, throwing magic while
baby yours grows within?" The accent and syntax were
pure Rover. The garlic-flavored armor shifted to include
Brevelan and Yaakke. Brevelan's spell dissolved.

"What? Who are you?" Brevelan and Darville asked in
unison.

"Healer I be. Baby asks my help. Curious he. Wants out
to come and see what do we." The old woman reached a
gnarled and trembling hand to the swell of Brevelan's stomach. "Almost time."

"Not yet, not for two more moons." Brevelan tried to
back away from the strange woman's touch and her own
fears left over from the premature labor triggered by
Shayla. The circle of magic and Yaakke's young body
stopped her.

"She only means to help, Brevelan. She won't hurt you."
Yaakke held her shoulders with comforting confidence.

"Boat have I. To safety you I take."

"Her name is Erda," Yaakke interpreted. "But we won't
all fit into her boat. She wants to take the princess with
her, too. His Grace and I can take my boat."

"How do you know all this?" Darville asked.

"Just listening . . . sir."

Respect for any elder, other than Baamin, had always been difficult for Yaakke. Brevelan allowed a moment of surprise that the boy had used any title at all in addressing his prince.

"I won't go anywhere with you, Darville," Rosie finally spoke.

"Nor will I," square-beard added. He raised a fist and smashed it against the unbreakable wall of magic. He continued to beat at it with increasingly frantic blows. "I can't stay here. I've got to get the girl away from the capital. He'll send me to the mines if I fail!" he wailed.

The old woman looked up from her examination of Brevelan to glare at the foreigner. "Choices, none you have, minion of the sorcerer king," Erda spat. "In boats, my men take all. Zolltarn likes not intrusion in territory his."

"Zolltarn!" Brevelan and Darville gasped together. The last time they had run into the king of the Rovers, he had attacked them and deliberately shattered Jaylor's staff at the behest of Lord Krej.

Suddenly, the crowd in the market square swelled in numbers. All of the newcomers wore black trews and vests, red or purple shirts, and multicolored scarves tied closely about their heads, the uniform of Zolltarn's clan. The tall, black-haired chieftain strode forward, sliding through Erda's armor as if it were nonexistent.

Zolltarn fingered the tiny metal earring Darville wore. "A pretty trinket, Prince of Wolves."

"Keep your thieving hands to yourself, Rover." Darville ground out the words painfully, as if his jaw were paralyzed.

"I can't allow old Baamin to trace you just yet." Zolltarn closed his hand around the miniature dragon.

"And I can't afford to separate myself from his protection." The prince forced his left hand onto the long dagger at his hip.

Strange hands reached from behind Darville, preventing him from drawing his weapon. Brevelan opened her mouth in warning as she took one step forward. Erda blocked her path.

"We have magic that is older than time. Learn now not

to defy us." Zolltarn yanked on Darville's earring. Blood dripped from the hole torn in his ear. Empathic pain ripped through Brevelan, blocking her vision and will.

Gone! The princess is gone. I knew I should have compelled her to obedience. But she grows resistant to the spell. The more I use it, the more I have to use it. Especially now.

Dragons only know what will happen if she comes into season while she is away from the palace and out of my control. That time is rapidly approaching.

I must find her. I will resort to the Tambootie. The leaves of the tree of magic will enhance my vision and calm me so that I may concentrate on my spells.

Chapter 21

"**J**aylor is the only person I know who can eat more than you do." Darville watched Yaakke gnaw the last taste of meat off a flusterhen bone. His third flusterhen, not to mention several helpings of tubers and squash.

The Rovers had willingly supplied the boy with whatever he wanted to regain his strength. Zolltarn's people had a magical task for him. But they hadn't specified that task, as yet.

Darville didn't intend to wait around long enough to find out. He continued his minute examination of the tent he and the boy occupied, seeking a hidden exit, a makeshift weapon, anything that would aid an escape.

He and the boy were in a large, family-sized tent, possibly Zolltarn's own. The interior was as exotically furnished as the exterior colors promised. Bright fabrics and rugs lined the walls and floors. Ropes of colored beads and bizarre statuary littered tables that could be folded and stored flat while traveling. The camp stools were covered in thick tapestry to rival the best furniture in the palace. And everywhere hung braids of garlic. The smell permeated the air and all of the furnishings. Was the herb hung so prominently for convenience, or as a ward?

A fire glowed in the center, giving off light and warmth. Smoke ventilated through an opening in the fabric ceiling. Evening was falling and so was the first rain of the autumn.

"Did Jaylor really eat this much before . . . ?" Even Yaakke, it seemed, was reluctant to speak of Jaylor's ordeal after freeing Shayla from her glass prison.

"He ate more; much more. He was bigger than you at your age." Maybe the boy could slip under the outside edge

of the tent. This back wall showed the promise of a loose-
ness in the guy strings.

"I imagine the Council will be searching for me by now,"
Darville mused. "Zolltarn doesn't have much time for whatever task he plans for you, Yaakke." He played with the tent
fabric to see if any guard was alerted by the activity.

He heard a shuffle of feet just beyond the tent. Then a
hand smoothed the wall from the outside.

So much for that idea. The entire circumference seemed
to be heavily guarded.

Now what? He had to get out of here and rescue the
others.

Brevelan and Rosie had been led to one of the smaller
shelters by the Rover women. Jaylor, hollow-eyed with
strain, but whole and strong otherwise, was heavily guarded
in another. Dragons only knew where Mica had gone. Darville hadn't seen the cat at all on the trek to the Rover
camp, here on the mainland, northwest of the capital.

And what about square-beard? Like the leader of the
band of raiders Darville had encountered in the field, the
man was likely an agent of King Simeon of SeLenicca. No
one from that kingdom had legitimate business in Coronnan. Darville would give his eyeteeth to know why his rival
monarch was so bent on kidnapping the princess. But did
he dare take the time to liberate the man from the Rovers?
Presuming that he got out himself.

"Zolltarn's going to ask me to summon Baamin here."
Yaakke quaffed a full tankard of ale. "Did you get the
sense we were sorta being herded to Last Isle, like so many
sheep?" Yaakke asked between bites of tubers.

"I hadn't thought about it. Seems an unlikely coincidence
that all of us should end up in the same confrontation with
an agent of King Simeon, just as Zolltarn waltzes in and
captures the lot of us."

"He wants to bargain something. I don't know what. He
keeps his thoughts closely guarded."

"With me as hostage, he's likely to get whatever he asks
for. But there are some who will gladly allow another to
remove me from their path." Darville threw a twig into the
fire and watched it glow and swell with heat before igniting.
Coronnan was in that glowing stage. Being kidnapped by
Rovers could be the final act before the entire country

blazed into civil war. The Council would blame him, of course. The Commune would blame the Council. Individual lords would attack their neighbors.

Stargods! Was there no end to the divisive bickering?

"You were an incidental prize. He's after something bigger. Much bigger. But I can't tell what."

"More of your 'listening,' Yaakke?"

"Can't help listening if people practically shout their thoughts." The boy shrugged. "Zolltarn has pretty heavy natural armor, though. Not much leaks out."

"You could be a handy person to have around. Who else knows of this ability of yours?" Darville turned his interest from fruitless plots of escape to the possibilities the boy presented.

"Old . . . Master Baamin knows. Brevelan suspects, but she's never said or thought anything about it, except that it's impolite to listen to people's private thoughts without an invitation. She can do it if she throws a spell."

"She doesn't need to with me," Darville admitted. "When we're close together, in the same room, she and Jaylor and I can read each other very clearly." That was probably why the Rovers had separated them, to keep them from plotting an escape.

"But you don't have any magic!"

"There are other magics, Yaakke. Magics that have nothing to do with spells and ley lines and dragons. Like friendship and loyalty and love. Especially love."

"These Rovers are the first people I've met who have natural armor. Most magicians have to throw a spell to put it in place." Yaakke shook his head in dismay. "I can hear the guard outside the tent pretty well, but he's young, only about my age. The oldsters send my thoughts in circles, and yet I can't smell any armor. Sorta like the drunk with the square beard. His armor was imposed on him. Couldn't get so much as a hint of his thoughts."

"You seem to have a nose for magic. Why were you so late in being apprenticed?" Darville was puzzled by the boy's history, or lack of one.

"Probably because I've been listening to people's thoughts and seeing ley lines for as long as I can remember. I didn't realize other people didn't do the same until I spent some time with Master Baamin. He was the only one who gave me real tasks—other than picking up after people and scrubbing dirty dishes. He was the one who noticed that I heard what he was thinking."

"Trust Old Baamin to discover something valuable that everyone else overlooks." Darville grinned a little as he used the more common description of the Senior Magician, rather than his proper title.

"Yeah. I won't need to actually throw a summoning spell with Old Baamin." Yaakke eased into the familiar form with an answering grin. "I could just speak to his mind with my mind. But I don't think we want Zolltarn to know I can do it." He picked up a horn spoon to delve into the pot of stew at his side.

"Good thought. Make the task appear a little harder than it is, if you can." Darville's mind began to plot. The boy could be a weapon, especially if he could communicate with their companions without throwing a summons.

"Have you smelled the Tambootie these people use?" Yaakke grimaced as he tasted the stew. "It's in everything, the fire, the food." Yaakke leaned closer to Darville and whispered. "I think even the bedding is stuffed with Tambootie leaves. Jaylor told me they put timboor, the dried berries of the Tambootie, into a lot of their foods."

"I can't smell anything but garlic."

Yaakke sat straighter and cocked his head as if listening. "Zolltarn has decided I've eaten enough to regain my strength. He's coming."

Brevelan pushed the seeking hands of Erda away from contact with her baby. She wasn't in labor yet and felt no need for the healer's touch.

"Where is my husband? I must see Jaylor, now." She tried to put a compulsion on the woman and met a . . . a blank wall. That was the only way to describe it. Usually when she reached out with her empathic powers, she could feel the winding paths of a person's emotions and guide those emotions to inner healing. Their thoughts became evident with the course of their feelings.

Erda had the same kind of armor Jaylor had. Only Jaylor's armor couldn't resist her loving mental touch anymore.

"Baby come. Soon." Erda shifted enough to throw a handful of herbs on the small brazier. She began a low chant, rocking her body back and forth in rhythm with her internal music. The aromatic smoke drifted through the tent, making Brevelan's head spin.

Timboor! How could she maintain control in the presence of that addictive drug?

"Must you pollute the air?" Rosie asked from the other side of the hot fire. They were all damp from the rain and the river crossing. But the princess seemed inclined to huddle closer to the warmth than either Brevelan or Erda found comfortable. "May I wash my hands and face?"

"Fetch the water from the river yourself, if you must. You know that. Everyone in this camp fends for themselves," Erda spat back at the girl. "No one is servant to another, told me yourself."

Then Rosie looked up from the fire. Brevelan felt the fear and bewilderment in the princess. There was an emptiness there, too. An emptiness that prevented her from understanding what was happening, why she had been kidnapped and was now a prisoner.

"By Simurgh the all-powerful, what have they done to you, child? You are not the Mikka I taught so many seasons ago." Erda shifted her attention from Brevelan and the baby to the princess. She crossed her wrists and fluttered her hands three times. "Bold the monster has grown in her quest for power. Stopped must she be."

Alerted by Erda's tone, Brevelan peered closer at Rosie, narrowing her eyes and vision. Awareness of the girl's true nature crept in slowly. "*Stargods*. We have to find Mica."

"Keep your magic in," Erda ordered. "Baby too curious. He come soon. Too soon."

"I will bear my child in my own home, at the proper time, with my own healer, and with my husband at my side," Brevelan insisted to Erda, though she never took her eyes off of Rosie.

"No healer have you. Just yourself. No man can help when baby becomes stubborn."

"Why do you care?" Brevelan wanted to get up and pace the confines of the tent. She was restless with unanswered questions and the unnatural lack of freedom. Her eyes kept going back to Rosie. The need to help the princess rose in her. If she could only touch her mind . . . if only she could coax Mica out of hiding.

"Baby is strong. Great Magician he be. We have few children. Baby will replace the one we lost."

"Not bloody likely!" Brevelan spat. "This is my baby. I'll not give it up to the likes of you!"

All of her attention arrowed in on the threat Erda posed to the baby.

"Keep you, too, if we must, to have the baby."

"You want to keep me prisoner, too," Rosie stated before Brevelan could protest. "You were pushing me to choose your tribe over being kidnapped by that foreigner. Why?" Some of the confusion cleared from her eyes. Some, not all.

"Zolltarn has his reasons. He will do much the plans of The Simeon to destroy. Mate with you himself, instead of the sorcerer king."

"I don't want to mate with anyone."

"You think that now. A few hours, a few days at most, you wait. Accept you will, any man who comes near you."

"Never!"

Erda laughed. An evil, knowing cackle that swelled and filled the tight confines of the tent.

"My price, Master Baamin, for the prince and his princess, unharmed, is a seat on the Commune of Magicians." Zolltarn dropped his demands upon his audience with studied casualness. His fingers touched the tiny metal dragon that now adorned his ear.

"No, Baamin. You can't allow a Rover access to our government, our armies, all of our secrets!" Outrage screamed from every pore of Darville's body. He rose to his feet in one swift movement so that he could stand taller than the seated Zolltarn. The Rover merely glanced up at him, then returned his gaze to the Senior Magician, seated on a chair on the other side of the fire.

"I could sweeten the pot by curing Jaylor of the warp in his magic," the Rover offered.

Baamin bit his lip in indecision. Darville paced a figure eight around the fire, looping around his companions. Yaakke continued to eat.

"You offer a great deal," Baamin stalled.

He ran his hands up and down his staff, caressing the texture.

"He offers you nothing," Darville spat. "He knows he can't hold me long, with the Council guards waiting just beyond the camp. How do we know he can cure Jaylor anyway?" he challenged.

"I have access to powers you have yet to dream of, Baamin. Elemental powers. Very old powers. My people threw magic long before the Stargods left behind their gifts within the blood of their heirs." Zolltarn leaned forward in his enthusiasm. "I will release the princess unharmed. If you force the issue, I will make certain that I am the one to mate with her when she comes into season."

Darville exchanged a worried look with Baamin.

Mikka had feared this outcome. Any child she bore was destined to become a pawn in a diabolical plot to control the three kingdoms—magically and temporally.

"How will you cure Jaylor?" Darville decided to avoid the issue of mates and births and inheritance.

"A binding spell," Zolltarn addressed Baamin.

Darville glared at the Rover. Zolltarn was ignoring him, just as the Council had time and time again. They saw him as ineffectual. The real power in Coronnan lay not in the hands of the monarch, but in the Council and Commune.

"Binding is only temporary. The spell needs things I couldn't translate to complete." A new voice joined the conversation.

Darville turned to face the man in the doorway, hand automatically reaching for his missing dagger.

"Jaylor," he breathed a sigh of relief. "Brevelan." Darville nodded to the slight woman who appeared at her husband's elbow. Behind her, like a shadow hiding behind a pillar of strength, stood Rosie.

"How did you get here?" Zolltarn stood so quickly his camp stool collapsed.

Jaylor stalked up to the rover chief. "I escaped. I am no longer your pawn, and neither are my wife and the princess," he hissed at Zolltarn. Two tall and powerful men, itching to strangle each other, stood eye-to-eye, nose-to-nose, strong will to stubbornness.

"Your magic is broken. You couldn't escape," Zolltarn protested.

"There are powers other than magic in this world." Jaylor lifted his clenched left fist and rubbed the raw knuckles with his right. "You set a magician to guard a magician. The poor boy outside my tent had defenses only against magic, not against brute force."

"He'll reinforce the binding spell with a ritual." Yaakke joined the conversation. There was no food left to divert his attention. The others stared at him in amazement. The boy just chuckled. "You'll be the focus of an eight-pointed star, Jaylor."

"How do you know this?" Zolltarn didn't remove his gaze from Jaylor for a single moment.

"You dropped your armor," the boy replied, searching the area around him. "I haven't had enough vegetables. Have you any more fresh greens?"

"Will the spell work, Zolltarn? Can you cure Jaylor?" Baamin forced his shorter body between the glaring men.

"It will work," the Rover confirmed.

"Then I agree to the exchange. Cure Jaylor and release your prisoners for a seat on the Commune."

"No!" Darville and Jaylor protested in unison.

"It's not worth the chance, Baamin. We know what kind of thieving scoundrel this Rover is." Jaylor gritted his teeth. "The last time we met he was employed by Krej to steal or shatter my staff so I would have no focus for the spell to free Shayla. He is desperate to rebuild his clan. Krej could have offered him a monstrous bribe to undercut Darville's authority. We can't trust either of them."

"Perhaps we would benefit from having him close at hand, where he can be watched," Brevelan offered. "Think, Jaylor, you could have your magic back, in full. Certainly you and Baamin and Yaakke could counter any wrongdoing."

"Ah, Yaakke!" Zolltarn sighed. "I will add half my wealth to this bargain for the boy."

"I'm not 'Boy,' anymore, Zolltarn. I'm an apprentice at the University. I make my own decisions." Yaakke stood to face the Rover.

"A child was stolen from us many years ago. You could assume his place at my side, as *my* apprentice and heir. But the price of that knowledge is to join my clan." Zolltarn's voice took on an enticing lilt.

"Master Baamin and Jaylor and Brevelan are all the family I need." Yaakke sat down again, staring resolutely into the fire.

"I repeat," Jaylor glared at each person in the tent in turn, "we can't trust his motives or his lies. My magic isn't worth the risk."

"Even though you are my designated heir?" Baamin quirked one eyebrow in question.

"Heir to what—your books and robes that won't fit me?"

"You have more experience of rogue magic than all of us combined. Therefore, you are the logical choice to become Senior Magician. I also choose to leave the University in your capable hands. The position of adviser to the king is Darville's choice, but since the two of you have been the best of friends since childhood. . . ."

"I value your magic and your friendship, Jaylor." Darville clasped his friend's shoulder. Emotion threatened to close this throat. "But the choice is yours. We'll find a way out of this mess one way or another. However, I prefer to see you whole . . . if you so choose."

Chapter 22

One breath, in three counts, out three counts. Second breath in, out. Jaylor focused his magic deep within himself. His lungs swelled the third time, deep and long. Reality faded and shimmered at the edges of his vision. A bright silver-blue ley line glowed and pulsed with magic from deep within the core of Kardia Hodos, fourth planet from the sun Helios. He shifted his feet to draw the maximum energy from the line.

"You are the focus, the center. As the planets revolve around the sun, our star pattern will revolve around you," Zolltarn intoned. The Rover, too, was hovering on the edge of a trance.

They stood in the exact center of a clearing—not the clearing on Sacred Isle, just an open space beyond the Rover camp, formed when a forest giant toppled. Remnants of the ancient, top-heavy tree lingered in sawed-up long benches around the circumference of the clearing. Smaller trees ringed them in a near perfect circle. Everblues, oaks, and alders and, Jaylor suspected, a Tambootie tree or two. Superstitious farmers had ceased planting their tithes of Tambootie under Krej's not-so-gentle persuasion. But home-loving citizens of Coronnan rarely ventured into mixed wooded areas where the trees of magic were already established.

Jaylor's attention wandered in a drifting pattern. Politics and the politics of magic twisted through his mind in a bright tangle. The void beckoned him into a deeper trance. Answers could be found in the void. But anytime he experimented there, a bit of the soul was left behind. Each journey through the intangible state of existence between planes of reality was harder to end. One day he would exist in both realities, but not truly in either.

He had to resist, at least until he understood the nature of this peculiar spell. Control came with understanding.

Erda shuffled through the clearing. She sprinkled colored sand in an intricate pattern that was evolving into eight points. She chanted the same words over and over. Words from the oldest language, forgotten and unused except in ritual. Magic swirled the star pattern in waves that increased with the depth of her song. With each of her steps, the aroma of garlic and timboor wafted to Jaylor. The scents threatened to tear his awareness away from his body and into the void.

Jaylor's trance heightened his senses. He recognized the form of Erda's magic, without understanding the words, a warding song, much the same as the ones Brevelan performed. The nurturing and healing most women invoked instinctively with their quiet tunes, Brevelan and Erda had perfected to an art form. Garlic and music. Brevelan and garlic. Love and music. Her inner serenity reached out and filled his body and mind with wonder.

She and the baby were safe, for the moment, outside the eight-pointed star. She and Darville and the princess huddled under a dripping tree, watching every move with distrust.

Mica hid in the shadows just behind them, a part of them, yet not. Jaylor saw much more than normal while hovering on the edge of the void. Light and dark, shadow and substance ceased to hinder his *Sight*.

The old woman's wards were on two levels. The first kept any not involved in the ritual outside the star. The second level was stronger. It would keep intruders out of the clearing and unaware of the activities within. Like the now dissolved magic border. Like the cloud of secrecy the Commune hid behind. . . .

Jaylor yanked his thoughts back to the star. He needed concentration to gain control of the spell and insure its proper completion. He needed knowledge as well.

Baamin and Yaakke had been drafted to fill two of the eight points of this ritual. Zolltarn and five of his met completed the pattern. Nine men—eight points and a focus—would bind Jaylor and his magic into a consistent whole.

The old woman shuffled out of her pattern to the ring of trees. "This is a spell of binding." Arms outstretched, she encompassed each of the nine men in her intonation. "All beings are one. All magic is one. The warped magic will be drawn out of this man's body, unraveled, and twisted back right, then the magic will be wrapped around and around his soul, until they are one and the same, complete again, whole again, right again. Only men can touch this magic. Only men will walk the star." Erda continued. Her eyes glazed over as if she, too, were in a trance.

"All creation carries magic. The dance is the water, ever moving—ever the same." The eight men began to weave their pattern around Jaylor.

"The candles—fire." Each man carried a candle. As they approached Jaylor within the pattern of the dance, their tapers shot to life; ignited by the magic that permeated the star.

"Incense symbolizes air." Erda threw a handful of aromatic herbs into the air. The candles ignited the flakes. Smoke filled the clearing, blurring vision.

"We ourselves are the kardia, created from dust by the great spirit; bound to the land during our lives, returning to dust at the end of our time." Erda clapped her hands four times, once for each element, and stepped out of the first circle. "Together, bound into one soul, kardia, air, fire, and water is the Gaia. One life, one soul, one mind, one magic!"

As the old woman's words faded into the evening mist, the men increased their tempo from a studied walk to a brisk glide along the lines of colored sand, widdershins along the path of the moon. Jaylor turned so that each of the eight came into his line of vision. He turned on the path of the sun. Turning, turning, faster, ever faster. He matched the pace of his ritual star. The careful steps became a trot, a hop, a dance. Whirling faster, ever faster. The rhythm invaded his being, the steps mimicked the great wheel of stars about the galaxy.

A strand of red and blue magic reached out to Baamin, another to Yaakke. Their thoughts became his thoughts. Yet another strand touched Zolltarn. The Rover's convoluted plans became clear.

In turn, each of the eight men drew a strand of magic out of Jaylor.

The braids of blue and red power twining out of Jaylor's

soul, were split and warped, just like his staff, exactly like his magic. With each circuit of the star, the strands straightened, unraveled.

Jaylor watched the threads of his magic as he spun around and around, faster, higher, ever higher. Up and up, always spinning, barely tethered to the ground by the unraveling strands of magic.

Above the clearing, above the hovering clouds, above it all until . . . until . . .

He burst free of Coronnan's gravity and into the void where a nimbus of dragons awaited him.

Jaylor grabbed hold of the wing spine of the big blue-tipped male dragon. Bigger than Shayla by half.

(I am Seaninn,) the dragon greeted him with proper dragon etiquette.

(I, Jaylor, greet thee, Seaninn.)

(I am Gliiam.) A young green-tip darted in front of them to lead the soaring dance. Everywhere Jaylor looked, there were dragons, hundreds of them. All of them had the luminescent pearl-colored fur that defied the eye to linger on it. Pearl with blue, green, red, yellow, and a rare purple running along the wing tips, ridges, and spines.

They were all males. Shayla, the sole remaining female in the nimbus was all colors/no colors. She had not come to greet him. Nor had she honored him when he had freed her from Krej's glass prison.

Some of the joy of his soaring freedom diminished. He had lessons to learn up here in the void. He'd best get to it and return to his body before the dragons tempted him to leave mortality forever.

A single copper strand of magic reached up through the tangle of blue and red. Even within the order of a ritual, Brevelan would not risk losing him.

He smiled.

Brevelan.

The last time he had soared with dragons, Brevelan's fragile tendril of magic had held him to reality, brought him home, saved him from the overdose of Tambootie.

Jaylor sent her a thought of reassurance. They had no need of magic tethers. As long as she waited for him, he would always return.

He took one last lingering look through the dispersing clouds at the clearing where eight men wove magic patterns with their footsteps around a strangely empty figure. His friends stood to one side watching. A small cat crept from the shadow of a prince into the lap of a princess. Even from the tremendous height of dragon flight, Jaylor heard her purring song joining in with the ritual of binding. The cat faded. The princess grew, enhanced, became complete.

The dragons lifted their wings in unison, then with a powerful downsurge, they all flew forward. Jaylor clung tight to Seaninn.

Time darted forward and back, forward and stalled in nonlinear form. Yesterday, today, and tomorrow had no form or continuity. Time joined the four elements of the Gaia. All was one.

The fierce wind took his breath away and refreshed his troubled mind and body. Coronnan spun below them in a myriad of greens and browns of the fields, zigzags of blue rivers and lakes, the whole crisscrossed with the bluey-silver lines of magic. The ley lines pulsed with power. Their color didn't seem as bright as the other time he had viewed them from this perspective. But he didn't have massive amounts of the Tambootie coursing through his system now to sensitize his vision.

The dragons swooped over a thick forest. A few scraggly Tambootie trees tempted them. All of the trees of magic needed cropping. Their distinctive flat tops were overgrown. Jaylor peered deeper at the trees. The roots were withering without the proper pruning dragons gave them.

A few bites from the huge maws of the male dragons, taken in flight, stabilized some of the trees. The largest ones were too far gone. Pruning sent them into shock. He watched the roots shrivel and die. The underground channels those roots had carved filled with copper. The ley lines running beneath those roots drained back into the core of the planet, to be replaced with gold or silver.

Jaylor searched the country with his FarSight. Everywhere that the Tambootie grew, the trees were dying, and with them the magic power.

Council and populace rejoiced. They had no need of magic. Precious metals brought them wealth and exotic trade.

Jaylor urged his dragon upward. He saw Hanassa to the

south, the refuge for outlawed magicians, Rovers, and other undesirables. Claimed by all, controlled by none, this haven sat within a huge caldera protected by high granite walls. Tunnels through the ancient mountain gave secret access to the hiding place. He blinked and knew those secrets.

The dragons flew northwest, back to Coronnan. From the capital islands nestled into the massive river, Jaylor sent his dragon escort west, up the Coronnan River. Where the river narrowed and climbed toward its mountain source, the ley lines ceased. So did all trace of the large Tambootie trees that fed dragons. This was the natural border with SeLenicca.

His dragon escort flew over that kingdom quickly and reluctantly. They told him the air was bad here. Great gouges marred once beautiful rolling hills, upland meadows and alpine lakes. Vast patches of land had been stripped of growth and minerals, leaving hills to crumble and rivers to overrun their banks. Beneath the surface ran black channels, burned-out power.

But those channels had not filled with valuable metals to be mined and exploited. These channels had been drained by a single blast of magic, so huge and volatile, they would forever remain empty.

The air disturbed Jaylor. Something shimmered, just beyond his perception, drawing his senses, but eluding them at the same time. He deliberately turned his FarSight back to Coronnan, back to the circle of men who were rebraiding his magic along the path of Helios.

Mica leaped from the wing of a middle-sized dragon with dark red wingtips onto Seaninn's back. She greeted Jaylor with a nudge of her head to his chin. Her body was barely a shadow and unreal.

Jaylor cuddled the little cat a moment. She radiated warmth and he was suddenly aware of the cold wind on his face and back. His awareness returned to his companions and to reality. The void began to fade around him.

Thought to thought, Mica urged him back to the ritual. Brevelan needed him.

Brevelan.

He felt the cramp in his belly at the same moment it touched her womb. The baby was coming. Early. Eager. Ready.

Brevelan needed him. She needed shelter and a mid-wife more.

Where? Where would she find those things among strangers in a Rover camp?

Seaninn gave him a thought and a spell. So simple. The answers were all so simple up here on dragonback. The dragons showed him how to lift his wife, cradling her vulnerable body, to the suite in the University. Darville and Rosie went with her. He might as well send Baamin and Yaakke to safety, too.

But they were bound up in the ritual star. A moment's more concentration and they were all deposited in the courtyard of the University. At the last moment he scooped Erda, the old healer into his massive spell.

His dragon swooped low and he slid back down the ropes of magic into the center of the intact star. He left a pathway for Mica to follow.

Chapter 23

Yaakke blinked his eyes. The courtyard stopped spinning around him. What had happened?

Chaotic thoughts buzzed through his head with blinding speed and disorientation. He blinked again, trying to sort through the assault of unarmored minds to find his own among them.

The massive stones of the University buildings came into focus. Yaakke stared at the cornerstone of the dormitory wing, forcing himself to read the ancient inscription. Only then could he center himself and armor his mind against the invasive minds of the other men.

A moment ago he had been walking his way through the ritual star in a clearing on the mainland. Now he was back at the University.

He knew he hadn't lifted up the entire star and transported them. Baamin didn't know how, and Zolltarn, even if he knew the trick of the spell, wouldn't bring them all here, to the middle of the capital. So Jaylor must have his magic back intact.

Jaylor? Where did he get to?

Yaakke searched the faces of the dazed men around him. Zolltarn and his five Rover magicians were in place, stumbling, mumbling, making the archaic flapping gesture against evil. Old Baamin was in place, just standing there, rigid and bewildered. But no Jaylor. That heap of damp clothing in the center couldn't be Jaylor! Could it?

The heap stirred and moaned, then lifted its head. Yes, that was Jaylor, and by the looks of him, he was exhausted, but triumphant. The spell must have worked.

Yaakee's eyes darted back to Baamin. The old man didn't

look well. Worse than Jaylor had looked last spring. Face waxy and pale. A peculiar gray color, peculiar even in this uncertain light.

Yaakke broke free of the magic that chained him to a specific position within the star and darted across the lines of colored sand to the side of his mentor, heedlessly scuffing the design.

"Master Baamin? Be you all right?" He slipped into the peasant syntax of his childhood as he slid a strong shoulder beneath the old magician's arm. Baamin's full weight landed on Yaakke. "Master!"

"My heart . . ." Baamin clutched at his chest with a spasming fist.

Rossemikka awoke in gradual stages. First she was aware of her feet, shod in uncomfortable shoes, resting on a cold stone floor. The rest of her body appeared to be seated in a stiff chair. Her feet and hands were damp and chilled. She needed to be petted within a warm lap.

The flicker of firelight caught her attention. In slow, wrenching jerks, she twisted her rigid neck to her right. She saw the outline of a large fireplace and mantle. A man stooped to feed the fire.

Something about the length of his back and the breadth of his shoulders stirred a memory. Her own back ached in sympathy with the curve in the man's spine. Every muscle and bone in her body ached as well, for different reasons. The movements of her neck sent tingles of dizziness whirling around her head. Her hands felt clammy.

Instinctively, she raised them to her mouth to lave them with a raspy tongue. A jolt of reality stopped her movement as her hand came into view.

No fur covered the five fingers.

This body was human. She was free of the curse. But for how long?

"Darville?" Her voice sounded hoarse, as if she were coming down with a cold, or she hadn't used it in a long time. She looked once more to the man at the fire.

"So you're awake." His tone was cold, matter-of-fact.

"Where are we?" She was hurt and puzzled by the distance of his reception. The last time they had been together they had shared the deepest intimacy. What had happened since then? Her memories were distorted and incomplete.

"The University. Jaylor's and Brevelan's suite. I've sent for a healer. Erda is with Brevelan now. The baby could be in trouble."

Slowly, ever so slowly, Mikka stood from her straight-backed chair, careful to keep the dizzying disorientation at bay. She reached a hand to touch her lover's back in mute sympathy.

He jerked away and stiffened.

"Darville, what is wrong? Why do you reject me?"

"A strange comment from you, Princess Rossemikka. This morning you ran away to a convent just to avoid marrying me." He, too, stood and glared at her. His long body unfolded in awkward spasms. His anger was barely controlled. "Your actions have caused no end of trouble. King Simeon's agents tried to kidnap you. Zolltarn of the Rovers took us all prisoner. His ransom is a seat on the Commune! And you dare ask what is wrong?"

"Darville, beloved, that was Rosie. This is me, Mikka," she protested. Yesterday he could tell them apart. Why not now?

"No, you aren't!" He grabbed her arm and roughly jerked her closer to the firelight. From a nearby table he fetched a polished metal mirror and shoved it in front of her face.

"Look at yourself, Princess," he sneered. "Your hair is streaked white at the right . . . the right temple?" His jaw gaped open in bewilderment.

Mikka looked into the mirror as commanded. Certainly there was white streaked across her temple. But across her left temple, not the right, and it was no longer solid white, more like a dotted line of ivory, mixed with the brown and gold and auburn of her natural coloring.

"Rosse? Where is the cat, Darville?" Panic nudged at her self-control.

"The cat?"

"Where is she?" Mikka searched the room in vain for the little bundle of fur. No sign of her. She stretched her senses and listened for any sound out of the ordinary. In days gone by, Rosse was never far from her. "Kitty? Here kitty, kitty, kitty." No answer.

"I haven't seen any cat since the market square. You were both clearly identifiable there."

Mikka turned her thoughts and awareness inward, seeking calm. She reeled and Darville caught her arm to steady her.

"Darville, I think we have a problem."

"Another one?"

"I think that I am both Mikka and Rosse. The cat is still in this body with me."

My princess is changing. She comes into season. Tonight, or tomorrow, she will be ready. The child she conceives will have the right to rule both Coronnan and Rossemeyer but only if Darville sires it.

This very night the marriage will take place. I have planted the idea into enough muddled heads that Darville will be forced to obey. Baamin is dying and can no longer interfere.

The coven's plans must be played out.

"This is an outrage!" Kevin-Rosse paced in front of the throne dais in the small audience chamber. "Where have you been, Prince Darville, all day and half the night with Princess Rossemikka, without the benefit of a chaperone?"

"You wouldn't believe me if I told you," Darville muttered. He leaned his head into his hand, propped on the broad arm of the lesser throne, to the right of the dragon throne. The Council still hadn't granted him permission to assume the official throne or the Coraurlia, the glass crown. He tried to appear interested in the furor that was raging around himself and the princess who was seated on a small chair just below him on the main floor of the room. He kept listening for the sound of footsteps behind him, for the messenger who would bring him news of Brevelan and the baby.

This labor was taking forever.

And so was the ambassador's hastily called conference. All of the Council, with all of their magicians, a larger than normal number of guards, courtiers, and officials from both Coronnan and Rossemeyer had squeezed into this little room designed to hold perhaps twenty people.

So much for keeping his day's adventures private. Janataea must have launched a loud protest at Rosie's absence.

"More intercourse with magic!" Lord Marnak the Elder sprang forward with his accusation, only to wince at his choice of words.

A slight smile touched Mikka's lips. At least Darville thought it was Mikka who was currently dominant. Half an hour ago she had scratched his face with those incredibly long fingernails, just because he had the audacity to touch her elbow when he escorted her back to her suite and her panic-stricken guardians. Those vivid parallel lines on his cheek were evidence that Rosie was ready to surge to the surface at any moment.

"You, Prince Darville, have sullied the reputation of our beloved princess." Kevin-Rosse wheeled to point an accusatory finger at Darville.

Mikka choked back a protest, or was it a chuckle. They both knew that for the last two years, at least, she had been anything but beloved by her uncle and his officials.

"The marriage must take place immediately," the ambassador continued.

"As soon as the banns have been posted," Darville agreed. That would give him three weeks to find a way to separate Mikka from Rosie and get them both back into their appropriate bodies.

"Tonight!" Kevin-Rosse demanded.

"Such unseemly haste, my dear ambassador, will cause more gossip than a day's adventures away from the palace. We will be married with all the appropriate pomp and ceremony as soon as the banns are posted."

"Tomorrow at the latest," Janataea demanded, stepping around Mikka's chair to face Darville. "Gossip runs through this palace like a wildfire on the plateau. By midnight the entire capital will know that our princess has been compromised. If word reaches her uncle. . . ." She paused and looked at each of the Council members in turn. "Regent Rumbellesth will have every reason to assemble an invasion force to punish you."

Heavy silence followed her pronouncement. So the threat was still there. Rumbellesth didn't want an alliance, he wanted an excuse for war.

A few days ago, before Darville knew the truth about Mikka and her cat, he would have welcomed the opportunity for returning the princess to her native land, signing a new treaty with SeLenicca, and massing his own army on the borders.

Now he couldn't do that. He loved Mikka too much. He looked forward to the day he would truly marry her— Mikka, not Rosie. How could he marry either while they both resided in the same body?

"Since you are all so concerned with gossip, why don't we just all agree never to speak of this matter again," Darville suggested. "The marriage will take place at the appropriate time and not a moment sooner—or later. When the banns have been posted."

"The marriage will take place tomorrow at noon!" Lord Krej marched the full length of the room to stand before Darville and the ambassador. "As Lord Regent of Coronnan, I command it."

"You aren't regent now, Lord Krej. And you will never be king," Darville growled.

"The Council backs me on this. Over half the army owes allegiance to me first, Coronnan second, and you not at all. You will not be king until you wed the Princess Rossemikka. My term of regency was voted to end on the day a new king is crowned. Refuse to wed her and you will be removed from the line of succession. Then I will be king. My troops will see to that."

Darville rose in challenge to his cousin. His hand automatically reached for the dagger Zolltarn had restored to him.

"Excuse me, my lords." Holmes cleared his throat behind Darville.

"The Lady Brevelan, Lord Krej's acknowledged daughter, has just give birth to a son." Holmes bowed his head in respect. "The baby is blond and promises to have golden eyes, sir," he whispered so that only Darville and Krej could hear.

Chapter 24

Mikka pricked up her ears at the aide's whispered words. There were advantages to retaining her cat senses. She heard every nuance of the last statement. The aide implied that Darville was the father of Brevelan's baby.

Depression threatened to overwhelm her. She should have known. She had been with Darville and Brevelan and Jaylor on that long quest last spring. The three of them had been inseparable, supporting each other, *thinking* for each other much of the time. And she, Mica, had been only a cat, a cuddly comfort on cold nights or during a brief moment of solitude.

Her truly close companionship with Darville hadn't come until Jaylor and Brevelan had retreated to the clearing. Mica had elected to stay with Darville, sensing he needed her more than Brevelan and Jaylor did.

Who needed her now?

Not Darville. He was still in love with Brevelan. She had never deluded herself into believing he would ever love anyone as completely as he did Brevelan. And now there was the baby to bind them closer.

Her brother, Rossemanuel, would achieve his crown soon. Perhaps he would make a place for her in his court. She was certain there would be no more marriage offers after she refused Darville. Not that she could ever marry anyone but Darville.

Mikka rose, cloaking herself with the regal bearing she'd been trained to since birth. Then she allowed Rosie's fear of Darville to come forward and voice the opinion of both. And with the fear came a reason. Every time Rosie had encountered Darville, he smelled different. To her sense-oriented brain, this made him undefinable and therefore untrustworthy.

To complicate her limited perceptions, the smells Darville emitted were all associated with Rosie's fears. On the barge there was the reek of magic. When she had gone to his office to apologize for her unwitting remark, he smelled of cat and she thought that cat was trying to kill her. Their next meeting was in the tunnels where he smelled of death after his brief battle with outlaws. Then, in the market square of Last Isle, he smelled of the river and a fear of drowning.

Mikka absorbed Rosie's sensations and wrapped them around herself self-righteously.

"I refuse this marriage." Her voice rang out across the crowded room. All of the buzzing speculation ceased. Every ear turned to her, cocked to make sure no syllable was missed.

"Your Highness! You can't. The treaty has been signed. We gave our word," Kevin-Rosse protested.

"Think, Rosie," Janataea hissed at her. "For once in your life, think before you speak." A tendril of compulsion followed the governess' words.

Mikka jumped away from the magic probe. She hummed just beneath hearing level to make sure her slight magic protected her. She had learned much about magic in the year she had lived with Brevelan, and during the six moons when she had protected Darville. Janataea would never penetrate her defenses again.

Carefully, she illumined Janataea's compulsion so that it was visible to everyone in the room, including the mundanes. Then, when the compulsion hit her invisible armor, it backlashed to the sender in a blaze of green light so deep in color it resembled a forest of Tambootie in deepest night. The nearly black light spread and engulfed Janataea in a prison of her own magic.

The acrid scent of burning Tambootie sizzled through the room.

"I renounce you, Janataea, for a witch of the highest order. You have kept me a prisoner of your magic and subject to your will for too long. This marriage was never my choice. I neither signed the treaty nor gave my word.

So I also renounce the betrothal and will return to my home. The treaty is null and void." Armor and dignity intact, Mikka glided down the length of the audience chamber, unhindered by the staring courtiers and guards.

"Stop right there, Princess Rossemikka!" Darville roared in his best parade ground tones. Lonely emptiness threatened to spread from the tight knot in his gut. He couldn't bear to lose her again. Not like this.

Mikka stopped her dignified retreat from the room, but she didn't turn to face him and her spine remained rigid.

"Compromise," he whispered to himself. "This is no time for injured pride." The presence of Rosie in Mikka's body complicated matters, but he'd tolerate it to keep his precious Mikka.

He marched, as rapidly as he dared in the crowded room, to stand directly behind her. With this many Council members, magicians, and soldiers present, he might as well be acting with every eye in the kingdom on him.

"Mikka, please stay," he pleaded. He'd learned long ago that orders slid over her without penetrating.

She didn't move.

"*Stargods,* woman, look at me!" Darville swung her around to face him. Moisture brightened her eyes. Other than that, there was no trace of emotion on her beautiful face.

"I'll not marry you. You don't love me, and all your pretty words of devotion and affection were as smoke, to drift away in the slightest breeze." A single tear teetered on the edge of her lashes.

Anger and desperation choked away the words that formed in Darville's throat. He could only act. He pulled her close to his chest with harsh hands as his mouth descended to hers in punishing need.

Mikka fought him—or was it Rosie? He couldn't be sure whose fists pounded his chest for release. Darville dug his fingers tighter into her shoulders, deepening his possessive kiss.

When he had drained her of response to the fierce plundering of her mouth, he lightened his hold. Gently, ever so gently, he allowed his tongue to caress her bruised and

swollen lips, begging for entrance. Satisfying warmth melted
his knees. She was so soft, so lovely. So very determined
not to yield.

He nipped gently at the corner of her mouth, tasting
the salt of her tears. "Don't cry, Mikka. Allow yourself to
love me."

Her lips slowly parted as her fists unclenched and clung
to him. He loosened his grip and slid his hands down her
back in loving remembrance of their night together. Mikka
reached to surround his neck with her arms, pressing her
sweet body close to his, molding her curves to him. Strength
returned to her grasp as she asserted her need for his love.

Darville clutched her tight against him, fearful lest Rosie
take over and she run away again.

"I am never going to let you out of my sight again," he
murmured when they came up for air.

Around them, he was dimly aware of buzzing gossip
and speculation.

"Does the treaty with Rossemeyer mean so much to you
that you will force this marriage?" Mikka closed her eyes
and leaned her forehead against his chest. She wasn't going
to allow him to see her eyes, read her thoughts.

"You mean more to me than any treaty. I will marry you
this night, even if the treaty is withdrawn and I find Coronnan plunged into war." He lifted her chin with gentle fingers so that she could read his conviction in his eyes.

"But you are still in love with Brevelan. She has just had
your son!" Mikka tried to protest. Her pupils started to
contract into a vertical slit, but she mastered the impulse
to allow Rosie dominance in this argument. Her eyes were
clear and fully human before he spoke again.

"Brevelan will always command a special piece of my
heart. But she has married another. I respect her choice."

"Will your heart be here with me, or longing for the
peace in her clearing, Darville?"

"I belong here. You can't imagine how boring that clearing can be." He quirked a knowing smile at her. "Or maybe
you can."

Mikka ducked her head a little to hide her smile of
remembrance.

"We have shared so much, Mikka. Who else can know
the humiliation, and the freedom, of being imprisoned in

the body of an animal?" he whispered so that only she could hear. "Who else has the audacity to bat my nose away from a meal with unsheathed claws?"

Her hand came up to trace the angry scratches on his face. The sting faded beneath her touch.

"I love you, Mikka, stronger and deeper than I have ever loved before, or will again. I promise I will always be faithful to you."

"And the child?"

"The report of one courtier who may be mistaken in his haste." Darville didn't dare say anything in this crowd about his suspicions of Holmes. The aide could still prove to be loyal and valuable. "Jaylor is the baby's father. As long as you give me strong sons and beautiful daughters, I have no need to seek an heir elsewhere."

"And if our children are weak and ugly?" A hint of her old mischief surfaced.

A smile tugged at Darville's mouth, too. "With you for a mother, how could they be anything but perfect little princes and princesses?" He bent his head to seal their bargain with another kiss.

"Find a priest." Darville finally addressed the crowd around them. "I agree to the wise decision of the Council." He suppressed a mocking smile. "Within the hour I will be wed and crowned King of Coronnan!"

"Yes, Your Grace," Lord Andrall proclaimed and left the room before the order could be contradicted by Krej.

"What of the governess, Your Grace?" one of the magicians inquired. "By our laws she is a witch and must be punished."

"By treaty she must be returned to her native land for judgment," Kevin-Rosse protested. "You have no right to punish her."

"Janataea," Darville turned to face the struggling governess who stood within a circle of magicians. Her captors had thrown some kind of barrier around her as soon as the green backlash had dissipated. She fought the new prison with fists and spells. But each time she managed to weaken one magician's portion of the barrier, another shored it up.

Teamwork. Not the joining and augmentation of dragon magic, just cooperation. That was the secret. If they could just continue to work together.

Lord Krej, Darville noted, stood back from the circle, arms crossed in an attitude of careful watching. The half grin on his face was too enigmatic to read during Darville's fast survey.

As the words addressed to Janataea penetrated her panic, Rossemikka's guardian ceased her useless flailing against the barrier. Her eyes narrowed malevolently, but she said nothing.

"You are accused of the crime of witchcraft. We have witnessed evidence of your attempts to manipulate my betrothed." Darville lifted his voice so that all could hear while he kept a proprietary arm around Mikka's waist. "How do you plead against this accusation?"

Silence. Janataea returned his unblinking stare.

"Can't you offer any defense, Mistress Janataea?" Kevin-Rosse tried to intervene on her behalf.

Silence. The accused stood rigid and controlled behind magic walls.

"By our laws, you will be treated with witchbane until a formal trial can be summoned," Darville pronounced. He turned his back on the woman. He had more important things to arrange tonight.

"Nooooo!" Janataea wailed. "You can't poison me without trial. I'll die if you force witchbane on me."

These stupid mundanes don't know that my rival has already found and used an antidote. I'll have it from him within minutes of their puny little dosage. Then they will know the full wrath of the coven.

Chapter 25

Jaylor pushed aside his lingering fatigue with a moderate replenishing spell, his fourth in as many hours. He couldn't keep this up for much longer. But he was needed in more than one place tonight. As husband, magician, teacher, adviser, and friend.

Very soon he must check on Baamin and Yaakke in another suite in the master's wing. Two hours ago the old magician had been weak, but stable. The heart attack that felled him was so massive it should have killed the old magician. Miraculously, he still breathed. A grief-stricken Yaakke refused to leave his side.

Good. Jaylor didn't need to worry about the boy's unpredictable activities if he were loose and roaming the palace and University tonight.

News of Jaylor's designation as Baamin's heir to both University and Commune had spread throughout the capital already. So far, Jaylor had kept the courtiers, servants, and sycophants at bay.

Darville needed Jaylor to stand at his side for the wedding ceremony within the hour. Pride and joy filled Jaylor at the prospect of seeing his friend married to a woman he loved as deeply as Jaylor loved Brevelan.

He took a moment to focus his priorities on the tiny scrap of humanity Erda had just placed into his arms. So small, so very small. Barely the length of his forearm. His heart ran the full spectrum of emotions.

Jaylor desperately wanted to love the tiny, tiny baby. But jealousy kept surfacing.

Was this truly his son?

Bathed and bundled into a warm blanket, the baby was

quiet for the first time since his untimely entry into the
world, almost an hour ago. By all accounts he shouldn't be
able to live after a mere seven moons of pregnancy. But
Erda had proclaimed his son to be whole and healthy, just
small and in need of extra care to bring him up to size.

His son. By law, at least, this unbelievably small person
was his. But by blood?

Jaylor's younger sisters were blonde. So this baby could
have inherited the common bloodline for that hair color.
But his eyes!

The baby blinked and stared up at him with unfocused
curiosity. At the moment, his eyes were the fuzzy blue so
common to newborns, giving few hints as to their eventual
color. In a few weeks they would begin to turn. Would they
be deep-bay blue like Brevelan's, or dark reddish-brown
like Jaylor's? Or possibly the smooth golden-brown of
Prince Darville?

Jaylor blinked back a curious probe, not quite daring to
search the baby for signs of magic, or for knowledge of
his birthright.

"I think we need to find a name for our son," Brevelan
whispered wearily. The furrows in her brow were pinched
white with strain. Yet her eyes glowed with overwhelming
love and accomplishment. She was tucked into the massive
bed in their suite, so small and pale as to be barely visible
beneath the mound of covers.

"What do you suggest?" Jaylor hedged. By tradition a
first son should be named for his paternal grandfather, or
at least a favored paternal uncle. But who was this child's
grandsire?

"The magic is strong in him," Erda pronounced from the
shadowy corners of the room. "Unusual for magic to be
strong, in one so young. He deserves an unusual name, a
name of power."

"For a child to inherit magic like this, it must come to
him from both parents," Brevelan reassured Jaylor.

He wasn't overly comforted. Darville's family was notoriously mundane. But there must be some potential for magic
linked to their metaphysical bond with the dragon nimbus.
Through Krej, Brevelan carried more magic than most master magicians.

The baby didn't need Jaylor's magic to add to his inheritance.

"Comes from his Mama throwing magic, willy-nilly. The child awakened early. Developed early. Needed to be born early." Erda shuffled over to stand beside Jaylor. One gnarled finger reached down to touch the baby on the forehead just above the bridge of his petit nose. "Curious is he. Needed to see what the magic was and who threw it. Wants to be a part of it even now."

The baby opened his tiny mouth and let out a pitiful wail. Jaylor jerked in surprise. "What did I do to frighten him? Am I holding him wrong?"

"Never, love." Brevelan chuckled as she reached thin arms for her child. "He's hungry. He needs to eat often, just like another magician I know." She winked at Jaylor.

As Jaylor released the infant to Brevelan, a trace of the baby's scent and weight lingered in the warmth on his arms. He knew a sudden emptiness. "Why don't we ask him what his name is?" he offered.

Both Brevelan and Erda looked a little startled at that.

"Well, why not? You ask animals what they wish to be called, all the time. Why not grant the same privilege to your son. Surely he's more intelligent than a rabbit or a greenbird?"

"Yes, why not," Brevelan mused, as she settled the infant to her breast. Her eyes lost focus a moment. "I can't penetrate beyond the need for food. I'm too tired. You ask him, Jaylor."

Jaylor wasn't sure if she really needed him to do the asking, or if it was just her way of strengthening his bond to the child, who might or might not be his.

With a deep breath, Jaylor marshaled his strength and dove headlong into the mind of the suckling child. He felt the warmth of a mothering body, the satisfaction of filling a tummy. A glow of comfort and protection surrounded him.

When he had absorbed the surface emotions, Jaylor allowed his inner eye to take over. Images assaulted him, devoid of color, but clearly defined. The clearing dominated them all. The clearing with Brevelan's distinctive protection enclosing the whole.

"Glendon." Jaylor removed himself from the engulfing

imagery. "The fortress in the glen." Where he was conceived. Where he would be raised.

"Put me down, Jaylor. I can walk," Brevelan protested halfheartedly. She enjoyed being cradled against her husband's chest as he carried her and Glendon down the long corridor to the Audience Chamber.

"No, you can't walk. You shouldn't be coming to this wedding at all," he growled.

Brevelan snuggled her cheek next to her husband's. "But I must be present. I cared for Darville and Mica for many moons without knowing who or what they really were. I need to see for myself that they belong together."

"Always the mother." Jaylor rubbed his face across the top of her head until he could kiss her hair. The movement shifted the careful illusion he had woven around his borrowed robes. The real fabric of Baamin's court regalia barely reached his knees. The illusion draped grandly to the floor. Magician blue robe over a rich tunic and fine cambric shirt, trimmed with delicate lace at wrist and throat. Only the Senior Magician could afford these clothes. Too bad they didn't fit the new Senior Magician.

Brevelan's heart swelled with love and happiness.

Moments later she was settled into a chair in the corner of the grand Audience Chamber. Most of the gathering crowd ignored her. She felt their uncertainty and understood they chose to overlook her presence, rather than commit a political breach of etiquette.

Brevelan chuckled deep within herself. In ignoring her, they were also ignoring the quiet glow of magic Jaylor wove around her and the baby. The mass of emotions emitted by this crowd would have sent her into empathic shock, otherwise. She really was too tired to be here.

She focused on Jaylor at the center of the knot of magicians. Even through her protection, she felt the concern radiating from the members of the Commune. Not all of those emotions were aimed at Baamin's serious heart condition. Many of the magicians were very wary of Jaylor, himself.

He was too young, too untried to be named Baamin's heir. This one-time inept might be their superior in a matter of hours.

Then, too, there was Jaylor's connection to Lord Krej. Concern colored the auras of some, that Jaylor would be a pawn in the hands of his father-in-law. Righteous glee tainted others. If they had to obey Krej, the natural order should be that Jaylor would, too.

Brevelan darted a look toward her father. He maintained a circle of courtiers around him, including his legitimate son-in-law and designated heir, Marnak the Younger. Lady Rhodia, Krej's scowling little wife, stood in a corner, barely suppressing a yawn. Her only companion, her oldest daughter, Rejiia.

Brevelan's half-sister had inherited her mother's cloud of dark hair and deep-set eyes that she artificially enhanced with kohl. There the resemblance to her plain mother ended. Instead of the sallow complexion and thin—or was it grim—mouth, her lips were lush and painted a deep red. Rose-red against a white background of flawless skin. Rejiia was a beauty. She could have won the hand of any man in the kingdom, even without her title and huge marriage portion.

But Lady Rejiia had one unforgivable flaw. She was as tall and big-boned as her father in a culture that thought women should be dainty and birdlike. Though only fourteen summers, she stood head and shoulders above her mother. She towered over her husband's slender figure. No wonder that slight young man chose not to stand beside her. Rejiia looked as if she could break Marnak's neck if he looked at her cross-eyed. No love spoke from either's eyes when they happened to glance toward each other.

Rumor suggested that Lady Rejiia trained with her father's guards rather than playing with delicate needlework in her mother's solar. Palace gossips tittered about Marnak's reluctance to bed his fierce bride.

An especially tall and thin magician leaned closer to Jaylor, speaking angry words. Jaylor glared back at the man, riveting him with his eyes. His concentration must have wavered, for the blue cloak with gold stars on the collar shimmered and shortened to his knees.

Brevelan suppressed another giggle as her husband's almost-clean country trews and boots showed beneath the actual length of the garment. Fortunately, Old Baamin had been very stout for his height and the borrowed cloak fit

Jaylor's broad shoulders adequately. A brief thought sent an image of Jaylor's appearance to him. He colored and the robe appeared to lengthen again.

Just in time. Darville entered the room from the covered doorway behind the throne. His court finery gleamed in the candlelight with jewels and gold embroidery on tunic and trews. A short cape of gold velvet hung from one shoulder, highlighting the amber stone in the hilt of his ceremonial sword.

Brevelan caught her breath. As emotionally close as she was to this man, she had never seen him dressed for court, never acknowledged the power that emanated from him. Long of leg and straight of back, the prince sized up the room with warrior keenness. Wary. Poised to pounce into action. The aura of a wolf lay comfortably on his shoulders. No wonder the Council kept him on a short leash. They feared his power more than any residue of magic that might cling to him.

A dozen aides and nobles rushed to surround him. The prince's eyes were restlessly scanning the room. His gaze lingered on Brevelan. Casually, he pushed aside the clinging courtiers and paced to her side. His soft, indoor boots made no more sound on the thick carpet than furred paws would on a woodland trail.

He knelt in front of her chair and delicately lifted the protective blanket from baby Glendon's face.

"He's beautiful, Brevelan," Darville whispered. Then he scanned her face with care. "Are you well enough to be here?"

"Of course. I couldn't miss your wedding." She reached to ruffle his hair behind his ears, as she would have when he was her wolf familiar. At the last second she hesitated and withdrew her hand. This was not the time or place to remind anyone of their past together.

"I hear whispers that his eyes are golden, that he is my son."

Worry creased his brow, even as pride radiated from his straight back and firm shoulders.

Brevelan almost didn't hear the words. But she felt his thoughts and their intensity. Thankfully, Darville could not read auras, hers or Glendon's.

"Glendon belongs to himself." She cloaked her thoughts from his penetrating gaze.

He darted a puzzled look and a frown at her.

A rustle at the back of the room drew everyone's attention. Darville rose with a gasp of awe as he greeted his bride.

Princess Rossemikka surveyed the room in all her majestic glory. Her long, multicolored hair was drawn into a braided coronet atop her head, emphasizing her long neck and graceful shoulders, as well as the extremely deep plunge of her bodice.

True to the custom of her people, the edges of her scarlet gown just barely covered her nipples and swelling breasts, then separated to a vee pointing almost to her navel. A thin lace of silver thread bound the gown together. Brevelan wasn't sure how the girl could keep the dress up, let alone float toward Darville's outstretched hand without tripping.

Silver embroidery on the red silk picked out images of plants and creatures from the high desert plateau in a wide band around the hem. A kahmsin eagle, the fierce hunter and protector of its young was symbolic of the warriors bred there and exported to fight the wars of the world. The barbed tumbler that never set down roots, but thrived on the arid volcanic soil, so like the nomadic herders of Rossemeyer. Swirls of thread represented the ever-present wind. And other images Brevelan couldn't recognize.

Draped over the whole, crown to toe, as a token of modesty to both cultures, was a veil of spun silver.

The couple stared at each other for long moments as the gathering waited in silence. Silence that stretched, grew impatient, and gave way to soft rustlings, throat clearings, and whispered comments. And still Darville stared at his princess. Love pulsed from them in ever widening circles, isolating them. They were two, soon to be one. No one else needed to exist.

Brevelan ducked her head to the sleeping baby in her arms. A tear dropped to the blanket covering his head.

Chapter 26

I laugh. I laugh at these stupid mundanes. They know nothing of the drugs they push at me. I can smell the antidote, even before Krej slips it to me.

So easy a remedy. Why did Maman wait until someone within the coven needed an antidote before giving us the recipe? A little of the blessed Tambootie. A lot of eel oil. Some garlic and common kitchen herbs. All bound together with black sand from the volcanoes of Hanassa. Our intense magic has penetrated even to the harsh soils of our land.

A look of fear, a scream of pain as they strip me and rub the witchbane into my skin, and they believe I am cured of magic. They could have put the drug into plain water or wine and poured it down my throat to make it work faster, less painfully.

But no, they had to take their pleasure in torturing me, titillating their perverse senses by pushing their noxious and useless compound into every pore and orifice on my voluptuous body.

I will endure the pain and Krej's laughter. I will endure because I will triumph over their petty punishment. They cannot know that the energy of the pain they inflict will feed my power. They have forgotten that witches of old used the pain and death of slaves as a source of magic.

They will learn what real torture is, before this night is through. My coven is with me. We will have our vengeance. Darville will never have the chance to father the child that will unite the kingdoms. Another will have that privilege. And then I shall kill them all. The pain they suffer before I allow them the release of death will endure through the ages, feeding yet more magic for generations to come.

The mundanes and traditionalists withdraw. They believe me powerless. Even the magic barrier is taken from this prison cell.

Fifteen minutes of loud weeping to lull their senses. They still hear the weeping. They still see my naked, shivering body within the prison cell.

I laugh. I laugh as I walk past their dicing guards. From behind, I smite the idiots with a lightning bolt. In the interest of time, I allow them to die quickly, without pain.

Rossemikka will be under my control again before dawn. And just to show them how weak they truly are, I shall have the babe as well. Magic is strong in him. He will bolster the coven as soon as he comes of age. He already recognizes me. He won't even miss his mother.

Jaylor opened one eye and peered at the door through his crusted eyelids. The raucous knocking that had awakened him sounded again. And again.

Behind the closed door to the bedroom, a baby cried hungrily.

"My lord?" a strange voice pleaded for entry.

"Lord? Since when am I a lord?" Jaylor muttered and rolled over. He pulled the pillow over his head, trying to block out the sounds that assaulted his too short sleep. He nearly fell off the cot he had set in front of the hearth. Brevelan had been sound asleep long before his duties were finished last night and he hadn't wanted to disturb her or the baby.

From the sounds coming from the bedroom, his wife and son hadn't slept any more than he had. The blasted brat had cried for nourishment most of the night. So what difference did it make where Jaylor parked his body after Darville's wedding?

"Master Jaylor, the Commune requests your presence immediately." The voice was sounding anxious.

Jaylor figured he'd best answer the door before someone broke it down.

Slowly he unfolded his body, wrapping the blanket around his naked middle. "Coming," he yawned. The baby cried again. Jaylor's hearing leaned more toward the bedroom than the corridor.

An apprentice stood in the dark hallway wringing his

hands. His eyes were wide with fear and awe, and more than just a little confusion.

"What?" Jaylor asked sharply.

"Master Jaylor, the Commune is in session. You've overslept and missed most of the discussion." The boy looked away from Jaylor's bare chest. He stammered and shuffled his feet as well. "And, sir, the council also requires you to sit in Master Baamin's place. They don't dare disturb the prince . . . er . . . the king, sir."

Jaylor groaned. So this is what it meant to be Old Baamin's heir. No sleep, no peace, and rival authorities demanding he be in two places at once.

What he wouldn't give to be able to do just that! With a hearty breakfast to fuel his body and the dragon's trick with a transport spell, safer than Yaakke's, he just might be able to appear to do that.

"Send me food, lots of it," he dismissed the apprentice. "And on your way to the kitchen, fetch Yaakke to me as well." Nothing like a few surprises to keep Commune and Council off balance until he figured out what they wanted.

He knew already what they wanted—Zolltarn out of the seat in the Commune he now claimed. That was probably the only issue the magicians would unite on this day.

A knock sounded on the door again. Jaylor thrust it open in his fatigue-ridden impatience.

His breakfast tray hovered at eye level. Bread, cheese, mush, and ale. Lots and lots of ale.

Someone in the kitchen knew how to fuel a magician's body against the stresses of long sessions with Commune and Council.

Interesting that the platter contained no meat. Jaylor hadn't eaten meat since his first encounter with Brevelan. Dragon magic, like the dragons themselves, required massive amounts of animal protein for fuel. Solitary magic, on the other hand, drew power from Kardia Hodos herself. Mixed plant proteins gave him energy now, flesh just weighed him down.

Who in the University understood this already?

Jaylor made a mental note to grant that servant a raise.

Mikka arched her back and stretched her arms over her head. A languid yawn escaped as she felt the smooth sheets of her marriage bed caress every inch of her naked body.

A faint ripple of enjoyment, deep in her center, reminded her that Rosie still lurked behind her consciousness. Mikka was learning to live with that. As long as the cat's persona didn't erupt without warning, she was in no danger.

She stretched her left foot across the wide bed to caress Darville's naked leg. Instead of hard muscle and springy hair, she met only more and more of the sheets. One eye popped open and scanned the expanse of empty bed. On the pillow opposite her lay a rose and a note.

Smiling, Mikka lifted the fragrant flower to her nose. Blood red and smelling of desert winds and roaring rivers. How like Darville to choose a rose from her own country as his first gift to his bride. Rossemeyer had reclaimed the desert in the deep river valleys. And on the high plateaus they cherished the freedom of the wind.

The note was scrawled hastily, almost unreadable. Something about the Council. Oh, well. She'd been raised to understand the demands placed on a ruler. Her training for her position as queen and chatelaine had been extensive—until Janataea had intervened. Mikka knew what was expected of her.

Palace Reveta Tristile had not had a chatelaine for many years—not since Queen Rebakka, Darville's mother, died nineteen years ago. Mikka wondered who had been in charge. The servants were obedient and food arrived hot and on time, so someone must give orders. There was no time like the present to find out who ran her new home, and how.

Rosie nudged her consciousness. First a bath, then breakfast. The bellpull to summon a maid was within reach of the bed.

Mikka rolled to the side so she could reach the bellpull. As her back raised up from the sheets, a sharp stinging pierced between her shoulder blades. She jerked around to look toward the window. The pain in her back sharpened and deepened. Her eyes lost focus.

A shrouded figure appeared from the balcony, outside the window.

Numbness flowed from her back, across her arms and down to her legs. Then the black tide of unfeeling raced to her eyes and mind. Just before she lost all control, the image of Janataea swam before her vision.

Rosie reached up and snarled through the drugs, claws unsheathed, and lashed at her nemesis. Long cuts appeared beneath Mikka's fingernails. Blackness overtook her.

Janataea laughed.

"Never will there be Rovers in the Commune!" screamed an elderly magician in a master's cloak, so old and faded it looked almost as gray as the man's hair and skin.

Jaylor ducked the candlestick the old man "threw" at his head with more magic power than his frail body should have been able to wield.

"You said the same about using rogue powers, Lyman." Jaylor settled back in the wide chair in Baamin's office. "Now we all are rogues. You seem to have adapted to solitary magic better than most." He smiled. He couldn't allow his temper to overtake his good sense the first time he presided over the Commune.

"But a Rover, Jaylor?" Scrawny asked. By age and seniority, Maarklin, known as Scrawny among his peers, should have been Baamin's heir. "Zolltarn and his tribe aren't even in Coronnan legally. How can we seat him in the Commune?"

"Would you rather have him running around the country, unchecked, unmonitored?"

"We'd rather he went back to Hanassa, or wherever it is he comes from," Lyman grumbled. "Rovers are great tricksters. We aren't even sure he can throw true magic."

"His magic is based on a different theory, but it is very powerful, gentlemen. Very powerful, indeed. Last night he worked a spell worthy of any master."

"And what spell is that? We detected no massive energy surges anywhere near the capital." Scrawny got up to pace beside the window. His gauntness must come from his ceaseless movement. Jaylor had never seen Scrawny sit still. Not for a moment. And lately, he was always by a window.

"The Rovers performed a ritual to bind me and my magic back together properly." Jaylor transported a cup of wine to his hand from the cellars with a blink of an eye. "Oh, excuse me, did anyone else wish for a cup?" He glanced around the crowded room with pretended innocence. "Two days ago, I couldn't do this." The cup vanished as quickly as it had arrived. "I'd have had two cups, one vinegar, one fresh fruit juice."

"I hadn't realized how powerful a spell you had thrown last spring, Jaylor," Fraandlor looked intently at Jaylor. In the old days, magicians never used their birth names. Instead they adopted, or were given a name that reflected their personality when they entered the University. Fraandlor was called Slippy, for his resemblance to the bay eels, slippery and poisonous if handled improperly. His temper was recorded as being vicious when roused. On all other occasions he was noted for his gentle healing touch and soft polite voice.

Baamin was known as "Toad Knees." He had ended the practice of adopted names for new apprentices.

It was on the tip of Jaylor's tongue to blurt out that his transformation of Shayla, from glass sculpture to living dragon, hadn't warped his magic—Krej had. But he'd made a solemn vow not to tell anyone, especially these magicians, that Krej had found an antidote to the witchbane.

"Zolltarn is a magician, of master strength. He has knowledge he is willing to share—as any master in the University is oath-bound to do. A seat on the Commune is his reward for healing me and increasing our understanding of new magic. Are we agreed?"

"No." The old man turned his face away from his fellow magicians.

Jaylor watched Slippy closely. He'd been assigned to traitorous Lord Krej since that lord had assumed governorship of Faciar. Not once in all those years had Slippy reported any of Krej's mysterious activities that were really a cover for his rogue magic. Had the magician absorbed the philosophy of his host?

"What other choice do we have?" Scrawny stopped pacing just long enough to utter his words. He next step began a new path all the way around the room, instead of back and forth at the window.

Jaylor watched his movements a moment before replying. Was Scrawny pacing an armoring circle?

"We have no other choice. Baamin and I gave our word."

"Look where it got Old Baamin. Who's to say his heart

didn't give out as a result of Zolltarn's poisons? He could have attacked our Senior Magician covertly because he knew you, Jaylor, are Baamin's designated successor and Zolltarn knows he can manipulate you." Lyman pointed a bony finger at Jaylor.

"That is possible. But if we deny him the seat, he and his tribe could attack each and every one of us until he is the only magician left."

"There's always the witchbane," Scrawny said.

Again, Jaylor wanted to inform them of the drug's uselessness. Zolltarn had worked with Krej before. The antidote could be given to him quite readily. "I hesitate to put too much reliance on witchbane. We have to find other alternatives for dealing with magicians outside the Commune. If we don't, we'll just be prescribing it every time we meet someone with powers we don't understand. Isn't it better to bring him into our circle and learn about the man and his magic?"

"A wise recommendation, Jaylor," Slippy commented. "I vote for his admittance."

"So do I," Scrawny added.

The remaining magicians nodded their agreement. At the very last, Lyman jerked his chin down once in reluctant agreement.

"Scrawny, would you admit our newest member and administer the oath? I'm due in Council."

"You're already late, boy," Slippy chuckled. "Are you going to transport yourself across the bridge, like you do your cups of wine?"

"Yes I am."

"What!" they all screeched in unison.

But Jaylor was halfway to his destination.

Chapter 27

Darville led his lords in to the opulent Council Chamber, back straight, eyes forward, and the Coraurlia, in its protective satchel, slung over his shoulder. The glass crown, forged from magical dragon fire, would not leave his person until the coronation at the next full moon. By that time, the crown would be imprinted with his aura and no other could wear it until after his death.

Full of pride and well-being, the new king strode to the head of the table. Today he would sit on the dragon throne and none could dispute his right to do so. Halfway to the throne, he stopped dead in his tracks.

The king's chair was not in its customary place. An ordinary seat, with straight lines and plain wooden seat, had been placed where the throne should rest.

Darville searched the room hastily. The elaborate carving of the throne wasn't in evidence.

"My lords." He whirled to face the men behind him. "Is this some kind of sick joke?"

"What, Your Grace?" Lord Andrall asked from right behind him.

Darville pointed to the common chair. Anger slowly rose to replace the contentment that had flooded his being upon waking to find Mikka beside him. He didn't want to lose the joy of his wedding night; didn't want to fall back into the games of mistrust and devious tactics with his Council.

"*Stargods!* Who is responsible for this?" Andrall glared at his fellow lords.

Confused babble broke out among them. No one wanted to take responsibility for the practical joke.

"Where is Lord Krej?" Darville hastily counted the men

within the room. His cousin wasn't among those present.
Nor was Krej's shadow, Marnak the Younger. "Fred, summon Lord Krej to the Council Chamber. We have business
to attend to," he called to his guard.

Just then, a servant in the maroon and green livery of
the Krej household pelted down the corridor, skidding to
a halt in front of the assembled lords.

"Your Grace, my lords." He bowed, never looking up to
the men he addressed. "Lord Krej is missing."

"What do you mean, Lord Krej is missing?" Darville
leaned across the Council table and glared at the cowering messenger.

"When I brought him his usual breakfast tray, his chamber was empty, Your Grace."

"I gave orders, days ago, that he was not to leave the
palace unescorted." Darville shifted his feet, resisting the
urge to pace the perimeter of the chamber like a caged
wolf.

"I questioned the guard on watch, sir. I knew his lordship
would be angry if he didn't get his breakfast on time. The
guard said he . . . he was es . . . escorted out of the city,
Your Grace. By his own men, sir," the servant stammered.
"At least, his wife and family were. No one remembers
seeing his lordship with them."

Darville couldn't make the liveried man look him in the
eye. "When? When did they leave the palace? And did
they have the dragon throne with them?" Darville straightened his back but refused to sit.

At least his cousin hadn't been able to take the Coraurlia
as well as the throne.

"Before dawn, Your Grace. His suite is empty. Empty
of everything, even the carpets and wardrobes."

Angry heat swelled Darville's face. The messenger
backed away from his king's wrath, but was stopped by a
glowering Fred.

"He can't have gone far with that kind of load, Your
Grace," Lord Andrall spoke soothingly. "Mounted troops
will overtake him with ease."

"Rogue magicians transport goods from place to place,
Lord Andrall," Darville reminded his oldest supporter.
"My cousin has finally stepped outside his carefully con-
structed disguise and revealed himself for a magician. I've

been telling you for moons of his power and you ignored me."

"But the witchbane, sir!" Another lord protested.

"And the people in his entourage. Magicians can't transport people."

"Krej has found an antidote to witchbane," Jaylor announced from the doorway. Clothed in his master's cloak and new trews and tunic, Darville's friend looked older, more mature and confident than the new king was used to seeing him.

Jaylor strode to Darville's side, his massive body stirring the air in the closed room. Power radiated from him. He seemed to glow with the remnants of yesterday's spirit journey with the dragons. The lords leaned away from his presence.

Darville stood eye-to-eye with his childhood companion. "How?" he asked simply.

"The references to witchbane that I found stated there was no antidote. The book was older than the Great War of Disruption. Magicians from Hanassa, Krej's mother among them, have had three hundred years to work on the problem." Jaylor shrugged. The breadth of his shoulders and the drape of the jewel-toned cloak only hinted at the energy glowing behind his eyes.

Darville wondered if Jaylor had been indulging in the Tambootie. After the events of the last two days, the man should be fainting with exhaustion.

"The magic border between Coronnan and Hanassa was the first to be breached when Krej destroyed traditional magic." Jaylor paced behind the place where the dragon throne should rest. That was his place now in the Council Chamber. He was Senior Magician and adviser to the king.

"Lady Janessa's family hailed originally from Hanassa, before they married into the royal family of SeLenicca. Lady Janessa was Lord Dratorelle's second wife, a political alliance. The brother of our king and the first cousin of theirs. Rumors have abounded for years of her bizarre religion and secret trips into the mountains. Who in Coronnan knows where she retired to upon the death of her husband? My guess is Hanassa, with the other rogue magicians."

Jaylor drummed his fingers on the tabletop, betraying his level of anxiety.

"You knew he had the antidote!" Darville accused.

"He made me swear on Brevelan's life not to reveal it," Jaylor excused himself, never dropping his eyes from confrontation with Darville.

"What made you break such an oath?" Darville breathed harshly through his teeth. His stomach lurched, and his heart beat faster. There was trouble ahead. A lot of it.

"He swore never to use his powers against the kingdom. I believe he has broken faith with all of us. Therefore, I am free to reveal all I know of his activities."

"How do you know for sure he has broken faith?" Lord Jonnias demanded.

"I just encountered another messenger in the hall. The witch Janataea has escaped. Krej is the only one who could have helped her."

"He was there in the cell when she was punished with the witchbane," Jonnias countered. "He helped administer the dosage."

"He could as easily slip her the antidote at the same time. If so, then my cousin has committed treason." Darville breathed heavily.

"Isn't that a bit hasty, Your Grace?" Sir Holmes spoke from behind Darville.

"Hasty?" Darville whirled to face his aide, certain now where the man's loyalty lay. "Hasty?" The list of Krej's crimes played over and over through Darville's head. Just his refusal to plant a tithe of land in Tambootie for the dragons was enough to remove him from the Council. Practicing solitary magic when such spells were illegal should have condemned him.

A twitch of an eyebrow sent Jaylor behind the retreating aide.

Darville pinned each of the lords to his chair with a look. The power of outraged betrayal surged through him, fueling his tirade. "I told you, time and again, that the beast-headed man who ensorcelled me into the form of a wolf could only have been Krej, or employed by him. With me trapped by his spells, he usurped the regency, and still the Council refused to call it treason. Now he has unleashed his rogue powers again and helped a foreign witch to escape. And you call an accusation of treason hasty?"

Freedom and power coursed through Darville's veins,

like the battle fever that took him when riding patrol against outlaws. He gestured his annoyance and produced his short sword without warning. His blood ran hot at the shock and fear in his opponent's eyes as he waved the tip of the weapon beneath Holmes' nose.

"Only another traitor would defend such a man as my cousin, Holmes. I watched you murder a spy from SeLenicca against my orders. Not only murder, but decapitate, so no magician could read his dying memories. I've watched you write reports of my actions—reports you said the Council requested, but which really went to Krej. You were the agent who corrupted the paymaster in order to divert the loyalty of my men. Now, you defend my enemy, the enemy of all Coronnan." Only a glare from Jaylor kept Darville from plunging his well-balanced blade into Holmes' heart.

"Guards! Arrest this man. Place him in a magically armored cell with a member of the Commune and an arms master in constant attendance. I'll not have my cousin and his witch freeing another traitor."

Pain stabbed into his back. Pain that lanced to his heart and numbed his limbs. Darville swung to face his Council. Accusations died on his lips.

All of the men in the circular room were in their places, all of their eyes were on Holmes.

The pain died as fast as it flared. Darville sought Jaylor's eyes for explanation.

A shriek of despair cut through his concentration. "Mikka!" he gasped.

"You have defied me for the last time, Rosie," Janataea hissed through oddly blackened teeth. Her body shimmered and shrank into the hideous form of an oily, green-black harpy. She raised extremely long, ragged-looking wings above a bloated bird body that retained her voluptuous human breasts. The nipples tightened with some bizarre excitement, that was echoed in her glowing red eyes. The same eyes that had pushed compulsion spells onto Rosie, yet oddly changed.

But the face was the same, superimposed upon the scrawny neck of this evil creature. Beautiful in bone structure, made ugly by her malicious sneer and the bleeding scratches Rosie had inflicted just before the drugged dart had taken effect.

Mikka's mind shuddered; her body had no sensations left within it to respond.

"Your willful ways have destroyed years of carefully laid plans. No more. You will come with me." Janataea's voice came from nowhere and everywhere. She reached out with long, hooked talons. "And you will pay for scratching me, Rosie. You will be punished, again and again and again!"

"Never!" Mikka fought the paralysis. Her body jerked and spasmed.

A new compulsion took over her muscles. Mikka's body sat upright. Her legs swung over the side of the bed. One resisting hand reached for her nightshift. Desperately, she tried to hold back. Inch by inch she willed her hand away.

Somehow she knew that her own safety rested in breaking this hold Janataea had over her.

"Release me, Janataea. Release me and I will request exile instead of death as your punishment." The words just barely squeaked through her numb lips.

"Janataea the governess no longer. I am Rhomerra, messenger of Simurgh," she cackled and flapped her wings.

Self-will dissolved within Mikka. Without knowing how or why, the shift flew over her head and settled over her body. She stood and waited.

Icily burning claws stabbed into her back. She jerked upward and back. Pain registered somewhere in her mind, then died.

"Take her away, brother," Janataea ordered. "I will join you in flight with our other prisoner."

"Don't take too long. I don't know how long I can hold this shape-change." A second harpy joined Janataea. Thick of body, with dangling human genitals, ugly in the black skin of the creature.

Lord Krej.

"What is happening?" Jaylor was already breathing deeply, preparing a spell.

"I don't know. Mikka is in danger!"

The room swirled around them in a blinding rainbow. Cold. Deathly cold, not of this world, blasted his body.

Black nothingness.

Sensation returned with blinding speed. Darville collapsed to the carpeted floor. The Council Chamber wasn't carpeted. But his apartment was.

He looked up, fighting the dizziness. Double images wavered and blurred, then righted within his brain. Jaylor paced, seeking and sniffing, seemingly unaffected by the rapid transport.

Darville searched the bed, where he had reluctantly left Mikka sound asleep. The sheets should have been rumpled and stained from their night of loving. The soft fabric had been slashed by a bloody knife. Rich tapestries hung in tatters around the bed. His note was shredded. And so were the pillows. Feathers littered the room. The fresh rose he had so lovingly placed beside his bride was wilted on the floor, crushed, as if ground beneath a vindictive foot.

"Mikka? *Stargods!* Where is she?" Darville scooped up the remnants of the flower. Its scent cloyed at his senses.

"Violent magic swept through this room, moments ago." Jaylor continued to pace the room. Each step moved him faster. Each sniff pinched his nostrils whiter.

"Mikka?" An emptiness yawned in Darville's middle, blacker and more desolate than the void.

"I can find no trace of her."

Brevelan sang a transparent bubble of gentle armor around herself and Glendon. "Such a hungry baby." She fondled his tiny head.

For a few moments, while he nursed, he was quiet and content. Their rocking chair seemed to find the rhythm of her tune and her heartbeat by itself.

"You are so special, my son. So wonderful," she cooed within her song.

The empty peace of her clearing in the southern mountains beckoned to her. She longed for Jaylor to finish his business in the capital so they could return to the quiet isolation of her home.

Jaylor had changed her entire perception of herself and her magic. With his love to support and nurture her, she could face the swirl of confusing emotions that beat at her armor in the city, without allowing them to swallow her whole. But it was hard work. She didn't know how long she could maintain control, and nurture her baby, too. Oh! How she longed for her clearing.

"Tall trees, Glendon. Lots of tall trees and soft ferns. A stream for fresh water and a bathing pool warmed by hot springs. The garden gets bigger with every season. There's more than enough there to satisfy us. You and me and your father. Just the three of us."

Glendon kicked and cooed as he nursed. She focused on her infant son and the emotions he broadcast so loudly.

Hunger. Sleep. Hunger. Too hot. Hunger. Too cold. Hunger. Hold me. Hunger.

Such a demanding baby. Barely a full day old and already he had grown. His personality was beginning to assert itself long before most infants. This was one life Brevelan could not separate from herself. Not for a long time, anyway. By absorbing his needs into herself, she could almost overlook the crowds of emotions that pressed against her careful control.

She caressed the downy head of hair and sang a stronger wall of armor. This was a special time with her son. A private time for creating lasting bonds of love and interdependence.

Women had sung this kind of magic for aeons without understanding the power they held. A gentle tune while stirring the stew blessed the meal. A lively whistle while hanging the wash ensured the sunshine through the afternoon. And tunes hummed in rhythm with a rocking chair, while nursing or mending or knitting, wove protection about the hearth and home.

All women had magic in their songs. But men, especially the isolated and often celibate members of the Commune, would never recognize it as magic.

Glendon interrupted his greedy feeding to stare into Brevelan's eyes. Unfocused, uncertain, he sought something/ someone that eluded him. He returned to his meal. If Brevelan didn't know better, she would think he was less satisfied with her milk than he had been a moment ago.

Since the night of Baamin's last summoning spell, when a strange and disturbing Presence had invaded the clearing, Brevelan had sensed her baby seeking, seeking, ever seeking something outside his limited perceptions.

Jealousy roared through her. Jealousy that another had reached to quiet the disturbed baby while she was out-of-body. She reinforced the armor yet again.

No one, absolutely no one, would be allowed to intrude on her bond with her son.

Beyond the perimeter of the magic armor, the bright sunshine dimmed. Brevelan looked up to see what had shadowed this bright autumnal morning. Clouds roiled across the sky, spewing lightning.

Darkness flowed between her and the window. A darkness with form and substance. A cloaked and hooded figure. Brevelan recognized the Presence immediately. So did Glendon.

Alarm replaced jealousy. She opened her mouth to scream. No sound exited her armor.

Chapter 28

Jaylor fought the disorientation of transport while extending his senses into every corner of the royal suite. Mikka might never have been in the room—ever, for all he could tell.

An oddity in the pattern of strewn pillow feathers drew his eyes back to the bed, again and again. Jaylor wanted to avoid the bed, so as not to embarrass Darville with the evidence of his previous night's activities. But he couldn't stay away from the whorls of feathers and soft linen, of blood and hair and . . . and. . . .

"A cat was in here," he announced. "A cat I should recognize, but can't quite place." Jaylor sniffed with his magic, as well as his other senses. The sense of alieness pervaded and clouded his assessment.

"Rosse?" Darville asked as he staggered upright. He clutched a chairback in white-knuckled anxiety. "What the hell did you do to me anyway?" The new king shook his head to clear it. Morning sunshine glinted off the movement of the miniature silvery metal dragon earring Baamin had given him. Zolltarn had reluctantly returned the jewel, but not until the Rover realized that by removing it from Darville, he'd alerted Baamin to danger.

Pinpoints of the reflected light stabbed Jaylor's magic-sensitized eyes. His ears were ringing, too. He refrained from shaking his own head. That action would stall the stabilization of his senses.

"Mikka's cat? I thought they were joined."

"They were. Could they have separated again?"

"Possible. I can't sense Mikka at all. Could they have shape-changed into the cat body?" Shape-change, possibly, but they couldn't separate. As far as Jaylor knew, the true cat body was still in the void with the dragons, waiting for a separation of the two souls who were trapped in one human body. Only then could the cat become properly animated. And if they shape-changed, which personality would dominate, cat or woman?

"Where? Who?" Darville was dazed and sinking into the lethargy of despair. "Mikka can't shape-change."

"Krej or Janataea is my guess." Jaylor bent over the puzzling pattern of feathers again. Some were just pillow down, others were dark and oily, almost scales. An old horror crept over him, the stuff of childish nightmares. But the memory was too deeply buried for him to pinpoint.

He caught a whiff of Tambootie tainted with the odor of Krej's magic, and something else, very like Krej, yet without the lord's distinctive stamp.

Someone else. "Or both!"

A new breeze pushed in from the open balcony window. The scents on the bed intensified within the dark wind. Jaylor strode across the wide room to the window in two huge steps. He sent a feeler of magic into the thickening clouds.

JAYLOR!

His mind swam with the telepathic call.

"Brevelan!" he screamed in fear. "Glendon!"

One breath, deeper than he knew how to take. Two breaths and he was halfway into the void. With a pass of his staff, he grabbed energy from the intensifying storm. A dragon wing dipped out of the void. He grabbed hold, hooked Darville with his staff, and took off. Three breaths and a *thank you* to the dragon sent him into his own suite within a heartbeat.

The void parted and dropped Jaylor and his hapless passenger. Jolted by the second transport, so close to the first, his balance and vision rebelled. Even as he staggered into a door, his magic was seeking contact.

"Guardians gather to the Coraurlia!" He broadcast the ancient rallying call on telepathic, as well as verbal levels.

Three hundred years ago that call had brought the Commune together in times of crises. It was a summons they had all been trained to respond to without question, without hesitation. Any University-trained magician, priest, or healer would follow the crown, and the king who wore it, into hell and back at that call. He hoped the glass artifact had had time to register enough of Darville's imprint for the magicians to find them.

"Brevelan!" Jaylor called with mind and voice and emotions.

No answer.

Anxiety clawed at him. Uncertainty delayed the rebalancing of his senses. He fought for calm. His vision cleared before the dizziness truly passed. Just in time, he spotted and ducked a bolt of slimy green-black magic, as it ricocheted off the tapestried walls of his suite. It was the same color as the oily feathers on Darville's and Mikka's bed. His rapid dive away from the bolt set his head spinning again.

There was a spell he could recite to steady himself. If only he could remember it. If only he had enough strength left to call up any magic. Two quick transports of two bodies, even with dragon assistance, had drained his reserves.

He ducked the bolt of magic energy again. The noisome thing bounced against a chair, turned, and sought his life force.

Once more he borrowed energy from the storm outside, lightning filling him with tingling strength. His body centered and balanced without an additional spell.

A gesture and three words contained the bouncing bolt of magic. Dark green magic, almost black. That must be from Janataea. Krej's magic was always a brighter green and deep red.

"Brevelan?"

His call bounced about the room, much as the magic bolt had. They had to be encountering armor somewhere. Otherwise, the magic and the word would be absorbed by carpets and wall hangings.

This time Jaylor sought armor, rather than a person.

There! In the corner, between the wardrobe and the wall. A bubble of "nothing" pushed his seeking away.

Jaylor fine-tuned his barb of magic into a gentle tendril of himself, with his enormous love for Brevelan emblazoned into the address.

The armor quivered, almost allowed the magic to penetrate. Then it firmed and rejected his touch absolutely.

"Jaylor, what the hell are you doing?" Darville had managed to rise as far as his hands and knees. He seemed steady enough, as long as he kept his eyes shut.

"I'm keeping you close to me, where I can protect you should you be the next target of our enemies." Jaylor helped his friend to his feet.

Darville leaned too heavily on his shoulder and still didn't open his eyes.

"*S'murgh it.* I forget you're mundane. You can't tolerate the void. I can just barely pass through it without losing so much strength I can't get out. Sit and empty your mind. The magic infection won't return, you're immune now, but who knows what damage the void will do to you." He pushed his friend into a large chair.

"Are we out of it? The void I mean." Darville supported his head with his free hand. Reluctantly, he reached to remove the heavy glass dragon crown and its satchel from his shoulder. The weight must seem an incredible drag on his back.

"Don't take it off!" Jaylor cried in alarm. "Protection was seared into the glass when it was forged. As long as you have the Coraurlia on your person, external spells can't harm you. And no other can wear it, unless duly crowned and anointed by the Commune."

Darville fingered his dragon earring. "Baamin gave me this trinket for the same purpose."

"The piece was keyed to Baamin. He can't help you in his condition."

Darville finally opened his eyes and looked at Jaylor. "*Stargods!* You aren't the same boy I grew up with. You're half transparent with fatigue, and still the power of magic glows through you." The new king shrank away from his lifelong friend.

Jaylor felt himself grinning inanely. If he didn't smile, he'd cry. "Nor are you the same boy who dared me to defy every rule set by my University and your tutors, Roy." Jaylor used their boyhood nickname to reestablish their old camaraderie. Age and responsibility was threatening to put tremendous distance between them. "Yesterday, you were a troubled prince who sought play to hide your frustrations. Today you are a king."

"And newly widowed, I fear. Krej couldn't exact a greater revenge upon me than to kill Mikka." Grief overtook the emotions racing across his face. His shoulders sagged inside the stiff tunic. The tall and grateful warrior seemed to shrink before Jaylor's eyes.

"Not quite a widower. If our enemies had wanted to kill your bride, they would have done so and left her for you to find. They took her, and they erased all trace of her presence so we couldn't follow. Krej needs her alive. I don't know why yet, but I assure you, Mikka is alive."

Darville only shook his head in denial. "I love her, Jaylor."

"I know." Jaylor turned away. Friends needed comfort in times of trouble. Kings needed privacy. Which was Darville at this moment?

The bubble of armor in the corner turned slightly opaque. A good sign. If that was Brevelan hiding in there, she was listening, possibly feeling Darville's grief. The healer in Brevelan would need to reach out and comfort Darville.

Jaylor sighed inwardly. His wife was responding to Darville's grief, but not to his loving need to protect her.

Footsteps pounding in the corridor diverted Jaylor's attention.

"Jaylor! What is the meaning of this unprecedented summons?" Scrawny stood in the doorway. Blue-robed magicians stood behind him, along with gray-robed healers and red-clad priests. All University-trained, all responding to the rallying cry.

"Member of the Commune, Guardians of Coronnan," Jaylor announced in his most authoritative voice. "Queen Rossemikka has been kidnapped. My wife, the Lady Brevelan, has been threatened."

"How in the hell did you manage to transport yourself and a mundane?" Scrawny seemed more interested in the magic than the current crisis.

Jaylor narrowed his eyes to really look at the man he had revered throughout his years as apprentice and journeyman. He was assigned to the court of Lord Andrall and had always, always supported king and Commune. The image of an exceedingly tall, gaunt man kept sliding out of his field of vision. His aura was nonexistent. A truth spell was inappropriate at the moment. Mistrust welled up in Jaylor.

"Krej!" Yaakke snorted in disgust, as he shouldered his way past the masters in the doorway, Zolltarn right behind him. "The room is thick with the smell of his magic. And someone else, too. Someone . . ." he sniffed again. "Someone related to him."

"What about Lord Krej?" Scrawny focused his accusatory tone on the boy.

"Was it Lord Krej who kidnapped Mikka?" Darville asked the boy.

"Seems likely. He's been in here throwing magic."

"Then my cousin has committed the ultimate treason, he has kidnapped the queen," Darville said. "I proclaim him outlaw."

"Will his troops follow him or you?" Slippy's question was more a sigh than a query. "I fear civil war will follow this action. We've tried everything to avoid it."

"Will you honor your vows to the Commune, Fraandlor?" Jaylor stepped between Slippy and Darville. The magician had been assigned to Krej's court for a decade or more. By using his formal name, Jaylor made his question a formal issue.

Slippy's honest. Yaakke's thoughts came into Jaylor's head. *Watch out for Scrawny.*

An echo from the bubble of armor confirmed Yaakke's opinion. Jaylor forced himself not to turn and face the space where he knew Brevelan must be hiding. If there were still traitors in their midst, he needed to protect her at all costs.

"Gentlemen," he addressed the Commune. "Please escort His Grace back to the Council Chamber. Protect him with your lives. And take that slimy bolt of magic with you. Find its signature and see if any of you can trace it. That may be our best clue to finding the queen. We are solitary magicians now, rather than communal. But with teamwork, we can persevere." Jaylor turned aside to his apprentice. "Go with them, Yaakke. Report anything amiss to me. And I mean anything out of the ordinary."

"But, sir, Master Baamin needs me. I can't leave him for long."

"Let him rest for a few hours."

The boy looked defiant.

Jaylor clamped a hand on his shoulder, tightening his

fingers until they dug deeply enough to insure the boy's attention. "I mean it, Yaakke. This is important. Stay with His Grace."

"And where will you be, Master Jaylor?" Scrawny accused. "As Senior Magician and adviser to the king, your place is in Council."

"There may still be clues here. When I have examined them and made certain no harm came to my wife and son, I will join you."

"Preposterous!" Scrawny protested. "Women have no place in the University. And magicians have no business taking a wife. An occasional mistress maybe, but not a wife!"

"Just shut up, you bloody bastard. Just shut up!" Yaakke was near to tears. The strain of the last day was telling on his youthful body and immature emotions. What little control he had snapped. "Brevelan's got more magic in her little toe than you've thrown in the last thirty years."

Jaylor pulled Yaakke tight against his chest, letting juvenile fists pound out pain and frustration. When the storm was over, the apprentice turned to face the stunned assembly of master magicians. "I won't apologize. Why should I? Scrawny's no longer a true magician and has no right to be part of the Commune. *His* magic is borrowed. Probably from Krej. He stinks of Krej."

"Yaakke, what are you saying?" Jaylor turned his apprentice to look directly into his eyes. Yaakke didn't have any tact or discipline and usually blurted out the truth without thought. He could keep secrets when he wanted to, though. What he saw with his wild magic talent was usually the best kept secret of all.

"His magic is borrowed, sir." Yaakke gulped around a new storm of emotions. "His aura isn't true and his thoughts are chaotic—like someone else is telling him what to do and what to say. There're others here, too, who lost their real magic when Shayla flew away. But they pretended, like, so they wouldn't be embarrassed."

"And just who is lending these men magic?" Lord Andrall entered the room. The Council was slower in response to Jaylor's summons than their magicians had been.

"Krej!" Zolltarn interceded for the boy. "My lords,

Guardians, our enemy seems to have left allies in our midst."

"His bastard daughter and her husband among them, perhaps?" Scrawny leaped toward Jaylor.

Scrawny's clawlike hands closed about Jaylor's throat before he could throw out his armor. Heat impaled his vocal cords. Air burned in his lungs, seeking escape.

The words of the spell wouldn't form. Blackness threatened. His vision elongated and fuzzed.

I am Jaylor. The solitary, Jaylor. He didn't need words. Words were indefinite. He needed images. Behind his bulging eyes he saw gleaming armor. Thick metal armor, hot metal armor slid around his throat and neck, up into a helm, down around his torso.

"Aieyeeeeee!" Scrawny screamed. Magic repulsion propelled him backward across the room in one mighty blast. Scrawny crashed against the wall with a sickening thud to his spine and bead. His sprawled hands were burned nearly free of skin.

Magic flowed out of him in visible sheets of pink—a muted shade of Krej's dark maroon magic.

"Out. All of you get out of my suite!" Jaylor ordered. He reached to massage his bruised throat. "We'll discuss bloodlines and true magic and traitors when my wife and the queen are both safe. Until then, remove yourself from my quarters. And take that . . ." He pointed toward the crumpled corpse of Scrawny with one hand, while the other continued to massage his injuries. "And take him somewhere where his body can be examined. We need information."

When they were all gone, the bolt of alien magic and the corpse with them, Jaylor spoke his thoughts. "Dragon dung! How did he break through my defenses?"

"He attacked with his body, instead of his magic. You weren't prepared for that from a master magician," Darville recited in a monotone. "You did the same thing to one of Zolltarn's guards. Remember?" He hung back, shoulders slumped, eyes lowered. His spine shuddered. Then he straightened and faced his friend with something of his old resolve and courage.

"I'll wait with you, Jaylor. Brevelan may respond to me," Darville offered.

"No, old friend. Your place is in Council. Yaakke and the Coraurlia will protect you until I get there. And don't worry. We'll find Mikka. We'll get her back for you."

"At least, leave Yaakke here to protect Brevelan," Darville protested.

"I'm sending her back to the clearing."

"No." Brevelan stood up from the corner, between the wardrobe and the wall. She reached to hug Jaylor close. "Forgive me for rejecting your touch. I feared the kidnappers would mimic your signature in order to lure me out."

Jaylor hugged her hard in relief. He kissed her hair, and then examined both her and the baby to make sure they were all right.

"Please go back to the clearing, beloved. You'll be safe there."

"I will stay here," Brevelan asserted. "Mikka will need me when she is found."

"How do you know?" Darville asked.

"The one who sought to steal my son entered the room in the guise of a harpy, the evil messenger of Simurgh."

"Stargods and dragons help us all," Jaylor sighed. "I do hope they haven't reverted to human sacrifice."

Chapter 29

Rosie clutched her thread cradle tight against her chest so that it wouldn't tangle. Softly, with a cat's stalking instinct, she tiptoed to the door of her windowless tower prison. The sparseness of the chamber reminded her of the days of her imprisonment at the hands of her uncle.

This incarceration, however, was much more dangerous, much more frightening than the last time. Her uncle was cruel and vindictive. But Janataea and her half brother were evil. So very, very evil.

Visions of Janataea and Krej shape-changed into giant harpies brought nausea into Rosie's throat. The ordeal of flight must have lasted many hours, many leagues. Her sense of time and distance were badly warped by the drugs shot into her by Janataea. All she remembered of the flight from the palace were the vicious vulture claws that encircled her shoulders, penetrating her thin shift and skin. Hanging, suspended in the thin, cold air, blood dripping down her body, she had lost all sense of up or down, right or left. Vertigo claimed her senses until, mercifully, her mind had closed.

The drug in her system had lasted just long enough to blot out the pain of the talon wounds in her back and shoulders during the flight. When she awoke, every movement of her arms and back sent sharp pains all through her body.

Now she was locked into a small room with stale air and minimal light. She wanted to sleep, but she hurt too much to rest. The strong and sensible person in the back of her mind seemed gone. No comfort there. No warmth anywhere. She needed reassurance and love. If only something, anything, in her prison smelled familiar, she could hope for an end of this nightmare.

Right now she would even welcome Darville.

Rosie held her breath and listened to the angry voices in the outer room. The words were incomprehensible through the thick panels of the door. But the tones were unmistakable. Janataea and Lord Krej were disagreeing again. Good. The longer they shouted at each other, the longer they left her alone. She could nurse and lick her wounds in private.

Hold your breath, Rosie. Don't let them hear you, the voice of the other person inside her head directed. *Open your ears. Listen like a cat in the wild.* Rosie pressed her ear to the wooden door. No help. The words were in a language she couldn't comprehend.

Help me understand, Rosie pleaded with the other person.

Mikka's frightened consciousness surged to the front, just enough to add intelligence and learning to the sensitivity of a cat. She dared not come further to the surface. When Janataea—in her own form—had pushed Rosie into this small prison, she had spoken as if she didn't know that both Mikka and Rosie were in the same body. Mikka wanted her presence, her intelligence, to remain hidden. That secret might make the difference in effecting an escape.

"What do you mean, you're impotent?" Janataea screeched. The accent was strange, but the vocabulary was one of the ancient tongues, from before the foundation of the three kingdoms.

Mikka, but not Rosie, had learned to read the nearly forgotten language as part of her classical education. But no one knew the exact pronunciation anymore. Or did they?

She'd heard the Rovers speak some of these words, and guessed a dialect had been adopted by the solitary magicians and exiles of Hanassa—a place where the wandering Rovers were welcome. Who were Krej and Janataea, that they used this archaic tongue so easily?

"Too much of the Tambootie does that to you. Maman warned me about the backlash of fatigue from Tambootie-augmented magic. Shape-change exhausts magic. Your princess might have been a cat during the flight, but she retained the full mass of a tall woman. Carrying her here took all of my reserves. I couldn't have done it without the Tambootie. But now I must recover," Krej apologized, meeker than Mikka had ever heard the self-righteous lord.

"Nonsense. A big man like you, in your prime. You're afraid of her cat's claws," Janataea sneered.

As well they should both be afraid. Rosie hoped her old governess would be scarred for life.

Mikka wondered if the wounds to her back and shoulders would heal cleanly. Both she and Rosie shuddered with the pain of the still seeping marks of harpy talons.

"Are you forgetting that I also stole the dragon throne and transported it here?"

"But you couldn't get the Coraurlia," Janataea lashed out at her brother. "If you'd gotten the Coraurlia, Darville would have been proved unfit to rule. You'd still be regent."

"Darville has already slept with her. What makes you think her body will accept my seed over his?" Krej sounded testy as he yawned.

Relief flooded through Mikka. If Krej were that tired, he might leave her alone long enough for her to escape.

"Rosie's body will accept you because she isn't in season yet. Tonight, or tomorrow at the latest, the cat within her will be ready to breed."

"She's a woman, for Simurgh's sake." Krej invoked the winged god who had been relegated to demon status, along with blood sacrifices, with the coming of the Stargods. "She becomes fertile every moon."

"She's also a cat who becomes truly fertile only once every six moons. The other flow is false as long as the cat is trapped in that body." Janataea paused. Soft footfalls indicated she was pacing closer to the door.

Rosie pulled back, seeking a place to hide in the bare room if Janataea chose that moment to open the door.

"Zolltarn reports that the cat, Mica, was lost in the void during their ritual," Janataea continued. "Mikka can never influence Rosie again. Therefore, she's more cat than woman. Trust me. Lay with her tonight and your offspring will rule the three kingdoms."

"I could rule the three kingdoms myself if I follow my own plans. Then maybe someone would let me sleep." He yawned again.

"Maman reviewed those plans and discarded them. The coven would still be outlawed by the Commune."

Janataea sounded near hysteria. That was when she inflicted the direst punishments against the princess. Rosie panicked, nearly losing contact with the other mind in her head. Mikka clung to consciousness, straining for mastery over the cat's instincts to hide.

"Damn the coven," Krej shouted. "The silly magic games you play have done nothing. The breakup of the nimbus of dragons, the distrust the Council holds for Darville, Simeon's marriage to Miranda, everything we have worked for was achieved through me. I am the real power in Coronnan. I have the dragon throne. I command all the troops. I will rule. And I will lay with the chit when I am ready, and not before."

Mikka shrank back from the door. She had to get away before Krej recovered. She'd kill herself before she allowed him to touch her.

"Master magicians," Jaylor confronted the members of the Commune outside the Council Chamber. "Before we enter this room, to serve as advisers and protectors of our lords, there is an issue we must address." Leadership and responsibility sat heavy on his shoulders. He didn't really want to do this. But he must.

Twenty pairs of eyes jumped from the open door of the chamber to the Senior Magician, standing several feet behind them. Jaylor wished he could read the thoughts behind those eyes. Then he wouldn't have to use this awful spell to unmask those disloyal to the Commune and Coronnan.

"I agree, we must deal with the apprentice Yaakke's accusation that some of us have borrowed magic. But not here, Jaylor." Slippy stepped to the front of the pack of magicians, arms crossed, face set in determination.

"This is a matter for the Commune, not the Council," Lyman reminded Jaylor.

"I disagree. The Council should have a say in the disposal of anyone who has borrowed magic from a rogue, a rogue with treasonous intent," Jaylor affirmed. And the Council needed to know the cost of supporting men who borrowed magic and advice from such a wicked rogue.

"Magicians have always been subject to the Commune only," Zolltarn reminded him.

"And so they will be. I ask only that the Council observe our justice and be advised." Jaylor stepped back a little more to give himself the space he needed.

The dragons said this spell would work. It had to. He had no other choice. If the Commune were going to survive, he had to root out the traitors now, no matter the cost.

He lifted his staff over his head, aiming the tip at the assembled Commune. Blue truth, fueled by Coronnan's elemental forces, darted from the end of his tool. The mist of the spell spread out into a cloud over the magicians' heads, then sank downward like so much blue rain. Magicians, priests, and healers were all bunched together. None of them could escape the truth.

Slippy and Lyman and thirteen others, including Zolltarn, stood straight, accepting the spell. The blue fog became a dust and settled lightly on their heads and shoulders and remained blue, intensely, vividly blue. As blue as the depths of the Great Bay in sunshine.

Five master magicians squirmed and twisted, trying to avoid the spell. The dust of truth turned fiery green as soon as it touched them, burning the truth out of them. None of them had enough magic to escape.

"You five, stand aside, lest your false magic contaminate the rest of us," Jaylor ordered.

The men in question looked to each other, looked to their former comrades, looked anywhere but at Jaylor and themselves.

"I said stand aside," the Senior Magician roared.

"We haven't done anything wrong!" the youngest of the lot, a man nearly forty, squeaked. The dust of truth burned his tongue. He opened his mouth to scream in pain, but no sound came out. Where the dust touched his skin, on face and hands, he aged decades before their eyes. His bones shrank and twisted with rheumatism. Dark auburn hair turned gray, then white and brittle. The more he protested and fought the truth, the older he grew, shriveling and dying before their eyes.

"I didn't think you had this kind of cruelty in you, Master Jaylor." Darville stared at Jaylor from the doorway, aghast at the torture the man endured. The Council hovered behind him, staring mutely at the horrifying sight in the corridor.

"*Stargods,* no man should be forced to tell the truth that way." Lord Wendray finally looked away.

"Should I have sent them all, innocent and guilty alike, to the dungeon, and allowed mundanes to torture the truth out of them?" Jaylor allowed his anger to surface, anger at himself for throwing the spell, anger at Krej for making it necessary. " 'Twas not my spell that caused the anguish of premature old age. 'Twas the nature of the magic they borrowed. That false power burned up their lives."

"Take them to the hospice. They no longer have magic of their own to escape a mundane cell, and they will need care." Darville bowed his head in regret for the loss.

The other four impostors stood absolutely still, not daring to protest the truth spell in any way.

"Send a loyal scribe to their rooms to record every detail of their confession. The truth is the only way these remaining four will escape the fate of their comrade." Jaylor lowered his staff and entered the Council Chamber, grateful to the dragons for giving him the means to expose these men. Sick with himself for having to do it.

Annoyed at yet another interruption to the day's work, Darville nodded for the breathless messenger to enter.

An obviously nervous priest eyed Jaylor as he edged into the Council Chamber. "Your Grace, my lords." He bowed to one and all. His eyes slid warily around Jaylor. "I have just picked up a distress call in my glass. The city of Sambol reports that King Simeon's troops have penetrated the outlying passes, as well as the main trade road into Coronnan, and are massing to besiege the city."

The priest backed out toward the doorway under a bombardment of questions. "I'm sorry, sirs. I don't know anything more. I only picked up the general distress call. It was sent out in all directions, to no one specific. A weak spell from an exhausted healer."

"You may return to your duties." Darville cut through the hubbub of voices. "Troop placements. How many? Exact locations? Supply trains? I need details!" he ordered the lords.

"Perhaps the kidnapping of your wife is for the best, Your Grace." Marnak the Elder stood by his chair, voice level and courteous.

"What?" Darville roared. "You think Lord Krej's treason a good thing?"

"You have fullfilled the treaty with Rossemeyer. Her kidnapping and slaying by magicians is beyond your control. We are now in a position to negotiate peace with King Simeon." Marnak continued to stand behind his chair.

"I agree," Lord Wendray rubbed his temples. "My city cannot withstand another assault. By the time reinforcements can be sent, even by forced march, Simeon will have a clear road up the Coronnan River, to the capital. We'd be better off abandoning the queen and treating with SeLenicca."

"And what of the ten thousand mercenaries from Rossemeyer that are disembarking onto our mainland as we speak?" Darville fought the outrage that nearly blinded him. Abandon Mikka for politics? Never.

And yet . . .

"Which of you wishes to explain to those ten thousand battle-hardened soldiers that we are abandoning their beloved princess, my wife, to the evil manipulations of a coven?" He half stood, the Coraurlia in its protective satchel banging against the table.

"Who says we have to tell them anything?" Wendray looked up with hope. "If we send them immediately to rescue my city, by the time they find out about the queen, we won't need them anymore."

"By that time, they'll be in the heart of Coronnan ready to turn on us. Do you want to try ousting ten thousand entrenched mercenaries?" Darville's voice and body shook with the myriad emotions he fought to control. How could they suggest such a thing? Shortsighted. Lumbird dumb. Murderous, self-serving. . . . The litany of curses continued on and on in his troubled mind.

He had to think. But images of Mikka danced through his head. He couldn't concentrate. Wearily he sank back into a chair, any chair that would take the strain from his trembling knees.

Mikka!

"I don't think we should allow those troops to set foot

on our soil." Marnak stood firm. "If we treat with King Simeon now, we won't need those mercenaries."

"If we treat with King Simeon at all, we reveal our vulnerability. He'll know we are desperate and cheat us of everything we hold dear," Jaylor interrupted.

"And I say we must. If the king and Council won't initiate negotiations, then I will." Jonnias stepped back from the table. "Who is with me?"

Three others, including Marnak the Elder, joined him. Marnak the Younger was still missing, along with the rest of Krej's household.

"Wendray?" Jonnias quirked an eyebrow toward the lord of the merchant city that straddled the main trade road out of Coronnan.

"I can't. If we treat, I'll lose my city, everything. Simeon wants control of the trade road. Sambol gives him that. I have to fight, though that is likely to destroy me and mine as well."

"My lords," Darville found his voice, weak as it was. "Please reconsider. If we divide now, we are likely to lose everything." Somehow he had to convince the Council that Coronnan must remain united. The carefully built network of trade, alliance, and protection was shattering before their eyes. They couldn't continue at half-strength. Half-wealth. Half-everything.

"Then join us, or be damned." Jonnias led his contingent out the door.

Silence lay heavily in the room, like a thick, sour-tasting sea fog.

"Magicians got us into this," someone mumbled loud enough for all to hear, but not so loud as to be identified.

"Perhaps we need to take corrective measures now, before the magicians get us into more trouble." Lord Andrall straightened his shoulders, as if shaking off the weight of indecision.

"What do you mean by that?" Darville lifted his face from his hands and glared at his most loyal supporters. Behind him, he sensed, the remaining magicians had focused their attention on Lord Andrall.

"Your Grace." Lord Andrall stood to be recognized by the reduced assembly. "King Darville, we of the Council have seen that the individual members of the Commune are vulnerable to uncontrollable greed and a lust for power they could not achieve in the old days, when dragons were the source of magic. We have seen trusted friends dissolve into monsters we can never know or understand." He looked pointedly at Jaylor. "We have seen the entire country divided and threatened by the question of the magicians. I recommend that henceforth, magicians be banned from Council. Furthermore, no lord may be a magician and no magician may be a lord."

"What?" Darville stared at his longtime supporter. "You can't eliminate the best educated men from their advisory positions. You've just voted to end three hundred years of proven working relationship." He leaned forward, hands flat on the table. Surprise and anger clouded his vision briefly. Then it cleared. Details focused with the sharpness of a knife edge.

"We can't take the chance that anyone in a position of authority will be manipulated by an unscrupulous rogue," Lord Andrall explained.

Like Krej.

"I agree," Wendray stood and moved beside Andrall. The remaining lords joined them in unanimous agreement.

"Until the Commune finds a way to prove the loyalty of every member . . ." Andrall looked directly into Jaylor's eyes in accusation. "And the test must be to the Council's satisfaction, not the Commune's . . . until that time, we forbid the presence of any magician in Council. We also terminate all advisory positions to the members of the Council."

Chapter 30

"**T**his thread goes here. Over and under. And take this one around and take two threads through," Rosie chanted the litany of her game.

Mikka allowed the cat within her to be occupied with the tangle of her threads. While their fingers passed through the intricate pattern again and again, her eyes peered into every crevice of the stone walls.

A careless servant had left Rosie's hairbrush and comb within the chamber. Janataea must still believe that Rosie could be lulled into docility by having her hair brushed. Mikka had bent and twisted the tail of the comb into a lock pick. Mikka couldn't fault the shuffling old woman for leaving behind the means of her escape. Where could a prisoner run to? Castle Krej was sealed shut in anticipation of a siege.

"I may not run, but I can hide until it's too late for Krej to rape me," she muttered to herself.

Narrow, dark corridors wound around and around the formidable fortress. The cat within her wanted to explore all of them—the deeper and darker, the better. Mikka suppressed the urge. This castle might have tunnels, but certainly they were not a likely means of escape. The defenses were designed around an impregnable position, carved out of a sheer cliff face, not an escape route that could be betrayed or discovered.

She found servant's clothing in a storeroom, stout trews and warm tunic, long woolen stockings, and indoor slippers to protect her feet. Warm and comfortable at last, she glided through the passages, as silent as a ghost.

All corridors in the building eventually led to the Great

Hall. This huge room was unlike any Mikka had run across in other castles. The dais, where the family and honored guests dined or held court, was missing. No armor, or sleeping pallets for men-at-arms lined the walls. The room was much less functional than a standard Great Hall, much more beautiful and very, very frightening.

A Tambootie wood fire glowed in a central hearth. Around that circle of stones, perched on appropriate pedestals, was Krej's renowned sculpture collection. In the moons since Shayla had torn a hole in the outer wall and freed the reanimated creatures, Krej had replaced most of his sculptures. Where Shayla had left the wall gaping to the elements now stood new stonework and a huge window to light his collection.

Mikka gasped at the cost of all that glass. No one had a right to own that much. Colored and clear pieces had been fashioned or cut to make a picture. Huge wings and enormous claws gave the impression of a dragon. Appropriate, since a dragon had created the space the window filled.

Then Mikka moved closer, staring in wonder at the morning sun streaming through the rare window. No dragon this. She was staring at an icon of Simurgh.

Quickly, she turned away from the blasphemous picture only to be greeted by the animals in the sculpture collection. A great gray bear in pewter. A wild tusker in ebony wood. The spotted saber cat in bronze. And several other creatures Mikka could not identify. There was a winged raptor, similar to the kahmsin eagle beloved in Rossemeyer, similar, but larger and more fierce. A pouched rodent, too preposterous to be real, raised up on oversized hind legs and thick tail. Its shortened forepaws seemed poised, as if prepared to engage its enemies in fisticuffs.

And yet . . . and yet the life of each creature glimmered beneath the surface of the sculpture. Resentment, anger, confusion, bewilderment assaulted Mikka. Was she doomed to the same fate? Once she had served Krej's and Janataea's purpose and borne the child they needed for their dynastic plans, would she be shape-changed into a cat, and then frozen in time in a prison of iridescent shale, the color of Rosse's fur?

Too frightened to think, she buried her consciousness deep inside herself.

Rosie tangled her thread into a hopeless knot. In frustration she ended the game and stretched the string into a long straight piece, with a huge Rover's knot just to the left of middle.

If only life were untangled so simply, a slightly recovered Mikka mused.

Then she saw it. In the wide place that had once contained a life-sized sculpture of a glass dragon sat a harpy, Rhomerra, the bringer of nightmares, plague and ill fortune. Whatever substance comprised the hideous form, it was amazingly lifelike. Filthy, oily feathers and scales covered a grossly fat bird's body. Long, knock-kneed legs ended in grasping talons, coated in dried blood and gore. Naked, pendulous breasts dangled from the chest. Set within the beak and beady eyes of a raptor was the face of Janataea. Her face wore the sensuously arrogant sneer so typical of the royal governess.

Was the creature real? Mikka dared a quick probe. No life resided in the carved stone. This was not one of Krej's prizes. It was an idol, with an altar in front of it. The offering was a miniature Tambootie tree in a priceless glass pot and a dead cat.

She couldn't look to see if the sacrifice was Rosse, the other half of herself.

"May we observe your spell of seeking, Master Jaylor?" Zolltarn asked.

He was more polite than Jaylor expected. Rovers were arrogant and suspicious and boastful, but rarely polite. What did this man really want? He'd passed the truth spell. But that didn't mean he didn't have secrets.

Jaylor unlocked the round meeting room reserved for the Commune with a pass of his hand and an image in his mind. The new spell gave him a chance to reinforce his status to the rest of the Commune, trailing up the long staircase. Only the Senior Magician could open the door alone. Any other master magician needed a second spell from another master to accomplish the same feat.

"I'm not sure I can work with an audience." Jaylor looked to Yaakke for confirmation. The boy lifted one shoulder, barely attentive. His mind was two floors below with Baamin.

"This isn't going to work at all if you don't pay attention, Yaakke," Jaylor hissed to the boy as he thrust the heavy door open. "I know you are concerned for your Master. We all wish Baamin well. But there are times when the welfare of the kingdom is more important than our individual concerns," he added more gently.

Jaylor needed to traverse the void in search of Mikka. Before he ventured into the realm of dragons again, he needed an anchor. Yaakke, his most familiar companion in magic, must serve that purpose.

"Entering the void is dangerous, Jaylor. We never had to do it with dragon magic. We're inexperienced. Is a foreign princess worth the risk, even if she is married to our new king?" Slippy argued.

"Rossemikka was kidnapped by magic. If we, the magicians, refuse to rescue her, then we only deepen the Council's conviction that all magicians are untrustworthy."

"Fat chance of convincing any of them that we are as loyal as they—maybe more so. They want power, not cooperation," Yaakke grumbled.

"Why is this apprentice here?" One of the younger masters tried to grab the boy's collar and usher him out of the private enclave. He had to jerk his hand away from Yaakke's shimmering armor.

"Because I need him to help me find the queen." Jaylor suppressed a smile. Skepticism glowered from a dozen faces.

"We can't join our magic to make the task any easier. Not like the old days, when dragons gave us power we could gather and amplify," Slippy groused.

"We can't join, but you can act as my staff, focus the spell, and feed my energy while Yaakke anchors me to this reality."

"It can't work!" Zolltarn looked as aghast as any of them.

"I did it once with Krej—before my magic was fully returned. I couldn't break Brevelan's link to the dragons, and it was killing her. I knew Krej couldn't be trusted, but he had the power and the link to Brevelan to help. The warp in my magic occurred because I defied him, mid-spell. He was too hasty. I would have killed both Shayla and my wife if I'd followed his orders. I realized then that I didn't have to blackmail him with the knowledge of his antidote to witchbane. He wanted a way to destroy the dragons once and for all."

"You violated your oath as a master to the Commune by assisting an enemy of the crown and the nimbus!"

"I saved my wife and son!"

"Gentlemen, gentlemen, we accomplish nothing if we bicker," Zolltarn soothed. "I am interested in this process. Maybe we can profit from it."

After a moment of grumbling, they all settled in their accustomed places at the round table. Black glass, solid and clear. The most precious object in the kingdom.

Yaakke shuffled beside Jaylor. There was no chair for him. Jaylor spotted the boy's problem. There were empty chairs, each upholstered in colors appropriate to a magician's magic. No master dared sit in the chair designated for another magician. Yaakke was only a lowly apprentice, with no status and no definition to his magical colors yet.

With a blink of Jaylor's eyes, a high stool appeared beside him—an appropriate seat for a student among his teachers. With an impudent grin, Yaakke perched in his new place.

"First, we must be physically linked." Jaylor reached for Yaakke's hand on his left and Slippy's on his right. "On my count we will enter a trance together."

"Sounds like the way we used to shore up the border."

"Similar. Once entranced, Yaakke will boost me into the void. You, as a group, will then push Yaakke after me."

"Like acrobats building a pyramid?"

"Exactly. I don't think you will be able to follow into the void as a group, but through my eyes you will be able to see what I am doing. Yaakke will monitor my actions and signal for my return, if I run into trouble. You, in turn will lend him your corporate strength."

Jaylor looked around the table. Each magician nodded his understanding and assent.

"On my count. One." They all inhaled deeply.

"Two . . ."

"Not without me, you don't!" Darville pounded up the stairs.

The spell collapsed before it had begun. The magicians

sank back into their chairs, gasping and shaking their heads clear of the almost-trance.

"Your Grace, you are mundane. You can't help."

"I'm strong, and I am involved. It is, after all, my wife you seek."

"The Council, Roy?" Jaylor brought his eyes back into focus.

"Dispensed to myriad duties in getting troops on the road. I may be missed. But I feel my place is here."

"And the magic infection, Your Grace?" Zolltarn intervened. "What if this triggers a recurrence? The Council would never forgive you, or us."

"The infection is cured. Never in recorded history has there been a recurrence or relapse after a cure." Darville reminded them it was their own books that had led to diagnosis and cure.

"Why not let the boy join us? Everything else about this adventure is extremely unorthodox. Take Scrawny's chair, bo . . . Your Grace." Slippy waved to the one opposite him. The orange and yellow covering was already fading. "And put on the Coraurlia. The magic embedded in it will give us something to link us to you."

"You know, Jaylor, if this works, we're going to have to find you a nickname. Messiah, maybe?" a master in healer's gray quipped.

"More like Mount Ohara by the size of him," Lyman murmured just loudly enough to be heard.

"Can we get on with this?" Jaylor glared at the magicians.

Once more they linked hands. At Yaakke's first touch, Jaylor sensed energy flowing strongly into his veins. "On my count. ONE." Blood tingled in the back of his neck, and almost hummed with tightly controlled magic.

"TWO." The singing flow of blood spread to his toes and fingertips and passed around the circle back into himself. "THREE."

The void yawned above him, waiting, calling, pulling him up and out of himself, out of Coronnan, out of life. Blacker-than-black emptiness reached on for eternity.

An almost physical shove launched him into the mind-numbing cold.

* * *

Yaakke paused long enough to catch his breath. The void was more beautiful each time he glimpsed it. Always he had sat on the threshold, uncertain where and how to proceed into the nothingness, unless he was zipping through it in transport. Now, with a strong link back to the Commune to pull him home again, he could afford to linger. He took his first tentative step forward.

Blackness swallowed him. Panic fought with his heartbeat. The silver umbilical of life that anchored him to the Commune quivered and tugged at him. He longed to follow it back to safety.

But Jaylor was out there, somewhere, searching for Darville's wife, the pretty princess who had smiled at him once.

"Jaylor?" He called with voice and mind and magic.

Nothing.

"Master!" His voice cracked.

Then he saw it, a red and blue braid, very faintly trailing back to him, caught within his own magic web. One hand on the braid, the other reaching out in front, as a blind man's guide, Yaakke floated forward with jerking irregularity. He had to force the image of his feet walking on solid ground. Moving through nothing sent his stomach roiling.

He looked back. His own silver umbilical was fading. The red and blue ahead was growing stronger, pulsing with vitality.

"Open your eyes, Yaakke, son of Yaacob." Not exactly a voice, not exactly a magic probe, either.

"I can't see anything."

"Open your eyes."

Yaakke thought his eyes were open. Maybe he was supposed to open all of his senses, including the web of magic armor that was always with him. He squinted and "saw" tiny pinpoints of light at each intersecting joint in the web. This was his protection, unique to him. He'd constructed it as a child, before he knew he had magic, as a defense from the older boys who taunted and jeered him for being stupid. He couldn't break that web. He needed it.

"Open, Yaakke. Break free of your armor or you won't survive the void."

Reluctantly, Yaakke separated two of the pinpoints of light and peered through to the outside. Rainbows and braids pulsed with life. Colors seen and felt, heard and smelled beckoned to him. He could get lost out there.

"Open the damn thing or go back to the Commune!" That was Jaylor's voice and mental probe.

Yaakke dropped the web, but he kept it close at hand. Those rainbows and braids were the essences of many, many souls. One never knew when those other lives would reach consciousness and reach out and grab him. He needed to explore this "place," not stay here permanently.

"Mikka's magic is akin to Brevelan's—elemental. Search for the colors of Coronnan. It will be linked to Darville's gold."

A golden filament hovered before his vision.

"It's bare. There's nothing linked to it." Yaakke scanned the umbilical as far as he could see in either direction.

"It shouldn't be. Brevelan and I should be entwined with him, and Shayla along with Mikka."

"I can't see any links in any of the cords. Each one is separate, not even touching another."

Someone yanked on Yaakke's silver life-thread, hard. Urgent.

"BAAMIN!" he screeched. "Don't die on me, Master. You can't die yet. I need you."

Abruptly he was sitting on his stool at the black glass table.

Darville flopped back in his chair, tired and hungry beyond belief. No wonder Jaylor and Yaakke ate so much. From the looks of the gathered Commune, all of the other magicians were as flagged as he was. They had poured all of their strength into Jaylor, and drained his mundane body, as well.

Except for Yaakke. His young body twitched with anxious energy.

"I have to go to him. He'll die if I'm not there!" Yaakke wailed and burst from the room with more energy than he had a right to have left over.

Jaylor reached a weak hand to restrain the boy.

"Let him go. He's useless in that state." Zolltarn closed his eyes. Fatigue drew new lines in his exotic skin. He looked in better shape than the others in the room.

"I didn't have a chance to find her. I've got to go back in." Jaylor began his deep breathing to repeat the spell.

"You can't," Slippy protested. "It's too soon and you are too drained. We might not be able to pull you back."

"That's a chance I'm prepared to take."

"I don't see how you expected to find one life strand in that tangle, Jaylor. Give it a rest. We can try again in a few hours. When we've eaten and slept." Slippy yawned.

"A few hours may be too late," Darville reminded them all. "Every hour we delay gives Krej that much more time to strengthen his defenses."

"Relax, Your Grace. We'll get Krej eventually. As for the queen, it was a political union, not like she was your mistress, someone you really loved." The ancient magician in a faded and threadbare cloak grumbled.

"None of you will ever understand!" Darville thrust back his chair. It teetered and fell over, as he pushed himself upright with an effort.

"Mikka is my wife. My *wife, s'murgh it.* How can any of you wrinkled old eunuches hope to comprehend what it is like to love a woman, to need a particular woman beside you as a companion, lover, friend, and adviser?" He glared at each one of them. Only Jaylor met his eye.

"I'm going back in. I'll find her for you. It would help if I knew what essence to look for. I couldn't find anything resembling Mica."

His mispronunciation of the name had to be deliberate. Jaylor knew the woman better as a cat than as the wife of his best friend.

"She is gold and copper, silver and lead. Diamonds, rubies, emeralds, sapphires, and opals. Kardia, air, fire, and water—all of the elements rolled into one. I caught just a brief glimpse of her as Yaakke pulled us out." Darville closed his eyes as he tried to describe the wonderful mix of life that comprised his beloved.

"A dragon could find her," Slippy grumbled.

"We don't have any dragons," Jaylor reminded them. "But we do have the dragon crown." He suddenly looked excited. "The crown is more than a protection against alien spells. It is part of your link to the dragons. I'll take you into the void with me. We'll find the dragons and make them help us find her."

"Wait!" Zolltarn cautioned. "You're too tired, Jaylor. If the void claims you now, you'll never come back. I won't be responsible for Brevelan's wrath if that happens."

"But I've been in the void with the dragons on two occasions. They know me. They respond to me."

"All the more reason not to go back again so soon. The dragons are possessive. They'll keep you."

"He's right," Darville agreed. "Remember the time you overdosed on the Tambootie?" He looked at his friend with a great deal of pain and pleasure in that memory. "We nearly lost you. While you soared with the dragons, you wanted to break all ties to Coronnan and your mortal body."

"Until Brevelan's love reached up and enticed me back."

Darville had been a part of that call, too. From the distance of several moons later, they were both too embarrassed to face the aftermath of that night—all three of them in bed together, Brevelan pregnant by one of them. Which one?

"Gentlemen, there is an easier way," Zolltarn announced. Every eye in the room turned to him. "We can construct a ritual that draws magic from all life, not just dragons. A ritual will require less than half the energy and will bind us all together so that no one gets lost in the void."

"Another eight-pointed star? There are thirteen of us here," Jaylor looked skeptical.

"All the better. Eight points, with a ninth for the center, taps ancient and arcane powers that require more of our souls than we are willing to give at this point. Twelve points, with a mundane center, is rooted to the very essence of Coronnan."

"What makes you think I trust you to conduct such a ritual?" Darville asked. "I don't doubt that you wish to find Mikka. But your reasons for helping us, when you and your people have been outcasts for generations, is beyond me."

"The void stripped us all of outer shells. Could any of you detect dishonesty in me?" Zolltarn spread his hands, palms upward in appeal to the other magicians.

"I wasn't looking," Jaylor admitted.

"I saw your loyalty to the spell, Zolltarn." Slippy leaned

closer to the Rover, peering at him with slitted eyes. A truth spell brushed them both, negated by the other's magic. "But you have other loyalties, as well."

"Lord Krej and his sister, Janataea, have betrayed me," Zolltarn defended himself. "I admit to ruthless ambition on my part, for me and my tribe. But even I will not degenerate into the ancient practice of human sacrifice to please the pagan god, Simurgh."

Terrified silence rang around the room.

Chapter 31

*W*hy *hasn't Rosie come into heat? The time has come and gone, but still she hides. Any normal cat would be seeking the company of a male, any male, rather than go through the torment of a mating urge without one. My weakling brother has retired again, rather than seek her out in the dungeons and tunnels of this rat's maze of a castle.*

Perhaps the shock of our kidnap has delayed Rosie's normal cycles. I shan't worry. She will come out when she is ripe.

The kidnap! What a glorious flight. I never believed in the god Simurgh, not like Maman did. Yet now, now he has granted me the power to achieve what I must. My faith is restored.

But Krej does not believe in anything. He uses people and gods for his own ends. He is becoming more and more like Mother's husband. I always assumed we had the same father. Mother loathed her husband. She returned to her lover, my father, in Hanassa often. My father should have been Krej's father. But now I wonder. Krej grows weaker of will, he strays from the purpose of the coven. That sniveling lord, Dratourelle, who married Mother, must be my brother's father.

I only need Krej a little longer. As soon as he impregnates Rosie, I shall offer him to the altar of Simurgh. I shall offer the entire coven in sacrifice. I don't need them any longer.

All I need is the Tambootie and Simurgh.

The door to Baamin's bedroom flew open with a bang. Brevelan looked up at Yaakke with annoyance. Not that the boy's careless and noisy burst of energy would affect

Baamin. The old man was even now sliding deeper into his final sleep.

"I can't let him die yet!" Magic radiated from the boy in visible waves. His aura extended toward the limp figure on the bed.

"You've got to let him go, Yaakke." Brevelan rose swiftly, grabbing Yaakke's shoulders. "His heart is worn out. He can't be healed, believe me, I've tried." She shook him to distract him from his projected spell.

"But I can lend him strength. I can support him until . . . until . . ." he broke off in a sob.

"He can't be healed, Yaakke. All we can do is wait and project our love so that he can die in peace."

"But I need him!"

"The entire kingdom needs him. But there is nothing we can do."

"Darcine?" Baamin called to his friend, Darville's father, who had been dead nearly seven moons. His voice was frail, barely more than a whisper.

Brevelan stilled her entire body in eerie surprise.

"Darcine?" Baamin called again. "I have seen her." A smile curved his bloodless lips.

Cautiously, Brevelan approached the bed. The old man's hand twitched. She grasped it lightly, pouring love and strength and healing into him.

"I have seen a dragon." He stopped speaking, but his lips kept moving.

Brevelan leaned closer to catch his whispers.

"All these years, I never saw a dragon. But I saw Shayla!"

And he slipped away.

Tears trembled in Brevelan's eyes.

"I can lend him my body." Yaakke grabbed Baamin's lifeless hand away from her.

"NO! Look what happened to the magicians who borrowed magic from Krej. They disintegrated very rapidly and very painfully. They are aging before the eyes of their guards. The remaining three will be dead by dawn. How much worse would it be to borrow an entire life. Do you want the same thing to happen to you? There is no way you can both survive." She choked back a sob as the pain crowding her heart suddenly burst and dissipated.

The last of Baamin's emotions passed through her. There was a moment of emptiness. Then, miraculously, a wonderful joy flooded her.

Brevelan looked at the wasted body of an old, old man, stunned. She had presided at a number of death watches. Her empathy had guided more than one spirit into the next plane of existence. Usually she encountered fear, loneliness, and regret. Inevitably, a little piece of her soul bonded with her patients and passed over with them. This was the first time she had felt such a wonderful anticipation and a restoration of her individuality—as though all the lives she had guided onward had returned the bits and pieces of her soul they had taken with them.

"Can you feel him, Yaakke?" she whispered. "Look at the smile on his face, Yaakke. Master Baamin wants to leave this reality. He's relieved to pass on his responsibilities to younger, more capable hands. You are a part of his grand plan for our future."

"He's going. I can bring him back. Really I can. I know the spell."

"How dare you!" She stayed his hand. "Such work is forbidden. You have to let him go."

"But . . . but. . . ."

"No. I don't care what you are capable of, Yaakke. Ability has nothing to do with right. You'll never be a true magician until you learn the limits of what you may and may not do."

"But I can do this."

"There is a difference between 'can' and 'may.' Look at him, Yaakke." She stood behind him, forcing his face to the bed where a slim shell of an old man was lost in the expanse of sheets and coverlets. "Really look at him and think about what is right for him. Not what is most comfortable for you."

The taut muscles of Yaakke's back crumpled. Tears streamed down his face. "What will I do without him, Brevelan? He's the only one who ever cared about me. He's . . . he's like my father and mother both. He's the only good thing that ever happened in my life."

"He gave you a wonderful gift, Yaakke. He gave you the right to think for yourself. He gave you the skills to make decisions. The time has come for you to reach beyond

Baamin and find out what your life is meant to be." She plunked down into her chair and picked up her knitting.

Calmly inserting her needles, she resumed her rocking. The rhythm of her chair matched the flow of tears down her cheeks.

Yaakke collapsed against the bed, crying so hard his breath came in jerky spasms.

Darville settled the Coraurlia on his head. His shoulders firmed and his chin came up as he found a new balance. The weight of the thick glass and gems became a natural part of him.

Around him, twelve magicians shuffled into their places. Each carried a candle. Twelve more unlit candles marked the edge of the smaller inner circle that defined Darville's space in the ritual.

Heavy incense smoldered in twelve censers around the circular subterranean room Zolltarn had found for this ceremony. Not a trace of the Tambootie was present.

"We are deep within the foundations of the University of Magic. Deep within the rock and soil of Coronnan. We bond with the kardia. If the one we seek rests anywhere on rock or soil, or in a building with foundations buried in the land, she is one with us and will be found," the Rover intoned. He moved two steps in. One step to his left he lit one of Darville's twelve candles from the taper he carried. The scent of newly plowed fields rose from the flame.

"Rossemikka we name her. She is flower and sunlight," Jaylor spoke his part of the ritual. He, too, moved inward two steps and one to his right. The candle he lit smelled of roses.

"A princess from the land of Rossemeyer. Her spirit soars like the kahmsin eagle of that land." Slippy's candle was more smoke than flames, smoke that lifted and spiraled around the chamber, like an eagle on the wind.

Each of the twelve spoke and lit a candle. Each portion of the rite defined Mikka, caught a bit of her essence.

By the sixth candle, Darville's senses were reeling. His vision faded in and out of focus. The eighth candle nearly sent him out of his body.

"Let go, Darville. Let the scents lift you into the void,"

a voice, perhaps it was Jaylor, or maybe Zolltarn, whispered into his mind or his ear. Or maybe he said the words himself.

"Dragons of Coronnan, gather to our plea. Lift us. Assist us. Set Rossemikka free!" Thirteen voices beseeched the creatures of the void.

Black nothingness. Numbing cold. Burning voices.

Darville opened himself to the void. Vibrantly colored threads tangled and wove about him. They pulsed with life, moved closer, wove away from him. A fat gold strand wound around and around him. He lifted it away from his face to better see whose life-thread intertwined with his own.

Dragons! Dozens of them, in all colors and shapes. Big and little, old and young. Invisible dragons with primary colors on their wing tips. Solid dragons that glowed with life and light and could be seen from leagues away. Every kind of dragon imaginable hovered in a glorious nimbus.

(Who do you seek and why?) The dragons spoke to him en masse.

"Mikka is the other half of my heart."

(Look to your left, the side of your heart.)

Darville turned his entire body to his left, toward his sword arm, and saw only more of the thick gold umbilical that was his own.

(She is your heart, not your strength. Look to your heart.)

He turned his body back to its original position. Then he twisted only his neck to look toward his left side. Something glimmered and beckoned, just beyond his sight.

(You will not find her outside of yourself.)

Why didn't they say so in the first place! He sought his beloved where he always knew she would be. From the time of his first dragon-dream in Shayla's cave he had known that Mikka was an essential part of him. During the moons that Mica had been his constant companion, he'd always been aware of where she was, even without seeing her. Since his first night in Mikka's bed, he had not been separated from her by more than a heartbeat.

Deep inside his soul, iridescent light surged upward. He grasped a hold on the essence of Mikka. An old blue-tipped dragon named Seannin flew beneath him. Darville caught the spine ridges of the leader of the nimbus in his free hand and flung himself astride. Together, they followed the glowing umbilical.

The void thinned ahead of them. Stars showed above, the foam of surf in the Great Bay splashed below them. Craggy hills rose straight up from the depths of the bay. Cliffs broke and crumbled into sharp pinnacles as the mountains marched into the sea. Carved into the northwest face of one of those peaks was a castle. The mountain above it was so steep and high, no one could drop into the grounds from above, not even from dragonback. There was only one pathway leading up to the closed gates from the village, at the base of the cliff. A daring climber might try to scale the sharp rocks to the castle walls. But the walls themselves were embedded with shards of knife-sharp volcanic material.

Castle Krej. Impregnable. The last stronghold of the rebels during the Great War of Disruption. Conquered only by the unified might of the Commune. A symbol of the civil wars that should never come again.

"We can bring Mikka out, or we can drop all of us in." Jaylor's voice cut into Darville's thoughts. "We don't have the strength for both."

When Darville looked around, he realized that all twelve of the master magicians were behind him, each on a different dragon.

"If we rescue the queen, we can then settle our score with Krej at our leisure," Slippy said.

"With Krej, there will be no leisure. We must end this battle here and now. Send me down to him." Darville closed his eyes and prayed that he had made the right decision. His actions might cost him his life, or worse, the life of Mikka. But if he died, he would take Krej with him. The kingdom would be safe.

For a while.

"Are you sure, Darville? We can get Mikka out safely," Jaylor argued.

"I've got to remove Krej from his seat of power. We'll never break his defenses with an army."

"The boy is right," Zolltarn agreed. "If we do not penetrate his base of power now, we will never again have peace from him and his ilk."

"Take us down, Seannin," Darville commanded his mount. "And give my regards to Shayla."

Mikka lifted her head and sniffed. Something was wrong, very wrong indeed.

There were a lot of things wrong in Krej's castle—that hideous altar among them. But this was something else. She sniffed again, with Rosie's help, for the difference in the air. Her latest hiding place, in the tiny cupboard underneath the back staircase, between the Great Hall and the dining hall, was too close to the kitchen. The scents of Krej's next meal overshadowed the smell of the individuals who passed by.

So far, she had seen only two servants in the entire castle: a man and a woman, old, nearly blind, and oblivious to all but their assigned tasks. The soldiers who lined the outer walls and marched in squads around the courtyard never entered the main building of the castle.

Carefully, Mikka edged toward the paneling that closed off her hiding place. She listened and tested the air for something different.

Roasting meat. Baking bread. Boiling tubers. Someone whipping cream for the sweet. Sliced cheese and apples for the savory. But no human scent near here.

She sent a tiny sliver of magic into the Great Hall with the tormented creatures trapped inside the sculptures. Janataea had been there twice in the last hour. Her boisterous prayers to Simurgh were not concealed. The servants avoided her and the hall. The room was empty now.

As were the dining hall and the offices behind it.

Did she dare risk a probe upward to the towers and bedchambers? Janataea would sense the magic and follow it back to Mikka. Better to slip up there, without magic, and hide somewhere new, somewhere Janataea had already looked.

She took the chance that the guards on the battlements would be drowsy. Perhaps they didn't know that she didn't belong there. She flitted past her tower prison, upward to the door and covered parapet.

Starlight and a faint sliver of a new moon outlined the shadows below her. Campfires in the distance. An army was camped out there. Darville's troops waiting to attack, or Krej's advance guard? No cloud marred her view of the heavens. Crisp salt air warned of a frost. All was quiet. Too quiet.

An air of expectancy hovered around the castle, as if the very stones of the castle watched and waited.

Darville wouldn't wait much longer. He must attack soon. A siege was useless against a castle with three internal wells and a year's worth of food in storage.

Mikka searched the walls again with her cat senses. There must be a way she could help her husband and his troops invade this bastion!

Then she caught a new scent on the wind. Sweeter, spicier than the salt air of the Bay. Colder than the winds on the desert plateau in winter.

She looked up. Starlight winked at her, then blanked out. Huge gaps occurred in the vault of the heavens. Blank places in the shape of giant wings. The black outline seemed the model for the stained glass window of Simurgh in the Great Hall.

Chapter 32

Darville slid down the blue-tipped dragon wing. Down, down, deeper down through the void, until his feet touched solid stone. The chill of the void burned through to his bones. He shuddered as sensation returned to his limbs. The aching dizziness passed more quickly than he expected.

Then he opened his eyes. He was alone in the Great Hall of Castle Krej. Alone, and yet. . . . The inanimate sculptures seethed with leashed emotions. Air gushed out of his lungs, weakening his resolve. All of these beautiful wild creatures had been released by Shayla last spring. Now they were imprisoned again, as if they had never been set free at all.

Were his own actions just as fruitless?

He couldn't allow himself to think in those self-defeating lines. For Mikka, for himself, for Coronnan and the dragons, he had to put an end to Krej and his evil schemes—today.

Something powerful disturbed the sculptures. Something powerful indeed, if Darville, a mundane, could sense their disquiet.

The dragons, perhaps? Or more of Krej's evil spells?

Cautiously, he unsheathed his sword. The rattle of metal against the scabbard set his teeth on edge. With barely a whisper of further sound he slipped behind the infamous spotted saber cat. No guard responded to the sound.

Darville stretched every sense to his mundane limits, stretched them further than he thought possible. He couldn't hear or smell any live person near this room. In imitation of Mica, he extended his tongue and tasted the

air. All kinds of flavors lingered, but none of them human.
He shifted his posture to an attack preparation and settled
his mind to think.

If he were Krej and planning the upcoming battle, the
guards would be on the walls, watching for an invasion
force. Defenses inside the castle would be magical and
geared to the known talents of the Commune.

What should he look for? Something he, a mundane,
couldn't perceive.

Perhaps that was his advantage. Krej was expecting the
magicians to transport in—especially Jaylor, not Darville
himself. The traps would be set for magicians. Mundane
servants and family members would have to move about
the castle unhindered.

Dawn sent bright slivers of light through the massive window in the southeastern wall. The central hearth had burned
down to embers. How long had they been in the void? One
day, two, or longer yet?

Darville straightened from his crouch behind the bronze
sculpture. One foot poised to step out, he froze. An un-
worldly buzz vibrated around the hall. The soft light flared
and greened, then it crackled in dozens of tiny bolts of
lightning.

If he'd been discovered, he might as well face his opponent head on. Sword arm *en garde,* he emerged from his
hiding place to face the focus of the magic trap.

"Hold, friend!" A swarthy figure dressed in black trews
and magician blue vest solidified within the lightning bolts.
Arms over his head in surrender, his eyes were wide with
alarm.

"Zolltarn." Darville lowered his sword. "Did I come out
of the void like that?"

"I don't know. I didn't see you emerge." The last of the
buzzing faded, and with it the weird light.

"Where are the others?" Darville searched the room for
signs that the other magicians had followed him.

"I lost track of them as we slid through the final folds
of the void."

"Can you locate them?"

"I don't think I dare risk a probe. Krej has probably set
traps for any flare of magic."

"Won't our emergence trigger them?"

Zolltarn shrugged in a classic Rover gesture. "I'll deal with that when I find out." Slowly he turned, surveying the Great Hall. "I see Krej has repaired the damage Shayla wrought last spring." He stopped his surveillance at the window. The restless Rover stood absolutely still.

"And improved. I wonder where he got the money for that window?" Then Darville saw it, too. A dragon pictured in colored glass. Only not a dragon. Simurgh.

"It's not real glass." Zolltarn touched one of the lower panes. He had to stand on tiptoe and extend his arm full length to just reach that piece of clear red. "He conjured it out of . . . I'm not sure. I sense blood and I smell the volcanic sands of Hanassa."

"Blood? As in sacrifice?" Darville turned away from the dazzling window and confronted the altar. "This is new!"

"They've finally done it. They've gone over the edge." Zolltarn joined him beside the hideous sculpture. "Notice the face."

Darville looked closer, trying not to retch at the stench coming from the decaying cat body at the base of the sculpture. "It looks like Janataea."

"Not quite. Janataea has a straighter nose and higher cheek bones. This is her mother. Krej's mother, the leader of the coven. I wondered what they did with her body after the rites of passing."

"They entombed their mother in a stone sculpture!" Hot, thick bile aimed for his throat. He didn't want to believe this hideous effigy was the late Countess Janessa, preserved for eternity as an idol for pagan worship.

"Wait a minute, Krej is the only child Janessa bore. His half siblings were all boys."

"Before her marriage to your father's cousin, the witch Janessa had two illegitimate children. One was Janataea, the other might be *the* Simeon. He claims descent from Rossemeyer's exiled queen, Safflon, and her daughter. That has never been proven."

"This is getting complicated, Zolltran. How do you know so much?"

"A very long tale, worthy of a campfire and two jugs of wine. I will enlighten you later. Right now we need to find our companions. If they were going to rematerialize in this room, they'd be here by now."

"I'll go up. You go down. We'll meet back here."

"Stay hidden."

"Be wary of magic traps." Darville checked his stride toward the servants' stairs. "Zolltarn, is that sacrifice the body of the cat Rosse?"

"Only our enemies know for sure. Pray that it is not."

We are discovered. I smell the invasion of many bodies. Curse the transport spell. Jaylor should have given us the secret. He owes Krej, and therefore the coven, the secret for saving his sniveling wife.

If I had the secret, I would take my princess to Hanassa. We would be safe there.

In the end, all things come to Hanassa.

Darville may invade, he may even rescue Rosie. But he will never truly rule until he faces Hanassa.

The shadows in the upstairs corridor were friendly. Darville hugged their shelter as he crept around the perimeter of the massive central keep. Closed and locked doors met him at every turn. Where was everybody?

On the road between Coronnan City and here. All of Krej's courtiers and family were elsewhere. The rooms were locked to keep the few remaining servants from disturbing the rooms, or stealing from them. Perhaps the locks were the traps Krej had set for an invasion of magicians.

He should have encountered someone, though. A servant, or one of the Commune, possibly even Krej himself. No one. He was beginning to think he had landed in the wrong castle.

An image of a man appeared before him. The beast-headed man of his nightmares. Long shaggy coils of red fur, the same color as Krej's hair, covered the saber's face and head. Clad only in a loincloth, the torso and legs rippled with strength. No body hair marred the sleek white skin.

This was the disguise Krej had worn when he threw Darville's ensorcelled body over a cliff and left him to die. This was the form the evil magician took when he entered Shayla's cave and imprisoned the dragon in glass.

Darville raised his sword, ready to attack.

"Looking for someone, wolf-man?" Krej's voice sneered from behind him.

The beast image hovered and wavered. That's all it was, an image. Darville's enemy was behind him. He dropped the sword slightly as he turned to face his cousin wearing another beastly disguise. This time, Krej had chosen the head of a wild tusker, but instead of the dark, lead coloring of a true woods prowler, this image, too, had red fur.

"I seem to have found him, Krej." No emotion quavered Darville's voice. He presented a blank facade to the magician. But the anger and outrage that had been building within him for nearly a year burned white hot and deadly in his gut.

"Have you really?" Krej's oily voice emanated from the opposite end of this curving hallway. At the same time, the wavering image of Krej appeared beside the more solid forms of the two beasts. Then they all faded into transparency, and back into their respective images.

Darville blinked but did not remove his stare from the form he believed to be the source of the kingdom's troubles.

"We've done this before, Krej. Just you and me. There's no one else to observe us. No one else to interfere. Only this time, I intend to win."

"You never learn, Darville. I am destined to rule Coronnan. I control the armies and the Council. I even control most of the Commune. There is nothing you can do to prevent me from killing you."

"Wouldn't you rather turn me into a golden sculpture?" Darville edged to his right. The image on that side seemed to be a false one. Krej's vision might be blocked by the figure.

"You'll make a magnificent addition to my collection. Thank you for the idea!" all three images spat, raising their arms to throw a spell.

"How powerful will you be when your followers realize the extent of your perversions, Krej? My people won't dismiss the Stargods for the bloodthirsty Simurgh. I've already removed your puppets from the Commune. Marnak the Elder and two other lords are in custody. Your power base is breaking down."

"I haven't time to waste on debate with you." All three images turned so that they still faced Darville fully. The left-hand figure of the saber cat stretched its neck ever so slightly more than the tusker and Krej.

The tusker lowered its head, as if to charge and gore Darville.

Darville focused his attention on the saber cat, ignoring the threat of the other two images. "Maintaining the illusions of your alter egos must be a terrible drain on your magic. You also have to keep your armor up. I could have brought reinforcements with me. Then again, I could be alone. You have no way of knowing." The tusker and man image wobbled and faded.

Krej emerged from the illusion of the cat. His eyes glowed with renewed energy. Lightning bolts of red and green erupted from his fingers.

Darville ducked the blasts of fiery magic, keeping his sword up. One by one, the weapon caught the flames with sizzling intensity. Each one crackled and sped the length of the blade, only to hiss and melt as it hit the guard.

Krej glowered at Darville's defense. A sword appeared in his outstretched hand. The weapon barely twitched, then fully engaged Darville's blade.

The shock of contact numbed Darville to the shoulder. He fought to maintain his grip. Krej shouldn't have that much physical strength. The power and agility must be augmented by magic.

Feeling surged back down Darville's arm in hot pulses. "You're no swordsman, Krej." He lunged and attacked with vigor. He couldn't allow Krej the time to throw a new magic spell.

Darville had spent a lifetime fighting right-handed arms masters. His dominant left arm was supposed to be a disadvantage. He'd learned more than one trick to make sword play awkward for his partners. He aimed for Krej's weak backhand.

"This one's for Shayla." Their swords locked and slid to tangle at the hilts. Darville wrenched his blade free and attacked again, without waiting for a reaction.

"This one's for the spotted saber cat." Darville pressed his advantage. Krej retreated, step by step, until his back was pressed against one of the many locked doors.

"This one's for Mikka." As the blades clanged again, Darville knew with utmost certainty that the body of the dead cat in the Great Hall belonged to Rosse. His wife and her cat were joined in body and soul forever.

The door behind Krej began to vibrate with life of its own.

Mistake! Darville was suddenly aware of the new energy filling Krej. Something or someone in that room was feeding him power. The next assault would be magic.

"Never again, Krej. I won't be your victim again!" The white-hot anger burning in his gut surged upward and outward. The sword vibrated. Or was it his hand shaking? The metal glowed and hummed. "This one's for me, Darville, King of Coronnan!" Krej's blade flew through the air and embedded in the door jamb opposite him.

"Golden wolf, frozen in time. Golden wolf, forever mine," the magician sang. Balls of glowing magic in marbled green and red appeared in each palm. He thrust them forward.

Darville caught the magics with his sword and flung them back to their source. Dragon fire from the Coraurlia, in every color imaginable, surrounded the red and green, engulfed Krej, swallowing and neutralizing his magic.

Without thinking, Darville thrust his sword forward again. He needed to make certain no more souls would be the victim of Krej's possessive greed. More molten light flowed from the crown on his head through the charged metal.

"No! You can't. You are mundane. You can't kill me," Krej choked. He writhed and screamed, as if burning. Burning within and without. His limbs became rigid, his body shrank and changed. His red hair lightened and faded. A feral quality filled his widened pupils. He opened his mouth and growled.

The primitive sounds echoed along the stone corridor in a fierce howl of rage and anguish.

The hair on the back of Darville's neck and arms stood up in eerie primeval distrust.

A rusty-gray weasel emerged from beneath the pulsing magic in Darville's weapon. A weasel frozen in cheap tin, gilded with false gold.

Chapter 33

"**S**et me down, Gliiam," Jaylor commanded the juvenile dragon beneath him.

The equivalent of a draconian laugh rippled through the long body. Sunlight glistened and reflected off his translucent fur and green wing-veins.

"I am not one of you. Set me down," Jaylor commanded with the full authority of the Senior Magician.

The dragon nimbus broke through the void, into the air above Coronnan. For a moment, Jaylor thought the winged creatures were complying with his demands.

Gliiam took wing and swept out to sea. On the swirling air masses of a gathering storm he dove and climbed, turned circles in a tail length, and sported with the waves below.

Jaylor searched the nimbus for Shayla. All of the dragons within sight wore a color on their wing-veins and horn tips. No all color/no color female dragon was present to help him, understand his plight, or control the exuberance of the young male he rode.

(*You are one of us now. Look at yourself.*)

Forcing panic down, Jaylor looked, really looked at his hands, where he clutched the green spine ridges. His skin was nearly transparent. Further inspection of his body revealed a similar fading of muscle and bone.

(*You ventured into the void once too often. You belong to us now.*)

"I am needed in Coronnan. You must let me go back to my duties." How many trips had he made into the realm of the magic in the last two days? There was the transport from the clearing to Coronnan City. That shouldn't count.

Yaakke had performed that spell. But there had been the ritual star, transports across the city, and two seeking spells for the queen. All necessary. None could have been avoided. Well, maybe one of the transports across the city.

(The king has taken care of our enemy.) The image of Krej shrinking into one of his own macabre sculptures flashed before Jaylor's mind. *(You are no longer needed there.)*

"We must still deal with the woman, Janataea. She is the deadlier of the two."

(That is true. But her brother is our enemy, not the woman. She did not arrange the destruction of the nimbus.)

"She will destroy Coronnan. You will never be allowed to return. Shayla wants to return with her young. I can hear her plaintive call."

(Shayla is unable to return.)

Something was wrong in that statement. Dragons couldn't lie, yet the word "unable" hung in the air around them with many meanings. He dismissed that argument until he'd had time to think on it.

"My wife and my son need my protection."

(And if he is not your son?)

Regret jolted Jaylor's heart.

"That makes no difference. The child needs me to guide him through a difficult life. He is a magician born. Coronnan is suspicious of all magicians. Glendon will be suspect because of his grandfather's evil. I love him. I must guide and protect him, regardless of whose seed started his life."

The dragons hesitated.

"My son is innocent. His mother is good-hearted. They need me, lest they be forced to follow the ways of Krej and Janataea because the mundanes refuse to understand them," Jaylor pressed his argument. "Send me back. I love them dearly."

(There are things you must see first. You may not wish to return to the troubles of Coronnan afterward.)

"I will always return to Brevelan."

(We shall see.)

Gliiam headed west, up the Coronnan River to the be-sieged city of Sambol. Time slowed. The combatants moved through the sluggish current of hours passing at less than half their natural rate. And yet, the strict forward movement of time seemed distorted and distended. Jaylor didn't know if what he saw was happening now, in ages past, or in some distant time in the future.

For that matter, what did "now" mean?

Jaylor saw death, fire, rape, and pillage. The river ran red with the blood of natives and attackers, innocent citizen and professional soldier alike. His heart swelled with grief at the sights and sounds of desperate war.

A war guided by the man who sat his war steed at a distance and watched. A man who licked his lips in eager anticipation of more and more bloodshed.

The dragons and their vision zoomed in on the magnificent figure on the hill. Long, straight nose, high cheek bones, florid complexion beneath bright red hair. Krej's face stared back at them. Krej's face, with a square-cut beard in the fashion of SeLenicca. Instantly, Jaylor knew the man to be the infamous King Simeon, and Krej's half brother. A sorcerer in a land that had no magic to feed his natural talents.

Dragon wisdom fed him the complex family tree that branched into every royal family on the planet. Patterns formed in the matings. Every birth was part of a huge plan to control every known government—not just the three kingdoms on this continent.

Beside King Simeon sat his queen, Miranda, a petite teenager with trusting eyes and a quiet nature. She wasn't watching the battle. She saw only her consort.

"She's bewitched," Jaylor spoke to his escort. "No wonder she granted him ruling powers and the title of king over the objections of her advisers and guardians. I can break the enchantment, make her see what this war is doing to innocent people."

(She will not believe you. She wants only to be in love with a strong and handsome man.)

Gliiam turned in a wing-length and flew east again to Coronnan City. The wide and muddy river absorbed the gray of the skies, the fading brown of autumnal fields, and the life blood of the people who lived on its swollen banks. The first of the fall rains fell on brick-dry ground and ran into the river without nourishing the land. Huge chunks of cultivated fields succumbed to the river's relentless force. Villages in its path were swept away. Harvests were ruined. More lives were lost.

Jaylor swallowed grief. "Many will go hungry this winter. For the second winter in a row."

In the city, the lords gathered in the Council Chamber and argued without resolution.

(Look at the Council. Do you truly wish to spend the remainder of your days battling their endless arguments? They will never agree with you, or with each other.)

The temptation to exile himself from the capital was strong. "Coronnan is my home, the land of my nurturing, my family, and generations of ancestors. For those I love, past, present, and future, for the good of the kingdom, I must pierce their self-centered power games."

Across a narrow footbridge, in the University, an old man surrendered to pain and died. The exotic poisons, given him by the coven and by the enemies of Coronnan, faded with his aura so that no one might know their origin.

Brevelan and Yaakke cried. Jaylor closed his eyes in sorrow.

"For all of our arguments, I loved Old Baamin. He trusted me when no one else did. I owe him much and grieve his passing."

The dragons, one and all, dipped their heads in salute to Baamin.

(He will be one of us shortly. His life has been honorable and his destiny not yet finished. His life spirit, his intelligence and his wisdom have been rescued from his poisoned body. A new form has been granted him so that he may finish his work. We grant him the right to wear blue on his wing tips, in memory of his previous life as a blue-robed magician.)

"I'm certain he will be honored."

Jaylor watched as Brevelan began preparing Baamin's body for the funeral rites. Yaakke was too grief-stricken to be of much help. Gently, she urged him through the final task, forcing him to accept a death.

Beside them, Glendon slept in his cradle. Jaylor saw the golden edge to the infant's aura. Evidence of Darville's blood, or of his own distinctive personality and magic?

(Do you still wish to return to Coronnan, to a life of fruitless striving against single-minded humans? You can be free of mortal concerns. Fly with us on the wind, live from moment to moment, with no responsibilities.)

He was tempted by the life of peace in the clearing with

Brevelan, not by the offer of near-immortality with the dragons. Jaylor wanted to grow old with Brevelan at his side. He wanted to share her dragon-dream of a large loving family who passed honorable magic down through generation after generation.

"Shayla promised Brevelan a passel of red-haired children. Only her firstborn is to be blond. By right of Shayla's dragon-dream, I demand that you return me to my own plane of existence. I must finish the work that I have begun. With Brevelan and our son by my side, I can succeed in the tasks the dragons have set for me."

(You have been tested and found worthy. You shall share the guardianship of the nimbus with Brevelan.)

An awareness, deep inside his heart, of every dragon alive, as well as those who had died, spread through him. Jaylor bowed his head in awe of the responsibility the dragons passed to him.

(Send the troops where they are needed.) Gliiam dipped toward the massive city. An army of fierce mercenaries gathered on the banks of the Great Bay, south of the city. *(We distort time. It is now near sunset on the day of the kidnap.)*

Jaylor sought the general from Rossemeyer. With dragon aid, he sent the image of a royal messenger to him. The troops that were part of Rossemikka's dowry must rescue their princess. Forced marches. Arrive at Castle Krej in two days, or lose the princess and the treaty.

"Take me to my wife," Jaylor commanded his transport.

(The king and queen have need of a healer. We take Brevelan with us. What of the babe? He is too young to be left.)

"Bring Yaakke. But allow Brevelan to carry Glendon for now."

A blink of the eye and Brevelan was caught up in a swirl of dragon wings. She cradled a squalling, blanket-wrapped bundle in her arms. A surprised Yaakke clutched the spine of the back of a red-tipped beast.

"Will the babe be altered by exposure to the void?" Jaylor demanded an answer of his hosts.

(He has been one of us since the moment of his conception. We are not yet ready to claim him.)

The truth hit Jaylor then. That night, the night he had tested Tambootie and taken too much, he was drifting with the dragons, needing never to return to Coronnan or his body. Brevelan, fueled by her love, and Darville, guided by his friendship, had sought him in the void and given him reasons to continue with the life granted him. Glendon had been conceived in the void. The babe belonged to no one but the dragons.

Blood pounded through Jaylor's veins again. His body took on substance. "Your love brought me back from the realm of the dragons once more, Brevelan." He hugged her tightly to his chest for the remainder of the ride.

"A nice trick, that," Zolltarn greeted Darville from the safety of several yards' distance. "Not everyone can back-lash a spell. Are you sure you have no magic in your family?"

"Not that I know of." Darville shook his head free of the vision of the spell. The crown weighed heavily on his brow. The figure of Krej, transformed, still sat before him. He hadn't dreamed that awful moment. "Perhaps the Coraurlia?"

"Poetic justice." Zolltarn moved to touch the rotten gilt flaking from Krej's metallic fur. "We have still to deal with his sister. I found the others. They are clearing the magic traps as they move upward from the dungeons."

"Is Jaylor with them? I'd like him at my side when I confront Janataea."

Zolltarn shrugged. "He does not appear to be within the castle walls. You will have to settle for me as your companion."

Darville eyed the Rover cautiously. "I've known Jaylor many years. We work well as a team. This last battle may not allow time to communicate my requirements to you. You know that my trust is still reluctant."

"Whatever else I have done to you, or will do for my own ends, in this mission I am as committed as you." Zolltarn shrugged again. "Lead on, Your Grace."

"Through here." Darville shoved at the locked door behind Krej.

"Allow me." Zolltarn waved his hand over the lock. The door opened smoothly. A long stairway circled upward into the tower.

"Mikka is up here." Darville sensed his wife as strongly

as he had during the seeking spell. "She's in danger." He rushed for the first step.

"Caution, Your Grace." Zolltarn stayed his impulsive ascent. "I smell magic, Janataea's magic."

Mikka gripped the edge of the parapet as vertigo filled her head. The world below her swung in awkward arcs, right and left and back to the right.

Eyes closed, she forced herself to turn away from the dizzying spectacle. Thoughts of flinging herself to the ground played with her common sense. She had to get away from here and the fascinating temptation to experience flight and death.

"I knew you'd reveal your hiding place as soon as the need overtook you."

Mikka's eyes opened of their own volition. Janataea stood over the trapdoor, the only exit from this half-open turret.

"You'll come along with me, Rosie. We'll take care of the ache that burns within you." Janataea held out her hand.

The oily persuasion of the governess' voice sickened Mikka.

"Rosie is gone, Janataea. I'm Mikka."

"NEVER!" The older woman screeched. She looked frantically about her for evidence of a cat. "We killed the cat. Krej assured me it was Mica."

"You sacrificed an empty body. Rosie and I are joined. But I am dominant. I am in control of my mind and my body. You will never again manipulate me."

Defiance died as the witch waved her arms in a grasping circle. An oily green-black miasma of magic flowed from her gesture.

Mikka watched, speechless, paralyzed, as the web of witch-born hate surrounded and lifted her body to the edge of the parapet. Desperately, she reached for the stone ledge that marked the boundary between life and a death plunge. Her arms remained lifeless at her side.

Slowly, the familiar acid of Janataea's compulsion ate at Mikka's consciousness.

"My mind is my own," Mikka shouted her defiance.

Janataea lifted her arms over her head. Mikka's body glided up over the edge of stonework. Her head and arms remained almost within reach of the wall, while her immobile feet dangled over nothing.

"I-will-not-allow-you . . ." Mikka ground out between clenched teeth.

Abruptly her feet flew up over her head. Magic suspended her upside down. The world spun crazily below her. She saw figures gathering in the stone-paved courtyard below. Mikka closed her eyes and gulped back the nausea of fear and disorientation. Rosie's need to have her feet down and head up clamored for attention inside her.

"Let Rosie come to the surface, Princess. Hide yourself behind Rosie and I'll save you," Janataea laughed. "There is still time to obey me."

"Never."

A sickening lurch dropped Mikka several feet. Rosie howled in the back of her mind.

"Will you let Rosie out now, Mikka?"

"If you kill me, you kill Rosie as well. You won't have either of us to fulfill your horrid plans."

"I have another body for Rosie. I'll pull her free at the moment of your death."

Mikka gulped as she dropped again.

"Free my wife or die, Janataea!" Darville burst through the trapdoor, knocking the Coraurlia askew in his haste. His eyes riveted on the desperate figure of Mikka hanging upside-down over the edge of the tower. Only a slim thread of magic tethered her ankles to Janataea's fingertips. Even as he watched, the magic was fraying.

"Make me, you trivial mundane," Janataea taunted him. She bounced Mikka up and down, like a ball.

"Return Mikka to safety." This time Darville pressed his sword to Janataea's throat, punctuating his demand by pricking her skin.

"How . . . how did you get past my armor, the traps set by my brother?" she croaked in alarm.

"The Coraurlia negates spells that threaten me!" Darville didn't dare shift his eyes away from Janataea. He needed to assess her every move by the shift in her eyes.

Mikka dropped again. Only her feet showed above the lip of the wall. Darville jerked his head away from the witch. His desperate move dislodged the crown further.

"Krej can't save you. He is the victim of backlash," Zolltarn gloated from the head of the stairs.

"Traitor!" she hissed at the Rover. "You have betrayed the coven."

"No, Janataea," Darville interrupted. "You have betrayed everyone, including yourself." He pressed his sword point a little deeper. Blood trickled from the nick in the witch's neck.

"I demand revenge for my brother. I'll kill Rossemikka."

"Kill the witch, Darville. She must die," Mikka cried from her precarious position.

"Mikka, I can't let you die!" Tears threatened Darville's clear vision. Even clad in ugly boy's clothing, her hair flying in the unruly wind, and hanging upside down by a slender thread, Mikka was the most beautiful woman in the world. His heart ached at the thought of being separated from her for all eternity.

"You promised to kill her, even if it means my death. You can't allow her to survive," Mikka argued with more resolve than Darville had.

"Give me a reason to hold on to her a little longer," Janataea laughed with malicious glee.

Darville looked to Mikka for an answer. Indecision clouded his vision.

"Can't think of one?" Janataea's flicked her wrist.

Darville reared back to avoid the tiny dart of magic poison. The slipping crown crashed to the stone floor of the parapet as the dart sped past his ear.

The thread of magic holding Mikka dissolved.

"I love you, Darville!" Mikka's cry soared downward.

"I claim your life in forfeit for my wife!" Darville rammed his sword deep into Janataea's throat. Blood sprayed outward, coating his hand and arm. Magic permeated the life fluid; magic generated from decades of rituals. The Tambootie she had ingested continuously for weeks sought a new host, like a parasite.

Darville jerked back his hand. The forgotten Coraurlia in the corner couldn't protect him. Janataea's tainted blood burned him to the bone, traveling upward seeking his brain and his soul.

Chapter 34

Images of Mikka's life passed before her mind's eye in agonizing slow motion, while the treacherous teeth of rocky pinnacles rushed toward her with increasing speed. In less than an eye blink, she saw her happy youth with her doting parents. Her father's death and her mother's retreat into tears stabbed her once more. The years with Janataea, and the night of her treacherous transformation flashed through her memory too fast for regret.

Then there were the many moons of travel southward to Brevelan's clearing. Contentment. Darville, as a wolf. Darville, as a man. Jaylor transforming Darville back into a wolf, as he leaped from their hiding place to defend his father's honor.

"I don't want to die," she sobbed. "I want to live for Darville!"

Transformation, Rosie reminded her.

Cats can't fly.

But a kahmsin eagle can.

Mikka spread her arms in a desperate attempt to slow her increasing speed toward death. Sharp spires of rock jutting up from the sea reached for her hungrily. The waves pushed closer and closer, ready to swallow her broken body.

Her injured shoulders protested the movement. The wind generated by her passing pounded against her, resisted her. She fought to extend herself. Desperate to survive, she forced every hint of magic in her life to obey her will. She twisted on a tendril of warmer air. Her limbs moved more freely this time.

"I *will* live!"

Power surged through her. Feathers replaced her garments and hair. Her eyes slitted and focused. Sharp talons retracted. Wings caught the wind, mastered it, and guided her upward.

The kahmsin eagle of Rossemeyer flew, as free as a dragon. She pushed downward, once, with huge wings and sailed higher, higher yet. The soft mist of a low hanging cloud greeted her. Wings leveled, she glided on a current of moist air.

Through the veil of cloud she spied the land below. Eyes focused on tiny details, a rabbit in the grass, a sparrow in a tree, bay crawlers on a shallow strand at low tide. Hunger assailed her. Neither the rabbit, the sparrow, nor the crab would feed her. This was something different, something special and wonderful.

Need filled her heart. Her mate called to her. Her mate needed her. Kahmsin eagles mated for life. If one partner should die, the other never sought another.

She must land. One particular perch called to her. The man's pile of stone looked intriguing. She dropped into a dive, wings tucked back against her body. As the opening to the aerie came level, she spread her wings to stop her flight.

Caution kept her back. She drifted on the currents of air while inspecting the figures who shifted in rapid jerky movements. She should be suspicious, hold back. Yet she needed to be in there. This was her aerie, she knew that. Her mate was within, and he was in trouble. The sparkling circlet in the corner needed to be attached to her mate before the trouble would go away. She seemed to be the only one to notice its absence.

A neat back wing and extension of her talons brought her to the ledge.

"Mikka?" her mate called weakly. He lay on the stones, injured. One wing was burned clean of coverings. He'd never fly again.

"Is that you, Mikka?" His weak cry tugged at her emotions.

"Aieeek?" She hopped down beside his neck and nuzzled him with her beak. *Get better,* she thought. *I can't live without you.*

Her mate fell back, no longer able to stay awake. The pain was too great.

Mikka cried her distress, fanning her mate with her wings. A man approached, she shied away in fright.

"Don't let her fly away!"

Blackness surround her. A net. A totally dark net covered her. Harsh claws gathered her into the folds of the dreaded net.

"Mikka?" Darville called weakly. The merciful blackness retreated and pain roared through his body. More pain as someone shifted and carried him. He thought he screamed. Perhaps that was only a dream, as well. The pain receded and so did his mind.

Candlelight burned behind Darville's eyelids. He swam upward to a level of awareness that acknowledged the pain in his arm and shoulder, yet not so far up that the sharp burning mastered him.

Voices whispered around him. He heard bodies shuffling through a room. Something sweet burning in the grate tickled his nose and beckoned him to a higher level of wakefulness.

"I hate using the Tambootie as a remedy for pain."

Was that Brevelan's voice he heard?

" 'Twas the Tambootie in the woman's body that caused the burn. Like to like, a poultice of the Tambootie to draw the magic poison from his wounds." That had to be Zolltarn's arrogant presumption that only he had an answer.

"The only thing that filthy drug is good for is dragon food," Brevelan argued.

Darville sensed the petite woman hovering over the bed where he lay. She would be facing the Rover, hands on hips, feet anchored, daring him to interfere with her patient.

"A boiled preparation of the leaves, mixed with eel oil, garlic, and mashed tubers works wonders on burns."

" 'Twas the Tambootie that drove Janataea insane. I'll not use it. All I need is a little quiet and a chance to work my own kind of magic. I've stabilized him, but he needs another session to promote his own healing."

"Mikka?" Darville croaked. He didn't need drugs or

healing spells. He needed to know that the vision of his wife saving herself with a shape-change was true.

"Bring the bird in," Brevelan ordered.

"The dust and mites in her feathers will contaminate the burns!" Zolltarn seemed adamant in his desire to be in control.

"She won't remain a bird long. As soon as she sees that her mate lives, she'll return to her own form voluntarily."

"And if he dies from his wounds?"

"He needs a reason to live. Seeing his love safe will give him one."

Quiet prevailed a moment. Darville risked opening his eyes a slit. He had been set on a soft mattress in the master bedroom. The master wouldn't be needing it anymore. Lush curtains in maroon and green protected the bed on three sides. The hangings were drawn back on the side facing the huge fireplace. Logs, as thick as his thighs, burned brightly, throwing warmth throughout the room. The Coraurlia rested on a feather pillow beside him.

The door creaked open. Carpets and wall hangings muffled any footsteps. Jaylor poked his head into the opening of bed curtains, keeping his body hidden. "You're awake."

"Barely." Darville's head and body throbbed with renewed pain by the effort of that single word. The darkness began drifting over his mind again. He willed it aside.

"Ready for company?"

"Only if it's Mikka."

"Your wish is my command, Your Grace." Jaylor moved slowly and carefully into view. On his outstretched arm—an arm misshapen by layers and layers of wrapped quilts—perched the largest eagle Darville had ever seen.

"When you were a cat, Mikka, I had to pad my shoulders from your claws. My tailor will have a fit if he has to protect my arms from those talons." He tried to chuckle, but his entire left side hurt too much.

"Dreeek?" The bird cocked her head and opened her eyes wide in question.

Darville patted the wide bed on his uninjured side. "Come, Mikka," he coaxed.

The eagle hopped awkwardly from her perch on Jaylor's arm to the bright coverlet. "Dreeek?" she asked again.

"My beautiful Mikka. Come back to me." Moisture gathered at the back of his eyes, tears of pain and loneliness, and tears of tremendous hope. "Come back to me, Mikka." The tears spilled and fell freely.

"We've got to hurry," Brevelan interrupted. "The Council and their troops are less than an hour away. They'll condemn Mikka in this condition. They'll condemn all of us for trade in black magic."

Darville had never before seen her wring her hands in agitation.

He'd conquered his enemies, and still he must fear his own Council.

"Jerook!" Mikka squawked and flapped her tremendous wings.

"Out, Jaylor, Zolltarn. They need privacy for this." Brevelan shooed the men with more frantic gestures of her hands.

"I'm a magician, I can help." Jaylor protested.

"You're a man and she's embarrassed. Don't you remember Darville each time he came out of a transformation?" Mischief glinted in her eyes. "I always had the decency to turn my back on his very naked body."

"Oh," he mouthed. "Well, yes, of course. We'll be just outside." They retreated behind the bed curtains.

Darville thought them gone when Brevelan emerged long enough to throw Jaylor's cloak onto the bed. He closed his eyes for strength.

The mattress shifted. The rope supports groaned.

He opened his eyes to a blur of colors. Gold, silver, lead. Ruby, emerald, diamond. Soil, clay, and sand.

His senses reeled in confusion. But he had to watch. The eagle grew in length, thinned in mass, stretched, and shifted.

"Thank heavens for Brevelan's good sense." Mikka sat beside him at last, long legs dangling over the edge of the bed, her glorious hair draping her arms and torso. In one deft movement, she twitched the blue cape around her. "What would this world be like without women of common sense?" Mikka's throaty chuckle surrounded the bed enclosure with love and hope.

Darville couldn't answer. He filled his eyes with the vision of his beloved.

She looked at him and smiled. "And if I know Brevelan,

she'll give us a moment to say hello." She leaned over and brushed her lips across his.

He couldn't help wincing, even as he sought a deep contact.

"Does it hurt much?" She was immediately contrite.

"Less since you came back to me."

She kissed him again, lingering over his mouth.

"The dragons told me to look to my left and I'd find you. I looked to my sword arm." He moved his injured arm and groaned with the pain. "I couldn't find you with my strength. I had to look to my heart. You are my heart, Mikka. And now you must be my strength, as well. This wound may be mortal."

"Not if I have anything to say about it." Brevelan bustled back into the room. Briskly, she swept aside the curtains and dumped an array of pots and bandages on the mattress beside Darville.

"You have approximately ten minutes to decide how you'll deal with your Council, King Darville." Jaylor was right behind his wife, the members of the Commune directly behind him. "While you've been unconscious, Krej's troops put up some resistance to the mercenaries from Rossemeyer. Andrall and a contrite Jonnias lead your thousand cavalry. With no true leader to push and guide the battle, most of Krej's men refused to face the combined armies."

"Suggestions?" Darville forced his awareness to the men in the room. Brevelan's ministrations were gentle, yet the extremity of his injury was pushing him toward unconsciousness again.

"Your queen has exhibited a rare and powerful magic talent. Your own feats this day defy mundane explanation. In their present mood, the Council may decide to enforce their new law against magicians and depose you." Zolltarn hooked his thumbs in his belt.

"Darville's backlash of Krej's spell may be explained by the action of the Coraurlia." Jaylor paced before the hearth.

"Has he worn the crown long enough to produce that violent a reaction?" Slippy asked from the doorway.

"I saw the backlash. I wasn't in a position to probe the source." Zolltarn shrugged his characteristic gesture. "The queen's talent probably sprang out of dormancy in the face of grave danger. That talent must now be dealt with or it will go wild—like Yaakke's"

"By Council decree, neither of you may rule." Slippy elbowed his way to the front of the crowd.

"We have decided to keep knowledge of your talents secret." Jaylor assumed command of the room again. "But we must have your word of honor—from both of you—that neither of you will throw a single spell until the Commune is reinstated."

"And when will that be?"

"When we get the dragons back."

Chapter 35

Yaakke viewed the cleared Great Hall of Castle Krej with awe. The members of the Commune had been busy. All of Krej's treasures were free. All except the former lord of the castle and the hideous harpy presiding over the sacrificial hearth. What would Jaylor do with them? Consign them to the sea, as Janataea's body had been—without any rites of passing?

The twelve magicians present stood around the two monstrosities, scratching their heads and arguing quietly among themselves.

"You sent for me, Jay . . . Master Jaylor?" Yaakke had to remember that his former friend was now Senior Magician of the entire Commune.

"Yes, Apprentice Yaakke, we did."

That sounded ominous. No one used "Apprentice" as a title, unless something of dire importance was about to happen. From the frowns that greeted him, Yaakke guessed the worst.

"We must discuss the matter of your abandonment of a superior in mid-spell." The magicians ringed themselves in a half-circle beneath the huge window. They held their staffs upright, extensions of themselves, gnarled symbols of their authority. Colored light sprinkled down upon them from the awesome window, turning their faces into masks of ancient deities—most of them malevolent.

Heat flushed Yaakke's face. His feet grew cold, and his hands started to shake. They were going to throw him out. He knew it. He'd be stripped of his powers and cast away, like the piece of rubbish he knew himself to be. His brief flirtation with magic was a dream the likes of him didn't deserve. He clutched his own nearly straight staff across his chest defensively.

"We could dismiss you from the University, Yaakke," Jaylor said, not unkindly. "You abandoned me in the void. You were a pivotal part of that spell. When you pulled away so abruptly, I could have died."

The dragons tried to keep me, Jaylor's thoughts added to Yaakke's mind. "You also endangered the life of our queen. We almost didn't find her in time."

"I'm sorry," Yaakke whispered. And he was truly sorry. He liked Jaylor, respected him, sort of. And the queen? Well if Jaylor couldn't find her, then Yaakke certainly never would have.

"And well you should be sorry, boy!" the oldest of them shook his staff at Yaakke. The old geezer was so ancient he'd retired to a monastery years before Baamin was elected Senior.

"It's just that Lord Baamin was dying and I thought I could help him," Yaakke defended himself. "I loved him." His words trailed off as grief choked him once more.

"We understand that." Jaylor cut off the old man's attempt to burst back into the conversation with a brief gesture of his own staff. "So you will not be dismissed."

Yaakke looked up with hope that died at the sight of the grim expressions of all assembled.

"There is no longer a University to dismiss you from," Zolltarn explained.

"No University? But there has always been a University. The kingdom depends upon it." That was the most amazing thought of all. He couldn't conceive of a world without the University. The massive stone buildings were the only home he had ever known, ever dreamed of knowing. "How will we fight the war? Who will advise the king and the lords?"

"That is an unknown we must all discover." Jaylor shook his head in dismay.

"Can't we just move it?" Yaakke looked expectantly to each of the masters.

"We have already begun to empty the University of all contents and remove ourselves to a new location, outside the capital." Slippy looked a little disgruntled at having to explain things to this boy. "The Council has exiled us from the government. We, in turn, will withdraw from the lords. Magicians will move out of palace, manor, and castle into the villages. They will be available to the people as healers and teachers. But we have forbidden them to provide any service—even a simple message relay—to a lord without the express permission of the Commune, as a whole."

"Wow!" Yaakke couldn't say anything else. Those were drastic measures. The Council probably didn't realize how much they depended upon magicians. The lords weren't going to be happy at losing one of their greatest privileges.

"As part of the new University policy, membership in the Commune, henceforth, will be secret. The Council knows about us." Jaylor pointed to the group, as a whole. "But new masters and students will be as unknown as our new location."

"What about the war, sir? We can't just abandon the army. Simeon's fighting with magic," Yaakke protested. Then he blushed in realization of his audacity in questioning these powerful masters.

"As soon as you show them how, four magicians will transport to the front. We believe King Simeon to be the only sorcerer at our western border. Four University trained magicians should be enough to counter any magical attacks he can launch."

"The Simeon is pulling energy from somewhere. It's got to be mighty powerful to work in SeLenicca. We shouldn't underestimate him, Jaylor." Zolltarn looked worried. "Are you sure four are enough?"

"To start. Simeon doesn't know the transport spell. We can send reinforcements before he can launch any attack our members can't handle." Jaylor looked more worried than he sounded. He and Zolltarn continued to stare at each other in a contest of wills. Zolltarn wanted to direct the defense of the kingdom. Jaylor had the authority.

"The king, sirs, and the queen, too? They've both got magic that the Council doesn't know about. Will they be rejected as rulers because of their magic?" Yaakke's curiosity was up and roaring.

"How I handle that secret will remain secret." Jaylor glared at him.

"What about me, sir?" Yaakke screwed up his courage to ask. He'd been summoned for a reason. Punishment?

Promotion? Or just a lot of work transporting people and things hither, thither, and yon?

"You have the greatest challenge of all, boy. Don't take it lightly." The oldest magician advanced on Yaakke as if he meant to strike at him with his staff.

Yaakke couldn't back away. But he did wince at the magician's use of his childhood appellation.

"I have a name now, sir," he challenged. "I was 'boy' when I was a nameless kitchen drudge with no magic and fewer brains. I'm an apprentice magician who can read and write and throw spells with the best of you. I've rights now, and a name is one of them."

"What? Oh, well, yes, of course you do. But you're still a boy." The old man chewed his lip. "You're all boys compared to me." He swung his staff to include the entire assemblage.

"My task, Lord Jaylor?" Yaakke's curiosity burned.

"Your quest, Yaakke, is to remain at my side, protect me if necessary, and learn all you can. When *I* decide you are ready, I will send you to find Shayla," Jaylor said with a tinge of envy in his voice. "When she is found, you will return to the Commune so that we, as a whole, can bring her back."

"A *quest,* sir?" Yaakke's voice cracked into an annoying and juvenile squeak. "A master's quest?"

The magicians broke out into a squabble. "No!"

"Yes!"

"He's too young."

"He's had no formal training."

"We'll see how you progress with your training and how well you behave." Jaylor ended the argument.

The huge courtyard within the palace grounds was filled to overflowing with rowdy lords and commoners alike. Mikka peered out at the crowd awaiting the coronation of their new king and his bride.

"Don't be intimidated by them, Mikka." Darville touched her arm with reassurance.

"They're exciting. I haven't seen anything this joyful since . . . since before Papa died." Carefully, she smoothed the clean lines of her golden gown. This regal outfit was cut more modestly than her spectacular wedding gown, but still showed more of her bosom than was considered proper in this conservative society. Oh, well, they'd reach a fashion compromise eventually.

"Is Rosie shying away from the noise?" Darville seemed overly concerned about her. She rested her hand on his arm lightly. He winced at the contact. The burns from Janataea's blood were healing slowly. There was only so much a healer could do for him—even a magician healer.

"Sorry, darling." She lifted her hand from his sleeve. His free hand covered hers and put it back on his arm, where it belonged.

"How's Rosie doing?" He repeated his question with genuine concern.

"Very well." She grinned.

"Will she jump out and repudiate me in mid-ceremony?" A smile tugged at the corners of his mouth.

"Meow?" Rossemikka ran a long fingernail gently along the line of the fading marks of a previous scratch on his cheek. "Does that answer your question, my love?"

Darville shifted just enough to kiss her lips long and lingering.

"We'd best get this show started," he breathed as they came up for air. "Did you see Jaylor and Brevelan in the crowd? They promised to be here."

"I didn't see them. I don't expect to. With the current mood against magic in the capital, they can't just transport in or announce their presence to one and all."

"I guess not." Darville looked disappointed. "But they are my best friends."

"Mine, too. They'll be here. We just haven't found them yet."

A blast of trumpets announced the beginning of the procession. Acolytes swinging incense burners led the way, followed by green-clad sisters of the stars singing hymns in six-part harmony. Priests in scarlet robes came next, intoning ritual prayers. Then followed the lords. Andrall led the way, carrying the Coraurlia on a golden silk pillow.

At the moment the dragon crown emerged into the open courtyard, the high overcast broke apart and a shaft of sunlight arrowed into the gleaming glass. Rainbows arced from the symbol of royal authority. Awed silence rang through the crowd.

"Dragon weather!" someone, who sounded a great deal like Jaylor, announced with awe. Murmurs and shouts of approval rippled through the crowd. This was a good omen.

"I believe that is our signal to follow." Darville gestured, then he and Mikka stepped out to greet their people.

The sun burst forth in sparkling autumnal glory. Everyone looked up. A speck in the distant sky grew and flew closer. No one moved.

The speck took on an outline, indistinct but huge. Mouths gaped open as the creature flew closer. Light shimmered around the winged form, teasing the eye, drawing vision out and around.

"A dragon!" The priests shouted with glee.

"A blue-tipped male dragon," Darville added.

The huge creature hovered over the courtyard, almost visible. It gave the impression of searching the crowd.

"Grrower!" it trumpeted with joy.

Sunlight touched the dragon's wings and arced downward. Rainbows of color filled the Coraurlia with life. Lord Andrall turned within the circle of prismatic light to face his king. His face glowed with wonder.

The dragon shifted. Rainbows followed his wing movement and bathed Darville and Mikka in magnificent blessing.

Epilogue

*T*he coven has failed in its mission. Our two strongest members have been stolen from us. The next candidate to be the focus has betrayed and deserted us.

But we are not broken. The Council has begun the campaign to outlaw all magic in Coronnan. As the mundanes rejoice with their maimed king and trollop of a queen, witches and magicians flock to the coven. They will work with us against the Council and our enemies in the Commune.

The coronation is but a mockery. The ceremony will never be completed. And while all of Coronnan turns its attention to the gaudy display of jewels and fashion, the coven will implement a scheme destined to restore the true balance of power.

THE
LONELIEST
MAGICIAN

Epilogue

This book is dedicated to the members
of the Portland Lace Society,
active and retired

Acknowledgments

I wish to thank the members of **The International Old Lacers** for helping me research this book over the last thirteen years, even when I was having too much fun to call it research.
Thanks also go to my editor, Sheila Gilbert, and her staff of miracle workers for turning my rambling prose into real books.
Most of all I need to thank my agent, Carol McCleary, for believing in me before anyone else did.

Prologue

*L*ord Krej and his sister Janataea are lost to the coven. Zolltarn, king of the Rovers, betrayed them both and deserted our ranks. No other has enough power to become the focus of our magic rituals. Our numbers are depleted; a miserable six when we need nine, and I am but half-trained. The Council of Provinces and their puppet king have triumphed.

But only for the moment. I am making plans for when we are a full nine once more. Then the Twelve will die for what they have done to us.

I have not the power or knowledge to break the reflected magic that transformed Krej into a tin weasel with flaking gilt paint. No honor for him, tricked by Darville and caught in the spell's backlash. If only our Lady Janessa could be revived. She would know how to release her son. But she died and was honored by being transformed into an idol at the moment of death. I sense that Lord Krej still lives within his statue prison. His life-spirit fades little by little.

I will have revenge. Before Darville is crowned, when all eyes are on the gaudy display of the coronation festival, my agents will kill the self-righteous king and his trollop of a queen.

The great winged god Simurgh will demand blood for the power needed to carry through with the plan. A mere slave will do for the initial spells. When all is done, I will need a triple sacrifice for the return of Krej. Yes! I sense the balances moving into place as I plan.

Jaylor is boon companion to Darville. His wife, Brevelan, is bastard daughter of Krej. And their babe is an innocent. They should die together.

Chapter 1

Apprentice Magician Yaakke downed the last of his ale, purchased with illusory coins. Sullenly, he elbowed his way out of the makeshift tavern and into the rowdy coronation crowd. He'd lingered too long.

Time never flowed at the speed he wanted it to, and now he was late. One more infraction of the rules to prevent his promotion to journeyman.

A crow scolded him from atop his perch on the tavern tent's ridgepole with raucous cries. Guilt and shame burned Yaakke's ears at the reminder of his tardiness.

He'd idled the hours with forbidden eavesdropping on the thoughts of drunken revelers. He liked to imagine these simple folk were his family, since he had none. Every farmer or merchant could be his father come to visit him during the week-long coronation festival. . . .

Now he was late.

"Disgusting filth!" A lean man of middle height spat a bite of meat roll into the gutter. His bright scarlet tunic with gold braid proclaimed him a senior member of the Guild of Bay Pilots. The wily boatmen were an integral part of Coronnan's defense. No one else could guide shipping through the constantly changing channels in the mudflats of the Great Bay. Invading navies had ceased trying to negotiate the mudflats centuries ago.

"That's good meat and pasty. How dare you insult my wares!" A young woman with blond curls escaping her kerchief glared at her customer. She planted work-worn hands on narrow hips, presenting a picture of outraged determination. "You took a bite, now pay up."

The noisy black crow swooped down from the ridgepole

of the tavern pavilion and devoured the discarded food in one gulp. Not a crow, a jackdaw. As it lifted its head and croaked in triumph, Yaakke noted the white tufts of feathers above the bird's eyes, much like the bushy eyebrows of an old man. The bird rotated its eyes before launching itself back to its high perch. The movement caused the white tufts to waggle, just the way Old Baamin's eyebrows had whenever he admonished his apprentice.

Grief threatened to choke Yaakke. The irritable old man would never again correct him for an error in magic or in manners.

The argument between the girl and the Bay Pilot drew Yaakke's attention back to the present. His telepathic senses amplified the anger, distrust, and fear that surrounded this typical market argument. He considered turning his back and slipping into the throng of revelers, unseen, unknown.

"Uncooked pig offal. I'll not pay to be poisoned." The pilot's hand reached for the long boat hook that dangled from his belt.

Violence spilled from the man's aura, infecting other members of the crowd. Warning prickled the length of Yaakke's spine. He searched the crowd for help, anyone with a hint of authority to intervene. A ring of avid observers formed around the arguing couple.

"Give the arrogant bastard what for, Margit!" one of the watchers yelled.

"Don't let the chit cheat you, Guildsman!" another voice answered from the other side of the crow. Violence simmered around them, inviting their participation with more than words.

The pilot looked over his shoulder at the crowd. Uncertainty flickered in his eyes and in his aura. Then the mask of arrogance, so typical of his kind, dropped back into place. He waved the boat hook in front of Margit. The girl didn't retreat.

Yaakke silently applauded Margit's courage. He'd had his meals stolen from him by bullies often enough to understand the girl's need to stop this one thief before another took advantage of her weakness.

"You'll pay or I'll have the guard on you!" Margit's eyes

grew large at the sight of the Guildsman's sharp boat hook. Her aura pulsed red. Anger or fear?

Power?

No. Her eyes were too clear and innocent for her to possess the sudden surge of magic Yaakke sensed in the air.

"What guard?" the boatman snorted. "Only my Guild keeps Coronnan safe!"

More jeers from the crowd, for and against the Guildsman.

Yaakke decided he'd better step in before a riot started. If he prevented a dangerous disturbance at the king's long awaited coronation, maybe the Commune would consider him reliable again. He also needed to track down that sudden surge of magic he'd felt. Maybe Jaylor would give him his journeyman's quest after all.

Yaakke sought the pilot's name within his mind. The information hid from a light probe. Yaakke concentrated harder. *Paetor.* Unusual. The syllables grated on his tongue like a foreign language. The Guild tended to be separate from the rest of Coronnan, inbred to the point of alienness. But the name was strange even for the Guild. Curiosity and admiration of Margit's courage propelled Yaakke forward.

He threw an illegal spell, a small delusion. The surge of magic didn't return to combat him. Reflection from the Guildsman's eyes showed the short apprentice as an army officer twice the man's height and double his breadth of shoulder.

"You'll pay for the pasty, or I'll lay you out as fish food," Yaakke hissed at Paetor, grabbing the haft of the boat hook with one hand. His little boot knife suddenly appeared in his other hand looking very much like a foot-long dagger tickling the pilot's throat.

Paetor's jaw opened, then shut.

The crowd edged backward, suddenly silent.

"She gave me refuse from the gutter to eat!" Paetor fingered his purse but didn't open it. Some of the arrogance slid out of his posture. His eyes darted to the thinning crowd.

"That's good sausage!" Margit protested. "If you don't like it, fine. But you ate it, now pay for it."

An angry tirade from Paetor's mind filtered through to Yaakke's mental ears, in a very foreign language. This was no Bay Pilot with a few strange ways, but a foreign smuggler up to no good. The strange source of magic must come from him.

Jaylor! Yaakke sent a telepathic plea to his new master, the Senior Magician. *We've got trouble.*

No answer. Jaylor's thoughts were normally easy to find and separate from a crowd. Something must be terribly wrong in the Grand Court, where the coronation was about to take place, if Jaylor didn't answer a message of trouble.

The smuggler wrenched himself free. He took off at a run over the bridge to the next city island. Yaakke followed him. He discarded his spell of delusion and became, once more, the undersized, nameless drudge from the University kitchens he had been until last spring. No one took much note of his running pursuit of the smuggler except to protest his jabbing elbows as he cleared a passage.

He lost sight of the smuggler in the crowds of dancing and singing citizens who thronged along the processional route. More tavern pavilions sprang up along the way, offering a dozen places for the man to hide.

Think! Yaakke admonished himself. *Think like a smuggler.* The docks were too obvious. Where else would a fleeing foreigner head?

Yaakke calmed his panic-driven heart rate and focused his psychic powers on one specific accent. The physical and telepathic din from the crowds dropped to a murmur. Two men thought with that peculiar clicking rhythm to their mental voices. Yaakke tuned in to them. One was at a distance, probably the other side of the capital. One was just ahead.

Yaakke fine-tuned his listening and heard surface thoughts in a foreign language. He probed deeper, seeking meaning in images rather than words. He encountered a little resistance, then the man's thoughts became clear.

I've got to get to the boat and close the cargo hatches, the accented mental voice hummed anxiously. *Can't let the guard find those* s'murghing *Tambootie seedlings before the assassination.*

What? Yaakke sought the source of that desperate thought. The smuggler had to be stopped. He had to discover who was going to be killed and when.

But the significance of the Tambootie bothered him more. If Coronnite Tambooties grew anywhere else, the dragons would seek it, and they'd never be enticed back to their homeland. Magic and magicians would be illegal in Coronnan forever without the dragons. The border to keep out King Simeon's invading armies would remain collapsed without dragons and dragon magic. Yaakke listened for the elusive mental voice again.

Nothing. Almost as if the smuggler and his thoughts had been swallowed whole by the void. Further probes from Yaakke's mind met a wall of resistance. Some kind of internal armor.

He sniffed the magic that surrounded the foreigner's mind as he edged his physical body closer. The magic didn't come from within the smuggler. Only a powerful and well-trained magician could impose that kind of subtle protection on another man. And this magic didn't smell like anyone in the Commune.

Carefully, Yaakke probed the "nothing" with a finely honed magic dart. In his mind's eye he saw the witch bolt of questing magic pierce the armor. The invisible arrow came up against an undulating wall of power and slid around it. Glaring white light filled the dart with explosive menace as it rounded the curve of armor and headed straight back toward its sender at double speed and intensity.

Yaakke recoiled in horror. If the probe pierced his mind, then the hidden magician who had placed the layers of armor on Paetor would know everything about Yaakke, about the Commune's secrets and the disguises used by the Master Magicians today.

Yaakke needed his staff to counteract the probe. If he opened his magic senses to keep track of the questing spell, his own power would attract it like a magnet. The staff was inert, unless charged by Yaakke, and could absorb the magic safely. But the staff was hidden, along with his pack, back at the inn. If he'd carried it today, he would have been marked as a magician and hustled off to gaol hours ago.

On the edge of panic, he ducked the speeding probe and ran, scattering diverting delusions in this wake. The dart of magic swung around to Yaakke's new direction, seeking the mind that had launched it.

Rejiia de Draconis peered at the coronation spectacle in the Grand Courtyard from behind a magical mask. Resentment of her cousin, the new king, colored her perceptions with black auras. Counting slowly, she controlled her breathing. "I have to see things clearly if I am to succeed," she whispered to herself.

Calm spread through her body. Knotted muscles in her back and shoulders relaxed a little.

The royal steward flung open the massive doors of the King's Gate, signaling the beginning of the coronation ceremony and a major interruption of Rejiia's plans to become queen.

A hush fell over the crowd. Gold- and green-clad musicians sounded the fanfare. Rejiia winced at the harsh sound.

"Do you think the king will actually show his face?" she whispered into the silence that followed the trumpet blast.

"Sshh," a woman held one finger to her pursed lips, signaling silence to her husband.

Rejiia smiled. The thrown-voice spell worked! "I heard Darville's face was horribly disfigured in his battle with the magicians," she commented louder, meaning for all to hear. King Darville's face hadn't been touched in the fateful battle with her father and aunt, but his sword arm was badly burned.

With mischievous glee she fed the mundane superstition against the outlawed magicians of the Commune. Her purposes were served well if the crowd believed all evil sprang from the Commune—especially the coming assassination.

Acolytes in white, swinging censers of burning incense, began the procession from the palace around the dais in the center of the courtyard. A choir of green-robed sisters of the stars followed next, bearing lighted candles. Their songs invoked blessings from the Stargods in six-part harmony.

Behind the women marched a bevy of red-robed priests, silently carrying the books of wisdom left by the Stargods. All three groups circled the cloth-of-gold-draped dais.

The crowd followed the clerics with their eyes. Rejiia was totally forgotten and ignored. Good. She could continue her assignment undisturbed. She faded backward, toward the protection of a guardroom.

The priests took up positions around the dais. The sisters and the acolytes joined them, alternating silence, song, and incense.

A ritual the Stargods stole from Simurgh. Rejiia felt the blood drain from her face as she realized the significance of the processional. Nine priests, nine sisters, and nine acolytes marched sun-wise around a place of reverence. *Widdershins, you fools!* she screamed within her mind *'Tis a ritual designed to raise power and inspire awe. Who knows what demons you will spawn by performing the ritual incorrectly?*

The incense thickened into a purple haze. Too sweet and cloying. Witchbane. Rejiia retreated farther from the dais. She had too much to do today to fall victim to her own plot. If any magicians hid behind delusions in the courtyard, the witchbane would cause their minds to wander aimlessly while their vision bounced and circled. If they tried to use magic to bring their senses back to order and restore their disguises, they would discover all power had deserted them, including their disguises. The mundanes wouldn't know anything was amiss.

Lord Andrall, most loyal to the crown of all the Twelve Lords of the Council of Provinces and a royal relative by marriage, emerged from the palace. He carried the Coraurlia, the splendid glass crown shaped into the head of a dragon. The crown that should have come to Rejiia. Costly rubies, emeralds, and star sapphires adorned the crown in gaudy splendor, none more precious than the rare glass of the crown itself.

Lord Krej almost had the Coraurlia while he was regent. But Jaylor and the Commune had interfered. She wanted the crown, the title, and royal authority so much her teeth ached. She unclenched her jaw and concentrated on her tasks.

"Aaah!" the assembly gasped. Many of them had never seen the dragon crown before.

But I have seen the crown before. I know firsthand the magic power embedded into the glass. The Coraurlia protected King Darville in his battle against my father. By rights it should be mine. 'Twill look hideous against Darville's golden hair and eyes. My raven hair and bay-blue eyes will enhance the glory of the Coraurlia when it is finally mine.

I will be avenged for Janataea's death and Krej's humiliating imprisonment. Darville has to have the crown on his head to invoke the protection. He won't live that long.

Chapter 2

Yaakke gasped for breath, pressing his back against the outside walls of the Grand Court. He had nowhere else to run. His lungs ached with each breath. Darkness pressed at the sides of his vision. How could he hope to escape his own probe turned malevolent?

He blanked his mind, as if preparing himself for a trance. The all-but-invisible magic dart paused, seeking. It avoided the mundane minds of the dancers as they leaped and spun with wild abandon. Musicians increased the tempo of flute and drum. The probe sped forward as if enticed by the whirling music.

Yaakke dove into yet another party of celebrants, letting their overt thoughts and conversations mask his mind.

"Can you imagine the audacity of the healer?" a fat ore broker protested to his clinging companion. "He refused to use magic to banish the pox. Insisted that only herbs were legal now!"

The companion-for-hire nodded and made sympathetic noises. She arched her back, displaying more of her bosom.

The ore merchant wandered off with his companion, leaving Yaakke alone in the crowd. The magic probe slid around and through the musicians straight for Yaakke's eyes. Nothing stood between the apprentice and the witch bolt.

A dark shadow flitted across Yaakke's vision. For a moment he thought the probe had found him. Then, miraculously, a large black bird dove between him and the glittering dart of magic.

The probe couldn't divert its path around the bird and plowed directly into the shining black breast feathers.

"Braaaawk!" the bird screamed. A cloud of tiny feathers burst from his breast. His flight faltered and the bird dropped heavily and clumsily to the ground at Yaakke's feet. The splash of white head feathers over its eyes rose and fell several times. Angrily the jackdaw stabbed at the wound with its beak.

"Yuaaawk!" The bird spat more feathers from its clacking bill in disgust as it danced in a circle. The bird's body jerked forward with each step in a rhythm peculiar to his kind.

Yaakke breathed a sigh of relief. The probe had found a victim. Wouldn't the armored magician be surprised when the only information revealed was a litany of abuse from a bird! A raw wound in the jackdaw's breast marred the smooth velvet of his coloring and reminded Yaakke of the sacrifice the bird made for him. What would happen to it now? Did a jackdaw have enough of a mind to be stripped by the probe?

"Thanks, bird." Yaakke saluted the cranky creature still preening and pulling damaged feathers from its breast.

"Corby, Corby, Corby." The bird cocked its head and repeated the sounds as if speaking directly to Yaakke. Its beady black eye probed him almost as deeply as the witch bolt would have.

"All right. Corby you are. I owe you one, Corby." Yaakke turned to push his way through the crowd toward the Grand Court entrance—where he should have met Jaylor over an hour ago.

"Owe me one. Owe me one. Owe me one," Corby repeated.

Yaakke paused a moment at the shift of the pronoun. The bird was just mimicking sounds. Wasn't it? Whoever heard of a jackdaw smart enough to speak? Unless the probe had given the bird the intelligence it would have stripped from Yaakke. He twisted his neck to look at Corby one more time. The white tufts above his eyes waggled again. The resemblance to Lord Baamin was so strong in that instant, he almost saw his dead master peering out of the black, beady bird eyes.

"No. You aren't Old Baamin. You're just a bird."

"Corby. Corby. Corby," the bird repeated as it flapped its wide wings and launched itself into the sky.

Yaakke dismissed the bird with a shake of his head.

Jaylor needed to know about the smuggler and the foreign magician running free in the capital, not about weird birds. Right away. Yaakke sent another message to Jaylor. Still no answer.

At the entrance to the Grand Court, Yaakke dropped to his hands and knees in the middle of the crush of people. He found paths between legs. He avoided trouncing feet with the skills he'd learned as a child while avoiding bullies and thieves. He dared not throw a spell of invisibility to let him pass through the tight crowd. One jostling elbow would rip right through the spell and get him into more trouble.

Already today he'd passed magic coins at the tavern, revealed his magic to an alien magician, and lost all trace of the smuggler. He really needed to avoid any other problems.

No one noticed his natural thin and ragged urchin body as he crawled between the legs of a cloth merchant and under the crossed pikes of the guards. All attention seemed directed toward the center of the courtyard where King Darville and Queen Rossemikka moved in stately procession toward the dais.

"But I provided the queen's gown. I have a right to view the coronation," the cloth merchant above Yaakke argued with the guard.

"You'll have to wait for the procession across the city bridges, sir," the guard repeated the same phrase he'd probably been saying all morning. "One more person in there and the whole court will sink back into the river."

Breathless and sweating, despite the autumn nip in the air, Yaakke crawled through the crowd to the wall of the court where it hung out over the River Coronnan. He tried to stand up, but couldn't force himself through the mass of legs and brocade robes, velvet slippers and leather boots.

"May you all wallow in dragon dung," he grunted as he pushed his back against the wall and inched upward. Stone and mortar scraped his skin through his simple homespun shirt. He ignored the burning scratches until he was fully upright, staring straight into the bay-blue eyes of a tall, black-haired girl with beautifully clear, pale skin. His heart almost stopped beating as he gasped at her beauty. Long black lashes framed her big eyes. She lifted a hand to sweep a stray lock of hair back behind her ear. Graceful. Elegant. She was taller than he by half a head or more and seemed to be about his own age. But those eyes spoke of knowledge and pain, and were old beyond her years.

Something about the set of her jaw and the penetrating look she gave him was familiar. Brevelan's eyes. Another of Lord Krej's get. The deposed regent had scattered his seed as indiscriminately as his magic. Which of his many daughters was she? Before he could remember, she turned and dissolved into the crowd. None of her thoughts were open to his telepathy. She didn't seem to be armored, just elusive. He watched the spot where she had disappeared into the crowd, hoping to catch another glimpse of her.

"I don't have time for this," he muttered.

Yaakke searched the crowd for Jaylor and Brevelan. All he saw was satin and brocade and jewels, fortunes in jewels. Wealth and prestige were the only things that counted in the Grand Court today. His everyday country trews and tunic, as well as his youthful face and small stature would mark him as an outsider and unworthy to attend the coronation. He draped a little delusion about himself, making sure that each citizen saw his tunic and trews as equal in cost and grandeur to their own.

And he'd better avoid the numerous guards scattered throughout the crowd. Palace guards were notoriously strong witch-sniffers. One whiff of his magic and he'd end up in the same dungeon cell as the hideous statue that Krej had become with a heavy dose of witchbane to keep him there.

"I don't mind King Darville wanting more money for the army," a lavishly garbed town dweller complained. "We've got to protect our borders since the magicians deserted us and took their protective barriers with them. But Darville thinks we should feed the poor, too. I say let the wretches find honest work or join the army. I have trouble enough keeping the wife in SeLenese lace." He and his equally elegant companion strained anxiously to see the king he discredited.

SeLenese lace? All imports and exports from SeLenicca were banned. Could that be where the smuggler aimed to take the Tambootie seedlings? Yaakke strained to follow the speaker with his eyes, but lost him among the throng of taller observers.

The mood of the crowd seemed to echo the speaker—half wildly enthusiastic for the king and half faddishly bored, unable to approve of anything.

With the slightly crossed eyes required for TrueSight, Yaakke scanned the courtyard for any hint of Jaylor. All he could sense was a tiny tune of peace and love just ahead of him. That had to be Brevelan, Jaylor's wife. An island of calm radiated outward from the delicately framed witch-woman. Her witch-red hair and magic were disguised. No one who didn't know her would suspect that the quiet tune she *Sang* to her new baby was really a spell to keep the overwhelming emotions of the crowd away from her empathic sensitivities.

Disguised or not, Jaylor wasn't beside her.

Yaakke climbed to the top level of seats erected around the central dais, almost to the top of the wall. He ignored Corby perched atop the wall ten arm-lengths away as he preened scorched breast feathers. Tendrils of black floated on the wind, like ash, with each stab of his sharp beak.

Scanning the crowd for anyone wearing a magic disguise or delusion—friend and enemy alike—Yaakke avoided jostling elbows that threatened to push him over the outside wall into the churning river that encircled Palace Isle. The jackdaw cackled laughter at his concern.

"Rotten weather for a celebration." A sergeant in the green-and-gold uniform of Darville's personal guard remarked beside Yaakke.

"Yeah, could rain any minute." Yaakke looked at the sky where the jackdaw now flew, rather than at his unwanted companion. He swallowed heavily and tried to ease away from the young sergeant.

"Do I know you?" the Palace guard asked, peering closely at the black-and-silver tunic Yaakke had chosen for his magic disguise. He thought it went well with his dark hair and eyes. Then he remembered the girl with raven hair and bay-blue eyes. She had been wearing black and silver too.

"I don't think we've met." Yaakke looked around nervously. He wished he could dissolve into the crowd like the girl had, without using any magic. This curious sergeant looked as if he might be trying to "smell" the presence of magic.

A bizarre purple haze clung to the area around the dais. Yaakke wrinkled his nose against the odor of the incense. Cautiously he eased a light shell of magic armor around him. The overly sweet smell subsided.

The sergeant opened his eyes wide and shoved his way down the tier of seats, like a boat forging upriver against a strong current, pushing noble and wealthy citizens aside without regard. Apparently he didn't like the smell either.

Yaakke watched, wondering at the sergeant's haste and determination. Then he saw what had disturbed the sergeant. One of the acolytes wasn't a young boy. Beneath a dissolving spell of delusion, he was a short, middle-aged man with a square-cut beard. No respectable citizen of Coronnan would wear a beard trimmed in the style affected by King Simeon of SeLenicca, the sorcerer-king who waged war against Coronnan.

A sorcerer-king who ruled a land notorious for the absence of magic, A dragon could provide Simeon with enough magic to work his spells. He'd need Tambootie trees to feed the dragons who had deserted Coronnan last spring.

Was the smuggler headed for SeLenicca and King Simeon?

Assassin! The outside thought came into Yaakke's head unbidden.

He sent an invisible probe into the false acolyte's head. *Poison.* The man was going to shoot poison into King Darville. Yaakke had to stop him.

But how? He was too far away to get to the dais before the assassin acted.

If he threw any magic at all—at this distance he'd have to summon power and focus the spell with gestures and a trance—the guard standing one tier away would arrest him for using outlawed powers. The guard might even think he, Yaakke, was the assassin.

Rejiia eased out of the guardroom toward the King's Gate. That magician boy had seen her. That meddlesome apprentice of Jaylor's, who seemed to melt into walls and fade into obscurity while listening to the most private of

conversations, was skulking around the coronation. She had
no doubt he could penetrate her delusions. Perhaps he
could eavesdrop on her private thoughts and telepathic conversations as well.

If he overheard, the coven's plans were in danger. The
safety of many depended upon her role in today's actions.
She darted into her new hiding place, just inside the corridor to the throne room. She peered around the edge of the
door to watch the coronation.

King Darville and his foreign queen approached the dais
with slow, measured steps. The gold of the king's tunic
seemed a perfect match to his barely restrained mane and
yellow-brown eyes. He knew how to manipulate the crowd's
loyalty by projecting an image of beauty and power. Rejiia
aimed for the same aura of authority with her black and
silver gowns and sapphire jewelry—though her husband dis-
approved of her dramatic clothing. When she was queen,
he'd not be around to scowl and whine at her.

The crowd's attention strayed from the majesty of the
new king to the audacious display of bosom by his queen,
Rossemikka. Her golden gown didn't dip nearly as deep as
her wedding gown had, but still, she challenged the modesty of all the other women present. Rejiia wished she
dared expose so much of her own breasts. Her meek little
husband and his father, Lord Marnak the Elder, had beaten
and bruised her the one time she'd tried. They'd pay for
that. Soon. When Darville was dead and she was queen.

If all eyes were on the queen, then no one would see the
magically armored assassin make his move.

One of the acolytes ceased swinging his censer. Rejiia
held her breath in anticipation as he lifted a small cylinder
from the center of his incense holder. The assassin's SeL-
enese beard poked through his disguise, making him look
much older. *Demon spawn!* The armor did not work in the
presence of the witchbane.

No outcry rose against the hired killer. Perhaps no one
noticed him amid the dazzle of the Coraurlia and the
queen's white breasts.

A tiny dart head protruded from the bottom of the tube
in the censer lid. The assassin held the tube up to his lips.
He took a deep breath to blow. Rejiia filled her lungs as
well, willing the poison dart to find its target.

Almost done. A few more seconds and she would be queen.

Hands reached out from beneath the dais and encircled the ankles of the assassin. One mighty yank from those hands and the hireling fell forward. *Thunk!* His face slapped the pavement with a hideous sound. He opened his mouth in a soundless protest and he inhaled the dart. The assassin's eyes rolled up and his mouth foamed as the poison penetrated the delicate membranes of his mouth and throat.

Another yank on the assassin's ankles by the person hidden beneath the dais and the body disappeared from view. No one in the crowd seemed to notice the slight disruption in the ceremonies.

Stunned by the failure of her plans. Rejiia stared at the place where her agent had disappeared beneath the dais. Jaylor, the youngest Senior Magician in history and King Darville's childhood friend, peeked out from beneath the platform. His eyes searched the courtyard and rested on the King's Gate where Rejiia stood.

"Dragon dung!" Rejiia gasped. "I've got to get out of here."

She turned and ran down the corridor toward the throne room.

Failed! We have failed to execute Darville. What kind of demon is he to pervert fate and remain alive?

Calm. I must force myself to accept the failure and find another plan. Sooner or later the king's luck will run out. The magicians protect him, even though I arranged for them to be outlawed. I must separate Darville from the Commune. Will they still protect him if he and Jaylor are no longer friends?

Today I must settle for rescuing Lord Krej from the dungeons. That should cause Darville some trouble. For only a magician can break the spells surrounding the cell, and the only magicians he knows belong to Jaylor and the Commune.

Yaakke slipped behind a broad-shouldered petit-noble. He watched warily as Jaylor peeked out from beneath the dais searching for someone in the crowd. If Jaylor couldn't find his apprentice, then he couldn't punish Yaakke for

succumbing to cowardice and failing to intervene against
the assassin. To protect the Commune, Coronnan, and the
king was the most sacred oath of magicians.

Yaakke suspected his journeyman's quest would be delayed once more because of his failure. A new commotion
stopped him.

"Look, up there. A dragon!" A sharp-eyed priest shouted
and pointed. All eyes lifted to the heavens.

Yaakke fought the compulsion to look upward as well.
A vision of the court wallowing in dragon dung brought a
smile to his face. He'd have to take more care how he
cursed. Best he slip into the city and get as far away from
his master as possible for the rest of the day. Jaylor had
peered right at Yaakke and known he hadn't done a bloody
thing to save the king. Maybe by nightfall he'd forget Yaakke's shortcomings.

He'd have to send a brief telepathic message about the
smuggler when he was a safe distance from Palace Isle.

"It's a blue-tipped male dragon," King Darville added to
the crowd's murmurs.

This time Yaakke couldn't resist looking up, as he eased
closer to the guardroom exit. The outline of the winged
creature hovered and shimmered in a shaft of sunlight over
the courtyard, almost visible against the dark gray sky. The
beast's crystal-like fur directed light and sight around him,
challenging the coronation crowd to look everywhere but
directly at him. Yet their eyes needed to linger and seek a
glimpse of the dragon.

"Grrower!" The gray overcast dissipated in the blink of
an eye, as if commanded by the dragon's trumpeting call.

Sunlight danced across translucent wings and arced
downward. Rainbows sparked the Coraurlia with life and
color. A giant aura spread around the glass dragon crown
for all to see.

This was the Coraurlia of legend; forged by dragon fire
to protect the rightful king and no other.

Lord Andrall lifted the crown high and turned within the
circle of prismatic light to face King Darville. His face
glowed with the same wonder Yaakke saw reflected in
every face in the court. Warmth and joy tingled from Yaakke's toes to his ears.

The dragon shifted. The rainbow followed his wing

movement and bathed King Darville and Queen Rosse-mikka in the light of magnificent blessing.

The young king and his consort mounted the six steps of the dais amidst applause and cheers. The dancing rainbows seemed to follow them, bursting into bright auras for all to see, magic and mundane alike.

Yaakke smiled and lingered outside the guardroom. Darville deserved to be king. The few times Yaakke had encountered him, the young ruler had been kind, almost friendly. Rossemikka had to be the most beautiful woman in the kingdom, maybe in the three kingdoms.

An image of black lashes surrounding huge blue eyes flitted across his memory. Well, maybe there was one girl, almost-woman, more beautiful than Queen Rossemikka.

The procession followed Darville and Rossemikka, ready for the ancient ritual to consecrate them monarch and consort of Coronnan. An overwhelming sense of pride and joy lingered in the court. In a tradition not seen in living memory, the dragons had validated Darville's claim to the throne.

(Come to me.) The dragon voice came into Yaakke's head.

"What?" Yaakke whispered. Only royals were supposed to hear dragons. He looked up again, searching the clear sky for a glimpse of wing or tail.

(You are needed.)

"Did a dragon speak to me?" Maybe the dragon spoke to someone else and Yaakke merely overheard. He eavesdropped on people's thoughts easily, why not a dragon's?

(Meet me in Shayla's old dragon lair. Above Brevelan's clearing, two weeks hence.) The dragon disappeared above the remaining fluffy white clouds.

"What would a dragon need me for?" He craned his neck in search of one last glimpse of blue-tipped crystal.

(I know of your parents, Boy. Come to me and we will discuss those who left you with no name and no heritage. Tell no one of our tryst. You must not be followed.)

"Two weeks? I only need that much time if I bother taking a travel steed. I have the transport spell. I can be there tomorrow." His parents? Maybe he had a real name after all and needn't borrow one from history.

(No. You use the transport spell too often. Danger follows it. Steal a steed if you must, but come in two weeks.)

"Steal? What if I get caught?" A thrill of danger almost replaced the awe of speaking to a dragon. A real live dragon who spoke to him and wanted to meet with him in secret.

(You will not be caught. I will tell you of your heritage two weeks hence. No sooner.)

"If I sneak out through the dungeon tunnels, I can be out of the city before sunset." Who would miss him? Yaakke lifted the latch on the guardroom door.

(Don't be late.) The chuckle in the dragon's voice reminded Yaakke of Old Master Baamin. Grief touched his eyes with moisture for just a moment.

Then he straightened his shoulders with pride. "I'll follow the dragon for your sake, sir," he whispered to the memory of an old man who had cared for him when he was nothing.

(Do it for your own sake, or you won't find the lair.)

Chapter 3

Katrina Kaantille halted her quest for a cup of milk or a cracker to stop her stomach growling. The door to the family kitchen was firmly closed. Raised voices beyond the door made her uncertain she wanted to overhear yet another fight between her parents.

Cold seeped from the floorboards into her feet. Winter had come early to Queen's City—to all of SeLenicca according to market gossip. Just a moon past the equinox and frost made the front steps slippery every morning. She should have stopped to slip clogs over her velvet house slippers. But she'd put down her study of geometric grids for only a moment. A sudden growth spurt had made her stomach clamor for food all the time lately. Often she couldn't concentrate for the discomfort.

"What do you mean there isn't enough money to buy Katrina's apprenticeship!" Katrina's mother, Tattia, hissed.

Katrina pressed her ear against the kitchen door to listen more closely. Her entire body shivered with apprehension.

Money was hard to come by all over SeLenicca these days. Yesterday the price of milk was twice what it had been last week. P'pa had dismissed the scullery maid, valet, and governess last week because he couldn't pay them. Cook would go next week.

But Katrina's father, Fraanken Kaantille, was a wealthy merchant. M'ma worked as the queen's Lace Mistress. Exporters and lace factory owners valued M'ma's new designs. Surely her father could find enough money for her apprenticeship somewhere.

Katrina loved the fine thread work that had become SeLenicca's primary export. She'd reached her thirteenth

birthday last moon, the age of apprenticeship. Only a few
weeks' more work and she would complete the entry requirements. That future now seemed in jeopardy.

"There will be enough money. Just not right now. Upon
King Simeon's request, I've invested all our money in a
ship," P'pa explained.

Katrina could almost see her father place a soothing
hand on M'ma's shoulder before her volatile temper
exploded.

"And just what cargo do you expect to put in the hold
of that ship? The mines are played out and the timberlands
are nearly barren. Lace is the only thing left to export and
the queen controls every shipment," M'ma argued. Her
voice was growing louder rather than softer.

Katrina nearly winced at the acid in her mother's tone.
Talented and highly respected artist that she was, Tattia
Kaantille had never learned moderation in her emotional
reactions. Lesser beings were expected to jump to her commands and bow to her superior knowledge.

"But what do you make your lace with, my dear?" P'pa's
wide and generous smile shone through his voice. That endearing grin usually soothed M'ma.

"Inferior cotton and short-spun linen. Since the war with
Coronnan, we can't get any decent Tambrin. Our own Tambootie trees are too small, too tough and irregular in their
fibers. And there's barely enough of them in a few isolated
spots to bother seeking."

Katrina breathed a little easier. M'ma's angry tones continued, but now her temper was directed toward the enemy
of SeLenicca and not her husband of fourteen years.

"How much would one ship filled with Tambootie seedlings from Coronnan be worth, *cherbein* Tattia?" P'pa used
an intimate endearment meant to soothe and flatter. His
voice lifted with pride and greed. "Seedlings that will grow
into thread-producing trees in a few years."

Katrina gasped. The long, silky fibers of six-year-old
Tambootie trees made the best lace in the world. One tree
supplied enough Tambrin to make a hundred arm-lengths
of finger lace, symmetrical insertions as wide as the queen's
ring finger was long. Of course, some of the trees would
have to be saved to produce seeds for the next crop. Even
so, a shipload of seedlings, once grown to proper size, but

before they were mature enough to sprout flowers and seeds, could save SeLenicca and make Katrina's family as wealthy as the queen.

But trade with Coronnan was forbidden. Military ships inspected every cargo. What if P'pa's ship was stopped? The entire family would be in deep trouble. He'd invested all of his money in that ship. All of it?

Too excited and frightened to be hungry anymore, Katrina returned to the workroom on the third floor of the tall, narrow townhouse. Vents from the kitchen fires kept this room warm enough for the entire family to pursue their daily occupations.

Dolls and miniature clothing lay scattered around the workroom floor. Katrina's two younger sisters had obviously used her brief absence as an excuse to abandon their lessons in keeping household accounts for playtime. The limited pictorial language of household ledgers might be all they ever learned to read, but women in the Kaantille family could add and subtract better than any merchant who might try to cheat them.

"Katey, Maaben says my dolly isn't as pretty as hers. Tell her it isn't so," six-year-old Hilza wailed and tugged at Katrina's long woolen skirt.

"Your doll is ugly and broken," nine-year-old Maaben rejoined. "Tell the truth, Katey. Tell her how ugly her doll is. Its hair is dirty and doesn't look blond anymore, and the eyes are dull, not blue like a real lady's. Only peasants and outlanders have dark hair and eyes. It's ugly," Maaben quoted the often-heard prejudice. "And peasants can't wear lace. Give my doll that shawl and cap!"

"Maaben, Hilza, stop it! Now get back to your lessons. I can't waste time on such stupid squabbles. I . . . I have to work at my lace for a while," Katrina brushed aside the grasping hands of her sisters. She needed the soothing thread work to banish the frightening argument she had overheard in the kitchen. What if P'pa lost *all* of his money?

She walked past the long study table to the cupboards beneath the single glass window—the greatest luxury in the house. Her agile fingers pressed the lock buttons in the proper sequence and the doors sprang open to reveal her finest treasure.

She caressed the tubular pillow stuffed with unspun wool,

from sheep bred half a world away. Her hand traced the dimensions of the pillow—as long as her forearm and as thick as her fingers stretched wide. Tucked inside the center of the tube was a compartment designed to hold the strips of stiff leather that were a lacemaker's patterns. Pinholes in a geometric grid covered the patterns, guides for the weaving of the lace. Katrina had inherited nearly one hundred patterns from her father's mother. Irreplaceable patterns that had never been duplicated and that she alone could legally work.

The velvet-covered pillow rested in a wooden frame that kept it from rolling. Gently, Katrina carried the precious pillow and frame to the study table. She placed it in the one spot the autumn sun brightened the most. Only when the pillow rested securely in place did she remove the loose cloth draped over the top to reveal an arm-length of a simple piece of lace. Two dozen spindles of carved bone wound with thread dangled from the unfinished end of the lace.

This lacemaker's pillow and the patterns were Katrina's thirteenth birthday present as well as her heritage and her dowry. Gentlewomen of SeLenicca had always made lace to adorn their wardrobes. In the last three generations, lace had been elevated to a national treasure. Only the export of lace could replace the money lost from the failing mines and empty timberlands. Only lace could buy food and wine and woven cloth from abroad, for the land of SeLenicca had never been farmed.

"Can we watch?" Maaben crossed the room on reverent tiptoe. Her blue eyes widened with wonder.

Hilza crept behind her sister, moon-blond curls glistening in the weak sunshine. The dolls lay abandoned in a heap.

"If you are quiet, you may watch. I can't think if you ask questions or argue." Katrina caressed the first two pairs of bobbins, thrilling at the texture and wonderful lace they would produce. Engravings etched some of the thin bone spindles. She examined tiny pictures of mythical animals or the names and birthdays of the relatives indentured to the royal family SeLenicca as lacemakers, including herself. At the bottom of each bobbin was a circle of precious beads, some wood, others metal. The bangles added weight to the slender bobbins and kept them from rolling and twisting the thread. Only the bobbins commemorating a Lace Mistress, like Tattia and Granm'ma, contained a single, priceless, glass bead within the circle.

Peasant women who worked in the export factories couldn't afford slender, beaded bobbins, light and smooth enough to work Tambrin and the finest long cotton and linen threads. The factory owners supplied their workers with heavy, barely sanded, wooden bobbins with fat bulbs on the ends, as well as pillows covered in rough homespun and stuffed with straw. The factory tools, including the pins, were so clumsy that only thread heavy enough so it wouldn't suffer damage from rolling bobbins and overtwisting could be used on them. The light in the factories was poor, restricting patterns to large, open, and symmetrical designs. Katrina pitied those women for a moment. Her family was wealthy. She would learn the art of lace and design at the palace, as well as how to finish the lace onto garments. She owned her own equipment and could work at home if she chose, once she'd finished her journeywoman's work. She also had a treasure trove of exclusive patterns to keep her work unique. These wonderful tools would grant her special privileges at court, and if she managed to design a truly glorious pattern, she could be named a national treasure.

M'ma was still working for that status. Granm'ma had achieved the prestigious title days before her death last winter.

Deftly, Katrina worked a stitch, double twist right over left in both pairs, single cross, left over right between the pairs, and push a very slender pin into the proper hole in the pattern that encircled the bolster. Then, another double twist of right over left and a cross of left over right to enclose the pin in thread. Set aside one pair of bobbins, pick up the next in line.

The ancient rhythm of the bobbin weaving settled into her hands as a work tune brushed her mind. She hummed the soft clicking rhythm of the song—the first lullaby she'd ever heard—in time with the movements of her hands. Double twist, cross, and pin.

This third of the beginning patterns already seemed too simple and she longed for a more complex one. The first few finger-lengths of this lace, where she'd made two mistakes, had become the disputed doll's shawl and cap. Katrina had started and restarted the pattern several times until the work was perfect. Two arm-lengths of lace from each of three patterns were the entry examination for apprenticeship. A few more days of concentrated work would finish the requirement.

She had more than a few days to finish. She had until P'pa's ship returned with its precious cargo.

Double twist, cross.

"When will you get to use Tambrin thread?" Hilza barely breathed her question.

"Not for years yet. I've got too much to learn before I can use anything but short-spun cotton and thick linen," Katrina replied. Double twist, cross, and pin. "Only lace-makers as smart as M'ma can use Tambrin. It's too expensive to waste on beginners."

Double twist, cross.

"Maybe by the time Queen Miranda's baby is of an age to marry, I'll be skilled enough to make the wedding veil out of Tambrin." Provided P'pa found the money for her apprenticeship.

Maaben and Hilza continued to watch, mouths slightly open, breathing shallow, and eyes fixed on the lace.

Double twist, cross. Double twist, cross, and pin.

Yaakke crept up the back stairs of the Bay Hag Inn to retrieve his staff and pack. Twilight had fallen early, along with a new onslaught of rain. He hadn't been able to communicate with Jaylor by telepathy all day. News of the smuggler would have to wait a little while. He had to get out of town tonight if he wanted to meet the dragon's deadline.

He munched absently on a thin slice of purloined meat stuck between two slabs of coarse bread. Not nearly as tasty as the sausage rolls Margit had offered him when he'd questioned her about the smuggler masquerading as a Guild Pilot. She'd thanked him prettily for intervening on her behalf. Her clear blue-gray eyes had offered him more than a pasty. He didn't have time or inclination to linger.

His eyes and mind focused on the essence of each piece of wood in the steps, picking out stress points that would groan and betray his presence to anyone in adjacent rooms.

Finding the creaks on the stairs with his magic was better than thinking about the half-cooked fat and gristle.

But what else should he expect from the Bay Hag? Isolated on the mainland from the river delta islands that made up Coronnan City, this was the kind of place where a man could rent bed space well away from prying eyes and ears, without questions.

The Bay Hag Inn seethed with life tonight. Mostly lowlifes who couldn't afford shelter from the rain in the city proper. Patches of fresh thatch dotted the moldering roof. Damp salt air from the Great Bay was hard on thatch. This nearly forgotten hostel beside the river didn't look prosperous enough to reroof with slate, or even wood.

Brevelan and Yaakke had both turned up their noses when Jaylor chose to lodge his family here. The Senior Magician had insisted it would be easy to guard Brevelan and baby Glendon against theft and physical attack at the Bay Hag. Protecting them from suspicious neighbors who might report the presence of magicians to the Council might prove impossible.

Yaakke extended his senses into the wooden planks and beyond. The loft where he'd hidden his staff and pack was empty of people. Maybe he should just transport them to his hand. He could grab them and leave right now. No, Jaylor and Brevelan were constantly reminding him that magic was for need, not convenience, and he'd wasted too many spells on inconsequential things today. Witch-sniffers might be on his tail already.

"If he needs healing, I must go to him. I can't return to the clearing yet." Brevelan's urgent whispers to her husband penetrated Yaakke's thoughts through the closed door at the top of the landing.

Why hadn't they answered his telepathic call?

"We don't dare stay in the capital any longer," Jaylor returned. "The witchbane is still in me. I can't whisk us out of here at the first sign of trouble. We have to leave on foot with the rest of the crowds before someone recognizes us."

Witchbane? That explained Jaylor's silence. Yaakke sent a tendril of self-healing through his body, searching for something wrong. Nothing. Wherever Jaylor had encountered the dreaded drug, Yaakke had escaped an accidental dosage that would temporarily rob him of his magic. He shuddered. Without magic he was just another nameless kitchen drudge.

"I'm not leaving until I see Darville and I know that he is well," Brevelan announced.

Yaakke knew from experience that Jaylor might as well give up his arguments when Brevelan used that tone of voice.

"NO!" Jaylor's denial echoed across the landing.

Baby Glendon set up a howl of protest at the angry words circling around the room.

The king must be very ill indeed if he needed Brevelan's special brand of empathic healing. He'd looked a little pale at the coronation, wincing when he jarred his injured arm. Not many people in the Grand Court looked beyond the joy of the coronation to see the deep creases in the king's forehead that suggested the pain was never very far away—a legacy of his last battle with the witch Janataea.

Yaakke was glad he wasn't an empath like Brevelan. The churning discomfort he felt in his gut from just listening to this fight was bad enough. To actually experience other people's anger and grief, their pain and illness, as Brevelan did, was more than his body and mind could handle.

Did he dare linger long enough to deliver his message about the smuggler, or should he wait until he was out of town and Jaylor free of the witchbane?

Yaakke stretched his ears a little closer to the closed door.

"Conventional healers can't help Darville. He needs me!" Brevelan said.

Yaakke bit his lip. He had never heard these two fight before. He knew nothing of how a marriage worked, even less of women and their moods. Could a loving bond recover from angry words? *Stargods*, he needed to be away from this argument.

"And just how do you intend to get close enough to the king to heal him? When do you propose to do this—before or after the witchbane wears off? You got a pretty good dose of that purple smoke, too. Don't deny it." Jaylor's voice started to rise. Then he dropped it to a hissing whisper.

Yaakke's toes began to tingle with the urge to depart.

He didn't want to stay here at the inn and listen to his only two friends argue and hurt each other. He didn't want to watch their bruised feelings dissolve their love.

He turned to make his way back down to the kitchen level. He'd have to risk retrieving his few possessions later by magical transport.

Jaylor threw open the door of his private chamber and grabbed his apprentice's collar. "Not so fast, Yaakke. Where have you been? You should have been back hours ago."

"How'd you know it was me?" Yaakke squeaked. He cleared his throat, almost glad rather than embarrassed by his lack of control over his voice. Maybe, just maybe, he was finally growing into manhood. Fifteen was kind of late for the change.

By tradition he couldn't face the rite of passage with the Tambootie smoke until his body entered puberty. He needed that trial to achieve journeyman status. Technically he couldn't leave his master or be inducted into the Commune of Magicians without the trial. He needed to set out tonight if he was going to reach Brevelan's clearing and the dragon in two weeks.

"I have eyes and ears beyond my magic." Jaylor closed the door to the bedroom, separating them from Brevelan and the now quiet baby. "You were supposed to report to me before the coronation began. Where have you been, Yaakke?"

"I—ah—I overheard—ah—" How did he explain how he heard the smuggler when he wasn't supposed to use any magic at all?

"Just this once, I wish you would answer a direct question. I'm not going to steal your dinner or beat you for impertinence."

Yaakke fought for the right words. His long habit of keeping his mouth shut and his mind sharp to avoid bullies and punishment stalled the words in his throat.

"*Stargods*, I'm not an empath like Brevelan. I can't read you," Jaylor ground the words through his teeth.

Yaakke hung his head. Fear of punishment clawed at his throat, killing the words. He had to try. He had to make Jaylor see how valuable he could be to the Commune.

"I overheard a smuggler. . . ."

"Criminals aren't my problem. I need your help now. Did the witchbane in the Grand Court affect you?"

"Witchbane?" Yaakke shuddered again at the thought of losing his magic and therefore his right to call himself anything but "Boy."

"The purple smoke one of the acolytes was dispensing instead of incense."

"I didn't like the smell, so I armored against it right off." Yaakke looked at the food still clutched in his fist. "The smuggler might be important to the king. He's taking . . ."

"That isn't important now. The king's health is. Is your magic intact?" Jaylor pressed for an answer.

"I guess so." He'd tell about the smuggler and SeLenicca and the dragons later, when Jaylor was ready to listen.

"Show me your magic."

Yaakke shrugged and brought a globe of witchlight to his outstretched palm. Shadows dissolved in the direction-less glow. He extinguished it with the pass of a hand before anyone from the kitchens below them could investigate.

"Good. You can eat on the way to the palace." Jaylor latched onto Yaakke's arm and pulled him toward his room.

Yaakke crammed the last of the bread and meat into his mouth. He didn't wait to swallow before he mumbled: "But, Jaylor, I've got to go . . . to tell you . . ."

"You need to follow my orders." Jaylor dragged him into the private room, still holding his collar. "We're ready, Brevelan." He grabbed his staff and headed back down the stairs. Brevelan slung a shawl around herself and Glendon, hurrying in her husband's wake. She didn't even notice the smell of the meat Yaakke had eaten. Usually the smell of an animal's death pained her.

"Where are we going?" Yaakke asked, swallowing the last bite of his hasty meal. He figured he'd need all of his strength for whatever Jaylor planned.

"The king is ill," Jaylor announced grimly, checking the back stairs for privacy.

"Did the assassin get him after all?"

"So you know about that."

"I'm sorry I didn't help, Jaylor. But I was too far away and there was a guard standing very close to me. I couldn't throw any magic without . . ."

"Never mind apologizing. Fred and I handled it. Now get a move on. We're needed at the palace."

"Fred?"

"Darville's personal bodyguard. The sergeant."

"Oh, him." Yaakke relaxed as if a weight lifted from his shoulders. "Is it okay if he sorta recognized me?"

"He's loyal to Darville first and the Council second. He won't betray us." They hurried into the muddy yard at the back of the inn. The hoarse caw of a crow or jackdaw greeted them, then faded with the last of the daylight.

Yaakke looked toward the roof of the ramshackle stable for signs of Corby, the jackdaw who seemed to have followed him all day. The lumpy thatch betrayed no unusual outline.

"Is the king's sword arm acting up again?" he asked to cover his search for Corby. If that was all that was wrong with the king, maybe he could get Darville to listen to his news about the smuggler.

"I'm afraid so. The wound, where the rotten magic in Janataea's witch blood burned him, is getting worse. If we can't reverse the damage tonight, I'm afraid he might die." Jaylor choked on the words.

"I need my staff." Yaakke "listened" to the loft. No one remained up there, awake or asleep. Another croak from Corby seemed to confirm the absence of patrons above the private rooms. Yaakke wondered briefly where the bird was, and if it truly was speaking to him.

The long walking stick appeared in his hand. Transporting things through the void from one place to another was easy—transporting people was hard. The distinctive grain of the oak staff from the Sacred Grove was already beginning to twist from the magic he had forced through it. "And our errand with the king is so urgent, I'll transport us." Yaakke halted in his tracks. He closed his eyes a moment and sent his pack to a concealed corner of the stable. He could retrieve it from there later without arousing suspicion. While he was at it, he might as well get an apple from the barrel in the cellar.

"No transports." Jaylor shook Yaakke's shoulder to keep him from sliding into a deeper trance. "The spell is too dangerous. The last time I used it, I nearly got lost in the void."

Chapter 4

Yaakke peered over Brevelan's shoulder as she stirred herbs into a steaming pot stolen from the palace kitchens. Brevelan and Queen Rossemikka knelt on the floor before the hearth in the royal bedroom. Whenever instructed, Yaakke repeated the words of a spell Brevelan gave him, infusing power into the words and thence into the healing mixture. The conversation between Jaylor and King Darville intruded into his concentration for making the hot poultice. He forced his mind back onto the symbolic power behind the words while still half-listening.

"You shouldn't have risked coming here tonight." King Darville sounded weary and excited at the same time. His coronation day had been a long series of exhausting formal rituals culminating with the dragon's blessing. By ancient tradition, he now ruled by Dragon-right. No one could contest his possession of the crown.

Yaakke desperately needed to start his journey to meet that same dragon. He also needed to impart the information about the smuggler—if anyone would listen. Flusterhen feathers quivered in his belly.

"Have you ever tried arguing with Brevelan?" Jaylor answered his king and friend with a chuckle.

"Not since Krej enchanged me into the body of a golden wolf and I tried to bring my freshly killed supper into her hut," Darville replied. Laughter tinged his voice, too.

"Then you know I had no choice but to sneak her in here by way of the tunnels." Jaylor's restless eyes surveyed the room.

Yaakke had already searched the room for signs of eavesdroppers. There weren't many hiding places left in the apartments since the new queen had cleared away the clutter of generations.

"Take off your tunic, Darville." Brevelan stood in front of him, a steaming bowl in her hands. Noxious fumes rose from the contents. Yaakke and Queen Mikka stood right behind her.

"Help him, Jaylor, please." Mikka lifted her slanted eyes to plead with the Senior Magician. Her pupils were round now. Yaakke had seen them slit vertically when her cat persona dominated her body. "My stubborn husband won't admit how much the burns still hurt him, or how difficult those fitted tunics are to get out of. Now if court fashion allowed him to wear a decent robe. . . ."

"The court is already outraged at your foreign costumes, my dear." Darville struggled upright, but his smiling eyes never left the expanse of bosom showing above her gown. A place Yaakke hadn't dared allow his own gaze to linger.

"And I have difficulty coping with the immodesty of unveiled hair and skirts that reveal the ankles! A woman's breasts are a source of pride. And when I have proved my ability to bear and nurse a child, I intend to decently and proudly display my breasts." Mikka stared her husband down, amusement tickling the corners of her mouth. Her fingers flexed and curved like cat's paws. Her very long fingernails scratched at the velvet nap of her skirt.

Mikka had participated in a binding spell to heal Jaylor's warped magic. By accident she had joined with her pet cat. Her dual personality was the Commune's most closely guarded secret—except for the transport spell.

Yaakke yanked his eyes away from Mikka's catlike caress of her gown to Darville. He noted how the king kept his injured left arm close to his body and used his right arm to brace himself against the chair arm. Darville paused before standing, as if gathering strength against the pain he knew would come. Jaylor hurried to assist him. Yaakke stood on the opposite side with a polite hand beneath Darville's elbow.

The king shook off any help from Yaakke while he leaned heavily on his best friend. Yaakke remembered the tales of mischief that still followed these two around the city from when they were adolescents. Ten years of close friendship was a long time.

Once he'd read a person's thoughts, Yaakke knew their selfish motives. He couldn't think of anyone he'd liked and trusted for more than a few moments. Well, maybe Old Baamin.

Tonight he made a serious effort not to read the thoughts of these two couples. He didn't need to know what it was like to be half-cat, or a new mother. He didn't want to develop jealousy of the love they all shared.

Darville winced as Jaylor lifted the stiff tunic over the injured arm.

"Now roll up your shirtsleeve. This poultice may sting for a while, but it should draw more of the poison out and allow your body to heal itself." Brevelan set the bowl on the side table and began soaking bandages in the odoriferous liquid. "I've shown Mikka how to brew the solution. Between us, we'll have you well in no time."

"I certainly hope so. It's getting harder and harder just to sign my name to the infinite number of documents the Council comes up with. Then there's the problem of eating like a civilized man." Darville shook his head. "Life was easier when I was just your 'Puppy,' Brevelan."

"But not nearly so interesting." Mikka smiled and bent to kiss him.

While Darville was distracted by his bride, Brevelan placed the first of the steaming cloths on the exposed black burns that snaked up Darville's arm.

"Yaiyeee! What is in that demon brew!" Darville gritted his teeth. The cords of his neck went rigid.

"You don't want to know." Brevelan's expression didn't change until she turned to look at Jaylor.

Worry furrowed her brow and whitened her naturally pale skin. The spray of freckles across her nose appeared darker in contrast. Jaylor placed a supporting hand on his wife's narrow shoulder. Fear crossed Jaylor's face.

Yaakke couldn't penetrate the wall of Jaylor's thoughts. The apprentice touched the bandages as if to check them. A raw tingle traveled from the wound up through his arms. The weird sensation turned to a burn and then a pulsing jolt that tried to push his hand away or invade his entire body. He wasn't sure which. He didn't like the magic scent that suddenly tainted the room.

"Do what you have to, love," Jaylor whispered to Brevelan.

"What does that mean?" Darville clung to Mikka while he fought the pain.

"There is magic in that wound, Darville. Dark and dangerous magic." Jaylor refused to look at his friend.

Yaakke suddenly found the pattern in the rug fascinating. He'd felt death in that wound.

"We know that. Janataea's blood was rotten with Tambootie and evil magic. Everywhere it touched me, it burned through clothes and flesh almost to the bone." Sweat dotted Darville's brow and his breathing became shallow.

"This is something more, my dearest friend. I'm going to have to *Sing* the magic out." Brevelan clutched her hands in her lap.

Her healing talent required her to take the alien magic into her own body as well as Darville's pain. Her healthy body would gradually absorb, then dissipate, whatever was eating away at Darville. Someday, her ability to heal just might kill her.

"I'll lend you strength." Jaylor sat on the floor beside Brevelan, where she knelt at Darville's feet.

"As will I." Mikka plopped down on Brevelan's other side.

Yaakke dropped to his knees behind Brevelan, hands on her shoulders. The witchbane was still in her. He'd have to fuel the magic for her *Song*.

"No, Mikka." Jaylor put up a hand to keep the queen beside Darville. "The Council would burn you and depose Darville if they ever found out you participated in magic."

"I'm not the one throwing magic tonight." Mikka planted her clenched fists on her hips and glared at Jaylor. Stubborn determination creased her brow and set her lips into a straight line. "Is lending physical strength magic?"

Jaylor didn't answer. Queen Rossemikka had a reputation for single-minded determination. Several headstrong servants reported she had the patience to outstare and outwait a stone statue.

"Well, is it?"

"Not by our definition. But it might be by the Council's," Jaylor hedged.

"He's my husband. I will help him however I can."
Mikka plunked herself down beside Brevelan.

Yaakke placed his hands on Brevelan's shoulders. They
took a deep breath in unison. The beginning of Yaakke's
magic trance extended through his hands to include her.
Jaylor and Mikka mimicked the calming exercise. Breathe
in three counts, hold, breathe out. Again. A third time. The
rhythm drew them all halfway to the void. Reality shifted
in layers of past and present.

As usual, the ritual sent Yaakke's mind above his body.
From there he could reach below the mask of the witchbane in Brevelan's body and tap her empathic healing ability. Her tune started low and melancholy.

Unusual. Brevelan's healing tunes tended to be light and
cheerful, replacing pain and illness with joy and life.

Except that one time last spring when Jaylor had poured
his life into the spell that released Shayla, the last female
dragon, from Lord Krej's glass prison. Brevelan had called
Jaylor back to life with a tune as soft and poignant as this.

Yaakke forced calm upon his mind. Panic and worry
would end the spell. If Darville's injury was as bad as the
tune indicated, then Brevelan needed every fragment of
help he could give.

The tune grew in volume. The melody took on a richer
more complex tone. Dimly Yaakke heard Jaylor's deep
baritone seeking the harmony of the *Song*. The apprentice
needed to add his own wavering voice in harmony an octave above Jaylor. The *Song* circled and wove and blended
around the three voices. Mikka's untrained alto voice
joined the spell, complementing Brevelan's piercingly
sweet soprano.

Colored mists danced around the room in rhythm with
the *Song*. The music lifted higher, enticing the poison out
of Darville's body, urging the blackness to dissipate into
the colored fog.

Darville dropped his head against the back of the chair.
Gradually the lines of pain etched around his eyes and
down his cheeks eased and flowed away.

Brevelan brought the *Song* to a glorious high note and
lingered there. Jaylor took his harmony to a complemen-
tary fifth an octave below her. Mikka found the third.

Communal magic, fueled by dragons, must feel like this. Unity, companionship, binding them all together.

Yaakke opened his mouth to silence. The large room in a stone palace faded and shimmered. Different walls, older, unhewn bones of the Kardia curved around a cave. Cold dampness. Loneliness and pain.

He fought the vision and shook it from his mind. Reality was here in Coronnan City. He needed his concentration and strength *here* to heal the king.

Darville opened his eyes in wonder, then screwed up his face in agony. His scream caught Brevelan's shriek as they all collapsed in utter failure.

"Shayla!" Darville and Brevelan breathed together.

Yaakke forced himself to rouse from the exhaustion of strong magic. Shayla was lonely and hurt in her self-imposed exile from Coronnan. Had his vision shown him where the dragon hid?

"Did you see the dragon in your vision?" Jaylor asked wearily.

"She's hurt, trapped by an injured wing, and she can't fly," Darville panted. The pain seemed to return with double intensity.

"We've stabilized your wound with this spell. But I can't heal you, Darville, or Shayla. This wound is more than Janataea's poisoned blood. Your body is tied to the health of the dragons. The Coraurlia and the dragon blessing compound the link of your royal blood to the dragon nimbus. As long as Shayla ails, you will, too." Tears flowed down Brevelan's face. "I should have tried this yesterday, when I was in full control of my talent, before the dragons sealed your ties to them."

"Then why aren't you hurt, too, Brevelan? Your blood is almost as royal as mine. Shayla is linked to you."

"My link with Shayla was severed, Darville." Brevelan hung her head in regret.

"If Shayla is hurt that badly, then I'd best go find her." Jaylor stood, his hand already reaching for his staff.

"No!" Brevelan and Darville commanded in unison.

"I'm Senior Magician. 'Tis my duty to go," Jaylor protested.

"And you are the only one who can hold the remnants

of the Commune together. You have to stay in Coronnan, Jaylor." Darville leaned back in the chair, cradling his injured arm against his body.

"A Commune that is now outlawed by your Council."

"All the more reason for you to stay. You have the strength of will and body to fight the Council. Our government is an intricate balance among twelve lords and the monarch, with the magicians as neutral advisers. That balance has been destroyed. Dragon magic allows magicians to join and amplify their powers by orders of magnitude to overcome any solitary rogue magician who won't obey the ethics of the Commune or laws of the land. Those restrictions have been shattered by the absence of dragons. Only you can hold the Commmune together and advise me until the balance is restored. Send someone else. I need you here, Jaylor, even if your counsel is given in secret."

"Who else could I send? My class of journeymen never returned from their quests. The Master Magicians agreed to my elevation to Senior because they are all too old or unfamiliar with solitary magic to guide the Commune. There is no one else. I have to go." Jaylor tapped his staff against the floor with each word for emphasis.

"Excuse my presumption, sir," Yaakke interrupted. He forced politeness into his words to mask his excitement. "You have an apprentice, sir. You could give me this quest, now, like you said a few weeks ago. 'Tis my quest when I'm ready . . . when I've proved I'm reliable."

"Reliable and trained," Jaylor countered. "And of an age to undergo the trial by Tambootie smoke."

Yaakke refused to be disappointed. Somehow he had to make Jaylor see that he was *meant* to take this quest. Tonight. Before he left for his appointment with a dragon. Maybe if he told them about the smuggler now . . .

"Excuse me, Your Grace." Fred slipped into the room unannounced through a mere crack in the doorway.

Darville sat up straight and alert. "Yes?" Only a dire emergency would bring the king's bodyguard into his private quarters unsummoned.

"There's a ruckus in the dungeons, sir. Someone has stolen Lord Krej."

Chapter 5

Child's play. The telltales Jaylor left around Krej's dungeon cell evaporated too easily. I wasted precious minutes looking for additional traps that weren't there. I watched him set the spells and knew some of their secrets. When I ran out of time, I took a chance and levitated the statue that is now Krej through my escape route.

Would that the spell enchanting Krej dissolved as readily. At least a member of the coven now has possession of his entrapped spirit. He will be kept safe by the one person who can guard him best while we research the nature of the spell.

"Every one of Jaylor's spells has been released." Yaakke announced as he examined the outside of Krej's now empty dungeon cell. "Whoever sprang the magic traps either did it before the coronation or while the witchbane was spreading around the Grand Court," he continued as he sniffed with his magic senses.

"Shayla is hurt so that I won't heal, there's been an assassination attempt, and now someone has liberated my enemy!" Darville paced the dungeon corridor, anger simmering just below the surface of his kingly posture. "This coronation day is not turning out particularly joyous."

Yaakke looked around for anything Jaylor's sharp eyes might have missed. He'd placed several balls of the shadowless witchlight in and around the cell to make sure no clue remained hidden. Krej's cell was empty; there was no straw on the stone floor, no bedding on the cot. Not even a chamber pot or bucket in the corner. Ensorcelled into a tin statue, Krej wouldn't have needed any of those bleak comforts.

Krej had been alive when his own spell to capture Darville into a sculpture had been backlashed by the Coraurlia, trapping the rogue magician in his own evil.

Had the magic reached Darville as intended, the king would have assumed the figure of a golden wolf—the image dictated by his aura. The tin weasel reflected Krej's personality.

"Who did this, Yaakke?" Jaylor asked. He searched for minute traces of evidence with his master's glass, a rare piece of magnifying glass, as large as a man's hand, framed in gold. Jaylor could use the precious instrument to direct spells, as well as enlarge cramped print and seek clues.

"Don't know." Yaakke breathed deeply and allowed his eyes to cross in the first stage of a trance. "Something's wrong. The little bits of magic left over are really weird, but I can't say why." The cell next to this one smelled equally strange, too, as if the thief had lingered there but hadn't thrown any spells within the room. The grisly statue of Krej's mother, Lady Janessa, was still there. She'd been dead when Krej and his sister Janataea had ensorcelled her into an onyx statue of a harpy. She couldn't be revived and was useless to the coven. Krej still lived within his tin prison. He might revive if they could figure a way to break his own backlashed spell.

"Well, if we can't tell who and how let's look at where," Darville ceased his restless pacing a moment. "Where could the thief expect to take Lord Krej when he's been transformed into a statue of a weasel?"

"Somewhere close," Jaylor pronounced. "The statue might be the size of a real weasel, but it contains Krej's full weight and mass. That much dead weight concentrated in a small form would challenge a very strong man."

"A strong magician could transport him," Yaakke interjected. That's what he would do.

"If the magician who sprang the traps doesn't have the secret of transporting a living being unharmed, I don't think he'd risk damaging Krej." Jaylor finger-combed his beard; a familiar gesture when he was deep in thought. "But he might try levitation. That's how Krej got Shayla back to his castle last spring after he'd turned her into glass."

Yaakke thought back to the magic probe he had dodged

this morning. He hadn't revealed the secret of the transport spell to the smuggler from SeLenicca. Nor the queen's dual personality. He was sure of it. But maybe . . .

A blush crept up from his toes to his hairline. In all the rush and excitement he'd forgotten to relate important information. A smuggler. A ship to SeLenicca. Were all the mishaps connected?

"Does this corridor lead to the tunnels and maybe access to the river or another part of the city?"

"It does," Darville said. Traces of suspicion crossed his eyes. "But only if you know the tunnels exist, how to get out, and which walls hide doors."

Jaylor and Darville looked at each other for a long moment. If Jaylor's magic weren't dormant, Yaakke would swear they were talking mind-to-mind.

Yaakke looked down the dark length of the nearly empty prison carved out of bedrock. He squinted his eyes for traces of magic. Patches of red-and-black mist glowed in the shape of footprints.

"Who's red and black?" Yaakke asked Jaylor while following the faint traces of a magician's path. Magic tended to take on the color of the magician's personality. No two alike, though shades of a color might be similar.

"Red and black?" Jaylor looked surprised.

"Maybe not black. Something very dark. And the red is bright, like blood." The footprints were small, the stride short. Traces of delusion faded in and out, altering the shape and length of the telltales. Who was this magician?

"The assassin in the Grand Court was short!" Yaakke exclaimed. "And his beard was cut square, like he was from SeLenicca. There's a smuggler's ship going to SeLenicca tonight!"

"What? Tell me everything you know, Yaakke," Jaylor ordered. "Why didn't you tell me earlier?"

"You wouldn't listen and then we got caught up with the healing and I forgot." Yaakke's mind and mouth closed with a firm snap. Survival depended upon keen observation and keeping his secrets. He hadn't really forgotten to relate this information. Long habits of silence had pushed the incidents to the back of his mind. Ten years as the smallest and weakest kitchen drudge had taught him that.

"This is too important for you to hide behind big innocent eyes and silence." Jaylor grasped Yaakke's chin and forced him to look directly at him.

Yaakke saw anxiety and authority in Jaylor's gaze. He also saw a potential for violence within this big man. But none of his anger and aggression was directed toward Yaakke.

"Tell me what you know, Yaakke," Jaylor pleaded.

Yaakke filled his lungs and forced himself to trust his master. Never, in the months they'd been together, had Jaylor raised a hand to him. Not once had he given Yaakke reason to doubt his intentions.

"Yes, sir." Carefully, Yaakke related his morning's adventure, including his first suspicion that Margit the pasty seller had thrown a defensive spell at the beginning of the argument, finishing with an assurance that he hadn't leaked the transport spell to a foreigner nor revealed the queen's potential for magic.

What if he had revealed that information without knowing it?

"Where is that damned crow now?" Jaylor asked.

Yaakke fell silent once more. One of the shadows in Janessa's cell looked suspiciously like a bird sleeping with its head under one wing. If Corby followed him, everything the jackdaw did was special. For years, all he'd owned were his secrets. He had to keep Corby to himself a while longer.

"More important, how were the smugglers planning to get through the mudflats to the Bay proper?" King Darville resumed pacing the dank corridor, more restless than Yaakke had ever seen him. He nodded to the hovering Fred to send troops to investigate any ship leaving the Great Bay tonight.

"Only Bay Pilots know the ever-changing channels, and they are the most arrogantly close-mouthed demon spawn I've ever encountered!" The king yanked the golden queue restraint from his hair and shook the mane free. Once more he appeared the barely tamed wolf. The theft of Krej had challenged Darville's kingship and done more to invigorate him than all of Brevelan's healing spells.

"Can we assume that the theft of Lord Krej is related to the abortive assassination attempt?" Darville pressed.

Sounds of merriment from the banqueting hall drifted down into the higher levels of the dungeon as Fred opened the door a crack and slipped back to watch over Darville. He nodded that his errand was complete.

"I can't afford to absent myself from the festivities much longer, Jaylor. Can you find other clues, anything?"

"Sir," Yaakke interrupted. "Whoever stole Krej was strong enough to throw a delusion over the assassin and armor another man who was headed for the smuggler's ship. That's a lot of magic to throw and clear the cell, too."

Soberly silent, the three of them turned their attention back to the slim pieces of evidence. Jaylor placed a few threads of black cloth on a pewter tray alongside some flakes of gilt. "When was Krej last checked?"

"There is supposed to be a regular check of every cell by the guards at least once an hour. Every cell, not just these two." Darville extended his pacing to bypass half a dozen unoccupied cells. A coronation pardon had emptied most of them. Only two foreign spies and a few of Krej's steadfast followers remained.

"Could the backlashed spell have worn off?" Fred asked from the shadows. Yaakke added more witchlight to the corridor to eliminate concealing darkness.

"I doubt it. Krej's original spell was meant to be permanent," Jaylor replied. "Krej himself would have to remove the spell, and he can't do it until he's animate again." He shifted his weight as if shrugging away an uneasy memory.

Yaakke looked at his master and knew he relived the scene in Krej's great hall last spring when Jaylor had freed Shayla from her glass prison. That spell was supposed to be unbreakable, too. The great effort of throwing the mighty magic had nearly killed Jaylor. Only Brevelan's love and healing *Songs* had brought him back from the void between the planes of existence.

Darville stopped square in front of his oldest friend. "Our thief must also know the tunnels. There are no maps of these passages. Few know they exist, fewer still know where they lead."

"I don't know who it is," Jaylor replied. "The magic signature doesn't belong to any of my Commune. *We* don't want Krej free to cause more trouble." He looked directly at his apprentice for confirmation.

Yaakke nodded, free of guilt. He'd thought about freeing Krej just to see if he could do it. For once he hadn't followed through. All of Coronnan, including Yaakke, was better off with Krej frozen into his tin weasel statue.

"I've got to get back to the banquet before people start asking questions." Darville ran a hand through his hair.

His right hand, Yaakke noted, not his normally dominant, but now damaged, left.

Jaylor reached his left arm out to clasp Darville's in friendship before they separated. Darville responded in kind. The lightest of squeezes on his forearm caused his brows to furrow and his shoulders to tense.

"We've got to do something about that arm," Jaylor whispered. Yaakke heard, but he doubted Fred did. "Maybe another session with Brevelan?"

"No." Darville stood firm. "I miss you both, terribly, but you have to leave the city before the Council guesses that you've been here."

"The Council of Provinces couldn't keep me away. I've awaited this day since I was twelve and you were fourteen." Jaylor's smile lit his eyes with merriment.

"The day I ran away from home to join your band of renegade boys. The best day of my life, even if it lasted only a few hours." Darville returned the grin. Much of the pain drained from his face with the memory.

Yaakke burned with jealousy. He'd never had a friend. Never had a family to run away from.

"I've got to go." Darville broke the hand clasp and took a decisive step toward his personal guard. "Jaylor." He stopped his progress. "I miss your counsel. I'm working hard to rescind the banishment of magicians."

"I know, old friend. I'm working hard at it, too."

"How? You're supposed to be in exile."

"Sometimes it takes an exile to find an exile."

"Shayla! You've got to find her." The king winced as his left arm brushed against Fred.

"I guess I have to send Yaakke on that mission."

"Everything will be fine, Your Grace, once I return with the dragons," Yaakke burst forth. He had his quest. Jaylor had forgiven his earlier shortcomings and given him his quest!

Dragons take them all! Almost we reached open water. Almost, we sailed free of Coronnan. Darville's men followed in a fast galley. They overtook us and shot burning arrows into the sails. Then they boarded my ship with unsheathed weapons. My captain and his crew fought valiantly for our freedom. When all was lost, I planted the idea of suicide into their feeble minds. Better they all die than betray my spell of invisibility. Darville must never know 'twas I who stole Lord Krej.

I can no longer flee to SeLenicca with my treasure. Where can I hide? Right under their noses, where they are least likely to look.

Black mists chilled Yaakke to the bone. Utter blackness that had never known light. All of his senses stopped. He'd shiver with fright if he had a body to respond to his mind.

All of his previous trips through the void had been brief—darting in and out in the middle of the transport spell. Familiarity didn't make a transport spell any easier or less frightening. If he slipped in his concentration for even as long as a blink of the eye (presuming he still had eyes), he could end up permanently lost in this black nothingness.

Yaakke fixed an image of Brevelan's clearing in his mind. He saw the one-room thatched hut in the center, with a new lean-to affixed to the back: The coop where the flusterhens laid their eggs and the goat munched on her hay. A new weed in the kitchen garden and the layers of mulch Jaylor had laid on the big field to protect the last of the yampion roots. The closest thing to home Yaakke knew.

Brevelan wasn't there to open and close the barrier around the clearing. He'd have to shape-change into a wild animal to slip through. Remembering to change back into his human form afterward was the hard part of that little trick. He hoped Brevelan never learned he'd found a way in and out of her protected home.

The blackness faded just a little. He pulled the image of the clearing into sharper focus and aimed his spell for the open space before the hut.

Pulsing colored lines crisscrossed the lightest patch of nothingness. Could that be a door out of the void and back to reality? He reinforced the image of the clearing. The web of lines brightened. A sensation of speed propelled him toward the colors and he braced himself for contact with solid ground.

He bounced against something soft. At least he thought that was the sensation. The only softness in the clearing might be the upper branches of a tree, or the thatched roof. But he hadn't visualized either as his landing place.

Carefully he scanned his surroundings with every sense available to him. Wild tangles of throbbing umbilicals, in every hue imaginable, wrapped around and around him like the tentacles of a giant sea monster. Between and behind the colored symbols of life forces the void continued, on and on. Nothing between here and eternity.

He pushed a few cords away from what should be his face. Memory struck him. The time he'd entered the void with Jaylor to search for Queen Rossemikka's life force when Krej had kidnapped her, these threads of life had encircled them both. During that spell, the sight of a magician's blue umbilical fading to nothing had told Yaakke the moment Baamin died.

The shock of the old man's death had dropped him out of the void and the spell, leaving Jaylor alone, without an anchor to his corporeal body.

Yaakke was stranded in the void now, body and all. He needed to find a familiar life and follow it out. He didn't care where he landed as long as it was out of this sensation-robbing blackness.

Dozens of life forces coiled around his body and tightened. Suffocation squeezed his mind to blankness. Desperately he clawed at the life-lines, seeking an exit. One shimmering white thread clung persistently. He grasped it to pluck it away from his heart. New images filled his head.

A girl with moon-bright hair braided in a foreign style fell to her knees crying. She clutched a tubular pillow to her skinny chest. Wooden spindles dangled from the pillow by slender threads. An older man with similar features and hair ripped the clumsy bundle from her arms. Her father? One of the wooden spindles broke free of the pillow and fell back into the girl's lap. She covered it with a fold of her dark skirt to hide it from the man. The well-dressed father then thrust the bundle into the greedy grasp of a tall, dark-eyed merchant. Money changed hands and the father grabbed the girl by the arm and dragged her away. She continued to clutch the hidden spindle.

Yaakke dropped that life-thread as if it were hot, sensing

danger to himself in the vision. Shame heated his mind as if he were responsible for the girl's distress. Who was she? He was sure he'd never met her, never seen a woman with two four-strand brands that joined into one halfway down her back. Why was her life wrapped around his as if they were soul mates?

He resisted the pull to view more of the girl's life. One more vision of her might answer his questions and quiet the longing that surrounded his heart. No time. He had to get out of the void.

Somewhere there was an exit. But where? Blackness and the coils of lives stretched on toward infinity.

Chapter 6

"**W**here can the boy be?" Jaylor paced the flat roof atop the central keep of the last monastery dedicated to the priests of the Stargods. Its remote solitude had, so far, left it untouched by the purges of all enclaves of magicians. He feared their safety was only temporary. When the extremists ran out of targets for their venom, they would remember that a man must first be a magician before he became a priest. Temples and monasteries might lose their sacred protection.

Jaylor glared at a long telescope mounted atop the crenellated wall as if the arcane instrument could provide answers. His concern for his missing apprentice demanded more immediate answers than his worry over political purges and the omens his study of the heavens offered.

Master Fraandalor, known as Slippy within the intimate enclave of the Commune of Magicians, shrugged his shoulders in reply and positioned his eye to look through his own priceless equipment. "A quest is by necessity a solitary endeavor," he said, still squinting through the lens toward the northeastern sky.

"But he left the capital alone, before Brevelan and I did. He didn't collect any drageen to buy supplies or wait for special instructions. I haven't been able to find him in the glass for weeks and I'm worried about him." Jaylor ran his left hand through his unrestrained hair, then finger-combed his beard. "He didn't have the benefit of the trial by Tambootie smoke."

"We couldn't put him through that, Jaylor." Slippy made a notation on a piece of parchment without lifting his eyes from the telescope. "He hasn't reached puberty yet. He wouldn't have survived the ordeal."

"What happens when his body does make the change and his magic runs as wild as his emotions?" Jaylor resisted the urge to slam his fist into the long black tube that had been bequeathed to the first magicians of Coronnan by the Stargods.

"I don't know what will happen to Yaakke, Jaylor. The ritual of the Tambootie smoke is older than communal magic. If there were any records of what happens when a magic talent runs wild at puberty—especially a talent as strong as Yaakke's—those records were destroyed. We lost so much knowledge by suppressing solitary magic." Slippy shook his head in regret and returned to stargazing, the time-honored duty of all men of talent: magicians, healers, and priests of the Stargods.

The knowledge gained by observation of the sun and moon and stars would become as scarce as true glass if the fanatics rallying around the Council of Provinces destroyed the Commune. The precious instruments could not be replaced. New ones made by the Sisters of the Stars never quite measured up to the originals. Only dragon fire was hot enough to burn the Kardia's impurities out of sand to make glass clear enough for lenses. Normal furnaces left the glass too muddy and brittle for much of any use. Dragons hadn't been cooperative or predictable for several generations. There were many reasons Yaakke had been sent to seek them.

"I stalled Yaakke's quest as long as I could, hoping he'd exhibit some signs of maturation while he learned something of responsibility."

"You did the best you could. He's a headstrong boy with a mind of his own. Almost as determined and imaginative as you were at that age." Slipppy chuckled without looking away from his telescope.

"He's at least thirteen, maybe as old as fifteen, and shows no sign of puberty. Do you suppose there's something wrong, that he'll never mature?" Jaylor asked the older magician.

"Sometimes that happens. Usually when the boy has been the victim of privation and cruelty as an infant. Or if his mother was the victim of those conditions during pregnancy. Sometimes it just happens."

"We'll never know if that's the case with Yaakke. He was dropped off at the poor house when quite young. We have no idea how old he was. One year old, based on his size? Or closer to three, based upon his manual dexterity? By the time he was indentured to the University no one thought to test him for intelligence because his language skills were retarded." More likely, he'd learned to keep his mouth shut in self-defense.

"I have heard of some distant races where maturity comes late—people who tend to live to very advanced ages," Slippy mused. "Could the boy hail from across the seas?"

Jaylor shrugged. Yaakke's thick dark hair, big lustrous eyes, and olive skin weren't common features in Coronnan, but they were not unknown.

"He'll turn up eventually, Jaylor. Now get back to work. This unexpected meteor shower won't last much longer. We need to record the data for interpretation later. Perhaps the unusual pattern is an omen of the dragons returning."

"Or a sign of disasters yet to come," Jaylor grumbled as he bent to look through his instrument. "I wonder if I could sniff for his magic in the void?"

"Don't even think about it!" Slippy looked up aghast. "The last time you ventured into the void the dragons almost kept you."

"Yaakke never feared that damned transport spell. Sometimes I wish my apprentice had never discovered it."

"Next time you wish that, remember how important the spell is in keeping the Commune and our scientific equipment safe from that new cult, the Gnostic Utilitarians. Whoever heard of preferring to earn something by hard work, study, and sweat rather than requesting it by magic?"

"Our enemies don't want knowledge and hard work, they just resent the fact that magicians have secrets and power beyond mundane control. I just hope our spy in the capital manages to stay out of their way."

Yaakke thrust the shimmering white umbilical away from his heart. As fascinating as the girl seemed to be, he had to find a familiar thread and follow it out of the void—no matter where it led.

He plucked the nearest coil of colored life away from his face. Cool and gold except for a black spot that looked as if disease burned into the shiny metal. This should be King Darville. A bright iridescent thread entwined with the gold one had to be Rossemikka.

Slowly Yaakke sorted the cords by the colors of the people who had come close to him. Copper for Brevelan, rusty soil tinged with magician blue must be Jaylor. He deserved the blue now that he was Senior. A silver line dangled from where Yaakke's belly button should be. An early lesson in magic theory tickled his mind. No one ever saw the true colors of his own aura until tested and found worthy by the dragons.

Could he follow his own life back out of the void? That might lead him right back where he started—into the suspicion-riddled capital. An abrupt materialization would earn him witchbane and imprisonment at the hands of the Council.

Then a grayish-green cord wrapped around his waist and squeezed until a sensation akin to belly cramp demanded his attention. More cautiously than before, Yaakke plucked at it. The keeper of the Bay Hag Inn appeared before him, thrashing around his filthy kitchen and pantry. He screamed and searched the cupboards. Though Yaakke couldn't hear his words, he knew the man needed bread and cheese and dried meat to supply the last group of travelers. Every cabinet, basket, and shelf was as empty as his cash box. Illusory coins passed and exchanged by Yaakke during the coronation festival had vanished. Behind the innkeeper stood a tax collector. Without the journey rations to sell to the travelers, the innkeeper didn't have enough cash left to pay his due. Yaakke had stolen a large portion of those rations for his fast trip away from the capital.

An unpleasant taste penetrated Yaakke's overloaded senses. He couldn't remember why he'd had to steal or where he was going. He thrust aside the innkeeper. The man was a cheat and overcharged for everything from his rooms to a single mug of ale. He deserved a hefty fine for overdue taxes.

Maybe Yaakke should search out the single crystal umbilical that was Shayla. Certainly the dragon would be willing to help him.

Help him do what?

He thrust his shadowy hand past another bluish cord. A
vision of Nimbulan, the greatest magician in Coronnan's
history, shimmered before him. The exhausted founder of
the Commune said a sad farewell to his beloved wife as
she left Coronnan for a lonely exile. All magicians who
couldn't gather dragon magic were banished from Coronnan at the end of the great War of Disruption. All women
of magic, led by Nimbulan's wife, Myrilandel, were included in that ban.

Yaakke knew what it was like to be alone.

Other scenes from Coronnan's past fled by him. He
watched, fascinated, as lives wove themselves into the web
that trapped Yaakke. Curiosity propelled him forward and
back through time. He caressed the umbilicals, searching
for . . . searching for . . .

He couldn't remember. Somewhere in the compelling in-
terplay of life, he lost track of himself. Yet something told
him he couldn't waste any more time here. He had to go.
But where? What was time?

The copper umbilical glided beside him. Copper. That
was important. Copper, a planetary element, anchored to
the core of Kardia Hodos. Copper for Brevelan and her
unique nurturing magic.

Partial memory lightened fading corners of his mind.
Brevelan, the first woman to care enough about him to
teach him manners and give him hugs without attempting
to pick his pockets. He had to find her clearing deep in the
southern mountains. From there he needed to make his
way to Shayla's old lair higher yet in those mountains.

He picked up the copper cord, seeking an image to guide
him back out of the void.

Instead of the clearing, he saw a cave. Jaylor and Brevelan. The two were frozen in time, reaching out in protest,
Reaching out to Shayla. Yaakke watched, horrified, as a
dancing Krej used his magic to transform Shayla into a
glass sculpture. Every transparent hair that cloaked the
dragon's gravid body changed into a real crystal. The elegant all color/no color wing veins and spines dulled from

natural iridescence to clear glass. The life within her and the lives of the twelve babies she carried stilled, stumbled, glimmered, just barely aware. Yaakke nearly dropped the copper thread of life in despair.

The images faded and something alive and wonderful died within Yaakke. One of Shayla's babies hadn't survived that spell. When freed of the magic prison, the dragon's anger over Krej's betrayal of the pact between Coronnan and the dragon nimbus caused her to fly away, leaving magic chaos in her wake.

Now it was up to Yaakke to find her again and restore the controls that existed only in dragon magic. Those controls would also end his own magic career. Because he couldn't gather dragon magic, the Commune would exile him or dose him with witchbane.

The blue-tipped male dragon had asked for a meeting in the very cave where Krej had worked his evil. Could he provide clues to Shayla's location?

Solid ground rocked Yaakke's body and jarred his teeth. Slowly he opened one eye. Did he have an eye to open, or was that an illusion of the void?

Morning light, slanting through the thick forest pierced his vision. By contrast to the emptiness of the void, the watery sun trying to break through the clouds and fog seemed blindingly bright. Cautiously, he checked around him.

The clearing! Familiar, homey, isolated. He gulped the fresh mountain air filled with the clean and natural scents of trees and ferns, of animals and life. Real scents and sounds, not the dulled echoes of memories tangled together in the void.

"Late. Ye'r late," a jackdaw's mocking greeted him from the bird's perch atop the hut's roof. White tufts of feathers above his eyes waggled in stern disapproval.

"Shut up, you stupid bird. How'd you get here so fast?" He'd given up questioning why Corby was so intent upon following him.

Yaakke's stomach growled. The tiny discomfort was a wonderful reminder that he lived. He reached for the journey rations in his pack. Gone. His pack hadn't survived the transport. Memory of the innkeeper's frantic search for something to sell so he could pay his taxes flashed before

Yaakke's mind. The sour taste returned to his mouth. Had he been responsible?

Food first. Think later.

Before leaving for the coronation, Brevelan had stashed a sack of oats by the hearth. The flusterhens would probably have laid some eggs in the coop. The goat would need milking. Enough to fill him up once he started a cooking fire.

His stomach growled and roiled at the same time. He was so hungry he almost fainted; so hungry the thought of food sickened him.

How long had he been in the void anyway? A day, a week, a year?

"*Stargods*, I hope the dragon waits for me. I can't afford to lose any more time." He thought about transporting up to the lair. Brevelan's copper life force had left an indelible memory of the cave in his mind to direct the spell.

Coils of colored lives, and one shimmering white one, enticed him back into the void, invited him to linger and learn.

"Ye'r late! Late, late, late," Corby reminded him again.

"I'll be later yet if I don't get something to eat," Yaakke protested. The blue-tipped dragon was right. Yaakke had used the transport spell once too often. Next time he might not have the will to leave the void.

"I'm still hungry!" Hilza whined, her voice little more than a whisper.

"We're all hungry," Katrina tried to soothe her sister. Was there any way to ease the pangs that gnawed at her belly? Two weeks of anxious waiting for the ship while bankers hounded P'pa for repayment of their investment; then two more weeks of small, meatless meals as P'pa scrambled for every coin he could gather to repay the bankers lest they send him to prison.

"Just try to think of something else, baby." P'pa looked at his plate as if by a miracle he'd left a tidbit to give Hilza. Flesh had fallen from his face since the day his ship hadn't sailed into port on time.

"Don't coddle the child," M'ma pouted. "She's old enough to learn that we are all paying for your mistake,

Fraanken." M'ma's face was still full and bright. Only P'pa made the effort to give some of his share to his children.

"There is still time, Tattia. The ship may have been delayed by storms," P'pa protested.

"Tell that to the bankers and King Simeon!" M'ma screamed.

Hilza wailed in fright. Katrina choked back her own fear. Fear that tomorrow there would be no food on the table. Cold and upset, she reached over and pulled her youngest sister into her lap. Every meal lately ended with someone in tears. At least Maaben had the sense to spend her afternoons with Tante Syllia and Oncle Yon so she would be invited to stay for dinner. P'pa's brother and sister-in-law were childless and doted on Maaben, but had no time for studious Katrina or timid little Hilza.

"I've tried and tried for an audience with His Majesty," P'pa explained. "He won't see me. He won't admit that he ordered me to invest in that ship or that he has already borrowed and spent his share of the profits. Profits that will never be. He won't accept any part of the blame." P'pa seemed to shrink within his altered robes.

Yesterday, Katrina had cut all the costly embroidery from her father's clothing and reshaped the fabric for him. The ornaments had been sold to buy tonight's meager supper of rice and stale bread. The price of the food equaled what a full banquet would have cost six moons ago.

"If the ship doesn't come tomorrow, the day after at the latest, we'll have to sell Katrina's patterns," M'ma pronounced. "Without the patterns to work, we might as well sell the pillow and bobbins, too. She'll never be accepted into the palace school without her own patterns. Do you want to be responsible for ruining your daughter's future?"

"Perhaps if you spoke to the queen?" P'pa looked hopefully to his wife.

"The queen dismissed me today and impounded my pillow and patterns." M'ma dropped her eyes and her voice. "Please, Fraanken, you have to do something before we starve."

Katrina had never seen her mother so reduced, so helpless. Always, Tattia Kaantille's talent and experience with lace had placed her above ordinary people, granted her privileges and secured her place in society. Now she was lost. Katrina feared they were all lost as well as hungry.

"What will it take to make the king forgive you, P'pa?" Katrina whispered around the lump in her throat.

"Too much."

"What, Fraanken?" M'ma raised her head, hope bright in her eyes.

P'pa stood so fast he knocked over his chair. "I will sell myself to the slave ships before I sacrifice any of my daughters to The Simeon's bloodthirsty god, Simurgh!"

Hilza wailed again in fright and hunger.

Katrina lost all heat from her already shivering body.

Chapter 7

"**T**his doesn't seem right, M'ma." Katrina shuffled her feet on the wooden sidewalk of Royal Avenue. This major thoroughfare ran straight through Queen's City on a true east-west axis. To the north lay the tall, elegant houses of the merchants. Beyond them on the hillside were the palaces of the nobles. To the south lay the commercial district and warehouses that fronted on the SeLenicca River. M'ma walked toward those warehouses.

"Right doesn't put food on the table, Katey. With King Simeon's threat hanging over our heads, we dare not add any more debt, lest he take you and your sisters as sacrifices. Last week he announced that he needs the deaths of all the queen's prisoners to fuel his next battle spell and win through the pass into Coronnan." Tattia Kaantille charged ahead on the crowded street. "If I don't sell this pattern today, we'll have to sell your patterns and pillow, then next week the house will go. Though the Stargods only know if anyone in SeLenicca has the money to buy it."

"Sell the house?" That would mean moving outside Queen's City. The homeless and dispossessed must leave this side of the river after sunset.

In recent months Katrina had watched the south bank of the River Lenicc become a veritable city of tents and hovels in its own right. Large numbers of desperate and destitute people fled there daily from all over SeLenicca as mines and timberlands closed.

Signs of a collapsing economy and the trade embargo with Coronnan affected Katrina's family faster than most residents of their neighborhood. No servant walked ahead of Tattia as a symbol of her wealth and favor with the queen. Katrina supposed the cook, the governess, the butler, and scullery maids were now part of the crowds who pressed against her, hands out begging, or attempting to creep into her pockets. There was nothing in her pockets to steal. Indeed the only signs that she and her mother had ever been privileged were the still sturdy black cloth of their skirts and cloaks and the two braids that started at their temples and joined into a single plait at their shoulder blades. Peasant women wore a single braid. Noble women wore three. Only the queen wore four plaits.

"But why must we tell the factory owner I designed the pattern?" Katrina hurried her steps a little so she wouldn't be separated from her mother by the press of people. They stepped off the sidewalk into a muddy alley.

"Because the queen has forbidden my designs. That's one of the prices we have to pay for your father's foolish investment." Tattia set her lips in a grim line. She scanned the narrow alley for unfriendly elements hiding in the shadows before proceeding farther.

"Do you think the factory owner will buy the pattern? He'll never believe that I drew it. I'm not even an apprentice—officially," she hastily added. M'ma had been teaching her at home, pushing her through the apprentice patterns and into journeywoman work faster than the palace normally allowed.

"No, but you are my daughter. We must make these men believe that you have inherited my talents."

"I'm not sure I can . . . I don't know enough about lace." Katrina bit her lip in uncertainty.

"Nonsense, Katrina. This is a simple T'chon pattern that uses twenty pairs of bobbins. I designed it for apprentices. It's so easy, the factory girls ought to be able to produce leagues of it for export. Just mention symmetry and geometric grids. They'll believe you. These are businessmen, not lacemakers!"

The alley suddenly narrowed and veered off to the right. Refuse grew thick in the gutter, as if it were some exotic plant with a life of its own. Shops with houses above gave way to warehouses—windowless, bleak, and huge. Empty. The air smelled of fish and garbage. They emerged onto a planked walkway beside the docks.

Katrina stared at the pier where P'pa's ship was supposed to rest at anchor, hoping for a miracle. If only the black-hulled vessel with red Kaantille sails bumped gently against the dock, all their troubles would be over.

"I don't like this district, M'ma." Katrina slipped her hand into her mother's.

"Who does? But thread has to be kept moist or it becomes brittle and breaks. The best place for a lace factory is near the river. These old warehouses are rotten with damp."

"I bet the lacemakers are, too."

"Yes, well, I suppose many of the women suffer from the cold and the damp. It's necessary. There wouldn't be any money in SeLenicca at all if we didn't have lace to export. Stargods only know if there will ever be any timber or enough ore to supply overseas markets again," Tattia whispered.

"Perhaps if we went to the temple first and prayed, M'ma. Not many people do that now. Maybe the Stargods have time to listen to our prayers."

"Don't even think that, child!" M'ma looked around hastily for signs of eavesdroppers. "We're in enough trouble with King Simeon. We daren't ask for more by being seen at the temple."

"But going to temple isn't forbidden," Katrina protested. Suddenly she felt an overwhelming need to kneel before an altar and release all of her family's problems to the Stargods.

"No, prayer in the temple has not been forbidden by the king—yet. But such action earns his extreme displeasure."

For centuries the people had believed a never-ending supply of resources to exploit was their gift from the Stargods. To nurture and replant the land was blasphemy—denial of SeLenese status as the Chosen.

Now the resources were gone and no one knew how to replace them.

King Simeon preached a new philosophy. The people of SeLenicca were the Chosen of Simurgh, not the Stargods. The ancient bloodthirsty god required feeding for SeLenicca to regain its dominance in world trade and politics. King Simeon said he would get SeLenicca new resources through conquest, not farming or praying. Those who agreed with the king's religion—at least in public—found favor at court and in the marketplace.

A dark-green wooden door suddenly appeared in the otherwise blank brick wall of a factory. Freshly painted, with shiny brass hardware, the doorway invited business people within. Tattia paused long enough to take a deep breath before turning the doorknob.

Katrina followed her into the murky depths of the entry with heavy feet and a lump in her throat.

"This is necessary," she muttered to herself. "We have to get enough money to buy food and firewood."

A tiny bell jingled above them as the door swung shut of its own accord. A man approached them from the open office to their left. Tall and thin, he moved with an odd grace.

Katrina thought anyone that tall and long-limbed should jerk and wobble his way toward them. Dark eyes burned from his gaunt face beneath a fringe of sandy-blond hair. He wore a square beard.

"Outland half-breed!" M'ma hissed through her teeth.

Katrina hoped the man hadn't heard the insult. Success today depended upon his goodwill.

"We are not hiring today." The man looked down his nose at them. A long way down.

"I do not seek employment." M'ma stood tall and straight. Every bit of her artistic superiority added majesty to her posture and highlighted the man's inferior breeding.

"Then why do you disturb my busy schedule?" The man didn't back down before M'ma's glare.

"I wish to discuss a matter of business with the owner." M'ma sniffed as if the hallway smelled as badly as the gutters outside.

"You do not have an appointment." The man withdrew two steps. He reached to close the office door with long, slender fingers. Katrina thought his hands ideal for making lace.

"Tell your superior that Tattia Kaantille wishes to speak with him."

The man's eyes widened a little at the name then closed to mere slits. "No man, or woman, is my superior, madam.

And I am the owner of this establishment. You do not have an appointment."

The door slammed in their faces.

"Hmf!" M'ma sniffed her disgust. "I'll have your father track down the true owner of this factory. That ungrateful peasant will be fired for his insolence to us. Everyone knows you can't trust dark-eyes. They are born stupid and dishonest."

"You shouldn't have insulted him, M'ma," Katrina whispered.

"I don't want to do business with anyone who hires out-land half-breeds." M'ma marched back up the alley. "No wonder the country is falling to pieces. First the queen marries a foreigner, and now inferiors are allowed positions of authority."

A few more twists and turns in the back streets brought them to another grim factory. This time the green door wasn't newly painted and the brass fittings needed a good polish.

The man inside the office was small, wiry, and as filthy as M'ma thought the outlander had been. He bought the design, but only after M'ma had sworn that no one else in the city had it.

"We will try the next two factories. That should give us enough money to last the month." M'ma smiled brightly as she secreted the coins inside her embroidered vest.

"But, M'ma, you just swore that no one else in the city had the design!" Katrina protested almost as loudly as her empty stomach.

"And no one else does. Yet," M'ma replied.

"Isn't that illegal?"

"This is a matter of survival, Katey."

"Oh, M'ma, this seems so wrong so . . . so dirty. Please, don't make me come back here."

"Lord Jonnias?" Rejiia whispered into her father's glass. "You could depose Darville and rule all of Coronnan if you destroyed the Commune. You know where the Commune hides." That piece of information had come to her with the cost of many spells and the lives of several informers—none of them Jaylor's spy here in the capital. Now she revealed the secret to Jonnias.

The image of the sleeping lord squirmed within the candle flame behind Rejiia's glass. The basic summons spell worked better than a compulsion with mundanes, if she spoke to them in their dreams. When they awoke, her words seemed her victim's own ideas and they didn't build up resistance to the spell as Rossemikka had to Janataea.

"Take a witch-sniffer, Jonnias. Take him to the ancient monastery in the foothills of the southern mountains." She waited a moment for that idea to settle in the lord's mind. "You will need the troops of Marnak the Elder and the Younger plus your own. The wife of the Younger will provide you with a copy of the king's personal banner to grant you authority. She will demand to go with you. Accede to her wishes."

The image of Jonnias smiled in his sleep. Pompous and arrogant he might be. But he wasn't stupid. He knew that Darville and Jaylor had been friends most of their lives.

"Jaylor will blame Darville for the attack when he sees the banner. If he survives the attack, their friendship will be broken. Then they will both be vulnerable.

"You have followers within the new cult. They will make you king if you destroy the Commune."

"Yes," Jonnias whispered in his sleep. "Yes."

Rejiia extinguished the flame, breaking her contact with the odious lord. She allowed herself a moment's rest before she repeated the summons to Lord Marnak the Elder. The two were easy to manipulate. Their inflated sense of self-importance made them vulnerable to her plans. When their conspiracy failed because they overstepped their abilities to lead, she would abandon them. Until then, they served a purpose.

A chuckle tickled the back of her throat. She wondered which one of them would be first to order a new crown made. The Coraurlia contained the taint of magic. They wouldn't be able to justify using it if they used the Gnuls to achieve their goals.

But the Coraurlia was the crown Rejiia sought. Its magical protection *Sang* to her in her dreams.

She caressed the tin statue that sat beside her chair. "Soon, P'pa. Soon I will be queen. Then I will be able to set you free. By then I will have learned more magic and you must recognize me as your equal. I will not submit to you demeaning me in public again. Until then, I must send you by fishing boat and other secret ways to a place of safety."

(You are late.) A deep voice bellowed the words from the depths of the cave through Yaakke's physical and mental ears. He stopped short before passing through the black entrance into the heart of the mountain.

"Ye'r late, late, late." Above him, the attendant jackdaw circled and echoed the dragon's proclamation.

Late? Yaakke knew he'd lost time in the void. How much time? Certainly not two weeks. Autumn weather hadn't deepened by more than a day or two at most. The sun had warmed his back quite nicely on his long walk from the clearing. When he'd discovered the barriers around the clearing were down, probably because Brevelan wasn't there, he'd started the trek uphill rather than wait to recover his strength for a shape-change. The single night he'd spent sleeping rough had been cold, but not intolerable as long as his campfire glowed within a bubble of armor.

"I . . . got lost in the void," Yaakke stammered his explanation.

(I told you not to use that spell.) Light shifted and distorted within the cave entrance. Star bursts of light exploded before Yaakke's eyes.

He blinked and refocused and blinked again. The brightness settled into sunbeams refracted off the faceted points of a huge oval jewel. He forgot the journey dust that clogged his throat.

Tremors traveled beneath the ground, telling of something heavy moving across the stony plateau in front of the cave. The jewel took on a more definite shape. A fold of a nearly transparent membrance closed over an all color/no color kaleidoscope.

A dragon's eye! Yaakke sighed in relief. The blue-tipped dragon had waited. But how long? Now for the first time, Yaakke wished he'd learned to center his magic so that it tracked time accurately.

Gradually the rest of the dragon emerged from the depths of the lair. Hazy, autumnal sunshine slanted off his crystalline fur, pulling Yaakke's sight around the dragon rather than directly toward him. He blinked and forced his mind to concentrate on the outline of the huge creature before his eyes tricked his mind into believing the dragon invisible.

Larger than Shayla, the dragon rested back on his haunches. Blue veins outlined the shape of wings folded against his back. More blue marched across his head and down his back in a showy display of horns. On his shortened forelegs, blue claws flexed, much like human fingers.

Yaakke waited, expecting the dragon to offer his name according to dragon protocol.

The dragon remained silent while surveying Yaakke with those penetrating eyes.

Yaakke squirmed in guilty self-consciousness. "I'm sorry." Finally he offered the apology he knew he owed the dragon.

(You have become arrogant with your power.) The dragon words came into Yaakke's head unbidden.

"I'm sorry," Yaakke's murmured again. "I should have guessed you have more knowledge of the void than I." He hung his head a little, peeping up at the dragon through lowered lashes.

(I hope your trip through the realm of the dragons taught you something useful.)

"I don't know . . . um . . . sir. What do I call you anyway?"

(Sir will do.)

"Anyway, *sir,* the images came so fast I didn't recognize half of what I saw." A memory of moon-bright hair and tears on a girl's pale face flashed through his mind. "Who is she?"

(You will learn that when your time reference catches up with what you observed. Time has no meaning in the void. Past, present, and future are all the same. Dragons observe it all and learn.)

"Why did you call me here?"

(Shayla needs assistance from the magicians.)

"Shayla!" Yaakke breathed through his teeth. His quest was almost over. He'd be the youngest Master Magician ever. Without ever having been a journeyman!

(Your journey is long, apprentice. Long in distance and long in maturity.) The dragon speared Yaakke with a com-

pelling gaze. *(There are things you must know before you face the dangers ahead of you.)*

The ominous tone of the words in the back of Yaakke's mind was so like Old Baamin, the boy automatically keyed all of his attention to the huge beast.

(Drink, Boy. Then we will discuss your future and perhaps your past.) The dragon gestured with his muzzle toward a crystal cold stream trickling down the mountain face beside the cave entrance.

"You promised to tell me about my parents, sir," Yaakke reminded the dragon.

(I know of your sire and your dam. The knowledge will be given to you at the appropriate time.)

"When will that be?"

(At the appropriate time. Drink and refresh yourself. You have much to learn in order to find Shayla.)

Curiosity flared. Yaakke was always eager to know more about magic. He'd taught himself to read so that he could steal books from the University library before he knew for sure he had any magic.

Yaakke knelt beside the little pool that formed in a hollow made by the falling stream. He cupped his hands in the water. Colors and images swirled before his vision, then faded to reflections of sunlight on water. He drank deeply, twice, then splashed his face and hair reasonably clean.

One more drink. He'd never known plain water to taste so sweet before. Head bent over the pool, he was about to dip his hands once again, when the dragon's reflection shimmered in the water.

The beast loomed behind him, magnificent head higher than two sledge steeds. Sunlight sparkled. Water reflected. Crystal fur shimmered and those huge, faceted eyes showed access to the void and all of those tempting umbilicals.

Chapter 8

Pinpoints of light speared Yaakke's eyes, then burst into a myriad of stars. Suddenly the dark cave entrance and the crystal spring disappeared.

A thundering cascade of water filled his ears. His gut reverberated in response to the deep *boom* of a river tumbling hundreds of feet into a deep pool. He shivered as cold spray dampened his clothes and drizzled down his face. A wall of algae-slick granite, older and paler than the jagged basalt near the lair, pressed into his face, but he didn't dare jerk away from the slime until he found secure footing. He glanced at his feet without moving his head. A narrow shelf of rock jutted out from a cliff side, barely wide enough to contain both of his feet.

Finger-length by finger-length, he eased his body around to face the roaring waterfall. Tiny droplets tumbled, joined, separated, fell hundreds of feet below him into a wide pool. Turbulence from the waterfall thrust small waves across a deep pool to a long rolling meadow. Steep walls on three sides defined a wide vale that narrowed at the far end into a canyon leading to the outside world. His only exit from this unknown mountain hideaway?

A wide undercut yawned deep into the base of the cliff behind the waterfall. He knew instinctively that a series of caves wandered back into the bowels of the mountain from that barely glimpsed opening. Shadow within shadow moved behind the lacy curtain of water. Was that the outline of a dragon head, its glittering eyes the same color as the water drops?

He'd found Shayla! But where?

Then Yaakke scanned the setting for clues. He looked

up. A black bird with funny white tufts on its head soared up the cliff a hundred feet above him. Scrubby everblues seemed to hang out over the edge. The water poured over the lip around and through them. Ferns, lichens, and wildflowers clung to the rocky face, adding spring vibrancy to the scene.

The waving grass in the open field appeared lush with moisture and new growth. Clumps of tall shrubs offered shade and shelter on this bright afternoon. More than just shrubs, stunted Tambootie trees. Dragon salad.

Above the hidden vale, sharp mountain peaks, still covered in snow, rose in undulating tiers into the distant, hazy horizon. Jutting out from closer crags and pinnacles, wind-sculpted lumps of stone pointed toward the cloudless sky. Dragons standing guard?

Yaakke sniffed the air and wrinkled his nose. "Woodsmoke." Alarm sent his heart racing. Corby cawed loudly in distress, then disappeared. Soon, the mindless destruction of fire unleashed would envelop this lovely glade. Tambootie smoke would poison all living creatures within two leagues or more.

He sought the magic power that should be entwined with the rock and soil of the cliff. No energy tingled through his body. "Rain. *Stargods*, I need rain to stop this!" Concentrating the failing reserves of his own body, he reached up into the sky for every drop of moisture available.

A small cloud formed. Then another. Tiny, fluffy white clouds. Not big enough or heavy enough to release a single drop of rain.

(Cease!)

Dragon thoughts sent him tumbling down, down toward the pool. Cold water numbed his mind and body. Pain lanced through his temple.

(You may not change a dragon-dream.)

Yaakke sat up from the plateau outside Shayla's old lair. "Dream? It all seemed so real." Delicately he probed his temple with shaking fingers. Aches spread outward into his jaw and ear. No sticky blood. Just a bruise from collapsing onto the ground.

(Reality changes from eyeblink to eyeblink. What you see is real until you disprove it with new perceptions.)

"Where is this place you showed me? Not in Coronnan.

The mountain shapes were wrong. Too jagged and bare of trees." Yaakke inspected the rest of his body for damage, glad that he hadn't ceased breathing because he thought he fell into a pool and drowned.

(Your quest ends in a place that appeared to you in the dragon-dream. The jackdaw will guide you.)

"Do I still have a quest? I left Jaylor without an explanation. I disobeyed you. Will anyone trust me after that?"

(Seek Shayla with your heart as well as your mind. She will trust your heart.)

"What is that supposed to mean?"

(Shayla's life depends upon you. Without Shayla the Nimbus of Dragons will die.)

"I need to talk to Jaylor first. He'll help me understand . . ." His voice trailed off. Yaakke wasn't certain what he needed to understand. His bizarre trip through the void followed by a dragon-dream seemed to have scrambled his insides as well as his thoughts.

(You may discuss this with me.) The dragon sounded sad or upset that Yaakke sought advice from another.

"You're just a dragon. You wouldn't understand."

Uncomfortable silence stretched between them.

(If only I could tell you.)

Was that a dragon thought? Yaakke wondered if he truly caught a glimmer of hurt and resignation in the droop of the dragon's muzzle and half-closed eyes. He shook his head, trying to clear it of confusion so he could be sure.

More silence.

(Jaylor's hiding place is on your way.)

"On my way where? Is Shayla hurt like King Darville? Can she fly?"

Yaakke twisted his neck to peer at the dragon. Gone! The dragon was gone, disappeared.

"I know you are nearly invisible, but this is too much."

Silence except for the distant call of a jackdaw. Yaakke staggered to his feet and blundered toward the cave entrance that had shadowed the dragon. With outstretched hands he examined the lair entrance. Nothing.

"Is this whole thing a dragon-dream?" No one answered but Corby. "*S'murgh it*, I could still be in the capital for all I know."

*   *   *

Jaylor squinted through his telescope one last time. The other Master Magicians had deserted him for the warmth of their beds hours ago. There wasn't anything particularly interesting in the sky tonight. But Jaylor needed the practice. And he needed some time alone.

A year ago, when he'd begun his journeyman's quest, all he'd wanted was to "Go see an invisible dragon" and earn the right to be a Master Magician. He had no idea, then, precisely what master status entailed. Now he knew.

Master Magicians charted the stars, tabulated the paths of celestial bodies, and searched for anomalies and omens. Closer to the mundane population, magicians used their powers to minister to the sick, communicate with distant outposts, test the soil, and advise the people about proper nutrients and crop rotation and efficient breeding of stock. The secret knowledge entrusted to them by the Stargods provided them with guides. They experimented with tools and inventions, striving for improvements in production. They kept records and wrote chronicles. In better times, magicians advised the rich and powerful about diplomacy, economics, and alliances.

Those responsibilities were child's play compared to Jaylor's duties as Senior Magician. Endless lists of supplies, maintenance and observation schedules, keeping track of every member of the diminished Commune, and placing the magicians where their talents could be maximized and their limitations augmented by others. And a constant monitoring of the defensive war being waged at the pass near Sambol. How many magicians dared he post there without raising superstitious fear among the troops, generals, and Council? The number had to be enough to counteract King Simeon's indiscriminate use of battle magic. Where did they get the power to wage war? Everyone knew there were no ley lines in SeLenicca to fuel magic.

These late hours on the roof seemed to be the only time Jaylor had alone, to think, to plan, to worry. He couldn't remember the last time he'd gone to bed at the same time as Brevelan.

His wife and son were always sound asleep when he crawled beneath the covers and still asleep when he rose before dawn to his morning duties.

He checked the position of the wanderer he had been

monitoring for twenty-one nights. Then he measured its position between two fixed stars. His eyes blurred and he placed the point of light on the wrong chart, in the wrong position.

His geometric calculations on the chart tangled.

One more time. A deep breath for calm. A second deep breath for clear vision. His third deep breath sent him into a light trance. With the aid of his magic, he looked, measured, and calculated once more. The numbers fell into place. The wanderer had definitely shifted its position relative to his location. Precisely what it was supposed to do at this time of year.

The calculations on the chart, combined with the recent meteor shower, predicted chaos. The same conclusion the other masters had drawn a week ago.

At last he'd done something correctly. He bent to touch his toes, stretching his back in relief. As he stood again, his shoulder bumped the telescope.

"Dragon dung. Now it's out of alignment." He looked into the lens, still maintaining his extended senses, to see how far off he'd knocked the sights.

Shimmering pinpoints of light responded to his magic senses. Not starlight. Too green, wrong shapes. He extended his TrueSight and hearing through the telescope into the distance beyond.

At the extreme limits of his magic, woodsmoke caressed his nose. The sounds of drowsy steeds cropping grass within their picket line tickled his ears. Jaylor drew upon FarSight and the scene jumped as close as the exterior grounds of the monastery. Seventy-five, no, one hundred campfires. One thousand men. Herds of war steeds. He spotted a sentry patrolling a perimeter.

An army camped out there, half a day's hard march away.

Whose army? His spy in the palace had said nothing to him about an army on the move.

He wished for Yaakke's listening talent, or for the boy himself. No word from him for nearly two moons now. Curse the boy for his secretive ways and stubborn disregard for others.

Jaylor sought and found a silvery-blue ley line filled with magic power, running through the foundations of the monastery. Slowly, he urged the magic energy to rise through the walls. The stones caught the power, resonating with their internal music. The magic picked up the natural harmonics and amplified them within the ageless bones of the land. Jaylor listened to the singing of the power. His body vibrated in harmony with it. Only then did he draw upon the power, forcing it upward when it wanted to dart out into the world through his fingers. Up and up into his neck and his mind. The *Song* of the Kardia grew. He *Sang* the magic into his eyes and his ears.

Only then did he look through the telescope again. Bright banners atop gaudy war pavilions came into focus. He identified the flags of Marnak the Elder from Hanic in the southwest and Jonnias from Sauria in the northwest. Neither lord was particularly fond of Jaylor or his magicians, but they had sworn loyalty to Darville.

A third banner caught Taylor's attention. Marnak the Younger of Faciar. Through his wife, Rejiia, that sniveling little upstart had claimed Krej's old province. He, too, had sworn loyalty to Darville, but only after Jaylor had purged the young man of all traces of Krej's magic manipulation. If Marnak and Rejiia hadn't been so young and naive about Krej's corruption, the Council of Provinces would have forced them into exile with Krej's wife and six younger legitimate daughters. No one bothered counting his bastards.

Rumor in the capital claimed the tall, determined, and still very young heiress to the province intimidated her shorter husband, and that the marriage had never been consummated.

Rejiia had tried to renounce her marriage along with her father when the extent of Krej's evil became obvious. But the Council of Provinces had held the adolescent marriage to be legal and Rejiia's husband governor of her province.

The three lords encamped beyond the next line of hills were an odd confederation to lead an army. None of them had ever shown interest in the arts of war before.

Jaylor puzzled over the implications, listening to the small sounds of night life in a military camp. He swung his vision around the perimeter of pickets and steed lines, tents, and provision sledges. One more large pavilion stood off to the side, but still within the perimeter of the camp, as if seeking privacy and protection at the same time. The royal banner of a dragon outlined in gold against a midnight blue field surrounded by silver stars flew from the ridgepole. A golden wolf stood in the comer of the flag.

Darville's personal emblem. The presence of the king explained the other three banners. None of those lords would be willing to remain idle in the palace when there was a chance to kiss royal ass in the field.

The tent flap opened and a shadowy figure slipped out into the fresh night air. A tall man, broad of shoulder, slim of hip, stretched and yawned. King Darville. Jaylor's best friend.

As Jaylor watched, the king walked to the perimeter, speaking with each of the guards. Darville's personal contact with his soldiers had won their loyalty and made him a better general.

Why would Darville bring his army within two days' ride of where Jaylor and the Commune hid from the Council of Provinces?

Jaylor yawned and stretched. He couldn't think straight until he'd indulged in some much needed sleep. Darville would never deliberately harm him. Time enough to puzzle this out in the morning.

He thought of Brevelan's warm body and inviting arms. Already he ached to hold her tight against his chest and sleep with her sweet scent filling him with her serenity and calm.

Hilza coughed and coughed again. Katrina looked up from her newest lace pattern to check her sister. Hilza's thin body collapsed jerkily with each new spasm. Dots of sweat popped out on the little girl's brow though the workroom was icy. The kitchen fires that heated the whole house had been extinguished right after a meager breakfast of thin porridge, in order to conserve firewood.

Hilza coughed again, nearly choking from lack of breath. Maaben dropped her tablet of figures and dashed out of the room, slamming the door behind her. Distantly, Katrina heard the front door bang shut. She knew that Maaben would seek refuge from the stress of little food and less heat, of sickness and short tempers, with Tante Syllia and Oncle Yon. Their relatives welcomed Maaben, fed and cosseted her, where they rebuffed the rest of the family. King Simeon's displeasure with P'pa had extended to anyone seen assisting the Kaantille family.

Tears streamed down Hilza's face. "I can't help it, Katey. I can't stop coughing. Why does Maaben blame me?" She choked out the words around a raspy throat.

"I don't know, Hilza." Katrina cradled her youngest sister against her chest, rocking her gently, humming an old lullaby to soothe her.

> *All is quiet, all is still,*
> *Sleep, my child, fear not ill,*
> *Wintry winds blow chill and drear,*
> *Lullaby, my baby dear,*
> *Wintry winds blow chill and drear,*
> *Lullaby, my baby dear.*

"Maybe Maaben is afraid," Katrina cooed to her now quiet sister.

"She hates me," Hilza whispered around a sniffle.

"Hush, little one. Hush."

> *Let thy little eyelids close,*
> *Like the petals of the rose;*
> *When the morning sun shall glow,*
> *They shall into blossom blow,*
> *They shall into blossom blow,*
> *When the morning sun shall glow.*

"P'pa is trying to raise more money. He'll come home tonight with bundles of firewood and a fat chicken for our dinner." Katrina's mouth watered at the thought of meat, so long absent from their table.

"And M'ma?" Hilza murmured drowsily.

"M'ma has made a wonderful lace shawl for the queen. If Queen Miranda accepts the gift, then M'ma can go back to work at the palace." M'ma had worked the shawl with weaving silk, a thread much heavier than most lacework. Yet the fibers worked up to appear filmy and frothy. If M'ma started a new fashion trend, then she would be in demand to design more shawls and maybe veils. The Kaantille family would be rich again.

"But the queen may not like the gift," Hilza protested. She partially roused from her sleepiness but didn't raise her head. The cords of her neck stood out rigid and hard under Katrina's caressing fingers.

"She must accept it, little one. No one makes lace like M'ma does. The shipments of lace overseas are fetching less and less money since M'ma left the palace. Queen Miranda has to take M'ma back." She hoped.

The lace factories had stopped buying M'ma's designs. She'd falsely promised exclusive rights to the patterns once too often.

The front door slammed again. A heavy reluctant thread on the steep stairs. That would be P'pa. If his steps dragged, then his mission had failed. There would be no chicken for dinner.

Another step behind P'pa. This one springier and lighter. A stranger. The door to the workroom opened slowly. P'pa stood there, a deep scowl on his face. Defeat seemed to drag his shoulders down, shortening, reducing him to a haggard old man.

"What is it, P'pa?" Katrina looked up at her parent, frightened and insecure. She kept Hilza's weary body cradled within her arms, face buried in her lap.

"Is your mother home?" P'pa looked around the room, peering into shadows He seemed to fear what he might find.

"No" Katrina answered.

"Good." Was that relief in his tone and the raising of his shoulders?

A tall, hooded stranger appeared behind P'pa, pushing to gain access to the room. "Almost as cold in here as it is outside, Merchant Kaantille." The thin man rubbed his long-fingered hands together, not with cold, but with some kind of eagerness.

Katrina had seen those hands before. "Take the blasted patterns and be gone!" P'pa bellowed impatiently.

"Patterns? P'pa, you didn't!" Katrina darted across the room to her lace pillow, heedless of Hilza. She clutched the velvet bolster with its cache of patterns to her chest, letting the bobbins tangle. Pins that held her latest lace into the pattern pressed through her clothes, pricking her skin.

"I'm sorry, Katey. I had no choice." P'pa looked at the floor.

"Give me the pillow with the patterns, girl." The thin man stepped closer, hands reaching for her treasure. His hood fell back revealing the dark-eyed owner of the first lace factory she and M'ma had approached. The man M'ma had insulted.

"No. I don't care how much money you paid him. The pillow and patterns are mine. My dowry. He can't sell it." She swung around so her back was to the stranger. She hated the gleeful revenge that burned in his brown eyes.

"Give him the pillow, Katrina. Give it up or watch your sister die of the lung rot and the rest of us starve or freeze to death," P'pa ordered. His voice was as weak and reluctant as his steps.

He was right. The patterns contained within the pillow with its engraved bone bobbins were the most precious things left in the house. Even the glass window in the workroom had been sold, the opening covered with scrap wood. M'ma's pillow and patterns had remained at the palace when she was dismissed and could not be retrieved.

"I can't, P'pa. If I give this up, I have no future." Katrina dropped to her knees, her legs suddenly too weak to hold her upright.

"If you don't, we'll all starve, Katey." P'pa pried her fingers up and yanked the bolster out of her arms. He thrust it at the eager stranger.

A single bobbin broke loose from the tangle of fine cotton threads. Katrina caught it within the folds of her skirt. The men wouldn't notice one bobbin missing. Not one lonely little bone bobbin out of forty pairs.

"Take it and be gone. I don't want to ever see your face gain." P'pa ushered the stranger toward the door.

The man shoved a fat purse into P'pa's still outstretched hand. It slipped through his fingers and dropped to the floor with a clank that echoed around the silent room.

Katrina glanced at the bobbin still clutched in her skirt. "Tattia Kaantille" the engraved letters spelled in a spiral around the slender piece of bone. She traced the letters from bottom to top. Something sharp caught on the threads of her skirt. The glass bead on the bangle had shattered in the fall.

Chapter 9

Rejiia listened through the night for magic on the wind. Not long after midnight, she sensed a spell of braided magic winding its way through the encampment like a ghost of stray mist, questing but not disturbing.

Red and blue. The Senior Magician was scouting the army with that spell. She had watched Jaylor work magic in the capital often enough to know his signature colors.

Silently she crept from her bed behind a heavy screen in the largest pavilion. Marnak the Younger, her husband, snored on a cot on the other side of the screen. A year of marriage and he still hadn't found the courage to join her in bed. A shiver of loathing coursed through her as her nightrail brushed against his cot.

She thought she might have more respect for him if he'd raped her on their wedding night, as her father had advised. But now? The weak little lordling was still dependent upon and submissive to his father. Rejiia would rather sleep with the sergeant who patrolled the nobles' section of the encampment than with her lawful husband.

Outside the tent, she sniffed for the magic again, clearer and sharper in the fresh air. Half invisible, she followed the drifting red-and-blue braid to the edge of camp. Earlier, she had ordered a single tent set up here. A delusion slipped from her fingertips. She smiled in delight as she transformed the miserable private's shelter into a huge royal pavilion with Darville's personal banner flying above.

The magic circled the delusion briefly then hesitated at the opening, scanning Rejiia's form. She gave the questing magic an image of Darville tall, blond, dynamic in his masculinity. The red-and-blue braid persisted, wanting reassurance.

Reluctantly, Rejiia ambled around the edge of the camp, cloaked in the image of her royal cousin. She paused and spoke to several of the sleepy soldiers, as the king would do.

Darville had stolen the crown that should have been hers. She hated him and resented his presence even in this imaginary form.

At last Jaylor's magic was satisfied and retreated to the monastery. It smelled of curiosity partially satisfied.

Rejiia hummed a joyful tune she'd heard the troops singing as they marched from the capital. More than slightly bawdy and confident, the song collapsed the delusions. Her body tingled with power. Maybe she should seduce the sergeant, right under Marnak's nose.

No. Not tonight. She should save her maidenhead until she needed its destruction to fuel a spell of real importance. Her bed and a well-deserved sleep enticed her back to the camp. "Perhaps I'll dream of looting and rape and fire. Tomorrow the Commune dies along with my bastard sister and her brat. Brevelan stole my father's love from me. Now she will pay."

Yaakke forced himself to walk west, away from familiar jagged peaks toward the more rounded mountains of SeLenicca. Shayla's hiding place was in a valley near rounded mountains, stripped of timber. The only mountains like those were west of Coronnan. He counted four more steps and then four more.

"Shay-la needs me. Shay-la needs me," he recited in rhythm with his steps.

The more space he put between himself and the dragon lair, the less worn and confused he felt. Every time he looked at his body, he was afraid he'd start to fade into transparency—like the dragons.

Hunger gnawed at him constantly. He'd devoured all of the food he'd been able to scavenge in Brevelan's clearing—including one of her precious flusterhens. Villagers were shy and suspicious of strangers in this part of Coronnan, so he'd had to steal a few provisions here and there, including a pack and cooking utensils. Still he ached with fatigue and emptiness.

How long had he been in the void?

He looked at the sky for some indication he'd chosen the right direction. A deep overcast didn't betray the position of the sun.

Corby the jackdaw cawed enthusiastically above him, dropping a smelly blob on the trail behind Yaakke. He looked from the bird to his deposit, then along the trail. Sure enough, Corby had spotted a crested perdix lurking in the scrubby grasses. The characteristic head bobbing and twisted topknot were not fully developed in the bird. Probably a youngster without the sense to migrate.

Yaakke stood hunter-still. His mouth watered at the thought of a true meal cooked over a campfire. A palm-sized rock appeared in his fist. Desperation enhanced his reflexes and trued his aim. He flung the stone directly onto the perdix's bobbing head.

"Thanks, Corby. I'll save you some!" Yaakke plunged toward his prey.

"Owe me one, owe me one," the jackdaw cawed.

Almost, Yaakke considered eating the meat raw, feathers and all. Then something deep inside him sickened at the thought. Methodically he sought a campsite.

One good thing about being a magician: he could start a fire even when the wood was wet. He settled his pack beneath an overhang where the soil was reasonably dry. His tin pot came readily to hand. It always did, no matter where he'd stuffed it.

He'd seen a Rover trick once that might help him find Shayla or Jaylor—or someone who might help him. He needed food and rest first. When he had some grains and the gutted perdix simmering nicely, he granted himself the luxury of a quick wash and a fresh shirt. As he ran his fingers over his jaw and neck, the texture of his skin seemed changed, coarser, rougher. Using a calm pool at the edge of the creek as a mirror he checked for cuts or rash or just left over mud.

Nothing quite so usual greeted his reflection. Dark shadows creased his jaw and upper lip. The beginning of a beard! A rather complete and dark beard at that. Well, several days' worth anyway. The facial hair seemed soft and fine now. Soon enough it would grow thicker and heavier.

At last!

About time.

"La, la, la, la," he sang, testing the quality of his voice. To his own ear the notes sounded his same childish soprano.

"Loo, loo, loo, loo," he sang again, on a lower tone. Much lower than he used to sing.

"La, la, laeeeeek," he tried the high notes and lost all control.

Good. By the time he found Jaylor, maybe he'd be through the worst of the change and be able to speak like a man. Jaylor could authorize his trial by Tambootie smoke and promote him to journeyman. Once promoted, he could claim a larger piece of glass for focusing his spells. The trial might also grant him a vision to guide him to Shayla.

"Shayla needs me."

Yaakke tried the notes again and didn't croak until almost two tones lower than last time.

Corby jeered from his perch atop the boulder at Yaakke's miserable attempt to sing.

"Your voice doesn't sound much smoother, bird!" Yaakke returned to his campfire, anxious to try the Rover trick.

Just before leaving Shayla's lair, he had seen something very frightening reflected in water. More than reflections. A vision, or another dragon-dream. Jaylor and Brevelan and the baby had stood in the middle of a raging inferno, desperately seeking escape.

The vision had ended before Yaakke had seen an accurate picture of *where* Jaylor and Brevelan were. He needed to know where, or what direction in order to direct a standard summons spell.

Yaakke knew deep inside himself that Jaylor and his family needed help.

He'd been granted the vision for a reason. He had to find Jaylor and warn him of the fire. Or help him escape.

If the trick worked.

The trap is set. By an hour after sunrise, the Commune will cease to exist. An hour later my agent will inform King

Darville how it happened and who was responsible. Jonnias and the Marnaks will never be trusted in Council again. When they realize the depth of the rift between themselves and their king, the three sniveling lords will revolt. The rest of the Council will blame Darville for the newest civil war. He won't be allowed to survive as king of a country tearing itself apart and he without an heir and with a witch for a wife.

Within a few moons Coronnan will be in such chaos, the coven will be able to step in and enforce law and order on their own terms. Soon, so very soon.

Four horsemen backed by a thousand soldiers rode up to the gates of the monastery. Jaylor watched the three noble banners fluttering above the lieutenants who each represented a lord: Jonnias, Marnak the Elder, and Marnak the Younger. Higher than the three fluttered a fourth banner. The man carrying the symbol of a crystal dragon and a golden wolf didn't wear a uniform of the royal household or army.

An aura of hate shimmered over the entire army.

"I don't like the smell of this," Jaylor growled to Brevelan who stood by his side at the window of their tower room.

"I sense a great deal of anger out there." Brevelan edged behind Jaylor, putting a physical barrier between herself and the roiling emotions of a thousand armed men. "Anger and fear. They do not come in peace."

"Can you isolate Darville in the throng? I want to talk to him privately before I face those emissaries at the gate." Jaylor leaned against the windowsill, trying desperately to find one familiar blond head among the battle-hardened men.

Brevelan's eyes closed in concentration. Her pale skin turned whiter; but shadows hollowed her cheeks and furrowed in her brow. Jaylor resisted the urge to reach out and offer her strength and comfort. If he touched her right now, her contact with the army below would shrivel.

"No. There are too many people out there to find one soul." She shook her head. Huge blue eyes, clouded with bewilderment and pain, looked up to his. "Our king is the one person I should be able to isolate at any distance. He hides himself from me."

A momentary pang of jealousy brought a red mist to

Jaylor's eyes and judgment. Brevelan might be his, Jaylor's, wife now. Darville might be very much in love with his own bride, Rossemikka, *now*. But he could never forget that little less than a year ago, Brevelan had made a very hard choice between the two men.

The possibility that the king's seed had fathered Glendon remained.

"You know it is you I love, Jaylor," Brevelan reached across the barrier of his emotions.

A hard spot in his heart dissolved. Her small hand sought his. With those few words the jealousy died and love reblossomed in his chest. He clung to her hand, the simple gesture binding them together.

"What do we do about them?" She gestured to the horsemen who were pounding on the gates for entrance.

"I know Darville's banner gives this army authority. But I cannot find any reason our friend would betray our location to those three lords. He might tell Lord Andrall—his loyalty has never been questioned. But those three?" He shrugged in disbelief.

"Could it have been a trick to disarm your suspicions. You would open the gate willingly for your king."

"Aye. But not to Jonnias and the two Marnaks."

The wind shifted slightly, carrying the babble of voices from the army. The aura of hatred intensified.

"I believe we have been betrayed, Brevelan." By whom? An agent of the fanatical Gnostic Utilitarian cult which decreed that all knowledge must come by hard work and experience, not magic? His best friend? Jaylor faced that painful possibility reluctantly. His spy should have told him about this army before it left the capital. Perhaps the Council had decided to secretly remove Glendon, the king's bastard son, from Jaylor's and Brevelan's custody.

Never! Jaylor resolved. "Show Master Fraandalor an image of Shayla's old lair and have him begin transporting the library and the telescopes there. The time has come to find a new sanctuary for the Commune." Regret hung heavily on his shoulders.

The sanctity of this remote retreat for aging magicians, priests, and healers should not be violated by an army bent on destruction. Darville should not have succumbed to any of the forces that wanted an end to all magic in Coronnan.

"Will we be able to protect everyone there?" Brevelan looked out over the undulating sea of soldiers that spread across the hills. The noise of their coming increased.

"If Krej couldn't find the path up the mountain without help, then this mundane army won't be able to either. There is shelter, water, and privacy." He snatched a quick kiss from her. "Go quickly. I'll stall the lieutenants at the gates." The ancient wooden barriers were beginning to buckle from the pounding of sword hilts on the planks.

Brevelan's departure emptied the stark room of warmth and sunshine. Jaylor emptied his mind and body of emotion, allowing keen thoughts to focus without distraction. Only by eliminating his beloved from his consciousness could he generate the spells necessary to save her. To save the Commune.

"Why, Darville? Why are you with these men?" he asked the wind.

Below him, in the courtyard, the gatekeepers peered out the viewing hole of the right-hand gate. Anxiety written in their posture and the wringing of their hands, they looked up to the tower window for guidance.

Jaylor uncoiled a thread of magic, linking him to the gatekeepers. He fed them instructions to keep the gates barred, but not to retreat yet.

The banner-toting envoys drew back a pace. "Yield this sacred stronghold of the Stargods to Darville III, by the grace of the dragons, King of Coronnan!" bellowed the man carrying the banner of Jonnias of Sauria.

"This enclave belongs to the Stargods, not to any mundane king," one of the two gatekeepers squeaked a reply. His frail old voice barely carried through the massive wooden barrier.

The lieutenants growled and consulted among themselves for a stronger command.

Jaylor directed the gatekeepers to withdraw to the safety of the library.

"Yield or be taken by force!" the lieutenant of Jonnias cried once more.

No one was left at the gate to reply.

The lieutenants hoisted their banners high, Darville's symbol highest of all, and returned to their comrades.

The ranks of soldiers lunged forward, anxious to begin.

A strange chant issued from a thousand throats. Waves of violent sound chilled Jaylor's mind. "Kill magic. Kill all magicians." The chant grew in volume and aggression, fed by a whiff of magic from some unknown source. Battle frenzy swelled, binding the men together for the coming fray.

"Kill magic. Kill all magicians."

Weapons drumming on shields took on the rhythm of a thousand hearts beating in unison; a thousand minds with one goal. Battle. Blood. Heat. Lust.

"Kill magic. Kill all magicians."

Determination rose and rose again as the chant became a shout and then a roar.

Horror ran before the swelling noise, growing like a living thing. Fear filled the tower chamber and laid a heavy pall of doom on the once-quiet monastery.

No spell could combat the power of unity and relentless drive generated by the chant. Anyone caught between the men and their objective would be torn limb from limb.

Small points of deadly fire bloomed on the tips of arrows. Bright blossoms of green flame became a hailstorm of destruction.

Chapter 10

Yaakke sat beside the creekbed, replete and rested for the first time since he'd left Coronnan City. He folded his legs under him, palms resting on his knees, open and receptive. He stilled the twitching muscles of his back and thighs. His mind opened reluctantly.

Three times he had dropped pebbles into the quiet pool at the edge of the creek. As the dropping rock created ripples in the surface of the water, raindrops had interfered with the pattern of ripples. He'd caught glimpses of scenes from his past. Yaakke and Baamin clearing debris from the cache of forbidden books in the tunnels. Yaakke in Brevelan's clearing with Jaylor, teaching him the secret of transporting live humans without danger . . .

But no glimpses of the future. The old Rover woman had sworn to Yaakke that the pebble always told what was to come within the next few hours.

Maybe if Yaakke could properly center his magic, he'd work the Rover spell correctly.

Fire. Smoke. His vision back at the dragon lair had been so real . . .

Corby perched on a rock in front of him, head cocked curiously at his strange inactivity. Yaakke resisted the urge to shoo him away. He didn't need an audience, but he had to remain still or lose his concentration.

Stargods! He hated meditation. He couldn't think of any other way to align himself to the Kardia. Knowledge of where he was and what direction he was headed in would follow. He hadn't seen the sun rise or set beyond the ominous cloud cover for days. His youthful confidence melted with each new onslaught of rain, until he was totally lost and disoriented.

Once he managed to center his magic, maybe he could sense Shayla's power. *Shayla needs me*, he reminded himself.

The urge to let his muscles move plagued his attempts at stillness. He resisted, forcing his mind to accept the wind and rain as an extension of himself. He heard only the creek rushing over stones. Then his heartbeat filled his ears just as loudly. He breathed deeply, listening.

Slowly his pulse and the rhythm of his breathing tuned to the rhythm of the land around him. He heard birds on their perches fluffing their feathers against the cold. He felt the sap drift sluggishly within the tree that sheltered him. When his body cried out for him to move, he concentrated on the worms opening new paths through the soil, seeking tiny rootlets.

Gradually a pull of energy tugged at his back. With eyes closed and a minimal shift of position, he turned to face the tug. This must be south, the nearest planetary pole. The world adjusted its orbit to include him. He merged with the four elements and the cardinal directions, one more piece of the whole.

Behind his eyelids, his vision centered. Mountains to the south and west. Rolling plains to the north. The Great Bay to the east. The creek flowed north and east. Therefore he must be in the foothills of the south.

A year ago, Jaylor had taken refuge in a monastery in this general vicinity, one day's hard walk from Castle Krej. Yaakke had helped Jaylor hide there while they protected an injured Brevelan and Darville, who pranced at his heels, ensorcelled into the body of a golden wolf.

This morning Yaakke had passed a boulder with a tall everblue growing out of a crack that nearly split the rock in two. He'd marked it, deep inside his memory, as a pointer during that adventure last spring. Now, as his consciousness floated free of his body, he remembered the landmark. How far away was the monastery? The last time Yaakke had come this way, he'd been on steedback, compelling the animal to move faster than normal. Distances were badly distorted in his memory.

Yaakke took a deep breath and roused himself from the silence. The rain had ceased and Corby was gone. His campfire smoldered within a ring of rocks three paces away. He fed it a few dry sticks. Flame glowed on the ends, then licked upward to consume the wood.

He set his pan of water before the fire, allowing it to settle. Green-and-yellow flames reflected in the water. Their gentle movement enticed Yaakke to look deeper into them. He dropped a smooth white pebble into the water.

Pictures appeared in the watery surface, more flames, bigger, hotter—destructive rather than friendly. Jaylor and Brevelan trapped by falling beams. Yaakke blinked and cleared his eyes of smoke.

Anxiously Yaakke fixed an image of Jaylor in his mind and sent it through the water to the monastery. He had no shard of glass to direct a summons properly since he'd lost his pack in the void. The reflective surface of the water would have to do. The vision of flames grew higher, fiercer. The Senior Magician appeared in their midst. Frantically Jaylor lifted a fallen beam from a crumpled form. Flames licked at his hands. He ignored them. The muscles of his broad back and shoulders strained, and he grunted as he moved the beam aside with brute force. Why didn't he use his magic?

Yaakke watched in horror as his master gathered the unconscious form of Brevelan to his breast, and then they both disappeared as another flaming beam crashed down on top of them.

Yaakke breathed deeply, sending his mind toward the void in preparation for transport.

"Naw!" Corby warned him from the top of a tree. Yaakke couldn't rescue Jaylor and Brevelan if he got lost in the void again. He cast around him for another solution. Smoke drifted on the wind from the west. He tried fixing his magic on Jaylor and Brevelan. He'd never transported two people at the same time before.

His magic darted around and around the images in the flames. There was no one to latch onto and transport to safety.

Yaakke took off at a run, over hummocks, around boulders and through a number of icy streams, taking the straightest route toward the smoke. Uphill he ran. Above him and to the left the land rose in a series of grassy plateaus. He crested the first ridge and pressed onward.

Familiarity tugged at his memory as landmarks flashed past. On and on he ran, until his lungs burned and his legs begged for collapse. Still he ran, stumbling, panting, crying.

Time and distance ceased to have meaning as he pressed his body to cover more and more ground. The only reality lay in the column of smoke that appeared beyond the next hilltop. He crested the steep rise. Terraced hills came into view half a league ahead.

The refuge of the Commune should be on the third level, set back from the ridge about two hundred arm-lengths. The smoke thickened in that direction.

If only he hadn't taken so much time to center his magic—if only he hadn't gotten lost in the void—

The smell of smoke was stronger here, sour and vile. Halfway to the third ridge, Yaakke slowed his pelting progress. He couldn't breathe. His legs and arms felt like jelled meat broth. His newly awakened contact with the wheel of sun, moon, and stars hummed a warning.

A pile of boulders, a hundred arm-lengths beyond, offered shadows and a view of the next ridge. He stretched and pulled himself up the rocks, seeking hand- and footholds by instinct. He barked his knuckles and scraped his shins in his haste. At last he crawled on top of the tumbled boulders. Lying flat, barely breathing, he scanned the horizon.

Ahead, above, and below him stretched an army of jubilant soldiers. Cadres of men capered and jeered as they tossed plunder back and forth in a vicious game of keep away with slighter, less aggressive men. Lean, battle-hardened men in well-used armor. Their evil grins gaped like bottomless pits in their smoke-blackened faces. One scarred sergeant made obscene gestures with a gnarled and twisted staff—the kind of tool favored by magicians.

The plaited grain in the wood looked suspiciously like Jaylor's staff—broken and mended by magic at three points. Yaakke sent out another mental probe addressed to his matter. His questions dissipated and died. No mind received or responded.

On the next ridge, smoke rose in a dense black column. The monastery was gutted, the roof collapsed, and the walls breached in a dozen places.

Incompetent fools! Couldn't those bumbling generals tell that Jaylor had whisked his Commune to safety before they entered the buildings? Not a shred of paper left in their library. None of their fabled viewing equipment shattered from the heat of the flames. NOTHING!

They used the transport spell. I will have that secret. As long as the Commune can jump from place to place without pursuit, none of the coven will be safe. We have to master that spell for our own escapes and secret raids.

Jaylor's escape is merely a setback, not a destruction of my goals. His suspicion of Darville's involvement must remain. I have broken their friendship. I have had a minor success.

I will not resort to the Tambootie to soothe my irritated nerves. That was the biggest mistake made by both Krej and his sister Janataea. Let us hope The Simeon doesn't stoop to the drug as well. I need him in the coven and I need his base of temporal power as a sanctuary for Lord Krej.

"Don't give up, Hilza!" Katrina sat beside the little box bed in the kitchen holding her sister's limp hand. Fever had dried the shrunken palm to parchment.

At least the kitchen was warm now. Last moon, P'pa had overcome M'ma's prideful objections and rented the upper levels of the narrow townhouse to street merchants, students, and artists. The money they paid Fraanken Kaantille bought firewood to heat the entire house and enough plain food to keep the family alive. But no amount of money could buy medicine to combat the lung rot that gripped half of Queen's City.

The rasping wheeze of Hilza's lungs was the only reply to Katrina's plea. Apprehension clawed at Katrina's heart. Her little sister had slipped into unconsciousness last evening as her fever soared.

Now, in the darkest hours before midwinter dawn, Hilza opened her eyes. Katrina bit her lip as she saw the hazy film covering her sister's vision. Hilza's breath grew shallower, more labored.

Katrina rolled a blanket and stuffed it behind Hilza's

head, propping her as upright as possible. Her sister's head lolled loosely on her weakened neck. Spasms racked her frail body as her lungs tried one more time to clear themselves of the accumulated fluid. Violent tremors passed through her limbs and bloody spittle trickled from her parched mouth.

"P'pa, wake up. I need your help!" Katrina called.

"I'm awake," Fraanken answered as he rose stiffly from the straight-backed chair where he had dozed fitfully most of the night. Sadly he lifted his youngest daughter, supporting her head on his shoulder.

Always, since the lung rot had grabbed hold of Hilza last autumn, P'pa's cradling comfort had been able to overcome the worst of the cough. Not tonight. Hilza continued to choke and bleed with the disease that killed its victims, young and old, hale and weak.

"Awaken your mother, Katey." P'pa stroked Hilza's back, trying desperately to soothe her.

Katrina ran up the stairs to the guest parlor on the ground floor that was now her parents' bedroom.

A lamp on the dresser cast a dim glow on the room. Frightened at this sign of negligence and waste on the part of her mother, Katrina hastened to extinguish the tiny flame. Her eyes strayed to the wide bed where her mother should be asleep. The down quilts—remnants of better times—lay flat and empty, undisturbed by any sleeper.

"M'ma?" Katrina searched the dim corners for some sign of her mother's presence. No flicker of movement or shadow out of place. "M'ma!" she called louder.

A cold draft made the lamp flame flicker. Katrina raced to the entry seeking the source of the frigid air. The inner door stood wide open. Beyond it, the outer door was closed but not latched.

"M'ma!" Katrina screamed in fear. She tugged on the outer door. Three filaments of white silk hung tangled in the lock. The finest yarn available that Tattia had woven into a lace shawl for Queen Miranda last autumn. A present the queen's husband had rejected as unworthy of his wife because it had been made by a disgraced Kaantille. Queen Miranda hadn't been allowed to view the gift and decide for herself to accept or reject it. Just yesterday, M'ma had tried again to see the queen and present her gift. She'd been evicted from the palace at the kitchen gate, before she reached Miranda.

Katrina stared at the threads. Her chin quivered in uncertainty. She returned to the bedroom, seeking some sign of her mother. Tattia's last woolen gown lay draped over the clothespress. Her cloak and shoes were in place. Nothing seemed missing except Tattia and the infamous lace shawl.

Tattia had worn the shawl as a badge of honor ever since the rejection by King Simeon. A merchant, unknown to Katrina or her father, had offered to buy the shawl several times. Proud Tattia had refused to let it go. Now she had gone out in the predawn freeze wearing nothing but her nightrail and the silken lace.

Katrina ran back to the kitchen. Her father gently laid Hilza's slack body on the straw mattress. Tears streamed down his careworn cheeks.

"P'pa?" Katrina choked on the fears that swamped her.

"There is nothing more we can do, Katey. Our baby is gone. We must be grateful that she is no longer in pain, no longer struggling for every breath." He stood over the body of his youngest daughter, shoulders slumped.

"P'pa, I'm frightened. I think M'ma ran away. She didn't wear her cloak or her shoes."

Fraanken looked up from his contemplation of death. His chin trembled with the effort to control himself. "Stay with your sister. One of us must watch over her until her spirit is prepared for passing." There was no one else. He didn't need to remind Katrina that Maaben no longer considered herself part of the family. "I will search for your mother. Perhaps she finally agreed to sell the shawl. She would have to go in secret because of King Simeon's ban on her work."

"M'ma would not have left the house at midnight without her gown, or shoes, or cloak if she merely wanted to sell the shawl."

A fierce pounding on the kitchen door roused them both. Katrina's eyes widened in greater turmoil. *Stargods!* What other disaster could plague them? For only the direst emergency would bring unannounced visitors to the basement door in the dead of night.

Fraanken yanked open the inner door and unlatched the outer with fumbling haste. A dour-faced man in the black uniform of the city guard glared at them. "Do you recognize this?" He held up a sodden and filthy length of lacy silk.

"M'ma!" Katrina gasped.

P'pa held the shawl as if it were a great treasure. He suddenly appeared old, shrunken, feeble.

"We found that floating in the river right after a passing member of the palace guard reported seeing a woman jump from the bridge."

Chapter 11

Yaakke concentrated on the clouds. He forced a clump of moisture to gather above the ruined monastery.

"You can't save them." A feminine voice interrupted his spell.

He whirled on top of his rock, almost losing his balance. A black-haired young woman, with incredibly beautiful white skin, stood at the base of the boulders, hands on hips, huge blue eyes angry and accusing. The skirts of her black traveling gown and the length of her unbound hair billowed out behind her in the rising wind.

Vaguely he realized his manipulations of the clouds and temperature had created the wind.

"I've got to try!" Yaakke returned to his task. The clouds above the ruins sagged, heavy with water. A little shift of the temperature beneath them and they dumped their load of thunder and lightning, but no rain.

Yaakke tried again, lowering the clouds into the ruins of the monastery. Still no rain, only a dense oily fog rolling through the crumbling masonry.

None of the soldiers noticed the strange weather. They were too busy mauling tapestries depicting the descent of the Stargods. Crude ale splashed from golden winecups. But no one burned a book or smashed delicate glass and brass instruments.

"Trying to smother the enemy with a mist?" The girl laughed, rich tones sliding up her white throat. "Like as not you'd have more success putting out the fire if you spat on it."

Yaakke blushed from his ears to his toes. "You destroyed my concentration." His voice cracked into an embarrassing squeak.

"You still can't save them. You're too late," she stated. "But you can exact vengeance from the lords who sent the army to destroy your precious Commune."

The clouds above the monastery thinned and drifted back to a more natural pattern. The wind faded with them. Once more Yaakke sought Jaylor's spirit within the ruins.

Nothing.

With mounting anxiety he probed for any member of the Commune: prickly old Lyman, wily Fraandalor, gentle Brevelan, or even her baby, Glendon.

No response.

"I told you, you're too late. But I will reward you mightily if you blast Lord Jonnias and the Marnaks—Elder and Younger—to hell and back again." Her eyes smoldered with fanatical hate.

"Who are you?" Yaakke twisted into a sitting position on top of the boulder. He rested his head in his hands, massaging his temples. Where were Jaylor and the others? They couldn't all have died. He'd have felt their passing, he was sure of it.

The barriers surrounding Brevelan's clearing had been down. Surely not because she had died! That was weeks ago.

How had the spell gone so wrong? He'd been careful to visualize rain, torrents of rain to douse the fire.

"Don't you recognize me?" The girl hiked her skirts and began climbing up to Yaakke's perch. She revealed an indelicate amount of ankle and calf beneath the black cloth.

"Danger! Danger, danger," Corby croaked, circling above.

"I saw you at the coronation," he muttered.

"I'm Rejiia." She sat beside him, mimicking his cross-legged pose.

"Krej's daughter?" He barely acknowledged her presence. Why hadn't he centered his magic and found Jaylor by summons as soon as he'd departed from the dragon? He could have reported everything and maybe received some more clues on where to look for Shayla. Jaylor would then have known where Yaakke was, so he could have sent a summons for help in time.

The barriers around the clearing were already down. How long had he been in the void? Long enough for all his friends to die?

"Aren't you going to ask why I want you to kill my husband, Marnak the Younger, his father, and their best friend, Lord Jonnias?" She sounded aggrieved that his attention had wandered away from her beauty. What good would he do helping Shayla if there were no more Commune to gather the dragon's magic?

Rejiia's pout dragged his attention back to her question.

"You must have your reasons for wanting those men dead. They don't concern me. I've got to save the Commune." Yaakke dismissed her. Why hadn't the king stopped his lords from waging war on the magicians?

"King Darville doesn't know this was their mission," Rejiia answered his unspoken question.

"You read my thoughts. Do you have magic?" Yaakke hastily erected some armor around his thoughts lest she read his lonely pain and find him vulnerable.

Yaakke started scrambling down from the rock. He had to see for himself that the monastery was destroyed and that all of his friends were dead.

"I have some magic," Rejiia said interrupting his descent. "Not enough to do more than a few parlor tricks. My father never saw fit to test or train me. He had no use for his daughters, except to marry us off for power and wealth."

"And now you want freedom from your chosen husband." Yaakke let his eyes wander away from her toward the mass of soldiers behind them, seeking a sign of Marnak the Younger, or evidence of Jaylor's demise.

"You won't find Marnak in the field. He directs things from the safety of his tent," she spat the words with disgust. "And yes, I want my freedom. Faciar is *my* province—from the capital to the southern mountains, from the Great Bay inland five leagues. All of it is *mine*. I won't let my husband destroy it with his greed."

"Why not destroy him yourself?" Yaakke completed his slide to the ground, prepared to fight his way up to the smoking ruins if anyone stopped him.

"I told you, I don't have enough magic to kill him with suitable subtlety and get away with it." She frowned petulantly. "What good is killing him if I am caught and burned at the stake?"

Yaakke dismissed her petty anger. She might have reason to dislike and distrust her husband, Marnak the Younger. Yaakke had the more immediate grudge. The greed of both Marnaks—Elder and Younger—as well as Jonnias' superstition, had destroyed the Commune. Yaakke's Commune. His friends and family.

A great ball of magic built within him on the heels of the grief turned to anger. Not enough. He found more magic beneath his feet. He pulled energy from a storm building to the east. His newly awakened alignment with the magnetic pole centered the magic. All he had to do was shape it into a weapon, address it, and send it forth.

"That's right, use your magic. Wreak havoc through this army of destruction," Rejiia coached in excited whispers. "Revenge is sweet." She licked her lips in almost sexual satisfaction at the power she gathered.

Yaakke didn't know why he hesitated. An image of a young woman with moon-bright hair and pale blue eyes reddened with sadness came between himself and Rejiia's excited face. Then a memory of the blue-tipped dragon superimposed upon his preparation to hurl the magic.

"There is never a right time or place to throw magic for harm." The dragon spoke with Old Master Baamin's voice, reciting the first rule of Communal ethics. "Magic is for health, for growth, for the benefit of Coronnan and all who live within our boundaries. Magic can never be used to destroy lest we destroy ourselves in the process."

"What does right have to do with this? They killed my friends!" Yaakke screamed into the wind. The magic fireball burned for release within his gut.

"Do it, boy. Do it and I'll take you to my bed. A bed where I never allowed Marnak to exercise his privileges." Rejiia's aura pulsed with sexual vibrancy.

He needed no reward, only vengeance. The magic came into his hand. He shaped it with anger and addressed it to the image of skinny, sniveling Marnak the Younger, Krej's puppet, whose loyalty landed wherever was most convenient to Marnak.

With a mighty thrust of his shoulders, back, and arm he

lobbed the magical firebomb into the air in the direction of the field tents behind the massed soldiers.

The magic sought the symbols on a standard raised above one particular tent. Through the air it flew, heedless of wind or missiles thrown to divert it, with Yaakke's mind close on its heels. Faster and faster the bomb flew. Yaakke became the magic fire as it fed on his mind. They gathered speed and intensity from the cries of fear and horror growing within the army; horror that invaded Yaakke. He tried to jerk his mind away from the bomb but found himself trapped within it.

The bomb slammed into the standard with crackling intensity. Magical blue light glowed from the flagpole and raced down, down into the tent. It consumed wood and fabric as it sped toward its target, greedy for more interesting fuel. Marnak, wearing light field armor, lounged against the tent pole. He rejoiced with his coconspirators, a cup of pilfered wine in one hand, precious altar linens edged in SeLenese lace in the other.

His smile turned to shock and then to agony as the firebomb leaped from tent pole to head, to hand, and body. Flames burst upward, followed by screams.

Indiscriminate screams gathered harshly on Yaakke's conscience and slammed him back into his body, but he still sensed all that happened within range of the bomb he had exploded in Marnak's face. The smell of burning flesh and cloth, of hot metal and pain beyond imagining, violated his senses. Rampant emotions from a thousand sources filled his mind, contorting his perceptions. He became the instrument of destruction and, in turn, was its victim.

Hate. Fear. Greed. Desperate prayers. Revenge. Mindless flight.

Every soldier, officer, and lord broadcast his feelings directly into Yaakke's being. No magical armor could block the intimate sharing.

The onslaught of foreign emotions tore at Yaakke's sanity. Who was *he*? Which thoughts were his own? Whose body did his mind inhabit? What did *he* feel? Painful wounds stabbed and burned into his heart.

Suddenly the riotous noise of a thousand men swelled within Yaakke's ears. The wind increased to a howl and seemed to stab his skin with the force of arrows. His blood pounded and roared within his body.

He had to get away. Away from the noise. Away from Rejiia. Away from himself.

Jaylor coughed the smoke from his lungs. Desperately, he heaved the fallen beam away from Brevelan where she had fallen when the roof collapsed. With blackened hands, he clutched his wife tightly against his chest and transported them out of the inferno that had been the monastery library.

The shocking cold of the void roused them both from the stupor induced by roiling smoke and blistering heat. Reality slowly formed around them. Still kneeling in the position he'd been in when he transported out, Jaylor coughed again and blinked his gritty eyes. He clung to the sensation of holding his beloved in his arms while he concentrated on maintaining his balance.

"Where's the baby?" Brevelan whispered, then coughed.

Other coughs and grumbles penetrated Jaylor's awareness. He counted bodies, eyes still too blurred to distinguish faces.

Forty-three. "Where's the baby?" he asked louder.

"Glendon?" Brevelan asked again.

"Right here." Elder Librarian Lyman stepped forward with a grimy bundle cradled in his arms. "Took to the void like he was born there. Little tyke never uttered a squeak." He clucked and shifted the baby against his shoulder, rubbing his back and cooing nonsense as if he'd always cared for infants instead of living the lonely, celibate life of most magicians.

Brevelan reached for Glendon before Jaylor could settle her onto the rough cave floor. Anxiously she removed the smoky blanket and checked her baby for any signs of distress. Little Glendon looked up at his mother, eyes focusing in his narrow field of vision. A slurpy gurgle followed by a toothless smile brought a sigh of relief from the entire gathering.

"My son wasn't born in the void, but he was conceived there," Jaylor murmured to himself. Stiffly he stood and faced the ragtail gathering. "We're all safe. Did the equipment make it through?"

"All except one shelf of books—duplicates most of them." Slippy surveyed the array of books and observation equipment littering the floor of the cave that had once been a dragon lair.

"It's damp here, Jaylor. Not good for my books," Lyman reminded him. "Not good for my old bones either. At least we're safe from those heathen lords and their troops. For now."

"There's a broad valley between here and Brevelan's clearing," Jaylor told them. In his mind he saw a meadow at the base of a cliff. A small waterfall tumbled down the cliff into a scattering of boulders. That same cliff Prince Darville had fallen over when Krej ensorcelled him into a wolf and left him for dead. Neither of them had known at the time that Shayla, the resident dragon, was so tied to the royal family by honor, blood, and magic that she would compel Brevelan to rescue the injured wolf from the snow-drifts. Jaylor could think of no better place to rebuild the University: to honor a now dead friendship.

"We'll begin building as soon as we have recovered from our journey and the weather warms enough to fell timber. By summer we'll have a refuge for all those who flee the persecution of magic. This attack against us smells like the work of that new cult, the Gnostic Utilitarians."

"The Gnuls have less of a sense of morality when it comes to magicians than the coven does," Lyman grumbled.

"I fear the attack on our monastery was just the beginning of some very hard times to come for our people," Jaylor said sadly. He had to contact his spy among Queen Rossemikka's maids. Surely the girl had eavesdropped on enough conversations to know what Darville meant by sending the army to the monastery. If Darville had authorized it at all.

Rejiia latched onto the boy's magic, sucking and feeding upon it as a leech draws blood from its victims. She had watched her father do this. A little giggle escaped her. She ignored the hysterical quality of the mirth. If the mighty and arrogant Lord Krej could see her now, he wouldn't dismiss her as worthless.

She had every intention of murdering the loathsome boy as soon as she'd drained him of his magic and his secrets. He wasn't hard to follow. The flaws in his magic screamed at her through the tentacle she'd attached to him. His power rose to amazing strength and then fell abruptly to nothing in unpredictable waves. He committed the ultimate folly by allowing his emotions to affect his magic.

She took a deep breath in preparation. At the next hint of a waver in his talent, she'd drop a compulsion on him.

He ran furiously. Legs pumping. Arms straining.

In her mind, Rejiia followed, feeling what he felt, seeing what he saw. She couldn't read his thoughts and his secrets yet. The power was still rising in him.

"Give me the transport spell!" she whispered through her tentacle of magic. "The coven will reward me well. They'll have to give me full membership if I discover the secret. I'll surpass my dear father in power and prestige. Then when I revive him, he will have to look up to me!"

"Spirits of the dead, spring forth in freedom from fleshly concerns," the magistrate implored as he released a sack of ashes into the River Lenicc. "As these last remnants of your corporeal bodies dissolve, so shall your attachments to this life. Your possessions are dispersed. Your families are reconciled to your passing. Your next existence beckons. Release your hold on this one!"

Dry-eyed and numb, Katrina watched as Hilza's ashes spread across the icy water like a gray blanket. The sluggish current caught the smothering cover of ashes, swirled them into an ugly soup, and dragged them down. All that remained of sweet little Hilza sank into watery oblivion.

A commoner's funeral. No expensive priests, no professional mourners. Not even a proper grave. Merely ashes of the dead cast into the almost-frozen river by one of King Simeon's officials. A duty the man had performed too often these last moons.

The ground was frozen deep. No one could dig graves this winter. There was barely enough wood for a single funeral pyre. So, the numerous dead—from hunger and disease—were heaped together in a common bonfire, their remains mingled, and their funerals held at the same time. There was no way to separate the ashes for the grieving families. The poor and the homeless gathered around the pyres in a morbid search for warmth, cheering as each new body added fuel to the noisome black smoke.

Katrina wouldn't have an urn to set beside the hearth to cherish, for either Hilza or Tattia. Tattia's body had not been found. All that remained of her was the lace scarf. P'pa had wanted to burn it along with Hilza's body. Katrina had cleaned the precious reminder of her mother and hidden it where her father and the persistent merchant would never find it. Why was the stranger so eager to purchase the piece, tainted as it was by Tattia's suicide?

Ten other families joined Katrina in mourning the loss of a loved one on this cloudy day. Families huddled together for warmth, comfort, and shared memories. No one stood beside Katrina.

Oncle Yon and Tante Syllia refused to be seen near the family of a suicide. Tattia's ghost would haunt her kin for five generations.

Lawsuits had been filed with Queen's Court and Temple to sever all bonds of blood and law between Fraanken Kaantille and his brother Yon. Maaben's name was included in the suits. Maaben would be kept safe and secure from this latest, and worst, scandal in the Kaantille family.

The river marched toward the sea. A few traces of gray ash clung to the bobbing ice floes. Gradually they passed out of sight, under the bridges, on and on toward open water. Nothing remained of the dead but the grief within a few hearts.

"Be warm, Hilza," Katrina murmured. She could think of no other wish for her little sister. It was the same wish most citizens of Queen's City prayed for.

The stranger who was eager to buy Tattia's shawl separated himself from the crowd of mourners. Katrina turned her steps away from him and the scene of the funeral. She ducked into a narrow alley wishing for the release of tears. Her eyes continued dry. Her grief built within her until she thought the pain would choke the breath from her.

Aimlessly she wandered until the tears flowed freely, releasing the paralyzing grief in her throat. Only then did she seek her own kitchen door.

"P'pa!" she called as the inner door banged behind her. "P'pa, I'm home." Silence rang through the cold and empty kitchen.

"Curse you, P'pa. The tenants will complain and refuse

to pay their rent it you let the fire go out." She gathered fresh kindling and a fire rock as she rushed to the stove that filled one whole corner of the room.

Since Hilza's death and M'ma's suicide, P'pa rarely moved from his chair by the stove, where he sat in morose silence. The loss of his wife and child preyed more heavily on his mind and spirit than all of his financial woes combined. He started in fear at every moving shadow and sharp sound. He was the first person Tattia would haunt and plague until he, too, joined her in self-inflicted death.

Only his fear for Katrina had prevented him from committing the ultimate sin.

He was not in the kitchen today and had not attended Hilza's funeral.

The bell on the front stoop rang, loud and imperious.

"P'pa!" she called again, as she fumbled with the kindling. The fire was more important than a visitor. Who would visit the disgraced Kaantilles?

The bell rang again, impatient as a sick old granm'ma.

Still no sounds from above or the front room. Where had P'pa gone? Katrina struck a spark and fed it enough fuel to keep it lit until she answered the bell.

She flung open the inner door. Harsh pounding rattled the outer door. Her heart leaped into her throat.

With shaking hands and trembling heart she opened the outer door. Three men-at-arms, in the gray uniform of the palace, stood on the front step. All the same height, all the same coloring and uniform. All with identical grim expressions.

The center man stepped forward. Two bands of silver on each cuff marked his rank as above the other two. "Katrina Marie, daughter of Fraanken and Tattia Kaantille, you are summoned to the presence of His Majesty, King Simeon the First, Lord of SeLenicca, Emperor of Hanassa, and rightful Heir of Rossemeyer."

Katrina swallowed the lump in her throat. It wouldn't go down. She swallowed again and almost choked on her fear.

"I . . . I must tell my P'pa, and I must damp the fire." Wildly she looked around. A million questions pounded at her. She couldn't make sense of any of this.

"Your hearth is cold, the tenants dismissed, and your

father is already in custody," the ranking soldier informed her. No flicker of emotion crossed his face, and his eyes stared straight ahead, above Katrina.

She backed to the inner door. *Flee*, her feet urged. *Hide*, her mind overruled. *Faint*, her heart joined the clamor of emotions.

A harsh hand gripped her arm. Pain shot up to her shoulder.

"You will come now," the soldier said.

She hung back. His fingers dug deeper into the muscles of her upper arm. Numbness spread down to her fingers and up into her brain.

"You will come, or you will die here and now." Knives appeared in the right hand of each of the three soldiers. Their blank faces awoke with ugly grins.

Chapter 12

"**Y**ou must flee now, boy. Escape before the troops turn on you. Teach me the transport spell, so I can flee with you," Rejiia whispered to Yaakke from behind.

Yaakke halted his flight from the scene of destruction and turned to ask her what she knew about the spell, the Commune's most closely guarded secret. Only a grimy soldier, gaping at the flames in the center of the camp stood there. A flash of black skirts, or maybe black feathers, flitted through the trees above him.

"Teach me the spell; I will take you with me!" Jaylor's voice demanded from the mouth of the grimy soldier.

"No," Yaakke formed the word without sound. The glare of the sun through the pall of clouds and smoke intensified. Pain lanced from his eyes to his mind.

"The transport spell. Give me the spell." This time Rejiia's haunting voice came from the jackdaw perched in the tree above him.

"Quickly, boy! Give me the spell." The whispers bombarded him from all directions. Rejiia, Jaylor, Baamin, and Corby. A compulsion grew within him, insisting he whisper the secret.

Frantically Yaakke opened every listening channel in his mind to find the source of the demanding voice. Was it Rejiia who haunted him, or a true magician using Yaakke's suppressed attraction for the Lady of Faciar to trap him?

Every mind in the army was firmly closed to him. Only the demanding whispers leaked through to his telepathy. They grew louder.

Sun and the fire he had unleashed blazed before his eyes. He closed them. Still the blinding light penetrated.

Then, suddenly, the wall between the thousand troops and his mind broke apart. A myriad of mental voices made a jumble of his thoughts and weakened his knees. His senses stretched beyond normal limits to include field mice, cats, and panicky steeds. Images of his firebomb exploding within a tent and burning all it touched with lethal intensity, including himself, replayed in his memory again and again. Mental and physical screams racked his aching body.

Pain, blinding light, noise, demands. Always the demand. *Give me the transport spell!*

Yaakke resumed his run uphill until his lungs burned. Away from the voice; he had to get away from the voice. The smoke from the monastery ruins thickened. Heat, trapped within the building stones, seared his hands when he touched them. He pressed his palms harder against a half-standing wall, ignoring the pain, seeking the lives that once dwelt within.

More pain, more screams: his own and others. Escape. He had to escape.

There was nothing left of his own thoughts or identity. Confusion. Noise. Pain. Bewilderment. Screams.

"I've got to get out of here!" Yaakke searched blindly for an avenue of retreat from the noise, from the light, from his own guilt. Quickly, he built a picture of cool, quiet, darkness around his stretched and oversensitive nerves. Three deep breaths into a trance. Another lungful of air whisked him across the void and plunged him down, down, down, into the bowels of Kardia Hodos, the living planet.

A guard on each side of Katrina held her arms tight and high, barely allowing her feet to touch the ground on the long walk up the hill toward the palace. Her knees were so weak with dread she doubted they'd hold her up.

Along the wooden sidewalk the men marched her, following in the rapid wake of their two-stripe leader. Merchants, shoppers, and homeless wanderers stepped out of their path, gaping at her.

"Where are they taking her?" a frightened housewife whispered.

"Hush. She's a Kaantille, getting what they all deserve. No doubt this is the last we'll see of that clan." Disgust colored a man's voice. "If King Simeon executes them all, then the ghost will be banished."

Katrina felt the blood drain from her head. *If King Simeon executes them all . . .* Images of dark, dank prison cells, torture, and death built tremendous pressure in her chest and sent her heart pounding. She lashed out with both feet in a desperate attempt to escape.

The relentless guards kept their grip on her arms, marching faster as they approached the villas of the nobility. At the end of the long Royal Avenue stood the palace and her doom.

Darkness encroached on her vision from the sides. Cold sweat broke out on her face and back. The burning grip of hard male hands on her arms deepened and spread. At the last moment of consciousness the uniformed men turned left away from the palace. Her mind revived slightly as questions rose within her.

Huge marble mansions lined the hill becoming more and more opulent farther away from the river. Evidence of the luxury afforded the nobility in the crowded Queen's City was revealed in the wider spaces of open land that lay between each of the homes, cropped grass and sculptured shrubs, and large gardens.

They passed between two of the sprawling mansions and proceeded to the back entrance of nearly the last villa before the end of the road and the beginning of the rolling hills. The two-stripe leader entered without knocking. Obviously, they were expected.

Katrina looked at her grim escorts, hoping they would allow her the dignity of walking on her own. Neither man varied his grip, his expression, or his rapid pace.

At a double door on the left of the long corridor, the leader paused and knocked lightly. A grunt from within responded. The door slid open without a touch from the guard and Katrina found herself carried into the presence of King Simeon where she was abruptly dropped.

Her knees buckled, and she scrambled, ungracefully, to an upright position. Through a swimming haze she focused on the carpet rather than the man who held her fate in his unpredictable and often tyrannical hands.

Her royal judge sat behind a large desk. Witchballs of

shadowless light sat atop silver stands. The room was nearly as bright as daylight. King Simeon need not squint and hunch over the parchment he wrote upon. He needed no inkwell, for his quill pen flowed with dark liquid at the precise level required. At his left elbow, in a place of honor, sat a life-sized tin statue of a weasel. Gilt paint flaked from its molded fur. Mouth agape in a vicious snarl, the weasel's teeth seemed to drip venom.

Katrina shuddered in repulsion at the sight of the ugly statue and the loving caress King Simeon gave it as he raised his deep blue eyes from his work. His gaze seemed to bore right through her, delving into her innermost secrets. An aura of power shimmered around him and extended to the hideous statue. The rest of the room seemed dim and unimportant compared to the broad-shouldered man with bright, outland red hair.

"So this is the last of the traitorous Kaantilles?" King Simeon leaned back in his thronelike chair. Hooded eyes continued to probe and appraise her body. "Remove her cloak," he ordered.

The guards whisked off the heavy oiled wool and stepped back. A chill rippled through Katrina as the king's penetrating eyes lingered on the budding curves of her body. A spark of interest flashed within the deep blue orbs and a mocking half smile touched the comer of his mouth.

Katrina crossed her arms in front of her, trying to hide from his gaze a body she was not yet familiar or comfortable with.

"Where . . . where is my P'pa?" Katrina whispered.

"Never speak until you are spoken to! I am your king. You must show respect." Anger propelled Simeon up into a half-stand behind his desk. He leaned forward, hands pressed against the massive wooden top until his wrists and knuckles grew white. A shudder coursed down his body from neck to arms. Then he seemed to relax.

The king sat again and dusted invisible specks from his fire green tunic. "Now, my dear, I have some news for you, some good and some bad."

She bit back her alarm and her questions.

"Very good, Katrina. You're learning respect. As a reward, I'll tell you about your P'pa. Your brave and smart P'pa who ruined me and himself with his investments." The king rose and sauntered around to the front of his desk. There he perched on the edge of the furniture, his thick and powerful legs thrust out in front of him, arms crossed on his chest in mocking imitation of her own stance.

Shoulders hunched, back curved, Katrina tried to huddle deeper into her arms. The solid presence of the guards prevented her from backing up to put more distance between herself and the king's penetrating gaze. She wondered if this acknowledged sorcerer saw through her vest and skirt, through her shift to her naked body. Lumbird bumps rose on her arms and chest. Beneath a loose breast band, her nipples tightened into yet more bumps. A ripple of fear and disgust added to her discomfort.

"The bad news first. Your esteemed P'pa has sold himself to the slave ships." Mocking amusement touched King Simeon's lips but didn't light his eyes. "In return for his five years of servitude, Fraanken Kaantille demanded I forgive his debts and allow you to inherit the house. He claimed you could earn enough to maintain yourself and the house by renting out the upper rooms. Of course he forgot that under the ancient laws of SeLenicca, the daughter of a slave—freeborn or not—has no rights and can possess nothing, least of all a valuable house in the middle of a respectable neighborhood."

"You can't turn me out!" she protested.

Cold. So very cold. The room, her body, the king's smile. Everything was so cold.

"Quiet, or I'll increase his indenture to seven years in the mines. Your P'pa might survive five years in my galleys. But no one survives the mines. No one! Do you hear?" the king shouted.

Katrina nodded, too frightened to do more. The tin weasel seemed to raise a lip to bare more teeth. She stared at it in shock rather than look at her king.

"Now then, the good news." King Simeon smiled in abrupt and capricious change of mood. He thrust himself upright from his perch on the desk and took two steps closer.

She didn't like his tone. Didn't trust his volatile temper. She feared the way he looked at her.

"Leave us." He nodded to the guards.

Behind her, Katrina heard the door slide open, footsteps

retreated, and the door whispered shut again. She was alone with the most feared man in the Three Kingdoms.

"My dear, I have a proposition for you." King Simeon walked around her, his eyes appraised her front and back, from her two plaits of blond hair to the hem of her skirt. "Only you can save your father. Indeed, I'm willing to forgive his debts and return him to a place of honor in the mercantile community. In return, all I ask is a favor from you."

She didn't dare ask the nature of that favor. Rumors followed this man. Rumors of black sorcery and sacrifices to a foreign and bloodthirsty god. No one dared repeat those rumors to Queen Miranda. According to Tattia, the hereditary ruler of SeLenicca was so besotted with her outland husband she wouldn't have listened to them anyway. She hadn't listened to her advisers when she granted Simeon all the rank and authority of a king.

Could Simeon have thrown a magic spell on his wife to force her to give him all her rights and power?

"Only you can grant me this favor, Katrina. Think of it, your beloved P'pa restored to his home and his fortune, your sister Maaben returned to the loving arms of her family. You can achieve this for them." He toyed with the lacing on her shift, tugging playfully until the neckline started to gape open; then he released the tie to finger the buttons on her vest.

"H . . . how?"

"My coven has need of a willing virgin." He uncrossed her protective arms with gentle hands and opened her vest with a swift movement she barely saw. "I presume you are still a virgin?" One mocking eyebrow reached nearly to his full head of red hair.

Her jaw dropped, aghast at the immodesty of his question and his actions.

"I see by your reaction that you are untouched, by your P'pa or any other man. Good. Good." His finger traced the line of her shift, opening it until her undergarment was revealed. His finger stopped on the tip of her breast.

How could he imply such a horrible thing? P'pa was good and kind and honorable. He would never do . . . do *that* to her. But the king could. The sensuous caress of that single finger rasped against her taut nerves. Hot shame vied with a need for him to continue his teasing of her nipple. Shame won.

"Did you know, my dear, that the next Vernal Equinox occurs on the night of the dark of the moon? 'Twill be a night of powerful magic. I will be able to build spells of such magnitude, all other magicians will be forced to bow to my will. But I need a virgin." His gaze captured her eyes and bound them together with alien power. His thumbs traced erotic circles on her breasts.

"A willing virgin."

"Wh . . . what will become of me?" She couldn't look away though she tried and tried. Lightning seemed to flash across her vision, then leap from his hooded eyes into hers. Of its own will, her body arched toward him.

Disgusted with herself, she fought the heated longing he built within her.

"There is power buried deep within you. With proper training between now and the Equinox, you have a good chance of surviving the ritual. At the end of it, you would no longer be a virgin, but your power would be released. Only I have a matching power that will bring yours to maturation, ready to be tapped. I might even allow you to bear me a son. A child raised to rule the coven as Miranda's son will rule SeLenicca." Finally he blinked and released her. The spell that bound them together slid away, and he retreated to the edge of his desk once more.

"And if I don't agree to this?"

"Then I will take you for my own pleasure—and yours, my dear—and your father will rot in the mines!" Anger exploded from him like a living being. Katrina recoiled from him.

All traces of longing for his renewed touch vanished, replaced with cold hate. "Then I have no guarantees that you will honor the bargain even if I give myself willingly to your vile purposes."

"You can trust me. I am your king, after all."

" 'Twas not P'pa's fault the ship was lost at sea. Why are you blaming him?" She blinked back tears of bewilderment.

"Fraanken Kaantille organized the plan and supervised the investment syndicate. If the ship had won through, he would have been a hero. But the ship was betrayed by a

dark-eyed magician boy. My agent barely escaped alive."
He petted the thin weasel once more, almost cooing to it.
"The plan failed. For all I know, Fraanken Kaantille may
have sold out to the agents of King Darville's Commune
of Magicians. So, 'tis only right your father be considered
a traitor for that failure," he stated evenly.

"P'pa would never sell out to an outlander. He loves our
land and our queen."

"Answer me now. Do you give yourself freely to my
coven for the Equinox ritual?" A sneer marred his handsome face. No spell bound them together this time. She
was free to make a rational decision.

"Never."

"Perhaps a few moons of humiliation and unrelenting
toil in a factory will change your mind. Did you know a
factory owner has offered to buy you from me? You, with
your moon-blond hair, fair skin, and blue eyes of a true-
blooded woman will be the slave of an outland half-breed.
He hates all true-bloods and will make certain you suffer.
And you condemn your father to death in the mines."

"No, I don't. You do."

"Remember my offer when hunger, cold, aching back,
dimming vision, and humiliation drive you away from the
factory. I'll wait for you, Katrina Kaantille. You will come
back to me."

"Simurgh save me!" Rejiia gasped. "Come back here,
Yaakke. I'm not finished with you. You can't do that. I
won't let you!" She stamped her foot in rage.

Gone. Without a trace. She flung a web of magic outward
to snare any life within her range. One very cranky crow
screamed at her as he beat his wings against her entrapment. Nothing else. The soldiers were too far away, all
rushing to douse the fire in Marnak's camp.

"Where are you, boy?" she screamed as she released the
crow with the funny white feathers on its head. She cast
the net again, more carefully and in a wider pattern. Still
nothing.

"What did I do wrong?" All her dreams of power faded.
Having probed his magic, she should be able to find him
anywhere on Kardia Hodos. Still he eluded her.

That kind of power was unheard of, outside of legend.

Only one of the Stargods could disappear so completely. "I'll get you yet, Yaakke. Then I will take you to the coven for judgment. And I shall preside as your judge and executioner."

Quiet. Blessed quiet surrounded Yaakke. Darkness soothed his eyes. He'd transported himself to some unknown sanctuary. Yet still he heard the echoes of thoughts and saw flashes of light.

The sound of dripping water penetrated his exhausted mind and body. His hands hurt, burned by the fire-blasted stones of the monastery. He opened his eyes to seek the source of water to soothe the burns. The light flashes continued to blind him.

Footsteps upon stone. Flickering light from lanterns. The harsh smell of lamp oil and stale air.

More voices. Real this time.

"Gimme the whip! Here's another one broken his chain. See how his hand is burned from the barracks fire? Have to make an example of malcontent slaves." A harsh voice spoke, made deeper by malice. "We'll have this mine up and running again in no time once we punish the leaders of this little rebellion."

"There are no slaves in Coronnan!" Yaakke croaked.

"Yeah, so you said 'afore you killed three guards. Tell that t' the army what sends us prisoners and t' judges what sends us criminals." The man laughed.

Yaakke looked up, a long way up into a craggy face and ugly harelip. An evil, malicious grin added another broken seam to the filthy face. This man enjoyed inflicting pain.

Frantically, Yaakke sought a spell, any spell to protect himself. Armor. Transport. Another firebomb. He had to be free to help Shayla!

His mind went blank and his magic died with the first bite of the whip across his chest.

Chapter 13

Time dragged forward. The man called Muaynwor—the dark mute—marked the passage of days in the number of breaths he could take during the one-hour sun break each noon. He measured days in strokes of the sledgehammer. He counted the stars as he marched with his fellow slaves in iron chains from mine adit to barracks.

Each day and each night he counted and wondered why. He'd stopped wondering who he was or how he had come to be a slave in the mines when slavery had been outlawed a millennium ago. Counting seemed safer than speaking or remembering. Remembering brought the lash across his back. A word to his chain partner for the day earned them both the sweat box.

Heft the hammer, breathe. Slam the hammer down, breathe. He found solace in the rhythm. Heft, breathe. Slam, breathe. One stroke, two and three, shift the spike. One, two, three. Four, five, six.

The familiarity of the count brought a tingle of awareness to his mind. Breathe in one, two, three, as he raised the hammer. Hold one, two, three, as he gathered his strength. Breathe out one, two, three, as he lowered the hammer. Hold one, two, three. Raise the hammer one, two, three . . .

He swung downward with the hammer. The force of his blow sent shock waves from the hammer head up the shaft and into his hands. His arms ached and his head threatened to split open with the backlash of pain.

Numbly he lifted the hammer again. One, two, three. Breathe one, two, three. Something wasn't quite right. The hammer was too light. He stopped his movement, mid-stroke, unsure how to proceed.

A guard patrolled the length of the cleared shaft to enforce the no talking rule. Muaynwor continued to stare straight ahead. What was wrong?

"Stupid slave," the guard grunted. "Broke your hammer and don't even know it." The guard bent and retrieved a different tool from the pile. He thrust a shovel into Muaynwor's hands.

The dark mute continued to stare. The new tool wasn't right either.

"You'll probably break that one as well. Get yerself a new handle. That one's too worn. You know how to do it." The guard pushed Muaynwor toward a pile of wood in various shapes and sizes.

Muaynwor hobbled the last few steps, anxious to avoid the guard's touch. The manacle on his right ankle dragged his chain partner with him. The partner seemed familiar, safe, unlike the guard whose touch sometimes brought pain.

He reached for a new handle. The first piece of wood was too thick and short, meant for a sledgehammer. The second piece was wrong, too. He discarded them both and reached deeper.

His hand curled around something smooth and straight. A long straight piece of wood. Power pulsed up his arms. He looked at the handle more closely.

A tree branch cut to the length of a walking stick, smoothed and polished. Good, solid oak. The grain was obscured by a thick layer of dirt. Warmth caressed his tired hand. The wood seemed to glow and pulsate with unnatural blue sparks.

Light. A glowing warmth just out of reach beckoned. Something huge and shinning and winged at the core.

"Ja . . . Jack . . ." he croaked at the urging of the shimmering presence in his mind.

"Hold your tongue, slave!" The guard flicked his wrist. The lash bit deep into Muaynwor's cheek. "Ain't spoke in nigh on three year. Don't need to start now."

Three years? Three years of counting hammer strokes and breaths. The oak staff shot a flame of awareness to his mind.

Jack, he thought. *My name is . . .* Not Jack, almost . . .

Jack closed his eyes and shook his head. When he opened them again, the glow in the staff intensified. The tingling warmth spread up his hand to his arm and tight shoulder muscles. The peculiar warmth invaded his toes and soothed his aching arches caused by the ill-fitting boots.

"Git back to work, y' worthless slaves. Fix the shovel, and start clearin' the debris around that *s'murghing* boulder."

The guard shoved Jack and his chain partner toward the rubble.

When the guard moved on around a bend in the passage, Jack examined the staff. Knowledge and memory jolted through his mind.

He'd taken innocent lives. He hadn't even stopped to offer healing magic to the victims. Shame and disgust for some unknown action washed over him.

"What do you remember?" his partner whispered, barely audible.

"Too much and not enough," Jack replied, still staring at the staff. A magician's staff. *His* tool and focus for spells. He didn't know if he had any magic left within him.

He and the staff had been separated for three years. His magic had been dead an equal amount of time. "Is it too late to find the power again?" he asked the staff.

Katrina sat before the rough factory pillow, an alien in the only world she knew. Her neat single plait gathered from the crown of her head to the nape of her neck, her plain dark skirt, and her meticulously clean hands and nails, showed how different she was from every other lacemaker in the cold and dark factory.

She was a slave and could never leave the building without permission. She had to wear the clothes provided for her by her owner and had no salary to spend on the cheap, gaudy jewelry the other lacemakers delighted in. The only similarity was her single plait. Unlike the other women, Katrina kept hers neat, tight, and clean. Most of the others merely clubbed their dirty hair together at the nape of their necks and braided it loosely.

Her owner, Neeles Brunix never ceased to remind her that her slavery was his revenge for the way Tattia Kaantille had insulted him that day three years ago when he refused to buy her patterns.

Katrina shifted in her straight chair, willing her bladder

to hold out a little longer. Another hour to the noon sun break. Three years she had been a slave in the factory, and she still hadn't learned to adjust her body to the daily routine. Another wiggle eased her back, a little.

She tried to dismiss the whispers and covert glances from the other lacemakers. Constant, disquieting murmurs filled the workroom on the third floor of the largest factory in Queen's City. Each exchange between two lacemakers was followed by a pointed look over a shoulder or across the room toward the coveted window position occupied by Katrina. She fought the urge to shift her back and ease the pressure on her bladder.

No work song lightened the long and tedious day. Katrina's soul cried out for music.

Alone in the world and in the factory, Katrina bent her head to her work. The heavy bobbins didn't fly through the pattern as her lighter, more slender bobbins had. Rhythm was difficult to maintain without music.

In defiance of factory rules, Katrina hummed an ancient work tune to aid her as she worked her pattern.

> *Meet together, crossing paths.*
> *Work together, twisting threads.*
> *Sing a little, friends are fast.*

The snickering whispers and slightly turned shoulders told her more than words how unwelcome any contribution from her would be. They would never be her friends.

Katrina flipped her right-hand pair of bobbins in a triple twist. The outside thread caught on the imperfections in the pillow cover, throwing her timing and tension off. The pin-hole in the pattern was out of alignment as well. The song died in her heart as the flow of work was interrupted.

"Ooooh! Not again," Maari, the newest lacemaker in the darkest corner of the Brunix factory, whined.

Katrina put down her bobbins with a sigh and crossed the large workroom to the new girl's pillow. Owner Brunix had given Katrina extra food and new blankets for her bed in return for helping the beginners keep their work straight and error free. After three years she had proved her skills above and beyond any of the free workers.

Somehow, someday she'd find a way out of this miserable

factory and back to her rightful place in society where she could wear two plaits again. Becoming the best lacemaker ever was the key to her survival and eventual freedom.

Brunix had offered many times to change her slave status to employee if she willingly shared his bed. That course was no more than another form of slavery.

"This pattern is too hard," Maari protested.

She sounded so much like Hilza before her last illness, Katrina had to restrain the urge to hug the girl to her breast. She hadn't allowed that wound to heal. The reminder of the deprivations inflicted upon her family by King Simeon kept her angry. Made her strong enough to survive and to resist Owner Brunix's sexual offers.

Allowing any man to take liberties with her body was too close to King Simeon's ugly demands for Katrina to agree to her owner's lewd suggestions. Why didn't he just rape her? He had the right. He owned her body.

She'd never give up her soul.

"There is nothing new in this pattern, Maari," Katrina explained brusquely. "I've added two extra pairs of bobbins to the fan and reversed the rose ground with the half-stitch diamond."

"But it *looks* different. And the half stitch is always tangled." Maari's lower lip stuck out. Hilza had pouted the same way. In a moment the girl would cry. Big fat tears that garnered sympathy but did nothing to mar her clear skin and sweet blue eyes.

Katrina hardened her heart lest she shatter three years of reserve and give in to Maari's sulks. Fixing the problem for her wouldn't help the girl overcome her lack of proper training. Nor would it give her the skills to survive in the fierce competition of factory life.

"Half stitch always looks tangled until you get four or five rows into it. Look." Katrina extracted a long pin with a costly amber bead on the head from the thickest part of her single plait. She was supposed to use this expensive gift from Owner Brunix to separate her growing clumps of bobbins into sections. It was more useful as a pointer. The tiny insect trapped in the amber was a constant reminder of the prison she had made for herself in accepting slavery in the factory over King Simeon's coven.

She laid the length of the pin along one thread running

through the questioned part of the pattern. The mistake jumped into view.

Maari nodded, eyes wandering around her pillow.

"Watch the threads, not the bobbins."

Maari's eyes jerkily followed the path of the pin along the threads.

"Oh!" Maari breathed. "I twisted twice instead of once." Hastily she reached for her bobbins to unweave the lopsided diamond.

Katrina halted Maari's hasty movements with a touch of the pin. "And never throw the bobbins! Lay them down neatly, in order. That is your true problem, Maari. You do not respect your bobbins or your work. You led a pampered life, and your teachers always rescued you. Now you have to take care of yourself and fix your own mistakes."

Maari had come from a wealthy mercantile family brought to ruin by the war and changing times, just as Katrina had. No one had helped Katrina during those early days in the factory as she struggled to keep up with more experienced lacemakers. No one had protected her from their cruel insults and sneaky tricks. Jealous rivals within the factory sometimes stole a bobbin from a pillow—usually from a place that required extensive reworking to add a replacement thread.

She jerked her head around to view her own pillow to make sure no one did that now. Taalia, one of the senior employees, stood halfway between her own work stand and Katrina's. She scuttled back to her chair at Katrina's fierce glare.

Katrina returned her attention to her pupil. "Tomorrow, I expect to see every half-stitch diamond worked correctly. I also expect to see your hands scrubbed and your fingernails *clean*." She retreated toward her own work.

"Did you give Owner Brunix the new design?" Taalia asked as Katrina passed by. Her tone was as breezy as ever, not acknowledging her previous attempt at trickery.

"Not yet."

"Afraid he'll notice there's more to you than lacemaker's hands and sharp eyes? I'll take him the pattern and claim it as my own. Maybe he'll offer me the same bonus he wants to give you." Taalia shifted in her chair, thrusting her bosom forward and wiggling her hips provocatively.

"I'll deliver the pattern when it is ready." Katrina bit her lip. Neeles Brunix's sexual innuendoes were getting harder to turn aside or ignore.

She wondered yet again why the owner hadn't forced her into his bed. He seemed to prefer his women willing—just like Simeon, who needed a willing virgin.

The most recent increase in privileges could be a bribe, or perhaps merely a reminder that Neeles Brunix controlled every aspect of her life. Why shouldn't she take a step toward earning her freedom by granting the owner a few favors?

Because the touch of his hand on hers reminded her over and over of the filthy suggestions made by King Simeon. She'd never give herself to any man without marriage, without respect. She didn't dare hope to find love.

"I'll give him the pattern during the sun break. He won't make lewd suggestions with all of the others around," Katrina said to herself.

"Don't underestimate him, Katey." Iza came up behind her. Iza no longer made lace. She was nearly blind and hunchbacked from a lifetime of working her pillow in dim light. She wound bobbins or straightened pins and did other useful, time-consuming chores. Working in the factory had deprived her of a life and family of her own. She was now too old and her skin too yellow, from the enforced restrictions on trips to the necessary during work hours, to catch Brunix's lustful eye. Iza had no other place to go.

"Brunix wants you, not just for your body. He wants to use your talents to gain the respect of the other owners. If he can flaunt a fair-haired woman with palace training as his mistress, then he believes the other owners will accept his dark eyes and dusky skin. Hold out for marriage." Iza urged Katrina back to her work.

"I don't want to marry Owner Brunix. Marriage to an outlander won't earn me two plaits. I've been betrayed by dark-eyed men before. I'll never let it happen again." A magician boy with dark eyes had betrayed her father's ship and ruined her entire family.

Katrina had never met the apprentice responsible for stopping her father's ship full of Tambootie seedlings, yet her hatred and mistrust of him grew with each year of separation from her old, comfortable, and stable way of life with a family she loved.

"Design is your entrance to the palace and out of this rat's maze," Iza reminded her. "Show him the design today at the sun break. I'll stand behind you."

"At the sun break," Katrina affirmed with trembling hands and quaking heart.

"Are you sure the queen is pregnant? So soon after her last miscarriage?" Jaylor asked the flickering image in the glass.

A slight tickle in his mind told him that Brevelan listened to his conversation with the Commune's informer.

Three years ago, on the night of Darville's coronation, he and Brevelan had been anxious to leave the capital before the Council discovered them. But he'd taken the time to recruit the spy. He needed information to keep his Commune safe. He couldn't risk talking directly to Darville or Mikka.

Though Margit had confirmed that Darville had not been with the army that attacked the monastery three years ago, Jaylor and his best friend had agreed to end all association and communication until prejudice against magic subsided throughout Coronnan. That couldn't happen until the dragons returned. Bringing control back to the magicians.

"I overheard her tell the king. She isn't well, Master Jaylor. She's as likely to lose this baby as all the others," the spy said. Her voice was clearer than her face.

Was it her lack of control of this spell or something else that interfered with the summons? Jaylor had only had time to teach her the basics of a summons and extending her listening senses when he recruited her.

Yaakke had noticed her carefully hidden talent without recognizing her as the source. After three years, her powers hadn't increased. She'd never qualify as an apprentice. She made a very good spy, however, despite her chafing at the confines of her work as a maid in Rossemikka's household. Her need to be away from people and buildings had prompted her to dress as a boy and follow the king on a wild tusker hunt the day he appeared to be outside the old monastery. Her unauthorized actions had given Darville a welcome alibi.

"Do the king and queen plan to announce this pregnancy?" Jaylor pushed a little of his own magic into the spell, though the girl had initiated it. Her image remained dim and flickered in and out of focus.

"Not for a while. She's miscarried so often, they're afraid of offering false hope of an heir." The girl paused. Swirls of gray and blue clouded Jaylor's glass. "I've got to go. The queen is calling for me. I wish you would allow me to find other employment in the palace. I hate being indoors all the time as much as I hate cats."

"I need you where you are, Margit. Take care of the queen. Try to make her stay in bed as much as possible. Brevelan says . . ." His glass cleared. All he could see through it was the candle flame, greatly magnified.

"I have to go to Mikka," Brevelan said from behind him. She grabbed several handfuls of herbs drying in the rafters of their home and stuffed them into her small satchel.

"You can't go. It's not safe, for you or for our baby," he replied. Gently he touched her slightly swollen belly where she carried their third child. "Our children need you here. You can't take Glendon with you. One look at him and everyone would know who his father is."

"I can help Mikka. I can prevent a miscarriage. I should have gone a long time ago." Grief and guilt crossed her face.

"What if you had gone and helped her through a full pregnancy? If anyone suspected her new midwife had any magic, the child would be removed from the succession. They'd suspect the child as a potential witch or, worse, a changeling. Mikka might be put aside, too. No. The fear of magic is too strong in the capital. I won't risk you. Darville won't risk the Council sending Mikka back to her brother. That might start a new war with Rossemeyer. We have to find another way to help our friends get an heir."

"Mikka loves Darville too much to allow her brother to start a war. She's close to Rossemanuel. He'll listen to her." Brevelan continued packing medicines.

"Rossemanuel may be king, but he's still very young. Their uncle's party rules Rossemeyer. They still control hordes of mercenaries anxious to fight. Coronnan is as good a target as anyplace."

"If they are so anxious to fight, why haven't they joined our war against SeLenicca? Maybe with their active support we could end this stalemate." Brevelan set her carry pack on the table, next to Jaylor's glass and candle. "I'll take the boys over to the apprentice dormitory. Your students need practice in controlling our two hooligans." A small grin touched the corners of her mouth. Three-year-old Glendon and his two-year-old brother, Lukan, managed to find more mischief than any ten normal boys combined.

"You must stay here, Brevelan. The journey to the capital is too long. I won't risk you and the baby." Jaylor picked up the satchel and began replacing the small crocks and vials of medicine on their shelves.

"Then send me by the transport spell." Brevelan returned her potions to the satchel as fast as he removed them.

"No! I have forbidden the use of that spell except for the most dire emergencies. We haven't any dragons to guide us through the void. I can't allow you to go." Panic sent his heart racing. The thought of losing Brevelan to magic or to those who feared her magic made his world bleak and empty. "Think, Brevelan. Think of the consequences."

"Then you will have to find us some dragons. Quickly. Mikka needs me!"

"I have no one to send in search of Shayla yet. The only alternative is to let me go, as I should have gone three years ago." Yaakke's death still weighed heavily on his conscience. When would he have the courage to send another journeyman in search of the dragons?

"I can't let you go, Jaylor." Brevelan clung to him, crying silently.

Queen Rossemikka seems to be barren. The Council looks elsewhere, outside of Coronnan to distant relatives of Darville, for an heir. Rejiia's son died at birth. Now she has deserted her husband and disappeared from Coronnan. Lord Andrall's son is mentally defective and hasn't been considered a possible heir to the Coraurlia for more than twenty years. The Council and the increasingly powerful

Gnuls will not countenance an illegitimate birth. If they did, they would have to look at witchwoman Brevelan as next heir. If they could find her. Krej acknowledged her as his eldest. If the Council insists on a male, they would look to Brevelan's oldest son, Glendon—likely a magician born and bred. She never claimed Darville to be the father. We all know he is. Descended from two royal lines, her son has the strongest blood claim to the throne—if the people of Coronnan could put aside their prejudice against magic.

The coven is so close, and yet so far, from achieving domination of the Three Kingdoms. I have waited years for events to move themselves. My patience is at an end. I must stir some mischief to move events forward.

Chapter 14

Mid-afternoon brought a thinning of spring clouds. All of the lacemakers gratefully grabbed their cloaks and trooped onto the narrow walkway that separated the factory from the river. Katrina wasn't sure where or when the custom of a sun break had begun, but it was now a time-honored tradition. Fines for denying workers their right to an hour of sunlight in the middle of the day—even when it was storming—could financially ruin an employer. Too bad she spent most of the time waiting in line to use the necessary.

The men who worked in the factory warehouse would have their sun break after the women returned to the workroom.

Katrina looked askance at the welcome sun. Neeles Brunix did not always join his lacemakers on the walkway. A break in the clouds almost guaranteed his presence. He was here today, ahead of the women. His long body leaning against the sand-brick wall of the factory, almost the same color as his hair, he stared at the rushing river. No flicker of his dark, hooded eyes acknowledged the presence of his employees until Katrina appeared at the end of the line. As soon as she threw back her hood and raised her face to the sun, Neeles Brunix stood straight and his eyes sparked with unconcealed desire.

The younger lacemakers scurried out of his way, not willing to have those intense eyes rest on their bodies.

"I hear you treated the new girl very harshly this morning." Brunix appeared at Katrina's side before she had a chance to gather her courage and take a deep breath.

"You make me responsible for her training. Therefore I

am also responsible for her mistakes and dirty lace." She looked at the river rushing past the levee. It smelled clean today, refreshed by snow melting in the hills. An unwelcome urge to follow her mother in the water's endless journey to the sea gripped her. To end the struggle. To know peace.

She didn't want peace. She wanted to avenge the wrongs done to her and her family by King Simeon and a dark-eyed magician boy. In her mind the magician looked very much like a younger Neeles Brunix.

"I would free you from slavery if you would add certain other responsibilities to your . . . work." His eyes opened as they skimmed her cloaked body.

Did he know she made certain her clothing was too large for her and that she bound her full bosom extra tight to disguise her figure from his gaze?

Just then, Taalia sauntered by, her wrap drooping on her shoulder to reveal the deep neckline of her bodice. Her heavy breasts swelled above the white cloth. A dusky shadow peeked out from the skimpy confines of her clothing in blatant invitation to Brunix. She rotated her hips as she walked, making little thrusting movements with her pelvis.

Katrina turned away, embarrassed.

Brunix never took his eyes off Katrina.

"This is the only additional responsibility I ask." Katrina thrust the new pattern under his nose so he couldn't ignore it. "I want to draw new patterns."

"I have no need of new designs. I have all of the patterns you inherited and I bought. I do need you to warm my bed," he stated as he took the pattern from her and examined the flowing lines of the floral motif.

"No." Katrina stood her ground, wishing she could turn him into a living torch like the witches of legend.

"I own you, Katrina Kaantille, just as I own your inheritance. I could order you to submit."

"But you prefer your women willing, just like King Simeon."

Brunix blanched at her comparison.

"I am not willing."

"Compromise!" Iza hissed as she pushed her frail body

between them. "The pattern is good and it is unique. You will make money from it, Brunix."

"It is also complex. Only the most skilled lacemaker could work it. I'm not certain Tattia Kaantille could work the design, let alone her half-trained daughter."

Katrina gasped at his audacity. By invoking her mother's name, he reminded them all of the taint of suicide that clung to Katrina. Tattia's ghost was said to haunt the workroom at night. Superstition claimed that Katrina, too, would become a ghost upon her death because of her mother's sin.

"We seem to be at an impasse," Brunix sneered at Katrina. "I will examine the design. If it is worthy, I will consider adding it to my stock."

"No." Katrina grabbed the pattern from him and walked over to the edge of the walkway. There she held the strip of leather over the rushing river. "I have many more ideas for new patterns—exporters always need new designs. All of my ideas are exclusively yours in exchange for my freedom. End my slavery, or I destroy it."

"That pattern is mine! And so are you." Brunix lunged to grab it away from Katrina. As his hands curled around her arm, she opened her fingers. A puff of wind caught the contested prize, swirled it, and then dropped it at Brunix's feet. He retrieved the strip of stained leather before the next breeze drowned it in the river.

"Stupid bitch. You'll pay for your insolence!" Brunix screamed. "I'll make a fortune from this design and the others. You owe me your life and I intend to keep you my slave for a very, very long time."

"I hope the cost of a license for Tambrin to work the design properly will beggar you." Katrina stalked back to the workroom alone.

Jaylor raised his head and listened to the clearing. "Someone comes," he announced to Brevelan across the open space where she hung the laundry.

"Another victim?" She cocked her head as if listening. "Build up the fire and start some water boiling. Fetch some bandages, too. I sense pain. Serious pain." She hurried toward the west path.

Glendon ran ahead of his father into the hut. Two-year-

old Lukan planted a reluctant lop-eared rabbit onto his hip
and toddled in her wake.

Light shimmered in a sense-lurching flash of colored arcs
as the forest shifted and the entrance to this hidden clearing opened.

A nondescript young man dressed in common trews and
homespun shirt used his sturdy staff for balance as he
dragged a smaller body up the hill.

"Another victim," Jaylor acknowledged, knowing his
wife had been correct in her assessment of the newcomers.
He hastened to set a cauldron of water to boil for whatever
healing herbs and poultices she might need. Bandages. The
stock was low. This was the third refugee in the past moon.
He sent Glendon to tear strips from the store of linen in
the loft.

The young man he recognized as Journeyman Marcus.
One of the few boys of talent who had remained with the
Commune since Baamin's death and the disbanding of the
University. Journeyman quests now revolved around rescu-
ing the victims of the Gnostic Utilitarians. In the last year
the cult's hatred had gained momentum. Why?

Whether the child with Marcus had true magical abilities
or was hounded away from his home because of unfounded
accusations of witchcraft remained to be seen.

More than two dozen refugees had found shelter in the
southern mountains with the remnants of the Commune.
Most of them had some talent; one or two had the potential
to become true magicians and join the continual fight for
the survival of the Commune.

Unfortunately, most of the girls who found their way to
the clearing were so traumatized by the rape gangs that
wandered villages in search of "potential" witches, they'd
never be brave enough to try magic. The mistaken belief
that only virgins could throw magic was just an excuse for
bullies to run wilder than magicians were reputed to.

"Good thing we started a new cabin to house apprentices," Jaylor remarked to the greenbird perched above the
doorway of his own newly expanded home. The cluster of
wooden buildings at the base of a cliff an hour's walk from
the clearing had grown from a single library to include Masters' quarters and now apprentice dormitories. The two
journeymen, Marcus and Robb, parked their weary bodies

where they could when they were about. Mostly they wandered Coronnan, supplying Jaylor with information and new apprentices.

Jaylor's biggest worry lately was to find ways to feed them all without arousing the suspicion of the countryside.

"News from the capital, Master." Marcus eased his companion onto a cot before the hearth at Brevelan's direction.

While his wife tended the pale and frightened boy, Jaylor ushered his two sons and the journeyman ahead of him, out of the cottage. "How badly is he hurt?" He handed Marcus the length of linen and gestured for him to start ripping it into bandages.

"A broken arm, I think. Straightened and splinted it as best I could, but I'm no healer. Lee's da threw stones at him when he stopped plowing and ran to help a steed in distress foaling twins." Marcus shook his head in dismay. "The boy was only trying to help the mare and save the foals."

"I know, Marcus. I know. 'Tis the same story we've heard over and over. The Gnostic Utilitarians have spread dire tales of the evils of magic. They encourage lawless vengeance against innocents. I wonder that King Darville allows it."

"I don't think he sanctions the Gnuls, sir. King Darville is a good king and Coronnan has prospered these last three years, despite the war. I think the Gnuls have invented evidence of evil magic to regain the followers who aren't afraid of magic now that life is getting comfortable again."

"Does this boy have true talent?" Jaylor changed the subject rather than dispute the issue with Marcus. The Gnuls claimed Darville had led the attack on the monastery three years ago. Revealing the truth—that Margit had followed him on a wild tusker hunt in the opposite direction—might jeopardize the girl's position.

"Can't tell what's talent and what's sensitive hearing. Lee feels guilty for having any magic. He's bottled it all up so tight I couldn't find it with my probes. But I think he must. The mare went into labor weeks early. She was pastured well away from where the boy was tilling. Yet he knew. Just reared up his head, nostrils flaring and eyes wide, like he felt the pain himself. Or heard her distress well beyond the reach of normal senses."

"Another empath? Brevelan does that."

"Good thing I was in the area. I 'heard' the boy cry out when the first stone knocked the wind out of him. If I hadn't thrown a delusion of Lee running away and diverted the attack, he'd be dead now. Good thing he's a boy."

A fearful father might have raped his own daughter to kill her magic. Boys were just murdered.

"Someone is compounding the ugliness. I've heard reports of animals being stolen from secure pens and being found slaughtered—throats slit, blood drained in a ritual manner—miles away." Marcus swallowed heavily as if keeping down bile.

"I've heard those rumors, too. No evidence, though. It's always in the next village."

"Now it's in the capital. I talked to a woman whose cat was stolen from her arms, on her doorstep, by a gang of older boys. She found the cat on her doorstep the next morning. She claims she saw a cloaked man in the shadow of the next house directing the gang. Later the boys involved each had a gold piece they had no explanation for earning. Some of her neighbors are calling her a witch now. Just 'cause she's old and alone."

"Hearsay again."

"I've alerted Margit. She's looking for hard evidence. I've tried to teach her new spells, but she can't seem to learn anything beyond a basic summons. She'll have to rely on her knowledge of Coronnan City."

Regretful silence followed while Jaylor tried to calm his fury at events in the capital. He hugged both his sons tighter, savoring their innocence. Glendon responded by wrapping one arm around Jaylor's knees. Lukan plopped his thumb into his empty mouth and snuggled into his father's lap.

"Any other news from the capital?" Jaylor diverted his thoughts and his anger away from the persecution of magic. How could he stop the torture and murder of innocents? The rumors of sacrificed animals had to stop before they amplified into tales of stolen children.

The time for the Commune to intervene and show that magic was not something to fear was fast approaching, with or without dragons. But their numbers were so few!

With luck and a lot more training, Marcus and Robb

would be ready to go on a real quest in search of Shayla within a year or two. Too late. Something needed to be done now. Before the Gnuls discovered the University in exile and murdered them all.

"The king still wears a sling on his left arm. But he attends banquets now and eats with his right hand. Until recently he hasn't been seen to eat in public since the battle with Janataea and Krej."

Jaylor knew that. Margit had reported the Council's complaints that the queen's miscarriages and subsequent illness shouldn't keep Darville from attending banquets and other festivities.

"There's something else you should know, sir." Marcus looked about the clearing as if seeking information.

"Did you find a trace of Yaakke?" He asked the same question every time either Marcus or Robb returned with reports.

"Not him. But sort of like him. Robb and I have noticed some of the outlying villages disappear."

"What?" Jaylor roared. His sons slipped behind him to avoid his wrath. He reached out and hugged them both, drawing calm from their innocence.

"Sometimes when we pass by at a distance we see houses and people, fields and flocks. And then as soon as someone spots us, we can't see them anymore. If we weren't stretching our senses looking for magic, I doubt we'd see these places at all. It's like this clearing. If Brevelan doesn't want the path open, ain't no way in Simurgh's hell anyone, magician or mundane, is going to find our refuge."

Darville walked the streets of Sambol on the old border between Coronnan and SeLenicca. The stillness in the air that foretold dawn enhanced the scents of spice and cut lumber, of salted fish and too many people crowded within the walls of the merchant city. All was silent, as if·Kardia Hodos held its breath in anticipation of the new day, the Vernal Equinox.

False dawn glimmered on the eastern horizon. The near-constant wind funneling down the mountain pass to the west returned.

The troubled king turned his back on the wind and the last bite of winter in the mountains. At the far end of the pass,

his army would be preparing for the first battle of the season.
A first battle that would carry the war out of the pass and
into SeLenicca, hopefully crushing the next invasion before
it began. He'd kept King Simeon's army out of Coronnan
for three long years. Now, at last, he was in a position to
end the conflict.

He didn't think he'd have been allowed to achieve that
advantage if Lord Jonnias and Lord Marnak still sat on the
Council of Provinces. Heavy fines for their attack on the
monastery and banishment from the Council until those
fines were paid had ended their dissension. For the first
time in too many years the Council worked with their king
as a team and the war progressed, however slightly. A defensive war only. Until now.

Both Coronnan and SeLenicca were exhausted and running low on resources.

Dark shadows still lay between the steep walls of the
pass. Night would linger longer there, hiding ambushes and
stalling messages. 'Twas one message in particular that had
brought King Darville to the city on the edge of the battlefront. His spies in the enemy army had sent a coded letter
by a long and circuitous route. The generals of King Simeon of SeLenicca were willing to discuss an armed truce,
with or without Simeon's approval.

Frost clung to the trees and paths this cloudy equinox
morning. But yesterday had been balmy. Any disarmament
had to take place soon, so that soldiers could go home in
time for spring planting.

Darville heaved a lonely sigh as he continued his ritual
walk. Fred, his trusty bodyguard and confidant, now that
Jaylor remained in hiding, was somewhere behind him, hovering protectively. Dawn was almost here and Darville had
yet to make the decision that drove him to walk the streets
at dawn.

"Jaylor knew before I did that I think better on my feet,"
he mused. Then he looked up to the sky and addressed the
wind as if it were Jaylor. "I miss you, old friend."

He lengthened his stride, almost hoping to lose Fred and
his loneliness in the tangle of alleys and warehouses. No
questions arose in his mind about the tentative offer of
peace. That he would grab.

But what would he do about the Council's request that

he put aside his beloved wife in favor of a woman who could bear him a son and heir?

More than three years had passed since his coronation, and Mikka had miscarried seven times. He feared her current pregnancy would also end in disaster. For her own health, she shouldn't have conceived again so soon. She had enough magic talent in her to prevent it.

But Mikka was a princess born and bred. She *knew* how much Coronnan needed an heir to provide a clear line of succession. The country wouldn't survive a dynastic war compounded by the exhausted reserves from the current war with SeLenicca.

He walked on. The tangle of alleys opened to a market square. In the center stood a proud Equinox Pylon decorated with the first greens and flowers of the season. As soon as the sun topped the horizon, citizens would be dancing and singing a welcome to spring. The celebration and fertility rituals would go on all day and well into the night. He should be with Mikka.

The wind shifted once again, and new odors assaulted the king. Death.

Recent death. And not a clean one. The hair on the back of his neck rose in preternatural fear. He cast about him for the source of danger, left hand reaching automatically to the short sword on his hip.

"S'murgh it!" he cursed as an aching burn snaked up his arm and his hand grasped nothing. "I'll never learn to fight right-handed." With a conscious thought he grasped his weapon with his undamaged hand.

"What is it, Your Grace?" Fred appeared at his left elbow, ready to guard his vulnerable side. Then he wrinkled his nose.

A flicker of movement by the Pylon drew their attention. No one stood near the focus of celebration, but an ugly brown nest of twigs at the base crackled with new fire. Atop the fuel lay the gutted body of a cat, intestines and blood feeding the growing flames.

Fred dashed forward to stamp out the fire before it spread to the Pylon and spring decorations.

"Who would sacrifice a cat?" Darville asked the air. Painful memories of Krej and his coven sacrificing the body of one particular cat came to mind. Thanks to their efforts, there was no feline body to receive the alien spirit sharing Mikka's human form.

He'd heard about ritual slaughter of livestock around the country. This was the first report of the carcass being found at a Pylon. The action brought back childhood horror stories of the days before the Stargods when Simurgh, the winged god of death, had reigned throughout Kardia Hodos.

Krej's old coven had worked to restore that bloodthirsty religion. They'd had three years to restore their numbers after the death of Janessa, Krej's mother, and Janataea, his sister. Krej himself had been locked into the tin statue of a weasel. And Zolltarn had deserted their ranks for the Commune. Had Krej broken free and restored the coven?

Had a cat been sacrificed this time because they were the symbol of a witch's familiar and fearful citizens targeted the poor animals? Maybe a malcontent chose a beloved pet to stir up fear of witches.

Or had the coven sent a warning that they knew Mikka harbored the spirit of a cat in her human body? If that knowledge leaked to anyone, Mikka would be named witch and exiled or executed. He didn't know if he had enough authority to save her.

"Looks like the work of the coven. I heard there was a village up north that found a sacrificed child by their Pylon at the last Solstice."

"Unconfirmed rumors," Darville said sharply, breathing through his mouth to reduce the stench. "I have to have hard evidence to confirm or refute these stories of human sacrifice. Remind me when we get back to the city. I'll have to send out a trusted agent."

"We'd best hide this before anyone else sees it and panics," Fred suggested. "The coven would love to involve you in suspicion of witchcraft, so's the Gnuls would depose you or start a new civil war."

"I wouldn't put it past the Gnostic Utilitarians to plant this fake sacrifice so I would lead a witch-hunt. When we get back to the capital, I'll find a spy to infiltrate that group, too." Darville found a sturdy branch among those gathered for the bonfire that would be lit at midnight.

Together the two men scooped up as much of the grisly

evidence as they could. "Throw it into the river, Fred. And not a word of this to anyone."

"Evil rumors have a way of starting without evidence."

"Rumors that must be squashed before they become fact. I'll not fall victim to the plots of either the coven or the Gnuls. I have had enough of my citizens becoming vicious, prying spies. Those lavish rewards granted to informers by the Gnuls must stop. People invent evidence of magic against their neighbors, family, and business rivals for money." And courtiers followed Queen Rossemikka, hoping she'd betray her rumored magic talent. Was that why the Council pushed him daily to put aside his queen?

Darville set his jaw in determination. No one would make him set aside his wife. Not even Mikka herself.

Chapter 15

"**G**ood thing the old commandant wandered off and drowned himself in a creek two inches deep," Jack's chain partner whispered out of the side of his mouth. "Died with a smile on his face, I hear."

Dragon-dream!

He'd heard of that happening before. Where? When?

Jack didn't reply until the black-uniformed guard making his rounds passed beyond them. Speaking was forbidden in the yard during sun breaks as well as in the mines.

"Why is it good?" He kept his faced turned toward the sun, absorbing as much warmth and light as possible. His body turned toward a natural tug, and he knew that direction was south. Without knowing why, he checked the position of the sun against the length of the shadows. The sun had just passed the Vernal Equinox.

"The old commandant would have ordered you whipped for disrupting the routine when you broke that hammer." The partner also continued to bask in the sunlight.

"Not my fault the equipment is shoddy and worn out," Jack protested, still in whispers.

"That was the old commandant. The new one knows that slaves are in short supply. Most criminals are sent to reinforce the army at the front rather than here. Now that Coronnan is setting up an invasion, Simeon doesn't have enough troops." News of the last battle had come with a private message to the commandant a few days ago. Two dozen of the youngest and healthiest miners were due to be shipped out when the pass cleared. Jack and his partner weren't among them, though both could bear the hardships of army life.

Something was wrong with Simeon sending slaves from this mine to battle Coronnan. Jack didn't know what.

"We live longer and work harder when the commandant feeds us and goes lighter on the lash," the partner finished.

"How long has the new commandant been here?"

"Two years. Maybe more. Hard to keep track of time in a place like this."

"Why can't we speak?" Jack muttered into his beard and turned his back on his companion as another guard strolled around them. He'd counted four uniformed men in the yard, armed with clubs and whips. Nearly one hundred prisoners—he refused to think of himself as a slave. The weapons were not formidable. Surely one hundred prisoners could overpower four guards and escape.

"Same reason chain partners are changed every few days. They don't want to give us the opportunity to plan an escape or learn to trust each other." The partner stretched his arms over his head as if offering prayers to the sun.

"Who needs plans? We're strong from hard work. Why can't we bash a few heads and break out?"

"Where would we go?"

That stunned Jack. He hadn't thought further than escape.

"CRAWK, Crawk, crawk, crawk . . ." A jackdaw, perched atop the commandant's quarters, mocked Jack's shortsightedness with a raucous cackle. He watched the bird preen himself a moment, absorbing the familiar movements in a memory that seemed to have been washed as clean as a cooking pot.

His hand hovered over an imaginary kettle as if wielding a dishrag. He'd washed pots before. But where or when?

"CROOAWK, Crooawk, crooawk . . ." the jackdaw cawed again, this time as if encouraging him to drag more memories out of his tired brain.

"So far, the guards have allowed me to stay as your partner for three weeks," his partner said, breaking into Jack's thoughts.

"Because I've been walking in my sleep for three years?"

"Probably. You haven't spoken or even acknowledged anyone with a flicker of an eye or a nod of the head. They don't consider you a threat."

"Hmf." Jack looked away again.

A slight, stoop-shouldered, man with a thin, patchy beard edged closer, as if listening. Jack turned his back on the man. The listener was new to the mine, new since . . . yesterday!

Jack smiled inwardly at this minor triumph of memory. Then he frowned. A newcomer eavesdropping bothered him.

He allowed his eyes to focus on the jackdaw with the white spots above its eyes—almost like bushy white eyebrows. Why did that thought resound through his body as if it were important?

"CRAWK, Crawk, crawk," the bird encouraged him again.

Jack suddenly knew he'd awakened to the same raucous call every morning since arriving in the mine. The bird was tied to him in some way. He longed to go back into the mine and hold his staff again. His tool of magic had to be the key to his memory. It was still lashed to a shovel inside the mine.

"Don't blame you for existing in a fog like that. We were all sent here to die. Not thinking, not remembering the pain we've caused others makes it all easier to bear," the partner said.

"I don't think I was sent here for that purpose," Jack said, more to the jackdaw then to his partner. "If only I could remember!"

"Don't force it. Memories are like quicksilver. They look solid until you try to grasp them, then they slip away just out of reach, still looking solid but more than ready to escape again. What are some of the things you do remember? Do you have a name?"

"Jack." That didn't sound exactly right, but it was close enough.

"I'm Fraank."

The jackdaw glided to a fence post on the south side of the yard. It cocked its head and looked at the pair as if listening to their muted conversation. Perhaps the bird had been a familiar. He knew he was a magician, so why not?

"Corby, Corby, Corby," the jackdaw called.

Jack had heard the bird speak in just that way once before. "Corby." He formed the word soundlessly. "Your name is Corby." He smiled at the memory of Corby scolding him, listening to him, spotting game for him.

"What else do you remember?" his partner prodded him.

"I remember things. I can't remember me. Look at me, I'm half a head taller than I think I should be, I'm strong instead of skinny, and this beard is full when I've never had a beard before."

"What things do you remember?"

"Things, like this is Coronnan and the Stargods outlawed slaves here a thousand years ago. So how can King Simeon of *SeLenicca* draw slaves from here to fight in his army?"

"This isn't Coronnan. We're in SeLenicca and King Simeon owns this mine."

"No." Jack shook his head. He knew that information was wrong. "None of the guards, nor the commandant, cuts his beard square. The guards speak both languages. Some of the prisoners might be SeLenese, but we aren't in SeLenicca."

"But I was sent here by King Simeon in punishment for my . . . for crimes against him!" Fraank protested.

"I know that when I fled to this place, it was within the boundaries of Coronnan. I know that in my bones. We are within the borders of the land once reserved for the dragons."

"Fled here? You came here by choice?" Fraank's voice squeaked in apprehension. "Jack, no one comes to this death camp by choice. Not unless you wanted to die or you were running away from something too hideous to remember."

Like me.

A death camp. No one left here alive.

What had he fled that a hard death in the mines was preferable to?

"Margit, would you summon my cousin the ambassador?" Queen Rossemikka looked up from sealing a long letter. "I wish to place this letter to my brother in the diplomatic pouch."

"Yes, Your Grace." Margit dipped a polite curtsy and fled the queen's study eagerly. Her lungs grew heavy and clogged every time she was alone with Rossemikka. If she didn't know better, she'd swear a dozen cats filled the room.

Margit hated cats. She hated them even when they provided a necessary check to rats and mice in barns. But at least she could breathe in a barn, cats or no cats. Maintaining her pose as a devoted servant to the queen was getting harder all the time.

Kevin-Rosse, the ambassador from Rossemeyer and Rossemikka's cousin, lived in a different part of the city from Palace Reveta Tristile. Margit breathed easier knowing she had a legitimate excuse to leave the crowded confines and stale air of the palace.

If only she were a real apprentice magician. Then she could live in the mountains with Jaylor and Brevelan and the other magicians. She could breathe clean air and sleep out-of-doors if she chose. Eventually she'd be given a quest and allowed to roam Coronnan freely like Marcus and Robb.

She hurried past the market square between Palace Isle and University Island. Three years ago, she'd sold sausage rolls and other savory pasties here, enjoying the opportunity to escape her mother's hot and stuffy shop every day. Then Yaakke, the strange magician boy, had sent Jaylor into her life. He'd tapped the power in her brain that she'd kept carefully hidden from the Gnuls and her mother. No one in her family had ever been tainted by magic. At least no one Margit knew about.

Jaylor had freed her from her mother's shop and opened many possibilities for the future. A position in the queen's household had seemed like a small temporary step upward. Temporary had dragged into a third year and approached a fourth.

She skimmed over three more bridges on her way to the ambassador's residence. The rushing waters between each of the city islands cleansed her of the weight of living in the palace. At the end of the next bridge, a line of heavily laden sledges blocked her way. She wove her way among them, speaking softly to the huge steeds harnessed in front of them. The placid steeds nuzzled her pockets for treats she didn't have.

"You'll have to settle for a scratch," she whispered to an

animal in the middle of the caravan as she ran her blunted fingernails up and down the center of its head.

The steed snorted and stamped with pleasure. The sounds muffled the approach of a merchant and the steed's wrangler. Their whispered words stopped her in her tracks.

"Do you have the poison?" the Rover-dark merchant asked the blond wrangler.

"I have it hidden." The wrangler touched the scrip at his waist, right next to his long dagger.

"As soon as the ambassador gives me the diplomatic pouch, I'll pass it to you. You'll only have a few moments while I distract him. Then we'll have to strap the pouch onto the courier's chest where it will stay for the duration of the journey. The queen's letter to her brother will be on top. The last item added. Will you be able to do it?"

"Three drops on the queen's seal will kill King Rossemanuel within an instant of opening the letter. He always caresses the seal as if touching his beloved sister. The poison will be traced to Rossemikka. She will be executed for murder."

Margit suppressed a gasp. She couldn't let them discover her now. She had to find out who wanted to murder the queen's brother and depose Rossemikka before she bore an heir to Darville. The delicate political balance among the Three Kingdoms would be terribly upset. Who would inherit the thrones of Coronnan and Rossemeyer?

"Ordinary poisons might not be enough. If the boy has inherited any magic talent from his mother's family, he could detect and neutralize it," the merchant protested.

"The ingredients were prepared by King Simeon's mistress. Who knows what magic she added to the formula." The wrangler shrugged, unconcerned. "She distilled it right after the Solstice when the coven's rituals created some very powerful magic for her to tap."

"Good. Once the little king is out of the way, his younger brother will pose no problem. His health was compromised years ago by Janataea when she was governess to all three Rossemeyer brats. The coven has agents in place to name Simeon the rightful king of Rossemeyer. We'll have control of all three kingdoms before the year is out."

Margit slid behind the huge sledge steed. Who did she

tell first? How could she keep the queen's letter out of the diplomatic pouch? Her first thoughts flew to Marcus, the journeyman magician who took her reports whenever he wandered into town.

No time for that. She had to summon Jaylor with a candle and a glass. No time. Ambassador Kevin-Rosse expected her. He could arrest these assassins. Unless he was part of the plot. He and Queen Rossemikka rarely agreed on anything, especially Rossemeyer's limited involvement in the war against SeLenicca.

Who could she trust?

Only herself.

A smile crept across her face. "I've never practiced the invisibility delusion on anyone but Mama. Maybe it's time to see how well it works on strangers," she said to the steed. The animal nodded its massive head as if in agreement. Probably only a beg for more scratches. Margit complied as she thought out her plan.

Three minutes later she replaced the tiny vial in the wrangler's scrip. He didn't react to her presence at all. Now the vial contained only plain river water.

She had leisure now to reveal the plot to Jaylor, and only Jaylor, on the next full moon when she summoned him.

"Look, there's the queen!" Iza tugged on Katrina's sleeve to watch the processional. The lacemakers and other factory workers had been given a day away from their work to celebrate the third birthday of Princess Jaranda.

"Queen Miranda does not look well," Katrina observed. Tight lines of fatigue and worry creased the hereditary monarch's eyes. Though barely two years senior to Katrina, the queen looked much older. Her body was too thin; her four plaits pulled so tight against her scalp her facial bones seemed devoid of flesh. The platinum crown set with priceless jewels was so heavy that Miranda's thin neck strained to support her head. Her white and silver ceremonial gown did nothing to enhance her complexion.

"She looks unhappy," Katrina murmured. The gradual hush that fell over the crowd echoed her sentiment. "So unhappy with her husband she's withdrawing the Edict of Joint Monarchy. Rumor claims she'll sue for peace with Coronnan when she deposes The Simeon."

Peace was an idea that met with mixed popularity. The unemployed and homeless, who flocked to the army, loved the war-effort. Merchants, who imported arms and supplies, profited. The widows, orphans, and other victims of the war hated it. Katrina couldn't forget the war had caused the trade embargo with Coronnan that led to P'pa's bankruptcy.

She fingered the lace shawl she'd retrieved from her father's house during her first year of slavery. The gleaming white fibers added a festive touch to her plain skirt and vest on this day of celebration. It should have adorned the queen.

"Oh, the little princess, all dressed in purple and silver!" Iza continued her litany of praise. "Isn't she pretty, Katrina? I think she's the prettiest little girl in the whole world."

A purple canopy carried by four half-naked slaves rose above the princess' open litter. She was too young for even the most placid ponies. The little girl smiled and waved shyly at the crowds of people gathered along the wide Royal Avenue.

A sickly child, Katrina thought. Waxy skin, too pale to be fashionable, and too small for three years old. Her hair shone in the sunshine, red highlights obvious in her four thin plaits, too short to join into a single braid below her neck. Queen's City hadn't seen much of the princess. The queen, too, had remained mostly in seclusion these last three years. King Simeon was the only member of the once-beloved royal family much in evidence. And he wasn't loved by many. Certainly not by the families of his Solstice victims or those who had lost men in the endless war against Coronnan.

Three once-proud men, former military heroes who had secretly sought peace with Coronnan, followed a troop of elite military guards in the parade. Raw wounds marred their naked backs. One man's face had been beaten until his left eye was permanently closed. He dragged his left leg painfully. Soon they would join the criminals sacrificed to Simeon's god at the next solstice. Unless Queen Miranda removed her husband from power before then.

Why had the queen tolerated his cruel religion all these years? Or was she so isolated in the palace she didn't know? More likely, Simeon had bewitched her so she couldn't intervene and outlaw his sacrifices.

Rumors from the palace suggested the bewitchment was waning, though.

Katrina had trouble maintaining interest in the parade of dancing steeds with ribbons plaited in their manes and haughty noblewomen flaunting three plaits and fortunes' worth of Tambrin lace on their gowns.

Katrina searched the faces of the slaves for Fraanken Kaantille. P'pa wasn't carrying the canopy. The little flame of hope died within her heart. Royal servants were born into slavery and knew their lot in life. They were treated well and trusted. Criminals, prisoners of war, and traitors, like her father, were sent to die in the king's galley ships or in the mines.

"I could buy your freedom from Neeles Brunix if you gave me that shawl," a man said quietly into Katrina's ear.

She looked around startled by his unsuspected presence. The man wore a hooded cloak that shadowed his face. The voice was familiar. Where had she heard him speak before?

"What?" Hope kindled a tiny light in her mind. *Freedom!* "Why?" She damped any possibility he could truly offer her freedom.

"That shawl is valuable. More valuable than your slave price." His voice barely reached her ears.

"Does this offer include employment once I am free of Brunix?" Once he released her, the factory owner wouldn't allow her to continue working for him. Not unless she shared his bed. What use freedom at the cost of the shawl, the only tangible link to her mother she still had?

"I have not the resources to help you beyond the purchase of your slave papers." The man bowed his head, increasing the shadows around him.

"I have no use for freedom without a promise of employment." Katrina dismissed the offer reluctantly.

"I may not be able to meet the price again. Think long and hard. I will try to speak to you again. Later." The man faded into the crowd, as if he'd never been there at all.

Iza continued to prattle, unaware of the exchange. "Look. Look, there behind the Lord Chancellor rides the king. So far back from the queen and princess. Do you suppose the rumors are true, that Miranda will divorce him and outlaw his hideous religion?''

Katrina returned her attention to the parade, deliberately pushing aside all thoughts of the strange encounter with the cloaked man. She sought the figure of the outland king who had bewitched young Miranda and mercilessly ruled SeLenicca ever since. What had happened to weaken the adoration that used to shine from the queen's eyes? Katrina didn't care as long as the man she hated was brought low and stripped of power.

"The outland woman riding beside Simeon, who is she?" Katrina asked. The tall beauty with black hair and blue eyes rode a sleek black steed draped in silver-and-black ribbons. Her black gown trimmed in silver lace dipped immodestly low into her bosom. Undoubtedly, steed and gown had been chosen to set her apart from the sea of blond citizens riding equally light-colored steeds.

"Her?" Iza spat. "His latest mistress. He calls her 'niece.' But everyone knows he has no siblings. Gossip in the city says he flaunted her at the palace once too often. Miranda threw him out. That's why she's going to rescind the Edict of Joint Monarchy."

"Simeon's niece looks pregnant." Katrina scanned the elegant curves of the tall woman. A noticeable bulge filled her black gown.

"She does, doesn't she? And Miranda isn't. The nobles call us workers immoral. They should look to themselves before they condemn us," Iza sniffed.

"Simeon can't be trusted. Someone should warn Miranda." Katrina eyed the man she hated. "He'll kill her before he relinquishes power."

"Don't be silly. Guards and councillors and lacemakers surround the queen day and night."

"Guards won't stop a sorcerer."

As if he heard her sneer, Simeon turned his burning gaze directly to Katrina. His eyes widened as he stared at her. Then his lips curled up in a mocking, self-satisfied grin. Insolently he blew her a kiss.

Katrina stepped back, shocked and revolted. Her hand reached to her throat in surprise. She gathered the lace shawl protectively around her. The king's gaze followed her hands. His eyes narrowed and seethed with emotion.

Why do you wait so long to come to me and meet your destiny, Katrina Kaantille?

The words echoed around her head. She hadn't really heard them. Her imagination had interpreted the flirtatious gesture and fed upon her fears.

"He saluted you!" Iza gasped. "You didn't tell me you knew the king."

"I don't." Katrina turned her face toward the head of the procession so she wouldn't have to look at King Simeon. "He's a notorious flirt."

Queen Miranda twisted her body to speak to the princess. Her steed chose that moment to shy away from the noisy crowd. A flash of blue light stabbed the skittish animal's hindquarters. The frightened mare reared high, screaming in pain. Miranda fought for control of the reins.

Another flash of blue light pierced the frightened steed in the chest. The animal reared again and circled, trying to bolt away from the magical dart. Miranda lost the reins and control of the headstrong beast. She bounced out of her saddle. She lay unmoving on the cobblestones, blood staining her four white-gold plaits.

Chapter 16

People screamed. Steeds reared and circled in confused panic. Princess Jaranda cried out. Noble ladies swooned. Guards rushed forward to form a protective ring around the queen. King Simeon pushed the converging crowd aside.

Hastily he knelt and cradled his wife in his arms, the picture of a devoted husband. Katrina watched him closely, not trusting the concern written on his face. He tested Miranda's pulse, then lifted his head, eyes searching the crowd. Briefly he exchanged a look with the black-gowned woman. She nodded slightly, knowingly.

Then Simeon looked up, directly at Katrina, as if he always knew where to find her in the crowd. His gaze locked with hers. A malicious smile played across his face.

Unbidden, his thoughts invaded her mind. *You won't get away from me this time, little lacemaker.*

Katrina shook her head and pulled the hood of her open cloak over her face to break mental contact with the sorcerer-king. Her mother's lace shawl seemed to squeeze the breath out of her as she hid from his gaze.

Queen Miranda moaned and stirred. Tension returned to her muscles. Her mouth opened on a silent scream. A look of panic crossed Simeon's face. He pressed his fingers to her neck once more as if testing her pulse. The queen slumped back into unconsciousness at his touch.

"Seize that woman! The one with the lace shawl," Simeon cried, pointing at Katrina. He held Miranda's face close against his chest, smothering any sound she might make. "She shot an arrow into the queen's steed. Seize the one in the black cloak and lace shawl!"

All eyes turned in the direction he indicated—to stare directly at Katrina. She shrank back behind Iza.

"I didn't," she whispered anxiously.

"Quick, leave your cloak. Take mine. Blend in with the crowd. Don't run," Iza directed as she slipped her ordinary brown cloak over Katrina's shoulders, obscuring the distinctive lace.

"I didn't do it," Katrina protested, too stunned to follow her friend's advice.

"I know that. Only a magician could throw an arrow made of blue light. Now drift away. Don't call attention to yourself." Iza shoved Katrina back into the depths of the crowd, then turned to face the grim guards converging on her. Katrina's thick, black cloak of oiled wool now draped Iza's shoulders, standing out from the cheap and ordinary coverings protecting working-class citizens. The same cloak Katrina had brought with her from her father's house three years before.

More aggressive onlookers elbowed Katrina aside. Shame and guilt warred with her need to put a safe distance between herself and the palace guards. What would they do to Iza, her only friend? She couldn't watch.

She had to watch. With renewed determination, Katrina pushed her way back toward Iza. The crowd resisted her efforts.

"Lose yourself quickly," an unknown woman whispered as she stepped in front of Katrina. "We can't hide you much longer."

"But Iza . . ." Katrina protested.

"Save yourself." The man who had spoken to her earlier picked her up by the waist and set her back down, facing in the other direction. He shoved her hard. "Lose yourself in the alleys; don't go directly back to the factory. I've searched for you and that shawl for a long time. I'll meet you by the side door of the temple," he hissed.

Katrina stumbled. Hands helped her up and eased her away from the center of the action.

The guards carried Iza away amidst bitter protests from the bystanders. Mud and rocks pelted the guards. More gray-uniformed men entered the fray, clearing a path for their prisoner.

Katrina was pushed farther and farther away from the

core of the riot. Tears streaming down her face, she allowed her anxious feet to speed her toward safety.

She ran and ran until her sides ached and her lungs threatened to burst. The temple loomed in front of her. The man with the shadowed face offered her safety, freedom. Where had she met him before?

I've searched for you and that shawl for a long time. His words burned into her memory.

Who was he? A friend of her father's perhaps. More likely an agent of King Simeon, sent to trick her.

The familiarity of Brunix and his factory beckoned her. Her life there was hard. But it was safe. She turned and ran again.

At last the familiar blocky outline of the Brunix factory loomed ahead of her. Grateful for the sanctuary offered by its dark corridors and damp rooms, she pelted headlong for the green-painted doorway.

Abruptly her flight stopped as she ran into the tall, lean body of Owner Neeles Brunix. He grabbed her shoulders and forced her to look up at him. Up and up she looked to his hollow cheeks and sallow skin. His dark, outland eyes captured hers in an angry gaze.

"The king's men will be here soon to search for you," he announced matter-of-factly as he escorted her inside to his ground floor office.

"I did nothing but watch!" she sobbed, trying to catch her breath. "I'm innocent." She leaned over the back of a single straight-backed chair to ease her heaving lungs.

"No matter. Simeon has decided to have you back. This time you will choose to participate in his ritual rather than suffer death by torture. He has violated his pact with me."

Katrina took a long series of deep breaths fighting the panic Brunix's words evoked. Finally her vision cleared and her pulse ceased pounding behind her eyes.

Then she saw an expensive, velvet lace pillow resting on a stand beside her chair. Dangling from one of her grandmother's patterns were a hundred or more slender, bone bobbins with bright bangles on the ends.

She peered closer, still bent over the chair. Her eyes focused on the bobbins while she gathered her thoughts and courage. She picked out a bobbin with a spiraled inscription and a familiar blue bead at the center of the

bangle. "K-A-. . . ." the next letters wound away from her.
". . . I-N . . . ." And above those letters "A-A . . ." was
visible. She didn't need to twist the slender spindle to know
that this bobbin along with the pattern was part of her
dowry, sold to buy food and medicine for Hilza.

Food and medicine purchased too late to save her little
sister.

Anger at King Simeon, who had brought her family low
and still pursued her, replaced her fear. Hot hatred filled
her veins and eased the pain in her lungs.

"Why does the sorcerer-king persecute you, Katrina
Kaantille? I know he wants your body as much as I do,
but there must be more. He has access to many women.
What makes you so special?" Brunix took the cloak from
her shoulders and hung it on a tall rack alongside his own.

"I don't know. He picked me out of the crowd as if he
were looking for me." She closed her eyes against the sight
of her own bobbins gracing this man's pillow.

"Perhaps he is anxious to retrieve something he consid-
ers his own. What passed between you the night you chose
slavery to me, an outland half-breed, rather than joining
his ritual?" His voice sounded devoid of emotion, as if he
calculated possibilities and advantages with the same scrutiny he weighed imported goods taken in trade for exported lace.

Katrina kept her eyes closed to help control the pain
memory of that night still brought her. "I have done him
no hurt, yet he pursues me and threatens me for a crime I
have not committed. He shot the bolt of blue light into the
queen's steed, not I. How could I? He's the only magician
in SeLenicca!"

"Perhaps he hunts you because you did refuse him. How
many women in SeLenicca would sacrifice much to become
the king's mistress?"

"Or be sacrificed to him?" she added.

Criminals and outlanders were routinely burned at the
stake as part of the king's rituals. So far he had not publicly
sacrificed one of the queen's citizens.

"I heard he likes his toys young and virginal, dismissed
as soon as they become boring." Brunix paced a circle
around her and the lace pillow. "Marriages are discreetly
arranged for the girls he ravishes. Those girls he rapes with-

out guilt. But you . . . you he demands must come willingly to·him. My contract with him forbids me to force you. As if he didn't know that rape is a most heinous crime among my mother's people. But I am supposed to . . . never mind. He has broken that contract." He fingered the lace still draped around her shoulders. Gently he removed it and hung it beneath the cloaks.

"He told me that if I survived his Equinox ritual, my power would be released and I would be worthy to bear him a son. But I must come to his altar willingly. He hoped the humiliation of being *your* slave would drive me back to him. Willingly."

"The black-gowned goddess!" he hissed. "She carries a child, conceived near the Autumnal Equinox. And she wears the aura of one with much power. Was she willing? Eager perhaps?"

Crashing footsteps on the wooden walkway, loud shouts, and angry questions brought Katrina upright. Her balance shifted to her toes, as she made ready to flee again.

"I can save you," Brunix stood between her and the door, the only exit from the room. Another man had offered her the same thing. He'd asked for her mother's shawl in repayment.

"What will it cost me?" She sought frantically for a window, another door, a place to hide.

"You know my price. Come to my bed *of your own free will.*"

The door buckled on its hinges from the fierce pounding on the painted planks.

Katrina bit her lip. There was no way out.

She nodded, too frightened to speak.

Brunix reached behind him to unlatch the door. Six broad-shouldered men wearing the gray uniforms of the palace guard filled the narrow hallway.

"In the name of His Majesty, King Simeon the First, I place you, Katrina Kaantille, under arrest," the leader, wearing three silver stripes on his cuff, informed them. He stepped into the office so his companions could flank him.

"What crime has my wife committed?" Brunix remained firmly in place between Katrina and the uniformed men.

"Wife?" Three-stripe raised an eyebrow in surprise. "I was told the girl is a maiden."

"My *wife* has been with me all morning, developing a new pattern." Brunix waved a hand at the bolster pillow. "What makes you think she is the person you seek?"

"The queen was struck down during the birthday parade. His Majesty picked that woman out of the crowd as the perpetrator. She was wearing a black cloak and a wide lace shawl about her neck and shoulders. We arrested another woman wearing her cloak, but not the lace shawl. She is being detained until we find the true culprit and the lace." The officer's eyes strayed to the hook where the cloaks hung. Brunix's outdoor garment was dark green. Katrina had been wearing Iza's brown. The shawl was draped beneath them both, not visible to the guard.

"How can my wife be guilty? She has been here with me all morning. And though we make lace to sell, who but the nobility can afford to wear it?"

"Your lies won't protect her, outland half-breed," Threestripe sneered. He raised his arm as if to backhand Brunix across the mouth.

Brunix caught the man's wrist well away from his face. He squeezed and twisted the guard's arm backward. "My father was a true-blooded citizen, my mother half," he ground out. Brunix's eyes grew darker with cold anger. "How much true blood runs in Simeon's veins? He is the outlander, and a sorcerer. Yet you trust him over me, a lawful citizen of the *queen*. How did he single out the name and address of one woman in the crowd, who was not there, as the assailant? Look to him for answers before you arrest and accuse innocent citizens."

He wrenched his hands away from contact with the guard as if the man were dirty. The guard hopped back a step, shaking his arm and wrist.

Three-stripe's mouth opened and closed without a sound. Indecision marred his posture. He suddenly seemed shorter and less imposing. The two men flanking him edged backward, toward the hall.

"We will be back." Three-stripe turned on his heel and retreated with less noise than he had come.

"And now, my dear, the time has come to pay what you owe me." Brunix gathered the cloaks and the lace shawl from the rack as he gestured toward the staircase.

Up the long series of steps to his apartment on the top floor.

"Hmm, distinctive design." He studied the shawl as if unconcerned with her obedience to his wishes. "Unusual concept. We will discuss payment for this design after I teach you the delights of sharing my bed."

"You are certain you can do it?" Jaylor asked Marcus for the fifth time. "Sensing a concentration of dragon magic is crucial in this quest."

"I'm certain, sir," Marcus replied tiredly. "I was gathering dragon magic before Old Baamin died."

Jaylor turned to his other journeyman. "What about you, Robb?"

"Master Jaylor, I was levitating winecups long before any of my class." The young man looked indignant at the question. "Successfully."

"Then I charge you both with the quest to go see an invisible dragon," Jaylor said quietly. Unconsciously he'd used the same phrase Master Baamin had spoken when giving Jaylor his journeyman's quest four years ago.

But Jaylor was Senior Magician now. So much had changed in the intervening years. Coronnan needed journeymen magicians to seek Shayla and bring the dragon nimbus up to full strength more than ever. Without dragons, Communal magicians could not combine and augment their magic by orders of magnitude to overcome the solitary rogues. Only with the enhanced power of several magicians joined together could the Commune hope to impose and enforce honor, ethics, and justice into all uses of magic.

Until then, judges, lords, and mundane citizens looked to the Gnostic Utilitarians to protect them from all magic, good and bad. Good thing the Gnuls and the coven hadn't worked together on their separate plots to depose Darville and his queen.

"I hope you are more successful in restoring the dragon nimbus to Coronnan than I was." Jaylor draped his arms about the shoulders of his journeymen.

"You freed Shayla from Krej's glass sculpture. That was a start," Marcus reminded him.

Jaylor paused a moment, remembering his lengthy recovery from that spell.

"You had better return as full masters of your powers, or I'll come find you to make you regret it," he added sternly, shaking them with affection.

"As if Brevelan would let you chase after us without her," Marcus mumbled.

"We know who really runs the Commune." Robb grinned at his partner.

"What did you say?" Jaylor glared at the young men.

"Nothing, sir. We'll come back. With the dragon." Marcus winked at Robb.

"Or if she can't fly, we'll summon Brevelan."

"Good. Now remember your instructions. Stay in touch. I want a summons every night at sunset." He'd said this all before, but it deserved repeating. "Keep together and blend in with the locals any way you can. You'll have to be doubly careful avoiding detection at the battlefront. SeLenicca is gearing up for a major push to drive our army back toward the pass. There is no magic in SeLenicca to augment your own reserves, so you'll have to keep your delusions to a minimum. And whatever you do, don't rouse King Simeon's suspicion. The battle mages report small concentrations of dragon magic across the border, but not enough for all to gather and combine. That convinces me that Simeon is holding Shayla hostage. He won't want to give her up. You will be executed as spies at the first suggestion that you come from Coronnan."

"We know, Jaylor." Robb patted the Senior Magician's shoulder reassuringly. "We've been over this a dozen times."

"Keep going over it. I can't afford to lose any more journeyman. Keep a look out for Lady Rejiia, too. She's been missing since her child died."

"But Queen Rossemikka is pregnant again. We don't need Rejiia as heir to the crown," Robb grumbled.

Jaylor bit back the bitterness of that news. Margit reported that Mikka ailed with this pregnancy. A few whispers had begun that the queen's inability to carry a child to term was clear evidence of witchcraft.

Between the whispers and the difficult pregnancy, Jaylor had decided to keep word of the plot against the queen's brother to himself. Mikka and Darville didn't need the extra worry. The plot had been temporarily foiled. King Simeon's mistress, whoever she was, would need time to replace the poison.

"Better off without Krej's daughter. I never trusted her," Marcus added.

"More reason to bring the dragons back, to protect the queen's baby—the long-awaited heir. Take care of yourselves." Jaylor saluted them with a fist clenched over his heart, then offered his left hand, little finger, and ring finger curled under. A mild shock of power that only another magician could feel went into the handshake—the new recognition signal of the Commune.

He watched the young men gather their packs and march toward the edge of the clearing.

"Will you keep an eye on Margit, sir? She's feeling kind of abandoned with both of us going off on quest." Marcus paused at the edge of the clearing barrier. "Maybe you can teach her to tolerate cats better. I really like cats."

"I'll make contact with her every week instead of every moon," Jaylor promised.

Marcus nodded and smiled his thanks as the edges of the clearing blurred and the journeymen passed through to the path.

Jaylor raised his hand, as if to delay their departure once more. Surely they'd forgotten something. He should call them back, delay their leave-taking a little longer.

"They are older than you were when you were given the same quest. And better equipped." Brevelan placed a gentle hand on his shoulder. "Those boys have scoured Coronnan for apprentices these last three years. They know how to live rough and fend for themselves," she reminded him.

"I guess I can spare the boys for a while. They must succeed where I failed. Coronnan depends upon them."

"Thanks to those 'boys,' you have ten new journeymen to take their place and fifteen apprentices eager to join them." Brevelan urged him away from the sight of the path closing behind the retreating steps of Robb and Marcus.

"We still don't have enough magicians to resume our traditional roles in society, if and when we are ever legal again. I wonder if I should leave the University in Slippy's care while I go with the boys?"

"Don't you dare!" Brevelan's hands fluttered trying to reach for him and curve protectively around her swelling belly at the same time. If the mundanes could see Brevelan and her children, they'd never again believe that witches couldn't bear children. That was an action he dared not allow.

Jaylor smiled anyway. Brevelan's dragon-dream was coming true. Shayla had promised her a clearing full of healthy children. In the vision, the oldest boy was as blond as King Darville, all the rest as red-haired as their mother.

Jaylor's eyes automatically searched the clearing for blond Glendon, now three, and his redheaded brother, Lukan. The boys were rolling around the freshly tilled kitchen garden, wrestling with a wolf pup. As usual they were filthy, healthy, and laughing.

"We have been blessed, Brevelan." He patted the evidence of their new child. A tingle of awareness shot up his arm. The child was already asserting its personality.

"Twins this time." Brevelan sighed happily. "Girls."

"What! I thought this was to be another boy. Next time is supposed to be twins. Dragon-dreams don't lie."

"We make our own future, dear heart. This time we made twins," she laughed at him and with him. "Gossip from the capital says that Darville is much better since he learned to sign his name and wield cutlery with his right hand. He's learning to live with the pain. His wound isn't worse," she continued happily.

"If the boys don't find Shayla and heal her, then Darville will always have a useless left arm," Jaylor reminded her. Memory of Darville's situation sobered the bubbling joy of impending fatherhood.

He and Darville had wrestled in the mud as boys, much like Glendon and Lukan. They'd been happy and healthy then, blond- and auburn-haired, just like Glendon and Lukan.

Yaakke had spent his childhood as a kitchen drudge, without much happiness, love, or companionship. Jaylor wasn't sure why his thoughts turned to his lost apprentice. Sending two journeymen off on the same quest as Yaakke must have reminded him of the boy's failure.

Had the wild fluxes of a maturing body caught up with

his unbounded magical talent? If so, perhaps he was better off dead. The massive, uncontrolled powers unleashed in such circumstances must have been lethal to Yaakke's spirit as well as his body.

"I am reluctant to authorize a full-scale invasion of SeLenicca, Andrall," Darville informed his most trusted Council member. He paced the small retiring room behind the Council Chamber.

" 'Tis sound military strategy, Your Grace," Andrall reminded him. "We control both ends of the pass through the mountains. Our position will be reinforced if we hold more territory on their side of the border."

"The battle mages we employ at the front fear there is not enough magic in SeLenicca for them to protect our troops from Simeon's mages. I would give a fortune to know where they get their power! Besides, invasion will put us on the offensive. If we keep to defensive resistance, we have leverage in convincing other countries to honor the trade embargo against SeLenicca."

"The Council of Provinces intends to push for an invasion, and override your veto if necessary, Your Grace," Andrall whispered, though no one had access to this room except through the empty Council Chamber.

"I need something to bargain with. Something that will . . ." Darville stopped in mid-sentence. A shift in the tapestry that separated them from the main room alerted him to the presence of an eavesdropper. Both men stood absolutely still, hands holding ceremonial short swords at the ready.

"Ahem, Your Grace?" Fred called from the main room.

Darville relaxed and thrust aside the wall hanging. "Yes, Sergeant?"

"I have someone important for you to interview, sir." Fred clamped his mouth shut and stared pointedly at Lord Andrall.

"You can trust His Lordship, Fred. Who claims my attention now?"

"The spy, sir."

"Which spy?" There were so many, in SeLenicca, in Rossemeyer, in the households of his lords, at the front . . .

He dared not trust anyone these days. Not with the Gnuls gaining influence with the Council and the Council paying people to spy on himself and Mikka.

"The one we sent from Sambol last year, sir. The one who knows about cats . . . dead cats."

A frisson of alarm ran from Darville's spine to his hands, making him itch to wield his sword. If ever he needed Jaylor's counsel, it was now. How did he deal with people who left gutted cats in places where he was likely to find them? The one he and Fred had found at the Equinox Pylon in Sambol was the first of many.

Every time he rode through the country, they found another. The placement of the corpses was no coincidence.

"Bring the man to my office. I'll fetch the queen. If I can pry her away from that nosy maid, Margit." Mikka was his best adviser since Jaylor had deserted him. Raised to be a queen, Mikka knew how to listen and observe. From a quiet place in the corner she often saw things that Darville missed, like gestures and postures suggesting lies and deceit. "We will discuss the military situation later, just before the lords regather, Andrall," he said as he dismissed the lord.

"They will be here momentarily, Your Grace," Andrall reminded him. They'd met here, behind the Council Chamber for that reason.

"Then tell them I am detained. I need an hour."

"Yes, Your Grace." Andrall bowed his head in grudging acquiescence.

Three years ago the Council might have taken advantage of Darville's absence to vote for invasion. Now, however, he knew they'd wait for their king.

Minutes later, Fred hustled a slim young man wearing the white robes adopted by the Gnostic Utilitarian cult into the king's office. Cut in the same manner as the red-robed priests of the Stargods, the white was symbolic of their purity from the taint of magic.

Mikka's eyes narrowed at first sight of the man. Her nose twitched with suspicion and she withdrew deeper into her window seat. If anyone had reason to fear this cult, 'twas the queen. Magic was still illegal in Coronnan and she possessed a great deal of magical talent. The cult had been known to denounce those who claimed to be the victims of magic as well the perpetrators. Knowledge of the cat persona trapped within Mikka's body would draw their outrage and fuel the pleas for Darville to put her aside as his queen.

So far he'd been able to avoid confronting the issue of her inability to bear him an heir. How much longer before he was forced by lords and populace alike to bring in a distant and foreign relative or divorce Mikka?

"Your Grace," the spy bowed deeply, but his eyes darted furtively into every corner as he moved. "I have not much time. I must either return to my dwelling before I am discovered missing or leave the country within the hour." He continued to search the shadows for any sign of listeners. His eyes lingered on the queen in the window seat, then darted back to Fred for reassurance.

"I will protect you . . . uh, your name was not given to me. Please sit down." Darville leaned back in his demithrone, adopting a position of ease. He hoped the spy would become comfortable enough to speak freely.

"My name is best kept secret from all but the Stargods. No one is safe from the Gnuls, sir. No one. They'll torture and kill me without hesitation if they suspect where my allegiance lies." His pale skin lost more color as he shivered inside his robe. He remained standing, poised to dart out of the room at the first sign of trouble.

"Then tell us quickly. What have you learned?" Darville sat forward, frowning. None of his appointed magistrates had the authority to overlook such outrages.

"Life has been quiet and prosperous for nearly three full years. People don't really fear magic when life is good, and the Gnuls have lost a lot of followers. The sacrifices at the Equinox Pylons have been engineered by the Gnuls to frighten the people. Cats and dogs at first. Pigs and goats will come later if they have to. They discuss bringing suspected witches and magicians to justice at the next holiday." He stared at the queen a silent moment. "But I've never found evidence of an innocent or a child becoming a victim. The evidence of human sacrifice always comes from someone in the next village who heard it from a cousin's sister-in-law, or some such." The last words faded away and he refused to look up from the floor.

"There is more," Mikka whispered. They all heard her

quiet words. "What do you fear telling us, Spy?" Her hands trembled as they stroked the nap of her gown.

The spy looked to the door again as if he needed to escape immediately.

"Tell me, Spy," Darville demanded. "What else have you learned?"

"Rumors only."

"Rumors! I hate rumors. Tell me so that I may squash them before they are lifted into the wind and become the truth for all who hear them."

"The queen, sir," he said so quietly Darville had to strain to hear him.

"What about my wife?"

"I have met with the leaders of one cell of Gnuls. They have orders to prove that she is a witch of the first order. Everyone knows that witches can't bear children." He swallowed deeply. "And . . . and they say she has bewitched you so you won't put her aside, just as King Simeon has bewitched the Queen of SeLenicca. Some say that Her Grace is in league with Simeon and that is why you won't invade SeLenicca and end the war. The leaders plan to drug the queen so that she will miscarry. Then they will present the deformed fetus as 'evidence' to the Council of Provinces in time for her to be exiled or burned at the next solstice."

Chapter 17

Fear for Mikka drained the blood from Darville's head and limbs. Shakily, he dismissed the spy with a handful of gold to buy passage out of Coronnan that very day.

"I must return to my brother's court," Mikka whispered. "For your sake, I must go." She rose gracefully from her window seat and the bright sunshine she loved. "If you wait to divorce me until I get there, I can persuade Manuel the fault is mine and he needn't invade Coronnan to avenge my honor."

"No." Feeling and heat began to return to Darville's body. "If you scuttle away now, like some beetle frightened of the light, then you have given the Gnuls control over our lives, over all of Coronnan. I cannot allow that to happen. I will not let them take you from me." He knelt in front of her window seat, clutching her hand between both of his.

"What else can we do?" She pulled free of his touch and buried her face in her hands.

Darville gathered her into his arms, holding her close against his heart, where she belonged.

"First, I will order your maids to taste all of your food before you do. Everything, even a cup of water. Then, I will set forces in motion to hunt down members of the cult who commit outrages against my citizens. No more will I bury myself so deeply in military tactics and trade agreements that I lose sight of what is happening in my own country. The Gnuls will be brought to justice."

"But their followers are many. They will not tolerate a banning of the cult. Executing the leaders will make them martyrs." Mikka raised her head, once more a dignified queen advising her husband.

"They will be brought to justice, not banned or outlawed. If they commit the crimes of kidnap, torture, and murder, then they will pay for their crimes, like any other citizen."

"That will not stop the rumors. I am still suspected of witchcraft."

"We will do what we must to put the rumors aside. Though I know in my head and my gut that the action is a tactical error, I will authorize an invasion of SeLenicca."

Military men must wear blinders. They can see forward only in a straight line. Darville has foolishly invaded SeLenicca. At first his troops penetrated deep into the interior along the trader's road.

But that movement outraged all of Simeon's citizens, even the ones who hate and fear him. They rally to defend their land. War fever grips them. The homeless and unemployed flock to join the army. Merchants double the price of lace overseas to buy more weapons and supplies. Outlanders react to the inflated value of lace by ordering even more and demanding greater variety.

Now Darville is in danger of losing control of the pass between the two countries. His Council will not tolerate defeat. They bring Jonnias and the Marnaks back into their ranks in defiance of Darville, though the rebel lords have not paid their fines or made public apology for burning the monastery all those years ago. The younger Marnak wears a ring with a black diamond. His wedding ring, presented by Lord Krej himself. Marnak does not know that the diamond is really precious glass. With a candle and my own glass, I can see and hear through the ring all of the Council's private discussions. I should have forced him to pay the fines earlier so I could spy on the Council.

Soon young Rossemanuel of Rossemeyer will receive his poisonous letter from his sister. His death, traced back to Rossemikka, will start a new war against Darville and Coronnan.

Events move closer to my goals. I need the chaos of war to make my form of peace and order look like a blessing.

Jack awakened gradually from his dream of a woman with pale blond hair, like moonlight on water. He'd dreamed of her often in the last three years, wondering who she was and why she haunted him.

He'd been reaching out to pull her away from something dangerous. But he couldn't quite touch her.

The sounds of men grunting and scratching, shifting in their hammocks and whispering quietly banished the last images of his vision. Several men coughed, long spasms that threatened to turn their lungs inside out. They were dying and they knew it.

They were all dying unless they escaped. The sense of having left something undone nagged at Jack and urged him to push forward his plans to escape—even before he had regained full memory and before the mountain passes cleared of snow.

He wondered if the tiny spell he had tried last night had succeeded and what good it would do if it had.

The gray light of false dawn seeped beneath the closed plank door. Knotted muscles in his shoulders protested every movement he made. Not that he could move very far or very fast with his right ankle chained to the post.

"Uhrrgh!" he moaned and rolled over. Another day of opening a new mine shaft. In a few minutes the guard with a harelip would slam the door open and glare at the thirty men. His small, deep-set eyes, would seek out the last one to remain in his hammock. That laggard would likely feel the tip of the lash all day long for the tiniest infraction of the rules. Harelip enjoyed seeing other men in pain.

Jack fingered the scars beneath his ragged shirt. All of them had been inflicted by Harelip. They didn't hurt anymore. The new one forming on his cheek still stung. Memory of the pain kept him wary and obedient.

"You awake, Jack?" Fraank whispered from the hammock above him.

"No," he replied.

"The birds aren't up yet. You have a few minutes to rest. Though I've never known you to be a slug-a-bed before."

"I've not been able to think about options before—or the lack of them."

"One way or another, we all chose to come here," Fraank replied.

"You're an educated man, surely you didn't choose this hell hole."

"I came here to die a slow death. My punishment won't bring back my wife and child, nor will it restore my family to wealth and honor. But perhaps Tattia's ghost will rest easier knowing I suffer for my sins."

"What sins?"

"A foolish investment. Greed and ambition above my station in life."

"All men make mistakes. Surely an unwise investment isn't a sin."

"King Simeon asked me to form an investment syndicate. He had plans to smuggle a shipload of Tambootie seedlings out of Coronnan. The fibers of immature trees can be spun into the most wonderful thread for lace. My wife was a lacemaker. The best in the kingdom. I wanted to please her with an unlimited supply of Tambrin."

"So?" Jack shivered. An almost memory tasted bad in his mouth. He knew something about this shipload of Tambootie. What?

"I borrowed heavily, sold almost everything I owned so I could finance the venture myself. I wanted to reap all of the profits. King Simeon would have taken half of the money as his portion for arranging the shipment. I didn't want to share the rest. I wanted to buy prestige for my wife. She deserved to be named a National Treasure."

"The ship didn't make it through the blockade," Jack stated. He could have guessed the fate of the ill-advised venture. But he knew. Knew in his gut that he had something to do with Fraank's fall from grace.

Fate or the dragons had brought him face-to-face with the consequences of his actions.

"And I lost everything. My brother disowned me and stole one of my daughters. Another daughter died of the lung rot. She died in my arms, too weak to cough, too worn out to breathe. I couldn't afford to keep the house warm enough to protect her. None of us had enough to eat to stay healthy. I couldn't . . ." he choked in his litany of grief.

Jack gave him a moment of silence to recover, sensing the man's need to tell someone of his internal pain.

"Tattia was dismissed from the palace. She was lost. If she couldn't make lace, she had no place in life, no identity, no reason for living. Because of my failure, she threw herself into the river. And now her ghost will haunt our descendants for five generations."

"You had another child to carry the bloodline?"

A burst of birdsong silenced the whispers of the men. Above the sweet trills that greeted the dawn came the hoarse croak of a jackdaw.

The door was thrust open so violently it bounced against the stone wall. "All right you miserable beasts. Up. Everybody up." Harelip stood outlined in the doorway, begging someone to challenge him so he could mete out punishment with is whip.

Why don't we just jump him? Jack thought. *Thirty men could strangle him before he raised the bloody whip.*

"Not ready," the jackdaw cawed. "Ye're not ready."

Jack slid his gaze toward the door. The stupid bird hadn't really talked to him, had it?

Still affecting a daze of incomprehension, Jack stood mutely beside his hammock while a second guard unlocked his chain from the post. Fraank stood beside him, patiently waiting to be partnered with him.

"You two been gettin' chummy, I hear. Can't have that." The guard with grime embedded around his neck like a necklace yanked on Jack's chain to lead him several paces down the line to a new partner.

They chained him to the scrawny newcomer with the patchy beard. Jack almost opened his mouth to protest. A warning glance from Fraank kept him quiet and docile. Harelip was watching for an opportunity to uncoil his whip.

Patchy-beard wrung his hands in anxiety, then scratched his face in a habitual manner. A few strands of mud-colored hair fell to the floor.

Out in the yard, the day crew marched through their regular routine. A trip to the privy—an open trench in one corner of the fenced compound. Then a bowl of thin gruel slurped from wooden bowls without benefit of a spoon. The food was enough to keep the men alive and working, but not energetic enough to plot or risk escape.

The jackdaw fluttered to the top of a fence post and watched the pot of gruel for an opportunity to steal some. The white tufts of feathers above its eyes twitched.

"Look. Look," the jackdaw mimicked words.

A guard laughed at the bird and held out his arm for it to perch on. The jackdaw ignored him and continued to instruct Jack to "Look, look."

Certainty that the bird was speaking to him alone, drew

Jack's gaze to the high wooden fence. Eight feet high at least. Smooth planks that would defy a man to climb. What was he supposed to look at?

"Through my eyes. Through my eyes." The jackdaw cocked his head and looked directly at Jack.

A wave of revulsion almost brought the gruel back up from Jack's stomach. Invading another creature's mind had to be the worst form of violation.

The jackdaw shook himself. Dust flew from his wings.

"Filthy bird!" Someone picked up a loose stone and flung it at him.

"Craaawk!" it squawked and jumped into flight. Two flaps of his wings and he perched on top of Jack's head. "Look," it repeated.

Jack remained absolutely still, as if he didn't know a black bird was tugging at his hair with a sharp beak.

"Always knew that Muaynwor was a scarecrow," Harelip guffawed, flapping his arms like grotesque wings. Jack looked right through his antics as if they didn't exist. He hoped the men wouldn't start throwing stones at him as well as the bird.

Without knowing how or why, his thoughts blended with the bird. The color spectrum shifted and he saw colors he'd never seen before. Colors that revealed temperatures. Men became layers of overlapping reds and yellows. Buildings revealed neutral grays.

His perspective shifted upward and then flew with the bird over the fence. He knew a moment of dizziness and spinning colors. Then the terrain below came into focus.

Trackless mountains still covered in snow, that revealed iciness in shades of blue, spread out to the horizon in every direction. Snow blocked the valleys between peaks and ridges. A few scraggly everblue trees appeared pink and yellow as sap began to flow and bring them out of winter dormancy.

Together, he and the jackdaw skimmed over black rivers and pale blue lakes still choked with darker blue ice. Ice that cracked and thinned as the rising red and orange sun touched it.

"Not yet. Not yet," the jackdaw reminded him. They soared upward, along another pass where the melted snow had filled the nearby river to overflowing. At the western end of the pass, a trader caravan camped. Their train of surefooted mules was loaded with supplies for the prison mine.

Escape needed to wait until Jack could load one of those mules with enough supplies to last him several weeks. By the time the caravan arrived, the worst of the storms would have passed. He'd be able to walk away from the mine and survive.

Jack's consciousness plunged back into his own body with an abruptness that sent his senses reeling. He forced himself to remain upright, still, blank-faced. Escape would be doubly difficult if the guards suspected he was aware.

Chapter 18

"**R**espond to me!" Neeles Brunix screamed at Katrina, withdrawing his hand from her naked breast. "I've had your maidenhead. You have nothing left to lose. Respond to me like the whore you are."

She turned her face away, biting her lip against her tears of humiliation. She wouldn't give him the satisfaction of evoking any emotion in her.

Owner Brunix heaved his long, naked body off the bed. Frustration radiated from him as he paced his private suite on the topmost floor of his factory. He seemed oblivious to his nakedness, concerned only with the emotions that roiled within him.

"You just lie there, pale and elegant, beautiful beyond imagination and numb. Making love to you is like fucking a corpse."

Katrina resisted the urge to recoil from his lecherous stare at the tuft of pale hair between her legs.

Brunix paused in his rapid prowl to stare at himself. Limp. As unresponsive as Katrina.

"All true-blooded women are whores at heart—titillated by sex because it is forbidden outside the bonds of marriage. But you refuse to show your true feelings out of some perverted need to punish me. You punish me because I have saved your life, fed you, clothed you, and allowed you to make lace for three years. Why should I keep a slave who can't satisfy me in bed?"

"Do what you will. I don't have to enjoy your rape of my body."

" 'Twasn't rape, Katrina. You came to me willingly, or out of duty, I don't care. But I didn't rape you, and you can't take this to my clan. Besides, you enjoyed it. Didn't you!"

She turned her face away from him. His touch reminded her too much of King Simeon's erotic caress and lewd suggestion that she might do this with P'pa.

"Tell me you enjoyed it!"

"How could I?"

"Like all true whores, you're holding out for marriage." He snapped his fingers as the idea occurred to him. "I could invoke the ancient laws of my mother's people, the natural laws that governed this land before the pale-eyed northerns conquered all. I told the palace guards that you are my wife, a clear declaration before witnesses. Your virgin's blood stains my sheets. The two make a legal marriage."

"I am required by law to make myself available to you. Marriage would not change my feelings," she whispered, afraid he would see her inner pain and become aroused by even that small display of emotion.

"I have no trouble with the whores I can buy on any street corner. I perform admirably with the other women in my factory. But with you, the only one I really want . . . nothing," he raised his hands over his head in exasperation and dropped them limply to his side. "I should have ignored my bargain with The Simeon and taken you the first day you came into this factory, taught you to enjoy my body while you were too young to know differently."

"A bar . . . gain?" Katrina tried very hard not to stammer. Hesitancy was an emotion Brunix could latch onto.

"The Simeon made me vow not to touch you so that you would return to him as pure as when he sold you to work in my factory. I have saved you from his ritual at least. He needed you virginal to tap some unknown power he sensed in you. A power my Rover instincts cannot find." To emphasize his words, he leaned over her and pinched her nipples hard.

She refused to flinch or recoil.

"But The Simeon has broken his part of the bargain in pursuing you." Disgusted, Brunix returned to his pacing. "Therefore, I do not have to honor my part of the bargain. You are mine by right. *Mine!* I have wanted you for a very long time, and I have had you and you don't satisfy me."

"I see." She remained stone still. Inside, questions plagued her. What had triggered this new round of persecution from Simeon? The man at the parade, was he an agent of the king? Perhaps he owned a lace factory and wanted to deprive Brunix of his premier lacemaker. No, if he wanted that, he would have promised Katrina employment.

"Is there nothing that excites you? Nothing that raises your passion?" Brunix leaned over her, his eyes nearly glowing red with his frustration.

Katrina didn't respond. She had worked so hard at controlling her anger and hatred toward Simeon and the fate that sent her into slavery that she doubted she could show her true feelings ever again.

"If I can't have your body, Katrina Kaantille, I will have your mind and your talents." Brunix pounded his fist into the mattress beside her naked body.

A faint glimmer of hope sprang to life deep in her heart. She didn't dare let it flare too high.

"That lace shawl you wear, the one your mother made for the queen . . . the one the king identified you by."

Katrina nodded her acknowledgment. He'd studied the piece of lace thoroughly, even tried draping it erotically around her body to evoke something within her. He couldn't know that this unique piece of lace was all that she had left of her mother. Wearing it kept her keenly aware of all that she had lost.

"You will make a pattern from this lace. A pattern that is difficult to duplicate. I will not have my business rivals stealing the design."

She didn't tell him his business rivals already knew about the shawl and offered her freedom in exchange for it.

"Will . . . will you consider my obligation to service you in bed canceled?" She couldn't look him in the eye.

"The pattern will postpone your obligation to me. You have until you finish making a sample shawl to . . . develop some enthusiasm for me."

"The pillow I use in the factory is engaged with another pattern. The homespun cover is too rough for the fine silk M'ma used for the shawl."

"You will use the pillow in my office."

Excitement flared deep within Katrina. A real pillow, covered in soft velvet, stuffed with unspun wool. And slender bobbins that clicked and sang as she worked. Some of those bobbins had been made for her. Just to handle them again was a reward beyond her daily hopes for escape from this man and his grim factory.

"Light? The workroom is too dark to see a fine pattern. And pins? They must be delicate, sharp, and free of rust."

Brunix narrowed his eyes as he gazed at her with longing and speculation. He nodded briefly. "If I am pleased with the design, if it makes me as much profit as I think it will, you may consider the pillow and the bobbins yours. The light and the pins I will investigate. White paint on the walls perhaps."

"Oh!" Katrina gaped at him in surprise and delight.

"So you do have passion within you, my dear. Passion for lace, true lace instead of the rudimentary garbage the others turn out. We'll see if we can translate that enthusiasm into gratitude to me." He grabbed her roughly by and arm, pulling her to stand close to him. He pressed the full length of his naked body against her as he ground his mouth over her lips in a cruel and possessive kiss. "Remember, Katrina Kaantille, you and your work belong to me, body and soul. And I will never let you go."

Queen Miranda lies near death. Her court is in chaos. The princess hides in her suite. Dour councillors and advisers cower in the lesser audience chamber, wringing their hands in panic. In Coronnan, the nobles would seize control and continue to govern with little or no interruption. Lucky for King Simeon that in SeLenicca a royal wish is absolute law.

Miranda's council doesn't know how to act, only advise and hinder decisive action as being too rash. Miranda hasn't had time to revoke her Edict of Joint Monarchy. Simeon is now in position to seize the throne for himself, without Miranda's dithering. Once in control, he can allow Miranda to die and remain king without passing the crown to Princess Jaranda.

The coven, through Simeon, is now in total control of one of the Three Kingdoms. My agents move into place. Soon the entire continent will be mine—except for Hanassa. No one can rule that haven of outlaws, rogues, and thieves. And Rovers.

*   *   *

An alien presence brought Jaylor to full wakefulness. No light of moon or stars crept through the smoke hole, around the shutter or beneath the door. Yet he could clearly see every object in the crowded cottage. Moving only his eyes, all his magical senses alert, he surveyed his home seeking the *thing* that had startled him out of a sound sleep.

A ball of witchlight glowed at the foot of the bed he shared with Brevelan.

Instinctively he raised armor around his sons sleeping in the loft. The ball didn't move or flicker. Jaylor risked a little probe into the light. His mental arrow encountered no resistance, no menace, nothing. The light just hung there, waiting.

Waiting for what?

Carefully Jaylor swung his legs over the side of the bed. The ball of light shifted so that it continued to face him. As he stood, Jaylor grabbed the extra quilt to wrap around his shoulders against the night chill. The ball of light didn't object or move.

"What are you?" he whispered into the darkness, afraid to rouse Brevelan or the children in case the light turned hostile.

No answer from the light.

Jaylor took one step toward the central hearth. The light moved with him, remaining a few feet in front of his face.

"Who sent you?" Jaylor probed with his mind as well as his words.

The light bobbed a little, as if the question almost triggered a response but not quite.

"Are you a message?"

The light quivered and wobbled, almost joyfully.

A strange summons indeed. Magicians were trained to send a flame through a glass to a designated person. What if Robb or Marcus were in trouble and couldn't build a fire or reach a glass? The witchlight might serve the same purpose. He had to give the boys credit for ingenuity.

"Give me your message," he ordered.

I AM YAAKKE AND I AM ALIVE!

A long-handled shovel came readily to Jack's hand. Several men had hefted it and discarded it without knowing why. The balance was wrong, the grip too large, or they preferred a pickax to a shovel.

Jack allowed himself a small, secret smile. His staff, fixed as the handle of the shovel, didn't like to be touched by anyone but him. The more he used it, the stronger his bond with this basic tool of magic became. Each day, the staff fed him memories and knowledge. Each night he practiced a spell or two. But still there was something he had to do. Something that compelled him to escape, beyond the need for mere survival.

The iron chain around his ankle resisted magic. He was still bound to a partner or a pillar. Patchy-beard remained his chain-mate, someone who was too observing, always touching him, distracting him from his act of blankness.

The supply caravan should be close. Soon Jack would have to take his chances and escape. He'd be able to complete . . . something. If he couldn't break the chain, he'd have to drag his partner with him. The scraggly little man with bowed shoulders and patchy beard would slow him down, hamper his movements. If he waited a few more days until he was rotated back to being Fraank's partner, his chance of survival improved. Fraank was trustworthy and still reasonably strong—though his mine cough worsened each morning. Patchy-beard made the hair on the back of Jack's neck stand on end.

Jack wished the cranky jackdaw would come back and show him how far the caravan had come, how much time he had to plan and work on a spell to unlock the chains.

Aided by the strength of the staff, Jack stabbed his shovel at the nearest pile of rocky debris. As the blade clanged against solid rock, a new perception opened to him. A sound, so faint normal hearing could not detect it, whispered to him. Then the merest inkling of a vibration trickled through his toes to the soles of his feet.

Something bright and shining hovered on the sides of his vision. He extended his senses with magic and sent them in all directions.

"Rockfall!" he yelled with three years of stored energy. "Get out *now*." Without waiting for orders he grabbed his chain-mate by the hand and lunged for the lift.

He broke the staff free of the shovel blade and tucked

his tool through the cord that held his trews around his waist where it wouldn't get lost.

Fifteen pairs of men followed him without question, tripping over their ankle chains in their haste. Two-by-two they squeezed into the lift designed to haul half that many men out of the shafts. Jack took a moment to make sure that Fraank was with them. The guard pulled on the bell rope signaling ascent. The lift stayed in place.

An ominous roar rose from the deepest portion of the shaft. Dread hovered over each man's left shoulder, like death waiting to pounce.

"Simurgh take you lazy bastards," the guard yelled up the shaft. "Pull us up!"

The rumbling beneath the shaft grew louder. The lift seemed to sway side to side within the wobbling mine walls.

Jack and his chain-mate, with surprising strength for such an elderly and scrawny man, reached for the emergency rope. Fraank and his partner on the opposite side of the crowded platform grabbed the companion rope. Together they hauled on the pulley device and lifted the crew an arm-length.

Dust replaced breathable air. Pulsing roars filled Jack's ears. "One, two, three, heave," he ordered. Four pairs of hands hauled again on the ropes. "One, two, three, heave." He may have lost his name, his memory, and three years of his life, but at least he remembered how to count.

"Three, one, two, heave," the guard ordered in a squeaky whisper.

Up an arm-length, then two more. Jack and his comrades found the rhythm and pulled in unison without the off-count commands of the guard.

Dust and smoke built to a choking density. Men coughed and sweated; hearts beat double time. No one spoke.

Arm-length by arm-length the platform rose. Louder and louder the protests of the inner planet swelled to enclose them, cut them off from reality. New tremors sent them rocking against the smooth walls of the vertical shaft.

The lantern dropped and extinguished itself. Direction became meaningless. There was only the burn of the rope upon sweating palms and the choking nightmare of once solid rock rippling like laundry in the wind.

And still the roar grew. Words lost themselves. Thought ceased.

Jack and his comrades pulled. *One, two, three, heave. One, two, three, heave*, he commanded them with his mind when words ceased to have meaning.

"Light, I see a light up there," someone croaked.

"Pulls us up," the guard yelled again to the men on top.

At last the grinding tension in Jack's shoulder's and arms eased as the crew on top took over with a winch. He felt slack in his rope. The platform jerked upward. He clung to his safety line, fearful lest the main pulley snap under the stress.

Faster and faster they rose to the surface. Thicker and thicker the dust filled their eyes and their lungs. Deeper and deeper grew the roar of collapsing rock and screams of dying men who hadn't had enough warning to escape.

At last the lift broke the surface. Torches still burned in the upper chamber. All but the pulley crew had deserted to the safety of outside.

Jack pushed older, weaker men ahead of him. He and his chain-mate lifted the cumbersome length of iron links and hobbled in their wake. *Find the rhythm. Outside foot, inside foot*, he commanded his partner with his mind.

As if he heard the mental order, the other man complied. Less clumsy, they sped toward light and solid ground. Smoke and collapsing tunnels followed.

Chapter 19

*T*he lacemaker hides with a Rover. That is what Simeon fears. If he crosses the factory owner, the man's entire tribe will curse the crown of SeLenicca.

I have little use for Rover tricks or Simeon's superstitions. Yet Simeon was raised in Hanassa, where Rovers are welcome. He knows more of their ways and their abilities than I do. I know only Zolltarn, the Rover king, and his treachery.

I must bring the lacemaker to heel so that I can end Simeon's obsession with her. The spells of the solstice will be useless if he cannot concentrate.

How to circumvent the mysterious connections of Rovers? I must force a confrontation with Zolltarn. He witnessed Krej's backlashed spell. He knows the construction of the magic. He also deserted the coven for the dubious honor of membership in the Commune.

Chaos reigned in the yard outside the mine adit. Jack assessed the situation with two quick glances. Most of the men, prisoners and guards alike, were running for their lives.

"Bring ropes and lanterns. We have to get the rest of the men out!" the commandant yelled from the center of the yard. "Come back here, you cowards."

No one heeded him. Jack dragged his sluggish chain-mate toward the storeroom for survival equipment. They hadn't much time.

Without thinking, propelled by his need to escape the mine, he whipped out his staff and tapped it against his leg irons. The manacles loosened. He bent and easily snapped them open with his hands. He repeated the procedure for all the other prisoners he encountered on his way to the storeroom.

"The gate is open. This way." Fraank dragged at his sleeve, holding him back. Fraank's chain-mate, in turn tugged Fraank toward the gate, toward freedom.

Patchy-beard pointed to his own leg iron in an appeal for freedom. "We've got to escape before the guards come to their senses."

Jack scowled at the man's pleas. "We'll never survive without food and warm clothing," Jack yelled at Fraank over the din of men screaming and the Kardia collapsing within the mine.

"Blankets and food. A pack steed if we can find one," Fraank agreed with Jack. "What about him?" He pointed to the still manacled Patchy-beard.

"He's a spy for the commandant. We'd better leave him."

Both Fraank and Patchy-beard gaped at him.

"You might as well remove the entire beard, spy. The glue won't hold it much longer." Jack continued his trek across the compound to the storehouse.

"How did you know?" The spy ripped the false beard off in one smooth motion, revealing clean, healthy, skin beneath.

"You listened too closely and kept trying to touch me in a camp where men avoid physical contact as much as possible in order to maintain some semblance of privacy. As we hauled the lift up the mine shaft, you pulled with too much strength." Jack selected blankets and new boots, coats, and a tarp for a tent while Fraank stuffed another pack with food.

"You won't get far in these mountains without help and a guide. Release my chains, magician, and I'll take you to safety," the spy said as he added water carriers to the supplies.

"What makes you think I'm a magician?" Jack tapped the end of his staff lightly against his thigh. Power shot from the end of the wood down his muscles to his feet. An aftershock tingled against his feet. Moments later the Kardia shook again.

"The staff." Patchy-beard clung to the door frame for balance until the tremor eased. "I felt a surge of power the

day you found it and came to investigate. Smart move
keeping it inside the mine where the commandant couldn't
sniff its power." The narrow-shouldered man straightened
to his true height. With shoulders back and chin lifted, he
was suddenly as tall and strong as Jack. And not much
older.

"You are more than a prisoner of war, or a criminal
culled from The Simeon's prisons," Jack said. He looked
behind the man's left ear, judging the colors of his aura.
The colors swirled and changed layers rapidly, defying interpretation. "I suspect you are a military officer on assignment. Perhaps you are one of the sorcerer-king's converts,
seeking sacrifices to Simurgh."

Jack looked around for anything more he might need
rather than make himself dizzy with the constantly shifting
colors of the man's aura. Nothing important appeared
nearby.

"We have enough. Let's go, Fraank."

"You haven't released me yet," the spy reminded him.

"You don't deserve release. You and the mine owners
and King Simeon should be thrown to the bottom of the
mine for what you have done to free men. No one has the
right to own slaves and work them to death in that hell-
hole!"

"If you release me and take me with you, I can take you
to the coven. They have need of men with your power.
They will reward you well."

"If you work for the coven, you must be a magician, too.
Release yourself." Anger filled him for his three lost years,
for the pain and toil of hundreds of men who had suffered
in the mines, anger at himself for becoming a victim of
King Simeon. He resisted the urge to plow his fist into the
spy's handsome face.

"Take me with you. I'm not a magician," the spy cried.
Panic tinged his voice as Jack dove out of the storeroom,
Fraank in his wake. "I'm only sensitive to power. And I
sense power in these mountains. The Simeon has hidden a
dragon in this region. If you are the magician sent by the
Commune to find the dragon, I can take you to her!"

Rejiia held her father's gold-rimmed circle of glass up to
a candle flame. Slowly she recited the words of a spell she'd

devised herself, pronouncing each word distinctly. The language was modern and didn't have the power of the ancient tongue of Simurgh, so she reinforced each syllable with magical energy from her mind.

The babe within her belly quieted his morning ritual of kicking and squirming, as if he knew the importance of magic and didn't wish to disrupt it.

Behind the glass, the green flame grew in size, broadened and stilled. The hot core of light surrounding the wick took on new colors. Gold and brown, mixed with ruby, silver, and pearl. Gold by itself. The colors became shapes. Reality faded. She sent her essence into the flame, to become one with the vision she called forth.

Rossemikka writhing in pain and grief. Darville silently holding her hand. Blood. Death?

Abruptly the vision ended. The present or the future? No matter. Rejiia had seen enough. She smiled. Something in the bizarre double aura surrounding the queen had caused the latest hemorrhage and kept her from giving Coronnan the long-awaited heir. She hadn't miscarried yet. But she would, and with enough damage to her internal organs she might never conceive again.

Plans appeared, full and complete, in her head. "I shall demand that Lord Krej's line be proclaimed heirs to Darville when I return to Coronnan in high summer. Why waste time with Simeon's pitiful efforts to rule through the coven when I can have it all myself?" She knew her child was male. As soon as he was born, she would arrange his betrothal to Princess Jaranda. That would put both Coronnan and SeLenicca firmly into her control.

Within the week she expected to hear of Rossemeyer's king being assassinated by poison. Poison on a letter from the young king's own sister, the queen of Coronnan. War would follow immediately upon the heels of that news.

Simeon had already proclaimed his right to Rossemeyer as the son of Rossemikka's father by his first and rightful queen. When the other Rossemeyer brat died of his long and lingering illness, the ruling party could turn only to Simeon to take the crown.

Rejiia had to make Simeon acknowledge her son as his heir to Rossemeyer. Once she returned to Coronnan as Darville's heir, she could afford to eliminate her lover. Her son would have Coronnan and Rossemeyer. Simeon's daughter would have SeLenicca. All three kingdoms lay within her grasp. She didn't need Simeon much longer.

The king had become so obsessed with finding one sniveling little lacemaker, he neglected all of his other duties to coven and country.

Her father would know how to manipulate the increasingly unstable king of SeLenicca. The two men had been raised together as foster brothers. P'pa knew Simeon's motives better than the king knew himself. Theirs was an intimacy Rejiia could never know as merely Simeon's mistress.

Simeon's mother, exiled Princess Jaylene of Rossemeyer, had died shortly after giving birth to him. Before she died, she had entrusted the care and education of her child to her best friend and the only person in attendance at the birth, Janessa. A few years later Janessa had married the brother of the king of Coronnan, taking Simeon and another foster child, Janataea, with her.

Some said Jaylene had died of a broken heart when she couldn't return to Rossemeyer. Others claimed she'd been poisoned by her midwife, Janessa.

Lord Krej knew Simeon as a brother. He would understand why the king was obsessed with one ugly little lacemaker when he had a city full of nubile virgins willing to dance upon his altar in return for prestige and safety for their families. Rejiia's father would know how the little lacemaker had escaped them at the birthday parade and where she hid. Or, he would know how to get that information.

Ask who protects her and why.

Rejiia looked closely at the tin weasel sitting on the table beside her candle and glass. Had her father managed to penetrate her mind with his thoughts?

Rejiia returned her InnerSight to the flame. This time she positioned the weasel statue on the other side of the candle. Krej's red-and-green aura writhed within a tight case of alien magic. She couldn't see any breaches in the spell that trapped her father. Where had the thought come from?

Once more she repeated the words of the spell, seeking the secret of the tin prison.

                    *   *   *

"Where are we, Spy?" Jack surveyed the break between two rounded peaks. A dry polar wind whipped down that trackless pass, chilling his bones and burning his eyes. Above it, Corby soared, feeding him images of more wind-swept waste ahead.

"I have a name," the spy reminded Jack, shivering beneath the blanket he clutched around his shoulders. His lips were chapped to bleeding and ice rimed his new growth of natural blond beard.

Something in the silent misery of the man touched a sad memory in Jack. He, too, had wrestled with the ignominy of being a nameless drudge. He'd had to earn the respect of others before they consented to refer to him as anything other than "Boy."

The spy had earned Jack's respect in his stalwart plodding through the mountains, a heavy pack of supplies on his back, in all kinds of punishing weather. Their weeks of trekking toward the dragon lair had left all three of them, Jack, Fraank, and the spy, hungry, lean, cold, and dependent upon each other for survival. Only Corby seemed to thrive in this treeless landscape. He taunted them now with his freedom to fly.

"Where are we, Officer Lanciar?" Jack repeated the question.

"I don't know where we are. Somewhere in SeLenicca, but so much of this land has been logged off and then eroded, all the landmarks look the same."

"Do you sense the dragon anywhere near?" Jack knew the lair had to be in the hills, at the bottom of a cliff with a wide waterfall. That kind of landscape didn't occur in the rolling plains and river valleys of SeLenicca proper.

"Sensing people with talent is easier. South, I think," Lanciar grumbled. He sank deeper into the folds of his blanket. There was no cover anywhere to shelter them from the punishing wind.

Lanciar's mind remained mostly closed to Jack. The secrets behind his mental armor still troubled Jack. Respect was there, but trust was a long time in coming.

"We should have stayed at the mine." Fraank edged closer to Lanciar seeking warmth or a windbreak. He didn't look well. His years in the mine had taken their toll.

"You sense power in people of talent," Jack turned his

attention back to Lanciar. "Dragons emit a kind of power. Look for power in the air, in the ground, in the living rocks of these mountains."

"Look yourself. You're the magician," Lanciar snarled.

"I cannot gather dragon magic," Jack admitted reluctantly.

"Then why bother seeking the dragon? You should have run back to Coronnan where you belong. Or let me take you to King Simeon. Maybe he'll take you to the precious dragon."

"Shayla is the only hope for saving Coronnan *from* Simeon. I must find a way to rebuild the Commune and erect the magic border again," Jack affirmed. For the memory of his friends, Jaylor and Brevelan, and his beloved mentor, Baamin. "That is my quest. I must complete it in order to complete myself."

Though once he'd done that, he'd be an exiled rogue magician or a nameless drudge again. Because he couldn't gather dragon magic.

"Come, we must find shelter before the sun sets. I believe I see a cave up there," Jack pointed to a dark spot in the hills that guarded the pass. "And enough scrub to build a fire."

" 'Tis early yet. We can traverse the pass before nightfall. There is bound to be shelter on the other side," Lanciar argued. "Villages used to guard the western end of passes. Not all of them were deserted when the timber industry died."

"I have much to teach you tonight, Officer Lanciar." Before they reached the bedraggled village Corby saw on the other side. "Tonight, by the light of a campfire, you will learn to center yourself and align your body to the pole. Thus anchored, your spirit will be free to search for magic in all its forms. Tonight you will find the dragon."

One thousand pins and counting. Katrina stared at her mother's lace shawl stretched out on an inclined work board. The cream-colored wood pulp paper beneath the lace was marked off in a precise grid to help her determine the proper angle of pin placement. The intricate lace did not conform to any predetermined angle.

Katrina's head swam with geometrical equations, trying

to discover the design. T'chon lace was worked on precise forty-five degree angles. Net-ground laces flowed at a wider angle. This piece defied geometry. She knew that science as well as her mother, or any lacemaker before her. She hadn't been taught to read but she *knew* mathematics.

She stretched her back and rose from her straight chair in the corner of Neeles Brunix's office. The owner was off on some errand, so she had the ground floor room to herself. She shuddered in memory of the night he'd taken her maidenhood. Her skin crawled whenever she thought of his hands on her face, breast, between her legs . . .

She deliberately pushed aside her revulsion. Dwelling on Brunix wouldn't draw a pattern from the shawl. Without his watchful eye pinning her to her chair, Katrina took the opportunity to walk around her new workstation and stare at the obstinate piece of lace from a different angle.

Spring sunshine filtered in through the two high windows covered with a mosaic of mica flakes. Fresh white paint enhanced that light and relieved the strain on her eyes. A stray beam broke through the heavy windows setting the lustrous silk of the shawl aglow in three dimensions. An entire garden of abstract flowers jumped to life before Katrina's eyes.

She tried to remember the weeks M'ma had spent designing the shawl. Tattia had tried to keep her work a secret, but during those days, the entire family had huddled together in the upstairs workroom for warmth and light.

A picture of Tattia bent over her design board flashed before Katrina's eyes. "She didn't use a straight edge! She drew pictures. Pictures of flowers connected by a variety of entwined braids and nets."

Inspired by this insight, Katrina perched over the board again, removing all of the one thousand and more pins she had used as markers. Carefully she placed each of the precious pins into a magnetized box. A new piece of paper beneath the lace and she started over.

Pins in the top corners and along the fanned edge across the lace. Then several more along the side edges to hold the thing in place. With a new vision of how the design flowed she traced the outside of each flower with pins at logical points. The center of each motif received appropriate pins, too.

Tediously she traced each flower, following the lines of

thread rather than any predetermined geometric pattern. The outside edges came easily. The inside motifs didn't seem to conform.

Again Katrina jumped up and paced the office, studying the lace from several new angles. The floral centers appeared too angular, too regular to match the rest of the design. They were almost like the ancient runes carved into the walls of the temple. Runes that represented the language before the Stargods brought the modern alphabet. The ancient writing was the foundation of the pictorial ledger language all women were taught to keep their household accounts. A forgotten language deemed too unimportant for those few men who needed to read.

The rune in the lower right-hand corner suggested something illegal. The one in the upper right-hand corner showed ashes. She knew the symbol as part of the recipe for making soap—ashes and lye. But it was different somehow. A mood of menace lingered in the runes.

How strange of Tattia to put such symbols in a gift for the queen!

The sun shifted. A shadow fell across the lace obscuring her insight.

"S'murgh it!" she cursed. "I need better light."

"You may not take the board to the workroom upstairs. I will not have the other lacemakers peering over your shoulder at the lace and gossiping about my newest venture." Owner Brunix placed a long hand on her shoulder and squeezed gently, affectionately.

"Oh, you startled me." Katrina jumped away from him. The hair on her arms and the back of her neck stood up in instinctive fear of his touch. She had been so lost in her work she hadn't noticed the sounds of doors opening and closing or footsteps.

Brunix frowned at the distance she put between them. He didn't say anything further until he sat behind his desk, in a position of unopposable authority. "You may carry your work to my apartment." The top floor windows of thinnest mica and a skylight of real glass—coarse and mottled but genuine enough to bring the sunshine inside—offered the best visibility in the district. How many fortunes had he spent on that luxury?

Katrina hesitated, reluctant to agree with him. He was

right about the lighting. But she hoped she had escaped the necessity of ever returning to the intimacy of his private rooms. She looked at her board and the waning shaft of sunlight that now spread across his desk.

"I'll not press you to share my bed until the piece is finished. You may work in silent peace." He scowled.

His eyes were on an accounting ledger rather than on her, so she couldn't tell whether she or the figures displeased him. She peeked at the ledger, upside down. Unlike her father and other merchants, Brunix used the feminine runic language to keep his books. Where had he learned it? Not from any normal teacher.

Without a word she gathered her supplies under her arm.

"You could thank me," Brunix reminded her, still not looking up.

"For what?"

"For saving your eyes from strain. For delivering you from King Simeon, twice."

Katrina remained silent.

"His Majesty thought the humiliation of being owned by a half-breed outlander would be greater than suffering through his perverted rituals." Brunix peered at her speculatively. "The Simeon thought you would choose him over me. He made the mistake of underestimating you. I will not make the same mistake. I find great satisfaction in owning you. Me, a dark-eyed half-breed owning a true-blood woman. I own a Kaantille, one of the greatest lacemakers in the world, and all of your work belongs to me. All of it!"

"You own my work, Owner Brunix. You will never own my soul. I couldn't respond to you, because you demanded it as your right, something you bought and paid for. When you ask me out of love, I will reconsider." She put more distance between them.

"Will you, really?" He stepped between Katrina and the door so fast she barely saw him move. "Will you give me your soul if I ask out of love?"

"Maybe. Maybe not. I said I would reconsider if you could ever raise your self-esteem high enough to risk *asking*." She looked up at his tight face. He stood head and shoulders taller than she—another indication of his outland blood. She didn't let his height or his authority intimidate her.

"Get out of my sight. Get up into the loft and work on that blasted shawl until you go blind. Work until your fingers are bloody and your back permanently curved. For I'll not release you from bondage until no one has any further use for your mind, your hands, or your body. Even The Simeon won't be able to use you."

Chapter 20

"**B**reathe in three counts, hold three, out three, hold three. Again," Jack instructed Officer Lanciar as he himself engaged the first stages of a trance. He wasn't about to send this unknown sensitive in search of a dragon alone. Jack intended to be right on his heels—psychically speaking.

"Still your mind. Breathe in, hold, breathe out. Again. Let go of your thoughts. Drift free of your body," he continued the monotonous litany.

The moon rose high and bright above the canyon. Frigid winds continued to howl and moan. Inside the long, narrow cave the three men were snug, almost comfortably warm. Corby crouched on a protruding ledge, head under his wing; oblivious to the proceedings. Fraank snored quietly on the other side of their campfire. The older man had feigned boredom from the long and repetitious exercises to cover his exhaustion. The mines had taken their toll on his lungs as well as his strength. If Jack didn't find the dragon soon, Fraank might not live to return to his daughter.

Lanciar fidgeted, like any first-year apprentice learning the basics of magic. Mental and physical disciplines were things he'd learned during his years in the army. But this control over heartbeat and breath was taxing his patience.

A vibration of power rippled from Lanciar. He had achieved the first stage of trance. His latent magic was set free of mental inhibitions. Jack's body hummed, seeking a resonance with the other man. When they were tuned, Jack was ready to follow wherever Lanciar led.

"Anchor your body with the *Kardia*. Make if one with the land beneath you so that you may achieve the *Gaia*. The oneness with all that lives and breathes and exists."

Jack did the same. Automatically his blood pulsed in accord with the living rhythms of the planet and homed in on the magnetic forces of the nearest pole.

Lanciar took a little longer, not yet confident enough to release his body to instinct.

"Let go, Lanciar. Let your body find the *Kardia*. From the *Kardia* you were conceived and born. To the *Kardia* you will return. It is your home, nurturer of all life. Release your body to the loving arms of the *Kardia*."

"It's too much like death," Lanciar protested. At least he didn't break his trance. Five times they'd gotten this far and four times he had fallen out of rapport at the moment of release.

"What is death but one more phase of life? Touch it now, and you will never fear it again. Touch the *Gaia*. Touch all life." Jack's blood sang with power and joy as he followed his own instructions. Never before had he achieved such a sense of unity with life. He released his grief over the deaths of all those who had touched him with love and friendship.

Without listening, he heard underground water gurgling, the stones breathed, the soil mourned for the loss of the tall trees that had once anchored it to the planet. Jack knew where every bird nested, every mouse hid her burrow. He smelled the beginning of new leaves on the bushes. He sensed the stars wheeling in the great dance of life. He heard the moon pass through the sky.

He was a part of it all.

Lanciar followed him into the unity of life, death, renewal. Together they soared through the universe with their homeland.

Power beckoned them from all directions. Every living mote contained power, eager to be tapped and joined with the thriving life of the magician. Great blue pools and rivers of power surged through the planet beneath them. The power altered its internal resonance to match Jack's unique life song. It flowed through him as if he were another conduit, just like the planet.

He reached out with his senses, seeking his destiny. The image of a woman with hair graced by moonlight flitted past his mind's eye. A woman bent over a worktable with a single four-strand plait of hair down her back. He recognized the girl he had seen once before in a vision and many times in his dreams. Now he saw her grown to womanhood. Sad beauty touched her features and his heart.

Their lives were somehow linked. How? Why?

The vision faded. The future was an element he could glimpse but not know.

A shimmering crystal of power winked at him. *(Now you are ready!)*

All of Jack's past, good memories as well as bad, returned to him. He winked back to the core of crystalline power tinged with blue around the edges and continued his journey.

Enhanced by the land, he pulled more power from the moon and the sun, growing beyond them to the stars and distant galaxies. He saw more planets circling their suns, felt more lives that would never touch his own in real time and space. He joined and became a part of all life and rejoiced in the fullness of being.

Gradually the crackle of a small campfire, the cool wind and his stiff back touched his awareness. He sank back into his body, refreshed and renewed.

Lanciar's return was less graceful. His body jerked and slumped. He twisted his neck stiffly and stared numbly at Jack, mouth agape, eyes wide. "No wonder you were able to sense the rockfall before anyone else. If that is a sample of who you are, no wonder The Simeon sent me looking for you."

"That's . . . I never . . ." How could Jack explain that this was the first time he had *expanded* himself so far and so fully? "I saw the dragons. I know how to find them," he said instead.

"I didn't notice a dragon. I saw only a shimmering haze around everything and lines of blue crisscrossing beneath us." Lanciar stared at the remnants of the fire, still stunned by his awesome experience.

"Beneath us?" Jack glared at Lanciar with magic-sharpened senses. "There is no power in SeLenicca. Every magician knows that." So he hadn't looked for it. Suspicion grew in Jack. The power dimmed within him in response to the negative emotion. He didn't care. There was enough left in his body's reserves.

"You saw it, too!" Lanciar protested. "Not all over like

in the rest of the planet. Pockets of power, raw power that hasn't been honed and fine-tuned by contact with magicians."

"We can't be in SeLenicca if there are ley lines. Where have you led us? We've twisted and changed direction often enough we could be in Hanassa for all I know." Jack controlled the urge to throw a truth spell over his companion. He wanted to know the depth of Lanciar's betrayal first.

"I swear to you, by the vision we both shared, that we are in SeLenicca. All you have to do is march to the other side of this pass and question the inhabitants of the village. They speak SeLenese. The men cut their beards square. The women braid their hair in four-strand plaits. This is SeLenicca!" Lanciar's aura flared with blue truth. He believed what he said.

"Then something very strange is happening in your land." Jack swallowed deeply while he organized his thoughts. "Nimbulan burned out all of the power in SeLenicca when he established the border three centuries ago. For three hundred years, none of the ley lines had begun to recover. Why would they now?"

"I hate this," Darville whispered to himself.

"Think of it as cauterizing a wound," Mikka whispered back at him. "If we do not cleanse the problem now, the poison will spread until all of Coronnan is diseased and crippled!"

"So fierce, my queen?" Darville kissed her hand, then placed it atop his forearm in preparation for their formal entrance into the lesser audience chamber.

"I enjoy trials and executions no more than you, beloved. Remember we seek justice not vengeance."

He was grateful for the gentle pressure of her fingers against his own. She gave him the courage to mask his anger. Justice. He had to remember that.

Margit, Mikka's maid, had detected an herbal combination in this morning's porridge. A healthy woman who wasn't pregnant wouldn't notice anything more than a strange taste to the cereal. Mikka would have miscarried, possibly with dangerous hemorrhaging if she'd eaten it. No one else in the palace reported anything strange in their breakfast.

The Gnuls had to be neutralized now.

The major officials of the court bowed as the royal couple

moved toward the thrones on the dais. Lord Andrall stood to the right of the thrones. Jonnias and the Marnaks to his right. Behind the senior lords, Fred and a cadre of Darville's elite troops blocked any retreat through the back door. Another cadre had orders to move into position by the main entrance as soon as the royal couple passed through it.

No one smiled. No hands reached out with petitions. The mood of the court reflected the grimness of Darville's purpose. The full court would not have been assembled so hastily except in a dire emergency.

"They all have to know what is happening to Coronnan. I can't keep this private within the Council of Provinces," he muttered to give himself the courage to face the assembly.

"The lords would hide the ugliness behind secrecy," Mikka reminded him. "None of them have any concept of the reality or the consequences of their petty schemes and manipulations. You must force them to face this issue."

"Bring in the evidence and the prisoner," Darville commanded when he reached the dais.

The guards shifted position enough to allow a stoop-shouldered man of middle years wearing hand and foot manacles passage to the center of the chamber. Two grim-faced guards in palace green escorted him on either side. A ragged hole in the prisoner's tunic, above his heart, revealed to all the place where his badge of office had once resided. Upon first examination of the man's crimes, in the chill hours before dawn today, Darville had ripped the insignia away in disgust and despair.

"Where is the evidence?" Darville reminded his men.

The sergeant opened his mouth as if to protest. Darville scowled at him, daring him to disobey. The sergeant signaled to the privates waiting in the corridor.

Expressions carefully schooled, the foot soldiers carried a shrouded litter between them into the audience chamber. All around them, gently born men and women gasped in horror and withdrew from the stench of a three-day-old corpse. Escape from the grim proceedings was firmly blocked by battle-hardened men.

"You will all hear this prisoner's tale." Darville lifted his voice to parade-ground levels. "You will all witness my judgment."

Grimly he whisked the sheet off the dead body for all to see the wreck of a once human face and form. Patches of skin had been burned away. Multiple stab wounds had ripped open his chest. Blood coated the open mouth where the tongue had been cut out and stuffed back in backward. One eye was missing.

The king covered the body once more before he lost control of the hot bile in his throat. From the sounds at the far end of the long room, others succumbed to their revulsion.

"State your name and your former office, prisoner." Fred stepped forward and faced the man in chains.

"Caardack. I was senior magistrate of the city of Baria in the Province of Sauria," he whispered, never lifting his eyes from his chains.

"Louder. Speak loud enough for all to hear." Fred prodded the prisoner with a short club.

Caardack almost doubled over at the touch of Fred's weapon. Evidence that he'd endured more than one beating since being taken prisoner. He repeated his statement a little louder.

"Tell your tale, simply and clearly. The entire court needs to know how far from law and order our people have fallen." Darville sank onto his throne. Mikka placed her hand on his and squeezed gently. He had to endure this. For the good of the country, Caardack had to name his confederate in public. The court needed to see the perfidy of one of their own.

"I have been magistrate of Baria for twenty years," Caardack said proudly. He stood a little taller and straighter as he leveled his eyes on the king. "Always I have striven to be fair and just and maintain the laws of my king and the Stargods."

"Why, then, did you proclaim this man's death an accident not worthy of further investigation?" Fred pointed to the corpse.

Caardack looked furtively around the chamber, keeping his mouth firmly shut.

"Tell us why, Caardack. I promised you leniency only if you named those who ordered you to ignore death by torture. Illegal torture. Death perpetrated by a small cult of fanatics against a man in my employ!" Darville barely kept his voice below the level of a scream. He couldn't let the court see him lose control. Not yet. Not until the true criminals were revealed once and for all.

" 'Tisn't a small cult anymore," someone muttered to Darville's right.

"Numbers of followers do not make the crime of murder acceptable, Lord Jonnias." Darville stared directly at the man who had plagued him for years.

"I was told that the spy was executed lawfully," Caardack defended himself. "I was also told to proclaim the death an accident so as not to panic the populace."

"If 'twas a lawful execution, why wasn't it carried out in public by the king's order?" Fred threatened Caardack with the club once more.

"I do not question orders from the nobility."

Gasps and murmurs rose through the court. Men and women eyed each other suspiciously. Mikka bowed her head in sadness.

"As magistrate you have the right to question anyone," Lord Andrall said softly.

Caardack looked in fear at the four lords standing to the king's right. "If I had questioned Lord Marnak, I would have died as hideously as did the king's spy."

"Don't be ridiculous," Lord Marnak the Elder protested. "Baria is in Sauria. I govern Hanic. What interest have I in your city?" He stepped backward, hand on his sword. Two guards grabbed his arms from behind. He struggled to free himself from their grasp. "Hands off me! I am an anointed lord. You may not touch me."

"My orders supersede yours, Marnak." Darville rose from his throne and stalked to stand in front of him. "Laws handed to us from the Stargods forbid taking a life without due course of trial. The dead man was under my protection." On the day he died so hideously, the spy should have been fleeing Coronnan with Darville's gold to save himself from the Gnostic Utilitarians he had infiltrated. "You had no right to bring him to trial without my consent, so you had him murdered."

"He was a spy," Marnak spat. "A filthy spy sent to betray the rightful worshipers of the Stargods. Keeping our temples pure of magic gives us the right to protect ourselves from such as he. And you!"

"Father, no," Young Marnak backed away from the accused lord. His burn-scarred face took on a more horrible expression than usual. With no eyebrows or lashes left, his wide open eyes gave him a fishy look. "Our loyalty to the crown must never be questioned. Rejiia . . . my wife . . . ah . . ."

Hot anger narrowed Darville's vision to the elder Marnak's haughty face. The room and the gathered court faded from his awareness. His fingers itched to draw his sword and plunge it into the man's wide body.

Control yourself. Mikka's voice invaded his thoughts. *Calm. Think quiet peace.*

Visions of softly flowing water through woodlands. Calubra ferns swaying in the breeze. Shy wildflowers peeking out from shady glades.

"Lord Marnak the Elder, Governor of Hanic, I order your immediate arrest for the crime of murder. I will investigate charges of treason at the same time."

"Not treason, Your Grace." Lord Jonnias positioned himself between Darville and Marnak.

"Treason," Darville repeated. "When Caardack's full story is told at trial, all of Coronnan will know that the Gnostic Utilitarian cult seeks to set aside the dragon-blessed monarchy and the Council of Provinces. They want to set one of their own on the throne as absolute ruler of Coronnan. Since my ancestor, Darville I, ended the Great Wars of Disruption, the only person who can dissolve the Council of Provinces is a monarch consecrated by the dragons." He turned and stared at the entire court. "All of you saw and acknowledged the dragon at my coronation."

Shuffling feet and rustling fabric were the only sounds in the room. The story of a blue-tip dragon blessing Darville's coronation had grown into a legend, sung in taverns and on street corners across the land. Most of the people in the chamber had witnessed the event.

"Does anyone question that an attempt to assassinate me or my family is treason?"

Eyes opened wide with alarm and chins dropped as reality struck the members of the court. This was no game of gossip and intrigue for power and influence. Darville raised the question of murder of one of their own! By one of their own.

"We believe otherwise," Marnak interjected. " 'Tis treason to allow you and your witch-queen to rule. We must reestablish rightful government from the temple. The dragons have deserted Coronnan. The old laws protecting magicians are no longer valid.'

"What right have you to accuse my wife of witchcraft? What evidence do you produce to back your claim?" A pulse pounded in Darville's temple. Not once in nearly four years of marriage had Mikka thrown a spell. Yet the rumors persisted.

"Everyone knows she has bewitched you."

"Everyone does not know that, Marnak. What everyone knows and the truth are rarely the same thing. I have had enough of rumors and whispers. There will be no more of them!" he bellowed, almost beyond control. "The next person to accuse the queen without evidence will follow you to the dungeons."

He swallowed heavily and breathed deeply, praying for calm. When the red mist cleared from his eyes, he leveled his gaze upon Marnak once more. "Speak no more until the trial, Marnak, lest you condemn yourself without the benefit of trial."

"I do not care for your petty justice, *King* Darville," Marnak sneered. "I shall die a martyr."

"Only if I let you die."

Marnak paled. Jonnias swallowed repeatedly.

Darville heard the gasps of dismay from the crowd. He didn't care if they believed him capable of the kind of torture his spy had endured. He wanted them to think about that horrible death and know revulsion against those who caused it.

"I promised Caardack a short term of prison and penance, instead of death, if he named the leaders of the Gnostic Utilitarians. I can offer you the same clemency, Marnak. But only if you tell us all who gives *you* orders."

"I take my orders from the Stargods."

"Perhaps you will tell us who you planned to raise up as ruler of Coronnan after my assassination?"

Marnak looked hastily toward Jonnias, then back to his king. Jonnias edged away, his skinny legs trembling.

"I have vowed to die before I reveal the identity of our sacred leader." Marnak bowed his head in submission to his fate.

"What about you, Jonnias? Have you taken the same

vow?" Darville drew his short sword as he whirled to face the other lord. He stopped the blade a hair's breath from Jonnias' convulsing throat. Two burly guards kept the man from retreating further.

"I know nothing of this," Jonnias protested. His voice cracked with fear.

"Then you did not commission a new crown of gold and rubies from goldsmiths in Jhabb? Their ambassador thought you had. He also showed me a contract, written and signed by you, for ten thousand mercenaries to invade the capital city upon my death. They are to take orders from no one but you."

Jonnias slumped.

"Are you the sacred leader of this cult, or do you take orders from someone else?"

Jonnias remained defiantly mute.

"Take them away," Darville said. Sadness and relief dragged at his shoulders. He looked back to Mikka, still sitting quietly on her throne. A brief, sad smile touched one corner of her mouth.

"A formal trial against Marnak the Elder of Hanic and Jonnias of Sauria will begin at dawn. If they are found guilty, I will sentence them according to the law." He knew he'd have to order their deaths.

Marnak was right; they would die martyrs. Without leaders within the Council of Provinces, the cult would fade for a while . . . until some other power-hungry fanatic rose among their ranks. Whoever truly directed the cult would not remain in secret isolation long.

"What about me, Your Grace? I had nothing to do with the conspiracy." Marnak the Younger tugged at Darville's sleeve.

The king stared at the offending hand clutching the black silk of his shirt until the young lord removed it. "We will discuss your situation after the trial. If you are not guilty of aiding an attempt to put me aside in favor of Jonnias or any other potential leader, then you have nothing to fear."

Marnak blanched and bowed as he stepped hastily away.

Chapter 21

Jaylor sat before a fire at the far edge of Brevelan's clearing. Years before he had cast a summoning spell from this very spot. Then he had held a multicolored cat in his arms. Mica's rhythmic purr had aided his concentration in guiding the tiny flame through the glass toward his mentor, Baamin, in the University of Magicians. Tonight he held a feisty tabby with a torn ear who was just a cat. No princess with magic in her soul had borrowed this cat body.

The purring tom dug his claws into Jaylor's thigh, bringing him back to the important task of stroking fur in rhythm with his breathing.

Mica had often done the same when she had aided his spells. For all of her human intelligence, Mica had adapted to her cat body and instincts very well. Rosse, the cat who had inherited the princess' body, hadn't been quite so adaptable.

And now the two spirits were joined in Rossemikka's human body.

He sighed, still missing Darville. The necessary silence between them had gone on much longer than either had expected. Margit's reports of the king's and queen's daily activities didn't feel the same as speaking directly with his best friend.

Enough speculation on the politics. Jaylor had news for his two journeymen. Yaakke was alive! The ball of witch-light had left a magic trace in the same direction Marcus and Robb had taken. He must contact the boys tonight, before they slipped around the armies guarding the pass and entered SeLenicca.

Jaylor had a feeling that his former apprentice was in

trouble. Otherwise he wouldn't have sent such an unorthodox message after three years of silence.

I am Yaakke and I am alive.

Alive but not well; not returning; not capable of sending a normal summons spell.

Jaylor added another branch to the fire, to keep it going for the duration of the spell. As the flames caught, he breathed deeply, once, twice, thrice. The void beckoned him. He ignored the enticement of sending himself instead of his thoughts into the spell.

His trance settled comfortably on his mind and body. Cat purred and kneaded dough on the fabric of his trews. The flames grew larger, more animate in his mind's eye. A hand that might have been his, but seemed unattached to an arm, brought a large glass into view. The gold rim of the precious tool sparkled in the firelight. The images seen through the magnification grew even larger.

Carefully, Jaylor plucked one particularly lively flame from its greedy feeding on the wood. A thought melded the flame into the spells surrounding the glass. Then a gentle nudge and the flame surged outward, seeking. Seeking another flame hovering within a glass.

Down the foothills, through the forest and across rich farmland the flame traveled. Southward toward mountains. Mountains that were once rich in ore and covered in trees but were now barren and mined out. The flame traveled along blue lines of magical power. The magic trapped within the planet gave speed and ease to the journey.

At the mundane border, the flame hesitated. All of the blue lines ended abruptly—burned out centuries ago. The spark hovered, looking south and north, looking west and east. It wanted to retreat, back along the magic lines. Jaylor pushed it forward. The flame sputtered and tried to die.

Sweat broke out on Jaylor's physical body while his mind guided and fed the flame. *Another bit of fire.* He urged the traveling spark of his spell to seek another flame, any flame to renew itself.

He cast his senses farther, in all directions. No presence touched him with magic. No living person lived within a league of the spot where the flame flickered and tried once more to die.

Impossible. Last night Marcus and Robb had been

camped on this particular ley line. Surely they couldn't have traveled farther in one day. Even if they had ridden fleet steeds, they should be within sensing distance of this summons.

He tried another direction. Hundreds of campfires dotted the landscape, separated by an invisible line. The front. Two armies faced each other in silent impasse. The flame brightened as it neared others of its kind. None of them were magnified by a glass, or a bowl of water, or a ball of witchlight. The flame flickered and hesitated.

Jaylor's body sagged, drained of strength. Hastily he pulled the flame back into his glass. He couldn't allow the spell to leave a telltale that could be traced back to him, should a magician from either army discover any residual power. The secret location of Brevelan's clearing must remain secret.

Robb and Marcus knew how to find the clearing and the sprawling buildings of the University just beyond.

Jaylor sent the flame seeking for a presence again. Nothing. What if the young men had been kidnapped or conscripted into one of the armies? Rovers or solitary rogues could overpower the two young men, not yet fully grown into their powers. Armor was easy to erect around magical minds. An adept rogue would know the boys were in touch with their master and would shield against future communication.

Jaylor looked closer for an *absence*. Sometimes the easiest way to find a person was to find the *nothing* they hid within.

The flame found vast acres of hills and river valleys, some lush, some barren. It skimmed around scrubby bushes and dipped into burned-out and charred power lines. Across and back it flew, still seeking. Together in spirit, the flame and Jaylor crisscrossed every inch of land within a dozen leagues of Marcus and Robb's last known camping spot.

The landscape was as it should be. There were no holes and no lives. The military encampment sheltered, among the soldiers of Coronnan, several latent talents who didn't respond to the whisper of the flame. Nor did the powerful magicians on the western side of the pass understand the address of the summons. Marcus and Robb had vanished, as if they had never been.

They had to have been kidnapped. By whom and how? Not just anyone could make two magicians disappear beyond the reach of the Senior Magician of the Commune. That someone was an enemy to be reckoned with.

How much coercion could the two journeymen endure before they revealed every secret they knew? Including Queen Mikka's magical talent. Secrets that could be sold to a frightened Council of Provinces and the remnants of the Gnul conspiracy.

With sickening abruptness, Jaylor dropped back into his body from his trance. No time now to cater to a bouncing stomach and reeling vision.

"I've got to hide Brevelan and the boys. We aren't safe here anymore."

Marcus and Robb! Jaylor choked a moment in grief. He was Master now. The safety and well-being of those two boys fell on his shoulders. He'd sent them on their quest too soon. Just as he had with Yaakke. None of them were ready for the responsibilities and rigors of a quest.

He rose to his knees and doused the campfire with dirt. He didn't have time for regret and sorrow. More lives than two journeymen who knew the risks were at stake.

"What have I done to you? Lost. Yaakke, Marcus, Robb. All lost." He sent a silent prayer for their safety even as he ran the length of the clearing to begin the work of moving his family and his University where no one could find them.

As Jack led Lanciar and Fraank down the far side of the pass, the wind died and the sun broke free of the early morning cloud cover. Corby squawked and sprang from his perch on Jack's shoulder into the air, flapping his wings noisily. His tail rose convulsively and let drop a smelly white blob, inches from Jack's boot.

"Filthy bird!" He stumbled slightly as he hopped to avoid the splatter.

"Crawk!" The bird answered back crankily.

"You're so ornery maybe I should call you *Baamin*," Jack mused.

"Newak," the bird gave a negative reply, almost indignantly. "Corby, Corby, Corby." He resumed his flight path and quickly gained enough altitude to catch a rising current of warm air. Gliding effortlessly, he soared in lazy circles above their heads.

For a moment, Jack envied the bird its freedom. If he could fly like that, he'd be over Shayla's lair in a matter of hours instead of the week he estimated the journey would take. Maybe longer if Fraank's breathing didn't improve.

Lanciar didn't look too healthy this morning either. His first foray into the realm of magic had left him limp and drained, too tired to eat. Without food he'd never replenish the energy that magic depleted. The dry journey rations in their packs were unappetizing on a healthy stomach. Maybe the mountain village just below the pass would feed them, give them warm shelter for a night or two.

Fresh meat. Milk full of rich cream. Bread hot from the oven. Jack's mouth watered and he lengthened his stride in anticipation.

Ten more steps, around a boulder and under an overhang, brought him to a point where he could see far out across the lower slopes of the mountain range. Hill after barren hill rolled out in a wide vista. Pockets of morning mist clung to the valleys. A few small and isolated trees struggled toward sunlight in inaccessible ravines.

And not a rooftop in sight.

Jack looked up at the circling jackdaw, trying to peer through the bird's eyes as he had once before.

"Croawk!" The cranky bird chose that moment to slip into a new updraft and out of sight behind the boulders.

Jack's probe went astray. "Dragon dung! How are you supposed to become my familiar if you won't stick around long enough to be familiar?" He shook his fist at the last place he saw the bird. Corby didn't return.

"Where's the village?" Lanciar asked. His eyes looked hollow and his cheeks gaunt. He nibbled on a piece of dry meat, but not fast enough to feed his fading reserves of strength. None of the pockets of ley lines seemed to have revived in this area to support the use of magic and restore a body's reserves.

And yet a vibration hung in the air, almost like a *Song*. He listened closer, and the sensation faded like a perfume dissipating in the wind.

"That's what I'd like to know." Jack stomped forward looking for the jagged line of two dozen homes that were here last night. Both he and Lanciar had *seen* the village during their mystic journey. The bird had revealed the location to him earlier in the day.

"Villages don't just up and move overnight," Lanciar protested.

"Ley lines don't either. They're gone, too." Jack scratched the dirt with the toe of his worn boot. "We haven't time to puzzle this out. We need food and shelter. This was once heavy timber country. Where there was one village there ought to be another not far away." He shifted the pack on his back to a more comfortable position.

"There's a river valley." Lanciar pointed west by northwest. "The harvesters used to float the trees down the rivers to Queen's City and other ports. Maybe we'll find something that way."

"I prefer that path." Jack pointed to a different valley farther south. Mistrust of everything Lanciar suggested rose in him like a creeping poison. There weren't supposed to be any ley lines in SeLenicca. None at all. But a slender one tingling with raw power suddenly sprang up beneath his feet, begging him to tap into it.

He didn't trust the line either. It could be an illusion. It could be a dragon-dream. *He* could be wrong in all his perceptions.

"The dragon is that way." Jack stepped toward his chosen path.

"But we'll find food to the west. We need to replenish our supplies," Lanciar protested.

"Then we'll hunt." Jack began walking. Fraank followed silently in his wake, too tired and hungry to make a decision on his own.

"Hunting takes time and energy." Lanciar stood firmly in place.

"So does lying and betrayal. How many of King Simeon's agents are waiting in that valley, ready to pounce on us and drag us to Queen's City in chains, or back to the mine?" Jack didn't bother looking at either of his companions. He expected them to follow; Fraank because he couldn't do anything else, Lanciar because his mission was incomplete without a magician to turn over to Simeon and the coven.

"I have to go this way!" Lanciar took a step in the opposite direction.

"Then you go alone." Jack turned his back with a hastily erected wall of armor around himself and Fraank.

Katrina knelt before the little side altar in the grand temple. Her hands folded in front of her, and head bowed, she hoped the crowd of petitioners in the main sanctuary believed her lost in prayer. Like so many in the capital.

Queen Miranda still lay deep in a coma. Her citizens trooped into the temples daily to plead with the Stargods for a return of their monarch's health.

Isolated in the factory, with little free time or opportunity to travel outside the industrial district, Katrina hadn't realized how neglected the temple had become in the last five years.

The belief that SeLenicca was the land of the Chosen, theirs to exploit, was falling apart as the mines gave out and the timber did not regrow. King Simeon preached that the duty of all true-blood SeLenese was to conquer other lands, grabbing resources as they went and leaving behind everlasting evidence of the supremacy of the winged god, Simurgh.

Since Simeon's marriage to Miranda, attendance at the temples and contributions had fallen to mere pittances. Mortar crumbled and mold grew on the walls. The few priests left were ancient. They trembled with cold and nursed painfully swollen joints. Like the bent old man who shuffled behind the altar where Katrina knelt. His hands were so misshapen from the joint disease, he could barely hold his taper steady enough to renew the candles.

Worship of the Stargods hadn't been forbidden, but it had definitely fallen into disfavor. Until their beloved queen lay near death and her husband had named himself monarch. Not regent for the young princess, but ruling king.

Katrina wasn't the only one who had seen the magical bolt of blue fire that caused Miranda's steed to rear and bolt. All who had seen knew who had launched it. No one dared accuse the king, or the king's black-haired, outland mistress. Such an accusation was an invitation to a torturously long death. Iza had returned to the lace factory from Simeon's dungeons, with numerous bruises but no broken bones. Her mind drifted aimlessly and she spoke no more. She still wound bobbins and straightened pins, the chores of a lifetime not easily forgotten.

Surprisingly, Brunix continued to allow her to live in the dormitory despite her growing clumsiness.

The populace returned to their neglected temples with apologies and prayers and offerings. The Stargods were benevolent. Simurgh would not restore their queen and depose the bloodthirsty king. The Stargods might.

New candles on the altar cast flickering shadows on the walls of this tiny and nearly forgotten chapel. The geometric shapes, carved into the stone, faded in and out of visibility with each shift of the light. Katrina peered at them until her eyes burned.

The motifs in the lace shawl's flower centers were the same runes that decorated this wall, variations of the limited ledger language. She'd studied the lace shawl often enough to know the symbols by heart. Three runes out of the hundred displayed resembled the words for illegal trade; none of the others were familiar.

What did they mean? No one understood this ancient language anymore. Tattia Kaantille must have known something of it, or she wouldn't have included the runes in the shawl. A message or merely an unusual twist in the design?

Surely not the latter. The runes were interesting and in a different motif could have been lovely. The flowers surrounding the runes were too soft and flowing to support the hard angles and straight lines of this forgotten alphabet.

An ancient priest wheezed as he slipped out from behind the little altar. He wobbled past Katrina to replace the sputtering candles on the stand at the opening to the chapel. His threadbare robes had once been fiery green, but the dyes had faded with time and too many washings to muddy brown.

"Excuse me, good sir," Katrina whispered to the priest. "Do you know anything of these runes?"

"Eh?" He bent toward her, cupping an ear with his hand.

"The runes." She pointed to the chiseled markings. "Do

you know what they say?" She raised her voice a little. Hope of a discreet inquiry and quick answer faded.

The old priest turned to face the wall, peered at the ancient writing, and shook his head. Then he bent closer, holding his lighted taper right up against the markings.

Sigils flared bright red against black stone as if gathering life from the flame. Seemingly random nines in a distinctive geometric pattern leaped away from the wall burning their image into Katrina's mind. The same symbols, in the same order as the ones Tattia used.

Katrina's eyes widened in surprise and excitement. The old priest backed away from the wall shaking his head. "I'm sorry, daughter. I can't see well enough anymore to read this wall."

"But you know something of the ancient alphabet, perhaps something of the old prophecy? Did you read the wall for my mother three years ago?" She rose in her eagerness to get to the bottom of this puzzle.

"Knowledge of the runes has been forgotten by most. Best you spend your time and energy praying for the queen." The priest wandered off again.

"Maybe the knowledge has been forgotten, but you read the wall, old man. I'll find the truth yet." She turned to follow, eager to pursue her questions in a more private place.

"A word, Mistress Kaantille?" A stranger restrained her with a whisper.

She knew that voice! The man who had offered her freedom for the shawl. The shawl had a message. For this man or another?

"Stay away from me." She backed away from him until the low altar rail pressed against her thighs.

"I can offer you freedom and passage out of SeLenicca in return for the shawl. Your mother promised it to me three years ago. But she died before she could give it to me. I have searched long and hard for it. And for you, Katrina Kaantille."

"The stranger who offered to buy the shawl? M'ma refused your offer. Why should I accept it?"

"Your situation is more desperate now. Your M'ma refused my first offer. Later, she promised to bring it to me.

I waited for her until dawn on the night she died. Would she have committed suicide on the night she expected to gain enough gold to feed you all for a year or more?"

Confusion clutched Katrina's heart and mind. She turned her back on the man and knelt at the altar again.

"Go away. I must think on this. I don't trust you." She bowed her head until she heard the man walking away.

A long-fingered hand grasped her upper arm in a vicious grip. She jerked away, ready to scream at the stranger to leave her alone.

"So this is where you hide." Owner Brunix knelt beside her, crossing himself in the accepted manner as he lowered his long body onto the stone floor.

"Not even you can deny me the right to say a prayer for the queen." Katrina dipped her head and closed her eyes. Her heart throbbed in her ears. Her skin burned where he had touched her. Had he seen her with the stranger? Would his jealousy drive him to such anger that he forced her to his bed again?

"Pray? Is that what you do for so many hours each evening?" he whispered in her ear. His breath fanned a stray tendril of her hair, just in front of her ear.

She shuddered and leaned slightly away from him.

"You have no reason to love our queen, or her outland husband," Brunix said. "They deserve your curses, not your prayers."

Katrina schooled her face to immobility, her thoughts whirling in confusion. Had her mother truly promised to sell the shawl? Who was the stranger and why was he so desperate to get the shawl?

Silence sat uneasily between them.

"You are an educated man, Owner Brunix. What do those runes on the wall tell you?" Did he know more of them than the limited feminine alphabet used in keeping mercantile records?

"Nothing. The Stargods wiped out all knowledge of that form of writing. They considered it a service to *Kardia Hodos,* along with eliminating a plague and erasing the cult of Simurgh. But the three who descended from the stars were ignorant and considered all of the ancient gods and their arcane knowledge as one with the bloodthirsty demon Simurgh. We lost many unique and special parts of our culture. A thousand years have passed and we are not likely to reclaim any of it."

"But surely there must be a legend of old text that preserves the meaning of those symbols, else they would have been plastered over or sanded into oblivion centuries ago," she protested.

"Legends about a prophecy of doom persist. Yaakke, son of Yaacob the Usurper, is supposed to bring about the disaster." Brunix shrugged. "Why are you so interested, my Katrina? I thought you were lost in prayer for our queen."

"Beauty and symmetry," she answered too hastily. "I would like to incorporate some of the runes into a design—bed hangings or perhaps a table runner." Deep inside her, Katrina knew the sigils conveyed a message. An important message. She had to be the first to interpret it so she knew who to tell and who to avoid.

"Not bed hangings, please. The prophecy of doom might carry over into . . ." Brunix rose hastily, turning his back on her. "City curfew is upon us. The factory curfew is long past. You will return with me now," he ordered. "I don't remember giving you permission to leave the factory."

"But you did! You told all of the lacemakers to say our prayers for the queen."

"I told my employees, not my slave. Such a flagrant disregard of the rules requires punishment. No breakfast for you tomorrow. If I dared, I'd deny you sun break as well." He grabbed her arm again, hoisting her to her feet. His fingers remained clamped just above her elbow as he propelled her out of the temple.

As Katrina stumbled in Brunix's wake his words echoed through her mind.

Yaakke, son of Yaacob the Usurper. A prophecy of doom?

What could be worse than what she endured now?

Chapter 22

Rejiia contemplated a water droplet on top of her viewing glass. The circle of gold-rimmed glass lay flat upon a tripod above a short candle flame. The water tended to enhance her visions of distant places and events to come.

Lately all she saw was death and destruction converging on a single point. There clarity ended and symbolism took over. Three feathers for the Rovers. A black bird for the dragon nimbus. Unnatural red flames must be the coven. What could the frothy sea foam covering it all stand for? Surely Rossemanuel's death by poison wouldn't be represented by that symbol. The eels that provided the oil to bind the ingredients of the poison lived in river bottoms, not in the tops of waves near the shore.

A summons spell hummed within Simeon's huge mirror on the wall of her private apartment before she found an answer. As tall as Rejiia, and nearly an arm-length across, the glass was incredibly valuable. Something only a king could afford. The images it revealed were imperfect, warped and wobbling, but better than polished metal and larger than the exact reflection from Krej's master glass.

Simeon kept the mirror in her quarters to feed his vanity. He spent more time preening naked in front of the mirror than using it to bring his ambitions to fruition.

"Since this tool was entrusted to me, I will answer the summons and act upon it." She stood awkwardly from her chair and faced the demanding mirror. The growing baby in her womb kept her from moving quickly or gracefully.

At the center of the glass, colors spun outward in a growing spiral until they filled the surface of the mirror. Greens and browns dominated the pattern. Gradually the spiral steadied and cleared. Lanciar appeared, life-sized against a barren landscape of scrubby hillsides.

Gray-green and greenish-brown were the signature colors of his latent magic.

Rejiia placed her hand against the glass in greeting, wondering where he was and who threw the summons spell for him. He returned the greeting with a raised hand, imitating her gesture image to image. She wished she could touch him across the distance of time and magic. Lanciar had such gifted hands. He was her favorite partner during the coven's ritualistic couplings.

"Lady, I have found a new magician. If we hurry, we can bring him into the coven." His voice sounded strained.

"Who? Where are you?" she asked. Excitement blossomed within her. A new magician. A new lover during the rituals. More power to funnel into her spells.

The face of a young man with Rover-black hair and beard flashed from Lanciar's mind to her own. Features fell into place. Long, straight nose, middle height, broad shoulders and burning black eyes.

"Yaakke!" she cried. Come back from the dead to haunt her. Her dreams of power faded. That wretched, incompetent boy had more power than the full coven.

"He seeks the dragon," Lanciar informed her. "He must not be allowed to reach the lair before we convert him to our cause. He might be able to break the spell that keeps Shayla captive in SeLenicca before he understands why she must remain."

"Yaakke will never willingly join the coven. We must kill him before he reaches the lair. Without the dragon, Simeon is nearly powerless."

"And so will be the others in the coven, Lady Rejiia. I will undertake the mission to destroy the magician. My magic has awakened and it is fueled by the dragon." Lanciar smiled in a sensuous way that sent Rejiia's senses lurching. He promised more in that smile than just magic. "Upon my return to the capital, I will request full membership in the coven. I will serve at your right hand to make certain you remain as the center of the eight-pointed star."

As long as Simeon believes the child you carry is his, he will be content to allow you to be the focus of the coven's spells. The unspoken words seemed to come from the tin weasel. Rejiia grinned, knowing her father had somehow managed to break through some of the barriers in his magical prison.

"My gravid body anchors the eight-pointed star to the Kardia as no other can," she replied. "I won't give up that position once your grandson is born." With Lanciar at full power to support her, she intended to remain the focus. Krej had fought for the center and lost it to petty bickering within the coven. Janataea, too, had been kept from the coveted role. Rejiia wouldn't relinquish it—especially to Simeon whose spells were increasingly erratic.

"The boy must be stopped, Lanciar. I shall send those I trust. Magicians from the coven who owe me much. Men who will not hesitate to kill the boy if he refuses to be recruited."

Jack heard the waterfalls before he saw them. Swollen by spring runoff, little creeks joined, became rivers and thundered over cliff tops in untamable torrents. Delicate mists drifted from the primary falls almost a mile up the valley. His ears roared as he entered the fog bank caused by cold, airborne water meeting thermal currents rising from the sun-warmed valley floor.

"Almost there, Fraank," he shouted to his companion over the sound of the booming cascades.

Fraank didn't look up from his concentrated trudging. Nor did he respond. All of his energy went into placing one foot in front of the other.

"Come, Fraank, you can't let King Simeon win. You've got to fight to get well."

Fever and lung-rotting mine dust dulled Fraank's upturned eyes. Sadly he shook his head and plodded forward, each step an effort.

Jack stretched his senses forward and back; a difficult task now that they were deep into SeLenicca and the pockets of rejuvenated magic were scarcer than the widespread villages. He sensed three large life-forms behind him, at least two days away. He couldn't tell if they were men, steeds, or deer. He didn't have enough magic to hone in on details and find out if Lanciar had summoned reinforcements.

Up ahead a different sensation sent his body tingling and humming with joy. LIFE! Vibrant, buoyant, joyful life. Dozens of lives, dominated by one, much larger than the rest. The primary mind picked up his probe and sent it back to him with greeting.

(Welcome, Magician. I have waited long for you. Come, eat, rest. There is much work to be done.)

Jack reared, propelled backward by the strength and clarity of the mental command.

"Shayla?" Jack asked the air around him. Who but a dragon could penetrate his armored mind?

(Who else would live behind a waterfall and play with a dozen silver dragonets?) The dragon chuckled. Her voice filled him with rich images of immature dragons frolicking in the rippling pool beneath the waterfall.

Feeling fresher and stronger than he had in weeks, Jack supported Fraank around the waist and marched the older man deeper into the rift between enclosing hills.

A path cleared by clawed dragon feet opened before them. Not a single pebble marred the surface of the packed dirt to trip them or lead them astray. Boulders had been pushed aside to allow passage of wide dragon bodies with delicate wing membranes. Above them, the mountain walls rose steep and sheer. What need had dragons of climbing upward when they could fly?

"Just a few more steps, Fraank. A few more steps and you can sleep," Jack urged his friend.

Half a mile farther, Fraank was drooping visibly, as if the end of the quest marked the end of his life. Stubbornly, Jack shouldered the older man's nearly empty pack, along with his own and continued to hold him up, almost carrying him as they penetrated the mist.

The valley corridor widened into a deep bowl ringed with cascades in many sizes. Sunlight struck water and sent rainbows arcing in all directions. Directly ahead, a huge waterfall thundered. The outline of a crystal dragon head pushed through the curtain of the falls. Sunlight struck water and dragon together, granting a wild array of colors to the mist.

Jack blinked. More of the dragon appeared outlined by the water. Rainbows danced around the crystal horns marching from forehead to tail. Then Shayla broke free of the main cascade of water. Droplets shone on her crystal-fur. Each tiny hair reflected the bright sunlight back to Jack's eyes, defying him to look directly at her.

And yet Shayla was so incredibly beautiful with her all-color/no-color fur, he couldn't look anywhere else but directly at her.

The male dragon who had shown young Yaakke a dragon-dream of this valley had been touched by blue along his wing veins and tips. Jack suspected the unnamed dragon's fur had held just a hint of color on the end of each hair too. But not Shayla. Every color visible to the human eye bounced off her body giving her the luster of pure, rare glass, a substance that could only be forged by dragon fire.

Gracefully, Shayla waded from her concealment behind the curtain of falling water through the pool to where Jack and Fraank stood. Jack watched her progress as the water lapped halfway up her side, splashing occasionally onto her wings and neck.

The pool was immense. And deep. At the shoulder, the dragon was twice as tall as Jack, and equally as wide. The pool was at least six dragon-lengths across. Shayla didn't seem to be swimming. Jack wasn't certain dragons could swim. So the water was at least as deep as he was tall, maybe more.

(We swim when the water is deep enough.) The dragon answered him before he could ask the question. *(We swam in the Great Bay often when we flew the skies above Coronnan.)*

Embarrassment tinged Jack's cheeks and the tips of his ears. He looked into Shayla's half-closed jewel of an eye. The whorls of spinning color didn't seem to mock him. Did dragons have a sense of humor? He clamped down on that question before Shayla could answer him.

She cocked her steedlike muzzle to one side as if puzzled by the closure of his thoughts.

(Don't you trust me to be honest with you?)

"Of course I trust you, Shayla. I'm just not used to having my thoughts read and my questions answered before I've thought them through." He looked away from the compelling jewel eyes.

The dragon loomed so high above him that the only place he could look without overbalancing was along her side to the folded wings. The transparent membranes fluttered slightly for balance as Shayla emerged from the pool.

A twisting black burn, as long as Jack's body and as wide as his two thighs pressed together, marred the beauty of the left wing. Charred by magic that snaked along veins and bones, the wing hung lower, heavier and more painful than its undamaged mate. Unable to heal herself and unable to fly to a healer, Shayla was trapped in the beautiful prison of this valley with the rainbow waterfall.

Jaylor studied the misty colors of the clearing's barrier with his magic-heightened senses. A tiny crack in the armor glared back at him. A crack that might admit an enemy. Since Brevelan refused to move her family or the Commune, Jaylor had to make sure the protections of the clearing were intact, impregnable.

"How are we going to explain this to your mother, Glendon?" he asked his son.

Sorry. The boy hung his head and stared at his feet. No words escaped him now. No words had ever come out of his mouth. What need had he of words when his mind relayed all the information he needed to impart?

"What were you and Lukan doing?" Jaylor shook his head in dismay. Brevelan was the chosen guardian of the clearing and the dragons. She had been the only person capable of opening and closing the barrier until Jaylor's spirit journey with the dragons. As Brevelan's husband, the dragons had granted him the privilege of sharing the guardianship. As far as he knew, the boys were not included in the privilege of opening and closing the clearing.

Stargods help them all if Glendon got loose to wreak his personal havoc and tricks on the world at large!

Wrestling, Glendon replied.

"Wrestling with what?" The image the boy relayed to his father didn't mesh with Jaylor's idea of normal little boy activity.

Dead silence surrounded Glendon. Nothing escaped his mind.

"Have you two been experimenting with magic again?" Jaylor tried to keep the panic out of his voice. He had gained early admission to the Old University at age ten because of his precocious talent. His sons were only three and two and they'd managed to crack armor that even their grandfather, Lord Krej, had been unable to weaken.

Krej had managed to come through the barrier by shape-changing himself and his followers into small animals, then transforming them back into normal form once they were through. Glendon and Lukan hadn't figured out how to shape-change, yet. Or had they?

"If you don't tell me, Glendon, your mother will extract the information from you. Do you want her mucking about with your feelings?"

Glendon had the grace to blush. Somehow he turned the expression into a scowl at the same time. Brevelan had a unique way of making the boys feel guilty and regretful for their infractions of rules. Her empathy projected her own hurt and disappointment into her children.

"Well, son, what were you wrestling with?"

Witchballs.

An image of giant globes, almost as large as Glendon, formed of moss and dirt and leaves, held together by a magic glue, formed in Jaylor's mind. He'd made witchballs for the boys—small ones—among their earliest toys. The balls had the advantage of being as light or heavy as a child could handle, easily replaced, never lost, and could be broken down with a thought before they crashed into some fragile object.

Who would have thought the clearing barrier was vulnerable to a witchball?

"How many rocks did you put into the center of the balls?" Jaylor had a brief nightmare of the boys forming their latest toy around a boulder and rolling it into the walls of the house.

No rocks, Glendon replied.

"Then what did you put into them?" Jaylor tried not to shout. Sometimes the boy's cryptic remarks made him wonder if Glendon might have been fathered by Old Baamin or maybe by a dragon.

Armor wrapped around Glendon and he seemed to fade into the natural colors of calubra ferns and everblue trees.

Jaylor concentrated hard on pushing his hand through his son's protection and grabbing the boy by the scruff of the neck. He wasn't Senior Magician for nothing. The boys had yet to figure how to keep him out. They tried, often, and he dreaded the day he couldn't break apart any spell they threw.

"What did you put into the witchballs, Glendon?"

Lightning probes.

Bolts of inquisitive magic whose sole purpose was to penetrate a given object or person for information.

"What did you learn from your probes?" Jaylor asked, trying very hard not to shake the boy and frighten him into silence.

Glendon panicked anyway. The armor around his small body thickened and thrust his father's grasp away with a jolt of energy. Before Jaylor could reassert his hold on his son, Glendon disappeared through the crack in the clearing.

Jack jerked his eyes and his mind away from the hideous wound on Shayla's wing, back to her face. She seemed to wince—as much as she could show expression—with each slight movement of her wing.

"Does it hurt?" he blurted, too astonished for tact.

(Yes.) She folded the wing abruptly.

Of its own volition, Jack's hand reached out to caress her long nose in sympathy. Inches from contact with her iridescent fur he pulled back, uncertain he had the right to make physical contact with her.

(You may touch.) The dragon dipped her head, butting into his still outstretched palm. He cupped his hand around her cheek and stroked the velvet softness. Instantly his shoulders relaxed and his mind stopped whirling.

The cranky jackdaw, absent for more than three days, chose that moment to circle and land on his head. A series of earsplitting croaks informed both man and dragon of his jealousy.

Jack reached up to pet the bird and received a painful peck on his hand in return.

"There's no pleasing you!" He brushed the bird away.

It hopped to Jack's foot, pecked at the loose sole of his journey-thin boots then leaped to Shayla's longest spinal ridge. That perch didn't seem to please the bird either. From Shayla's back, Corby flapped noisily into flight up the cliff walls to one of the irregular knobs standing sentinel over the valley.

Knobs of rock or crouching dragons?

Almost invisible against the darkening sky, the jackdaw
hovered over a looming shape, voicing his displeasure with
life in general and Jack in particular. Finally Corby landed
and quiet reigned in the valley once more. The jackdaw
began to preen, seemingly quite satisfied that he had thoroughly upset everyone.

"King Darville has a burn on his left arm that won't heal.
It looks just like that." Jack pointed to the ugly black
wound. "At least I presume it still looks like that. I haven't
had any contact with Coronnan for three years," he bab-
bled, unable to avert his eyes.

*(My king still wears the Coraurlia. His body continues to
bear the wounds of his battle with the evil ones. He will not
heal until I heal. He has learned to live with his pain, as
have I. We both grow weary of the burden.)*

"I'm not a healer, but I have observed Brevelan. I helped
her once when she tried to draw magic out of King Darville's wound. Maybe I can do something with the wing—
enough to let you fly home."

(That is why I sent for you.)

"I'm sorry I took so long getting here." Jack hung his
head. If he hadn't unleashed that terrible firebomb in Marnak's camp . . . if he had sent a summons to Jaylor
earlier . . . if he hadn't been so arrogant and gotten lost in
the void . . .

A million "what if's" couldn't change the past or bring
back the dead. He could only try to improve the present.

*(You were not strong enough, or wise enough to heal any-
one when my mate set you on your path. The passage of
seasons has been long, but not without rewards. When you
and your magic were mature enough, the dragons revived
your mind so that you would once more seek to finish
your quest.)*

"My staff? The dragons put the staff into my hand?"

*(We kept the staff hidden. It would have sought you ear-
lier, but you were not ready to awaken. When your mind
had healed enough to understand your mistakes and accept
your destiny, we allowed it to find you.)*

Jack smiled as he fondled the length of twisting oak. The
staff was a part of himself, linked to his magic. Of course
it would have rolled through the mine seeking him when
they were first separated.

Only then did he notice the dozen silvery shapes hiding in the shadows of smaller side falls that fed into the pool.

"You mated again! Or are these little ones three years old?" A smile spread through Jack at the sight of the pretty cublets, all silvery and dainty, climbing onto rocks to sun themselves. He counted ten little dragons—if one could consider a winged creature the size of a pack steed to be small—with pale colors beginning to emerge on spinal ridges and wing tips. Two each of blue, green, and red, the usual colors of dragon males. Still clinging to the protection of tumbling mist sat a shy pair tinged a rare purple. The last two dragon children who swam to Shayla's side showed no trace of color of their own. The immature females reflected light; sun and water shimmering into a myriad of rainbows.

(My other children seek lairs of their own and will mate at the end of the next century.) A note of maternal pride colored Shayla's mental voice. She seemed brighter and her eyes more colorful as images of the eleven older cublets grown strong, flashed into Jack's mind.

"Two purples in this litter?" Jack asked. "Isn't that supposed to be impossible to have two purples alive at the same time?"

Shayla hunched her shoulders in a dragon shrug. *(Destinies I cannot control determine the colors of my children.)* She glanced at each of her offspring. Love seemed to radiate from her in almost visible waves.

(I do not wish to birth a third litter in this land. When you have rested and eaten, we will begin the healing.)

"We don't have long," Jack informed her. "Someone approaches from the south."

(The Simeon comes but once a year to renew the pain.) Shayla's eyes grew dull. *('Tis not time for him.)*

"Unless his spy summoned him. He seeks new recruits for the coven. He wants me to fill an opening."

(Do you wish such a fate?) No emotion touched Shayla's voice. Yet Jack felt the great anger filling her to near bursting. He didn't want to be on the receiving end of her fury. Stargods help Simeon when she broke free of this beautiful prison.

"I have no love for King Simeon or his coven. They wreak havoc with each spell they throw." Jack affirmed.

(Then come behind the waterfall. There is time for you to

dine and sleep. We begin our work at dawn. When the agents of my enemy arrive, we will be long gone.)

"If I can remember the spell," Jack muttered to himself as he gathered the two packs and assisted the drooping Fraank around the edges of the pool. On the far left side, a narrow path led to a deep undercut behind the waterfall. A perfect hiding place or a dead-end trap?

Chapter 23

I have found the lacemaker. She hides within an enclave owned by a Rover. She possesses knowledge damning to Simeon. Which does the king fear more, the knowledge or the Rovers? Zolltarn's clan does not frighten me. I will have the knowledge and the lacemaker. Then I will have control over Simeon, king and sorcerer, as well.

Fraank looked better already. He sat, huddled over a fire—ignited by an attentive baby dragon showing off his newly learned trick of blowing fire. The older man absorbed warmth while a meal of venison and tubers roasted over the coals. A red-tipped dragonet crouched beside the weary man, much like an oversized puppy anxiously protecting its master.

This was no puppy. Rufan, as Shayla had named the dragonet, stood nearly as tall as Jack and probably weighed twice as much. His wings were wide enough and strong enough to support his body mass while flying. The hooked talons at wing elbow, wing tip, and on all four feet could flay man or crush the neck of a goat. He was not yet telepathic with humans.

Jack watched his traveling companion lean against Rufan's flank. Tension left Fraank's spine and neck as his body slumped further against the dragonet. In moments Fraank was asleep against his warm and furry pillow.

Relieved at the ease Fraank had finally found, Jack relaxed against a nest of dried leaves and blankets, easy in mind and body for the first time in years. For a while they were safe, warm, and dry. He could turn his mind toward matters beyond survival.

"Your mate, the blue-tipped dragon who showed me this place in a dragon-dream, promised me information when I found you."

(You desire to know of your family.)

"I have a right to know my own history!" The familiar anger of his youth began to curl within Jack's empty stomach. He clamped down on a temper he knew could soon boil out of control.

(Are you certain you want to know these things?)

"I must. How can I know who I am if I know nothing of my parentage and childhood? I need to know if the name I chose for myself is truly mine and I am worthy of it."

(You make your own life, your own future.)

"But my past shaped me."

(At moonrise, you may climb to the second highest peak above the waterfall. The dragon who wears magician blue on his wings and spines will speak to you there.)

"Is there a path, or must I levitate up there?" Levitation took more energy than Jack thought he could muster right now.

(A staircase exists. You must use your special gifts of sight beyond sight to find it.)

Sight beyond sight. That meant magic and only his bodily strength to draw upon. Time to refuel. "I think that venison is cooked enough."

Fraank woke up as Jack approached the fire pit. Rufan looked at them both with a sparkle of mischief in his eye. Maybe it was just a reflection of the firelight. The baby dragon eyed the venison and then cocked his long head at the two men. Jack caught a glimmer of a thought.

"Don't you dare add any more char to *my* roast!" Jack lunged to restrain Rufan from breathing more fire upon the deer carcass. He wrapped both hands around the silvery muzzle.

Rufan's surprise jolted Jack off his feet. Telepathic communication dribbled into Jack's mind as Rufan scooted backward on the cave floor, closer to his mother. A few incoherent thoughts and a gibberish of dragon language fed a confusion of images. Still Jack clung to the dragon's muzzle, afraid to let go, lest he be the next target of fiery experiments.

Shayla appeared at his side, looming tall and protective over her youngster. Jack cringed away from her powerful talons.

(You seem to have awakened the boy's mind. Now we must teach him to speak in words instead of baby pictures,) Shayla chuckled. With a nudge of her muzzle against Rufan and a wink of her enormous eye at Jack, she sent the child to his nest for the night.

"Sight beyond sight," Jack muttered to himself as he stretched his hands above him, seeking the next handhold on the cliff wall. The moon rose above his left shoulder, nearly full in a hazy sky. Diffuse light washed the cliff in a uniform pearly gloss. "I need eyes in my hands and feet for this climb." He clung to the next narrow indention.

Tired and panting, he pulled himself up another step. If the "stairs" were a little wider, he'd probably crawl. As it was, the indentations weren't wide enough to support one knee let alone two. The ledge he'd stood upon during his dragon-dream of this valley had been this narrow.

The moon rose higher. An irregular knob appeared above Jack, outlined in an eerie shimmer of magic and moonlight. A halo of deep blue hovered around the form. The dragon who wore magician blue.

Jack took another step and another, and then he was within the blue aura.

"Sir?" Jack tentatively probed the slumbering dragon with mind and words.

(You are late again, Boy.) The huge male didn't stir from his crouched pose, muzzle buried in a pillow of forepaws and encircling tail.

"I ran into some problems along the way," Jack defended himself. He wasn't a naive adolescent any more to bow to just any authoritative voice and manner.

(Did you learn anything from your brash mistakes?) The dragon opened one eye briefly, as if to verify his presence. Faceted points caught the moonlight and sparked with emotions Jack couldn't read. Then the translucent membrane dropped and the dragon seemed to slumber once more.

"My experiences taught me many things about the man I can be. Only you have the key to the child I was."

(You won't like the story I have to tell.)

"I don't like not knowing more. I have a right to know who I am, where I come from, what my true name is."

(Jack suits you fine; more honestly than Yaakke.)

"But what name was I given at birth? No mother would leave a child unnamed. You promised to tell me when I found Shayla!"

(The lack of this knowledge burns deep within you. That yearning must be satisfied or you will not have the concentration to work the healing spells. Come.) The nameless dragon heaved himself up onto his hind legs in a curiously graceful undulation for so large a creature. He stretched his spine and reached his shorter forelegs toward the night sky as if embracing the moon. Once more his eyes were open, light lancing from the facets.

(Observe, Jack. Watch your past and learn from the mistakes of others.)

Cold swirls of blue, green, and red light closed around Jack. He fell through the dancing star points of the jeweled dragon eyes into a void. Falling, falling, farther and farther away from himself through the lives of dozens of people and into the past.

Endless moments flowed through the wheel of the stars. And still he fell. His body learned the streams of movement through this strange void, stretched out and flew.

(Now you have enough of the dragon within you to observe the past. Remember the dragon within you and within every magician when next you have a need to visit with those who have gone before. Watch!)

"Observe what?" A strange/familiar landscape took shape around him. He'd been here before. But not at this moment in time. The trees were not quite the right shape and the sledge-ruts in the road were too deep. "Where are we?"

He looked around again, sensing and smelling familiarity rather than understanding it. There was a road running toward the southern border, just outside Brevelan's village, that looked something like this. He scanned the horizon. Yes. The creek plodded along its path beyond the dip in the meadow and on toward the Great Bay.

The water was clear and clean, not choked with mud and debris from the floods that had plagued Coronnan when last he saw this place. Birds sang in the fully leafed oak trees that should have their roots underwater but sat back from the bank by several steed lengths.

He measured the angle of the sun against the length of the shadows. Early morning, past the summer solstice. Jack and Fraank had left the mine just after the Vernal Equinox, only a few weeks ago.

"Maybe I should ask, 'When are we?' "

The dragon said nothing. Jack looked over his shoulder to where he sensed the beast hovered. All he saw was the dim outline of an old man in colorless flowing robes. Then he looked at himself. Almost transparent and wearing the black trews and vest of a Rover. His shirt appeared to be pale yellow, but so much of the green fields around him shone through the fabric and his skin, he couldn't be sure.

(Watch and listen,) the dragon ordered.

Just then a man and woman riding double on a fleet steed appeared on the road, coming from the north. The steed was black and sleek, bred for speed. Sweat shone on its glossy coat. They might be proceeding at a stately pace now, but just recently, the riders had pushed the steed in an all-out race.

The man in the front, clad in shiny black leather to match his mount, kept looking over his shoulder for signs of pursuit. The woman, perched behind the saddle, clung to his belt. She rode astride with her brightly colored skirts hiked up above her knees. Shapely legs and bare feet clutched the heaving sides of the steed.

"Rovers," Jack spat. Three years ago, Jack had a few encounters with Zolltarn, king of the Rovers and his tribe. Rovers had their own codes of ethics and honor that had little to do with the rest of civilization. Jack was convinced the entire race of wanderers would gladly slit a man's throat just to prove they could.

(Dragons observe and learn. We do not judge.)

"But . . ."

(Observe.)

The mounted couple moved past Jack and his guide seeking all around them with their eyes. The young magician started to greet the passing pair and offer them directions. A heavy hand on his shoulder stoppped his angry words. A human hand in shape and size. Prominent blue veins stood out on the backs of that nearly invisible hand, much like the colored veining on a dragon's wing.

(We are ghosts in this time. Our souls dictate our forms. They cannot see you. We cannot interact. Only observe.)

"Who are they?" The couple must be important or the dragon wouldn't have brought him to this place and time.

(The woman is your mother.)

"Mamam?" Jack dredged up a baby memory of the name he called her. He took a step as if to follow her. His body didn't seem to move. "My mother is a Rover? But Rovers keep their children, even half-breeds and orphans. I was abandoned at the poorhouse." Confusion dominated the churning emotions within him.

(Observe her past. You are not yet born in this time frame.)

"Does she have a name?" Anger and curiosity warred within Jack. Mamam looked so very beautiful. He'd been deprived of that beauty, and her love, all his life.

She had abandoned her infant son! He tried to keep his anger dominant and failed. She was so beautiful.

(Her father is Zolltarn. He named her Kestra for the kahmsin eaglet he spotted at the moment of her birth.)

"Kestra." Memories began to tickle Jack's mind. He knew that name. Somewhere he'd heard of a missing Kestra and her mythical child. Was he the lost child the Rovers searched for through all the lands?

The scene changed before Jack's eyes. The road twisted and dipped into the deep shadow of trees. His ghostly senses allowed him to see the shapes of hidden men within the darkness. Men who killed for pleasure and for the few small treasures carried by travelers.

Bandits were rare in Coronnan. Travelers, the natural prey of the lawless, were almost as rare. After the Great Wars of Disruption, villagers retained their suspicion of strangers and fears of marauding armies. Merchants passed from city to city, stronghold to village, in large caravans. Other citizens remained home, where they belonged.

Where had these desperate men come from?

(Hanassa,) the dragon answered him. *(These outlaws know the magic border is already crumbling in this remote sector. The Commune is not yet aware of how far or fast their magic decays.*

(Nestled in the mountains is the deep caldera of an extinct volcano. Lava tube tunnels and secret pathways lead into this hidden city. Exiled magicians, outlaws, and mercenaries live there and watch all three kingdoms for signs of weakness. Outsiders are not allowed in or out of the stronghold alive.)

The name of the forbidden city struck dread in Jack's heart. Legends of the harsh life there and the cruelties of its inhabitants were the stuff of nightmares.

His nightmares.

Sometime in the past he'd been there.

The bandits raised a thin rope across the road. The Rover steed stumbled to his knees, twisting and bucking wildly to recover his balance. Kestra fell to the ground, rolling, instinctively protecting her belly.

Unable to aid the woman his heart reached out to, Jack watched helplessly as the bandits pulled Kestra's man from the steed and slit his throat. His pockets and saddlebags were emptied before he was fully dead. Three men wrestled the girl to the ground and mounted her again and again, barely waiting for a comrade to finish before the next took his turn.

Kestra lay there, barely moving, not fighting lest her struggles lead to her death. Tears streamed down her face.

Disgust boiled in Jack's stomach as pain choked his throat and brought unwanted tears to his eyes. Despair made the air, his life and his body too heavy to manage.

"Which of the bastards is my father?"

Even as he spoke the words, the bandits carried Kestra off into the woods and across the already crumbling border, leaving her Rover guardian and the magnificent steed gutted in the middle of the road.

(None of them. She was pregnant before she left Coronnan City.)

Jack looked back at the dragon/man. Hope lifted his chin and his spirits.

"Who? The dead Rover there?"

(No. She was ordered to lay with a great magician. The child was to give the tribe the magical power to open the border for the Rovers. They still seek that child.)

"Zolltarn is my grandfather. My grandfather still lives! What about my father. Who is my father?" Jack tried to grab the dragon/man's shoulders and shake the information out of him. His hands slipped through air rather than touching solid flesh.

An aura of sadness clung to the old man. His eyes closed heavily. His long white mustaches dropped into this limp beard. *(You have much to learn before you can know your father. When the time is right, you will be able to look within your heart for the answers you seek.)*

Chapter 24

Jack awoke to the predawn twitter of birds. The air around him smelled damp and chill. But he was warm and dry, his head pillowed on the foreleg of a dragon. A wide blue-tipped wing covered him better than any woven blanket.

He opened one eye to find the probing depths of a dragon eye staring at him.

(You slept well?)

"Yes, yes, I did," Jack replied, surprised to find his body free of stiffness and chill and his mind refreshed by deep, dreamless sleep.

A thousand questions assaulted his mind as he huddled next to the dragon for warmth. "Why do Zolltarn and the Rovers still seek the missing child of Kestra?" he asked the dragon. The magic border had totally disintegrated the moment Krej ensorcelled Shayla into a glass sculpture. When Jaylor had released Shayla from her prison, she had left Coronnan because Krej was still a power to be reckoned with on the Council of Provinces. The Commune hadn't been able to restore the border since. Rovers could come and go without Kestra's child to break down the magical barrier.

(Rovers keep their own close. No one within the tribe is abandoned, exiled, or orphaned.) The dragon answered.

"So how did I end up in the poorhouse as a toddler— maybe as old as three or five? Why wasn't Kestra rescued?"

(Zolltarn was told that his daughter died after the attack. He mourned her but didn't have the heart to seek further news. Yet rumors of the child persisted. Zolltarn seeks to keep Rover magic within his Rover tribe.)

"Those years in Hanassa must have been hell for my mother."

(Kestra escaped through trickery. She fled with you into the teeth of a wicked storm. Merchants found her frozen to death on the road. You were still alive, sheltered by her dead body. They took you to Coronnan City, to the poorhouse, where you were cared for until you were big enough to work in the University kitchens. The merchants guessed you to be about a year old, based upon your size and inability—or unwillingness—to communicate. In truth, you were nearly four.)

Now Jack couldn't banish the memories of cold and fear, of loneliness and bewilderment that his mother wouldn't wake up and feed him. Grief clogged his eyes and his throat. "She did love me!" he asserted. "She must have loved me to give up her life protecting me." Anyone could love a baby. Who cared for Jack as a boy and a man? Now that Brevelan and Jaylor were gone, he had no one except for Fraank's reluctant companionship and a cranky jackdaw who acted as a familiar only when the bird chose.

Shadows flickered across the dragon's eyes. Jack closed his own sight away from the shifting points of light lest he be enticed into another dragon-dream. The vision of his mother had shaken him more than he thought possible. For a few brief seconds he'd experienced a moment of kinship with her, a rarity in his lonely life.

He'd been abandoned again when Baamin died. The old man had given up on life too easily. Had Kestra given up rather than face the memories of rape and despair?

"I guess I'd better find Zolltarn when I've finished the healing spell." He resigned himself to facing the wily Rover.

(The Rovers will keep you with them, bind you to their cause, but you will never be fully a member of the tribe.) The dragon appeared suddenly alert. His wings spread slightly, almost protectively over Jack. *(You have not been raised to their ways. The* geas *they will impose on you to keep you close will resemble the magic poison in Shayla that keeps her prisoner in this valley. A beautiful prison with ample food and space to breed, but she is chained here by pain and coercion, like a slave.)* The blue-tipped horns above the dragon's eye ridges seemed to glow in the dark-

ness. Unnatural blue sparks flared from each of his spines and wing veins.

"I have known slavery," Jack mused. "I will never succumb to that evil again. Nor will I allow another to. At dawn I will do my best to heal Shayla no matter the cost."

(You may need more strength and wisdom than you are able to give.)

"I'd rather die trying to help Shayla than be a slave again," Jack resolved. "Shayla's health and well-being affect more people that I ever will. Who will miss me if I give my all to this spell?"

(The time has come for you to descend to the lair. Eat and drink well, for you will need all of your strength, and mine as well to throw the necessary magic.)

"I can't gather dragon magic," Jack replied sadly. That inability had caused him to be rejected and shunned at the University. Because he couldn't gather the ethereal component of magic he had been considered retarded, denied any rights, even the right to a name. He saw that, too, as a form of slavery.

The nameless dragon lifted one eye ridge in silent query. For a moment he looked just like the cranky jackdaw when he lifted those odd white feathers above his eyes, or like Old Baamin cocking a bushy eyebrow at an errant apprentice. Jack dismissed the image as he took the first steps down the almost visible staircase.

Jack paused, one foot extended toward the first step down. "Why didn't Shayla or one of the other males give Simeon a dragon-dream to lead him astray?"

(He is immune to the visions we weave, as are all descendants of Hanassa.)

"Simeon was born in Hanassa, son of the exiled princess of Rossemeyer," Jack sighed. He'd been born in Hanassa, too. Why wasn't he immune? His Rover blood perhaps?

The dragon didn't offer any more explanation.

"Shayla must be able to fly away before the next solstice." Jack recognized the growing need within him to confront the power-hungry king who had brought so much pain and suffering to the Three Kingdoms. "I will deal with The Simeon when I have healed Shayla and seen her safely home," he promised himself.

Halfway down the stairs, a sense of vertigo overtook him.

The smell of woodsmoke on the wind and the rising sun over hilltops dumped him back into the dragon-dream he had experienced three years ago, the first time he had met the unnamed blue-tip. He sniffed the air, agitated that the fire might sweep down Shayla's valley and destroy her refuge as well as the pristine beauty of the place.

"I have been here before. In my first dragon-dream."

('Tis friendly fire.)

"Friendly?"

('Tisn't wild.) The chuckle behind the mental voice stopped Jack more than the command.

"Explain, please." Jack continued to stare out across the hills, seeking the source of the fire and the presence of the strangers who approached.

(Villagers slash and burn to clear fields for planting. Not the most efficient means, but all they know. They defy The Simeon's policy of exploiting the land for export. That way leads to starvation for all—human, animal, and plant life. These people begin to work the land, to nourish it with crops and with their toil. A friendly fire can be the beginning of life.)

"Margit! Damn it, girl, where are you hiding?" Darville yelled as he carried Mikka to their bed. "Margit!"

Mikka moaned and clutched her belly.

"Easy, my love. I'm getting help."

"Why now?" Mikka sobbed. "Why must I lose the baby now. I carried her so long, nearly five moons." She clung to her husband, not letting him leave her on the bed.

"Margit!" Darville gently disengaged Mikka's hands where they clutched his tunic. He rubbed at the raw wound in his left arm, newly aggravated by carrying Mikka from her solar where she had collapsed in a pool of pain and blood.

A sneeze betrayed Margit's arrival before she spoke. The only time the girl didn't sneeze was when she was out of doors.

"Yes, Your Grace?" Margit dipped a curtsy as she skidded to a halt in the doorway. She breathed heavily as if she had run from the cellars.

"Summon Jaylor and Brevelan. We need them now.

Hurry, girl." He shoved her toward the alcove where she slept.

"What? What am I supposed to do?" She turned big innocent eyes on him, gray-blue and wide as the Great Bay.

"I haven't time for your deceptions, Margit. I know you are Jaylor's apprentice and summon him on a regular basis. Now do it again. We need Brevelan here. The queen will lose the baby if she doesn't get here quickly."

"How'd you know, sir?" Margit asked as she fumbled with a firestick to light the candle. Frustrated by her hurry, she snapped her fingers and brought flame to the wick.

"I've been dodging Jaylor's tricks and magical pranks since I was fourteen. I knew he had a spy around somewhere. You're the most logical person."

"Yes, sir." She closed her eyes a moment. When she opened them again, they were slightly glazed, looking through her tiny shard of glass into far distances.

"Darville, she mustn't. It's not safe for Brevelan to come," Mikka protested weakly from the center of the bed. Her face had no more color in it than the white pillow slips.

"I don't care. Brevelan is the only healer I trust to help you. If anyone can save you and the baby, 'tis her." He didn't dare think about the possibility someone had slipped her another abortive, deliberately murdering their baby.

"Shayla, can your brats . . . um . . . children sing?" Jack gently pushed an inquisitive green-tipped youngster away from his pack. The dragon extended his lower jaw in a good imitation of a pout.

As fast as he separated one baby dragon from the packs, another breathed fire on the coals and burned the warming remains of last night's dinner. One of the purple-tipped dragonets scooped up a mouthful of water from the chuckling stream that ran through the cave, and sprayed it over the now blazing fire.

Jack nudged the helpful baby aside with his knee. A curious sensation of affection spread through him at the brief touch. He dismissed it. The dragonets were cute.

Then he fished the soggy, charred meat out of the coals, wondering just how hungry he really was.

(Sing? Why do you wish the children to sing?) Shayla

spread her undamaged wing in a gesture to gather the dozen curious youngsters to her. The females and the shy purples came readily to her side. The more aggressive males lingered around the fire, packs, and pallets.

A sharp, high-pitched command, almost above human hearing, from the mother dragon sent the reluctant children scuttling to her.

Jack almost heard the order to behave in the back of his head. He pushed aside the compulsion to join the baby dragons under Shayla's wing. Another directive from Shayla nearly sent him outside with the dragonets for the morning's hunt.

Only one purple-tip remained, hidden behind his mother's flank.

(Why do you wish my brats to sing?) Shayla captured his gaze with her compelling jeweled eyes. No rancor dwelled within the sparkling facets, only a mother's good humor.

"The only healing spell I know is the one Brevelan used on Darville. *Song* is her medium. I was hoping the little ones could aid in the spell by carrying the harmony."

(Alas, dragon songs are not for human ears. Your hearing would shatter should they lift their voices and they are not yet old enough to control communication between minds. However, you should be able to gather a little extra magic from this one.) With her muzzle, she nudged the shy youngster crouched behind her. The purple-tip dug in his claws and refused to budge.

"Let him stay hidden, Shayla. I can't gather dragon magic."

(Anyone can gather magic from a purple-tip, boy. Even you!) the unnamed blue-tip bellowed into Jack's mental ears. *(That's why they are so rare and only one lives to adulthood. The fate of our two has not yet been determined.)*

Jack cocked his head skeptically, staring at the shy dragonet. "Can I really?"

The baby dragon inched forward with more prodding from his mother. Jack reached out to gently pet the sensitive knob of his unformed spiral horn in the middle of his forehead.

(Amaranth,) the baby dragon nearly purred with pleasure.

Faint traces of power tingled beneath Jack's fingertips. Just like tapping a ley line!

"How much magic can I take from Amaranth without damaging him?"

(*As much as you can. You will not damage him. However, he is only a baby and you have no other magician to combine with you. You must remain in physical contact with him at all times during the spell,*) Shayla informed him.

"I'll take whatever help I can get."

"I used to be considered a decent tenor." Fraank roused from his pallet. A coughing fit overtook him. He rolled to his knees, slumping forward weakly until the racking spasms passed.

"Think you can support a note for the duration of a spell?" Jack asked skeptically. He waited for a reply that didn't come.

Fraank hung weakly in his kneeling position, drenched in cold sweat, panting for breath.

"When this spasm passes," he gasped, still too weak to stand.

"What about your mates?" Jack asked Shayla, not willing to accept Fraank's offer.

(*They may listen and try to support your* Song. *Human music is not a dragon talent.*)

Jack hastily swallowed a few more bites of his breakfast for fuel. Surprisingly, the meal wasn't ruined. He ate some more and washed it down with fresh, cold spring water and added a handful of dried fruit from his pack.

"Let's get started," he announced loudly, hoping a few of the male dragons might be listening. If they could harmonize at all, they'd help.

He knelt beside Shayla, touching her damaged wing with his left hand while his right arm draped around Amaranth's neck. A first deep breath cleared Jack's mind. The second breath on three counts sharpened his vision and brought out the auras surrounding everything within the cave, animate, plant, and mineral. The third breath triggered his trance and gave him access to the void.

Awareness of sight and sound, place and time faded. Only Shayla existed with him. She entered his mind, he became the dragon, they melded into one being, one knowledge, one soul. The horrible burning wound engulfed them both.

After the first jolt of sharp pain, awareness of the wound receded to a constant throbbing burn.

Jack sounded a deep note to counteract the hot ache and residual dull misery left by Simeon's evil.

A major fifth above the first note centered the black pain to a single location in his left arm. No longer did it radiate and infect his entire body.

Behind, above, and within him a second voice found the tenor note above his bass. Yet another male voice brought in the harmonic third.

A distant memory of Brevelan's clear soprano soaring through a melody lighted within Jack. He echoed the *Song* in his own vocal range.

The tune slid around and under the black burn, encapsulating it in magic. The wound lifted clear of delicate wing membranes, a visible entity pulsing and angry, yet contained by the magic of the *Song*. The wound sought to break free of the spell, sending new roots toward the dragon wing. Jack pushed it farther away, commanding it to dissolve. It resisted and drained strength from the *Singers*.

Jack fought the urge to collapse and forget his spell. He drew strength from Amaranth. He pushed on the living entity that sought to return to Shayla's wing, the source of its nourishment. A new root snaked free of the magic. He needed to send the blackness back into the void from whence it came.

He pushed harder with Amaranth's help.

The tenor notes cracked in a sputtering cough.

The second bass soared upward, beyond human hearing trying to compensate with a winding harmony. The ear-splitting shriek of a dragon voice *Singing* shattered Jack's concentration. Amaranth broke free of his touch.

Jack fell, fell, fell, away from the void, out of unity with Shayla, back into his shuddering body. Shaking hands covered his ears in a futile attempt to shut out the new pain in his physical ears. He rolled into a fetal ball.

Blackness descended upon him as the black wound crashed back into Shayla's wing.

He had failed.

Chapter 25

Jaylor and Brevelan crept quietly along the dank tunnels beneath Palace Reveta Tristile. Jaylor brought a ball of witchlight to his right hand. His twisted staff, held in his dominant left hand, hummed quietly. Wariness crawled along his spine like a swarm of dormant bees—ready to turn violent at any wrong move.

Brevelan inched behind him, drawing her shawl closer around her shoulders against the chill, subterranean dampness. Both of them stretched their senses for the presence of Council guards or witch-sniffers who might reawaken the zeal of the Gnostic Utilitarians.

"Mikka needs us. We have to hurry." Brevelan strode forward, ahead of the witchlight and Jaylor's protection.

"Slow down, Brevelan. Are you sure the transport spell didn't hurt you or the baby?"

"I'm fine. Now hurry. I sense her pain." She grabbed the witchlight from him and stepped forward with a determination that shouldn't have surprised Jaylor.

He shook his head in bewilderment. Only a true emergency would pry Brevelan away from the clearing and her two sons. She wouldn't move when he believed their secret location compromised. But Mikka's health demanded her immediate attention.

Three determined apprentices watched Glendon and Lukan back at the University. Hopefully the apprentices wouldn't have to call in reinforcements to keep the boys under control and within the confines of the apprentice dormitory.

Jaylor gestured silently at a branch in the tunnel; their pathway lay to the right.

None of the ever-present algae marred the stone steps leading up to the hidden doorway behind a wardrobe cabinet. Recently scrubbed or well used? Since his teenage escapades with Jaylor's band of renegade town boys, Darville had been one to seek regular and anonymous escape from his royal duties. The tunnels had provided him with easy exits from almost every part of the palace.

How did the king pass unnoticed among his people now, with his damaged left arm in a sling?

Three raps on the thick door with the butt of Jaylor's staff, followed by two more short knocks, signaled their arrival. Only a few moments had passed since Margit had summoned them. A few desperate words, then she'd broken the communication to help the queen.

The heavy wood portal slid aside slowly and silently. Jaylor hesitated before stepping through the portal. No friendly face greeted him.

"Go on, Jaylor." Brevelan pushed him through the small opening. "I can't sense Mikka's emotions, only Darville's."

Cautiously Jaylor poked his nose through the opening, ready to duck beneath his armor should any menace greet him.

"At last!" A very pale Margit grabbed his arm and pulled him through the tangle of gowns and scarves that cluttered the cabinet. Worry creased her brow.

Jaylor turned back to give Brevelan assistance through the wardrobe. The presence of twins in her womb made her bulkier and more awkward than usual.

His eyes sought Mikka and Darville as soon as Brevelan planted both feet on the carpeted floor. Mikka lay on the bed, pale and unmoving. Darville knelt beside her, holding her hand as if he could will his strength into her.

The queen's rich gown of rusty-brown silk revealed only the barest traces of the baby she had carried almost five full moons. The neckline dipped considerably lower than most thought modest, almost to the nipples. She was so proud of her pregnancy, she had reverted to the fashion of her home country, Rossemeyer. Among the desert dwellers who knew death's constant presence, a woman's breasts were considered a symbol of life. Mothers were granted the privilege of exposing their bosoms.

"At last. Brevelan, you've got to do something. Save her.

Please!" Darville released his wife's hand and began pacing around the bed with his characteristic restlessness. His golden aura spread outward, swirling with the red and indigo of suppressed energy and serious thought.

Jaylor retracted his armor a little at a time while he watched Darville. Brevelan opened her satchel before she reached Mikka's side.

"Hot water, Margit. Fresh linens, and bowls to mix some potions. This isn't going to be easy. Maybe you'd be more useful keeping inquisitive courtiers out," Brevelan said to the maid. She rolled up her sleeves as she took Mikka's wrist, examining her pulse.

Margit left quickly, with a sigh of relief.

"She's afraid of cats," Jaylor whispered to Darville.

Concern shadowed Brevelan's eyes. She looked up at Jaylor and gestured for him to take Darville away.

"We're in the way, Roy." He guided his reluctant friend into the anteroom. Only Fred waited there, standing guard by the door. "Leave us, Fred. And keep everyone away. The king and queen need privacy."

The sergeant nodded and retreated. Quickly he brushed tears from his eyes before closing the door behind him.

"About time you two showed up," the king muttered. "I think someone poisoned Mikka to make her miscarry." The black linen sling, dyed to match his clothing, hung limply about his neck. Over the last three years, the support for his injured arm had become an accepted part of his wardrobe, almost a badge of honor. The constant pain had taken its toll on Darville. Much of his joy in living had faded. He no longer resembled the bouncy young wolf Brevelan had rescued from a snowstorm. He had become an impatient, prematurely old king.

"Who would do such a heinous thing?" Jaylor asked. Immediately his armor snapped into place. He lowered it deliberately to allow his TrueSight to seek traces of an alien presence.

"I don't know! Margit found traces of an abortive in her porridge a few days ago. Everything she eats is tested before she puts it into her mouth." Darville ran his hand through his mane of golden hair, forcing himself to deliberate calm. "We had word of a Gnul plot. I thought we'd taken care of them."

"The coven also has access to obscure poisons." Jaylor decided the rest of that story could wait.

Silence hovered between the men. The easy silence of long friendship. Even after three years of separation, the old companionship bound them together.

Darville flexed and moved his injured arm stiffly up and down, trying to restore movement and circulation.

"Sit down, Roy. You're making me nervous. I'll get you some wine." Jaylor pushed his friend into the nearest chair.

"No. I need all my wits about me. This isn't the first miscarriage. But this one is more dangerous. She hasn't been well." He ran his hands through his hair again. They met resistance at his queue restraint. He ripped it off and flung it into a corner.

"I've had reports." Jaylor handed him a cup of wine. "Drink. You aren't helping Mikka when you're near to hysterics."

Darville sipped at the cup and put it aside. He returned to rubbing his arm.

"Does it itch?" Jaylor asked. "That's usually a sign of healing."

"I irritated it carrying Mikka in here from the solar. Fortunately she was alone. None of her women will summon a mundane healer or the Council until I order it."

"Let me look. Maybe I can ease the discomfort a little." Jaylor rolled up Darville's sleeve, being careful not to brush the black wound with the fabric. He focused his sight beyond sight onto the twisted black wound. A vibrant tingling and disorientation swamped his senses. In the distance, a soft echo of one of Brevelan's healing *Songs* teased his hearing.

The difference between this *Song* and the one brewing in the royal bedchamber bothered him. Deeper, less certain. What was happening?

"What are you doing?" Darville stared at the burn that snaked up his arm, almost from wrist to elbow. "I feel weird, something akin to when you used to transform me back and forth between man and wolf." The king rested his head on the back of the chair.

Jaylor's eyes lost focus. He closed them and shook his head clear of the dizziness. He looked again at Darville's wound. The blackness lifted several finger-lengths above the level of his arm. It shifted and writhed within some kind of barrier. Slender rootlets stretched out toward the living tissue it fed on. Some broke off and dissolved in the air. One, thicker and stronger than the others, almost touched the arm before quickly withdrawing into the black mass.

"What's happening?" Darville stared at the raw muscle on his arm where the wound had resided for three years.

"I don't know. Don't move." Jaylor pushed at the blackness with his finger. An envelope of magic pushed back.

A scream knifed through his mind and his ears. The blackness dropped back onto Darville's arm.

"Mikka!" The king was halfway to the door before he doubled over in pain.

"Not Mikka." Jaylor supported his friend back to the chair.

Brevelan appeared in the doorway. Her eyes asked her questions.

Jaylor shrugged his answer.

"Mikka?" Darville looked up from his deep contemplation of the wound that had become a part of him.

Brevelan shook her head. "I can't save the baby. If we're lucky, she'll recover." Her jaw clenched and released.

Jaylor watched her effort to control her emotions. Death always robbed her of vitality. He worried that the death of Mikka's child might affect the unborn twins.

"You're healing, Darville! Thank the Stargods for some good news." Brevelan rushed to his side and grabbed his arm.

The king winced and jerked his arm back.

"Not completely," he said through gritted teeth.

"But it is better," Brevelan said. "The wound is smaller, the edges ragged as if scabs had begun to peel away. Is this tender?" Brevelan touched some pink and healthy skin right next to the blackness.

Hope blossomed in Jaylor's chest. If Darville's wound healed, what was happening to Shayla?

Darville fidgeted as if he needed to continue his wolflike prowl. He kept looking toward the inner room, toward Mikka.

"Stand still, Darville," Brevelan commanded in the same voice she used on her young sons—the same voice she had

used to order Darville about when he was enchanted into
the body of a golden wolf.

"That still hurts, Brevelan." The king grinned weakly in
acknowledgment of her authority.

Jaylor peered over his wife's shoulder to examine the
evidence of healing. His extended senses caught a scent of
rotten magic beneath a clean aroma of growth. So different
from the whiff of magic-gone-awry coming from the bedroom.

"The strangest sensation came over me." Darville flexed
his arm once more and resumed his pacing.

Jaylor propped up the door with his back, his staff at
hand, ready to focus any spell he might need to throw in
a hurry if anyone else responded to the unnatural scream.

"Then my arm stopped aching," Darville continued.
"That was really weird, suddenly losing the pain after all
these years. I almost missed it. It's become so much a part
of me. . . ." The king's gaze drifted toward his bedroom
and his wife. Then he frowned in worry.

"Evidence suggests you got caught up in a magic spell
directed at someone else. I wonder who? And where?"
Jaylor moved to a small writing table and pulled out his
glass. "Shayla is linked to that wound. I need to know if
my journeymen found her."

Darville stared at the injured limb again. "Shouldn't you
be with Mikka?" He looked from Brevelan to the inner
room once more. Then he stepped decisively through the
doorway.

"The wound is smaller, Darville. Not all of it returned
to you. Whatever dissolved is gone for good," Brevelan
said as she followed him back to the bed where Mikka lay
pale and thin. "It's possible that the brief removal of the
poison allowed more healing to take place underneath."

Mikka shifted uneasily. Brevelan shifted, too, as if experi-
encing the same discomfort as the queen. Then her head
came up sharply and she turned her full attention, physical
and empathic, onto Darville.

"Stop looking at me as if I am your patient, Brevelan.
Mikka is the one who needs you." Darville knelt beside
the bed. Mikka reached a hand out to him. He clasped it
gently, kissing her fingertips.

"What happened out there, Darville?" Mikka asked weakly. "What sent Brevelan running to you?"

Mutely, Darville showed her his arm. "We think one of Jaylor's journeymen found Shayla and tried to heal her."

"I've had a sort of message from Yaakke. He'd have the strength and ingenuity to try a healing. I have no idea how to find him, I only know that he lives." Jaylor shook his head in dismay. "I knew I should have gone after Shayla myself."

Brevelan shot him a wrathful glance. He didn't pursue the subject.

"You have to locate the boy." Mikka turned her face away from her husband. A single tear trickled down her cheek. "We have to help him." She rolled to her side painfully, and curled into a ball. "So Darville can be well. So we can . . . I must . . ." She stopped abruptly. Tears choked her.

"Mikka!" Darville gathered her into his arms, heedless of his still painful wound. She buried her face in her husband's tunic. A brief shudder of her shoulders and a quiet sob betrayed her tears. When she finally turned her face back to Brevelan, she was calm and her tears dried. "I have to know, has the poison in Darville's blood affected our babies?"

"I don't think so." Brevelan's hand began a rhythmic rubbing of her belly, as if the babes she carried had become unusually active.

"Is it the black magic in my body that kills our children?" the king reiterated the question.

Jaylor stood back to study their auras while Brevelan asked more personal questions about the nature of the previous miscarriages. His vision clouded a moment as he thanked the Stargods for both his sons.

Sadness and love for Darville and Mikka threatened to dissolve his objectivity. Images of him and Darville working together, laughing together, playing together slid around his control.

He brought clarity back to his magic sight and found Darville's aura. The layers of colors were familiar, healthy but for the one black spot on the left side. The evidence of Janataea's malice was reduced in size and intensity.

Mikka's aura bothered him. Double layers represented herself and the cat spirit who had shared her body for over three years. The joining of the two souls was an unexpected side effect of a major spell thrown that fateful autumn of Darville's coronation. At the time, Mikka's two auras were distinct with separate layers and colors reflecting two individual personalities. Now the edges were blurred and blending together.

" 'Tis not the magic in Darville that hinders the growth of your babes in the womb," Brevelan said quietly.

"No, please, no!" Mikka cried.

Jaylor caught Darville's gaze as he stroked Mikka's unbound hair. The two men nodded to each other in acceptance of the inevitable.

"Do you wish the truth, Mikka?" Brevelan asked. "Or do you need to wait until you are stronger?"

Darville brought Mikka's right hand to his lips. "I love you, Mikka. No matter the cause, I would never do anything to hurt you. We have to know the truth if we are ever to overcome it."

She nodded, once more the proud, decisive queen. Only the paleness of her face against the pillows betrayed her physical weakness.

"The presence of the cat in your body, Mikka, interferes with your natural rhythms and humors. You cannot achieve the balance necessary to nurture a babe until you are separated from the cat," Brevelan said sadly.

"Then you must force the cat out of me. You had to leave the capital too quickly three years ago when it happened. You must do it now."

"The cat will not leave you willingly, even if I can find a host body for it. The two of you are bound together in an intricate interdependence," Jaylor protested.

"Do it, Jaylor!" Mikka demanded. "I don't want to share this body with anyone but my children."

"I will need time to research the spells and find a host body. I'll have to find Zolltarn, because he directed the original binding spell. You need to rest and recover your strength. Think about this decision for a time, Mikka. It may cost you your life."

"Then my husband will be free to find a new wife to bear him the heirs necessary to secure the peaceful succession of

he dragon crown. We cannot allow Coronnan to be thrown
nto civil war again for lack of a clear succession."

"No, Mikka. I can't allow you to risk your life. There
nust be another way," Darville protested.

"Who will give you an heir?" Mikka asked. "Who in
our family line but Lord Andrall's retarded son is left
live with royal de Draconis blood? Do you honestly want
Rejiia, Krej's daughter, to rule after you?"

They both looked at Brevelan and Jaylor. Darville
nouthed a name: "Glendon."

Numbness spread from Jaylor's gut to his head. How
ould Darville even think of Glendon as his heir? "No. Oh
lease don't ask this, Darville," he muttered over and over,
haking his head.

"My son is not your heir, Darville." Brevelan stiffened.
'I will never give him to you."

"You have proof that Jaylor is the boy's father?" Darville challenged her with equal stiffness.

"You will never take my son from me, Darville. Not you.
Not your Council. Not anyone." Brevelan marched toward
he wardrobe. She paused and turned to face them, proud
nd defiant. "King Darville, I will take my son to Hanassa
before I allow you to strip him of his magic and turn him
nto a coddled and captive prince."

"We must return to the clearing." Jaylor clasped her
hand in his own. He couldn't believe his friend could ask
such a thing. Even making allowances for Darville's grief,
he didn't think him capable of such a request.

"Is Glendon my son, Brevelan?" Darville demanded.

She stepped into the wardrobe without answering.

"You have another child, Brevelan. You are destined to
bear more. Please, can't you share one little boy with us
who have none?" Mikka pleaded.

Some of his friends' empty pain invaded Jaylor. Darville
and Jaylor had shared their youth and many dangers and
wondrous adventures since. They'd shared Brevelan's bed
on that long summer quest four years ago. They'd risked
their lives for each other and for Coronnan. Could either
of them deny Coronnan an heir because Jaylor loved the
child with hair and eyes as golden as the king's?

"If you can't separate my wife from the cat, Jaylor,
Brevelan, then we need Glendon. The boy should be raised

here, to learn all he'll need to know as the next king o'
Coronnan." Darville reached a plaintive hand towar(
Brevelan.

"No." Brevelan retreated to the tunnels and the rout(
home.

Chapter 26

"Forgive me, Shayla!" Jack lifted his heavy head to plead with the dragon.

(Forgive me, Jack,) the blue-tipped male dragon apologized.

"Sorry, Jack, I couldn't stop coughing," Fraank croaked hoarsely.

Amaranth whined in distress, seeking shelter behind his mother again.

Shayla said nothing. Her steedlike muzzle drooped almost to the floor of the cave. Wings sagging and eyes nearly closed, she swayed and stumbled to retain her balance.

The spell to heal the dragon had failed utterly.

Silence reigned in the lair while Jack continued to crouch, nurturing what little strength he had left.

"Brawck! Strangers come. Strangers come," Corby croaked. He swooped into the cave, circling and flapping in an agitated frenzy. Harsh caws echoed around the lair with penetrating shrillness.

"Where? When?" Jack asked the bird, head throbbing with each new sound. He stuck out his arm, hoping the jackdaw would land and cease his noisy complaints.

Corby dropped beside Jack, pecking anxiously at his clothes. "Brawck. Strangers come. Strangers come," the bird repeated over and over.

(Get up, son!) the blue-tip added his urging to the jackdaw. *(You have only a few hours to get out of the valley!)*

"Who comes?" Jack shook his head to clear it. "Why must I run?" How could he run, as exhausted as he was?

(The agents of Simeon ride this way in haste. They will enslave you again if they find you.)

Lanciar, the spy from the mine, had found reinforcements!

"I can't desert Shayla. They'll hurt her. I have to try to heal her again, so she can escape." Jack rose to his knees. A wave of nausea overtook him. He dropped his head into the cradle of his arms as black spots swam before his eyes. "There is no one else left to do it."

(You cannot heal me while we are within the realm of The Simeon,) Shayla said. Her mental voice was weak with weariness and pain. *(There is not enough magic to support your spell and you do not know how to gather the magic we provide.)*

"I can't leave you here," Jack protested. "If only you could fly to Coronnan. With one strong ley line beneath my feet I could draw enough magic to work the spell."

(You have helped the pain a little. Not enough to allow me to fly.)

"What you need is a patch," Fraank offered.

"A patch?" Hope brightened within Jack. His stomach settled and his vision cleared. "A patch. Something light, but dense so it will float on the air like a kite, but strong enough to support the wing. What can we use?" Mentally he sorted through the contents of the packs they had stolen from the mine storeroom. An extra shirt apiece for himself and Fraank. A rectangle of rough canvas for a tent in rainy weather. Some food and cooking oddments.

"We don't have anything like that with us, Jack," Fraank told him needlessly.

"In the villages we passed through, the women were weaving. If we coat the fabric with a spell to resemble candle wax?" Jack tried picturing the looms and cloth. "Too coarse and loosely woven," he dismissed that idea.

"What you need is a piece of lace," Frank suggested. "Lace made from Tambrin!"

"Tambrin?" Jack's mind sped faster than he heard and comprehended.

"Thread spun from the inner bark of Tambootie seedlings. It's very rare and expensive, but it makes the best lace in the world."

"Tambootie seedlings," Jack groaned. Memories of his triumph at stopping a smuggler's ship full of immature trees weighed heavily on him. He remembered a long conversation with Fraank about the investment syndicate and the seedlings. If the ship had won through to SeLenicca three years ago, then the precious thread, with magic potential imbued in its fibers, would be plentiful now.

But if the ship had won through, Fraank probably wouldn't have gotten into trouble with King Simeon and wound up in the mines beside Jack to give him that precious information now.

(You must travel to Queen's City, Jack,) Shayla ordered. *(There you will find what you need. You will find your destiny. Find it before The Simeon comes again at the Solstice.)*

(She is correct, son. Today the servants of The Simeon come for you, not for Shayla.) The dictatorial tones of the blue-tipped male brooked no argument.

"That's barely two moons from now!" Jack protested anyway. "Fraank and I will need nearly a full moon to get to the city."

"Then you must leave me behind." Fraank straightened his shoulders with pride. His throat convulsed with a suppressed cough. "You'll make the journey in a week or less without me holding you back."

"I can't leave you for Simeon's men to find and enslave again." Jack stumbled to his friend's side.

(We will protect your friend as one of our own.)

"I won't live to see my home again, Jack. We both know I'm dying. You must seek out my daughter, Katrina, when you reach the city. She will help you find the right piece of lace."

"Will she be able to get this Tambrin thread?"

(You must take gold to buy the thread,) Shayla advised.

" 'Twould be easier to transport the trees to Queen's City for spinning than to find gold," Jack muttered.

(Not a bad idea, son,) the blue-tip added with a draconic chuckle. *(But dragons have gold. We treasure it nearly as much as humans do. I will fetch you some from our secret hoard.)*

"I have a name, Master Dragon!" Jack nearly stamped his foot in frustration.

(You chose a name out of legend, the name of a man who saved Coronnan more than once. To use the name 'Yaakke, son of Yaacob the Usurper' you must earn it. Bring back a suitable piece of lace made of Tambrin before midsummer.)

That was why he hadn't dredged his name out of his memory upon first awakening in the mine, nor used it since: he hadn't earned it yet.

Curses on Darville and his queen. They have named my sister's oldest son heir to Coronnan. A proclamation of legitimacy has been dispatched throughout the land. Curiously, the boy is to be left with his mother because of his young age. I wonder if Brevelan and Jaylor are unwilling to give up the child.

The rift in their friendship continues. They cannot join forces against me.

I am next in line to the throne. I must be heir, me or my child. I know the babe I carry is male. If I return to Coronnan and my hideous husband before the birth, Coronnan will be reminded of the true heirs. The people will support me and a child they will come to know over the distant bastard who is rumored to have great magic. Danger lies in the journey so close to my time. If only I had the transport spell!

Simeon has become useless to me. He is obsessed with the little lacemaker. Night and day he plots and schemes for her death, neglecting his royal duties and his place in the coven. If he is not careful, Queen Miranda will awaken from her coma and denounce him.

I have not the time to puzzle over this.

"You cannot forbid me my right to worship in the temple!" Katrina screamed at Owner Brunix. "Even slaves have the right to worship in the temple."

" 'Tis not I who forbids, but King Simeon," Brunix replied. "I have had this day a letter from him. If you leave the confines of this building for any reason, you will be arrested for treason."

"Treason? What am I supposed to have done? All day, every day, I am here, working." She paced a circle around her pillow stand in the center of the owner's private sitting room. Sunlight spilled through the real glass in the skylight. More precious light filtered into the room from the thin slices of mica that covered the windows. "From dawn to sunset, I sit here, making lace. I sit here until my back refuses to straighten and my eyes are full of sand. I work until my hands cramp from holding the bobbins hour after hour. I work here in silence without even a time-honored song to relieve the strain."

"I have not been privileged with the exact charges against you." Brunix's eyes strayed to the nearly finished shawl on Katrina's pillow. "Perhaps your treason has something to do with this?" He lifted the free end of gossamer lace made from silk spun almost as fine as the best linen.

"King Simeon rejected the original shawl as unworthy." Katrina wandered to one of the windows, unconsciously putting distance between herself and the owner. Her owner.

"Yet he offered to forgive your treason and eliminate the restrictions placed upon me in your articles of enslavement if I will give him the original shawl, the pattern, and any copies we have made. I have also had an anonymous offer to purchase the shawl for a vast amount of money."

"What?" Katrina's mind whirled.

The runes! Each symbol told an entire story. Tattia must have woven information into the design, information damaging to the king. She had to find out how to read the ancient language.

How? She couldn't even go to the temple anymore to seek out a priest who could read the strange symbols.

"What is in the shawl, Katrina? I can tell by your eyes that you know something." Brunix closed the distance between them. His tall frame loomed over her. An implied menace rested in his clenched fists.

"I do not know."

"Do not lie to me, Katrina Kaantille." He grabbed her arm and dragged her to the corner window. "Look down there, Katrina. Look at the palace guard who stands watch on my doorstep. His companion stands at the river entrance ready to arrest you on sight. What does Simeon fear from you and the shawl?"

"I . . . do not know." She shrank back from the window lest the guard see her.

"You need not fear him *yet*. I have summoned a band of my relatives and warded the building with Rover symbols. Enemies know better than to violate tribal sanctuary."

"The three yellow feathers tied with black string!" She had noticed the strange adornment hanging over every door on the ground floor yesterday on her way to the temple.

"Tell me what you do know before I summon those guards inside."

"You would lose your best lacemaker and all the designs that are still in my head." She couldn't trust Brunix. His ambitions and resentments ran too deep and complicated. Katrina had no idea if he would use the knowledge of a secret code woven into the original shawl—but not into her new pattern—to help or harm her.

"But if I arrange your death, or turn you over to the king, the ghost of your mother will cease to haunt my factory. The ghost of a suicide always follows blood kin to their death. Without Tattia Kaantille floating through my workroom, I could hire better lacemakers and designers. Her presence frightens off all but the most desperate. I have tolerated the ghost for three years in hopes of possessing you, body and soul." Still holding her arm he captured her mouth in a savage kiss. The heat of his body, the moisture of his mouth and the fierceness of his grasp brought shudders of revulsion to her knees and shoulders.

She wrenched free and turned her back to him. Hastily she wiped her mouth dry. The taste of him lingered.

"Why is it that everyone in your factory has seen the ghost of my mother but me? I have heard she might have been murdered by the palace guard and not committed suicide." Katrina refused to look at him. "Tattia is supposed to haunt me, not your workroom. And yet I am the only person who has not seen or felt her presence. Perhaps she haunts those who enslave me?"

"That, my dear Katrina, is a question only your mother can answer. And perhaps King Simeon. Would you like to ask him about it? Tell me the secret of the shawl!"

Jack stopped off a transport barge cloaked in a delusion of sandy blond hair and watery blue eyes. The few people he'd met on his journey south to Queen's City had taught him early that dark-eyed strangers were not trusted in SeLenicca.

Men who talked to birds weren't trusted either. Corby had instructions to keep his distance on this trek.

Jack had made good time, once he found the River Lenicc. People and goods moved down the river on a daily basis. Hardly anything or anyone moved upriver. Almost as if the waters drained the interior of life along with its soil as it roared to the sea.

No timber remained to hold the soil in place. Without the timber to cut and float down to the capital for sale, the people had no livelihood. They hadn't the knowledge to nurture the cleared land and turn it into crops or pasture land. Only a few had the courage to try.

So Jack joined the flood of people pouring into the capital looking for work, for food, for hope.

The streets and pathways nearest the docks were crowded with swarms of hungry people. Ragged children held up pitifully thin arms, entreating a bit of bread or a coin. Skinny young girls with eyes too large for their faces exposed their breasts in the age-old invitation to sell their bodies in hope of earning enough to keep them alive one more day.

None of them wore lace, wove it, or spun thread. He hadn't time to help all those who tugged at his heart with their pleas.

Swiftly he moved away from the river district and the grasping poor. Two streets inland brought an entirely different scene. Steed-drawn litters moved up and down broad thoroughfares. Elegantly dressed ladies with servants strolled along clean wooden sidewalks. Shops displayed the wealth of the world for sale to the few wealthy nobles.

Jack observed from the shadows. Lace abounded in this district. On clothing, decorating windows, as coin in the shops. All of it was attached to something or someone and none of the pieces was large enough to patch Shayla's wing.

When he looked closely, he realized that large numbers of the people were trading well-used pieces of lace for food. Few others bought or sold any of the bright trinkets or furnishings on display.

He headed uphill toward the palace. Fraank had said the best lace was made in the palace—supervised by the noble ladies of Queen Miranda's court.

Two men wearing the black uniforms of the city watch fell into step behind Jack. His spell of delusion covered only his hair and eyes. He didn't want to waste energy cloaking the rest of his body. What had seemed decent quality clothing in the country was too rough and simple for this wealthy neighborhood.

Too late to change the spell. The guards increased their pace to overtake him.

Jack stopped and turned to face the men. "Good sirs," he greeted them politely. "I've been sent with a message for one of the palace lacemakers. Perhaps you could direct me?" He refrained from tugging his forelock. That subservience seemed out of place.

The black-garbed men halted in confusion.

"Country folk aren't allowed in the palace," the taller of the two guards informed Jack.

"Give us the message and we'll pass it on to the palace guards. They'll see the lady receives your words," the other man added as he eased behind Jack, fingering iron manacles that hung from his belt.

Jack shuddered at the small clinking sounds the chain made with each movement the guard made. He'd had enough of manacles to last two lifetimes.

"I must speak to Mistress Kaantille myself, good sirs." Jack sidestepped to keep both guards and their hideous manacles in view.

"Kaantille!" the tall guard hissed in angry alarm.

"No daughter of a suicide would be allowed in the palace. Her father's a traitor, enslaved for his crimes." The manacles clanked as the shorter guard pulled them free of his belt.

"What kind of criminal are you that you need to speak to *her?*" The tall man tried to capture Jack's wrists.

Jack turned and ran, revulsion deep in his throat. He'd never submit to chains again.

"Stop him!" the short guard yelled brandishing the manacles. "Bring him to the gaol. King Simeon wants to know about anyone who has any connection at all to the Kaantilles."

Chapter 27

No magic sprang to Jack's hands for defense. Without ley lines to augment his natural reserves, his mild delusion took most of his talent. But he couldn't allow himself to be captured and dragged before King Simeon. His quest was too important.

He dropped the delusion that masked his staff. Instinct brought the tool up against the guard's chin with a resounding crack. The stout man staggered backward, fighting for balance and consciousness. Before the staff completed its upward arc, Jack swung it down and around into the tall man's chest.

The guard ducked back from the blow so the staff merely brushed the buttons of his uniform. In return he lashed out with a foot to Jack's groin. Jack deflected the kick into his thigh. Bone-numbing pain sent him staggering backward. His delusion slipped.

The black-clad man gasped and stared at Jack's dark hair and eyes.

"You want street fighting?" Jack ground out between clenched teeth. "I grew up fighting for scraps in alleys!" Almost recovered, Jack took advantage of the man's momentary distraction. He stood from his crouch, bringing the staff upright with him.

Right, left, right, and down he struck the guard. Step by step, Jack pushed the tallest man into a narrow passage between two houses. In the shadowed privacy of a hedge he let his fists fly to jaw and gut. He caught his opponent behind the knee with a foot in a blow meant to damage the hamstring.

In moments the fight was over and Jack was running

back the way he had come. Running toward the river district, where he could blend into the crowd and disappear.

As he rounded a corner, he heard the shorter guard gasp, "A magician! He changed his hair and eye color. A dark-eyed magician. He's the one with the price on his head. After him!"

Jack increased his pace. He elbowed merchants and shoppers aside in his headlong run. His foot caught the support pole of a market booth. Wooden poles and canvas awnings collapsed in the road behind him.

Guards stumbled. Ladies screamed. Men cursed.

Shadows from tall buildings invited Jack. He wrapped the growing darkness around him while he caught his breath. A cough born of mine dust threatened to choke him. He held his breath and melted against a brick wall.

The guards called for other men in black to assist them. A troop of seven stomped down the alley where Jack hid. He willed himself into silent immobility, knowing that color and movement caught the eye. His pursuers passed him by without a glance.

When the city watch turned a corner, Jack drifted away in a new direction. He had three more broad streets to cross before he reached the crowded industrial area. He tried a new delusion. Silver hair, stooped shoulders, a fine green cloak. His staff became a cane to assist his shuffling steps.

None of the agitated citizens looked at him twice. He crossed the first street. Large shops gave way to smaller stores with dwellings atop.

He crossed the second street and caught a glimpse of the marching troop of the city watch, now grown to twelve. He paused to cement the delusion in place.

The dozen men in black turned back onto the same route Jack followed. One man in the lead sniffed right and left, his right arm straight out before him. His nose wrinkled and he tested the air again. "There!" the witch-sniffer cried and pointed. "That old man, he's a magician."

"King Simeon has offered a year's pay for his head. Two years' pay for each of us if we catch him alive!"

Jack dropped the energy-draining delusion and ran.

The crowds increased. Jack found himself pushing and shoving innocent bystanders into the filthy gutters. Footsteps pounded hard behind him. The city watch gained on him. He needed a hiding place.

Large stone factories and warehouses crowded the narrowing streets. Shadows reached out to encircle him. He smelled the damp of the river and the tar used to coat ship hulls. Memories of Coronnan City assaulted and confused him. He stumbled on unfamiliar cobblestones up a curb into a green-painted door.

The latch was open and he fell into a narrow corridor. An unseen hand closed the door firmly behind him.

"A rather unseemly entrance for my new night watchman." An extremely tall and gaunt man dressed in fine black tunic and trews glared at Jack.

"Sorry, sir, I tripped on the curbing. I . . . I thought I was late and ran too fast," Jack stammered. His years as a drudge had taught him to dissemble rather than catch hell for imagined crimes and misdemeanors.

"Well, you are late. And you are short. The Rover chieftain promised me a strong man who could frighten off intruders, thieves, and spies."

Spies and Rovers? Jack wondered what he had stumbled into. Was escape from the city watch worth the risk of an even more dangerous situation?

"Oh, but I am strong, sir," Jack found himself saying. He flexed his arms to show off his muscles. Three years of wielding a sledge hammer had added considerable bulk to his shoulders and chest. "And I know how to fight." To emphasize that point he put on his most intimidating expression and stared into the eyes of his potential employer. Eyes that were as dark as his own and full of Rover deceit.

That boy is here!

I cannot blame the mundanes of the city watch for losing him. He outsmarted me before with his transport spell. Lanciar lost track of him a week ago. How does he find enough magic in this cursed land to support such a spell?

I shall find out. Simeon must be forced to turn his attention to finding the boy. I have not the strength. The babe draws all of my energy and concentration. Perhaps I shall have to force an early birth so that I can devote my time and strength to something else. My father's wife will welcome the opportunity to raise my child in secret exile.

*   *   *

"Do you have a name, young man?" The dark-eyed factory owner asked.

"Jack." He'd learned at least that this was a factory, and rival factory owners had been trying to steal designs from the tall man who bore the heritage of the Rovers in his eyes. Just as Jack did.

"Jack What?" One long sandy-blond eyebrow rose above the dark eyes so that it looked like a sideways question mark.

"Just Jack."

"A bastard, eh." The owner shrugged and led the way down the long corridor. "Here on the ground floor are my offices and the warehouse." He flung open a white-painted, wooden door on the right to reveal crates piled high. The storage area took up most of the building surrounding the stark and utilitarian office. A much wider double door opened from the back of the building directly onto the docks. Six men milled around an open crate while stevedores from a waiting ship lounged upon more crates.

"Why aren't you men at work?" The factory owner's voice dripped disdain for his employees.

"Sorry, Owner Brunix." One nondescript man of middle age separated himself from the others and approached Jack and the owner.

Now Jack had a name to attach to his new employer.

"Sir, this crate is short three reels of lace. That new design you wanted me to check special. It was in with the rest of the shipment yesterday when I packed it. But now it's gone."

"Cursed thieves!" Rage darkened the owner's skin to a dark sunburn. *Too stupid to respect Rover wards!*

The thought leaked through without Jack opening his mind. No further explanation followed the one angry explosion.

Owner Brunix's mind closed up once more. Rover tribes tended to have natural armor around their thoughts. What was so important about the wards that his thoughts leaked out?

So this was a lace factory. Luck or the Stargods had led him to a place to start looking for Mistress Kaantille. Or lacking her, he would have access to the delicate fabric he needed for Shayla.

His eyes searched every corner of the warehouse for clues. When the sealed crates revealed nothing but shadows, he allowed his other senses to open. "Listening" was much harder here, but easier than true magic. He only allowed himself to eavesdrop when he had no other course of action.

The stevedores were laughing among themselves at the free leisure while the warehouse crew puzzled over the theft. The men who worked for Owner Brunix quaked inwardly in fear that they would lose their jobs. Work was hard to come by in SeLenicca. The only alternative to homelessness and starvation was the army. That life might provide a man with food and a tent over his head, but it provided nothing for his family unless they became camp followers. None of these men wanted their wives and daughters in so vulnerable a position that they could fall into the role of prostitute for an entire troop of battle-hardened men.

"I sent word to our chieftain that I needed a night watchman. Someone special who can stop these thefts. That will be your job, Jack." Owner Brunix closed his mouth as tightly as his mind. His eyes, too, searched the cavernous room for unseen thieves. Then his expression softened a little. "I had to fire the last night watchman. He drank and fell asleep once too often. I believe my rivals provided the whiskey."

"Whiskey has never crossed my lips, sir, and probably never will," Jack affirmed. And it hadn't. In Coronnan, the thick, sweet—and potent—beta'arack, distilled from treacle betas in Rossemeyer, was the preferred hard liquor. Grain had more profitable and practical uses in Coronnan—uses like bread and winter feed for cattle; it wasn't wasted on whiskey. Since Queen Mikka from Rossemeyer had married King Darville and increased trade without tariff between the two countries, SeLenese whiskey was much more expensive than beta'arack.

SeLenicca never traded with the desert homeland of Queen Rossemikka, so they wouldn't have beta'arack. Indeed, Queen Mikka's marriage to King Darville had precipitated the war between SeLenicca and Coronnan.

"I have no uses for drunkards, Watchman Jack. Remember that and report to me if anyone offers you a bribe. You," Brunix pointed to the warehouse foreman, "complete the order for that crate with the reserve reels of lace in my office. The rest of you, get back to work!" Brunix turned on his heel and marched out of the warehouse.

Jack followed the owner's rapid steps up a rickety wooden staircase to the first floor. Again he was met with a long narrow corridor running the length of the building. Two doorways on each side broke the bare walls.

"Male employees sleep on the right. The far door is the bath." Brunix gestured to the appropriate door. "Move your things into any empty bunk as soon as we finish this tour of the factory. Be ready to report to work at sunset."

"What are the doorways on the left, sir?" Jack hurried to keep up as they headed for yet another wooden staircase at the opposite end of the building. These steps were in better repair, painted and secured with a smooth railing.

"The women's dormitories." Brunix paused halfway up the stairs. "Flogging and dismissal is the punishment for any man who enters those rooms. Even I must ask permission. Remember that if any of *my* women tempt you."

The possessiveness of the owner's attitude grated on Jack. He wondered if Brunix owned the women like he owned the factory. Suddenly he disliked Brunix. Any sense of kinship he might have felt with his Rover heritage evaporated.

"The workroom is above the dormitories on the second floor. You will patrol this area after the women retire for the night, as part of your rounds. Stay out at all other times. Touching the lace or the patterns is forbidden."

Jack stalled a moment to watch the two dozen women bent over their work stations. He'd seen loom weaving often enough, but this process of moving threads on slender spindles mystified him, defied all logic. Yet the delicate fabric spilling off the bolsters gleamed with life like gossamer strands of magic.

A last ray of setting sun broke through the oiled parchment window coverings. Light set the strands of lace glimmering like moonlight on a dragon wing.

Fraank was right. The patch must be of lace. This wonderful airy fabric seemed akin to Shayla's iridescent membranes.

"Is any of this lace made of Tambrin?" he asked casually. There was enough lace in this room to purchase a kingdom.

"No." Brunix squinted his eyes as if caught in a lie. "Only palace lacemakers are licensed to work with Tambrin. We make lace for export. It needs to be as inexpensive as possible, made with common threads. Palace lace is made for our own nobility and no one else."

If Tambrin added expense and value to lace, the women Jack had seen promenading through the shops each wore a king's ransom on their gowns.

Brunix walked to a woman who sat close to the long row of high windows. In spite of the extra light from the windows, her work space, like all the others, was illumined by a candle lantern at the head of her pillow stand. Brunix examined the length of finished lace as wide as a man's palm. He unrolled at least three arm-lengths from a second, small bolster dangling from the larger workspace.

Owner Brunix produced a pair of scissors from a concealed pocket and snipped the finished length from the roll. "Take this to the foreman and have it added to the shipment going out tonight," he instructed the woman as he pocketed the sharp scissors and returned to Jack.

Together they mounted the last flight of stairs.

"This is my private apartment." Brunix flung wide the door. Brilliant sunlight flooded the room from six standard windows of mica and a skylight of decent-quality glass.

Neither the University nor the palace in Coronnan City boasted a single window with as much glass as that pane. The only bigger piece Jack had seen was the black glass table where the Commune of Magicians used to confer.

"You will have no need to enter these room unless I summon you." Brunix reached to close the door again.

Movement in the corner of the sitting room caught Jack's attention. He willed the door to remain open a moment longer. Brunix seemed to have difficulty pulling the heavy, soundproof panels shut.

A young woman stood up from another workstation set between the windows. Moon-blond hair shone in the setting sun. Delicate fingers caressed a loose bobbin.

Her! The girl of his vision when he was lost in the void.
The girl all grown up into a beautiful woman. The woman
who had haunted his dreams when nothing else was real
during those endless years in the mines.

"Go back to work, Katrina," Brunix admonished. "We
will not disturb you."

"Your wife?" Jack asked still staring at the woman.

"My slave. You are not allowed to speak to her. Ever.
She is mine. Do you understand? MINE!" Brunix finally
managed to close the door, separating Jack from the
woman of his vision, returning him to reality.

Chapter 28

Katrina checked the corridor outside the dormitory for any signs of the new night watchman. She didn't trust this dark-eyed stranger any more than she trusted Owner Neeles Brunix.

Three nights running she had tried to slip up to the workroom when sleep refused to overtake her. Each of those three nights the stranger had appeared at the end of the corridor as if summoned by her presence.

The first night he merely nodded to her, acknowledging her right to be in the building. The second night he'd followed her to the workroom, then returned to wherever he spent the night hours. Last night he'd slipped silently in and out of the room, watching her work for a few moments every hour or so.

Lumbird bumps rose up on her arms as she thought of his ghostly movements through the warehouse. What would he do tonight? Ask for lessons? She shivered in the chill darkness. Why did he watch her so intently?

She refused to admit that each time he left the workroom, a terrible loneliness overcame her. Loneliness worse than that she had endured these last three years.

The corridor and stairway were empty. Soundlessly, and without benefit of a candle, Katrina slipped upstairs. She knew every creak in every unstable board in the building. She'd learned them well in three years. The watchman had learned them in one night.

She needed to lose herself in her work and find a kind of peace. Firestone brought her smokeless work candle to life. The bobbins came readily to hand. She caressed them and hummed lightly to herself. The old work songs sprang to life in her mind. She'd never let them die. In all these years of working in grim silence for Brunix, she'd gone over the songs in her mind, letting the gentle rhythms guide her hands.

Only at night, when she was alone and surrounded by darkness, did she allow herself to voice the words and tunes, very, very quietly. Brunix didn't believe in songs in his factory. Lacemaking was work and song made it seem like play.

The factory owner must know she worked alone at night, for he allowed her to keep a second pillow here in the workroom as long as the work was obscured from view by a large cloth during the day. A good pillow, covered in soft velvet, with bobbins as slender and graceful as the pattern she worked. The lace spilling off the bolster was the first design she'd given him. Other skilled women in the factory also worked the pattern. But they used a fine linen thread suitable for export. Katrina used Tambrin, as the design demanded.

She didn't know how Brunix acquired the thread or who purchased her lace. Did his Rover clan smuggle them in and out of SeLenicca? She didn't want to know, for if the palace ever discovered a factory using Tambrin, the owner would forfeit his license to make any lace at all.

The faintest whisper of sound reached her ears. Her eyes widened in alarm as she searched the shadows for signs of her mother's ghost.

"Don't you ever sleep?" the watchman asked directly behind her.

"Oh!" she gasped a little too loudly. "You frightened me." His presence always startled and intrigued her.

"Sorry, Mistress Kaantille. You are Katrina Kaantille aren't you?"

"I am mistress of nothing. Didn't Brunix tell you I am a slave?"

"He told me. Your father told me you were to be accepted as an apprentice at the palace and allowed to retain the family home. He wouldn't have sold himself to King Simeon otherwise."

"P'pa? You've seen my P'pa?" Wild relief and bitter anger roared through her heart, vying for dominance. Carefully she closed down all those confusing emotions, just as she had numbed herself the night she was forced into the owner's bed.

"Fraank Kaantille sends you his love. He wasn't well enough to come with me, but I'll take you to him when I've finished my mission here in the city."

"Then P'pa survived his years in the slave ships. I wondered if he would return when his servitude ended. That isn't supposed to be for another two years."

"Slave ships? Fraank and I met in the mines. And his sentence was life. If we hadn't escaped, he'd be dead with the mine rot by now. As it is, he's probably dying."

"The mines!" She shuddered. A long and bitter death. In her mind, Fraanken Kaantille had been dead for three years already. The reality of his condition brought new tears and a lump to her throat.

"King Simeon can't be trusted, even with his own laws." Her eyes blurred. Anger, born of three years of bitterness, covered her vision with red mist. Simeon was an outlander, just like Brunix and this new watchman. She couldn't trust any of them.

Neither said anything for a moment. She shouldn't see or speak to this dark-eyed outlander. She ignored the impulse to open her thoughts and emotions to him well beyond the realm of safety.

Katrina bent her head to the pillow, pointedly ending the conversation.

"Is this thread Tambrin?" the watchman changed the subject abruptly. His fingers came close to the finished length of lace, as if to examine it more closely. Then he jerked his hand away.

"What difference does it make?" she returned rather than answer with a lie.

"A great deal of difference if you work at night, in secret, with a thread that is forbidden."

"Hadn't you better go back to your job, guarding the warehouse?" She stared at him, willing him away.

"If you are worried about another theft, don't. No man will get past my . . . er . . . traps."

"You have been forbidden to speak to me. Go back to your work and let me continue with mine."

"Or what? What can you do to me?"

"Report you to Owner Brunix. You will be dismissed, if he doesn't kill you first."

"But I am not a slave he can murder without question. You shouldn't be either. How did this come about?"

"Go!" She couldn't relive that humiliating night when The Simeon gave her a choice between slavery and a torturous ritual. Nor could she allow this outlander to discover all that went on between her and Brunix.

Perhaps he already knew. They were both dark-eyed outlanders. Only Brunix would dare hire another outlander when there were so many true-bloods out of work and homeless.

"Ssshh!" the watchman hissed. He extinguished her candle with a pass of his hand. "Stay here," he said so quietly Katrina wasn't certain she actually heard him or merely understood from the press of his hand against her shoulder.

Jack listened with all of his senses for the faint sound of movement. Nothing. Puzzled, he crept back down the stairs to the warehouse level.

He'd left Corby perched on top of a stack of crates in the corner, a ball of witchlight in front of him to keep the complaining bird awake. If anyone but Jack entered the cavernous room, Corby would set up a fuss loud enough to wake the entire factory.

Corby was quiet. Too quiet. Almost as if he slept. But birds did not sleep in the presence of light and they did not sleep with their heads erect, standing on both feet.

Jack stopped in the doorway, willing himself into invisibility. As his eyes adjusted to the shadows of the warehouse, he opened his senses to alien sensations. His nose itched, as if to sneeze. The scent of magic hovered in the air around him. A very small amount of magic, and it carried the distinctive musky flavor of dragons.

The softest of footfalls behind him brought his hand up to still any further noise from Katrina. His enhanced awareness of the building and all who dwelled within it told him she had followed, even before she descended the first step. He found her mouth with his left hand and gently covered it in a signal of silence.

With another thought, his staff sprang into his hand. Silently he moved into the warehouse, nose alert for a concentration of magic.

Light flared from the end of his staff, illuminating the room in a shadowless light and wrapping armor around Jack. He broadcast a very mild delusion of an ordinary lantern in his hand and another beside Corby. Best not to betray his magic with the obvious witchlight.

Every crate in the warehouse, empty or filled with reels of lace, stood revealed to his sight. Bent over one of them was a man dressed in the dark gray of the palace guard. Gleaming white tendrils of lace spilled from his hands.

Someone too stupid to respect the Rover wards at the doors? Or was he too strong a magician to worry about them?

Startled by the light, the intruder looked up, unblinking in the new brightness. Corby awoke from his trance at the same moment and set up a strident fuss guaranteed to bring Brunix and his burly employees running.

"So, since the queen is ill, has the palace stooped to stealing lace rather than making it?" Jack asked. He couldn't alert this barely talented man to his own magic.

He had to act fast and turn the matter over to Brunix, before his armor faded. Unable to replenish his magic from ley lines or from dragons, he had to rely on his own bodily strength to support his spells. Years of heavy mine work had given him muscles and stamina. These were not infinite.

"I seek a piece of lace more important than any of this paltry export trash. A piece made of Tambrin and designed by that girl's mother!" The magician in gray challenged Jack and Katrina. "King Simeon would give a life's pension for that lace. The coven will give even more!"

"How valuable is a life's pension if my life only lasts a day beyond giving over such a piece of lace—if it exists?" Jack returned.

"The piece exists. We have, this night, captured a Coronnite spy who seeks the same lace. I believe he offered Owner Brunix a great deal of money for it. He won't live until dawn. Our leader has seen the lace in the glass. A magnificent and unique piece."

He'd said *Our Leader,* not *The Simeon.* Interesting.

Katrina said nothing in reply to the man's statement,

which sounded almost like an accusation. But Jack could feel her trembling in fear behind him. She was either very brave to remain there in the face of so much fear, or too stupid to know she could run.

Run where? The thought occurred to Jack that Brunix might not offer her the haven she needed. Her fear of her owner could be as great as her fear of her despotic king.

"I dispute The Simeon's ability to see anything in a magician's viewing glass. Else he'd know his enemy's movements ahead of time and would have conquered them years ago," Jack taunted, hoping the magician would reveal more.

"Simeon does not rule the coven."

"His black-haired mistress!" Katrina spat, coming out of her fear-induced paralysis. "*She* is responsible for Queen Miranda's illness. *She* leads the coven and corrupts the queen's government."

A clatter of footsteps on the stairs signaled the arrival of reinforcements. Good. Jack's reserves were growing thin. He'd held the armor too long after several hours of stretching his awareness far beyond his normal limits.

Corby ceased his noisy fuss and swooped from his high perch to Jack's head. "Nasty man," he quoted. "Dragon man. Nasty man. Not a dragon."

Jack reached up to soothe the bird's feathers. He wished fervently that Corby would learn to keep his thoughts to himself. "Some familiar. You cause more trouble than you help me get out of," he whispered under his breath.

"Trouble, trouble, trouble," Corby repeated.

"What is the meaning of this disturbance?" Brunix burst into the room. He glared fiercely at Katrina. A gesture of his head toward the stairs dismissed her.

His dramatic dressing gown of black and purple draped around his elongated figure, and the arrogant gesture toward Katrina reminded Jack of Zolltarn, the Rover king, dressed in black and purple. Whatever blood kinship Jack might share with the two unscrupulous men, his armor remained firmly in place without conscious reinforcement.

The intruder in the gray of the palace guard seemed to assess the true authority in the factory within a heartbeat. Immediately all of his concentration turned to Brunix.

"I search this factory with a warrant from the king,"

the magician announced. "Rumors of the forbidden use of Tambrin have reached the ears of the palace lacemakers."

"Then search openly and honestly," Brunix defied the man. "I dare you to find anything in this building that is not authorized and approved by the king personally."

Really? Jack wondered. What about the Tambrin on Katrina's pillow? What about the mysterious piece designed by her mother?

Now that Jack had felt Tambrin, he knew he'd never mistake any other fiber for the shimmering white thread that glowed with magic. Katrina's lace sent tingles of power up his arms. His fingers had never made contact with the lace. He didn't need to get any closer to it than a finger-length to recognize the energy stored within the depths of any Tambootie tree. A tree that was poison to mundanes and led magicians into irreversible insanity. Only dragons consumed it with impunity.

Jack faded into the background. Let Brunix and the agent of King Simeon settle the issue of the warrant between themselves.

He found himself standing beside Katrina in the dim hallway. A faint tingle of power pulsed from the ground beneath her feet. He squinted and detected traces of silvery blue. A ley line? Interesting.

He edged closer, seeking the source. The girl or the land?

"Do not touch me!" she hissed so that only he could hear. "You are a *magician*. A dark-eyed magician. I saw the witchlight and your delusion! There cannot be two such as you. 'Twas *you* who interfered with the shipment of Tambootie seedlings. 'Twas *you* who bankrupted my father, killed my sister, and drove my mother to suicide."

Chapter 29

"**D**id King Simeon plant you in this factory to spy on me, to find some new way to torment and destroy me?" Katrina backed away from the magician. The anger and hatred she'd carefully nursed for three years burned cold and clear in her mind.

"The sorcerer-king is more my enemy than yours." He followed her retreat, never allowing more than two steps between them.

"I doubt that. Who has lost more, suffered more at his hands than I?" One step up the stairs. He closed the distance. She could feel the heat of his body, see a pulse beating anxiously in his neck. His pet crow had flown off when Brunix arrived. Now it landed two steps above her. She couldn't retreat much farther without disturbing the noisy bird and drawing more attention to herself.

"The soldiers who die by the dozens, cold and hungry, bogged down in mud up to their knees, with disease plaguing their ranks more than the enemy ever could, have lost as much. That goes for both armies. All because ruining SeLenicca isn't enough. King Simeon has to conquer more."

"We need trade to stay alive. Coronnan is rich with farmland and resources but has repeatedly denied us access to them, even though we pay for them!" The argument was old, repeated often. "Coronnan has to be responsible for the food shortages, the unemployment, the . . ." Her words trailed off.

"SeLenicca could grow its own food, become self-sufficient if Simeon would let you."

"No. 'Twould blaspheme the Stargods. *We* are the Chosen. The resources were provided for us to exploit."

"In Coronnan, we believe ourselves to be the Chosen and our duty is to nurture the land and ourselves, in memory of the bounty bestowed by the Stargods. SeLenicca has been methodically stripped, rather than nourished, for a thousand years. But this political argument doesn't settle the conflict between us. Why do you accuse me of the king's crimes?"

"King Simeon did not stop the shipment that caused P'pa's bankruptcy. You did."

"I stopped a foreign spy from escaping *my* country. A spy who had organized an assassination of my king on the day of his coronation. Would you have done less?"

Katrina had to think about that. Hatred of the man who had caused her poverty, hunger, grief, and humiliation had focused her desire for revenge. In the first years of her slavery, little else had kept her from following her mother into the river. She needed to nurse that hatred back into life. She had nothing, was nothing without it.

"What makes you think Simeon would have allowed your father to profit from that shipment of Tambootie seedlings if it had won through?" He mounted the step to stand beside her. In the cramped space, only a hair's breadth separated them. His quiet words caressed her ear while the closeness of his body threatened her senses as Brunix's lovemaking never could.

"There is only one use for Tambootie. Simeon needed my father to market the fiber for lacemaking."

"Tambootie feeds dragons. Simeon has a small nimbus of dragons to supply magic to the men of his coven. The palace guard arguing with Brunix gathers dragon magic. He admitted to being part of the coven. None of that Tambootie would have been made into thread."

"Dragons? Where?" Fear, or was it the watchman's nearness, sent shivers through her body.

"Your father is protected by the dragons. My quest is to send them home so that Simeon no longer has a source of magic. Without the dragons he can't work his evil on SeLenicca anymore. Without his magic, Queen Miranda will recover."

Jaylor opened the fragile book with tender reverence. How many times had he passed it by in the library of the new University of Magicians? He wondered if he ignored the book just as someone searching for the clearing would walk right past the proper path.

But the crack in the clearing barrier widened daily. Brevelan still refused to move. Jaylor feared that soon an outsider would stumble into the clearing without knowing he shouldn't be able to. An agent of the Gnostic Utilitarian cult would be as happy to find the clearing as to find the hidden University with its priceless library of magic secrets. The Council of Provinces and the coven had been trying to penetrate the Commune's defense of secrecy for years.

Darville knew how to find the clearing. Mikka could open the crack and snatch Glendon away. . . . Jaylor couldn't dwell on that possibility. Fear of losing the boy paralyzed all thought.

The library had grown during these years in exile because a few educated men feared for the safety of their private book collections during the height of the Gnul's fanaticism. The Gnuls didn't believe in learning to read. Since the skill to interpret the marks in books into language had been the exclusive right of magicians for many generations, the cult had decided reading was another form of magic and therefore evil.

Rational men who could not embrace the cult but found it politically expedient not to oppose it had found ways to insure the safety of their collections of books. Secret messengers left bundles of them buried in protective wraps near abandoned Equinox Pylons—festival landmarks that had been revered in Coronnan for so long even the Gnuls would not desecrate them. Only the coven did that.

Jaylor enjoyed quiet time in the library, meditating and planning. Physical and psychic quiet was a rarity in the clearing. Glendon and Lukan didn't believe in quiet, unless they were asleep. Lukan screamed at everything, with delight, anger, or frustration. Glendon tended to blast minds with his telepathic shouts. Anything done quietly, to them, was work. The same task or game completed with as much noise as their two young bodies could muster, was play.

So Jaylor sat quietly in the library and stared at this slim volume that had lain hidden in piles of books, overlooked, pushed aside and forgotten time and again.

"A book that doesn't want to be found might contain a

spell that obscures a place," he mused. "Like the clearing." Since he couldn't persevere against Brevelan and make her move, he had to find a way to heal the barrier. If this book contained the spell that had originally set the protections, he might be able to analyze it and reset it.

Page by page he skimmed the volume. The penmanship flowed with delicate swirls and loops indicative of a feminine hand. An apprentice of old, recording for her teacher and mentor? Or Myrilandel, the fabled wife of the magician who tamed the dragons and the first known inhabitant of the clearing, perhaps?

If he could create his own protective boundary elsewhere, perhaps Brevelan would move and he needn't worry about that damned crack.

"It's worth a try." He ran his finger down a page and stopped on a poem entitled "Invisible Gate."

> *Spirit of air lift me high*
> *With the dragons let me fly.*
> *Protect us with a steady wind*
> *That blows nowhere but here within.*

> *Spirit of fire glowing green*
> *Descend from air and wind unseen.*
> *Heat my heart like purest gold*
> *Cast off dross of lies untold.*

> *Spirit of water, blessedly cool*
> *Drop by drop fill this pool*
> *Refresh my mind from life's pain.*
> *Wash me clean of greed and gain.*

> *Kardia gather with the other three*
> *Root me through a mighty tree.*
> *Anchor me with your knowing love.*
> *Free to choose in the world above.*

> *Altogether, the Gaia you are*
> *bound as one, near and far.*

The poem danced through Jaylor's mind with a familiar lilt. More a song than a chant. The words were similar to

the spells the Rovers had used to bind Jaylor and his fractured magic together long ago, before Darville's wedding
and coronation. Combined with a ritual of candles and
dance, the massive spell had drawn magic from the fabric
of life rather than simply from the planet below or the
dragons above.

"I'm starting to think in song!" he protested to himself.
"Brevelan sings her magic. Krej chanted his spells. There
is power in the music, power in the singer."

A tune he swore he'd never heard before, yet was haunt-
ingly familiar, trilled through his mind as he repeated the
words of the spell. His tongue began to tingle and his feet
vibrated in time with the pulsing life of the land beneath
his feet. Too soon. The song only bound the singer to the
four elements. He needed the spell for the boundary
around the clearing before he unleashed that power.

Carefully he clamped down on his mind and pushed the
humming magic back where it came from, but not so far
away he couldn't tap it again.

He turned the next page of the book and read carefully.
"Six eggs gathered this morning. One-and-a-half buckets
milked from the goat. Strung a line between the lower
limbs of the everblues to hang washing." Jaylor nearly
slammed the book closed. A bloody list of daily chores!

"One more page." Then another, and another all the
way to the end. More lists. The author of this book was
methodical in keeping records. Every person who visited,
every cure dispensed, stores of herbs and catalogs of clothing washed and mended.

Jaylor nearly threw the book down in disgust. "Why do
you work so hard at being ignored?" he asked the hand-
written pages. "Maybe the spell itself is hiding just like the
book. Hiding in an obvious place that I'm sure to overlook."

Carefully he pulled some magic into his eyes and lit his
senses. Looking obliquely for patterns rather than reading
individual words, he thumbed through the book again.

On the next page, the laundry list dissolved into a similar
pattern, revealing words written by magic beneath the mundane chores. The poem leaped out at him.

> *Circles within circles.*
> *Elements combined*
> *Protect from eyes*
> *Of the prying kind.*
> *Keep this place safe for me and mine.*
> *The Gaia's secrets carefully hid*
> *Recited in order from bottom to lid.*

Something of the writer's humor slipped through to Jaylor. With a jaunty air, whistling the tune that bounced from the first poem to his mouth, he returned to the clearing.

Just before the boundary, where the path's perceived direction wound around and around the widening crack, he halted and opened the book to the poem. In his joyful baritone he sang the poem backward, one line at a time—from bottom to lid.

The power of life tingled through his feet to his body core to his limbs and mind, opening every sense and pore to the elements. The boundary appeared before him as a humming wall of swirling metallic colors—copper, silver, gold, lead. In answer to his request, the drifting patterns coalesced and parted into an open gate.

Jaylor stepped through and sang the spell lid to bottom. The gate dissolved behind him and the colors disappeared. He reached out and touched a solid wall, invisible once again to his eyes and his magic. Just to make certain the clearing was once more inviolate, he wiped the spell from his mind and ran his hand along the barrier.

His fist fell through a chink in the wall wider than the crack left by Glendon.

Chapter 30

Jack followed the girl up to the workroom as quickly and as quietly as the rickety planks would allow. The sounds of the argument in the warehouse seemed to be winding down, and he expected the palace magician to come looking at the lace pillows for anything incriminating.

"What is Simeon looking for?" he asked Katrina.

She stared back at him without answering, eyes bewildered and accusing.

He could pluck the answer from her mind. He wouldn't. Not anymore.

"You magicians are all alike. How do I know you aren't in league with Simeon and that man downstairs? How can I trust anything you say?"

"You can't. But by the Stargods I hope you will trust me. Now, is this the only Tambrin in this room?" He gestured to the pillow where she had been singing and working earlier. If only he knew how to give back that joyful song rather than the ingrained bitterness she projected.

The stairs creaked and groaned under the weight of men climbing.

"It's the only piece I know of. I've got to hide it!" She looked anxiously around for concealment. There was only one door in or out of the room and the palace magician would soon block it.

Jack closed his eyes and sent the entire workstation, pillow, frame, stool, and candle deep into the warehouse. The magician wasn't likely to search there again. Corby flew after it. Jack caught an image from the bird's mind of plucking hairs from the magician's head as he swooped past him on the landing.

A screech and a curse confirmed Corby's mischief.

Jack stepped into the place where the pillow had been to disguise the blank spot in the orderly rows of workstations. Tendrils of raw power licked his feet—extensions of the ley lines he'd glimpsed on the ground floor. Katrina's workstation sat directly above them. Again he wondered at the source of regenerating power.

"What did you do?" Katrina gasped.

"I hid the evidence." He smiled and then drew the power into himself and faded into the woodwork. No transport for himself. A little invisibility would allow him to eavesdrop on the magician. The little blue ley lines beneath Katrina's work place fed him all the power he needed.

As an afterthought he drew Katrina into the circle of his spell. *If you move or utter a sound, he'll find us both,* he said into her mind. Then he draped his arm around her shoulders to keep her close and protected—something he'd wanted to do since his vision of a girl with pale, blond hair crying over the loss of her first pillow and bobbins.

Later he'd ask why she'd changed from the distinctive two braids to one.

She squirmed a little under his touch. He increased the pressure of his hand on her shoulder. She stilled, but he sensed her unease.

Filling his physical senses with her scent, her warmth, and the wondrous feel of her body next to his, Jack drew more power into himself in preparation for eavesdropping on the intrusive magician from the palace.

"Search for the Tambrin, search every corner of this building and you will not find any." Brunix threw the door to the room open with an expansive gesture of his long arms.

"Of course I won't find it. Your whore has had plenty of time to hide it." The thin magician sniffed in disdain.

Katrina stiffened beside Jack. He felt her indignation nearly as strong as she. Then her posture wilted in resignation. He pulled her closer, attempting to impart reassurance, respect, whatever emotions she needed right now. She didn't respond.

"You don't search, because Tambrin alone is not what you truly seek." Brunix narrowed his eyes and hunched his shoulders as if he were a vulture examining a particularly tasty morsel.

Jack has seen Zolltarn, king of the Rovers, assume the same pose of intimidation. It usually worked.

"I was sent," the magician leaned closer to Brunix as if imparting a great confidence, "to find a particularly fine piece of lace woven by the late Tattia Kaantille."

Katrina jumped. Jack stilled her movement and wondered at the guilt that seemed to pour out of her.

This was the second time the slightly built man had asked for that piece of lace.

Where is it? Jack whispered into Katrina's mind.

An image of Brunix's private sitting room, a secret wall panel that only the owner could key. The power engulfing Jack was enough that her thoughts flowed easily back into his mind without a conscious probe on his part.

Jack had yet to meet a lock or secret panel that refused his mental touch. He'd find the lace. If it was big enough, it might suffice as a patch for Shayla. Then he could leave this insufferable city and the sly, unreadable factory owner without delay.

He'd also have to leave Katrina. He was fairly certain she would not follow him to Shayla's lair.

You may not have it! Katrina's mind screamed at him.

How could she know he planned to steal it? In opening himself to her thoughts, he must have allowed her free access to his own.

"I know nothing of Tattia Kaantille's work. All of her designs were left at the palace, along with her pillow and bobbins, when she was dismissed by King Simeon," Brunix replied to the magician. His aura shot high white bolts of lightning filled with lies.

The glare from those lies left spots before Jack's physical eyes. He closed off that portion of his magic sight.

"Perhaps you should ask the ghost of Tattia Kaantille. She was a suicide and haunts her daughter here in this workroom," the owner continued.

The magician blanched and searched the shadowy corners for signs of a hovering spirit. His gaze slid over Jack and Katrina as if they weren't there.

"Th . . . there is no ghost here." He shrugged his shoulders as if dismissing his instinctive fear along with the ghost. "When King Simeon gave the girl to you, your duty was to pry her secrets from her. Three years have passed, and the lace is still missing."

"Nothing was said of secrets at the time. I was told to humiliate and frighten her so that she would be ripe for the coven's rituals. You are a member of the king's coven. You must know why he has not had the girl murdered so that her secrets die with her."

"He thought the lace lost with the body of Tattia Kaantille. But the girl wore it not a moon ago, at Princess Jaranda's birthday celebration. He saw it then. I saw it and so did our leader. We won't take action against Katrina Kaantille until the lace is turned over to Simeon or he sees it destroyed."

"If I were married to the girl, she would have the protection of my tribe. The king would not risk the wrath of the Rovers, I think."

"A knife across the throat would kill you as surely as the girl. This factory would then be forfeit and His Majesty could search for the lace at his leisure."

"My premature death would bring Rovers into the city bent on revenge more surely than the death of the girl. No. The king will send his thieves in the dead of night searching for the lace."

"*Where* is the shawl?"

"Only the ghost of Tattia Kaantille knows for sure."

"I . . . I sense no ghost. She isn't here. But she must be here. A suicide always haunts blood kin for five generations." The magician crossed his wrists and flapped in the ancient gesture of warding. Then, against royal policy, he invoked the cross of the Stargods. "With my head and heart and the strength of my shoulders I renounce the evil carried by this ghost." He scuttled out of the room and down the stairs like a beetle frightened by a predatory jackdaw.

Katrina hung her head. One of her tears touched Jack's wrist.

He sent his magic sight all over the room, followed by every sense he could summon. *There are no ghosts here.*

Katrina reared her head back so violently she almost shredded the spell of invisibility. *M'ma must haunt me. She threw herself into the river. Her spirit cannot pass into a new plane of existence until . . .*

I'd know if she were here. There is no trace of a ghost now or the recent past. Perhaps your mother did not suicide.

Katrina was silent a moment while Brunix followed the magician at a more dignified pace. Jack kept her within the private circle of his arms and his spell, marveling at the telepathic rapport he had found with the lacemaker. The intimacy of the moment was deeper and more profound than the lusty satisfaction Rejiia had once offered him.

Perhaps my mother was thrown from the bridge by an agent of her enemy, King Simeon. The spy who dies tonight from torture suspected murder. M'ma was wearing the shawl that night. It was retrieved from the river by the City Watch. I washed the shawl and hid it lest P'pa burn it. It was all I had left of her. M'ma's body was never recovered.

If the lace had been around the woman's neck and shoulders, then why did it float free while the body sank? Unless Tattia had put up a great deal of resistance before entering the river, loosening the lace. The fall into the icy water had probably sent her into shock so that she couldn't climb out again. Only Tattia herself and the agents of King Simeon knew for certain how and why the lacemistress had died.

Jack added that piece of information to his list of tasks to complete before he left the city.

Katrina fingered the nearly finished shawl of her own design. Her usual patterns of edgings and insertions did not yet match her mother's in uniqueness and elegance. This piece surpassed the original. Mostly because the floral centers flowed with the weaving lines of the petals. She doubted any of the lacemakers in the Brunix factory could figure out the convoluted thread paths of the runes in Tattia's shawl.

But then Tattia had incorporated the runes for a purpose, never meaning the design to be duplicated. If only Katrina knew the message in those runes. After last night's invasion of the factory by a spying magician, Katrina had no doubt that her only chances of survival were to keep the shawl and its secrets hidden, or to learn those secrets and spread the information to the right people.

Was Jack the right person? Part of her wanted to trust him and accept his friendship. Another part of her didn't dare.

King Simeon must know the meaning of the runes, or he wouldn't be pursuing the shawl so diligently now that he knew it had not been destroyed. If he didn't know, he wouldn't have prevented the queen from seeing it when M'ma first offered it.

The murmurs of talk from the workroom below her rose to a roar of speculation. Brunix had not seen fit to disclose to his workers why the factory had rocked with arguments and pounding feet last night. Katrina hadn't bothered to explain her late return to her bed—though most of the lacemakers presumed she had been servicing the owner. Jack had not yet been seen today.

Jack. Those few moments wrapped in his arms and his spell had shaken her carefully-layered suspicion and mistrust. He had allowed her to eavesdrop and learn the depth of Brunix's involvement with the king.

She wondered briefly if the glimpse Jack had allowed of his own mind was the result of the invisibility spell he had wrapped around them, or another trick to win her confidence. He wanted her help in completing his mission. She knew that much. What kind of help and how dangerous would it be? There had to be danger or he'd have given her more details.

A special piece of lace, made of Tambrin. Was he, too, after the shawl? That piece was made of silk. Wasn't it?

Katrina needed to examine the piece more closely, looking specifically for evidence of Tambrin spun with the silk. Owner Brunix wasn't about to remove the shawl from its locked hiding place so soon after the palace magician had searched for it. She didn't have the key.

Jack might be able to open it with magic.

Her circling thoughts came back to the dark-eyed stranger again and again. She had to trust him if she was to find the answers.

Yet she knew she shouldn't trust the outland magician who had stopped the ship containing the precious Tambootie seedlings.

He claimed to know her father, to have aided P'pa's escape from the mines.

Brunix treated him as if he were a cousin—another untrustworthy Rover.

Jack had vowed his mission would deprive Simeon of magic and therefore his power over SeLenicca.

The arguments wove back and forth and around like a

giant spiderweb. Katrina was the fly trapped at the center, waiting to be consumed, knowing her death waited just beyond the next heartbeat. Just like the insect trapped in the amber bead on her divider pin.

"I am tired of being a victim!" she shouted to herself, and the Stargods and anyone else within hearing distance. "If I am ever to cleanse myself of this web of lies and deceit, I have to take a risk."

Jack offered a solution as well as an escape. Brunix promised safety within the confines of slavery. How much longer would he wait to exert his rights over her again? Simeon offered nothing.

"I need Jack," she told herself. "I can use him as I have been used. I don't have to trust him." *But I do like him. I felt so complete, so right when he wrapped me in his arms.*

Decision made, she touched the single plait of hair hanging halfway down her back. With deft fingers, she rapidly released the tight weaving. A few moments later she had restored the two plaits she had missed for three long years. Assertive action began with simple gestures.

Tonight, when the factory slept and Jack was on duty, she would seek him out and offer her help. Until then, she would do what she did best—finish the shawl.

Rejiia watched through tired eyes as the Rover wet nurse fed her newborn son.

"Your son is strong but very small, born two moons early," the young woman commented on the infant's vigorous suckling.

Rejiia smiled in satisfaction. Too many plans relied on her strength and agility. The last two moons of pregnancy would have hindered her actions.

Old Erda, the Rover matriarch and mistress of all herbal medicines and the best midwife in the three kingdoms, wasn't available to assist her. But one of her apprentices had come with the tribe of Rovers that lingered on the outskirts of Queen's City. The bitter herbs Rejiia had drunk last night had forced the child into early birth.

"Your tribe will protect my son until I claim him," Rejiia commanded the young wet nurse.

"We will guard him as one of our own," the Rover woman murmured. She did not lift her gaze to meet Rejiia's.

"Only until I can claim him!" Rejiia hadn't the strength to compel the woman, so she pushed as much authority into her voice as possible.

"We will welcome you when you claim him." This time the woman met Rejiia's look in a token promise of compliance.

"Your name, girl. Tell me your name so that I may find you again."

"I am called Erda."

"Nonsense. There is only one Erda."

"Each of us who nurtures a child can claim the title Erda."

"Your true name, then. What name were you given at birth?"

"No outlander may know my true name."

"Enough of this evasion. Give me your name so that I may find you when the time is right to reclaim my son." Panic generated enough energy to draw a tiny spell into her words. Erda squirmed in resistance.

"Ask for Kestra. All of the tribes of Zolltarn know of Kestra."

"Good. The prematurity of the boy's birth is our secret. No one in Coronnan must suspect that my husband, Marnak, is incapable of fathering a child. By law we are still married and the child legitimate."

"That belief suits the needs of the Rovers."

"Then take the child. I will inform the king that his son is stillborn."

For now I must garner my strength so that I am ready for the Solstice Ritual.

I will use the power of the Solstice to kill Darville through the lingering wound in his arm. Coronnan expects him to die from that witch burn. I shall hasten the process and step in to claim the throne for me and my son.

I am too weak at the moment to investigate the disturbance in the magical energies I sense within the city. I need a familiar to aid my search. Jackdaws aplenty nest near the palace. More intelligent than mere crows, their ability to mimic will develop into limited speech through the bonding spells. I will subvert one to my will. Tomorrow. I must sleep now.

Chapter 31

"Ley lines don't exist singly. Nor do they appear spontaneously," Jack mused as he wandered Queen's City shortly after dawn.

Cloaked in the face and body of the slightly built palace magician, he peered easily at the land beneath his feet with every sense available to him. His magic had recharged during the time he had spent standing above the pocket of power in the workroom. A relief from the weeks of weakened abilities.

Burned out ley lines rotted at every street intersection. If the land did not heal soon, the old channels would collapse, taking building foundations and street paving with them. Jack foresaw a shift in the riverbed and upheaval in the hills behind the city. Death and chaos would follow.

Simeon deserved whatever destruction the Stargods visited upon him. The innocents of the city didn't.

Everywhere he saw the sings of decay, heightened by the short-sighted belief that the land's resources were unlimited and meant to be exploited. When the belief proved false, no one knew how to rectify matters. Abandoned shops and houses. Dirt and crumbling mortar strewn through the streets from the collapse of a warehouse, and no one with enough energy to clear it away. No refuse for dogs to scavenge. And everywhere, the haunted eyes of the hungry and the hopeless citizens. Only the nobles seemed unaware of the lifeblood of the country bleeding into the river along with the land that no longer had trees to hold it back.

Having lost all sense of the Kardia, SeLenicca, its people, and culture were dying. Only the export of lace kept the economy alive. Lace was not enough to employ an entire nation.

Nowhere in his day-long search of the city did Jack discover any active ley lines. The city was as dead magically as it was economically. Shayla was King Simeon's only source of power. Did he and the members of his coven know how to combine the magic and make the power grow well beyond anything a solitary magician could throw?

Jack already knew he was incapable of gathering the dragon magic. After last night's confrontation with the palace magician, he had little hope he could complete his mission and escape without detection. In a magic duel, Jack's only chance of survival was one grouping of hair-fine ley lines beneath the warehouse.

If only he knew why the ley lines had sprung up beneath Katrina's workstation and nowhere else. Once he mastered that puzzle, he might be able to force more lines to grow and feed his magic.

Katrina was the answer. Katrina and the lace she wove for the love of the shimmering threads and the patterns that bloomed beneath her hands while she sang little tunes in the dead of night; not the lace she made for the owner to exploit.

Her gentle little work tune danced through his mind and gave his feet a lighter step. He hummed it lightly as he prowled the city. His mind cleared of puzzles and worries.

A crowd gathering on the bridge ahead of him caught his curiosity. The black robes and tall hat, crowning a city official, flapped in the wind like the wings of a jackdaw. Wearily the clerk intoned a prayer and scattered something into the water. Jack merged with the solemn listeners.

Two middle-aged women wept. Their sharp chins and close-set eyes suggested a strong family resemblance. Between them stood a tight-lipped man, probably husband to one, grinding his teeth in his effort to restrain his own tears.

A funeral, Jack decided. An all-too-common occurrence in a city where food shortages were a constant worry and lack of firewood kept buildings chill and dark. The customary sun break at noon seemed to be the only source of joy left in Queen's City.

Jack pushed past the funeral goers. He might as well

check out the slums on the far side of the river for some trace of magical activity. The homeless and unemployed might have a better relationship with the Kardia than the elite of a mercantile city.

A winter chill filled his body with atavistic dread. He came to an abrupt halt. The day had been warm with a gentle breeze two heartbeats ago.

He scanned the center of the bridge with his already extended magical senses. A woman in soaking garments stood directly in front of him, flailing her arms as if fighting to the surface from the depths of the river. Her double plaits streamed down her back, dripping water. No drops or puddles formed on the wooden planks. For a moment Jack thought he was staring at a vision of Katrina grown into the beauty of maturity.

Only then did he notice the knife protruding from the woman's breast and blood staining the front of her gown. None of the mourners seemed aware of the injured woman or her plight. Instinctively he reached to withdraw the knife.

His hand passed straight through the woman. The hairs on the back of his hand and arm stood straight up. Lumbird bumps danced down his spine.

"The ghost of Tattia Kaantille," he whispered.

The apparition nodded at the sound of her name.

"Murder, not suicide?" Jack asked in a silent whisper.

Again the ghost gestured the correctness of his assumption.

"Who? Why?"

A shudder of effort seemed to pass through the spirit of Katrina's mother. She opened her mouth to speak, but no sound emerged.

Jack concentrated on the shapes her lips formed around soundless words.

"Simeon. Runes," he repeated the two words back to her.

She smiled and faded to wisps of water vapor.

"You were talking to that new man, Katrina. You are not to speak to any of the men I employ. And now you revert to the two plaits I forbade you to wear. To impress the new watchman? I'll not have it, Katrina. Why do you disobey me?" Brunix stood behind her left shoulder so he wouldn't cast a shadow on the lace shawl that grew beneath her fingers.

Katrina knew from experience she was not to interrupt her work while answering him. Lace provided the income that kept the factory going. Lace was more important than any of the workers within the factory. If a lacemaker fell short of her daily quota, Brunix would dismiss her without a second thought. If Katrina displeased the owner or made him angry he would sell her—possibly back to King Simeon.

"I was working and heard a noise," she explained. "I knew about the thefts and investigated. The watchman was already there."

Brunix moved in front of her, blocking her light so she had to look up to him. "The watchman was supposed to be there. You were not." He slapped her across the cheek, hard.

Pain lanced through her eyes to her jaw. The blow set her ears ringing and brought involuntary tears to her eyes. His violence shocked her senses and numbed her thoughts as his lovemaking had not. Never before had he hit her. The world centered on her pain and his burning anger.

" 'Tis not your position to put yourself into danger. You are *mine. My* slave. *My* possession." He backhanded her again across the face.

She tasted blood. This new blow jerked her head back, twisting her neck awkwardly.

"You are not to speak to any other male. You are not to venture below to the warehouse without my express permission." His long fingers grabbed her shoulders and he shook her, hard, rattling her teeth. "Do. You. Understand. Me?"

Katrina couldn't force words past her clenched jaw and reeling senses.

"Do you understand!" Brunix demanded again.

"Y . . . y . . . yes," she ground out.

"Good. I will find another watchman. This one broke my rules when he spoke to you." Brunix released her, seemingly oblivious to the blood that dripped from the corner of her mouth and the bruises forming on her cheek.

Katrina touched the back of her hand to the blood on

her face, careful not to stain her fingers which might transfer blood to the nearly completed shawl. She had to think, had to overcome the shock that closed down her senses.

Brunix couldn't dismiss Jack. She needed the outland magician to decipher the runes. He was the only person who could help her bring about King Simeon's downfall.

"Before the evening meal, you will move all of your things into my quarters. I am tired of waiting for you. Henceforth, you live with me, eat with me, and sleep with me. I can make you feel pain. You will respond to me, if only in pain. Only one-quarter of my blood is Rover. I have observed their prohibition against rape more than one quarter of my time with you. I would take you now, but I have business that will not wait. This apartment and the workroom are the only places you have permission to be." Brunix stalked to the door of his apartment. "Do you understand, Katrina?"

"Do I have the right to a sun break?" she asked calmly, though her heart beat so loud and fast she could barely hear her own words. She couldn't allow him to see the panic rising to choke her.

"You will take your sun break with me. I allow you outside the building only because the law requires I must and a complaint from one of your friends would bring me ruinous fines." He left her alone, slamming the door behind him. A heartbeat later, the lock clicked, sealing her inside.

"I can't read runes," Jack muttered to himself. "I wasn't at the University long enough to learn that skill. Where would I find runes, if I could read them?" He trekked back across the bridge into Queen's City. A glance over his shoulder confirmed that the ghost of Tattia Kaantille had vanished once her message had been passed along to him.

His growling stomach reminded him that he hadn't eaten since last night's supper, and the day was half gone. He must return to the factory in time to share supper with the other male employees—after the women had eaten and retired safely to their dormitory. He had almost no chance of seeing Katrina before midnight.

The official with the tall black hat, who had presided over the funeral brushed, past Jack. His black robes flapped in the wind, reminding Jack once more of a giant jackdaw.

The flowing sleeves of the black robe caught briefly on Jack's belt buckle. As the man tugged the fabric free with a deep frown of disapproval for Jack, the black embroidery on the black robe caught the magician's eye. Straight lines and slashes jumped into his perspective.

A primitive form of writing.

Runes!

This was no government clerk or judge, but a priest. Old temples sometimes had runes decorating tombs and icons.

Jack fell into step behind the man, thanking the Stargods as he kept a discreet distance.

A temple constructed of huge stone blocks, each as tall as a man, loomed before Jack. Bigger than the Palace Reveta Tristille, he'd never seen anything like it before. In Coronnan, the temples were small, little larger than a house, and scattered throughout the city for the convenience of each neighborhood, mostly taken for granted because they were an everyday part of life. This place of worship demanded attention by its imposing height and impossibly huge building stones. Men could not have built this place. It seemed designed for the entire population of the city to gather at once. The priest strode up the two dozen steps with the ease of long familiarity.

Jack followed him, stretching his legs to mount each broad stair. A long line of people dressed in sober colors filed into and out of the sanctuary. Jack joined them.

Inside the impressive structure, darkness ruled. No windows allowed daylight to penetrate beyond the porch. Hundreds of lighted candles lined the walls in banks of nine rows and nine tiers. The building was so massive in size, the candles lit only small areas around icons dedicated to one of the three red-haired Stargod brothers, or the painted canvases of the queen before her ailment. Nine tall candles in each of nine candelabras drew Jack's eyes to the altar.

One solid piece of lace spilled over the focal point of worship. Soft light reflected from the shimmering threads of the design. From the distance of one hundred armlengths, Jack knew the lace was made from Tambrin. The magic inherent in the Tambootie tree vibrated inside his body like a finely tuned instrument ready to sound the most beautiful note ever heard.

But it was a power he dared not draw into his body.

Dragons were the only beings who could safely digest any part of the Tambootie. Madness trod the path of the Tambootie. Simeon's obsessive search for Tattia's lace shawl exhibited some of the signs of that insanity.

The line of worshipers in front of Jack moved forward. To his right, a series of tiny chapels bulged outward from the main sanctuary. Some were no wider than a single person. Others could accommodate three or four kneeling side by side before altars dedicated to images Jack couldn't identify. Incense hung heavily in the air.

A sneeze tickled in the back of Jack's throat. He held his breath. The sneeze subsided along with the thick perfume of burning herbs. Priests used incense in their rituals in Coronnan. Jack had never heard of them saturating the air with it, nor of using such heavy and exotic scents. Like so many things in this decaying city, the incense sought to hide unpleasantness rather than cleanse it.

He looked up, way up, to see how high the cloud of incense hovered. Four or five stories above the center of the sanctuary, the bowl of a huge dome separated the worshipers from the weather. Painted night skies with stylized stars decorated the interior of the dome. Most of the constellation groupings were inaccurate, broken by seams. Ah, the priests did do something traditional in SeLenicca. The panels in the dome opened, by a series of just barely visible pulleys and ropes, for observation of the night skies.

The architecture seemed to be centered on that dome. Did the entire temple date from the time of the Stargods or was the open dome added later to accommodate stargazing?

He sidled out of line to examine the side aisles and their stone tombs. Jack guessed the stonework was much older than the religion of the Stargods and the efficient alphabet introduced by the three divine brothers. The ancient runes should still adorn places considered sacred through all the changes of dynasties and worship. Somewhere in this vast building there must be some runes and he intended to find them.

Then he'd worry about a translation.

Katrina paced the circumference of Brunix's sitting room. Two burly warehousemen carried her trunk of personal possessions between them into the bedroom beyond. A third employee hauled her extra pillow up the stairs.

"Where you want it?" he asked, not daring to lift his eyes to meet hers.

"By the window." She pointed to a cleared space beside the pillow where she worked the new shawl. Since the factory owner's uncharacteristic violence this morning, she hadn't been able to work, to concentrate, to think of anything but the night to come. The nights to come. For as long as Brunix desired her, she would have no peace.

"Think *he'll* let us have a go at her when he gets tired?" The two men with the trunk giggled and nudged each other.

Katrina felt all heat and sensation drain from her head to form a knot in her stomach. Brunix had promised her pain in order to force a response from her. Would he add the degradation of being mauled by these thugs as well?

The third man lifted one shoulder in a shrug. "What can I do?" he mouthed. His eyes pleaded for forgiveness from Katrina.

She didn't know how to reply to the man. Any attempt to help her escape Brunix tonight, or any other night, would result in his own dismissal from a job he sorely needed.

"Get Jack," she whispered. A ray of hope opened before her as soon as she whispered his name. Jack who persisted in his quest despite the dangers. Jack who held her tenderly and granted her the unique privilege of reading his mind as readily as he read hers.

If he had any secrets left, after that special rapport they had shared while eavesdropping on Brunix and the palace guard, those secrets were no danger to her.

"Gone, all day." The man ventured one step closer to her, casting about to ensure the other two weren't watching.

"Send his pet bird!"

"I'll try."

The three men filed out without a backward glance to Katrina. A loud click proclaimed they had followed orders and locked her in once more.

"Come quickly, Jack. I need you."

Chapter 32

"**D**amned birds!" Rejiia cursed the flock of black birds that circled away from her window.

The aerial display of the flock separated and settled into individual birds. For the fifth time this morning, Rejiia concentrated her mind probe on a bird. Slowly she merged her consciousness with the creature. Her vision tilted, shifted colors to reflect heat patterns, and distorted to the perspective of one high above the city.

A moment of euphoric flight filled her. Contact with her body diminished. "Almost. Almost total blending." A thin silver tendril of magic tethered her to the person in the window. She absorbed more of the bird.

Eebon, the bird announced his name.

Mistress, Rejiia said. *You will call me Mistress.*

He was ready. Another moment and the crow would be her winged familiar, bound to her for life.

She tugged on the tether. The bird banked and circled back. Another tug and he flew faster toward her.

Rejiia regained enough of her own body to stretch out her arm as a perch for her new pet. Eebon extended his talons to encircle her padded wrist.

"Newak!" a second bird screamed. The menacing jackdaw with white tufts over his eyes dove between Rejiia and Eebon.

The slender silver tether shredded from the force of the bird's descent. Eebon jerked away from the villa window squawking his confusion.

Together the two black birds turned and flapped until they caught an air current that took them away from Rejiia.

"Simurgh curse you, bird," she screamed in frustration.

Every time she made contact with a bird, the interloper shattered the spell. Who controlled the jackdaw? Only another magician could direct a wild creature to do such a thing. Who?

That boy! Yaakke had to be the jackdaw's master. "He's the only magician strong enough to thwart me. I'll have that bird. I'll torture it to death and enjoy every moment."

Jack wound his way among the alcoves as if seeking an unoccupied corner for private prayer. As he paused by each small altar, he examined all of the decoration for signs of the distinctive lines and slashes chiseled into the stone.

The sight of a pair of large boots sticking out from beneath a familiar robe halted his progress. A tall man knelt in the next alcove. Owner Neeles Brunix had worn a similar sleeveless green robe over his black tunic and trews when he descended to the warehouse in dignified silence this morning. His orders had been brief, almost as if his words were gold and he a miser.

Jack had seen the owner's aura flare with the red of suppressed, violent emotion as he viewed the scene of last night's intrusion. His reaction to Jack's presence had generated near flames in his spiking aura, but his face and tone had not changed. When the owner retreated to his office, he'd closed the door with precise control. Jack suspected Brunix might rip the painted planks from their hinges if he vented his true emotions.

That was when Jack decided to absent himself from the factory for the day. His next encounter with Brunix might end with Jack unemployed and no more access to Tambrin lace and Katrina. Keeping Katrina close and safe suddenly seemed as important as finding a patch for Shayla's wing.

Jack turned to go back the way he had come. Brunix would recognize his current disguise and the crowd was too thick to alter the delusion spell without drawing attention. The crowd was also too thick to allow him a safe retreat. Forward, toward the main altar lay the only open path.

On tiptoe, as silently as possible, he edged past the factory owner. Brunix remained on his knees, eyes fixed ahead of him. But he wasn't praying. His hands copied the wall etchings onto a sheet of parchment. Wall etchings that duplicated the runic embroidery on the priest's robes.

Surprised, Jack nearly stumbled over Brunix's feet where they protruded into the main aisle. There was little chance of coincidence that Tattia Kaantille's ghost would tell Jack to seek out runes on the same day that Brunix—who owned Tattia's daughter—would copy runes in the temple.

Brunix stirred from his fascinated study of the carved message. Slowly he levered himself up to his full standing height, using the altar rail as a brace.

Jack sought a hiding place amid the crowd.

A priest renewed a sputtering candle two alcoves along the aisle and then disappeared behind a tapestry. Jack pursued the old man in black robes, rudely elbowing his way through the throng of people waiting for the kneeling space Brunix had just left.

Peering from behind the woven portal covering, Jack watched Brunix stuff the parchment into an interior pocket of his sleeveless overrobe. The owner peered about him with a smile of contempt for those who prayed for the queen's recovery. His eyes gleamed in the candlelight and his aura flared once more, this time in a bright orange.

The man knew something important.

Following in Brunix's wake was easier than forcing a new path through the crowd. Jack itched to remove the parchment from its hiding place. The factory owner kept a proprietary hand over the concealed pocket. He'd notice if the crackling bulk suddenly disappeared.

Very slowly, Jack allowed his delusion to shift. Bit by bit, he absorbed the face and demeanor of a nondescript man he passed in the wide temple porch, shedding his old disguise in the same order. When he plunged after Brunix into the bright spring sunshine, no trace of his previous delusion remained.

Brunix stood unmoving on the top step, blinking rapidly until his eyes adjusted to the sunlight. Jack used those two moments of distraction well. He gathered the tattered remnants of extra magic left in his body and concentrated on the copied runes.

The single sheet of parchment weighed a ton inside his mind. It refused to budge from the fold of fabric that protected it.

Jack pushed his magic deep, struggled, and sweated. The

cords of his neck stood out with the strain of moving the burden.

Brunix blinked and twisted his neck in preparation for moving down the two dozen stone slabs that formed the steps.

Near panic that his quarry might escape, Jack "grabbed" the parchment with a spell and dumped it into his own pocket.

The factory owner stepped down into the milling throng.

Jack's knees turned weak in fatigue and reaction to the hasty spell. Barely able to keep a delusion of light-colored hair on his head, he sought a quiet corner at the edge of the open square before the temple.

Very soon, he must return to the factory and stand above Katrina's little web of ley lines. A good meal would work wonders at restoring his talent, too. But first a brief nap beneath that clump of bushes.

Eyes still on Brunix's progress across the broad square, Jack edged toward his chosen refuge. The tall man strode in the direction of the factory, never turning around or looking back to see if he was being followed.

Still five stairs from the paved square, Jack caught sight of a pair of men in palace-guard-gray scuttling behind Brunix. A knife flashed in the sunlight.

"No!" Jack screamed as he dashed across the square. King Simeon couldn't succeed with this murder. If Brunix died, then the sorcerer-king could confiscate the factory and all his property, including Katrina.

The men in gray disappeared, as if they had never been behind their victim.

Screams erupted from the throats of a hundred people. A wide circle formed around the crumpled body. Blood stained the fire-green robe and black tunic an ugly and lethal red.

Jack skidded to a halt beside the groaning figure. Cautiously he extended his hand to the carved bone of the knife hilt. The outline of a winged god glared at him, defying him to remove the knife from the wound.

He'd seen that outline before. Lord Krej had created a huge stained glass window of Simurgh in the great hall of his castle. Not true glass, but a magical simulation formed of blood and the volcanic sands of Hanassa.

Jack's hand shook as it hovered above the instrument of death. A ritual knife. Wielded by the coven.

Frantically, Jack sought a healing spell, anything to slow the bleeding, repair enough of the damage to keep Brunix alive.

"Get a healer!" he yelled to the watchers. They stared mutely at him, unmoving.

Why waste a healer on an outland half-breed? The stray thought penetrated Jack's mind.

Outraged at the arrogant prejudice of these people, he found a small spark of magic lingering within him. Instinctively he sought to draw more magic from the burned-out ley lines beneath his feet. Blue sparks shot from his hand into Brunix's gaping chest wound as the empty ley line shuddered from the strain of his tapping.

Brunix's eyes fluttered opened, unfocused, filled with pain. "Save the lace!" he whispered. "Save her. . . ."

Jack leaned closer to catch the man's dying words. A long-fingered hand grasped the neck of his tunic in a futile attempt to communicate.

"Katrina. Save her and the lace from Simeon." A death rattle choked Brunix and he collapsed, staring into the nothingness of the void between the planes of existence.

The stone paving of the square trembled as if a hundred war steeds galloped toward the murder scene.

Jack looked up for the source of the disturbance. The instability of the Kardia beneath his feet faded to nothing. A sense of the familiar rocked his senses.

Just before the cave-in at the mine, a similar vibration had told him of the impending disaster. Had his instinctive reaching for power caused the ley line to crumble?

Instead of the prison of tunnels dug deep within the planet to trap him at the time of disaster, he faced a ring of grim-faced palace guards.

"You are under arrest for murder." The magician who had invaded the factory last night stepped forward, a pair of iron manacles in his hand.

"He removed some outland garbage from our city!" protested an onlooker. A verbal protest only. No one stepped forward to defend Jack.

Praying that his protective delusion of blond hair wouldn't

evaporate, Jack visualized his armor snapping in place. Then he activated the spell with memorized trigger words.

Cold iron enclosed his wrists.

There was no magic left in his body or in the land. His staff was hidden back at the factory. Once more he was a prisoner and unable to save himself.

Hands slapped his body, roughly, in search of hidden weapons. The parchment crackled.

"What have we here, evidence of conspiracy with magic?" The slight man chortled at his public display of accusing Jack of more than just murder. He held the unrolled parchment up to the light for all to see.

Black ink sprawled across the page in a jumble of rectangular shapes and straight slashes. Under observation and bright sunlight, the runes flashed into unnatural red sigils. The parchment thinned. A bright circle of sunlight at the center charred and burst into flame.

Gasps of superstitious awe and fear rose from the crowd. A dozen hands signed the cross of the Stargods. Two dozen more crossed wrists and flapped their hands in the more ancient ward against evil.

In seconds, the parchment disappeared into useless ash.

"A trick with a glass," Jack murmured so that only the magician heard.

"Perhaps," he shrugged and scattered the last of the ashes across Brunix's lifeless body. "Tricks keep the peasants afraid and cost no energy."

The magician gestured for two burly men, easily a head taller than Jack, to take him into custody.

"Lock him in the warded dungeon. The rest of you come with me. We still have to capture the girl."

Katrina wiggled the long divider pin that had been a gift from Brunix into the tiny crack between two wall panels. The hidden safe was deep in this wall. The door would open under pressure upon a secret trigger at the same time as a key released the lock. The long pin would have to be her key while her fingers sought a sensitive place at the top of the crack.

In another portion of the factory, the sound of a door being thrust open with violence startled her. The vibrations

from the wooden panels shattering against the wall traveled
all the way up to the top floor. Katrina's feet tingled as the
entire building shook.

A few more moments of privacy and she would know if
the precious shawl had been made with Tambrin, or if Jack
and King Simeon sought a different piece.

Heavy boots pounded upon the first flight of steps to the
dormitory level. She almost didn't hear the click of the
hidden lock over the noise.

Brunix would be anxious to claim her when he returned,
but surely his large boots wouldn't make that much noise
in his own factory.

The panel swung open. Glimmering lace spilled·out. Reel
after reel of precious white lace, ivory lace, and ecru. Slender insertions, square mats, round doilies, fans and flounces
as wide as her spread fingers.

A fortune spilled out of the cavity. All of it made of
Tambrin. Enough to hang the owner who cached the forbidden treasure.

The footsteps slowed as the stairs steepened between the
dormitory and the workroom. A few screams from startled
lacemakers rose through the flooring.

Hastily, Katrina fumbled through the vast mound of lace
seeking the familiar texture of her mother's shawl with her
fingertips. At the back of the safe, beneath a stack of fans
she found it. Sensitized by years of thread work, she knew
without looking that the shawl had Tambrin spun with the
silk. Both fibers were so fine they had blended together,
neither distinguished from the other unless examined
closely by an expert.

A particular creak indicated someone had left the workroom and now sought the top floor of the factory.

Katrina bundled the spilled lace and shoved it into the
cavity. There was so much of it, she couldn't hold it all in
place while she closed the panel.

The lock on the outer door rattled. A fist hit the immov-
able panels.

Heedless of damaging dirt and tangles she crammed the
reels together, held them in place with her foot while she
closed the panel.

An alien foot slammed against the locked door.

The secret panel clicked closed.

She returned the long pin to its customary place within one of her plaits.

The door to the apartment crashed to the floor. Six palace guards crowded the landing.

Katrina backed up, hiding with her skirts the telltale tendril of shimmering white filigree peeping from the crack in the wall.

"Restrain her," the slender man who had searched the warehouse last night ordered.

Fear robbed Katrina of speech and will. Two men, much taller than the magician in charge, stepped toward her. The manacles looked puny dangling in the massive paw of the broadest of the guards.

At the last moment she stepped back, coming up against the wall abruptly.

"Owner Neeles Brunix holds me in slavery. You must have his authority to—"

"Owner Neeles Brunix is dead," the magician interrupted. "Murdered by one of his outland kin. At least we presume the night watchman in his employ is kin," he dismissed her protest. The magician's gleeful grin killed whatever hope Katrina might have had. "You belong to King Simeon now. Or the coven. Take your choice, Slave Kaantille."

"Brunix is dead?" Katrina didn't know what else to say, wishing only to stall. She had no doubt Jack had a good reason for committing murder. Like preserving his own life. But he was too smart, too powerful a magician to be caught so easily. Unless he didn't do it. Unless . . .

The cold iron of the manacle slapping her wrists drained the blood from her head and the strength from her knees. White spots appeared before her eyes, as cold sweat broke out on her back.

All these years of keeping Brunix at bay, of avoiding Simeon and his evil rituals were for naught. The Solstice was mere weeks away.

What will Simeon do to me when he finds out I'm no longer a virgin?

"Yes, Brunix is dead. I made certain of it when I twisted the knife before removing and cleaning it," the magician gloated as if he had committed the murder himself. "Now where is the shawl, Slave Kaantille?"

"What shawl?" she asked. Her eyes darted to the just completed piece on her pillow. Never would she betray to anyone but Jack the hoard of lace inside the wall.

"This shawl." The magician lifted the lace gingerly between two fingers, as if afraid of being contaminated by it. "You aren't a very good liar, Slave Kaantille. Don't bother trying to fool me. A truth spell will force proper answers from you. Painfully if necessary. Bring her," he ordered the guards as he sauntered out of the apartment, a sneer of contempt on his face, the lace held delicately away from his body.

Katrina screeched and struggled against her captors.

They ended her thrashing by simply lifting her by the elbows and carrying her between them out the door. Never once did the palace guard look behind them at the scrap of lace betraying the secret wall safe.

Chapter 33

Jack's ribs exploded in pain. He slumped against the manacles that chained him to the wall of the dungeon. His resistance to imprisonment evaporated with white hot agony.

Hope died.

A gap-toothed jailer smiled, fondling an iron bar as long as Jack's outstretched arm. "Want more?" the man in black leather grinned at Jack. "Just keep up yer hollerin' and ye can have all the tickles Old Mabel here can give."

Old Mabel? The cretin actually had a name for his crude weapon. The coven must love this man. The Commune believed that Lord Krej and his sister had learned to use pain—in others or themselves—to create magical energy.

Jack wasn't desperate enough, yet, to dive that deeply into black magic. Blood magic. Simurgh's magic.

Blackness encroached upon his vision. The tip of the iron bar caressed his side, cold against the spreading fire of crushed ribs and laboring lungs.

"Don't pass out on us now, boy," the jailer coaxed with an almost seductive voice. "King Simeon and his lady have questions to ask ye. Ye be polite now and stay awake. Otherwise Old Mabel will need to wake ye up again." With a parting chuckle, the jailer exited.

Jack invited the darkness of his unlit cell to soothe the blinding ache behind his eyes.

Little creatures scurried in the straw at his feet. He jerked back awake. The blood on his face and side had attracted rats. If he fell asleep, the disease-ridden rodents might take it as an invitation to feast on his still living flesh.

"*Stargods!* What did I do to deserve this?" he moaned.

"You chose to interfere with my dragon," a quiet voice answered from the doorway.

For a moment Jack thought he was hallucinating. The newcomer appeared to be Lord Krej returned to life. His red hair was a little duller with the passage of three years. His square-cut beard hid the shape of his chin. But the bay-blue eyes that peered at Jack with lusting evil were the same. Even his red and green aura was the same.

The magic permeating his body smelled different. Still filled with Tambootie, but overlaid with something else. Something Jack couldn't identify.

"Who broke the backlash spell, Krej?" Jack asked, his curiosity overcoming his pain, for a moment.

"KREJ!" the man yelled. "How dare you call me Krej? That insignificant son of a weak and petty Coronnite. I am *King* Simeon of SeLenicca and Hanassa, true heir to Rossemeyer and soon to be conqueror of Coronnan. Do you understand me, boy?"

"If you aren't Krej, then you're his twin brother," Jack accused. So this was Simeon the Sorcerer, King of SeLenicca. *Simeon the Insane,* judging by his reaction.

"Nonsense, utter nonsense." A new voice, calm and feminine and familiar, moved into Jack's field of vision.

"Rejiia," Jack whispered. Pale skin, smooth as ivory, black hair pulled into a sleek knot at her nape. Long and graceful body clothed in elegant black. There was a new sensuousness to her walk, maturity in her ample bosom and a seductive pout to her full, red lips. If anything she was lovelier than ever.

And taller. Rejiia at fifteen had been nearly as tall as her father, Krej. At twenty she topped the red-haired man beside her by a finger-width or two.

She deposited a lump of metal by the doorway. Jack squinted his aching eyes to focus on the talisman she had levitated to this cell. A tin weasel sculpture with flaking gilt paint. Krej.

"*Lady Rejiia* to you, boy," she lifted her arrogant little chin in contempt. Her nose wrinkled at the same time as she caught a whiff of the odors of the dungeon. She caressed the head of the statue before moving into the cell.

"Adding incest to your sins, *Lady* Rejiia?" Jack quipped, tired of their need to add insult to injury with the appellation "boy." Suddenly he was beyond pain, and fear. All that was left of him was a glimmer of hysterical humor and that wouldn't last long.

"What do you mean by that, *boy?*" Rejiia approached Jack, looking as if she would spit on him. Anger blazed from her eyes and some of her control slipped, changing her beautiful face into a mask of ugly hatred.

"I mean, that if Simeon isn't your father, then he's your father's brother. He's obviously your lover, you stink of him. Or don't you care about such things?" With the clarity of pain and knowing he wouldn't survive much longer, Jack saw it all.

Queen Rossemikka, who had been a victim of Janataea's and Krej's manipulations, had warned the Commune of the coven's dynastic plans. Royal marriages and births throughout the world had been arranged and scheduled along with appropriate assassinations. Generation after generation of alliances came down to one or two people eligible to claim multiple thrones.

Simeon claimed descent from Rossemikka's much older, exiled, half sister. Thus he should rule Rossemeyer. His marriage to Queen Miranda of SeLenicca had produced a princess who could claim both thrones. If she married the heir to Coronnan, the entire continent would be united under one crown.

Rejiia shared a common great-grandfather with Darville of Coronnan. She, or her child, could claim the Coraurlia, the dragon crown, if Darville and Mikka had no children. Jack wished he'd taken the time to catch up on current events since leaving the mines. He had no idea who was alive and well and who wasn't.

What seemed most important, now, was that the coven would control Queen Miranda's daughter, Jaranda, and whoever inherited Coronnan. Stargods help them all if Rejiia passed off a child of an incestuous relationship as heir and mate to Jaranda, another incestuous relationship.

Greedy madness shone in Simeon's eyes. He, like Krej, was too ambitious to wait for the coven's plans to come to fruition. He wanted to rule and exploit for himself and not the coven.

I have to end this madness, Jack thought. *No matter the cost, I have to stop the coven.*

A jolt of memory rocked his mind away from Rejiia's spitting indignation. Years ago, Jack had claimed the name of "Yaakke." A name out of legend. A name of power and great reverence.

A thousand years ago, Yaakke, son of Yaacob the Usurper, had united three clans in northern Coronnan to form the first kingdom. Yaakke had met the Stargods in the sacred clearing and vowed eternal fealty and reverence if the three red-haired brothers would save his wife and child from the plague. The plague was banished and Yaakke charged with the duty of eliminating the power of the winged demon Simurgh. He had succeeded but only after bitter and bloody battles. Yaakke died two days after the last battle.

Now Simeon's coven was attempting to reestablish the bloody rituals of Simurgh as the one true religion. Once more, the duty of preventing the deaths of innocents fell to a man named Yaakke.

If he was ever to earn the right to a name, Jack had to complete this quest, even if it brought him an ugly and painful death.

Katrina tripped on the slimy steps into the dungeon. Her guards grabbed the chain binding her wrists and yanked her upright. The strain on her arms and shoulders made her cry out.

"Careful o' t'at one. His Majesty wants her undamaged," warned a jailer who was missing at least three teeth. He caressed a long iron bar in his arms, as if it were a beloved pet.

"I know. I know," groused the guard who still hauled upward on the chain. "Won't be no cuts or bruises. Just enough pain to keep her in line." He pulled hard on the chain and Katrina stumbled forward in his path.

She had been brought to the same manor house on the outskirts of the city as she had been that night three years ago when King Simeon gave her to Owner Neeles Brunix. Apparently the king didn't want to soil the palace with dungeons and torture chambers and prisoners who would eventually be sacrificed to the coven.

The odors of sweat and fear, of midden that had never

been flushed clean, and blood—lots of blood—assaulted all of her senses. She swallowed heavily to force calm on her stomach.

She stumbled again. This time she dropped to her knees, unable to hold herself upright any longer. Her hands rested on the straw-covered stone floor. A vibration passed through her hands, much like the one that had shaken the factory just before she was taken by the guards.

Alarmed, she looked up at the grim-faced men, who seemed to be hovering outside one particular cell. None of them seemed to notice the shaking. The hideous statue of a weasel that had once been in Simeon's study rocked with the trembling Kardia.

Before she could analyze the nature of the vibration, her guard lifted her by the elbows and thrust her past the snarling statue, into the cell.

"Never utter your blasphemies again, boy," King Simeon screamed at a man, hanging by his wrists from the wall. "My mother was Jaylene D'Rossemeyer, exiled daughter of the late king. *Jaylene,* not Janessa. Janessa's children are all bastards and not a drop of royal blood in them." Spittle dribbled from the king's mouth and his eyes showed more white than color.

"Tell that to your aura," Jack defied him.

Jack! Oh, poor Jack. Katrina looked closer at the magician who had vowed to help her. He had shielded her from Brunix and the palace magician last night, and opened his mind to her. Her heart shrank and burned for him. If only she could ease his pain.

Blood and bruises spread an ugly stain across his left side up into his naked chest, and probably his back, too. His bare feet looked swollen and raw. More bruises marred his jaw and wrists. Arms stretched wide by the rings holding his manacles, he seemed to cling to consciousness by the barest of threads.

Death was the only way to ease pain now. There was no escape from Simeon's dungeons. Just as there was no escape from his mines.

But Jack and P'pa escaped the mines, a tiny thought whispered into her mind.

"What do you mean about his aura?" The black-haired

beauty who was always at Simeon's side these days thrust
the king aside and stood squarely in front of Jack. None
of them seemed to notice Katrina.

"I mean that Simeon's aura is almost identical to Krej's,
and his magic smells just like Janataea's. He's brother to
those two, which means you've been sleeping with your
uncle, Rejiia."

Rejiia reared back in alarm.

"And borne him a child," Katrina added from across the
cell, noting the woman's now flat belly. "An abomination
by anyone's standards."

At last they all looked at her. She almost wished she'd
kept her mouth shut. The malevolence dripping from Simeon's and Rejiia's demeanor echoed that of the weasel,
and was almost enough to physically push her back into
the arms of her guard. A disgusting thought, almost as unpleasant as the thought of Simeon sleeping with his niece.

"You can't prove that!" Simeon defended himself. "My
servant destroyed the runes that Brunix copied. I have the
shawl with the runes woven into the flowers. I have unraveled it and burned the threads. No one will ever prove that
Janessa was my mother. Therefore, I decree that it is not
so. It is treason to say otherwise."

"You're insane," Jack breathed. His chest heaved and
he winced in pain. "As insane as Janataea was just before
she died. The Tambootie has rotted your mind."

Katrina agreed with Jack. She didn't know the people
Jack spoke of, but she saw Simeon's eyes and knew that
madness lay behind them.

"We will discuss this later, Simeon," Rejiia ordered. She
edged away from her lover as if she, too, believed he had
lost control of his mind. "These two must be kept alive and
reasonably healthy until the Solstice."

"I can't allow him to spread treason," Simeon protested.
"Tattia put the runes into the shawl to warn the queen.
But I had the lacemaker murdered and the shawl destroyed
with her. But the shawl survived to haunt me. I have finally
burned it and all who know of it must die. I want him dead
now. Guard, slit his throat. Now. I demand his death.
Now."

Chapter 34

"**D**on't be a fool, Simeon." Rejiia brushed the mewling aside as she faced Jack once more. "He has the transport spell. While he is in pain, and hungry—totally vulnerable—I will strip his mind and have the secret. I will also learn where the Commune hides. This *boy* will be the instrument of their destruction!"

Jack bit back a retort. Why waste energy asserting his right to a name? He'd need all of his strength to combat Rejiia's mind probes.

Then he made sense of her statement. Some of the Commune had escaped the fire at the monastery! Fervently he prayed that Jaylor and Brevelan and the baby had been among them. If they had, then the remnants of the Commune might have retreated to the clearing or Shayla's lair. He had a place to send Shayla for final healing.

If he managed to save himself long enough to patch her wing. If he managed to think of something else during Rejiia's spell. He didn't dare consider what would happen to Katrina. He had to somehow survive until he was sure Katrina was safe.

"I am the king," Simeon asserted. "My will rules. This kingdom exists to serve *ME*. Kill the blasphemous boy."

"In this house, by your own decree, the coven rules," Rejiia returned. "And I am the focus of the coven." She stared at the red-haired man with contempt.

Good. Division within the coven reduced their power and purpose. And Rejiia was female, she couldn't gather dragon magic. She, too, was limited by her body's reserves.

"You were the focus only while you were pregnant. I allowed you to take the focus because of your connection

to the *Gaia*. You aren't pregnant anymore, and you lost
the child, so I take back the focus." Simeon pouted like a
little boy. The reek of Tambootie on his breath intensified.

Jack guessed the leaves of the dragon tree had finally
inflated Simeon's sense of superiority beyond all limits of
reality. The same thing had happened to Krej and Janataea.
Neither believed themselves mortal anymore and had left
their bodies open to physical attack.

"Don't push me, Simeon. The coven looks to me for
leadership," Rejiia warned. Then she turned her attention
back to her prisoners, authoritative and purposeful.
"Loosen the girl's chains so she may sit or lie against the
opposite wall. Then clear this room. I need space and
concentration."

The guards obeyed, fixing a long chain between Katrina's
right manacle and a ring in the wall. Then they backed out
of the cell. Simeon refused to follow, but he did station
himself against the door, leaving Rejiia free to work inside
the damp stone room. She planted herself between Jack
and Katrina.

An advantage to Jack. If he couldn't see the girl cowering
in the far corner, then he wouldn't be distracted by her.
Wouldn't allow his thoughts to linger on her and draw Rejiia's attention to her under the influence of the probe.

Jack blanked his mind, trying desperately to think of
nothing at all. If Rejiia's spells had nothing to latch onto,
perhaps they'd fly in one ear and out the other.

"What about this?" A new man wearing the uniform of
an army officer entered the cell. Lanciar, the spy from the
mine, who had helped Jack escape and then betrayed him.
He carried a dead bird by the feet in his outstretched arm.
His nose wrinkled in distaste.

"Ah, the familiar. Throw it into the midden," Rejiia dismissed the man and his burden.

"No!" Jack howled. "You murdered Corby. You've
taken my only friend in the world." Once before he'd scattered a mind probe into erratic bird thoughts. Maybe he
could do it again. If they believed his grief and panic.

"That's right, boy." Lanciar smiled. "You have nothing
left to live for. You might as well give up your secrets so
you may die in peace. But before you die, I want to thank
you. That little session we had searching for the dragon

opened me to my full powers where the coven's rituals couldn't. I am now a master magician, one of the coven and eager to watch this spell so that I may learn to use it interrogating prisoners of war at the newly activated front. We won a stunning victory last week and captured or killed at least half of Darville's troops."

"Not Corby!" Jack yelled again, ignoring this latest disaster. *Think like a jackdaw, remember the bird's scattered thought patterns.*

"We've done this before, boy. Three years ago, at the coronation. That time, the stupid bird intercepted the probe. Now he's dead. There is only you and me and my magic." A small dart of glowing dark green appeared in Rejiia's hand. As dark as her magic, almost black. The same color he'd found in another dungeon, back in Coronnan. Rejiia had broken Jaylor's wards and stolen Krej from his cell. Krej, who lingered in his tin statue form at Simeon's side, blinked at Jack with knowing eyes.

Can't think of Krej and that one hint of animation. Can't think about Jaylor or Coronnan. Think like the bird. Random. Meaningless.

Rejiia lay the probe on her outstretched hand, murmuring an incantation. Eyes half closed, her face became a mask of emotionless concentration.

The probe grew in length. Its sharp point broadened into an arrowhead, big enough to hunt wild tusker. Wide. Sharp. Barbed. Impossible to remove once it caught on meat. The meat of Jack's mind.

The hot sweat of pain turned icy on his back. The burn of scraped skin beneath the manacles numbed. All discomfort gathered in his brain, a concentrated mass of terror.

"This will only hurt for a little while, boy," Rejiia cooed. The lines of her face softened into sensuous pleasure. Her breasts strained against the rich fabric of her gown. Her body radiated seduction. "Give me your thoughts. Join your mind with my mind, your body into my body. Share with me the ultimate intimacy."

Jack's breathing deepened against his will, until it matched Rejiia's heavy rhythm of passion. His heart pounded in his ears and his body strained to fulfill her promise of the sexual delights.

His thoughts returned to Katrina and the few moments

of openness they'd shared within the shelter of his armor. Sweet, innocent, honest. Reluctant to give herself to any man without love, with less than total commitment from both of them. A sweetness he'd never know.

Rejiia had offered herself to him once before. Not from passion, but in payment. She was a whore. A filthy, amoral, spiteful, selfish whore.

Sickened by her, Jack's body and mind lost all interest in Rejiia. But he continued the litany of her vile attributes. "Incestuous bitch! Adulteress. Traitor. I will kill myself before I betray my Commune. The transport spell dies with me as it should have died with the passing of the Stargods."

"I love to rape innocent *boys*," Rejiia sighed with pleasure as she blew the pulsing probe from her hand as if sending a lover's kiss. "They learn to revel in the *pain!*"

Jack slammed his eyelids closed, praying that the probe wouldn't gain entrance to his mind through a vulnerable eye.

A slight whirring sound circled his head. Pressure built, squeezing his skull, demanding he open himself. More pressure until he thought his head would explode with it. His eyes seemed to bulge and his ears filled with a roar of unnatural sound. He fought the urge to cry out, to open any part of himself.

Think of quiet. Peace. Solitude. A gentle brook babbling down a mountain side. Hot springs filling a pool with enough warmth to bathe. Calubra ferns screening the path . . . the path back to the clearing.

"The clearing . . ." he heard himself say. "Brevelan's clearing."

Katrina watched in fascinated horror as Jack twisted and writhed as much as his bonds would allow. He fought the slimy black arrow of magic with eyes closed and muscled hunched.

She knew the moment Rejiia's spell penetrated Jack's defenses. His body relaxed, his face lost all expression and he began to speak. Incoherent words, gibberish, or a foreign language.

Rejiia flushed with embarrassment at this failure in communication. Then she screwed up her face into ugly contortions, concentrating her will on her victim. His words finally made sense.

"To find the clearing, take the path behind the pub, up hill to a large boulder split in two. The path seems to go around the boulder. You must step through the broken halves . . ." Jack recited in a monotone.

"Yes, yes, but what pub? Where?" Rejiia stamped her foot in frustration.

"Fishing village of no name. Step through the two broken halves of the boulder, under the fallen tree and onto a game trail . . ."

"Where is the fishing village?" Rejiia screamed. Her hands reached for her perfect hair as if to tear it from her scalp. At the last second she thought better of her actions. "Fetch me some Tambootie, Simeon. I must press him harder."

"No name village south of the capital. The game trail ends at a creek. Wait for the opening. Brevelan opens the path to those in need of her healing." Jack sagged against his chains as if unconscious. Sweat ran in rivulets down his cheeks and chest.

Katrina hoped he'd passed beyond the pain and guilt of succumbing to the spell. When he awoke, he'd be chilled and she wouldn't be able to comfort him.

In frustration she yanked at her chains. Simeon glared at her for quiet. His lips curled in a feral snarl, exactly like the expression on the face of the tin weasel. Katrina ceased her struggle.

"We will come back to Brevelan's clearing, boy. Give me the transport spell," Rejiia demanded. A fat oily leaf as broad as her palm appeared out of nowhere and drifted into her outstretched hand. She nibbled the tip of the leaf and licked droplets of oil from the vein.

A smile crossed her face and her hands began to flutter with new animation. Katrina hadn't been aware of the sagging in the woman's shoulders until this new resurgence of energy.

Jack looked puzzled and upset at the newest question. He did not respond.

"The *transport* spell. How is it done?" Rejiia urged, more patient now that she had consumed the dark green leaf with pink veins. She snapped her fingers at Simeon to indicate she needed another.

The king pouted and folded his arms across his chest in defiance of the order. Rejiia's eyes rolled up in exasperation. Without taking her eyes off Jack, she pointed to one of the men hovering outside the cell. The short magician who had visited the factory last night responded. In the matter of two heartbeats, three more leaves appeared in Rejiia's hand.

"Dangerous. Too dangerous. Lost in the void," Jack mumbled. His eyes snapped open and several emotions crossed his face in rapid succession. Fear of the spell fought Rejiia's compulsion to recite.

"I will risk the void. I will risk a confrontation with the dragons. Give. Me. The. Transport. Spell."

Words that meant nothing to Katrina, but delighted Rejiia and Simeon, poured from his mouth. Words of time lapses, visualization, deep breathing, and trances. And then a lilting series of words to trigger the spell. When the last syllables dribbled from him, like drool on a baby's chin, he collapsed against his chain, knees unable to support him any longer.

"Wake up, boy!" Rejiia slapped his face.

Katrina winced at the sharp sound. No response from Jack.

"Very well. I have what I came for. Guards, loosen his chains so he may lie down and die."

"Wouldn't want to take a steed up this path, Your Grace." Sergeant Fred de Baker checked the backtrail for signs of followers. Margit, dressed in comfortable leather trews and tunic and looking happier than Darville had ever seen her, signaled that no one followed.

"It's been a long time since I ran back and forth from village to clearing without a second thought. I'm not in condition for this." King Darville paused for breath in their upward trek. He held out his good right hand to assist his queen over a rough spot. Thanks to Brevelan's healing spells, Mikka had recovered rapidly from the last miscarriage.

She had said little since they left the capital. No stronger wall could stand between them than this endless silence.

"We were friends, Mikka, when we considered Brevelan's clearing our home," he said quietly.

She looked up then, her eyes steady and clear. Hope sparked between them.

" 'Tis Brevelan and Jaylor's friendship that worries me, love. How could we let this one issue destroy the bonds we forged? There must be another way," she said quietly.

"Our enemies have sought long and hard to shatter the friendship of a lifetime. We withstood those assaults only to fall victim to our own pride and ambition. Come, Mikka. We have to settle this, no matter how difficult for all of us."

"Promise me, Darville, that if we find no solution to the succession, you will put me aside and remarry."

"I won't even consider it. I'll match your strong will against my stubbornness. We will find a solution." He kissed her palm with loving tenderness. The wall of silence crumbled but other walls threatened to rise up.

"You sure this is the right path, Your Grace? Seems to fade into nothing more'n it goes forward," Fred asked.

Margit moved up beside him and giggled. "The clearing wouldn't be secure if just anyone could find it." She strode forward with a masculine swagger.

"This is the right path, Fred." In more ways than one. For the good of the kingdom, Darville realized, he needed to make peace with Brevelan and Jaylor over Glendon. More important, Mikka needed to settle the issue of the cat persona sharing her body.

Only Jaylor and Brevelan could help. So the royal couple had journeyed to the southern edge of Coronnan in search of the magicians.

They had left their military escort in the foul-smelling pub of a fishing village near the foothills to the Southern Mountains. Fred and Margit were the only ones allowed to accompany them on the long climb up hill.

Both Darville and Mikka knew the trail well. Four years ago, they'd traveled it often enough. He'd been a golden wolf then, and she a multicolored cat, familiars to a red-haired witchwoman.

Now he was a king, with a kingdom straining toward stability and she was his barren queen. An heir to the throne would give the people of Coronnan the confidence to continue their quest for peace among themselves and with their neighboring kingdoms.

Darville had acknowledged as heir his own bastard son, Glendon, over the claims of Rejiia de Draconis, daughter of his father's cousin. Rejiia's husband had petitioned the Council of Provinces time and again to proclaim his wife heir. But Rejiia had been absent from the capital for nearly a year. Rumor placed her variously in SeLenicca, in Hanassa, and in her home—locked up and beaten regularly by her jealous husband.

Rejiia's claim was tainted by her father's involvement with a forbidden coven of Simurgh. Glendon might never be allowed to ascend the throne because his mother was an acknowledged witch and illegitimate as well. So far, Darville's acceptance of the boy as heir had met with only minor opposition from the Council of Provinces. They still hoped the king would put aside his barren wife and make a new alliance to produce a better successor to the Coraurlia. Few outland kingdoms had come forward with prospective brides, but the lords themselves had dozens of noble daughters.

The broken boulder that signaled the approach to the clearing appeared before him. Both Fred and Margit marched around the split rock in the direction the path seemed to follow. Darville stepped between the two pieces, on the left-hand side of the tree that had grown between the halves. Fred and Margit were immediately lost to sight.

Twenty paces beyond the boulder, the path crossed a creek and died.

"Look over there, Darville." Mikka pointed through the trees.

"I don't see anything." He squinted his eyes to peer closer in the direction she indicated.

"The barrier to the clearing. There's a big hole in it. We can walk right in without Brevelan opening it for us."

"Come on." He grabbed her hand and dragged her toward the barrier. "Something's terribly wrong. We've got to get in there!"

Rejiia left in a sweep of black skirts, the men following in her wake. The door slammed closed behind them. The click of the lock tolled Jack's doom like a bell in the remaining silence.

Darkness descended upon the cell until the torches further down the corridor filtered light through the bars that formed the wall. Once Jack's eyes adjusted, he picked out the details of Katrina's huddled form on the pallet opposite his. The single chain binding his left wrist to the ring in the wall was obscured by shadow.

The building grumbled beneath his weary body. Every joint and muscle screamed at the least movement.

"Oh, Jack, are you alive?" Katrina whispered. She crawled toward him, as far as her chain would reach. When she could get no closer, she stretched her free hand, as if to smooth his brow. Inches separated them. He couldn't move closer to accept her gentle touch.

"Not sure," he breathed the words, careful not to jostle any part of his body.

"I'm sorry you had to go through that. It was awful to watch. I can't imagine how horrible it must have been to endure."

Her sympathy reached across the space between them, even if she herself couldn't. A little of the pain lifted free of his mind.

"Don't try to imagine it. You'd hurt more than I want you to have to endure." The thought of the girl's plight suddenly pained his heart almost as much as the jailers' blows hurt his body.

"She didn't have to kill your bird. I know he meant a great deal to you. That just added insult to injury so you'd be more vulnerable."

As soon as Jack was certain the others were out of earshot he flexed his now unbound right wrist to check for damage and grinned to himself in the shadowy twilight that settled in the cell. "Don't be sorry for me. That wasn't Corby."

"How can you tell?" Astonishment and the smallest measure of hope shone through her words.

In Jack's imagination she'd never looked or sounded more beautiful. Even knowing her face was marred with bruises didn't diminish his gladness that his imprisonment was lightened by her presence.

"That was a crow, bigger and no white spots on his head. My bird is a jackdaw. His white spots look like an old man's bushy eyebrows. I sent Corby back to the dragons this morning. He shouldn't be anywhere near the city."

"He obeys you so well?"

"He is my familiar." Jack shrugged and regretted the movement. As a magician he needed no other explanation for the bond that now existed between himself and the bird. "How'd you get those bruises?"

"Brunix. He slapped me for speaking to you last night." She paused a moment, rubbing her jaw. "Is he really dead?"

"Yes."

"Did you kill him?"

"No. Did you care so much for him?"

"I hated him. But life with him was better than death during one of Simeon's rituals. I don't care that I have a power the king wanted to release. If having power means being like him or Brunix, I don't want it."

"I've been a slave, too, Katrina. I know the limited choices you've had. But if Brunix left you a virgin, then he was a better man than I hoped."

She bit her lip and turned her head away in embarrassment. "What will Simeon do to me when he finds out I'm not?"

A new pain awakened in Jack. Brunix had raped her. Like all Rovers, the factory owner had no respect for anyone not of his race and clan.

"Brunix only took me once. Mostly to prove he could after Simeon violated some private agreement between them. But Brunix grew tired of waiting for me to come to him willingly. He promised to rape me tonight, after he finished his business. I wasn't as important to him as his business and his money."

"The business had something to do with the runes in the temple. They cost him his life. The coven murdered him in the temple square. I wonder if they knew what he'd done to you, and death was his punishment?"

Further conversation ended with the rattle of the door again. The gap-toothed guard with the iron bar entered with a bowl of gruel and a cup of steaming liquid. Light from the corridor chased away some of the shadows.

"Dinner time, sweetheart." He bent and placed the meal at Katrina's feet. "Ain't ye gonna thank me?" He reached out and pinched Katrina's breast hard.

She winced and closed her eyes but said nothing. Then

a mask of total blankness descended upon her. No emotion betrayed the pain and humiliation she must be feeling.

"Frigid bitch," the guard spat and left. He made a great show of locking the door behind him, making certain the prisoners knew he was free and they were not.

"You need this more than me." Katrina shoved the bowl and cup as far as she could reach. By pushing gently with her toes, the food inched to within reach of Jack's finger-nails.

"Just a sip of the broth." He grimaced and held his stomach. "Take the rest, you've got to keep up your strength to survive whatever Simeon plans for you."

"If I don't escape, I'll make sure I don't live long enough to face his rituals!" Hesitantly she fished the long divider pin from her tousled plaits. The thick portion, gathered close to her scalp from temple to nape, had hidden the tool during the guard's earlier search for weapons. Even when they knew her to be free of anything dangerous, her captors had continued to paw her breasts and between her legs.

How would she do it? A slash across the wrist and slow bleeding to death? No, the guards would find her and stop her. A stab to the heart? Her hand shook as she held the sharp pin up for inspection.

"We'll get out of this, Katrina. I don't know how yet. Simeon's insanity and Rejiia's arrogance can be turned against them. If I push Simeon hard enough, maybe he'll admit that he's a bastard and not descended from Jaylene of Rossemeyer. That will end his influence in SeLenicca and in the coven. They need his claim to Rossemeyer. But we have to stay alive to escape." He stared at her pin with eyes that speculated and evaluated even as he pleaded with her. "I don't think I told her everything."

"We'll share the food." Determination to survive replaced her earlier despair. "You've got to eat, Jack. I don't know how long this will take, and that bitch may return at any moment. They got the wrong shawl. If we can get out of here I think I have proof that Simeon is a bastard, with no royal blood and has no right to rule. M'ma coded a message to the queen into the shawl three years ago. Queen Miranda and her councillors would have annulled the marriage, and set Jaranda aside as heir, if they thought Simeon a bastard. I know where the shawl is hidden and I intend to use it."

She'd picked one lock today with this pin. The manacles shouldn't be that much more difficult.

"Rejiia is probably hoping that watching you eat will make me hungrier and weaker, hasten my death." He sipped at the cup and coughed, nearly retching. The spasm went on and on, wrenching his body and draining him of even more energy. At last he lay back groaning. His face flushed with the onset of fever from his injuries.

Katrina bent to her task with the pin. They didn't have any time to lose.

Chapter 35

Jaylor stood before Darville and Mikka in the middle of the broken barrier into the clearing. With his arms crossed sternly, and his face totally blank of expression he presented a formidable barrier himself. Years ago, the king would have been able to read his friend's emotions by his posture. Too much time had passed. The bond of trust had been weakened.

"I come with an apology and a need to consult the Senior Magician, my chief adviser," he stated simply. Beside him, Mikka nodded her agreement with the statement.

A little of Jaylor's rigidity melted.

"You haven't needed to consult your 'chief adviser' very often in the last three years," Jaylor returned. "Why now?"

"I miss your friendship. I miss your wisdom. Most of all, I miss you and Brevelan. The thought of losing you forever pains me deeply." Eye-to-eye, he and Jaylor stood, assessing each other's strength and sincerity. So they had challenged each other time and again since adolescence. Each time they had ended with laughter and stronger bonds. This time . . . ?

"Could you please address the problem of Mikka and her cat? If we find a solution, the question of my heir might no longer exist."

"You have the right of it, Darville. The cat is the problem, not custody of Glendon. I think you need to meet my sons to know why." Jaylor turned and gestured at the impenetrable wall of the forest. Abruptly, the path appeared before them, straight and smooth. The three of them stepped forward, not quite side-by-side, not quite separated.

The open meadow, the planted garden, the flusterhen

coop, and the goat wandering beneath the line of laundry were as familiar as yesterday. But the one-room hut that had sheltered an ensorcelled wolf, a witchwoman, and a strange little cat had grown into a large cottage. Two rooms below, a large loft above, and a shed attached to the side.

"You've made improvements," Darville commented, more to break the silence than to express himself.

Mikka smiled for the first time in weeks. Hope returned to Darville. The clearing had always offered healing to those in need.

Jaylor nodded toward the biggest improvement of all. Behind the coop two little boys stalked a beleaguered flustercock. The younger of the two, boasting a full head of red hair, clutched a bright tail feather that could only belong to the cock.

"He . . . they are wonderful, Jaylor," Mikka gasped, an anxious hand to her throat.

It was the older of the two, with golden hair and eyes, longer of leg and narrower of hip than his brother, who caught their attention. As they watched, Glendon launched himself in a flying leap onto the cock's back. He came up giggling and dusty but triumphant, a long tail feather clutched in his grubby fist. The flustercock squawked, flapped, and announced to the world his long-suffering displeasure.

Both boys dusted themselves off and ran back to the laundry line. Brevelan appeared from behind damp shirts in three sizes. She knelt on the ground to gather them both in a big hug as they showed off their treasures.

Darville smiled. This was his son, happy, playful, and handsome. He was growing up secure in the knowledge that both his parents loved him. Darville had not had such security. His parents had been monarchs with mountains of duties. As a young prince, he had been entrusted to a series of tutors and guardians, each more interested in his position at court than Darville's happiness and welfare.

How could he and Mikka take the boy away from all of this love?

"I can't get it, Jack," Katrina whispered some hours later. She shook her manacles in frustration and put the long pin back into her hair.

Jack roused from a fitful doze. He was sure the perverted
guard with his pet iron bar named Mabel had broken some
of his ribs. The hot stabbing pain all across his chest and
into his back never dulled. Cautiously he tested his breathing. Painful, but not wheezing. Perhaps he had escaped a
punctured lung.

"If I had any magic left, I could open all the locks with
a thought." Now would be the time to do it. After midnight. The jailers were drowsy, the torches in the corridor
guttered and burned low.

The only things keeping the manor awake tonight was
the irregular trembling of the Kardia beneath them. Something strange was happening in Queen's City.

Jack's time sense remained true and his alignment with
the pole and all directions seemed intact. He had access to
magic, just no strength to throw it. Rejiia's probe had failed
in one sense: she'd viewed information but she hadn't
tripped his mind as she threatened. And she'd had to
renew her spell twice with Tambootie.

If only he were back at the factory and that little puddle
of reactivated ley lines. Lines that grew beneath Katrina's
workstation—the place where she sang as she worked in
the dark of night.

His memory called up scenes in villages between the
mine and the capital. Women singing as they went about
their daily chores. Songs of joy, of love, of nurturing.

In those villages the ley lines had glowed with life, like
newly planted fields of wheat. There had been a few areas
where the magic was stronger, where there were supposed
to be villages—groups of homes and people visible to
Corby, but not to Jack. Could the women have *Sung* a kind
of armor around their homes?

Brevelan *Sang* all of the time and her clearing had the
best protection of any place he'd encountered. Except the
time he'd visited there on his way to and from meeting
the blue-tipped dragon. The barriers had been down then.
Because she was dead? He prayed that merely her pro-
longed absence had opened the clearing to him.

Men protected their families with brute strength. Women
were more subtle, and perhaps stronger, in their forms of
protection. Nurturing and strengthening from within.

"*Sing* something, Katrina."

"What?"

"At the factory, you created a pool of magic benea
your workstation. You *Sang* the magic into life. That's t
power Simeon sensed within you. But you awakened it l
yourself. Please *Sing*." He levered himself to a half-sitti
position, balanced on his right elbow, the side that didr
hurt quite so badly.

"I have no magic," Katrina protested. But she lean
forward, almost eagerly, to listen closer to him.

"You are a woman. Therefore you have the stronge
magic of all, even if you can't throw it in specific spell
Sing me a lullaby. A healing lullaby."

Just then the foundations rumbled for the tenth tin
since Jack had been captured. The sense of a series of sma
collapses in the land filled him with a new anxiety. The
hadn't much time before the burned-out ley lines gave w;
to the pressures of the abandoned and exploited surface.

> *All is quiet, all is still,*
> *Sleep, my child, and fear not ill,*
> *Wintry winds blow chill and drear,*
> *Lullaby, my baby dear.*

Katrina's thin voice whispered into the darkness. SI
nearly choked on the last line. "The last time I sang th
lullaby was to my sister Hilza."

"The one who died?"

She nodded. Then she lifted her tear streaked face an
sang again, stronger, surer.

> *Let thy little eyelids close,*
> *Like the petals of the rose;*
> *When the morning sun shall glow,*
> *They shall into blossom blow,*
> *When the morning sun shall glow.*

> *Then the little flowers I'll prize*
> *Then I'll kiss those little eyes.*
> *And thy mother will not care,*
> *If 'tis spring or winter drear,*
> *And thy mother will not care,*
> *If 'tis spring or winter drear.*

Jack concentrated on the air surrounding Katrina. He didn't need magic to read an aura.

Healing green shimmered around her in increasing layers. Palest green of new willow shoots accompanied the first lines of her *Song*. Then a darker green of grass marked with dew at sunrise grew between the willow and the white afterimage surrounding her like a halo.

When she began the second verse, the white burst into yellow and the next layer, the color of mature ivy, climbed from the stone floor into the glowing colors.

Katrina came to the end of her melody and the colors dimmed but did not disperse.

"Again," Jack coaxed, awed at the controlled power contained within this woman who knew only the magic instinctive to her gender.

> *The dark-eyed Rover came over the hill*
> *down through the valley on May-day.*
> *He whistled and he sang 'til the city rang*
> *and he sought the heart of a lady*

Katrina's aura renewed itself with the first five notes of this slow and mournful tune. The layers deepened and Jack's magic reached out to embrace her power. He sensed the twisting of the lock on his manacles more than heard or felt the release.

He lay back and listened, renewing his strength and his magic. Eyes half closed, he watched for any further change.

> *Her father forbade the Rover's suit*
> *Her mother wept a malady*
> *They cried and they blamed 'til the rafters rang*
> *Never could he love the lady.*

> *They ran away to the forest's lure*
> *They refused her parents pity.*
> *But they wept and they died, alone and poor,*
> *Ne'er to return to the city.*

The last note of the *Song* hung in the air, an almost visible souvenir. And then she *Sang* the words again. The meaning of the lyrics penetrated Jack's weary mind. A love song. A man and a woman of different class and culture separated by loyalties and responsibilities greater than themselves. Typical of SeLenicca, the ballad was sad, pronouncing dire fates to young people who valued love over money.

In Coronnan, the song was joyful, and full of promise for the lovers. 'Twas a song he'd like to sing for Katrina—in better times and in a better place.

He allowed himself only one moment of poignant regret. Katrina sang it correctly. She could never love him. His life as a magician was destined to be more solitary than that of a Rover. Superstition would push him to the fringes of civilization, make him an outcast. Katrina deserved better.

The song built an ache in his heart as the notes climbed and lingered near the top of Katrina's range. The dark blue-green of an everblue in moonlight pulsed at the depth of her aura.

More blue burst forth and filled the gaps. Like quicksilver, the blue energy molded and flowed up and down and around. It slid into the floor and quickly filled the gaps in the paving stones, spread and formed a network of fragile ley lines.

Baby lines that needed love and care and nurturing to grow and fully integrate with the four elements to become part of the *Gaia*.

Katrina brought her song to a close and slumped against the wall. The power of her spell vibrated in the air. Some of the glow in the new ley lines dimmed, but they continued to pulse and throb.

"Can you see what you've done, Katrina?" Jack gasped.

"I sense nothing different. Only another tremor. But this one is smaller."

A crash and rattle of broken shutters and cracked wooden panels above them belied her words.

"Not smaller. You have stabilized the ground directly beneath us, for the moment." He continued to stare at the ley lines. His need to be free called to them. One tiny flash of blue stretched toward him, like a feeder root seeking water.

Jack stretched out his foot to touch the line. His skin crawled as if a hundred ants swarmed up his leg.

"Ah," he sighed in relief. He allowed the power to nourish him.

"You can open your chains now," he said to Katrina, still drawing the magic into his starved and battered body.

The rocking tremor increased in intensity. The iron bars rattled. Shouts of alarm echoed along the corridor. Torches fell from their brackets and smoldered in the damp, filthy straw.

"I think we'd better make a break for it, Jack. This room might be stable, but the rest of the city is likely to collapse on top of us." Katrina hastened to the door, rattling it to see if the lock had sprung.

Jack pulled one last bit of power into himself, as if drinking the last few swallows of ale after a meal. He gestured the door open and crawled to his feet.

No part of his body was free of pain. Each breath stabbed in his chest. His vision blurred and shifted focus, spinning his head in six directions at once. He used a little of his careful store of magic to reduce the pain to manageable levels.

"Don't pass out on me now, Jack. We've got to get out of here." Katrina hauled on his arm toward the exit.

He groaned from the pressure on his ribs.

The last of the blue lines withered as a nearby building collapsed in a tumbling crash.

Katrina draped Jack's right arm around her shoulders, careful not to touch his wounded left side. Witches were supposed to be left-handed—that was one way to tell a witch from a normal person. So the guards had concentrated on Jack's left side, to weaken him further. She knew he was right-handed. Another superstition broken by fact.

Half-dragging his weight, she stumbled into the deserted corridor. The only light came from a fallen torch and the smoking straw beneath it.

As she watched, the filthy mess ignited.

"You've got to help me, Jack. I can't carry you," she pleaded with him. The twelve steps up to the next level of cellars appeared a mile high with his weight holding her back. She remembered how slippery and narrow the stone slabs were and how easily she had tripped on the worn centers.

Dutifully, Jack tried steadier steps. His right, her left, they wobbled and nearly fell.

"Together, Jack." She paused to regain her balance. "Right, left." They took two steps together and remained in rhythm.

They traversed the short corridor with relative ease. The stairs seemed another matter. Jack's bare feet recoiled from the cold stone. Katrina's torn indoor slippers didn't insulate her feet much either.

"If I had my staff . . ." Jack looked around him.

"Here, use this burned-out torch as a cane." Katrina picked up the nearest fallen brand. About as long as her arm, the handle was sturdy and whole. The oil-soaked rags wrapped around one end had ceased smoldering in the damp straw, but made a decent base.

Katrina stepped onto the first stair. Jack followed. They paused. She climbed. He climbed. Haltingly they rose to the next level.

"I don't like the sound of your breathing, Jack. You sound kind of wheezy." She paused while he took short shallow breaths, wincing with every intake.

"Got to keep going. Worry later." Grimly he took another step, putting as much weight on her shoulders as he did the improvised walking stick. "I can't waste magic on myself. Got to conserve it for the tasks to come."

The cellars above the dungeons were deserted. Barrels of dried goods and casks of ale lay on their sides, some still rolling against a new tilt to the floor. Ropes of onions and garlic had been flung from their ceiling hooks. One barrel of flour had burst when it collided with a wall. The white powder was scuffed and filthy from running feet.

"Looks like a band of Rovers wreaked havoc in here," Jack surmised.

Katrina just grunted and hastened to the next flight of stairs. She didn't like the way the outside wall bulged and water seeped through the gaps in the stonework.

These steps were easier, because they were wide enough to hold an entire foot and had recently been scrubbed clean of cellar-damp slime. But there were fifteen of them and Jack was already tired.

As she placed her foot on the first wooden plank, another quake shook the floor. They didn't bother counting stairs or pausing until they were at the top.

Jack's weight dragged against her shoulders. She loosened her grasp and he slumped to his knees. A new round of coughing claimed his strength. When he was done, he collapsed into a fetal ball on the kitchen floor. Each intake of air sounded like a boat whistle.

"Please get up, Jack. Oh, please. We haven't much time," she pleaded.

His eyes opened. Fever bright and unfocused he mumbled something. "Water," he repeated the sound, a little closer to a recognizable word.

Mercifully a pitcher remained upright on the long work table in the center of the kitchen. A cup rolled on the floor, handle broken, rim chipped, but the bowl was intact.

A few sips, most of which dribbled from Jack's mouth along his cheek to the floor, seemed to revive him. He rolled to his knees but didn't have the stamina to rise further.

Katrina placed the fallen torch into his hand once more and crawled beneath his other arm. Straining her back and thighs, she heaved him upright. They proceeded to the back door.

More painful steps up into the garden. Then a level path to the street.

Noise assaulted Katrina's ears as soon as they rounded the end of the manor house. Everywhere, people ran screaming. Children cried. Steeds wailed and dogs howled. Fires burned out of control. Houses gaped and split, while near neighbors remained intact.

A stream of frightened citizens clogged the broad street. All headed out of town toward the hills and safety.

"The river's broken its dike."

"Rovers fighting the palace guard."

"Flooding in the factories."

"Fire in the slums."

"Rovers looting the shops."

Comments flowed around them. How much was fact and how much was rumor?

She turned into the crowd, hoping the press of bodies would carry them.

"Turn back," Jack ordered.

"Don't be a fool, Jack. We've got to get out of town."

"I have to go back to the factory. I have to get some Tambrin lace to patch the dragon's wing." He wrenched free of her grasp, staggered and nearly fell beneath the feet of a frightened steed.

The rider hauled back on the reins. The beast reared. Iron-shod hooves lashed out.

Katrina dove for Jack, rolling with him out of harm's way. "Idiot. You'll be killed. You can't make it alone."

"Got to." He heaved himself upright again and pushed his way to the edge of the mob.

Katrina clutched his hand rather than be separated from him. "A piece of lace isn't important enough to risk your life. We'll come back when this is over."

As if to emphasize her words, the Kardia shook again. The roof of the manor they had just left collapsed, taking the walls with it.

"My life isn't important anymore. The dragons are. I've got to send the wing patch to Shayla now. Before Simeon can get to her again."

Fear tugged Katrina back into the crowd and the path to safety. But something more bound her to Jack and his cause. He was right. Their lives meant nothing if they allowed Simeon to continue in his insane path. The sorcerer had to be stopped. The only way to do that was to remove his dragon from SeLenicca.

"This way. I know a shortcut back to the river. If the flood hasn't destroyed the building. If Simeon hasn't found the stash of lace already. If we aren't killed along the way . . ."

All is undone. The land rebels against Simeon. His insane obsession with the lace shawl prevents him from stopping the earthquakes. The shawl he stole did not contain the runic message he fears will prove him a bastard—not even a royal bastard. While he screams and strikes out at all near him, the walls crumble. He has drained SeLenicca and its people of life. They can no longer serve him.

I would abandon him and this cursed land, but I still need him. He can gather dragon magic in great quantities. I cannot. His dragon magic must be turned back upon its source to destroy the dragons once and for all. Only then will I feel safe enough to return to Coronnan and demand my rights as blood heir to Darville.

Chapter 36

Jack endured the trek back to the lace factory in a haze of pain, eased only slightly by Katrina's unfailing support. Broken cobblestones tore his feet. Panicked citizens jostled his smashed ribs. Each collapse of an old ley line stabbed through his magic into his heart. He lost all sense of direction and time. Purpose alone carried him to the edge of the river.

He wished he dared summon a purple dragon. But the collapsing city and frightened citizens would be a greater danger to Amaranth than they were to Jack.

"We'll have to use the warehouse door," Jack grumbled as he eyed the rubble, including half of a wall from a neighboring factory, piled against the once proudly clean front door of Brunix's factory.

Inside, all was confusion. Laborers looted the crates of lace intended for export. Barter goods against hard times to come. Two stories up in the workroom, lacemakers rushed about, packing their pillows, bobbins, and patterns—the most precious possessions they could claim. With lace equipment and patterns, they could earn a living in any city in the world.

"Brunix cheated me time and again, snipping off arm-lengths of lace and not counting it in my wages," one woman screamed. "I claim the velvet pillow and bobbins in his flat!" She dashed up the last flight of stairs.

"The outland bastard demanded I sleep with him time and again without extra pay. The law says he had to pay me extra. I claim the patterns he hides up there!" another woman said as she, too, headed up the stairs.

"No," Katrina protested. "They'll find the stash of Tambrin lace!" She abandoned Jack to race after her rivals.

Just then, another tremor rocked the city. The staircase shook and the railing split. The lacemaker highest on the flight clutched at the cracked wood for balance. Her weight broke the remnants of the railing. She flailed her arms and crashed to the landing by the workroom.

Katrina and the second lacemaker stopped dead in their tracks. With the railing gone, neither dared test the stairs for stability.

Jack limped over to the fallen women. He didn't need to test her pulse to see if she lived. The awkward angle of her neck and the blankly staring eyes pronounced her dead.

"Katrina, I need the lace shawl made of Tambrin. We've risked our lives to get here for it. Where is it hidden?" he asked in the mildest voice he could muster. She couldn't freeze in panic now. They had to finish this.

She looked at him with wide anxious eyes. "Up there." Her head gestured slightly toward the apartment that covered the entire top story of the building.

One more flight of stairs, broken in places but passable, if one avoided the splintered railing. Surely he could manage one more. To free Shayla he had to endure one more flight of stairs. "I'll get it. Meet me in the workroom."

Lift one foot, put it down. Lift the other a little higher, put it down. He kept one hand against the wall, the other outstretched for balance. The world narrowed to the staircase and the pain in his side.

Two steps. Then three more. He collapsed, nearly blind with dizziness. A broken rib had moved and pierced his lung. He could hardly breathe.

"No, Jack. I'll get the shawl. Wait for me in the workroom." Katrina dashed up to the landing and disappeared into the flat. Her rival lacemaker took the steps more cautiously behind her.

Jack lay still a moment gathering breath and the will to move. The well of magic was behind him. Nurtured by *Song,* the blue lines were firmly anchored in the Kardia. He had to return to them.

Like a bay crawler he edged backward on all fours. When his feet touched the landing, he braced himself against the wall and heaved his body upright. The effort almost knocked him unconscious. "Ley lines. I need the ley lines." Just thinking about the restorative power of the latent magic spurred him into the chaos of the workroom.

Oblivious to his presence, the lacemakers fled in groups of two and three. By the time he reached the window, the room was empty.

The magic filled him at first touch. He drank greedily from the well. Strength and stability first. Then he pushed his ribs back into place and repaired the tiny hole in his lung.

His body demanded more. He dared not take it. This little puddle of magic had to transport Katrina and the lace to safety. He dared not drain it to help himself.

"The factory doors are blocked." Rejiia stared at the pile of rubble as if it were responsible for all of her problems instead of just one of them.

"We must enter by magic." Simeon announced.

"The spell will cost me too dearly," Rejiia warned, as she glared at him. He had learned the secret of the transport spell at the same time as she. He also had the dragon to give him extra magic. "You must work the spell of flight. The power within me is not enough," she ordered.

Another earthquake set the rubble trembling. Simeon jumped back from the danger pouting. Panicked gibberish leaked from his mind.

"If you told me what the real shawl looked like, I could grab it with magic and use my remaining reserves of power to escape this cursed city," Rejiia shouted at him. He didn't appear to hear. His hands fluttered over his heart as he anxiously searched a multitude of shadows for his enemies.

"The Kardia itself rebels against me. Why has Simurgh deserted me?" he wailed.

Rejiia repeated her question rather than screech her frustration. Simurgh was only a means to an end, not the all-knowing deity the coven believed. She had realized that the moment her father and aunt had fallen to Darville, a believer in the Stargods.

"I can't tell you! Only I must know the shawl's secrets," Simeon said around tight lips. His eyes rolled away from her direct gaze.

He wouldn't release the information even under coercion.

She had to try the spell. Carefully she replayed the magician boy's rambling instructions.

Three slow breaths brought her close to a trance. Three more and the void beckoned. Carefully she visualized the place she must take herself and Simeon. The office on the ground floor. She'd been there before with a bribe to Brunix for making the silver lace she preferred on her black gowns.

A quick grab at the power of the void and a quicker release. Visualization of their bodies three heartbeats before the beginning of the spell, but inside the building.

The air around them shifted and shimmered. Blackness, cold, no sense of body or self. Five heartbeats she endured the sensory deprivation. Then the image of the neat, white painted office wrapped around her and Simeon. She landed heavily, body and head spinning. Her passenger began searching the office before she had fully recovered.

Katrina didn't waste time sorting and choosing lace. Making a basket of her skirt she gathered the shawl and as much of the Tambrin lace as she could carry. Her pillow, the one P'pa had sold to Brunix, fit under her arm, the patterns tucked neatly inside the cylinder.

Her coworker, Taalia, staggered into the flat, more intent on loot than her own safety. Katrina barely spared her a glance. There was a second pillow and piles of lace for any who cared to grab them. She hated the thought of this greedy, spiteful woman claiming anything. With Brunix dead and the city collapsing around them, possession didn't seem to matter any more.

In moments she was back in the workroom.

Jack stood beneath the window where he had sheltered her from Brunix and the palace magician. An expression of relief, bordering on bliss, filled his bruised and filthy face.

"I'll need you to *Sing* again, Katrina," he said. His eyes were closed and his chin lifted as if listening to something far away.

"What . . . what are you going to do?" She couldn't bring herself to stand next to him. His entire body seemed to glow with an eerie blue light.

Ghosts were supposed to look like that. Once more she looked for signs of her mother's spirit. Half relieved and half disappointed at not finding her, she turned her full attention on Jack.

Sounds of more buildings crashing together outside dominated her senses.

"We're cut off. I have to transport you and the lace to Shayla," Jack stated.

Fear pressed against Katrina's chest. Transport? Magic! Where did he get the strength and the will?

"Now listen closely. Shayla is large and formidable. But she won't hurt you. Don't be frightened. You must secure the lace to her wing with touches of glue." He held out a pot of spirit gum he'd liberated from Brunix's office on the way to the workroom. "Small touches of the glue, just enough to hold the lace in position."

"I can't do it alone, Jack."

"You must. I have to stay here to keep Simeon and Rejiia from following you. I sense them coming closer. *Sing* while you patch Shayla's wing. *Sing* like you did in the dungeon. The dragon will take you and your father to safety."

"You have to come with me, Jack. I can't let you die here." She rushed to his side, dropping her pillow at their touching feet so she could grab his arm.

"I'll follow when I can." He opened his eyes and looked at her with longing. "Remember me kindly, Katrina. Now *Sing* as if your life depended upon it."

The only tune that came to mind was the work tune she hummed to herself as she worked alone at night. A few hesitant notes rose within her. Then certain that her songs gave this magician power, she opened her mouth wide and let the notes soar with her heart. If he needed more power to come with her, then she'd give it to him.

Jack felt another major ley line collapse. His preparation for transport faltered. The void appeared and disappeared before him.

Someone had thrown a powerful spell very close.

Rejiia or Simeon? How close were they?

He sent his awareness in a quick dart around the building. Two lives filled with purpose approached.

"The shawl is near. I can feel it. The runes threaten me!" King Simeon's voice.

"Upstairs. The source of power is directly above us," Rejiia said.

The king's mistress was close. Too close.

Jack faltered in his deep breathing. The memory of the pain she had inflicted upon him sent his heart racing. His mind went blank. He had to get away from her!

"Jack, what's wrong?" Katrina tugged at his arm.

Reality and purpose broke through his instinctive panic. "Rejiia and Simeon. Let go of my arm so I can send you to Shayla."

"No. She'll kill you this time. You must come with me." She held tighter as she changed her *Song.*

Jack ignored her plea and accessed the void. From memory, he built a mental picture of the field outside the lair. He added the waterfall and the pool, tall cliffs and clumps of stunted Tambootie trees. The dragonets and Shayla climbed into the picture of their own volition. Lastly he added the big blue-tipped male, Fraank, and Corby.

Then, he drew on all the power of the ley lines as he moved Katrina and her bundle of lace into the field, an arm-length from the edge of the pool. He'd better send her pillow, too; she'd risked much to salvage it.

He barely noticed the feminine arm clutching his shoulders. He heard only the love ballad Katrina *Sang* with renewed vigor.

"There they are!" Simeon called out. "She's got the shawl. We have to stop them!"

Cold blackness engulfed Katrina suddenly, painfully. She cried out but no sound emerged. For several heartbeats she lost contact with her body and her senses. Jack seemed to dissolve beneath her grasp.

Before she could panic, awareness of her feet returned. Spongy grass beneath her ragged slippers. Birds chirping. A roar in the background.

Instinctively she ducked away from the sound, expecting the ceiling to crash around her. Then she realized 'twas only water rushing from the mountains toward the sea. Were they on the riverbank?

Bright sunshine pierced Katrina's closed eyelids. Shivering and scared, she continued clinging to Jack. His body felt solid once more beneath her grasping hand.

Cautiously she opened one eye a tiny slit. A lush meadow filled with wild flowers sparkled with dew in the first kiss of the morning sun.

Bees flitted from flower to flower. A pool fed by a mighty waterfall lapped at her feet. Bushes rustled, and she was certain someone or *something* watched her with predatory instincts.

Born and bred in the city, she'd never seen anything like this wild valley.

"Jack?" she whispered. "Jack, where are you?"

He, too, opened one eye. "*You* are where you are supposed to be, outside the dragon lair. I'm supposed to be back in the city, preventing Rejiia and Simeon from following you."

"I . . . I . . ." Katrina stammered and blushed. Only then did she become aware that her arm was still wrapped around his naked shoulders. His arm held her close against his side as if he never intended to let go. A hair's breadth separated her mouth from his. Their hearts beat in unison as they breathed in counterpoint.

A long moment of awareness awoke within her. She stared at the curve of his full lips surrounded by a sensuously thick beard and mustache. A part of her needed to know if the silky hair was as soft as Tambrin.

"Jack! You're back," a quavering male voice called. The man, thin and stoop-shouldered, appeared from behind the curtain of the waterfall.

Jack stepped away from her and turned his head toward the man. A chill of foreboding planted itself in Katrina's mind as Jack removed the warmth of his body from contact with her—though only half an arm-length separated them.

Something familiar in the approaching man's voice brought Katrina's gaze away from the wonder of Jack's mouth to watch the man pick his way around the pool.

"What happened to you, Jack? You're a mess. Worse than in the mines. And who is this with you?" The man shielded his eyes from the increasingly bright sun with his hand. He blinked several times and then stumbled over nothing. "*Stargods,* is that you, Katrina?"

"P'pa!" Had his hair and beard always been so thin and gray? "Oh, P'pa," she rushed to his side, still cradling the treasure of lace in her skirt.

Father and daughter stared at each other for long moments, drinking in the sight of a long-lost loved one.

The pain and the anger against P'pa she had nursed for three years faded at the sight of his frail body. What she had suffered at the hands of Brunix was nothing compared to what he must have endured in the mines.

Jack had lived through the same anguish as her father and emerged strong and resourceful.

Her father had wasted away. Dark purple shadows made hollows of his eyes. Knots of pain gnarled his finger joints. His shoulders bent under the weight of the world.

"Katey, how you've grown! A beautiful woman now, tall as your M'ma and more beautiful than ever." Hesitantly he gathered her into his arms. Tears flowed freely from both of them.

"I never thought to see you again, P'pa. I never hoped to find . . . to find . . ." Her thoughts clumped in her throat unable to get around three years of unshed tears.

He doesn't know that you were sold into slavery also. Spare him, please. Jack spoke directly into her mind. His pain at having to watch his only friend waste away in a long death became her pain.

"But for Jack I wouldn't have survived. I owe him my life. I owe him more for bringing you to me." P'pa coughed. A great shuddering exhalation.

Katrina, with her ear pressed to her father's chest, was reminded of the tremors beneath Queen's City.

"P'pa," she moaned, holding him close. Frantically, she prayed that he had escaped the mine in time, that fresh air, sunshine, and rest would heal him.

"Fraank, Katrina, I must tell you that Tattia did not commit suicide," Jack said sadly. He didn't want to talk about death now. His own hovered too close. But he had to give these two people, the only people in the world he dared call friends, the slight comfort of the news. "Simeon had her murdered."

Fraank swallowed deeply several times as if Tattia's death had just happened, not three years ago. "How do you know?" he finally said.

"Her ghost sought me out. She was stabbed with a ritual knife by one of Simeon's coven. The same knife that killed Brunix."

Katrina hung her head briefly, then looked up. Relief smoothed the lines of grief on her beautiful face. "Thank you, Jack. I suspected as much. There is a little comfort in knowing she did not take her own life."

"Do you remember, the night before she died, Katey. She was almost happy that night. She acted as if she had found something to hope for." Fraank dashed a tear from his eyes.

"Sorry to interrupt with bad news. You can reminisce later, Fraank. We've work to do and enemies on our tail," Jack reminded them. A shirt appeared in his hands. He winced as he slid his arms into the sleeves. "Where's Corby?"

P'pa shrugged his shoulders. "Haven't seen the bird."

"I hope he's all right. 'Tis a long flight from the city." Worry furrowed his brow and marked his posture as he scanned the picturesque vale for signs of one noisy, black bird.

Chapter 37

"**O**h my!" Katrina whispered.

Jack watched her eyes grow round and her mouth open in wonder as two dragonets, Rufan and Amaranth, glided into the valley and landed at his feet. As tall and as long as he, either of the two were enough to frighten away most predators. Only the silvery softness of their fur and the ill-defined edges of babyhood made their appearance less intimidating.

Rufan greeted him with a joyous nudge of his steedlike muzzle. A nudge that nearly toppled Jack into the pool. The knob of Rufan's unformed spiral horn pressed painfully into Jack's still damaged side.

Amaranth tried to ease Jack's grimace of pain by fanning him with his silvery wings. The resulting wind sent waves of water from the pool back into the waterfall.

"Hi, 'gnets. Where's your mama?" Jack hooked his arm around Amaranth's neck, effectively curtailing any further pranks. And while he touched the purple-tip, he gathered as much magic as he could to repair and replenish his body.

He also looked through Amaranth's memories for the remains of last night's hunt, properly roasted by dragon fire. A thought brought a hunk of meat, big enough for him and Katrina to share.

He smiled at Katrina's rapidly changing expressions. First she tried to giggle at the eager antics of the baby dragons. Then the rippling sound died aborning as Shayla emerged from the lair. The vastness of her crystalline outline reminded them that Amaranth and his companion were still babies after all. Momentary fear, then awe widened Katrina's eyes until he could see cloud shadows in them.

(Welcome.) Shayla nodded her head in greeting. *(The children missed you, Jack.)*

"I missed them too, Shayla," Jack said around a mouthful of meat.

Katrina dipped a hasty curtsy. Her eyes were still glued to the dragon and her mouth slightly agape. But the beginnings of a smile tugged at her lips.

"I . . . I brought you some lace, ma'am," she stammered. "How do I address a dragon?" she whispered aside to Jack. A little of the strain of the last few days showed in the tight cords of her neck and glazed eyes.

(We prefer the use of names, Katrina.)

"Yes, ma'am . . . I mean, Shayla."

"Our enemies will follow shortly," Jack interrupted. "We have to set the patch without delay." He scanned the skies uneasily for signs of Corby. An entire day and night had passed since he'd sent the bird. How far could one lonely jackdaw fly in that amount of time?

While Katrina spread her treasure of Tambrin lace out on the grass, Shayla hunkered down close by, wings slightly spread. Katrina kept looking up at the dragon as if she expected to be eaten at any moment. Fraank knelt beside her. Jack paced wearily, stretching his senses for any sign of Rejiia and Simeon.

"No need to fret, Katey," Fraank soothed his daughter. "Shayla and her family hid me from Simeon's agents. They've fed me and kept me company. They'll not hurt you." The older man fingered the lace.

Jack scanned the skies once more. He allowed his gaze to linger on the irregular knob atop the cliff. The blue-tipped male still perched there, surveying the vale.

(I will keep watch, Jack. You may work your spell and then we will all flee to safety,) the blue-tip said.

What about the babies? Can they fly well enough to reach a safe haven? Jack kept half his attention on Katrina and Shayla as they examined the lace. He kept munching the meat, refueling his body, even after the venison had lost its first savory appeal.

(We've been practicing flying in the void. Don't worry about dragons. Worry about yourself and your lady.) A chuckle rippled from the male dragon's throat.

Jack was about to contradict the dragon about his status

with Katrina and changed his mind. Arguing with dragons just wasted breath. They never changed their minds.

Where's Corby? he asked, focusing his mental words on a tight line to the dragon.

(I cannot find him.) The dragon sounded puzzled but not worried. *(He is a wild bird and did not bond with you easily. He fought my compulsion to aid you with many temper tantrums. He may have returned to the wild now that your quest is nearly finished.)*

"I hope so. I'd hate to think Rejiia managed to capture him after all. She is the more powerful of our two enemies. Simeon's obsession with the runes within one piece of lace has narrowed his power. He sees only one objective and ignores all other possibilities and dangers."

Dragon thought exploded in Jack's mind. *(Runes! What runes?)*

"Part of a design Katrina's mother wove into one of those pieces." Jack gestured toward the selection of lace spread out on the grass in a prearranged pattern for attaching to the wing. "Nothing important."

The blue-tip spread his wings and glided from his perch into the meadow. The wind from his passage scattered the array of lace like sea foam on the beach of the Great Bay.

Shayla stretched her undamaged wing protectively over Katrina and the frothy lace. Her high-pitched hiss of reprimand pierced Jack's ears. He slapped his hands over the offended organs.

Too late he realized the temporary deafness obscured another sound born on the wind.

But the dragonets heard it and greeted the invasion of their peaceful vale by a flock of noisy crows with mock anger. Ten baby dragons took wing, eager for a new game of chase and harry.

The crows were being herded by a purpose more fearsome than a dozen playful dragons. Scout birds broke away from their arrowhead formation and flew in the opposite direction, screeching defiance. The dragonets left the main flock to pursue the individuals. Deep within the birds' ranks struggled a wounded member of the flock. They all dived together for the pool at the base of the waterfall.

"Quickly, Katrina, get the patch set. Anchor it with a *Song* and the glue. Shayla, as soon as you can get air under that wing, take Katrina to safety. Brevelan's clearing will shelter you until it's healed. One of your mates can carry Fraank. Take the babies with you. Especially Amaranth and his twin. We can't take a chance that Rejiia will trap them and gather their magic!" Jack barked orders right and left as he erected his personal armor and settled himself for the battle of his life.

"What about you, Jack?" Katrina asked as she shook out the largest piece of lace in the collection. The shawl wasn't large enough to cover the hole in Shayla's wing. She would need many of the smaller pieces to complete the patch.

"I have to delay Rejiia and Simeon here. They're right behind the birds. They probably followed the trail of our earlier transport. They can't be allowed to follow Shayla." He turned his back on the patching procedure.

The squawking flock of black birds zoomed downward with increasing speed. They were close enough now for Jack to pick out the weakest member. A larger, stronger bird flew directly beneath it, preventing it from falling when its wings failed. Other birds circled it in tight formation, protecting it from the worst of the wind.

As the mass of birds, a hundred or more, swooped low, Jack fought the urge to duck. At the last moment he opened his armor and caught the wounded bird with a touch of levitation. It dropped into his hands, exhausted and shivering. Above its eyes were two bald spots where tufts of white feathers should be.

"Corby?" Jack caressed the sleek black head with a gentling finger.

The bird tried to tuck his head beneath his wing. The effort of movement seemed too much. "Caged! Caged, caged," he croaked. "Big light."

"Someone caught you and caged you. They left you in the sun? Without water?"

"Reji comes, Reji, Reji." The last words drained the jackdaw of energy. He collapsed in Jack's hand, a heavy, inert weight.

"Don't you dare die on me, Corby!" Lonely tears swelled his throat. Through all his pain and years of toil only Corby had remained from his days as Jaylor's apprentice—the only time in his life he'd been happy and cared for. Loved. Until now. He had Katrina now. Maybe.

Light shimmered and distorted not six yards in front of Jack. He needed to cuddle and protect his companion, but urgency prevented that. Hastily he spared the magic to send the unconscious bird into a pocket between two spines on the blue-tipped dragon's back.

"Please keep him safe, sir," he pleaded as he ducked the first bolt of magic thrown by the now solid forms of Rejiia and Simeon.

"Take all your dragons out of here, Shayla," he yelled. "Without dragons, Simeon has no magic!" A flash of blinding white light followed his words.

Katrina held the last round doily in place over the edge of the ugly black wound in Shayla's wing. Never had she seen anything to match Simeon's cruelty in maiming this magnificent dragon. She counted carefully to ten for the glue to set while her heart hammered rapidly.

The skin on the back of her neck crawled with the sense of impending danger. She smelled the difference in the air when Simeon and his mistress materialized. A sharp scent of foliage beginning to rot.

(Now!) Shayla commanded. *(We must leave now.)*

"But it's not set. The patch will come off when you fly." Katrina held the doily in place, willing the liquid wax to congeal faster.

(No more time. I must fly as it is. Come.) The last word commanded the babies as well as Katrina.

The lacemaker wasted no more time. Shayla was too weak to take her. With a prayer and a leap she clambered onto the blue-tipped male dragon's back. Two spinal horns cradled her like a saddle. Corby lay between two smaller spikes in front of her, a black spot of reality in this fantastic adventure. She scooped the bird into her lap to keep him safe.

"P'pa, climb up behind me!" she called. Her father continued to stare at the three magicians.

"P'pa!"

(My mates will see to him,) Shayla explained. *(I must leave now.)*

Huge shoulder muscles stretched beneath Katrina as the male matched Shayla's movements. They spread their wings.

Some of the dragon's joy in the movement filtered into Katrina's mind.

(Too long since I have flown,) Shayla groaned. Her wings faltered in their upward movement. Before they quite reached the peak of the arch, Shayla thrust them downward and gathered her legs beneath her. *(Not enough strength. We'll have to run for it.)*

Katrina's dragon moved into position behind Shayla, encouraging and protecting her at the same time.

Above them, the dragonets fluttered and chirped. Higher still, more dim outlines circled. The sense of urgency pressed on Katrina like a weight.

Rejiia raised her arms in preparation for an assault on Shayla. Simeon's spell was aimed at Jack.

Shayla and her mate sprang forward in unison.

"Look out, Jack!" Katrina screamed into the rushing wind.

A blast of magic fire burst from both dragon mouths, directly at the sorcerer-king. Rejiia's attack faltered as she diverted her spell to protect Simeon. Dragon fire ringed them both, beat at invisible armor and died out. Neither of them flinched.

Both dragons ran past Simeon, gathering speed with each long step. Two more steps, two more sweeps of the huge wings, and Katrina felt the rush of air flow beneath her. A sudden release of the weight that held her to the Kardia and she knew they were airborne. A sense of wonder filled her as the vale diminished in size beneath her.

She looked down one last time. P'pa appeared as a heap of rags collapsed by the pool side. A ball of dark-green flame crashed through Jack's armor toward his eyes.

The blackness of the void engulfed her senses and her heart.

Chapter 38

"We cannot deny you access to the child, Darville," Jaylor said quietly. "But taking him to the capital now would cause more problems than it would solve." The two men faced each other, arms crossed, similar grim expressions on their faces.

"Don't you think that once Glendon is away from all these magicians, these receptive minds, he would learn to speak?" Darville gestured to the pair of apprentices who occupied the children.

"Possibly. But not before the Gnostic Utilitarian cult had sniffed out the presence of his magic. The law forbidding magicians from being lords and lords from being magicians has never been revoked," Jaylor reminded him. "Legally, Glendon can't be your heir."

"Legally, Glendon is already my heir. No one on the Council has questioned that he is my illegitimate son."

Brevelan called the boys to their breakfast from the doorway of the cottage. She glared at the men, warning them not to bring arguments into her home.

Both men turned to drink in the wholesome beauty they had both loved for so long. Darville looked away first, seeking Mikka.

"If we do not find solutions to our problems, Mikka will not stay with me," Darville mused. "My love for Brevelan is strong and special. But it cannot compare to the soul-deep love I bear my wife. I am nothing if she leaves me."

"I have assigned a team of magicians to the problem and summoned Zolltarn, since it was his binding spell that caused the problem," Jaylor reminded his friend.

"Shayla!" Brevelan called, startling both men out of their preoccupation. "Shayla's come back."

Mikka appeared behind Brevelan within the hut, hair unbound, and a glow of relaxed joy on her face.

Jaylor looked in the direction Brevelan pointed. A hint of a shadow passed between the sun and the clearing.

"Are you sure it's Shayla?" Jaylor called as he bolted to his wife's side.

"If she isn't certain, then I am," Darville confirmed. He stared at his left arm, eyes wide and mouth agape.

"What?" Mikka rushed to his side. Without waiting for an answer, she freed his arm from its sling and rolled up his shirt sleeve.

"Darville, your arm!" Brevelan gasped. The twisting black mass of the old burn faded and shrank before their eyes.

"If my dragon flies, then she must be healed, and so must I." The king smiled as he searched the sky for signs of the dragon.

Suddenly the air was filled with dragons. Big and small, tipped with color and luminescent pearl. The central figure glided in lazy circles around and around the clearing. Each pass was narrower and closer to the ground.

"Someone's riding the blue-tip," Jaylor announced at the same moment the others pointed to the human outline atop the nearly invisible dragon. "Suppose it's Yaakke?"

"No, it's a woman. Shayla is tiring. She's going to crash!" Brevelan shouted. She dashed forward to rescue the two little boys standing in the center of the meadow, watching the spectacle.

Jaylor was faster. One son under each arm, he dashed for the safety of a bank of saber ferns. Sharp, jagged leaves stabbed at his ankles and dragged against his trews. But the boys were safe.

Two heartbeats later, Shayla stretched out her claws and grabbed tufts of grass. Her legs buckled and her nose nearly hit the ground. Her distress was evident in the drooping half-furled wings.

"Where are we, Shayla? Are we safe? Who are all these people?" Katrina scrambled off the male dragon's back to check Shayla's wing.

The male extended his wings in preparation for flight. Katrina grabbed Corby and cradled him in one arm before the dragon took off again.

Shayla didn't answer. Exhaustion dragged nearly transparent eyelids over the jewel of her eye.

"We are friends," the blond man spoke hesitantly in a strange accent. "I know a little of your language."

He was tall, with a commanding presence, Katrina shrank away from him. The solid wall of Shayla's side prevented her from retreating further.

(Trust them.)

Katrina gulped back some of her fear. Outlanders. Her ingrained distrust rose. Jack was an outlander and he had proved himself more a friend to SeLenicca than her own king.

The man was blond, like a true-blood. Only his golden-brown eyes betrayed his lack of citizenship. The woman who stroked Shayla's muzzle and crooned a healing *Song* had proper blue eyes, but her red hair and something about the shape of her chin made her look too much like Simeon. The other tall man, holding two small boys under his arms, looked the friendliest, but his hair and eyes were almost as dark as Jack's.

"Do you know a man named Jack? A dark magician." She formed her words carefully to make sure they understood her.

The dark man spoke a few words in a strange language full of lilting, singsong phrases.

"Speak freely." The blond man smiled reassuringly. "The blond child understands you and translates."

Katrina stared at the squirming children. She hadn't heard them speak. Jack didn't need to speak. Were these people magicians as well?

"Jack sent us here for healing."

"Jack?" All three adults shook their heads.

"Yaakke!" proclaimed the dark man after exchanging a long stare with the blond child.

"He said his name was Jack." Her Jack wasn't part of a legend, though he'd performed some pretty miraculous feats. He hadn't brought about the prophecy of doom. Simeon had.

(Jack, Yaakke. Same man. Different attitude,) Shayla interjected.

"Where is the man you call Jack?" the dark-haired man asked slowly but in perfectly accented SeLenese.

"I fear King Simeon and his witch killed him. They killed P'pa too. And they killed SeLenicca. Queen's City is in ruins," Katrina cried. Tears fell down her cheeks unchecked. "All is lost."

"The Simeon destroyed his own capital?" the blond man asked anxiously.

"Jack thinks . . . thought . . . said that the influx of magic put too much strain on the burned-out ley lines. They . . . the lines collapsed. Earthquakes. Fire. People trampled to death. Rovers looting everything." Suddenly the horrors she had witnessed during the last two days caught up with her. Her teeth chattered with unnatural cold. Her body trembled uncontrollably. She nearly dropped Corby. The second woman, the one with hair the colors of a calico cat, took the injured bird from the basket of Katrina's skirt. She caressed him gently, cooing and murmuring soothing phrases.

(They come!) Shayla proclaimed. The anger and fear in her mental voice proclaimed the approach of foes.

Jack felt more than heard an audible whoosh of wind and a crack of the sky opening to the void; the signal that Shayla had successfully departed the valley.

The resulting vacuum dragged the breath from Jack and destroyed his balance. Rejiia and Simeon seemed equally disoriented; balance off, eyes unfocused.

Jack used the distraction and the falling sensation to duck out of his armor and roll behind a scrubby willow shrub. He left the protective spell in place, around a fuzzy image of himself. Rejiia's next magic attack crashed through the armor but found no target.

The black-haired witch recovered with amazing speed. She held up two white feathers. A wicked smile played over her lovely face.

A magician was tied to his familiar beyond the simple bonds of a pet. More than that, the stupid bird was the only friend and companion Jack had ever truly known.

S'murgh it, she was beautiful, even when she personified evil. Rejiia de Draconis enjoyed watching others suffer.

Rejiia wove a complicated gesture around the feathers, summoning the owner of those feathers to return to her.

But Corby was unconscious. He couldn't move. Would the spell levitate him back to Rejiia? Or worse yet, would it force Shayla and her mate, who carried him, to return to the vale?

Jack didn't wait to find out. An arrow-shaped probe formed in his hand. He threw it at the feathers and dove for a clump of tall grasses, armor returned, before Simeon found the spell to launch a new missile. The sorcerer-king looked dazed and distracted. His eyes kept wandering toward the sky.

The probe found the feathers, latched onto them, and yanked them from Rejiia's hand. In the blink of an eye, spell and feathers disappeared into the void. Hopefully they would find Corby and keep him in place.

Rejiia looked tired. She hadn't many spells left in her. But Simeon was still strong and filled with the need for vengeance. He'd conserved his spells for the lace shawl. His obsessive gaze landed on the heap of inert rags laying by the pool that could only be Fraank. Alive or dead?

Dragon magic was still in the air. Simeon gathered it and returned his attention to Jack. He stalked his prey, vision narrowed to one purpose, face set in grim determination.

If I can divert one more attack, Jack thought. *Just one more assault, then Simeon will have used up the last of the dragon magic.*

A blinding flash of sunlight on crystal flashed between Jack and Simeon. The big blue-tipped male dragon had come back. A huge supply of magic was at Simeon's fingertips while Jack's internal reserves were dwindling fast.

Then the bits and pieces of cloth and flesh moved, revealing Fraank's face. Neither the king nor Rejiia seemed to notice the man they had brought so low. The morning sunlight didn't reflect off the dull iron of the knife blade in Fraank's hand.

"You are bastard-born, an incestuous adulterer, and a traitor to your own kind, Simeon," Jack taunted, keeping the sorcerer's attention away from Fraank. "Even if you kill me, the coven will destroy you. You will have gained nothing."

Fraank staggered to his feet two paces behind the king. Jack had to distract the madman for two more paces.

"You betrayed the ship full of Tambootie," Simeon growled. "You were responsible for the economic disaster that followed. If the ship had won through, SeLenicca would have thriving exports once more. Food and jobs would be plentiful. The people would love me so much they'd welcome Queen Miranda's death so that I could rule!"

"Idiot!" Rejiia admonished. Her breathing was ragged and the strength had drained from her shoulders. "Stop talking and throw the *s'murghing* spell."

Simeon's armor flared a warning. If Fraank plunged his knife through the magic shielding, he'd die in an instant of blinding fire.

Jack flashed a warning to Katrina's father, his friend.

I'm a dead man already. The lung rot has worked into my bones and my heart. Let me kill this thing before I die.

Fraank raised the knife above his head.

Simeon whirled to face the new threat. With a flick of his wrist he dismissed the knife and its wielder. "No mundane can dare attack a magician, a king, a priest of Simurgh!"

Fraank staggered back a few steps as if struck, still clutching the knife. With the grim determination of a martyr he regained his footing and leaped forward. "You are a traitor to your country and my queen. Die like the miserable cur you are."

"Cease your attack or die!" Simeon screamed just before the iron knife plunged into his heart.

His armor had been set against magical attack, not a physical penetration. The armor ignited. Blood spurted. Smoke and flame and the stench of rotten Tambootie took them both into the void.

Not even a flake of ash remained of either man.

Jack flinched from the backlash of pain and death.

Rejiia absorbed it and swelled with a new source of magic. She seemed to grow and swell with dynamic power.

"Now it is your turn to die, boy."

(His name is Yaakke!) The blue-tipped dragon's bugling pronouncement echoed up and down the valley piercing mental and physical ears. *(Grab hold of my spines, Yaakke. Shayla and the little ones are safe now. I'll take you away*

from SeLenicca and the evil spawned by Simeon and this female.)

"I can't leave. I have to finish this." Jack poured his remaining strength into his armor.

(Another time. Your life is too important to waste on such as she.) The dragon reached out his strong forepaws and clamped Jack around the waist without touching ground.

With a massive sweep of wing and a blast of dragon fire, they lifted free of Kardia's gravity and into the void.

My enemies have done me a favor. Simeon can never cast doubt on the rights of my son and Princess Jaranda to marry and together claim the Three Kingdoms. No one must know that Princess Jaylene's child, the true Simeon, died at birth, replaced by Janessa's bastard, also named Simeon. Jaylene's link to Rossemeyer is the key to dynastic unity. That wretched piece of lace with the runic message is attached to the dragon's wing. I must find Shayla and destroy the lace before the Commune has the opportunity to read the secret.

Shayla will most certainly fly to the Commune. Fortunately the boy told me how to find Brevelan's clearing. If I take my sister or her children hostage, the dragon will surely give up her wing patch.

Glendon would be the best hostage. He is tied to the dragons through his father's blood as well as his mother's. And if I eliminate the child, then I clear the way to name myself and my son heirs to the throne and the Coraurlia—the glass dragon crown.

All sensation fled Jack's body as darkness closed around him. Panic rode at the edge of his awareness.

(We wait in the void,) the dragon told him.

"Why?" The dragons knew the void better than any human. Maybe they wouldn't get lost this time. Maybe.

Colored umbilicals, symbols of life forces, drifted past him. Gold and crystal, copper and blue. His own silver entwined with white. White for lace and moon-blond hair. Jack and Katrina.

As he watched, the silver umbilical of his own life took on a glow of purple. "Just like Amaranth, my colors are silver and purple. I've seen my own aura color!"

A rare achievement among magicians. Only those tested

and found worthy by the dragons were granted that privilege. He searched the glowing umbilicals for traces of his friends.

(Come look. See the future and the past.) The colored cords of life called to him.

He resisted the temptation. He'd been lost here once before. The last time he'd indulged in glimpses he'd seen things he wasn't meant to know.

(But you saw Katrina. You recognized her in your heart,) the dragon reminded him.

"What good will that do me? We've shared an adventure and both escaped. Now we must go our separate ways. Magicians aren't meant to share their lives with a mate. Our path—my path—must be solitary." Some of his happiness at finding his magical signature faded.

(Look again.)

A tangle of colors wrapped around Jack and a new vista opened before his eyes. The clearing. But not the clearing he had known. The house was bigger. Two boys wrestled and played in the meadow. Brevelan *Sang* as she stirred a hearty stew of yampion and legumes. Jaylor came up behind her, wrapping his arms around her gravid body.

Love and caring filled the clearing.

"But they're dead!" Jack would have cried if he knew where his body existed.

(Are they?)

"The monastery was burned out. A soldier played with Jaylor's staff."

(Many magicians passed into a new plane of existence from that monastery, over many centuries. Their staves were hung on the chapel wall in memory of their work. Magicians with the transport spell needn't be trapped by their enemies. The Commune escaped intact, Yaakke.)

Hope blossomed inside Jack.

"Why didn't you tell me before?"

(Would you have persevered to the end of your quest if you thought another magician could do it for you? Besides, you didn't ask. You assumed.)

Jack had to think about that a minute. Would he have endured the hardships of the trek from the mine to lair, the betrayal of Lanciar, the disasters in Queen's City?

"I think I might have, dragon. I may not have been as

willing to die for the quest if I knew I had friends waiting for me. But I would have continued to the end."

(Then you have truly grown into the rank of Master Magician.)

"Why are we lingering here? I need to warn my friends that Rejiia has the transport spell and directions to the clearing." Friends. What a wonderful word. His heart swelled within his chest. He needed to see his old friends, walk on familiar ground, speak his own language.

(We wait so that the daughter of Krej cannot follow our trail through the void.)

"How long?"

(Time is not measured in the void by the passage of the sun. Time flows forward and back and sideways in the void.)

Sideways?

(Between dimensions.)

"Great. So how long? I want my body back."

(You don't want answers?)

"I don't know what the questions are anymore." He'd escaped alive—so far. He hadn't planned to live beyond the magic duel with Rejiia and Simeon. Shayla had returned to Coronnan, Katrina was safe, and Simeon's tyranny had ended. Jack . . . Yaakke's quest was complete.

(You have accomplished much. For your self-respect and peace of mind, you had to do it alone. Dragons are not allowed to interfere in these matters. But you are not complete yet, Yaakke. You have earned a name. Yet you still know only a portion of your heritage. I am allowed to tell you the rest now that you have succeeded in your quest.)

"I'm half Rover. No matter who my father is, I can't overcome the prejudice against Zolltarn and his clan. They are thieves and malcontents, amoral nomads. Isn't that bad enough? Why should I want to know more?"

(What if Baamin was your father?)

"Baamin? My old master! Impossible."

(Why is it impossible?)

"Because it is. The old sot never . . . I mean he couldn't . . . he wouldn't. . ."

(Perhaps he did. Kestra was ordered to seduce a powerful magician. Who more powerful than Baamin on the night before his installation as the Senior Magician of the Commune?)

"But he would have told me!"

(Not if he didn't know.)

Sadness and joy threatened to split Jack in two. He and Baamin had been close. The old man had befriended and trusted Jack when no one else thought him smart enough to deserve a name. Of all the men he had known, Baamin was the one he would have chosen as a father.

But he had not known, had not done the things a father was meant to share with a son—the kinds of things Jaylor was doing now with his two little boys.

(Will you deny your own children the right of a father?)

"In case you hadn't noticed, I don't have any children. I haven't even . . . well, you know. Katrina's the only woman I know and we haven't gotten that far."

(Yet.)

"Not likely to either."

(Time will tell.)

"Not to change the subject or anything, but while we are sharing these intimate thoughts, how come you've never given me your name. Dragons like names, use them all the time. But you don't seem to have one."

(I have a name. The time was not right to tell you.)

"When will be the right time?"

(In another life I was called Baamin.)

Chapter 39

Weakness assailed Rejiia's limbs and mind. "How can I follow that wretched boy and his dragons? I have no magic left for the transport spell."

There is Tambootie here in the vale, a voice whispered in the back of her mind.

"P'pa?" She looked at the tin statue resting on the grass beside her. Sometime during the battle it had tipped onto its side. Flakes of gilt paint littered the grass in a circle around the sculpture. Very little paint was left.

Set me upright. The imperious tone, without the whine Simeon had developed these last few months, told her the owner of the voice belonged only to her father.

"At last you recognize that I have some purpose." She stared at Lord Krej without moving him. "You are now dependent upon me, Father."

And you must depend upon me to replenish your magic in time to follow the boy and the dragons.

"How?" She edged a little closer to him, not certain how she should feel toward him. "How are you speaking to me?" she amended her question.

The backlash wears thin.

"How?" she asked again. Her curiosity vied with her need to have her father acknowledge her as his equal in magic.

For many moons, I struggled against the spell. It fed upon the fight. I planned the spell to be self-renewing because I knew my intended victim would never give up. Once I realized this, the magic had no energy to feed it. Little by little it wears thin.

"How long before you are free?" Suddenly, Rejiia wasn't

certain she wanted him animate, arrogant, ordering her and everyone else to heed to his slightest wish. Besides, if he was animate again, he might try to steal the Coraurlia from her.

I cannot tell. Once we have dealt with Yaakke and the dragons, you must take me to Hanassa. My mother's people might help us.

"Us? What if I decide to leave you here? I am a full magician, more powerful than any in the Commune. What if I don't need you?"

You need me, child. Because I am your father and you will never be happy until we face each other and prove ourselves equals in magic and cunning.

"You are right about that, Father. I'll eat of this stunted Tambootie and the food left behind by the dragons. Then we will confront our enemies."

She welcomed the chill and the darkness of the void after the heat of the magic battle with Yaakke. The sensory deprivation ended the residual fatigue and the little aches and pains of her corporeal body.

We cannot linger here, Father. We must finish what I have started.

She didn't regret Simeon's passing. In Hanassa, she could find sufficient believers to form a ritual star again. Lanciar could be persuaded to join her. He was such a magnificent sexual partner, she'd regret losing him to another.

The fishing village with no name must be near the foothills of the Southern Mountains. She chose a spot near the decaying Equinox Pylon. P'pa had brought his entire family here the summer she turned ten. He didn't usually tour the forgotten reaches of his provinces. She'd forgotten what brought him here—something to do with witchwomen and dragons. The steep cliff down to the gravel beach and the Dragon's Teeth—a wicked rock formation in the cove—had stayed in her mind.

No one seemed to be active in the village yet. The fishing fleet would have left at dawn. Anyone else with sense was still abed.

The path behind the pub was easy to see. Many feet had pounded the dirt into reasonable smoothness. What was the boy's next landmark?

A boulder split in half by a tree.

The memory had been clear and precise in his head when she tried stripping his mind. Carefully she recreated the image of the broken boulder and launched herself and the tin weasel into the void.

This landing was more graceful. Practice, she told herself. Great magic took practice.

"Step through the split boulder, don't go around it as the path seems to indicate."

She lifted her skirts free of the dirt and moss that brushed against her and stepped through to a new path. Eight more steps and the path ended at a creek.

Bewildered, Rejiia searched the area with all of her senses. The boy had said to wait for Brevelan, but she didn't have time. She needed to find her way into the clearing on her own, without alarming the inhabitants.

Power tingled at the tips of her fingers, not quite entering her body. She reached out to find the source of energy. An invisible wall pushed her hand away. Finger-length by finger-length she followed the wall around, back to her starting place by the creek. Lives pulsed beyond the wall. The lives of her enemies.

She had found the Commune. And Darville. Her rival's presence taunted her, renewing her thirst for possession of the Coraurlia. "If he dies today with only a witch child as an heir, then I can put forth my claim to the throne without opposition." She giggled as she clenched her fist and pounded against the barrier, seeking access to the king who had stolen her crown.

Her hand and arm plunged through a hole in the barrier.

Ten dragonets landed in an awkward flurry of wings and dragging pot bellies. High-pitched squeals of distress pierced Jaylor's ears as the young dragons all tried to rush to their mother for protection and reassurance.

The clearing just wasn't big enough to contain them all without a talon or tail piercing the already damaged wall of the barrier.

A sparkle of black-and-purple lights announced the arrival of a magician by transport. "How dare you snatch me from my morning meal!" Zolltarn, king of the Rovers, bellowed before his body was fully formed. The tall man

with silver streaks within his blacker-than-black hair raised
a clenched fist and shook it at a vanishing shadow in the air.

"I summoned you the day before yesterday," Jaylor informed his colleague.

"And I was preparing to come. But a dragon snatched
me from the privacy of my tent while I was still eating!"

*(You will be needed today, not next week when you would
have arrived if left to your own schedule,)* a dragon voice
announced.

There were so many dragon bodies in the clearing Jaylor
couldn't tell which one had spoken. But the voice sounded
familiar. Maybe Seannin, the green-tip he'd ridden once.

The reek of Tambootie smoke dragged Jaylor's attention
away from Zolltarn, the frightened young woman, and the
crush of dragon bodies. Green flames licked the edges of
the small hole Glendon had made in the barrier. Jaylor's
armor snapped into place without conscious thought. This
was the stench of evil he had been reared to guard against.
This was the signal that all of Coronnan faced danger from
rogue magicians.

Zolltarn crouched defensively, his knife at the ready, as
well as a spell in his open palm.

The hole burned bigger; oily smoke poured through it.

"Brevelan, summon the rest of the Commune. Darville,
where is your sword?" As he asked, Jaylor remembered
the sight of Darville's long battle sword in its plain leather
scabbard propped upright beside the cottage door. He
transported it to the king's hand. Fred and Margit had
spent last night in the dormitory, an hour away. Not much
help unless he wasted energy on a transport.

"Boys, into the cottage!" Brevelan commanded. No one,
especially not small boys, disobeyed that tone of voice.

(I must flee. I cannot stand against her.) Shayla gathered
her remaining energies.

"Her?" Darville and Jaylor asked at the same time.

*(Rejiia. Daughter of Krej, mistress of Simeon, witch of
Hanassa.)*

"And mother of the next king of Coronnan!" The figure
of a tall, slender woman, dressed in elegant black appeared
in the flaming arch. Every sleek dark hair in place. She
exuded calm confidence.

Overconfident, Jaylor reminded himself. Her father and her aunt had been defeated by their lack of wariness.

"Her!" Zolltarn spat. "She has been stripping SeLenicca of gold and power, and men of talent."

A shimmering sparkle of light rolled and gathered beside Rejiia. The tin weasel that was Lord Krej materialized at her feet. The statue's mouth opened a fraction and drooled venom.

"My father must watch the final destruction of his enemies," she announced. "But Zolltarn I will only maim until he reveals the reversal of the spell that holds Lord Krej captive." With her words she wove her hands in a complicated pattern. A dark green, almost black, lightning probe surrounded her.

"Stargods, she's going to burn the rest of the barrier." Jaylor ran to stop her as the stench of burning Tambootie choked him. Three dragonets blocked his passage.

Rejiia laughed at his clumsy and useless progress. "You'll not stop me, University man. Dragon magic is nothing compared to the powers I control."

But she stood *between* two of the six ley lines that met at the center of the clearing. Jaylor nudged a purple-tipped dragon out of his way with a knee and planted his feet at the join. Zolltarn joined him. Shoulder to shoulder they stood, united in purpose. The magic welled up in Jaylor, eager to be woven into the fabric of the *Gaia*.

One small blond head appeared among the milling dragon backs, between Jaylor and his target.

"Glendon, into the house!" he ordered. Curiosity touched Jaylor's mind. The boy knew no fear.

"Glendon, come to me. I will show you what makes the barrier and what destroys it," Rejiia coaxed.

Jaylor used the magic filling him to throw a wall between Glendon and the witch. The spell hit a shiny metallic surface and bounced back to him. He ducked the backlash and prepared a new protection for Glendon.

Zolltarn threw the next spell. It, too, backlashed.

"Give it up, Rejiia," a new voice commanded. A strong and assured baritone voice with hints of familiarity in it thundered around the clearing.

*   *   *

Jack slid off Baamin's wing from the edge of the void into the center of the clearing, right beside Jaylor, his old master, and Zolltarn, his grandfather. Affection and a sense of homecoming almost pushed the menace of Rejiia out of his thoughts.

"Jack, you're alive!" Katrina squealed in delight behind him. The baby dragons stepped aside so that she could run to him. She plunged the last few steps into his arms.

He held her tight for two heartbeats, allowing her joy to fill him with purpose. He couldn't afford the distraction of her greeting. Drawing renewal from the living ley lines he sent a spray of magic water to douse the flames still in Rejiia's hands.

Amaranth and his purple-tipped twin joined Katrina in a jubilant rush to get to Jack. Balance askew, Jack's spell dropped just short of his target.

His hands landed on the back of the purple-tipped baby dragon.

Iianthe. The dragonet's name appeared in Jack's mind without warning.

Amaranth, the other reminded him.

He stroked the silvery fur once in greeting and gave back his own name. Dragon magic jolted through his hands and up his arms. He gathered power from both dragons.

Energy from the ley lines rushed to greet and twine around the power granted him by dragon. The two magics combined and filled him to overflowing. Jaylor placed a hand on his left shoulder. Zolltarn touched his right. Dragon magic reached out to him and amplified both energy sources. A sense of overwhelming completeness and belonging flooded his being.

He was home, and this was his family. He didn't stop to analyze his emotions. He needed a massive counterattack.

Katrina's healing *Song* rose within him. A love song. Rejiia's evil was the only thing keeping Jack from Katrina's side. He *Sang.*

> *They ran away to the clearing fair*
> *They ran away to fight magic.*
> *They whistled and they sang 'til love overcame*
> *an enemy evil and tragic.*

A flash of magic counteracted the fire eating away at the barrier. The flame withered.

"NO! You can't do this to me. You're only an untried boy," Rejiia screamed. From the folds of her gown she drew a wand, a miniature staff. She pointed the tool of focus directly into Jack's eyes.

Black arrows of magic sped from the tip of the wood.

> *They whistled and they sang 'til the clearing rang*
> *Filled with love and magic.*

Katrina raised her voice in *Song*. Beside her, Brevelan and Mikka joined her. Jaylor and Zolltarn raised their arms with a new spell fed by ley lines, dragons, and *Song*.

The offending black arrows dissolved into ashes.

Rejiia renewed the stream of magic.

Jack raised a wall of armor in front of them.

Rejiia's black arrows bounced off the armor and circled in confusion. Anxiously the witch stabbed at her spell with the wand. The arrows withered and fell back into the Kardia.

Jack raised a whirlwind of sparkling magic to circle around Rejiia and the statue of her father. Leaves and soil, moss and small rocks rolled into the tornado. The wind increased and lifted its burden free of the Kardia's gravity.

Everyone in the crowded clearing ducked and shielded vulnerable eyes from the blowing debris.

> *He whistled and she sang 'til the clearing rang*
> *Filled with love and magic.*

The magic storm winked out, taking Rejiia and Krej into the void. The burning arch collapsed and puckered, forming a ragged scar around the now-closed wound in the magic barrier.

Chapter 40

Magicians and dragons filled Shayla's old lair with life and energy, laughter and love. Jack watched the flames from the campfire dance around the circle of rocks. He closed his eyes in contentment.

He stretched out his legs and shifted his back to a more comfortable position. Home at last, with a family of magicians gathered around. Katrina sat beside him on a nest of old blankets. Jaylor approached them, an odd bundle held close against his chest. Jack squeezed Katrina's fingers in reassurance, then stood to face the Senior Magician.

"Don't know why we kept any of Master Baamin's old robes." Jaylor kept one eye on the blue-tipped male dragon who embodied all of the knowledge, wisdom, humor, and spirit of the former Senior Magician. "But it seems fitting that his master's cloak be yours now, Yaakke."

Without much ceremony or ritual, the current Senior Magician handed Jack the cloak of fine blue wool with silver stars embroidered on the collar.

"My name is Jack." He looked around at the gathered assembly with pride and a swelling sense of family. His eyes lingered on Zolltarn and then Baamin. "Yaakke was a name chosen by a child to prove to the world that I was worth something. I don't need that name anymore. I'm Jack, just plain Jack."

A ripple of nervous laughter passed through the gathering.

"Knew you'd lose that childhood arrogance once we turned you loose." Old Lyman, the eldest member of the Commune, slapped him on the back.

Jack remembered hearing the old man saying that

Yaakke should be locked up, for the safety of the kingdom, until he learned humility. He didn't correct him. He didn't need to.

"Yaakke is a name of power, for a man destined to lead great peoples. As my grandson, you will one day lead the Rovers!" Zolltarn pronounced in a voice that echoed throughout the lair.

"You have sons and other grandsons more deserving than I, Zolltarn. I have not been raised to Rover traditions and won't tolerate a lot of your ways." Jack didn't look away from his grandfather's piercing glare.

"What traditions won't you tolerate? We are an old and honorable race!"

"I won't steal for a living. Nor will I rove the countryside. I want a home. A wife. Children." He glanced down at Katrina.

She blushed but didn't turn her head away.

"And now that you are a full Master Magician, Jack," Jaylor took command of the meeting again. "I have an assignment for you."

"If you want me to find Marcus and Robb, I'm sorry. I don't think they can be found until both armies are pulled back from the front and fully counted, magician and mundane. There have been some pretty strange things happening out there lately." Jack shook his head in dismay.

"I claim that quest, Jaylor. If anyone is sent to find Marcus, its me." The pasty seller from the coronation market jumped up from her place among the apprentices.

Jack recognized her, even dressed in boy's leather trews and vest. If she had any magic talent to earn her place in this gathering, she hid it very well.

"You aren't going anywhere, young lady, until you've earned journeywoman's status." Jaylor frowned at the girl, then turned back to Jack. "I do want to find my journeymen as soon as possible, Jack. I have sent word to the battle mages at the front to look for them. If necessary, I'll send a journeyman in search of them. The task I have for you is closer to home and of some urgency."

"Tonight? Don't I get an opportunity to get drunk and sleep off the hangover with the rest of you?" Jack cocked an eyebrow at Baamin. "Seems that even my father had one night of rebellion before he accepted the saddle of responsibility."

More snickers. Jaylor gathered Brevelan and the boys close to his side, clear evidence that he, too, took some time away from his responsibilities.

"We must sing and dance to celebrate the return of my grandson!" Zolltarn looked ready to dance circles around the fire.

(Enough, youngster,) an affronted dragon commanded. If a dragon could blush, Baamin appeared to.

Jack drew Katrina up with him, wrapping his arm around her shoulders.

"Tomorrow or the next day will do, Jack," Jaylor chuckled. "Before His Grace is ready to return to the capital, we must deal with Queen Rossemikka's pesky cat." He winked at the queen, who looked very much at home in the rough camp. She'd made a comfortable nest for Corby out of her veil and left her hair loose around her shoulders as she dished stew from the communal cauldron.

"I knew she had a cat hidden somewhere," Margit muttered. "I hate cats."

"That's not going to be easy, sir. I'll need some time to study and experiment." Jack turned his gaze away from the grumbling girl apprentice and the smiling queen. Her double aura fascinated him.

"I can't be away from the capital much longer, Jaylor," Darville reminded them.

"The spells need to be thrown here, so we can guarantee privacy. Magic is not yet legal in Coronnan," Jaylor said. "For now, I'll send Jack with you, disguised as Sergeant Fred's assistant. You can all return here when you are ready, Jack. But you'll have to shave that beard. Square cuts aren't very popular in Coronnan City."

Jack fingered the growth of hair on his face. He liked the image of himself as a bearded, exotic foreigner. Katrina seemed to like touching it. Maybe he'd just trim it to a more rounded shape.

"You can also advise me about new ambassadors to Se-Lenicca, Jack." King Darville stretched and took a long sip of his ale.

"The best way to establish peaceful relations with our

neighbors is to help them rebuild," Jack said more to Katrina than his king.

"We will no longer be enemies?" Katrina interjected. She fingered a bright agate in the palm of her hand. Jack had placed a translation spell into the stone to help her communicate.

"We'll be friends, allies. Family." Jack gazed deeply into her eyes. "We can begin breaking down the barriers right here and now. If you will be my wife, Katrina, you won't be alone anymore."

"Do the dragons come with you as part of the family?" A tiny smile touched the corner of her mouth, belying the glistening of tears that glazed her eyes and the trembling of her chin.

"Amaranth and Iianthe do." Jack reached to pet the purple-tipped dragon heads. Neither dragonet had been out of reach since the incredible swelling and combining of three forms of magic he had experienced in the clearing this morning.

Rufan grunted in jealous displeasure. The red-tipped dragonet butted his head between Margit and Fred into the sergeant's lap, begging for similar pets.

(My boys are not yet ready to leave the nest,) Shayla insisted. She stretched her wing and shoulder stiffly as if to gather her young to her side. A trail of loosened lace drifted to the ground from her hasty bandage.

Katrina hurried to rescue the doily. Jack followed her across the cave. He couldn't let her go without an answer.

Brevelan and Mikka stood beside him, looking over his shoulder at the damaged wing.

"I think we should remove the patches and work a proper healing for both Shayla and Darville," Brevelan mused. She began working the loose edges free.

Katrina reached to help. Her fingers seemed more concerned with preserving the lace than protecting the delicate membranes beneath.

"Don't bother," Darville laughed, waving his left arm freely. "I think the patch worked a miracle on both of us."

"We'll see about that, Darville." Mikka looked closely at his arm. "The blackness is completely gone!" she gasped in amazement, then turned her attention back to the lace-covered dragon wing.

Bit by bit the ladies handed Jack the lace. Square pieces. Round doilies. Yards of edging. Amazingly, it was all as white and pure as when it was first made. The Tambrin fibers vibrated mildly, reminding him of the power within.

"The wing is healed!" Brevelan and Mikka gasped together.

"Told you so," Darville smiled. The women grabbed his arm again and compared the newly pink skin against the dragon wing. All traces of black burns were gone.

"With our Tambootie and your lacemakers, we'll all be rich." Jack turned away from the healers and their patients. "Our farmers will replant the devastated trees if they can see a profit from selling the fiber to SeLenicca. The dragons will have Tambootie to eat. Coronnan will have a strong nimbus again and we'll all have peace!"

"And the Commune will have dragons to make magic legal and controlled again," Jaylor added.

"And Katrina will have the most beautiful wedding ever," Brevelan sighed as she lifted the last piece of lace from the wing. The shawl came free in a single piece, stretched beyond its original size into a frothy veil. Carefully she settled the lace onto Katrina's hair. "That is, if she ever gets the courage to accept Jack's proposal."

"We barely know each other, Jack." Katrina put her hand up to remove the veil.

Jack covered her hand with his own. "I feel like I've known you forever, Katrina. I hope you can come to care for me, a little. Please say you'll at least think about it."

"Having a lair full of dragons as part of my family will take some getting used to," she said with a shy smile and a wink of mischief. "When I was alone and friendless, you offered me help and love without conditions. I'll always love you for that. I think I'd like to share my life with the dragons, and you."

Jack gathered her into his arms.

"Well, prove your Rover blood, boy . . . I mean Jack. Kiss her!" Zolltarn shouted with joy.

A blush galloped from Jack's toes to his face. He wanted desperately to kiss his love. But they were all watching.

Shyly Katrina lifted her face. Again that glint of mischief in her eyes. "This is what having a family means. Sharing love and happiness as well as sadness. I never thought I'd have family again. Thank you for sharing yours with me," she whispered to him.

Accepting the inevitable, Jack lowered his mouth to her in a quick gesture of affection.

"Put more heart into it, boy!" Zolltarn laughed.

"Later," Jack whispered. "When we're alone."

The waning flames in the center of the lair highlighted denser sections of the lace shawl framing Katrina's face. Jaylor reached to examine the lace more closely. A puzzled frown crossed his face as he read the runes encoded in the lace. Then he threw back his head and laughed.

"What's so funny about a prophecy of doom?" Jack asked.

(The runes name Simeon's true parentage, as the sorcerer-king feared.) Baamin peered over Jaylor's shoulder, also reading the runes. *(But they continued with the legend of Yaakke riding a dragon to the last battle that destroyed the coven of Simurgh. Tattia copied all of the runes into the shawl because she didn't know for sure which ones went beyond the intent of her original message. Seems we fulfilled the prophecy, Jack.)*

"I brought the dragons home. Coronnan will learn that magic can be honorable and controlled. I fulfilled my quest. That is enough legend and adventure for one lifetime. Now I want only to be a Master Magician in service to my Commune and king. And a husband and father." He smiled at Katrina, still within the circle of his arms.

(That's all we ever asked of you, Jack.) Baamin winked at him again.

"Soon," Katrina replied.

Jack captured her fingers with his own, lacing them together. "Soon."

"Best if you take your vows before I send him to SeLenicca as ambassador to help rebuild your country." Darville remarked.

"Ambassador?" Jack choked.

"I'm willing to bet that the power in the shawl's runes severed the magical connection between Simeon and Shayla. He couldn't protect himself against that last attack because he couldn't gather any more dragon magic." Jaylor scanned the lace once more. "If we present it to Queen

Miranda, as it should have been three years ago, this shawl could sever the magic that holds her in a coma."

"Who better to deliver the magic than Jack?" Darville pounded him on the back with his restored left arm.

"First he has to find a way to take care of my cat," Mikka reminded them.

"No problem," Jack shrugged, never taking his eyes off of Katrina.

"What makes you think the queen's cat will be no problem?" Jaylor asked.

Katrina smiled and kissed his cheek. The world brightened around him and his magic swelled in response.

"I'll have to study the problem a while." Jack continued to stare at Katrina, wondering if he dared kiss her right now, in front of the entire gathering. "I want to show Coronnan City to Katrina and rest my magic while I seek an answer. But if there is no spell in existence to solve the problem, then we'll have to improvise."

(You do too much of that, boy. When will you learn proper procedures?) Baamin glared at him as he had in the old days when he was Senior Magician, training a wayward apprentice.

"When you learn that I'm no longer a nameless boy, *Father?* But I won't have to work the spell alone. I have the whole Commune—my family—to help. I'll never have to work alone again."

Epilogue

*T*he void does not frighten me. In the black nothingness, all pain, bindings, and disguises slip away. I see my father as he truly is, still alive, still thirsting for vengeance. His vitality fades along with the backlash. The nature of the spell surrounding his physical body becomes obvious. 'Twill eventually drain the life from him.

From the sanctuary of the void we flee to Hanassa. There we can research the backlash spell. Now that the void has revealed the secret, I can find a way to reverse the transformation. And I shall bring Lanciar to join me and my son.

Hanassa harbors others of our kind who long for an end to Coronnan and the dragons. We must entice Darville and the Commune into coming to the secret stronghold buried in the mountains to meet their destiny.

In the end all things come to Hanassa.